By ARTHUR MEEKER, Jr.

The

IVORY MISCHIEF

He [Aristotle] used to say that personal beauty was a better introduction than any letter; but others say that it
was Diogenes who gave this description of it, while Aris-
totle called beauty 'the gift of God'; that Socrates called
it 'a short-lived tyranny'; Theophrastus, 'a silent deceit';
Theocritus, 'an ivory mischief'... (DIOGENES LAERTIUS,
The Lives and Opinions of Eminent Philosophers)

HOUGHTON MIFFLIN COMPANY · BOSTON

The Riverside Press Cambridge

1942

The Riverside Press
CAMBRIDGE . MASSACHUSETTS
PRINTED IN THE U.S.A.

PREFATORY NOTE

None of the characters in this novel is imaginary.

Contents

Contents

Charles d'Angennes,   m.   Marie du Raynier-Droué
Baron de la Louppe   (d. 1679)
(d. before 1650)

Catherine-Henriette [Cateau]   m. (1652)   Louis de la Trémouille, Comte d'Olonne (b. 1626 — d. February, 1686)
(baptized June 16, 1634 — d. June 13, 1714)

Magdelaine [Magdelon] *   m. (1655)   Henri de Senneterre, Maréchal de la Ferté (b. circa 1600 — d. September 27, 1681), created Duke in 1665
(baptized May 8, 1635, d. March 15, 1714)

Henri-François, Marquis de la Ferté   m. (1675)   Marie-Gabrielle-Isabelle-Angélique de la Mothe-Houdancourt, Mademoiselle de Toucy (b. 1654 — d. 1726)
(b. January 23, 1657 — d. August 1, 1703) Duke in 1678

Louis, Seigneur de la Louppe (b. May 2, 1659 — d. May 7, 1732). Entered Society of Jesus in 1676. Became Jesuit Father in 1693.

Catherine-Henriette   m. (1688)   François de Bullion, Marquis de Villiers-Longchesne
(b. 1662)

Annibal-Jules (b. August 6, 1665 — d. October, 1702) Knight of Malta

Cécile-Adelaide   m. (1693)   Louis-César, Comte de Rabodanges
(b. October 2, 1673 — d. January 6, 1720)

Marie-Angélique   m. (1689)   Gaston-Jean-Baptiste de Lévis, Marquis de Mirepoix (b. 1660 — d. July 26, 1699)
(b. November 2, 1676 — d. March 31, 1713)

Catherine-Louise, Mademoiselle de Menetou (b. 1680)   m. (1698)   François-Thibaut de la Carte (b. 1669). Created Marquis de la Ferté after his marriage

* By her liaison with Charles-Paris d'Orléans, Duc de Longueville (b. January 29, 1649 — d. June 12, 1672) Madame de la Ferté became the mother of Charles-Louis d'Orléans, Chevalier de Longueville (b. circa 1671 — d. November, 1688).

BOOK ONE

MAGDELON

(January — April, 1655)

Chapter I

CALCULATE AS ONE WOULD, IT WAS NOT MORE THAN FIVE-AND-twenty leagues from La Louppe to Paris. Five-and-twenty leagues — that is, two good days' journey, especially with the roads knee-deep in mud and half-melted snow. Moreover, Madame de la Louppe's coach was lumbering and old-fashioned, and the four stout bays that pulled it had, like their burden, the more prosperous part of their careers behind them.

Still, thought Magdelon, they could quite well have managed it. The very next evening she might have been sure of kissing her sister Cateau, in the latter's new house in the rue Neuve-Saint-Augustin — but for Aunt de Marville.

It was bad enough, as it was, to be chaperoned by her instead of by Maman. Maman, with all her manias and moods, could be exceedingly amusing at times; whereas Aunt de Marville was never anything but a pious little bore. Not that she was actually more religious than Maman. No one, Magdelon was sure, could possibly be that. But Aunt de Marville merely prayed a great deal, with her round small nose buried deep in a black-bordered handkerchief; went to Mass twice a day all week, and three or four times on Sunday. On the other hand, Maman's fits of devotion displayed themselves in more diverting ways. She was forever burning candles to Saint Anthony or the Blessed Virgin, making improbable vows, and living on lentils and sour-cabbage salad for weeks during Lent. Besides, she was quite as apt to consult the local soothsayer on the state of her conscience as the parish priest; and when she shut herself up in her oratory, as she frequently did, for hours on end with that weazened, duck-eyed little Father Denis, Magdelon was by no means certain that they were actually praying all of the time, nor even, when they were, that it was God who was being addressed. Rumours were occasionally wafted about the house of brief but fascinating interviews with departed spirits, who had come back to earth via Father Denis to leave all manner of absurd and unexpected messages. Papa, for instance, it appeared, had talked with them more than once, as well as Grandpapa, Maman's father, Monsieur de Droué, who had been dead more years than one could count, and both of Cateau's and Magelon's uncles, the Sieurs du Raymier and de Marville.

As a matter of fact, it was after one of these ghostly conversations that Maman came very late to the dinner-table one day in January, her pale grey eyes popping with excitement, and announced that she had had 'word' from Uncle Jacques that Magdelon was to be sent to her sister in Paris.

Magdelon looked up with a startled smile, then dropped her gaze again and said nothing. But Aunt de Marville laid down her knife and fork to clap her hands, and rummaged round in her pocket till she produced, with an air of triumph, a letter from Cousin Julie de Montausier, saying that she and her mother, the famous Madame de Rambouillet, were in residence at the moment at their castle, and expected to remain in the country for at least six more weeks.

So, of course, there was nothing for it but that the ladies must plan to stop the first night of their journey at Rambouillet... and who knew how much of a delay *that* might entail?

'It would be a most delicate attention,' said Madame de Marville, her voice hushed, her blue eyes solemn at the mention of their august relative's name. 'To tell the truth, if our Cousin de Rambouillet were later to learn that I'd passed so close to their house without doing myself the honour of presenting Magdelon to her and Cousin Julie, I dare say she'd never forgive me. And quite right, too. Such a very, very distinguished woman!'

And she looked about the dinner-table as if she had made a clever remark, while Magdelon recalled that Cateau always maintained that, if Aunt de Marville lived to be a hundred, she would never forget the glory of her achievement in marrying into the Angennes family — of which both the Rambouillets and the La Louppes were branches. (Though, really, why a Pommereuil, the widow of an Espinay, was not every bit as good...)

'Well, of course,' said Madame de la Louppe, in her husky drawl, 'now that the Marquis is dead, and that hunchbacked son of hers as well, she is the titular head of the tribe. A pack of women — that's all that's left of us! I suppose you had better go to see her. God bless her soul! I've always thought her a tiresome old nuisance!'

She gave a shrill squeal of laughter, while Madame de Marville's crabapple-pink cheeks flushed scarlet, and she pursed up her mouth till it resembled a small rosy O.

Magdelon laughed noiselessly in her napkin, so that Aunt de Marville should not notice, and thought: 'That's why one really can't help loving Maman. She comes right out with things that everyone thinks, but no one dares say.'

They went on eating in silence for a few minutes, the only sounds being the scrape of the cutlery on the second-best silver service and the squeak of André the butler's old red Russia-leather shoes on the carpetless parquet.

No one lingered over a meal in this kind of weather. The castle of La Louppe, an angular stone pile, relic of the reign before last, had few modern comforts to recommend it. It was bitterly cold in the great dining-hall. The light slanting through the high uncurtained windows was harsh and cheerless; the very portraits of long-dead Angennes seemed frozen in their frames on the marble walls. Even two fires, blazing briskly at either end of the room, could do little but take off the edge of the chill. They really gave less of an impression of warmth than the figure of Magdelon in her cramoisie velvet. She bloomed like a rose between the two elder ladies, who, by contrast, in their widow's caps and sombre robes, looked as lifeless and flat as the family portraits.

Magdelon's big black eyes brimmed with vitality. Sparks of it seemed to snap in her hair, which fell in a dark curly cascade over her shoulders, burnished bronze where it was touched by the light. Her lips were almost as red as her gown, her cheeks faintly pink over the wonderful pure pallor of the celebrated 'du Raynier skin.' ... 'The girls get their complexions from *my* side of the house,' Madame de la Louppe was wont to observe with complacency. 'I was the same in my day. Lilies and snowdrops, they called it!' (But she was wrong about that: it was a softer, subtler hue, like new ivory, that gave Cateau's and Magdelon's faces their delicate finish.) Several well-known artists had striven unsuccessfully to fix this marvellous colour on canvas; what was, on the whole, the best of the various attempts, a double portrait of the sisters, one as dark as the other was fair, a three-quarter length by Juste d'Egmont, hung now in the drawing-room at La Louppe. It had never been quite paid for.... Some dispute had arisen about the size of the pearls Cateau was wearing, the angle of Magdelon's eyebrows.... Still, there it was, for visitors to admire — and Monsieur Juste had long ago given up writing letters to Maman, since they were always promptly consigned to the fire.

It was conceivable that Cateau, at court, was fully aware by now of the power of her charms. But Magdelon, as far as one could tell, did not seem to know that she was lovely.

She sat demurely in her place, her mind wholly fixed on feeding her spaniel, Madam Mouse, who was under the table, without attracting Maman's attention.

Madam Mouse was strictly forbidden the room during meals. She knew this perfectly well and remained tactfully out of sight beneath the long damask cloth. But she kept her curly brown head wedged against her mistress's knee, her chestnut eyes fixed on the latter's face; and from time to time Magdelon managed to drop a bit of beef into the waiting pink trap that never missed. It was a simple game that had amused them both for months.

After a while Madame de la Louppe stopped eating, leaned her elbows on the table — something she had never permitted her children to do — and said to Madame de Marville, exactly as if they had been carrying on an argument on the subject all along: 'But really, Françoise, Cousin de Rambouillet is a most affected, self-important old creature! As for family feeling, she hasn't a shred of it, outside of that flock of plain, gawky daughters of hers. Poor things! They all squint, and Clarisse has red hair and freckles as well. No wonder most of them have ended in convents! But you can't have forgotten how their mother acted the year I took Cateau and Magdelon to Paris to be presented at court. . . . Five years ago it was, the first of the winters we shared that house in the rue Férou. Naturally I thought, as cousins of Monsieur de Rambouillet, the least his wife could decently offer would be to give them the run of her house. As it turned out, she did ask them in to one or two of her stupid literary afternoons. I made the girls go — they didn't in the least want to, poor lambs! — because of course I supposed Madame de Rambouillet would see to it that they met some eligible young men. And, my dear, if you'll believe me, there wasn't a soul in the place under sixty, and all that happened was that Corneille read one of his cumbersome Greek tragedies, and they all sat about afterwards sipping hippocras and making jokes about *books!* . . . Oh no, if we'd had to depend on the Rambouillets to help us, Cateau would not be married today. Say what you will, it wasn't in their poky Blue Room she met the Comte d'Olonne! . . . Ah, well, it's a long time ago now: let bygones be bygones. And since the road to Paris goes directly by their castle, by all means pay a call on the old woman. Spend the night there, if you like. She'll give you a shocking bad dinner, and a room as cold as the grave to sleep in; but you'll hear all the news, especially if Julie de Montausier is stopping with her. It might be a good idea, before getting to town, to find out what's been happening at court. For instance, if the King is really going to marry one of those Mancinis, I'd want Magdelon to meet them at once. . . . This ragoût is tough: Can you eat any more? If not, come with me to my room for a few minutes; there's something I want to discuss with you. Magdelon, child, go practise the lute in the music-room. There's a fire laid, and I've just received a package from Paris, containing some delicious new gavottes by that clever Lambert. Come, Françoise!'

Madame de la Louppe pushed back her plate and sprang up, tall and commanding in her flowing sable draperies. She linked her arm in that of her sister-in-law — who cast a longing look at the pastries André had been on the point of handing round — and drew her out of the room, Aunt de Marville's podgy feet pattering along in a feeble effort to keep pace with Maman's quick, nervous stride.

Magdelon, left alone, felt far too much excited to finish her dinner. She waved André and his platter of pastries away, and as soon as he was safely out of sight called Madam Mouse from under the table and made her a present of the remains of the ragoût.

Oh, what should she do now? If she were unable to eat, still less could she stomach the idea of spending an hour by herself in the music-room, strumming the lute with frozen fingers. Gathering up the voluminous skirt of the cramoisie velvet — her Sunday dress, last remnant of Paris grandeur — with a hand that trembled with eagerness, she chirruped to Madam Mouse, and together they raced up the grand staircase, then up a second long flight of steps to her bedroom.

They ran as fast as they were able, for, if it had been chilly in the hall, it was positively arctic on the stairs. That was the worst of the country in winter: one spent one's life in a series of shivering rushes from one fire-warmed refuge to the next.

Magdelon's room was at the top of the house, in the tower to the right of the main entrance. It was the same one she and Cateau had shared as children, and now that she was grown up she steadily refused Maman's amiable offers to give her another apartment more suitable to her years and position. She loved the white, round, rather empty chamber, with its alcove hung with faded brocade curtains, screening the canopied oak bed. And, in Magdelon's opinion, there was no view in the world to compare with that from her windows, which overlooked the slates of the roof, a fantastic forest of towers and chimneys, carved garlands and gargoyles. Below lay the terrace, hedged and gravelled, shut in by the moat; beyond that, the park, the huddled tiled roofs of the village, and, in the distance, a glimpse of the gently rolling Norman countryside.

In summer the prospect was verdant and smiling: white and gold water-lilies starred the green scum of the moat, where dragonflies flashed and flitted all day; while the roof was peopled by pigeons. The first sound Magdelon heard in the morning was their cooing. She could remember, as far back as she could remember anything, waking to those soft, incessant notes and turning to find Cateau's yellow head beside her on the pillow. No matter how early it was, Cateau was sure to be awake, her enormous blue eyes staring fixedly at her sister ... 'Stupid, I thought you were going to sleep all day!' ... But in winter savage blasts rattled the casements of the tower room; the moat froze grey and solid; the glittering dragonflies were all dead; even the pigeons deserted their playground and cuddled for warmth in the cote in the farmyard.

Magdelon paused for a moment on the threshold, breathless after her climb, red lips parted, eyes wide and shining with excitement. She felt as she often had lately, half stifled with an emotion she could neither name nor express. Oh, what was it? What could it be? What made her...? Life really was... *what?*... She longed now to dance, to sing, to shout at the top of her voice, to hug some-one hard — someone, *anyone* — to give vent to her feelings. Yet that wasn't enough, after all. Was there not something else, some-thing new, something very much better that, if only she could find it, would make everything that puzzled her quite clear?

Madam Mouse, replete with ragout, received her mistress's im-pulsive advances with languor. And Polidore, her pet sparrow, was napping on his perch, his feathers all ruffled, a grey film of sleep drawn over each eye.... Oh, dear, was there nobody, *nobody* in the whole world...?

Fortunately, at this point the faded curtains in front of the alcove parted, and an old woman, in a shapeless brown woollen gown and a high ruffled white cap adorned with mauve ribbons, appeared.

Magdelon seized the old woman, spun her round thrice, while the bows on her cap bobbed up and down, and then embraced her so violently that the victim cried out for mercy.

'Oh!' cried Magdelon. 'Thank goodness, you're here! If someone hadn't come, I feel sure I'd have burst. Mahaut, just think what has happened: Maman is sending me to Paris to live with Cateau!'

The old woman looked at her with shrewd, deep-set eyes, like round black marbles sunk in her skull, and nodded her head slowly several times. When one examined her closely one saw that she was really not so old, after all, not more than fifty, perhaps — scarcely older than Maman. But her back was gnarled and bent, as if from years of toil; she had long ago lost all her teeth, which gave her jaw a sinister, shrunken look; and her face was heavily seamed, in token of a life of hardship. As a matter of fact, this appearance was de-ceptive. Mahaut had been born in the village at the castle gates, and taken into the household as a very young girl to fill the post of chambermaid. Later she had been nurse to both Cateau and Magde-lon, a title that was still nominally hers, though she had not done a stroke of work in years. She spent her time stirring up trouble in the kitchen, criticizing the other servants to her mistress, and gossiping with Magdelon... 'which only goes to show,' as Madame de la Louppe often said, 'once a peasant, always a peasant.'

'Do you hear me, Mahaut?' demanded Magdelon, with a touch of impatience at the other's silence. 'I'm going to Paris to spend the whole winter, maybe longer than that. Let's look over my clothes right away and see what'll do for the journey.'

'I hear you, mademoiselle,' replied the old woman, in a cracked and ancient voice that sounded as though it were produced by ma-chinery. 'And in a great hurry you seem to be in to leave us, I must say!'

'Well,' said Magdelon, 'you know Maman. Once she's made up her mind to a thing, it's as good as done. So we might just as well be prepared.'

'It's dancing and gaiety you're after,' remarked Mahaut gloomily, 'and Lord knows what sort of depravity. Well, well, 'tis only natural, at your age. The country's no place for young things, that's true. Your Maman never could bear it when she was first married to your Papa. She couldn't get it into her head why he'd rather stay at La Louppe and look after his properties. Many's the time she'd stamp her foot and say she'd rather lose the revenues of ten farms than the carnival season in Paris. . . . Yes, say what one will, it's a very fine city. I liked it well enough myself when we lived there those two winters in the rue Férou. I've never heard, nor do I hope to hear again, this side of Paradise, such elegant sermons as the vicar of Saint-Sulpice preached, the same as married Mademoiselle Cateau to that young Monsieur de la Trémouille.'

'Oh, Mahaut,' said Magdelon, 'how many times must I tell you? — Cateau's husband *isn't* Monsieur de la Trémouille. He belongs to the Trémouille family, true enough, but to a younger branch: his own name is Louis, Comte d'Olonne, and his father's the Marquis de Royan, Grand Seneschal of Poitou — don't you remember that fat little man with the very red face, who drank so much champagne at the wedding he had a dreadful fit of coughing and had to go home? Their house was just across the street from ours. And Louis is cornet of the King's Light Horse Troop. And Cateau doesn't live in the rue Férou any more. She's got a lovely new house in the rue Neuve-Saint-Augustin; that's in the parish of Saint-Roch, I think.'

'Well, well, what does it matter? Whatever's her name and wherever she lives, I pray she may still be a good girl and not forget to tell her beads and go to Mass every morning. Nor don't *you* forget it, either, Mademoiselle Magdelon. Paris is a godless town, for all of its churches, full of protestants and freethinkers — and worse!'

'I know all about Paris, nurse. I was there just as long as you were, you know.'

'A child you were then, my cabbage, an innocent babe in its cradle.'

'I wasn't a child at all,' retorted Magdelon quite crossly. 'Don't be so silly, Mahaut. I was sixteen the last time we went there to live, and eighteen past when Cateau was married. I was her bridesmaid at the wedding. And I was presented at court, and danced in two of the royal ballets, and went to dozens of balls besides. I remember everything quite as well as you do.'

Indeed she did. She could review every detail of her life in those exciting months of the civil wars as vividly as if it had taken place last week. (Could it really be three years since the Fronde had ended and the gay operatic pageant suddenly faded away?) Magdelon herself had had little idea of the significance of the long struggle of the nobles against Anne of Austria, Queen Mother of France, and Cardinal Mazarin, her prime minister. But she paused now, in the midst of her irritation with Mahaut's stupidity, as she recalled what had happened the day the war had come to an end. She and Cateau had gone with their friend Mademoiselle de Montpensier to Madame de Choisy's house, which had a window looking towards the Louvre, to watch the boy King Louis make his triumphal entry into the city that had barred its gates to him for years. They had been uneasy and depressed, a little band of women whose gallants had marched away with the rebel Prince de Condé and left them defenceless and alone. (For Mademoiselle's father the Duc d'Orléans, though chief of the party, was no help at all; he had taken to his bed and was pretending to be ill!...)

Mademoiselle, determined to brazen it out till the very last, had put on a face like a dauntless sheep; she leaned far out of the window while the procession was under way, and called to a street vendor who was selling coloured-paper lanterns à la royale: 'Have you none à la Fronde?'... But Madame de Choisy, in a twitter of nervousness, had screamed: 'Jesus! Would you have me beheaded?' and slammed the window shut as quickly as she could. And though they had gone back to the Tuileries afterwards, at Mademoiselle's invitation, and had supper and listened to her string orchestra play their favourite gavottes and sarabandes, and pretended to be having a good time, it had been a melancholy evening. The pretty dance tunes reminded them of the partners who had squired them so gaily during those last merry months, and who were all gone, some, alas! never to return. Half the ladies were in tears before supper was over. Even Cateau and Magdelon, who knew nothing of politics, and had flirted impartially with royalist and rebel alike, shared the prevailing air of dejection. Magdelon remembered that she had been particularly struck when her sister, who never cried, broke into sobs in the middle of Boësset's new minuet and exclaimed: 'Oh, I can't *bear* for everything to be over!'

Mademoiselle had lifted her head, looking more than ever like a dauntless sheep, and replied: '*You've* nothing to worry about. *You'll* be all right. Your husband's a royalist. Didn't you see him this afternoon, at the head of his Light Horse Troop?'

'Yes, oh, yes!' said Cateau. But she went on crying even harder than before; and Magdelon had known it was because she was not really sure yet whether she was going to like being married or not. How could one tell, after only twenty-four hours? That was all she had had, so far; for the Count had been sent for to join his regiment the day after their wedding.

He appeared at the house in the rue Férou early next morning, dapper and smiling, to claim his bride. Cateau, who by that time had recovered her composure and was even smiling a little, too, had departed quite willingly; and the day after that Maman made up her mind, without warning, that they'd been spending far too much money, and had better retire to the country and economize for the rest of the season.

And here they had been ever since. . . . 'No, Mahaut, please . . . the *other* chest . . . that's it: the walnut one in the corner.' . . . Maman had explained frankly that she had been so overjoyed at Cateau's having made such a brilliant match that, in her resolve to impress the La Trémouilles at any cost, she had given her elder daughter twenty thousand francs down instead of the ten she had originally intended, besides settling both Canteloup and Saint-Pierre-du-Joncquet on her, instead of Canteloup alone, as she had first meant to do. Magdelon did not mind: it was exactly the sort of gesture she would have made herself. . . . 'There, now, nurse . . . lay everything out on the bed.' . . . She had not even minded leaving town and going back to the country . . . at least, not very much. She would hardly have minded at all if it hadn't meant leaving Cateau, too. For Magdelon seemed to be contented wherever she was. She had been happy in Paris, and she was happy at La Louppe. Once they had settled down in their old home she went back to the rural pursuits of her childhood as naturally as if she never had left them. She tended her rose-bushes, fed the pigeons, played with Polidore and Madam Mouse for hours every day; rode miles on her dashing black mare through the neighbouring woods and fields; paid visits to the peasants in the village with Maman and Maman's new steward, Monsieur Braye. In the evenings she practised the lute, or did tapestry-work by the fire in the great hall, while Maman and Aunt de Marville took turns reading aloud from *Le Grand Cyrus* or the new romance, *Clélie*. . . . 'Mahaut, dear, the bodices on one side, the skirts on the other!' . . .

Sometimes, too, the coach would be harnessed, and the three of them, dressed in their best, would drive in to Chartres for the Easter holidays or at Whitsuntide, to attend services at the cathedral and a few local assemblies as well. But the festivities of provincial Précieuses had small attraction for ladies accustomed to life in the capital. Magdelon, perhaps, left to herself, might have enjoyed herself more. She was so very fond of dancing that whenever she found a good partner she really could not help falling a little in love with him . . . at any rate, while the music was playing. But she was conscious always of a warning satirical eye upon her, and during the long drive home afterwards Maman would cheerfully tear hosts and guests alike to pieces, mimicking the ornate rusticities

of their manners so irresistibly that Magdelon, and often Aunt de
Marville as well, would collapse on the cushions in fits of helpless
laughter.

By this time Mahaut had succeeded in making an incomparable
mess of her young mistress's belongings, which were strewn in gay
coloured heaps over the bed, half a dozen chairs, and the adjacent
floor. Furthermore, her beady, acquisitive eye had marked as her
prey many a ribbon and scrap of lace Magdelon had by no means
made up her mind to part with; and the latter, good-natured as she
was, grew distinctly irritated by the reiterated mutters of 'You'll
not be needing *these* again, mademoiselle,' or 'My pigeon, I know a
poor girl in the village who'd be right glad of this taffeta!' (Poor
girl in the village, indeed! Magdelon knew better than to believe
that story.)

In the circumstances it was really a relief to be interrupted by a
knock at the door, which opened for Madame de la Louppe to thrust
in her head with her characteristic arch discretion, as if loath to
break in on an amorous interview.

'Packing already, my child? Are you so eager then to leave
home?'

'Oh, no, Maman, you know that I'm not! I don't want to leave
you at all. Why can't you come with me instead of Aunt de Marville?'

'Ah, love, if I could! If I could! It's only my duty to my two
poor fatherless babes that keeps me buried alive in the country. I
promised your Papa on his death-bed I would guard the family
fortune with my life, if need be — and so I have done from that day
to this. Besides, there's a new steward arriving this week, and if
I weren't here to explain his duties to him, goodness knows what
might happen! Françoise is a fool; she knows nothing of farming.'

'A new steward? Is Monsieur Braye going away? But I
thought ——'

'He has already gone, child,' replied Madame de la Louppe, with
dignity, seating herself on the edge of the one armchair in her daughter's room and pinching her thin lips together with an alarming
assumption of outraged virtue. 'I was willing, I own, to put up
with a good deal from that impertinent young man on account of
his ailing old father, whose sole support he asserted himself to be.
No doubt I have acted very weakly and foolishly. A really clever
woman could have told, months ago. . . . But some things were a
little too strong, even for my spirit of Christian magnanimity. And
when I caught him kissing Paulette . . . But that's neither here nor
there, dear. That's not at all what I started to say.'

Magdelon caught a wicked gleam in Mahaut's eye: the tales one
had heard in the servants' hall about Maman and Monsieur Braye

were then only too true. Magdelon had not been especially shocked
by them, merely somewhat surprised, because, to her, Monsieur
Braye had not seemed in the least attractive. . . . Poor, dear Maman!
It was the same story with her, over and over. One must hope that
the new man would prove more satisfactory in every way: she was
always so much better-tempered when she was deep in an intrigue
with her steward. . . . But what was this she was saying now?

' . . . Your aunt and I have talked things over, and we've decided
that you may as well go to Paris at once. Tomorrow, in fact, if the
coach can be got ready in time. There's nothing to keep you here,
and if you're going at all, it had better be now, while the carnival's
on. Poor lamb! You've been patience and goodness itself, these
two empty years in this moth-eaten prison! I'm sure you deserve a
little pleasure as your reward, if anyone does. Cateau can have you
as well at one time as another. And she can chaperon you to the
balls, and see that you meet some presentable young men. I've
written a letter to Cateau, giving her the fullest possible instructions. There'll be no excuse for any mistake.'

'Mistake, Maman? You mean . . .?'

Madame de la Louppe suddenly held out her arms, and pressed a
consecrating kiss of deep emotion on her daughter's dark curls.

'I mean only, my darling, that you're more beautiful than ever.
And that's all that matters for a woman. Remember it always:
Nothing's ever too late, while one still has one's beauty.'

Magdelon looked up, in quick, pleased surprise, only to intercept
once more an ironic glance from Mahaut. The old woman, bending
on trembling knees over the walnut chest, nodded meaningly to her
charge; and Magdelon, following the direction of the nod, saw her
mother's image reflected in the glass on the dressing-table, simpering
self-consciously with eyes as bright and silly as a bird's.

Chapter II

MAGDELON COULD NEVER HAVE GUESSED THAT SHE WOULD BE GLAD
to find herself at Rambouillet.

However, after an entire day spent in the coach with only Aunt de
Marville and her maid for company, it was actually a relief when,
just before dusk, the familiar red towers appeared through the trees
of the blue and misty park.

The drive across the barren, wind-swept plains of the Beauce had
been long and exceedingly dull. The carriage jolted over the rough
country roads, which, even for this time of year, were in a shocking
condition. Very likely they had not been repaired since the end of
the war. Most of the small farms they passed looked tumble-down
and deserted; they, too, had not yet recovered from the effects of
four years of the Fronde. Aunt de Marville, moaning at the devasta-
tion, told her rosary and brooded, like a hen, over the charcoal foot-
warmer. Célie, her maid, a pig-faced little peasant, snored, with her
mouth open, the whole day through, waking with an uneasy start
and a gusty 'Pardon, madam!' whenever they stopped to rest and
water the horses. Magdelon, on the back seat beside her aunt, sat
up very straight with her hands folded in her lap. She was wearing
a mauve velvet mantle with a peaked hood of the same material,
beneath which her eyes sparkled with suppressed animation. It was
cold in the coach, although the leather curtains were fastened tightly
on both sides, and so dark that Magdelon wished she dared suggest
stopping and changing her place for one up aloft next to Robin, the
coachman. There, at any rate, there would be something to see. . . .

As this was obviously impossible, she fell to wondering whether
Madam Mouse were missing her sadly, and if Mahaut would remember her promise to see that Polidore had fresh water and seed
every day — for she had had, alas! to leave both her pets behind:
the spaniel was too lively and too little trained for city life, and Magdelon had been afraid that the sparrow, which she might well have
brought with her, would catch cold on the journey.

She leaned forward, and peered through a chink in the curtains at
the dreary brown fields and the low dove-grey sky, from which a few
flakes of snow were idly falling.

'Aunt, if a band of brigands were to attack us . . .'

'Brigands? Lord save us! What put that idea into your head?'

'Or the Prince de Condé and his Spanish troops? That would be very much nicer, wouldn't it? I do like the Prince: he'd give us a picnic lunch, as he used to do when we went to see the army manoeuvres during the war.'

'Child, the war's over now.'

'Not really, aunt. We're still fighting Spain, are we not?'

'Not about here. And not in wintertime, *anywhere*. It's much too cold now for anyone to fight,' replied Aunt de Marville, with finality. '*Ave-Maria-gratia-plena-Dominus-tecum* . . .'

Even Rambouillet was more cheerful than this. It was pleasant, for one thing, to be greeted at the gate by Maître Claude, the porter, an acquaintance of old Paris days, who hobbled smiling out of the lodge with his cap in his hand, to open the drawbridge, so that the coach could pass through. It was agreeable, too, to get out of the cold: their cousins' house, though even older and less convenient in some respects than La Louppe, was richly and comfortably furnished. There were heavy stuff curtains hanging at all the windows, and soft woven carpets covered the floors. The Rambouillets, by no means millionaires, were nevertheless a good deal better off than anybody else in the family.

There were not, unfortunately, nearly enough fires lighted, and Magdelon remembered, as they followed a lackey down the long, vault-like entrance hall, that Cousin de Rambouillet had never been able to stand being near any kind of heat. Even the sun's rays were said to be too violent for the extraordinary delicacy of her skin: when exposed to their influence, she maintained — and the doctors at length had reluctantly agreed with her — that her blood could be seen to boil in her veins.

The Marquise was in her room, the lackey told them, but would see them later at dinner. Meanwhile, Madame de Montausier would receive the ladies and conduct them to their chamber.

A tall, sallow, scrawny-shouldered woman rustled out of an antechamber at the end of the hall. She was wearing an unbecoming green taffeta house-dress and black lace mitts on her hands, to ward off the cold; and when she caught sight of her guests she screwed up her slanting dark eyes and gave two small screams of ladylike rapture.

'My dears!' she exclaimed, in a high, toneless voice. 'What a pleasure! I bid you both heartily welcome. We are furiously glad to see you.'

Cousin Julie kissed Aunt de Marville's hand, and pressed a hard, perfunctory peck on each of Magdelon's cheeks. 'My mother,' it seemed, 'was in bed. . . . No, not ill, only resting. They themselves had arrived but four days ago, and at *her* age, one mustn't forget, all dis-

placements were cruelly exhausting. Besides, she had not been at
Rambouillet since before Papa's death — no, not since the winter of
'forty-nine — only fancy! One could imagine what painful emotions
were stirred by revisiting these scenes of the past. Julie herself had
thought it unwise for her parent to make the effort. 'But you know
my mother: she's nothing if not determined! And she's been saying
for years she wanted to see Rambouillet once more before she died.
. . . As for me,' added Madame de Montausier, lowering her voice
and casting down her eyes with a self-conscious air, 'I should really
be laid up, myself. It was only a week ago that I had the misfortune . . . Well, my dears, I don't put it in words, but you'll follow me
when I say there were hopes. . . . One had prayed that Marie-Julie
was to be blessed with a brother. . . .'

Magdelon glanced in bewilderment at her cousin, whose age, by
the kindest computation, could not be a day under eight-and-forty,
and decided that Julie had not improved since last they had met. . . .
That old maid! . . . Why, she had been well past thirty-five when she
married Monsieur de Montausier — after a courtship of thirteen
years, too: not even the long-winded romances of Mademoiselle de
Scudéry could supply a more astounding case of fidelity! — and most
people, Maman always said, considered it a miracle she'd had even
Marie-Julie . . . without being silly enough to pretend that another
. . . Oh, well, let her pretend, if she wanted to!

Madame de Montausier led the travellers to a large, tastefully
furnished room, hung with tapestries depicting pastoral scenes from
the novel *Astrée*, and blue velvet curtains embroidered in gold thread.
In the doorway she curtsied with a supple grace that recalled the
days when she had been famous as the best dancer at court, and said,
in her high, toneless voice: 'Till seven o'clock, my cousins, in the
Grand Saloon.'

'What a charming woman!' cried Aunt de Marville, directly the
door had closed on their hostess's back. 'My dear, *there's* a model of
elegant manners to set any young girl of good family!'

Magdelon perversely did not answer; she made a show of looking
out the window at the dusky snow-clad park.

Dinner turned out to be surprisingly good, in spite of the gloomy
prognostications of Madame de la Louppe. It was served in the great
hall, which was also hung with tapestries and, though fireless, not so
cold as Magdelon had feared.

The Marquise de Rambouillet was already in her place when her
guests were shown in. She sat enthroned in a high-backed oak chair,
its arms carved to represent a pair of snarling griffins, which stood
on a small platform about the middle of the table.

She held out a very white hand, blue-veined and laden with diamond rings; smiled sweetly, not only with her lips, but also with her

dark, wise, heavy-lidded eyes; and asked them how they did in a voice like a violin.

No one would have guessed that Cousin de Rambouillet was sixty-seven years old. She told everybody her age; indeed, she was rather proud of it. And why not? — when her beautiful face was almost unlined, her ash-brown hair as abundant as ever! True, its colour was due now to something out of a bottle; her mouth, also, was artificially reddened; her head and hands trembled ever so slightly in repose. But there was fire still in her eyes, a store of untapped energy in her voice. She held herself as erect as a queen — after all, she was treated like one! — and in the flattering candlelight of the great hall she looked actually younger than the attenuated Julie. Only her gown, a brocaded satin of the fashionable shade known as 'dead leaf,' trimmed with quantities of Flemish lace, betrayed, by the long, stiff lines in which the bodice was cut, that its wearer had belonged to the court of Marie de Médicis.

During dinner Madame de Rambouillet plied her little cousin assiduously with questions concerning her tastes and pursuits, by no means in the usual perfunctory manner of an elder relative addressing a very young girl. She never interrupted, paid careful attention to Magdelon's replies, and seemed to be much interested in everything the latter said. One had to steel oneself resolutely against the assaults of this extraordinarily compelling charm by remembering that its possessor was not really listening at all: she was merely following a formula. She had asked Magdelon these very same questions the last time they had met, and doubtless would repeat them the next.

Cousin de Rambouillet appeared to be especially pleased to hear about Maman's plan of sending Magdelon to spend the winter in Paris.

'I am only sorry not to be there, myself, for the moment,' she said, 'though as it's years since I've been to court, I doubt whether I could be of much use to you. Julie, here, would be very much better; but unfortunately, she's off in a fortnight to join her husband at Angoulême. My youngest daughter, Clarisse, is in town, though — perhaps you remember her?'

Magdelon said cheerfully that she did, very well — omitting to add that they had loathed each other on sight.

'I shall write to Clarisse by tomorrow's post, to tell her to call upon you at your sister's,' continued the Marquise, with a nod of her stately head. 'Madam, my cousin' — this to Aunt de Marville — 'you do not taste of the fish? It's only a carp boiled in white wine, at this season all one can manage to get in the country; but I fancy the chef prepares it quite well. Is there anything else you'd prefer?'

'Oh, no, thank you! No, no, indeed! I'm sure it's delicious! I mean, madam, this will do very nicely,' cried Aunt de Marville, flushing all over her round little face.

She hastily helped herself to the carp, choked on a crumb of bread, and subsided into an awestricken silence.

Cousin de Rambouillet herself seemed to eat scarcely anything. She nibbled a morsel of cheese with languor, and from time to time sipped a little of the old very rare Burgundy that stood in a handsome Venetian cut-glass decanter in front of her place at table. But she was solicitous of her guests' appetites, and pressed a succession of tempting dishes on them with hospitable insistence. Her manners were so exquisitely polite that they bordered on the insincere. About Madame de Montausier's there could be no doubt: they went definitely over the border. She had become a kind of elegant caricature of her mother. With *her*, civility had been aggravated to the proportions of a disease. During the whole of the meal she poured forth a string of extravagant compliments addressed impartially to both their guests. She praised their clothes, their looks, their wit, their charm; vowed that Magdelon would be a colossal success at court, and archly rallied Aunt de Marville, who had already buried two husbands, on the probability of her securing a third, till the poor lady was speechless with confusion.

As soon as dinner was over Cousin de Rambouillet, leaning on a shepherd's crook — more, one felt, because she thought it looked picturesque than because she needed its support — trailed her way into a smaller room adjoining the dining-hall, where a fire had been laid. She herself sought an alcove at the end of the room farthest from the fire, and settled herself on the bed, with a robe of bear's fur, which she said was a present from Marie-Louise de Gonzague, Queen of Poland, across her feet. Cousin Julie, with the air of performing a religious rite of immense significance, solemnly swathed her mother in a number of shawls, until the latter somewhat resembled a cocoon.

'I become deaf on Saint Martin's Day,' remarked the Marquise, with a deprecating smile, 'and only recover my hearing at Easter.'

Cousin Julie and Aunt de Marville, to whom the little jest had long been familiar, smiled conventionally as they seated themselves on either side of the bed and toasted their toes on the foot-warmers a lackey had placed before their chairs. They then produced their needles and tapestrywork. Magdelon, feeling slightly superfluous, curled up in a corner of the divan in front of the fire. There were several new books on the table beside her, but she was not a great reader at any time and, in any case, was too tired now to consider them.

The elder ladies had begun to gossip. They talked about people they had known long ago, many of whom were now dead. Cousin de

Rambouillet, who had made her début at the court of Henri IV, had known Paris society under three reigns. Her memory was remarkable. She had none of Madame de la Louppe's inclinations towards a visionary communication with the past, but she spoke about those who were gone as if they were still there. Her husband, her son Pisani, Mademoiselle Paulet, her dearest friend; Voiture, the poet, and scores of others passed in review while she talked, as vivid and human as they had been in life.

Magdelon, who had known none of them, laid her head back in her nest by the fire. The heat, her fatigue, the rich, heavy dinner, combined to make her feel drowsy. She yawned several times; then, as her aunt and her cousins seemed not to have noticed, pillowed her head on a cushion, and presently fell fast asleep.

When she opened her eyes again, some minutes later, the ladies were still talking, but the subject of their conversation appeared to have shifted. Their voices, instead of being droning and measured, were, though even lower than before, now eagerly excited. Listening, yet half asleep, Magdelon's attention was caught by her own name, and her sister's, uttered in a dramatic *sotto voce* by Cousin Julie. . . . 'Magdelaine . . . buzz-buzz . . .' Then 'Magdelaine' again and 'Catherine-Henriette' (that was Cateau) and 'What their mother can be thinking of . . .'

Cousin de Rambouillet said something in so inaudible a tone that Magdelon failed to get it; but it must have been 'Hush! She may hear you!' because Aunt de Marville replied at once: 'No, no, she's sleeping! Pray do go on!'

Then Cousin Julie began to speak, in a hoarse, emphatic whisper quite unlike her usual purring soprano: she hissed as venomously as the curling tongues of flame in the fireplace at Magdelon's feet.

'Well,' she said, 'you needn't, my cousin, say anything you choose not to admit. But my mother and I aren't fools: naturally we know as well as you do why you're taking Magdelaine to Paris. The girl's a great age already — quite one-and-twenty, for all she's so simple; and husbands aren't found, we imagine, growing like apples in the orchards of Normandy. No, no — but that's all right; that's none of our business. What *is* our business is to warn you of what lies ahead of you, for, from what you've been saying, I don't believe you have the faintest idea of the true situation. All I can say is, I should not dream of allowing any daughter of mine to live at the Olonnes'. Why, their house is no better than a gambling saloon — if not something very much worse! I tell you, Monsieur de Montausier and I went there one day last winter to call, out of pure kindness and family feeling — and Catherine-Henriette wasn't even at home!'

'Why, then, how do you know ———' Aunt de Marville was beginning; but Julie cut her short with an unaccustomed lack of ceremony.

'Wait till you hear: the Count *was!* We walked upstairs and found — well, I know not how to tell you! Mixed the company was, decidedly mixed! When I say that Madame de Choisy was the best of the women in the room, you can guess what I mean; for we all know how little she stands for in the community.... But the *men!* There they all were, a crowd of the worst idlers at court — Gramont, Saint-Evremond, Bussy-Rabutin, the Commander de Souvré and his nephew Boisdauphin — you know the set I mean. Freethinkers, steeped in vice up to their necks, every one of 'em! They hardly looked up when we entered, they were glued so fast to their card-tables. Olonne, they said, was in the kitchen, helping the chef prepare a mushroom sauce for supper. Someone sent for him to tell him we were there; and in he came, as cool and smiling as you please, with his coat white with flour — he'd not even stopped to wash his hands! I'm informed, on the best authority, that all he does, from one year's end to the other, is play reversi, feed half the town, and waste his cooks' time inventing entrées!'

'My dear,' said the Marquise gently, 'that's not quite fair. You know he did try to get the post of captain in the King's Light Horse Troop.'

'Well, what of that? Because he didn't get it, what did he do but send the Cardinal such an impudent note he's forbidden the court for a year for his pains! His Eminence showed me the letter himself; I blushed to read it and to think that the writer was a family connection!... Then, after that, out of pure pique, he resigns from his regiment. Monsieur de Montausier did his best to prevent it, but the young fool wouldn't listen to him. Think of it! Finished! Ruined! His career gone up in smoke before he is thirty! And it's his wife's fault quite as much as his own. If she'd a spark of ambition in her make-up, this could never have happened. When I said so to Catherine-Henriette, begged her — with tears in my eyes, positively! — to try to use her influence with her husband before it was too late, she only smiled — you know that irritating way she has of smiling and saying nothing — and when I pressed her for an answer, all I could get out of her was "Influence? My dear, I haven't any!"'

Aunt de Marville clucked like an anxious hen, and shook her head in perplexity.

'Poor Cateau! Yes, we knew — but, after all, that wasn't criminal of her.'

Cousin de Rambouillet sighed and said gravely: 'Madam, I fear there's more to it than that. Pray, my daughter, continue.'

'More! I should think there was more!' exclaimed Julie, almost breathless with spite. 'She's twenty times worse than Olonne! Catherine-Henriette may say what she pleases; she may even be

speaking the truth when she declares she has no influence over her
husband — but she has plenty of influence over other people's!
Half the men in Paris are in love with her. Why, I don't know —
she doesn't lift a finger to attract 'em; she's the most indolent creature alive. One never sees her at the Louvre; the Queen must think
it very strange, I'm afraid. . . . But the crowds of gallants that follow
her wherever she goes! Why, she's made a court all her own! As far
as I can make out, she has no women friends at all. But men buzz
round her morning, noon, and night — I can't think why, really!'

'My dear,' said her mother, 'Catherine-Henriette is a very beautiful woman.'

'Beautiful? Fiddlesticks!' said Julie. 'Oh, well, that may be' —
Magdelon knew without looking precisely how her cousin's sallow
face was drawn up into creases as she pronounced this verdict. 'Not
my style, of course. Still I'm willing to admit she has a good figure,
and her complexion's not bad, considering the late hours she keeps.
But you can't tell me it's her looks alone that makes her success.
And it certainly can't be her wit. She never glances at a book, nor
makes a clever remark, that I've heard of. In fact, she only opens
her mouth to laugh at some silly thing other people have said!'

'Perhaps that, in itself, has a certain originality,' suggested Cousin de Rambouillet; but Julie would not listen to her.

'No, no! It's not for her beauty, nor for her mind — for I'm sure
she has none, to speak of — that she has such a vogue. What the
secret of her attraction is, I don't pretend to explain. But I've my
own ideas on the subject.'

'My dear madam' — Aunt de Marville's voice sounded puzzled
and distressed — 'do you mean to insinuate ——'

'My dear madam, I insinuate nothing. I merely give you the
facts: you may draw what conclusions you please from them.'

'We need not be unduly alarmed,' said Cousin de Rambouillet
tactfully. 'Catherine-Henriette is a little imprudent, that is all.
No doubt it will correct itself with time.'

'But then,' Julie continued, with horrid relish, 'her gowns, her
jewels, her terrible extravagance! I know she received a very large
dowry; larger, indeed, than her mother could afford; the Count,
besides, is the eldest son of a wealthy man. But really, my dear, to
spend what she does on her clothes! Why, they say she never even
uses the same pair of gloves twice! And some of her toilets are
frightfully extreme. Last year, for instance, in the royal ballet —
it was *The Wedding of Peleus and Thetis*, an exquisite thing of Benserade's: you must have heard tell of it, even in Normandy — when
she appeared as Melpomene, muse of tragedy, her costume alone
cost quite five thousand francs. Did you ever *hear* —? And the way
it was cut — well, all I can say is, very little indeed was left to the

imagination. I did all I could to keep her from wearing it. Yes, and Monsieur de Montausier did all *he* could, too. He went to her after the dress rehearsal and spoke to her about it, naturally in the very *nicest* way. . . . But she did nothing but laugh, in that senseless manner of hers; and though he did succeed in making her promise to think the matter over, in the end she wore the dress, after all, just as I knew she intended to do from the beginning. It was the scandal of the evening. How the men stared! How the women whispered and giggled behind their fans! I didn't know *where* to look! And what the Queen thought, I can't bear to imagine! You know how exceedingly correct she is.'

Cousin Julie paused to take breath, and to let the weight of her accusations produce their full effect. There was a short silence. Then Cousin de Rambouillet said, with an air of deliberate tolerance:

'We mustn't blame the poor child too much. After all, she's very young yet — how old? Not more than twenty-two or three, I fancy — and we should remember the unfortunate bringing-up she has had. Her father died when she was little more than a baby, and my Cousin de la Louppe is an agreeable woman, but lax, very lax! From the time they were able to walk both girls were allowed to do exactly as they pleased. No proper supervision at all, and no education worth mentioning, if we except those two years at the convent in Caen. Ah, if Marie had been willing to take my advice, she'd have left them there permanently! In these troubled times a religious life is the happiest solution for girls of good family. Look at my three blessed little nuns!'

But this was more than even Aunt de Marville was able to accept with equanimity. After all, she had had quite as much to do with her nieces' bringing-up as their own mother; and her affection for Cateau and Magdelon was stronger than her timidity in the presence of the awe-inspiring Marquise.

'Madam,' said Aunt de Marville boldly, 'my sister-in-law's case is different from your own. You have five daughters; Marie has but two. And thanks be to God, He's seen fit to give them beauty enough to make possible marriages second to none, though their dowries may not be so large as some girls' I might mention, who've no pretensions to looks.'

'Well,' said Julie maliciously — for this was an obvious reflection on the Mesdemoiselles de Rambouillet — 'be that as it may, my last word to you is this: if you want a husband for Magdelaine, don't look for him in the Olonnes' drawing-room! It's no place for a young, inexperienced girl. What the men there are in search of, I don't presume to say. But it's certainly not a wife!'

'Ah,' sighed Cousin de Rambouillet, 'Paris is sadly changed since I was a girl! The tone of the salon has altered, I fear very much for

the worse. In my day elegant conversation was considered an indispensable art, both for men and for women; but young people no
longer seem to care for it.'

'In short,' Julie concluded, 'all they think of nowadays is gambling and guzzling and flirting, from one day's end to the next.'

'What is society coming to?'

'Holy Mother, madam!' cried Aunt de Marville. 'There I agree
with you. What, indeed?'

Both elder ladies made ticking sounds with their tongues.

One of the logs in the fire broke in two and fell into the grate with a
shower of sparks.

Magdelon, startled, sat up suddenly, blinking her eyes; and Cousin Julie dropped her tapestry-needle with an affected little shriek.

'Jesus! The child has been listening to all we've been saying!'

'I assure you, my cousin, I have not heard a word.'

'Poor darling! She's been sound asleep,' said Cousin de Rambouillet. 'It's high time she was tucked up in bed. Come, love,
give me a kiss and bid me good-night. Oh, what a warm, rosy cheek!
Just think, dear, this time tomorrow you'll be in Paris with Catherine-Henriette!'

'Sweet child!' murmured Julie. 'Do give her my love!'

'Promise me one thing, little Magdelaine,' said Cousin de Rambouillet, fixing the young girl with her grave, heavy-lidded dark
gaze. 'You will find yourself in the city surrounded by many temp-
tations. Catherine-Henriette, you know, belongs to a very gay circle.
But remember this: while much is permitted a young married
woman, a well brought-up girl who is proud of her family, and wishes
her family to be proud of her, will hold her virtue — nay, even the
report of her virtue — above rubies. Need I say more? For you, my
child, are as clever as you are pretty, are you not? And you are going — of that I am assured — to be as wise as you are clever: isn't
that so?'

'But, my cousin, *of course!*' said Magdelon, with wide, wondering
eyes.

Chapter III

MAGDELON AND HER AUNT DID NOT SEE COUSIN DE RAMBOUILLET again. She was still sleeping when they left next morning for Paris.

Julie appeared to bid them good-bye, looking bilious and ill-tempered, but with manners more honeyed than ever. She was accompanied by her daughter, Marie-Julie, an undersized child of nine with a hoarse voice and a pert expression in her big dark eyes, which would have resembled her grandmother's had they not been, alas! slightly crossed. (One must remember that detail, to report to Maman.)

Little Mademoiselle de Montausier was as tiresomely spoilt as the only child of rather elderly parents could hardly help being. She talked incessantly, with her mouth full of fragments of a sweet sticky bun she was munching; made embarrassing personal remarks, and insisted, though neither of the guests displayed the least eagerness to hear them, on reciting some verses about her pet parakeet, which she said she had made up herself.

The verses, unfortunately, were quite clever.

Cousin Julie smiled proudly while this impromptu performance was in progress. When it was finished she kissed her small daughter on both cheeks and said: 'That was charming, my dear. Now run along and set about your tasks, and Mother will join you as soon as she can.'

After that, it seemed politic not to delay one's departure any longer than necessary.

During the second half of the journey Aunt de Marville was as silent as she had been during the first half. She prayed harder than ever — 'probably for Cateau,' Magdelon conjectured — and held her handkerchief to her face as if suffering from cold.

Magdelon sat quietly in her place and thought for a very long time about her sister. She had said nothing to Aunt de Marville about the conversation she had overheard the night before in the drawing-room at Rambouillet. What was the use? To begin with, she would have had to confess she had eavesdropped, which everyone knew was dishonourable. True, she had not meant to do it, but Magdelon was not sure whether that lightened the offence — erase it, nothing could. Furthermore, out of loyalty to Cateau, she shrank from discussing the latter's misdeeds.

When she came to reflect on the matter Magdelon decided that, in spite of all the hateful hints Cousin Julie had dropped, she had been unable to lodge any serious complaint. Cateau was extravagant; but there was nothing wicked about that. She could not help it if men fell in love with her. Men had always fallen in love with her since she'd been old enough to talk; Julie herself had admitted that Cateau did nothing to make them. And, certainly, she could not be held responsible for her husband's shortcomings.

On the other hand, Magdelon felt she knew very little about what had been happening lately to her sister. She loved her more than anyone else in the world; she knew that Cateau loved her in the same way. For eighteen years they had not been separated a single day; they had grown so close to each other that they were almost like one person. Even Cateau's marriage, at first, had not seemed to make any difference. She had left them for only twenty-four hours.

There had been one moment of awful embarrassment between the sisters, the day that she returned, looking, strangely, much the same as before. Alone in their bedroom, Magdelon fiddled with the bows and buttons on her dress, and said a great many things that didn't matter at all. Finally, casting down her eyes with a shame-faced air and blushing furiously, she had ventured the question: 'What is it like, my sister — being married, I mean?' And Cateau, also looking away, and scuffing the floor with the toe of her shoe as busily as if her life depended on it, had answered quite fiercely: 'Simply horrid! Now *what* are you going to wear to Mademoiselle's concert tomorrow?'

After that, their relations continued as happily as ever. She and Magdelon had gone on sharing their room, their bed, their prayers, their meals, just as they had always done.

But when the Count came back from the war, and Maman an Magdelon left for La Louppe, the old life had broken abruptly two.

Cateau and Magdelon had been overcome by grief when the came to say good-bye for good. They cried and clung to each and Cateau exclaimed again and again, through her tears mind you write, darling — *mind* you write! And I'll do every week, without fail!'

But, of course, she had not done so. Magdelon had no pected it. Cateau was, indeed, very nearly incapable of name. How she had toiled and suffered, those tw the convent in Caen, over the weekly epistles the them to send to their parents! In the end, as often lon composed her own and Cateau's as well: h guessed? ... Cateau, her sister was sure, was mu the two: she could talk by the hour, gaily, ch

liantly — but she simply was not able to put her feelings ⸤
Magdelon understood, and was sympathetic; for she ha⸤
labour of writing, herself. In fact, neither of the girls was⸤
least literary. They seldom read books, never wrote verses, th⸤
bouts rimés and the fashionable enigmas a waste of time, and⸤
no opinions worth quoting on the rival merits of Voiture and B⸤
serade. Cousin de Rambouillet threw up her hands in despair. .⸤
Who would have guessed that relations of *hers* . . .? But Maman ha⸤
not appeared to take it to heart: after all, what did it matter, as⸤
long as her daughters never lacked a partner for the sarabande,
whether they knew the difference between a distich and a tristich,
or even thought that Corneille was a kind of bird? . . .

Since Magdelon's return to the country she had received three or
four short scribbled notes from Cateau, usually at Christmas time
or on her birthday, and invariably accompanied by handsome
presents of perfume or laces or jewelry. But of her life they told
nothing that could not be ascertained by any subscriber to the
Court Gazette. The Comte and Comtesse d'Olonne had dined at
Monsieur A.'s, supped at Monsieur B.'s, spent a week in the country
at Monsieur C.'s. Cateau had danced in the royal ballet, which
was pronounced 'delicious.' So were Boisrobert's new comedy, the
sermons of the Abbé de Roquette, and the terrace Alonne had designed for the court of their house in the rue Neuve-Saint-Augustin.
Of her feelings she seldom spoke.

Magdelon was aware that her replies were probably equally
unsatisfactory. She wrote a little more often because she had a
great deal more time, covering two or three sheets, every few
months, with her painstaking, very black writing — but then, she
had even less to report. Four calves had been born last week. The
vicar was coming to dine tomorrow. Maman's new steward was
having a quarrel with Mahaut. . . .

So now, though she was sure they had gone on, all the time they
had been apart, loving each other as dearly as ever, they had not
been able to tell each other so, nor, indeed, to say anything they
wanted to say for so long that it was almost as strangers they would
meet. As persons they had ceased to exist for one another, temporarily: they were only *ideas* of persons.

As this thought struck her Magdelon fidgetted in her seat and began patting the ends of her curls under the mauve velvet hood with
nervous fingers. Two years . . . why, two years were an eternity!
More than likely, Cateau was no longer wearing even one dress
Magdelon had seen her in.

This, somehow, was the most disturbing possibility that had
curred to her yet.

Now they were almost in Paris. For some time, dull as the day

was, it had been visible on the northern horizon, a grey jumble of towers and church spires, with its background of low green hills spotted with windmills. The highroad began to be filled with vehicles of all sorts; Célie, whose first trip to the city this was, hung open-mouthed at the window, pointing and exclaiming in spite of Aunt de Marville's frowns and disapproving shakes of the head. . . . 'Jesus, madam! There's a lady shut up in a box being carried like a parcel, for all the world as if she had no feet of her own! See the coach painted silver, and the lovely white horses with feathers on their heads, just like madam in her court costume! And oh, the tiny little donkeys, with baskets on their backs, all in a row! Did you ever! Oh, dear me! I don't know which way to look!'

The rue du Faubourg-Saint-Jacques, the old Roman road from the south, by which they were entering, ran for miles through the gardens and vineyards that belonged to the great religious houses of Paris. One by one they passed them: the Feuillantines, the Ursulines, Great Carmelites, Port Royal des Champs, the Val de Grâce, and many another. Magdelon shuddered at sight of their massive stone buildings, austere in the cold light of the short January afternoon. Even the gardens, pleasant enough in summer, looked drab at this time of year. . . . How lucky she was, not to be shut up behind those grim walls like many girls she had known, no less pretty and lively than she and Cateau! Nowadays most parents turned their superfluous daughters into nuns, whether the latter showed signs of vocations or not. Magdelon had met numbers of them, in her visits to various convents, in Maman's wake, or her aunt's, to look up poor dear Cousin This or poor dear Cousin That. These ladies seemed quite resigned to their fate. They were invariably cheerful and chatty, full of gossip about the great world outside, though apparently content to remain in the small one they had made for themselves. From such a world, it was but a step, one gathered, to heaven. Death seemed matter-of-fact, easy, desirable even, void of all terror. . . . 'But oh,' thought Magdelon, 'how can they bear to wait for it to come, when they know that all the time, at their very doors, lies — *Paris!*'

They were inside the gates at last, rattling along over the cobblestones in the midst of a screaming, jostling mob. Magdelon had forgotten how noisy and crowded the city was. She, too, hung at the window, as much excited as Célie herself, straining her eyes for familiar landmarks as they forced their passage through the aggressive lines of carriages and sedan-chairs, men on horseback, and pedestrians. Old Robin, though no doubt inwardly quaking, was steering with skill and aplomb.

Now they were on the Pont Neuf, the very centre of Paris life. Here the crowds were worse than ever, undeterred by the fine, cold rain that had begun to fall. Beggars and pedlars, jugglers and street singers, clamoured competitively for attention. The rabble was filthy; the din they made, deafening; the wares of the pedlars, tawdry; the songs of the singers, unspeakable.

But Magdelon drew a long breath of joyous anticipation. If this were not life, then what *was?*

Suddenly, just as they were passing the water-clock of La Samaritaine, Robin reined in the horses, and brought them to a full stop with a jerk that sent Aunt de Marville spinning forward to her knees on the floor of the carriage. What could be the matter?... Célie was crossing herself ... Dear Lord, why had she been in such haste to leave home?

Magdelon, peering forward to see what was holding them back, perceived that the way was blocked by a heavy gilt coach drawn by six coal-black horses with scarlet plumes on their heads. Whose it was, she could not tell; for the men on the box were wearing a livery that was strange to her.

The driver, purple with rage, was shouting to Robin to back up his horses, to make way there for Monsieur the Maréchal. Robin, however, held his ground obstinately. He was not easily moved at any time, and he knew that, in the circumstances, it would be impossible for him to turn: they were almost across the bridge, while the Maréchal's coach was just approaching it from the Quai de la Mégisserie: the latter, not Robin, would be obliged to retreat.

The stream of foot-passengers flowing past them, shouting conflicting directions, now to this side, now to that, only added to the confusion. A bird-catcher, upon whose shoulder perched a red-and-blue-and-yellow macaw with a very long tail, pushed his head in at the window of the La Louppes' carriage, laughing and saying something in an unintelligible dialect. The bird began to laugh, too, and uttered a piercing shriek in a voice so nearly human that Célie, with a moan, sank in a heap and covered her face with her hands.

At the height of the uproar the curtains of the big gilt coach were parted hastily, and between them appeared a head so fearsome that even Magdelon quailed, feeling that all must surely be lost. It was a handsome head, but a beast's rather than a man's: huge and shaggy, with rough, curly black hair and beard, and eyes as fiercely rolling as a bull's. Upon his matted crown was set a hat of yellow velvet, trimmed with plumes of the same scarlet as those his horses were wearing, which trembled as he shook his great hairy fist and roared in a voice of thunder: 'Oddsblood! Who dares block the road of the Maréchal de la Ferté, Governor of His Majesty's Province of Lorraine?'

Immediately a silence fell over the crowd. No one dared speak a word; even Robin and his antagonist stopped yelling at one another.

Madame de Marville, blanched and mumbling, was incapable of rallying her forces to make a reply. To tell the truth, Magdelon was almost as frightened as her aunt. However, mustering what courage she had left, she leaned forward, pushed back her hood, and thrust her face out of the window.

'Sir,' she began, in a quavering tone, 'I know not how ——'

But she was unable to proceed with her tremulous explanation. The Maréchal swept off his hat with the scarlet plumes, rolled his untamed animal's eyes more wildly than ever, and smiled ... at least, Magdelon supposed it must have been meant for a smile: one could be sure of nothing through that dark, tangled forest of beard. He then bellowed an order to his coachman. The latter promptly pulled in his horses, and started backing them; the great gilt coach, creaking and swaying, slowly reversed its direction, to the accompaniment of a burst of approving cheers from the crowd.

Before they realized it the danger was past. Robin whipped up his bays, and they trotted off smartly, not without a final grotesque salute from the bull-man, which Magdelon was far too much startled to acknowledge.

For some minutes the three women were speechless with emotion.

Fortunately, after this threatened accident, all went smoothly. It seemed no time before they were in the rue de Richelieu, skirting the long walled gardens of the Palais Royal, where the exiled Queen of England lived. A little farther on they came to the Palais Mazarin, the Cardinal's house; here Robin turned off into the rue Neuve-Saint-Augustin.

The street was a new one, not much built up as yet. Stately hotels surrounded by spacious gardens lined it on either side. To the left, at the back, rose the hill of the Butte Saint-Roch, crowned by twin windmills looming mysteriously through violet mist. In the fading light the snow that clung to their arms looked violet, too. Though it was only the middle of the afternoon, dusk was already folding it over the city.

The Hôtel d'Olonne was not hard to find: there was a row of carriages and sedan-chairs outside the entrance, and a blaze of light streaming from every window.

Without knowing how it happened, Magdelon found herself and her boxes deposited at the door. Aunt de Marville, it seemed, was not coming in, after all. Friends, she declared, were expecting her at the convent of the Daughters of Holy Mary in Chaillot. She would drive in to town tomorrow to see how her nieces did. Moreover, Cateau appeared to be having a party. ... Here Aunt de Marville contracted her lips, turned up her eyes, and shrugged her shoulders as only a relative could.

The coach drove away down the darkening street, leaving Magde-

lon alone on the threshold, full of feverish excitement. There was
no time any longer to wonder or hesitate: she was *there!*

Before she could raise her hand to knock the door was opened by
the Olonnes' Swiss porter in mulberry livery trimmed with gold....
'Mademoiselle...? You desire...?'

Past a double line of lackeys, bowing low before her — up a
flight of marble stairs (how her heels clicked on the polished surface!) — Magdelon was led. She paused at the top, partly for
breath, partly because she hardly dared proceed farther. She was
standing at the entrance to the Grand Saloon, which was already
so full of people that it seemed impossible to squeeze in even one
more.

It was like looking at a scene in a play, where the stage was so
crowded and lively that one had scant attention to spare for the
background. Magdelon had a confused impression of much white
paint and gold leaf; of scores of candles, winking like stars in their
sconces; and of a great sun of a crystal chandelier blazing in a pink-
and-blue sky full of flying cherubs. Tall gilded Venetian mirrors on
the walls gave back the light, and so multiplied the figures of the
actors that, to the bewildered senses of the young visitor, it appeared
that half Paris must be assembled in the Olonnes' drawing-room.

At first sight, Magdelon thought there were no women present.
Then she saw that there were two of them, standing together in
front of the fire: one, dark and rather stout, with a turned-up nose
and twinkling eyes; the other, pale and plain, with protruding teeth
and a wealth of lustreless auburn curls. Both were waving small
gauzy fans like captive moths and laughing at something a fat old
man, with a face as red as his satin suit, had just said.

Men, however, were everywhere — all kinds of men: soldiers in
uniform, with capes and spurs; languid gallants, beplumed and be-
ribboned, with curling tresses; a mincing abbé or two, in sober black
coquettishly relieved by lace. Men laughing, men talking, men eating, men drinking, men playing cards, men walking aimlessly up and
down, trying to make up their minds whether to laugh or talk or
eat or drink or play, themselves. Above all, men swarming about
the alcove at the end of the room farthest from the door. Magdelon
could not see the centre of attraction of that eager, excited little
knot; but she did not need to see, in order to guess what it might be:
Cateau's loud laugh, oddly mirthless and jarring, had not changed
with the years....

But how to get to Cateau? How make oneself heard above that
happy hum of voices? — how dare breast the endless, shifting sea of
faces?... Magdelon, still poised for flight on the threshold, glanced
wistfully at each in turn, hoping to find at least one that was familiar. No one paid any heed to her; no one seemed to know who

she was, nor care that she had arrived. Even the lackeys had
melted away.

Magdelon's lip was trembling; two big tears gathered in her
frightened dark eyes, waiting till she turned her head to roll down
her cheeks. But at this moment the merriment was redoubled; it
attained such proportions that it broke like a wave and fell into
pieces, in a series of small explosions, that rolled away to the four
corners of the room. At its impact the company divided in two;
thus bisected, it gave Magdelon a sudden glimpse of the alcove at
the end of the white-and-gold saloon. This alcove was almost entirely filled by a gilt-and-crimson bed; on the bed, propped up by
cushions, a lady was lying. The lady was tall and slim, dressed all
in gold, with a long train gracefully disposed in gleaming metallic
folds so as to cover her feet. But neither her dress, nor the blaze on
the hearth, nor the gilded walls, nor the candles in their sconces —
no, not even the lights of the great, glittering sun-chandelier itself
— were as golden as her hair, which, falling in a bright cascade to
her waist, shone with so triumphant a radiance that it appeared to
be the primary source of all the illumination in the room.

Five or six courtiers were crowded into the limited space in front
of the bed, all of them saying something at once to try to capture
the lady's attention. And the lady was laughing loudly, showing
her very white teeth as she laughed, and tossing back her head with
complete disregard for decorum. Could it be...? It was so like —
and still so unlike... Yes, after all, it *was*...

Magdelon's heart was pounding; she felt suffocated with emotion, and quite unable either to move from the spot where she stood,
stupidly staring at this luminous apparition, or to call out, for her
voice died away in her throat.

Suddenly the lady stopped laughing — when she stopped, everyone stopped — turned her head quickly — as she turned, everyone
turned, too — and caught sight of Magdelon. She then tumbled
off the bed, picked up her train, made a little rush across the room,
and flung herself into the latter's arms.

'Darling!' cried Cateau, in a high, mewing voice her sister had
never heard before. 'You've come at last! Oh, I thought you would
never get here!'

'And I thought,' said Magdelon, looking up with a tremulous
smile, 'that you'd never know I had come!'

After that, the spell was broken: Magdelon, too, became part of
the play. Cateau kissed her a dozen times, and exclaimed, over and
over — still in that odd new voice — how happy she was. (It was
a little puzzling, perhaps, that though her great wide-open blue
eyes gazed straight upon her sister, they did not seem to *see* her.)
Then, with a protective arm clasped round Magdelon's shoulder,

the hostess made a circle of the room and a series of introductions. She rattled off a bewildering number of names... 'The Marquise de Montglas... the Baronne de Montmorency-Fosseuse... the Comte de Bussy... the Chevalier de Gramont... the Marquis de Boisdauphin... the Marquis de Sillery... the Commander de Souvré...'

Magdelon soon stopped trying to keep them straight in her mind. She smiled at everybody, curtsied charmingly to the ladies, and said that she was very glad to find herself once more in Paris.... No, she was not tired: they had taken two days for the journey, having spent the night at Rambouillet with 'our cousin, the Marquise.'

'That old bore! Is she still living?' said Madame de Montmorency, in an audible stage-whisper. (She was the pale, plain woman with the prominent teeth, and spoke as though she had a reputation for making 'downright' remarks.)

Madame de Montglas said hastily: 'Hush!' — and there was a general ripple of laughter.

All the young men present bowed low before Mademoiselle de la Louppe, stared at her hard, and began paying her strings of flowery, quite undiscerning compliments. The Commander de Souvré, who turned out to be the fat old man in red satin, leered at her like Silenus, and took advantage of his position as an officer of the Knights of Malta to lay a benevolent hand on the young lady's head and press on her brow a kiss that smelt strongly of Burgundy.

The Abbé de Boisrobert fluttered up in a state of twittering delight. He was even older than the Commander, but his face was very prettily rouged, and his ribbons and laces were adjusted with feminine elegance.

'My dear, dear child!' said the Abbé, who managed to sound cordial in something halfway between a lisp and a squeak. 'To think that I once blessed you while you lay in your cradle! And fed you sugar-plums by the score! Well! Well! Time flies. No doubt today you could do without the blessing — but perhaps I can persuade you to let me offer you a little refreshment?'

'Thank you very much,' said Magdelon. 'Yes, I am rather hungry.'

Boisrobert disengaged his arm from that of the blond young man he had been embracing, and offered it, with a splendid flourish, to Mademoiselle de la Louppe.

As they moved away the blond young man scowled at her undisguisedly: he looked very young indeed, not more than seventeen or eighteen, and had rather flat features and sulky, opaque greenish eyes.

'The Marquis de Manicamp,' murmured Cateau rapidly — but

not as if it mattered much whether Magdelon remembered *his* name or not. 'My dear, you must be starved! Forgive me. And you've not seen Olonne yet, have you?'

'Why, no,' said Magdelon, suddenly recalling her host. 'Where is he?'

Cateau and Boisrobert looked at each other and laughed.

'Where?' said the former. 'By the buffet, of course. Where else could he be?'

The Abbé led Magdelon into the next room, followed by Cateau, who, in turn, was trailed by half the rest of the company, as though attached to her by strings.

Here they came upon a great many more people, gathered about a long table laden with all kinds of refreshments. There were tureenfuls of soup, both thick and clear; and joints of meat, hot with gravies or glacés and adorned with patterns of truffles. There were fishes and lobsters, pheasants and partridges, ortolans and plovers' eggs; mushrooms stewed in cream; mounds of bright-coloured salads; tarts and pastries in endless array; candied fruits and platters of various sweetmeats. Wines without number stood in a large silver cooler; lackeys were circulating with trays of liqueurs and warm spiced hippocras; the air was heavy with conflicting odours of good things to eat.

The Count appeared without warning at Magdelon's side, plump and smiling, proffering a glass of hippocras for her to taste.

'Welcome, my sister!' he said. 'You must take us just as you find us — potluck, as the peasants put it. I trust I'll be able to turn up something you'll fancy. Now what shall it be? The roasts, I know, have stood too long — the fish I fear's uneatable: how was the salmon, Boisdauphin? — and that rascal Saint-Evremond has just polished off the last of the peas. Sweets in the afternoon I myself consider deadly unwholesome. Dear me, I wonder *what* ——'

He tripped away on absurdly high heels to cast an anxious look at the festal board. The Comte d'Olonne was a handsome young man, almost as blond as his wife, with neat, small features modelled as delicately as porcelain, a pink, pouting mouth, and slits of eyes sunk so deep in his high cheek-bones that it was difficult to tell whether they were blue or grey.

'Don't be so fussy, Olonne,' commanded his wife. 'Magdelon's brought a fine country appetite with her to Paris: of that you may be sure. Only find her something, and quickly — it matters not what!'

'Madam, you demand the impossible,' observed an ugly little man, with bright, intelligent eyes and a huge nose defaced by a wart midway down its bridge. 'Would you have him turn traitor to the precepts he's made his rule of life?'

'I despair of his doing so, unless I can persuade *you* to turn traitor first, Saint-Evremond,' replied Cateau, 'since you know he calls you his philosopher, and if there are any rules in the world he respects, you must have made them.'

'What time is it now?' asked the Marquis de Boisdauphin, who looked like a worried small rat in court costume. He consulted a jewelled watch concealed in the laces of his collar. 'Half-past three — nay, nearly a quarter to four. I should recommend the young lady to take, at this hour — much too late to dine, still too early to sup — a small cream tart — *two* cream tarts, if her stomach demands them — with a glass of the wine of Ay, vintage of 1649, if possible, served at room temperature, or if she choose, slightly heated. But only *very* slightly.'

'Or Auvilé, if she prefers,' said Saint-Evremond. 'Or even Sillery. What matters it, so it be a good natural champagne?'

'And paid for by somebody else,' added, in a spiteful undertone, the Abbé de Boisrobert, who could not bear to lose, even momentarily, the centre of the stage, and, besides, perceived a certain irony in the fact that both gentlemen, notorious gourmets as they were, had never been known to offer so much as a biscuit to their friends.

'I disagree with you entirely,' said Olonne vigorously, who had meanwhile returned to his guest. 'I *never* heat my wine, unless it's to be mulled. Doctor Patin says ——'

'King François I had his own vineyard at Ay,' said Saint-Evremond, with equal animation, 'and according to his vintner's records, which I have carefully perused, there is no mention of his ever having drunk the wine at any but a natural temperature. The same is true of Henry VIII of England. And, if I mistake not, of Pope Leo X. On the other hand, the ancients maintained — you may find it in Horace and Petronius ——'

Magdelon burst out laughing, and threw up her hands.

'Gentlemen, gentlemen,' cried Cateau, putting her fingers to her ears, 'a truce, I beg of you! Will you stand there arguing all afternoon, while my sister starves to death?'

At this, there was a concerted rush towards the banquet table by all the young men, and Magdelon presently found her plate heaped high with dainties enough to last her a week.

She was at first slightly nonplussed to find that she was expected to eat before a semicircle of watchful, admiring eyes; but, after all, it was long past dinner-time, and she was exceedingly hungry.

While she ate Cateau sat by her side, making candid comments about some of her guests, exactly as if the latter were not in the room. . . . 'Do you remember the Montglas creature? She was a Cheverny, a cousin of Olonne's; Mademoiselle used to have her about a lot, but she's grown so fat I doubt if you'd recognize her.

I ask her here on Bussy's account — they're having an affair.....
The Montmorency's no fool — but take care of her tongue! On the
whole, she's the one woman I know who doesn't bore me to death.
Sillery's a nice little man. So's Gramont — only he cheats at piquet.
The Commander's great fun: I adore him! He's a fearful old lecher,
and gives the most marvellous supper-parties in his house at the
Temple. Olonne goes to him at least twice a week. I wish he'd
ask *me* — but he says women don't know how to eat!... Darling,
that reminds me, when you've quite finished — but don't hurry,
for Heaven's sake, take time for all you want! — whisk upstairs
and slip into an evening frock. I've a box at the Petit Bourbon
for the Italian comedy. We've missed half the long piece already,
but that's no matter: it's the farce at the end I'm dying to see. They
say it's very amusing and quite, quite ... What luck Aunt de Marville didn't stop! She'd have never ... Have you a thing fit to wear?
No, don't tell me — I know — the cramoisie velvet! Poor angel!
Never mind, it doesn't make any difference; no one looks at you at
the play. And we're supping afterwards at Madame de Bonelle's,
where it's so dark people can't possibly tell what you've got on.
But tomorrow we'll go shopping together.... There's a wonderful
woman in the rue Saint-Denis, who'll do anything to please me —
and Maman's sent me a nice little sum to spend on your clothes —
did you know?'

'No!' said Magdelon, much touched. 'Did she really? How
sweet of her!' (And how like Maman, to plan to surprise her!)

Cateau narrowed her eyes, and looked at her sister for the first
time since they had met as if she were really seeing her.

'Darling!' she said again. 'Your hair — it's all wrong! You must
let me fix it for you. One of my maids is a treasure, with the cleverest hands: she can do anything I tell her to. I'll come up with you
now, and we'll plan your coiffure together. You didn't bring Mahaut, I suppose?'

'No,' said Magdelon. 'What would have been the use? She'd
talk all the time and not do a thing.'

'Precisely,' said Cateau. 'You did perfectly right. Now, if you're
sure you won't take another cake ——'

'My dear, I couldn't!'

'Well, then, make your adieux, and we'll get away from this mob.
Oh, by the bye, say good-night to Olonne; you'll not see him again,
I dare say.'

'Why shan't I?' asked Magdelon, in surprise. 'Won't he go to
the play with us?'

'Oh, dear, no!' answered Cateau carelessly. 'He never budges
from the house, if he can help it. Besides, he's giving a medianoche
this evening, a man's affair, for the Commander.'

'Cateau!' cried Magdelon. 'After all they've had already, don't tell me they're going to eat any *more!*'

'My dear,' said Cateau, 'I see you don't know your brother-in-law. Why, they've just begun! These things that you see are only hors d'oeuvres, to help them work up an appetite. They won't start their *serious* eating till the crowd has gone. Then they'll have the table set over again, and sit there guzzling till all hours of the night. It's the same story every day, the whole winter long.'

'Dear me, don't you mind?'

'What good would it do if I did? Besides, the arrangement works well for both of us. I always know where he is — that he's happy and well taken care of — and he doesn't care where I am, as long as I get home eventually. Which, so far, I've managed to do,' concluded Cateau, rising. 'Now, dear, if you've quite finished? ... We've to call for that tiresome old Choisy, and though she's never been known to be on time, I dare say tonight, just to spite us, she'll be ready and waiting in her war-paint, on pins and needles because we're not there.'

'But,' said Magdelon, as she followed her sister back into the Grand Saloon, accompanied by their suite of cavaliers, 'Cateau, I don't quite see ... If Brother Louis is not coming, who, then, will call for us?'

Cateau swept the assembled company a splendid curtsy.

'Ladies and gentlemen, I bid you good-evening!' she said, once more in the lilting and languishing tone she seemed to have forgotten while she talked with Magdelon.

She drew the latter with her out of the room, and in the hall pressed her hand and smiled like a mischievous child.

'Hush, darling! You'll see, all in good time,' she whispered. 'My dear, I've a *lover!*'

Chapter IV

AT THE FOOT OF THE STAIRCASE CATEAU AND MAGDELON CAUGHT HOLD of each other's hands and ran up the steps as fast as they were able. This was something they had loved doing ever since they were children.

They arrived at the top breathless and laughing, without exactly knowing why.

The apartments of the Countess occupied the whole front of the second storey. They were lavishly decorated — as, indeed, the whole house was — with much gold leaf, many mirrors, magnificent tapestries, rare porcelains, and other ornaments, all disposed with perfect taste. It was more like a museum, though, than a private dwelling, Magdelon thought as she followed her sister along the hall.

'Your rooms, dear, are just opposite mine,' said Cateau, 'on the other side of the court. Olonne's on the floor below, thank goodness — no doubt to be nearer the kitchen — so there wasn't the least difficulty about arranging that. We must share our dressing-room — d'you mind?'

'I shall like it heaps better,' replied Magdelon.

In Cateau's dressing-room a fire was burning, and two maids in rose-pink dresses and frivolous lace caps were waiting to attend their mistress.

They were sisters, also, Quentine and Quinette, blue-eyed, apple-cheeked girls from the country. Their drawling Norman accents made Magdelon feel quite at home. At first she was afraid it might be impossible to tell them apart; but she soon discovered that one of them smiled without ceasing, while the other just as consistently frowned — though whether it was Quinette who was grave and Quentine who was merry, or the other way round, only time could determine.

Cateau slammed the door shut and flung herself on the couch in front of the fire.

'Now,' she said to Magdelon, 'we shall be quite, quite alone.' (This was odd: for there were Quentine and Quinette.) 'We must have a long talk,' Cateau continued, 'about Maman and Aunt de Marville, and everything at home. There are a thousand questions I am dying to ask you.'

But there were some matters of moment to be settled first. The Countess was supposed to be dressed for the evening. Suddenly, though, she decided that the gown she had on would never do, and tore it off with impatient hands; while Quinette (or Quentine?) submitted a score of others for her mistress's approval. In the end, after lamenting a great many times that — no, really, it was a shame! — she simply had *nothing* to wear, she reverted to her original choice.

Then she spent certainly half an hour in front of her looking-glass, having her golden curls brushed and perfumed and arranged by Quentine (or Quinette?), and fussing about with little boxes of Powder of Cyprus and Pommade of Florence, and flasks of virginal milk and thousand-flowers-water.

Meanwhile, Magdelon's modest box had been unpacked and its contents displayed to Cateau's critical eye. After inspecting the cramoisie velvet Cateau declared it was not good enough, even for the theatre. She proposed instead that Magdelon wear one of her own frocks, a yellow satin costume that had only just been sent home from the dressmaker's, and was to go back next day, as the bodice was a trifle too loose. But that, Cateau thought, might in this instance be an advantage, since Magdelon was, if anything, slightly plumper than herself.

The sisters had almost identical figures, high-waisted and slim as dryads, with long necks and elegantly rounded shoulders.

When Magdelon had put on the yellow satin and Quinette, frowning fiercely — it *was* Quinette, Magdelon was sure, for she had heard Quentine call her by name — had brushed out the black curls, under her mistress's expert direction, and disposed them in waves like Cateau's blonde ones, the resemblance between the two young women was seen to be extraordinary.

Quentine, who was of a sentimental turn of mind, clapped her hands and exclaimed, eyes upturned in her enthusiasm: 'Madam, the goddess of the sun and the goddess of the moon are met at last!'

'Nonsense, my girl!' retorted Cateau promptly. 'The sun's a god, not a goddess!'

But she did not look displeased at the compliment.

Magdelon would willingly have prolonged the hour indefinitely. Here in the intimacy of the dressing-room Cateau dropped the last traces of her fine lady's languor and became once more her old brisk, decisive self. She was, furthermore, bubbling with good-natured excitement over the transformation in her sister's appearance, and bent on essaying all possible refinements to add to the success of her creation. She sprayed drops of thousand-flowers-water on her ears, accentuated the arch of her eyebrows with a black pencil, and, as a finishing touch, leaned over the back of Magdelon's chair, while the latter still sat at the dressing-table, to fasten a rose from her bouquet in the gold fillet binding the lustrous dark curls.

'There!' said Cateau. 'That's much better. That's perfect, dear. Never let them frizz your hair so tightly again. You looked like Madame de Longueville, or one of those other worn-out old battle-axes of the Fronde!... Now, a necklace or not?... I think, on the whole, *not*. After all, you're not married — yet!' (But Magdelon knew that was not the real reason: she always, alas! lost every jewel she owned, sooner or later; and Cateau no doubt remembered it. It made no difference, really. She was perfectly happy without a necklace.)

To show that she was, she smiled at Cateau in the glass — and Cateau smiled back at her.

Even their smiles were exact duplicates of each other. Both had the same small heart-shaped mouths, the same even rows of very white teeth. In the flickering candlelight the two faces were so marvellously alike in every detail that it seemed as though they must belong on opposite sides of the mirror. But who was to say which was the original, which the reflected image?

Magdelon was convinced that Cateau was the most beautiful woman in France. So, indeed, was Cateau. But, to tell the truth, she thought Magdelon only a little less beautiful.

'Darling!' said Cateau. 'You're lovely!'

'So,' said Magdelon, 'are you — darling!'

They smiled at each other once more, because they could not help it, and Cateau blew a kiss with her finger-tips to their twin shining reflections.

For years afterwards, whenever Magdelon thought of her sister, the picture her mind presented to her was of Cateau as she had looked at that precise moment, leaning on the back of the chair, and laughing, because they were young and pretty and gay and glad to be together.

Scarcely had their toilets been completed before a valet knocked on the door, to say that the Marquis de Beuvron was waiting below with his carriage and begged leave to send word that if the ladies did not soon put in an appearance, the comedy would be ended.

Magdelon looked up in sudden trepidation. She had almost forgotten, in the pleasure of being alone with Cateau, that they were going out.

As they rustled through the door, which was held open for them by Lindor, the Countess's minute cherubic page-boy, Magdelon turned to her sister and whispered: 'The Marquis de Beuvron? Then *he* is your... I mean, the man who ——'

She paused, unable to finish her thought aloud.

Cateau laughed, and patted her hand consolingly.

'You mustn't mind Beuvron,' she said. 'He's a very good sort, on the whole; I don't know what I'd do without him.'

'But is he ...? You said ...'

'Of course, he's in love with me,' said Cateau composedly. 'Up to his ears, as a matter of fact. Why shouldn't he be? If he weren't, I'd like to know how I'd manage to get about at all.'

'Then *you* ... '

'Not in the least, child. I said that only to tease you. I'm afraid Olonne has only too little cause to worry about me. Besides, Beuvron is married himself, you know. His wife was one of the Le Telliers. She dresses so well I thought when I first met her she'd be sure to be amusing, but on the contrary — a perfect idiot, my dear! How he stands her, I really can't think. Fortunately, she's always ailing and seldom goes out, so I don't have to cope —— Ah, Marquis, good evening!'

'You are late, madam.'

'I am, sir: what then?'

Beuvron made no reply. He was a tall dark man, with deep-set eyes and an air of melancholy gravity Magdelon found attractive, after the chirping flippancy of her brother-in-law's friends.

He bowed over her hand and murmured a graceful greeting that might have meant almost anything: it was not quite all of a sentence. But his eyes rested on Cateau with an eloquence that needed no words.

At the door his lackeys were waiting with torches to see the ladies into the carriage.

The rain of the afternoon had turned into a light snow: flakes were falling as softly and indecisively as butterflies in the grey windless night; but, for all that, a pale moon showed through the clouds above the windmills of the Butte Saint-Roch.

Just as they were on the point of leaving the Abbé de Boisrobert tripped out of the house, to be met by a pair of blond pages with pretty, simpering faces, who were carrying lanterns to light their master home.

'A perfect afternoon, my divine one,' he called out to Cateau. ''Pon my honour, never was anything more furiously successful!'

'Why aren't you supping with Olonne?' said Cateau. 'I thought that, of course ——'

'Alas, my beloved, I can't! Utterly impossible! Ninon's expecting me to take her to the Fair of Saint-Germain. I'm an hour behind-hand, as it is. Too, too tiresome — but what can I do?'

'A propos, Abbé, a thousand thanks for the verses you sent me.'

'Madam, don't mention it. How did you find them, by the way? Were they to your taste?'

'Delicious,' said Cateau, in flute-like accents. 'Simply delicious.'

'Which did you think more gallant: the sonnet of the captive nightingale, or the rondeau on the distress of the sun eclipsed by the shining of your curls?'

'Impossible to choose. They were both the last word in elegance. Once more, a thousand thanks, dear friend!'

She offered her finger-tips through the window, which Boisrobert seized and kissed in ecstasy before flitting away down the street with his pretty pages, whose lamps glimmered wanly through the falling snow.

As the coach drove off Cateau turned to her companions with a smile.

'Not,' she remarked, 'that I remember the slightest thing about either one. In fact, it seems to me Quinette lighted the fire with 'em yesterday, before I'd got round to opening the packet.'

Magdelon giggled.

'Then why mention them?'

'Oh, well, my dear, he's always writing verses — it's safe to assume there are some in the house.'

For some reason, this struck Magdelon as funny. She began to laugh, and once she had begun found herself unable to stop.

She laughed all the way to the Hôtel de Blainville, where Madame de Choisy lived; she was still laughing when Monsieur de Beuvron handed that lady into the coach. But then her mirth died away as abruptly as it had started, for Madame de Choisy, who appeared in her best dress with a towering arrangement of cherry-red plumes on her head, was in a very bad temper.

She hardly took any notice of Magdelon or the Marquis, so busy was she telling Cateau how long the latter had kept her waiting.

'Well, dear! If I'd known, if I'd had the least idea how late you were going to be, I'd have given you up and simply run right round the corner,' she kept saying, in an aggrieved tone. 'The play will be almost over now. I don't know why we even bother to go. And it was a piece I was *particularly* anxious to see. Well, well, never mind — only I must say, if you had warned me, I could have run round the corner by myself, as well as not.'

Magdelon felt it might have saved a deal of trouble if she *had* run round the corner, for the Hôtel de Blainville *was* almost next door to the Petit Bourbon.

They were at the theatre before anyone else had been able to get in a word.

The principal play of the evening was just drawing to a close.

It was not Cateau's fault that it did not come to a full stop then and there. She appeared to make it a point to make as much noise as possible on entering their box. She laughed out loud several times, and dropped her bouquet; and, even after she had taken her seat, went on rustling her dress and throwing herself about.

Everyone in the theatre was looking at her. Presently the actors began to notice her, too. Scaramouche, who was playing the villain in the piece, in a chalk-white make-up and a fantastic costume half-way between a bat and a dragon, stepped out of his character long enough to pay a compliment to the 'golden queen' who had come to reign over them.

Cateau smiled and kissed her hand to him. A few minutes later, as he continued weaving admiring references to her charms into the text of the comedy, she plucked a rose from the bouquet she was holding and tossed it over the heads of the crowd in the pit onto the stage. Scaramouche caught it neatly, and pressed it to his heart with an extravagant grimace.

Magdelon glanced at Madame de Choisy, wondering how the latter's mood would support these marked attentions to another. To her surprise she found that the good lady had quite got over her recent attack of ill-humour, and was bridling with pleasure and nodding her head so that the topknot of feathers, which gave her a distinct resemblance to an exotic elderly pheasant, trembled perilously.

'Ah,' said Madame de Choisy, 'I *thought* Scaramouche knew I was here! Dear fellow, he never forgets me!'

She flourished her hand regally towards the stage, and with a satisfied smirk sat back in her chair between the two young women: the pheasant had begun to hatch!

Magdelon herself was slightly embarrassed, though interested, by the commotion they seemed to have caused. She tried to fix her attention on the stage, but found it hard, as the subject of the comedy was strange to her and it was acted in Italian, of which language she knew only a few words.

Cateau leaned across Madame de Choisy and pressed her sister's hand with an encouraging smile.

'Laugh when I do,' she whispered. 'Then you'll be quite safe. I used to follow that plan myself, till I found out what it was all about!'

The play was over before Magdelon had time to become seriously bored.

During the pause she found amusement enough in staring at the audience. It was not a 'court night'; still, Scaramouche always drew a fashionable crowd, and the boxes were filled with celebrities of the town. Madame de Choisy, with her lorgnette glued to her eyes, kept up a ceaseless flow of disparaging remarks concerning those of her female acquaintances who had the ill-luck to come within range of her glass. According to her, every woman she knew was either old, ugly, dressed in bad taste, or in doubtful company. Many of them seemed to be all four of these things at once.

Magdelon looked in artless amazement at their old friend, whose face was a mass of wrinkles, and so emaciated that the great nose that dominated it thrust itself forward like the prow of a ship; whose tired eyes were underscored by sagging pouches of loose yellow skin; whose hair, beneath its jaunty crown of cherry-red plumes, was of that awful blackness the secret of which was known only to vendors of certain small flasks in the rue Saint-Denis.

There seemed, really, to be nothing one could say.

Cateau enlivened the entr'acte by jumping up and down and changing her seat several times, to make sure that all who had not already seen it might have a good view of her gown. She sent one of Beuvron's lackeys to fetch her some syrup to drink, and when he had brought it made a fuss and said it was the wrong kind and sent him back to change it. Beuvron himself, who watched her with helpless, suffering eyes, she hardly addressed at all; and when their party was joined by the Marquis de Sillery and his nephew, the young Prince de Marsillac, she flatly turned her back on her gallant and began laughing and waving her fan and flirting with the new arrivals.

Beuvron looked at once so patient and so dejected that Magdelon felt truly sorry for him. She would have liked to say something comforting, but could not think how to begin.

Soon the mob streamed back into the hall, the curtain rose, and the play began once more.

The tailpiece of the evening was a knockabout farce of the broadest imaginable description. Scaramouche, dressed as Harlequin, and two very pretty girls were involved in a series of compromising situations, delivering themselves meanwhile of a number of jests that caused the pit to roar with laughter.

Cateau laughed, too, somewhat metallically; so did Sillery, screwing up his eyes and showing all his teeth — he had an acute, triangular face like a fox; so, too, did Madame de Choisy, who, Magdelon was sure, knew no more Italian than she herself did. At length, however, the young girl, not to be out of it, dutifully joined in the merriment, as Cateau had told her to. This course she pursued till she became conscious of young Marsillac's solemn stare fixed upon her: he was an awkward calf, still in his teens, with a heavy jaw and an eye combining a certain obstinate shrewdness with its look of adolescent perplexity.

'Do you understand what it's all about?' he whispered.

'No,' Magdelon whispered back, over her shoulder; 'I haven't the faintest idea. I only laugh when my sister does.'

Marsillac snorted at this, and looked hastily away; and Magdelon gave a cheerful giggle.

Nevertheless, she was beginning to wish that the play would come to an end. The air in the theatre had grown very close; it smelled strongly of patchouli and candle-grease and, what was worse, of sweating, tightly packed human bodies.

When the curtain fell on the final tableau of Scaramouche in bed, with a pretty girl on each side of him, Magdelon felt relieved.

On their way into the theatre the foyer had been deserted, as the performance had been going on. On the way out, however, there was a crowd about the entrance, and the ladies were obliged to wait just inside the door a few minutes, while Beuvron's lackeys ran to find his coach.

Everyone stared at Cateau, and Magdelon heard several men say, in an admiring undertone: 'There goes the Olonne!'

Mademoiselle de la Louppe, also, received her share of appraising glances. She was at first rather frightened to feel so many bold eyes turned upon her. Though it was undeniably stimulating, she could not keep from blushing a little; it was impossible for her to look as sublimely unconscious of the gallery as Cateau did.

Afterwards in the carriage, on the way to the supper-party at Madame de Bonnelle's, Madame de Choisy peered sharply at Magdelon, as if she had only just discovered her, and said, in her fussy way: 'Child, where have you been keeping yourself all these years? Come to supper next Thursday with your sister.'

At the Bonnelles' there were many more people whom Magdelon had never seen before. (Society seemed to have changed a good deal since the days of the Fronde.) The house was by no means so new or so splendid as the Olonnes'. It was small and rather dark, and appeared to be already uncomfortably crowded.

Cateau and Magdelon were pounced upon with screams of joy by their hostess, a fat little woman with bulging eyes and no neck, who dragged them off to the dining-room, where an elaborate meal was served.

Cateau continued deliberately during supper to flirt with Sillery.

Magdelon, at the other end of the table, tried to divide her attentions with scrupulous politeness between her host and Monsieur de Beuvron.

Bonnelle, an insignificant scrap of a man with a too-curly brown wig, who looked half asleep, devoted most of his energies to consuming his very excellent supper. Occasionally, between courses, he would pause to point out to his guest, with a reflective fork, the frescoes on the ceiling of the dining-room, a series of paintings by Simon Vouet depicting the history of Ulysses (who looked, strange to say, exactly like Monsieur de Bonnelle's late father, the finance minister Claude de Bullion).

Beuvron was able to eat nothing; he crumbled a morsel of bread and toyed with his silver merely for convention's sake. His wretchedness, however, did not prevent him from taking charmingly good care of his young companion. He talked to her seriously, sensibly, with an air of weighing his words that Magdelon instantly approved of; listened to her few shy-spoken remarks with interest; and answered her questions about life in the capital in detail, instead of turning them off with a laugh and a sugary compliment, as a younger man might have done.

Yes, he told her, court circles were much altered since the days of her former residence in Paris. The nobles kept less to themselves than in the early days of the Regency. The civil wars had somehow shaken classes together, and introduced quite a new, semi-bourgeois note into society. Moreover, after the Fronde, Mazarin and the Queen had resolved to make a clean sweep of the old insurgent element. Its chiefs had been deprived of their posts without ceremony, many of them exiled as well. There were, of course, exceptions... 'Our friend, the Choisy, for example, whose husband was Orléans' chancellor. But then no one takes anything amiss from Madame de Choisy!'... The new leaders were men who had remained loyal to Mazarin through thick and thin: the Chancellor Séguier, little old Senneterre and his son, the Maréchal de la Ferté.

'La Ferté?' said Magdelon. 'I've seen him: a horrid great beast of a man!'

'Yes, mademoiselle, a beast if you will — but a damned important beast! Next to Turenne, the King hasn't a better general in the field. You may well see him here tonight; he lives just across the street at his father's house, when he's not with the army or at Nancy, the seat of his government in Lorraine, and he often plays cards at the Bonnelles'.'

'A brute!' said Magdelon, shaking her head decidedly. 'I'd much rather not meet him. Pray, sir, if he comes, don't present him to me!'

Beuvron inclined his head courteously and replied: 'You shall meet no one, mademoiselle, who hasn't the good fortune to please you.'

After supper the company made a rush for the next room, where rows of card-tables had been set up, and fell to playing hoca and reversi with passionate eagerness.... The Hôtel de Bullion, said Beuvron, was the best-known gambling resort in Paris. The cleverest players of the court and the town assembled there, night after night. Obviously, it was no place for novices, although Madame de Bonnelle, who had been a devotee of reversi for twenty years without ever winning one hand, might almost have been considered in that light.

However, nothing seemed to discourage her. She staked appalling sums again and again — fortunately, Bullion's daughter-in-law could afford to lose! Her shrill cackling laugh kept on ringing out punctually like the chime of a clock; and as the evening wore on, though her staring doll's eyes nearly started out of her head with fatigue and a network of wrinkles appeared under them on her raddled cheeks, neither her persistence nor her optimism showed the least sign of flagging.

Madame de Choisy was also an inveterate and rather reckless gambler, unpleasantly inclined to berate her opponents and to embark upon endless disputes about very small points of procedure.

Cateau did not care much for cards. She drifted about from table to table, still with Sillery in attendance, staking a louis here and there. But sometimes she scarcely waited to see the result of her wager.

The fiddles had struck up in the Gallery of Ulysses, and Magdelon, who loved to dance, found herself in demand as the only young unmarried girl at the party.

Thank goodness, fashions in steps had not changed in the last two years! Here was something she knew she could do as well as Cateau. ... Oh, who could describe the rapture that filled her senses at the fiddles' first plaintive notes? the strange sweet thrill that possessed her when her partner led her out for the opening branle? There was a moment surpassing all other moments when, having sunk to the floor in a stately curtsy, she hardly dared rise or look up again, for this time — she was sure of it — Prince Charming was waiting at last. It was he — it *must* be he! — the answer to all her vague hopes and dreams. Indeed, while the music was playing, any young man, any young man at all, *was* the answer to them. Magdelon gave him her hand and moved, faint with ecstasy, through the complex routine of the dance. She could not falter, she could not make a mistake: she was enchanted. ... Not till the last soft chord had died away did she wake from the spell and gaze with startled, dewy eyes at the stranger by her side.

In the intervals between dances servants passed preserved fruits and sweetmeats, and it was necessary to manufacture a little gallant conversation. Magdelon could not, unfortunately, rally her partners as Cateau did, and make clever remarks to them. But she soon discovered that it answered just as well if she smiled and lowered her long black lashes and *looked* as though she'd made a clever remark.

There was no doubt about it: Mademoiselle de la Louppe was a ballroom success. All the older women present, like her hostess and Madame de Choisy, glanced at her approvingly as she floated by on some dashing viscount's arm; most of the younger ones, including Mesdames de Montglas and Montmorency, who had appeared together, arm-in-arm, rather late in the evening, looked as if they could cheerfully kill her.

This, of course, was delightful.

In fact, Magdelon's evening, slow at the start, was ending as a complete triumph. All the young men were in love with her; she was in love, in turn, with all the young men. And the Maréchal de la Ferté, the one man in Paris she felt it would be impossible to love, had not come to the party, after all.

Everything, in short, had been blissful, except for one moment's uneasiness — and even that moment had been concerned, not with herself, but with her sister.

For some reason Cateau did not come into the ballroom until late in the evening. When at length she made her appearance it was on the arm of the Comte de Moret, a handsome fellow who looked like a good-humoured bird of prey. He had, it seemed, just arrived from the Louvre, where he had attended the coucher of the King.

A buzz of excitement arose as they entered, out of all proportion, as far as Magdelon could see, to its cause. After circling the hall once or twice the couple disappeared, Magdelon supposed to go back to the gambling-room.

At all events, she did not see Cateau again on the floor.

Several hours later, when the fiddlers at last had stopped playing, it was Madame de Choisy who suddenly glided into the doorway, beckoning to Magdelon peremptorily with her fan.

'Child,' she said, 'it's very late; we must go home at once. Your sister wants you.'

She was in a very bad temper, having lost fifty louis on the last hand to the Marquis de Manicamp, whom, she said, she particularly disliked.

'It would,' she remarked, 'have to go to that little weasel. Of course, I've no intention of paying him — but it's the principle of the thing! Where's your cloak, child?'

Magdelon said she would go upstairs to fetch it, and asked where her sister was.

Madame de Choisy did not reply, and Magdelon had no need to ask again, for just then she caught sight of Cateau in an anteroom, a small chamber half hidden by curtains on the other side of the entrance hall.

Monsieur de Beuvron was with her. Magdelon could not see her sister's face, which was turned away from the door — but his she saw clearly: it was haggard in the bright candlelight, but his eyes were no longer miserable: they were angry and accusing. He did not seem in the least to care that his voice was perfectly audible to everyone in the hall.

'It's quite enough to be treated like the dirt under your feet,' he was saying loudly. 'That I don't mind. I ought to be used to it by now. I don't even mind your making an ass of Sillery — God knows it's easy enough! But to have to stand back and watch you strike your infamous bargain with Moret — pah! the puppy! I wonder he's not ashamed to play such a part. His master's go-between — no more, no less! I've half a mind to call him out for it. As for *you*, madam ——'

'Nonsense!' said Cateau, interrupting him. 'Nonsense! I won't even listen to you. It's too base — too low — how you can suspect me of such a thing . . .'

She appeared to be quite as angry as Beuvron himself — but she would not turn to look at him.

'Suspect?' cried Beuvron. 'I tell you, *I know*. Didn't I hear you, myself, say that you'd meet your precious princeling tomorrow night, and then it would be for him to take what measures he would? The shame of it! The cold-blooded infamy! Oh, to think — only three months ago ——'

'Hush!' said Cateau. 'I'll not hear another word. You must be mad, to say or even think such a thing. I'm going home now. No, don't come with me: my sister and I can take care of ourselves. Sir, I bid you good-night.'

She dropped him a mocking curtsy, and slipped out of the room straight into the arms of Magdelon and Madame de Choisy. When she saw them she raised her eyebrows and laughed a little, but showed no embarrassment, though it must have been obvious to her that they had overheard what had passed between her and her gallant.

'Oh, there you are,' she said, in a tranquil tone. 'I was looking for you both. It's time to go home. Beuvron's been acting too tiresomely — we'll have to find another escort, I fear. Sillery's no good; he hasn't a carriage of his own.'

'Ah, but this evening I have,' said Monsieur de Sillery, who came out of the gambling-room in time to catch this remark. 'My brother-in-law La Rochefoucauld's coach is at my disposal. And if the ladies will deign to honour me . . . The sooner we get out of this den of thieves, the better!'

So, after all, it was quite easily arranged.

Everyone was silent as they whirled home by torchlight through the dark, frozen streets.

It was late: they were all tired and dispirited. Sillery and Madame de Choisy had lost at cards; Cateau must have been suffering, one supposed, from the effects of her scene with Beuvron, though she was careful to conceal it; and Magdelon, who had danced herself into a state bordering on collapse, was upset because she felt her sister was upset. . . . So much had happened in the last few hours! Could it really be only this morning she had left Rambouillet? — but no, of course, that was *yesterday* morning now!

A sleepy servant in a nightcap admitted them to the Hôtel d'Olonne.

Still in silence they stumbled up the half-lighted stairs. At the top they were met by Quentine with a candle; the little maid was yawning, rosy after her nap.

'Quinette will be waiting for you in your room, to help you undress,' said Cateau. 'Darling, I hope you'll be comfortable, and have everything you want.'

'You know that I shall,' said Magdelon. 'Darling, good-night; it's so wonderful to be here.'

'It's wonderful to have you,' said Cateau.

She kissed Magdelon affectionately, and smiled as if she meant what she said. Her eyes were big with fatigue, almost drained of expression. Then, still smiling, she picked up her skirt of gold and trailed along the hall to her own door, followed by Quentine with the candle.

Magdelon spied them a moment later, through the window that gave on the court. Cateau, looking back, saw her, too, smiled once more, and kissed her hand. Then Quentine pulled the curtains, and all grew dark.

Magdelon, turning to enter her room, was arrested by a sudden rustle outside the hall window. Peering into the violet gloom of the court, where snow was still softly falling, she found that a pigeon had fluttered down from the roof and was perched on the sill, gazing up at her through the glass, as if pleading to be let come in. Its friendly plaint, recalling her pets in the tower room at La Louppe, comforted her and made her feel at home.

She stretched out her hand to open the window; then drew it back, she knew not why. Something in the bird's eyes, remote and expressionless as Cateau's own, seemed to repel her.

With a little shiver she turned away and entered her bedroom.

Chapter V

NEXT MORNING MAGDELON WOKE TO THE SOUND OF BELLS, PEALING clear and gay through the still, cold air. They rang from the church of Saint-Roch and from the neighbouring monasteries of the Feuillans and the Jacobins.

Quinette was standing by her bed, drawing back the curtains of heavy scarlet brocade. She had already unmasked the windows, through which shone the winter sun, a round red ball suspended in mist. . . . The Countess's compliments, please, said Quinette, and she hoped mademoiselle had slept well and would join her at breakfast in her dressing-room directly.

Magdelon yawned and stretched in the great gilt bed. . . . So soft! So warm! She felt as if it might still be the middle of the night.

'Oh, Quinette, what time is it?'

'Past ten,' replied Quinette. 'The Countess has been up for an hour or more. I believe she intends to go shopping this morning with mademoiselle.'

'Oh, yes, of course, I forgot. Dear me! I don't want to keep her waiting. Fetch my slippers and dressing-gown, please; I'll make my toilet later.'

Quinette made warning half-hoops of her eyebrows.

'I think,' she remarked austerely, 'mademoiselle would do well to robe herself now. The Countess is not alone.'

Half an hour later Magdelon, in her best street costume, tapped on the dressing-room door, which was opened by Lindor. Breakfast for three was laid on a small table in front of the fire. On one side of the table Cateau, wearing a frilly rose-coloured robe-de-chambre, posed picturesquely on her couch; on the other, ensconced in a snug armchair, sat Monsieur de Beuvron.

Apparently last night's quarrel had been quite forgotten. The pair were chatting cheerfully as if they had not a care in the world: Beuvron was reading aloud items of interest from this week's edition of the *Gazette de France*, while Cateau, smiling amiably, spread jam on a slice of bread of Gonesse for her guest.

'Darling!' she said, when she saw Magdelon. 'Good morning! I hope you slept well?'

'Perfectly,' answered Magdelon, stooping to kiss her sister and giving her hand with a smile to Beuvron. 'I'd have been sleeping yet if Quinette hadn't called me.'

'My dear, I am sorry. But we've such a lot to do today, I thought it was important to get an early start. There are all your clothes to be ordered, you know; and I want, if possible, to have something run up in a hurry for you to wear tonight.'

'Tonight . . . what's tonight?'

'Oh, it's the première of the King's new ballet. I'm not dancing in it this year — it's sure to be deadly dull,' said Cateau complacently, as if stating the same fact in two ways; 'but I feel, don't you, that Maman would like you to go to the Louvre? As a matter of fact, there's a much more amusing party at Madame de Nouveau's. Perhaps we can slip away later and look in there, too. On the other hand, you know the line Maman always takes about bourgeois balls. I'm not sure whether I *ought* . . . Darling, are you getting enough to eat? Drink a cup of hot bouillon; it's so good for the nerves. There's fruit, bread, spice-cake . . . what you will. . . . But if there's anything else you'd prefer, Lindor will fetch it for you. And in just a minute I'll be with you, and we'll start the serious business of the day.'

Cateau's minute expanded into something little less than an hour before they were actually ready to go.

As soon as breakfast had been cleared away there were numerous servants to be interviewed: the cook, the housekeeper, various valets, the Countess's equerry, the Swiss porter, who appeared with a batch of notes on a silver tray. These Cateau opened while she sat at her dressing-table, having her hair arranged by Quentine. Now and then she would pause to read a bit aloud out of one of them to Beuvron. Once she laughed to herself, and then frowned, and then brusquely tore the square of paper twice across before tossing it into the fire.

Magdelon was much impressed by her sister's way of dealing with the servants. Cateau's commands were brief and to the point: she always knew exactly what she wanted people to do, and though she smiled a good deal, none of her staff would have dared disobey her.

A milliner was next introduced, with boxes of hats to try on, as well as a man who had invented a new kind of sweetmeat, for which he was soliciting the honour of the Countess's patronage, and a shifty-eyed Moorish gentleman, who had little dogs and monkeys in cages to sell.

Cateau retired behind a screen with Quentine and the milliner and most of the dogs, to which, judging by the sounds that ensued, she was feeding *all* of the sweetmeats — and called out to be 'patient, please,' that she would be dressed *directly*.

Beuvron caught Magdelon's eye, and they shared a smile. . . . The Marquis had remained seated all this time in his place by the fire, viewing the bustling proceedings with tranquil good-humour. He seemed to be so much at home that it never occurred to Magdelon it was odd he should be there at all.

Cateau at length reappeared in a blue velvet street dress trimmed with ermine. She had adjusted her mask, and was just drawing on a pair of scented Russia-leather gloves, when a servant announced that Madame de Marville was below.

'Heavens!' said Cateau. 'I forgot all about her, didn't you? Show her up at once.'

Aunt de Marville's temper had not, it was evident, been improved by her recent sojourn with the Daughters of Holy Mary in Chaillot. She made a lugubrious entrance, swathed in penitential black, bestowed a kiss apiece on her nieces, with an air of grudging charity, as if she were dropping pennies into an alms-box, and cast a dully disapproving eye on Monsieur de Beuvron.

'And where,' demanded Aunt de Marville, in a funereal tone, 'is my nephew, the Count? I distinctly said at the door that I wanted to see you both.'

'Dear aunt, Olonne never gets up until noon,' said Cateau carelessly. 'I am so sorry; I never thought.... Of course, you would like to see him, wouldn't you? Shall I send Lindor to tell his valet to call him?'

'Oh, no, no, dear, not on *my* account, pray!' said Aunt de Marville. 'I wouldn't encroach on his rest for the world. So he never gets up until noon, eh? Dear, dear, I should have thought a strong young man like that ... Well, it's none of my business, Catherine-Henriette — but if he lies abed till such an hour, how does he manage to get to Mass?'

'Why, aunt, as a rule, he attends Vespers,' said Cateau, with great, innocent eyes — which reply caused Beuvron to snort audibly behind his hand and poor little Lindor to choke and run out of the room, to explode in hysterics in the hall.

Cateau, however, was determined to see that her aunt's visit went off well. She made a tremendous fuss over Madame de Marville: kissed and embraced her a number of times; sent Lindor to the kitchen for a fresh cup of bouillon, which she insisted on the good lady's drinking; and plied her with pressing invitations to dinner, to supper, to spend the night — all of which were unequivocally declined.

Aunt de Marville held out as long as she could — but there was no resisting Cateau when the latter exerted herself to please.

All might have been saved had not Madame de Montmorency, unluckily, chosen this moment to pay a morning call on Madame d'Olonne.

Aunt de Marville had never met Madame de Montmorency, but she had 'heard things' about her. Most people had, at one time or another. But they were all things that Madame de Montmorency intended them to hear. She was a young woman much impressed by a sense of her own importance, as wife to the head of the eldest branch of what had certainly been the most illustrious family in France. The fact that the dukedom was extinct, that her husband was only a baron, had no fortune to speak of, and was personally perfectly obscure, did not shake Madame de Montmorency's faith in her exalted position. She had the airs, if not the looks, of a great beauty; dressed better than she could afford; changed lovers punctually every six months; and had never been known to make a charitable remark.

This morning, attired in purple plush and sables, she sailed into the room with a high small scream of laughter, and launched immediately into a detailed recital of the 'latest' about Ninon.

The 'latest' was a horrid little story, involving a purse of gold louis, a suit of boy's clothes, and a midnight supper at a rather disreputable cabaret in Saint-Cloud.

Cateau smiled and frowned, and tried to indicate in pantomime to her friend that this was perhaps not the ideal audience for such anecdotes — but the Montmorency paid no heed to her warning signals, and continued unabashed to the end.

She was about to embark on an even more scandalous tale, when Aunt de Marville rose to take leave of her nieces, with a frigid smile and as much majesty as it was possible to muster, standing five feet in her very highest heels. . . . No, on no conditions could she stay any longer: they were expecting her at the convent in Chaillot for the midday meal, and as soon as dinner was over she purposed setting forth on the first stage of her long journey home.

'Catherine-Henriette, I bid you farewell. Magdelaine, child, I commend you to God's care.'

'Not to mine, my dear aunt?' inquired Cateau, with a wheedling smile. 'Am I then not to be trusted?'

But Madame de Marville was past being cajoled.

'I am sure, my dear, I hope that you are!' was the best they could get out of her — and she kissed both young women coldly and scuttled out of the room and down the stairs with an unanswered 'Love to Maman!' floating after her.

'There, now!' said Cateau. 'You've done it this time, Isabelle!'

'Done what?' inquired Madame de Montmorency, with an air of false innocence that deceived nobody.

'You know perfectly well what,' retorted Cateau, without rancour. 'But come, there's no use in wasting the whole morning, is there? Magdelon and I are going shopping. Would you like to come with us?'

Magdelon hoped that Madame de Montmorency might say no.

She found the latter's manners trying: it was obvious that her sister's friend considered young girls in general negligible quantities, and Mademoiselle de la Louppe in particular of no importance at all.

But the Montmorency replied that she would be delighted to make one of the party; there was nothing, she said, she liked better than helping to spend other people's money.

As the ladies were donning their masks and cloaks the bells of Saint-Roch rang out even more loudly than before. Nothing was said about going to Mass, and Magdelon did not like to mention the subject to Cateau in front of strangers. She muttered a hasty prayer on her way down to the carriage, thinking how wicked she was, and that she had not been in Paris even twenty-four hours without breaking one of God's laws.

Monsieur de Beuvron had not been asked whether he cared to go with them. But it seemed to be taken for granted that he would accompany Cateau.

Magdelon rather wondered what pleasure the morning's excursion could afford him, as he was left alone in the coach a good deal of the time, while the ladies disappeared on various errands.

Cateau, in extraordinarily high spirits, promptly took charge of affairs with her customary air of capability. They drove first to the Maison Gautier, in the rue des Bourdonnais, where they purchased yards of silks and satins, gold-and-silver-embroidered brocades, at prices that staggered Magdelon. ('But there's no good economizing on *materials*,' Cateau said firmly. 'The best is the cheapest, in the long run.')

Armed with their spoils — it took little Lindor and two brawny lackeys to carry the bundles — they then approached Maître Thomas, Maître Baudelet, and two or three other dressmakers in the fashionable Palais Royal quarter, to see who would make up the gowns at the lowest price.

Here Cateau displayed unsuspected powers of bargaining. There was not a tradesman in Paris who would not have sold his soul for the privilege of securing the custom of the Comtesse d'Olonne. This she was well aware of, and was not above turning to account for her sister's benefit. She screamed, and stamped, and said, again and again, that they were robbers, and were only trying to take advantage of a poor little girl from the country. But would Madame permit it? Certainly not! A thousand times, *no*! If Monsieur didn't care to meet her figure, there were plenty of others who would. Fortunately, he was not the only tailor in town.... 'Come, my sister, we shan't stop to argue with these harpies. I've an admirable address in the Place Dauphine....'

Thanks to these ruthless tactics, it was not long before the poor little girl from the country found herself well on the way to possessing an extensive and elaborate wardrobe. A dozen dresses for every conceivable occasion were being rushed to completion by expert hands; one beautiful flame-coloured brocade promised that very evening, for the ball at the Louvre. Hats, gloves, laces, and ribbons were also purchased in reckless profusion. For these Cateau resorted to the booths of the Palais, the law-courts on the island of the Cité near Notre Dame, where from time immemorial the best haberdashers in Paris had driven a thriving trade in a hall especially set aside for their use.

Here, also, Madame d'Olonne seemed to be very well known, and so anxious were the merchants to sell to the reigning queen of the mode that she was able to take what she wanted at almost her own price.

It was very clever of Cateau, Magdelon thought; and no doubt she was right in saying that nothing she bought cost very much. Still, trifles mounted up, if one kept on acquiring them — and she ended by ordering as much for herself as she did for her sister, encouraged in this extravagant course by the Montmorency, who was continually crying: 'Darling, how adorable you look in green!' and 'My dear, that bonnet is *you*, all over!'

By the end of the morning Cateau's carriage was full, but her purse was quite empty.

Beuvron and Madame de Montmorency were forced to refuse her cordial invitation to dinner, as they both had made other engagements, but they promised to call later in the day.

In the dining-room Magdelon met her brother-in-law again for the first time since the previous afternoon. He appeared to be in an excellent humour, asked her kindly what she and Cateau had been doing, then forgot all about her in his anxiety over a new kind of soup, the recipe for which the Commander had given him only the night before.

The soup was admirable, but Magdelon was really too much excited to eat: there were so many men in the room!

They sat down to table twenty-four strong. (Did Louis and Cateau give a party like this every day?) No women were present save Magdelon and their hostess. The guests were the same little group of men that had been at the house yesterday: Saint-Evremond, Souvré, Boisdauphin, Bussy-Rabutin, and the rest. Apparently they all knew one another very well, for the conversation was sustained on a comfortable note of intimacy without strain.

Magdelon felt too young and too shy to be able to contribute much to it; she noticed that even Cateau, who usually had a great deal to say for herself, confined her efforts to smiling sweetly on everyone and laughing at all the clever remarks that were made.

The clever remarks were countless. These men seemed to know

something about everything, and to pass on questions of taste with an air of gracious omniscience that left no room for retort. They talked about books and music, politics and people, just as Cousin de Rambouillet and her friends used to do; but the tone of the company was quite different. There was none of the stately, slightly cumbersome grace of the Blue Room in its days of glory: here everything was said lightly, quickly, as if half in jest, with a strong undercurrent of satire. No one was safe from the shafts of their wit; neither royalty nor religion seemed sacred — for the King, the Queen Mother, the Cardinal, even the Pope himself, were in turn the objects of more or less scandalous quips. The one thing, Magdelon discovered, about which they refused to be funny was their food: the supremely important business in life was to make sure of a really good dinner. And this, at the Hôtel d'Olonne, could never be a matter of doubt.

Although properly grateful to their host for providing it, the young Count's guests treated him rather like a charming spoilt child: he was only geographically the centre of the dinner-table. Neither was the position of leader granted to handsome, dashing Bussy, who kept the party convulsed with his malicious sallies, nor even to the Commander and the Abbé de Boisrobert, whose years and social importance might have been supposed to demand it. No: the core of the assembly was little Saint-Evremond, poor and personally insignificant as he was. Whenever he opened his mouth Magdelon noticed that the others fell silent, 'for fear,' as the Marquis de Boisdauphin whispered to her, 'of missing some excellent thing'; and his opinions were accepted as laws by everyone present.

When dinner was over Olonne carried the men off to his own apartments for a time, while the ladies retired to change their gowns. After that, Cateau returned to the drawing-room and took up her post on the great bed in the alcove, with her sister on a tabouret beside her.

A good many more people arrived, and the rest of the day was spent as the day before had been, in gambling and joking and desultory conversation.

Cateau and Magdelon were approached by group after group, being flattered and flirted with in a mild, conventional way, and tremendously enjoying their distinction as the only women in the room.

'I ought,' said the former frankly, 'to take you out to pay calls. That's what Maman would like me to do; that's what every woman in Paris does every day — except me! But oh, my dear, those dull drawing-rooms! And that terrible, would-be-literary chit-chat! Calling their mirrors the "councillors of the graces" and their chairs "the indispensables of conversation"! What nonsense! I had enough of the Précieuses at Cousin de Rambouillet's to last me a lifetime, didn't you?'

'Dear me, yes!' said Magdelon, looking frightened. 'Don't let's go anywhere where we have to be clever!'

When it came time to dress for the evening it was discovered that the Count had no intention of attending the ball. Beuvron had promised to call for the ladies, but they needed another man to complete their quartet; and Cateau, after surveying the company with a calculating eye, walked up to Saint-Evremond, who was deep in an argument with the Marquis de Sillery about the rival merits of Lucian and Petronius, and put her hand through his arm with a confiding gesture.

'Dear Chevalier,' she said, 'will you grant me a favour?'

Saint-Evremond smiled, showing all his big horse-teeth.

'Madam, when you look at me like that, I cannot find the heart to refuse you anything. What may I do for you?'

'Take my sister and me to the Louvre tonight.'

Saint-Evremond looked surprised, and rubbed the great wart on the bridge of his nose.

'What, young ladies! You desire my company, when Paris is full of gallant youths who would swoon with joy at the very idea of squiring two such exquisite goddesses! Fie, madam, fie! Your taste is deplorable.'

Cateau shook her head.

'You — or no one,' she said obstinately. 'Young men bore me. They all have only one thing to say.'

'So you want to see what an old one will do, eh?' retorted the Chevalier. 'Madam, madam, I thought you had more tact!'

But he smiled once more, and glanced at her kindly with the great jewel-like eyes that were his only good physical feature: obviously the Countess had won her point.

Magdelon looked almost as much surprised as Saint-Evremond, and a little disappointed as well. Young men did not bore *her*; she had certainly expected her sister's choice to fall on dapper Bussy or gay, elegant Boisdauphin.

But afterwards as they were going upstairs Cateau squeezed her arm and said: 'Now everything's going to be *perfect!* You'll see later why.'

Dressing for the ball at the Louvre was even more thrilling than it had been the night before, with only the Petit Bourbon and Madame de Bonnelle's supper in prospect.

Magdelon's flame-coloured brocade had come home from the dressmaker's and was pronounced a perfect fit; while Cateau arrayed herself in another pompous creation of pure gold — she seldom wore anything else after dark, on account of her hair — so stiff with metallic embroidery that it could almost have stood by itself.

Quentine and Quinette, who had caught the prevailing mood of excitement, fluttered from one glittering figure to the other, fastening a shoebuckle here, smoothing a fold of silk there; and, in honour of the occasion, Cateau had called in Champagne, the most fashionable hairdresser at court, whose conversation was as fascinating as his fingers were skilled; for he could tell one exactly what all the ladies were going to wear. (It was delightful, for instance, to hear that the Comtesse de Noailles' curls were quite false and that the Maréchale de l'Hôpital, who was as plump as a turkey, had insisted on squeezing herself into a twenty-four-inch waist and fainted dead away on the spot.)

As soon as Champagne had bowed himself out, with a string of parting raptures over his clients' appearance, there was a tap at the door and Olonne thrust his head in.

'*E permesso, signore?*'

'Magdelon, my dear, you don't mind, do you?' said Cateau. 'When I go out in state he always likes to see for himself how I look. And I must say no one has a surer eye for details than Olonne.'

It was, thought Magdelon, rather pretty to see them together: Brother Louis so obviously proud of his beautiful wife, and Cateau revolving gravely before him like a golden angel, glancing up half shyly, half saucily, for his approval.

After a minute inspection Olonne dropped his eyeglass on its silken cord and smiled in a satisfied way.

'Dear madam,' he said, 'my best compliments! You look perfectly charming.'

Cateau gave him her hand with an answering smile.

'Thank you, sir,' she said. 'My pleasure would be doubled were I only to be honoured by your company.'

'Ah, my dear, there, alas, we must draw the line! Nothing,' declared the Count, with candour, 'would induce me at my time of life to expose myself to the trials and tediums of one of Her Majesty's crushes. It is, however, a source of infinite pride to me to realize that the family will be so worthily represented. Now let us see how matters stand with our little sister.'

Laughing and blushing, Magdelon revolved in her turn before the critical glass.

'Exquisite! Exquisite!' said Olonne, after a moment of breathless suspense. 'Sister Magdelaine, all I can say is, you are a credit to the Countess. Higher praise no young lady could expect to deserve. This is *your* handiwork, my dear,' he continued, turning once more to Cateau. 'Allow me to congratulate you on your consummate taste, exercised, I observe, as freely for others as for yourself. Madam, you are as benevolent as you are bewitching.'

He bowed, and kissed her hand again; and with another bow to his sister-in-law left the room.

Magdelon laughed in mingled embarrassment and relief.

'Brother Louis is so kind,' she said. 'Isn't he, dear?'

'Kind?' said his wife. 'Oh, well, yes, I suppose he is, as long as it doesn't cost him anything. But it's not kindness that brought him here tonight. He looks upon me as one of his possessions, you know — something a trifle dearer than the bibelots in the drawing-room, almost as vital to his well-being as a new kind of saucepan! So naturally he likes to make sure that I shan't disgrace him. I must say, he has the most perfect taste imaginable — in food, in clothes, in everything! This house was all of his designing; I hadn't a word to say about its decoration. What little I've learned since in that line I owe to him. And if *he* says I'm looking well, why, I've nothing to fear! At least,' added Cateau, holding out her arms while Quinette clasped a cloak of pure white swansdown round her mistress's shoulders, 'not on *that* score!'

Magdelon's recollections of the evening later resolved themselves into a kaleidoscopic jumble of lights and colour and music, given meaning and movement by an underlying surge of hectic, mounting excitement.

She had never before seen the Louvre in festal array, for in the days when she had been living in Paris it had been dark and deserted, while its owners wandered disconsolate through a war-torn countryside.

Tonight, however, it was ablaze with candles and torches, so grandly illuminated that it cast a glow far and wide through the streets of the quarter. The rue du Louvre was a jam of carriages, all moving at a snail's pace in the same direction; and when at length they drew near the entrance to the palace it was impressive to find the doors guarded by double rows of Musketeers in dress uniform.

Magdelon glanced enviously at a few privileged carriages that, instead of depositing their occupants at the main gate, drove on through the court to a private door some distance beyond it. She said to Cateau that it would be fun to be a duchess and enjoy the 'honours of the Louvre,' but Cateau replied unconcernedly that duchesses always seemed to have big feet, or thick ankles, or both — and, for her part, she infinitely preferred being herself, even though it meant having to walk a few paces farther.

Inside the palace the crowd on the grand staircase ascending to the ballroom was suffocating. Magdelon was glad Monsieur de Beuvron and the Chevalier were there to lend them their arms; but, as it turned out, everyone was willing to make way for Cateau, whose arrival attracted general attention. A wave of spontaneous admiration followed her wherever she went, and seemed to sweep her triumphantly up the steps on its crest.

In the ballroom the sisters were soon surrounded by a little group of gallants. Cateau appeared to know every man in the room, and every man in the room who could made it his business to have a word with her, or at least to be seen in her vicinity.

She did not say much to any of them: merely smiled and turned her golden head now this way, and now that; but Magdelon thought her deportment most effective, and copied it as faithfully as she was able.

Shortly after their arrival a murmur arose of 'The Queen! The Queen!' — whereupon the phalanx of courtiers divided itself neatly into two, and, with a rustle of silk, every woman present sank to her knees, as if mowed to the ground by a sudden puff of wind.

As Magdelon rose trembling from her curtsy she beheld Anne of Austria, pale and majestic in black, lifting her waxen hands in a gracious salute to the court. The Queen was flanked by her lady-in-waiting, the old Marquise de Senecé, a rheumatic relic of the last century, and by her mistress-of-the-robes, the young Comtesse de Noailles; and followed by a bevy of beauties, the maids-of-honour, the names of the prettiest of whom Cateau retailed in a whisper.

Anne had aged a good deal, Magdelon thought: her face had grown heavier, and its paper-white pallor was accentuated by a frame of flat reddish curls; but she seemed cheerful and serene.

In the wake of the royal party the crowd pressed forward into the Hall of Apollo, which was to serve as the theatre. The Queen had with her her sister-in-law, Henrietta Maria of England, who Magdelon was surprised to see had turned into a bent old woman, and the latter's small daughter, Madame Henriette, a pretty, scrawny child, all eyes and beak like a young thrush. (It was odd not to find their old friend Mademoiselle in her accustomed post as first princess of the realm.)

Behind the royal family sat the Princesses of the Blood, in chairs with backs but without arms; then the duchesses, on their uncomfortable but coveted tabourets, settled in order of seniority by the gentlemen-in-waiting, who ran about flourishing silver wands excitedly.

The rest of the company was supposed to take care of itself.

Cateau, by dint of smiling continually and an adroit push or two, succeeded in obtaining excellent places for herself and Magdelon and their escorts.

Magdelon had imagined earlier in the evening that Saint-Evremond was obviously destined to fall to her lot; she had been somewhat alarmed at the prospect, remembering his prowess as a wit, though the little man had smiled at her from time to time all day with the kindest eyes in the world.

But Cateau sat down between the two men, with the Chevalier on her right at the end of the row, so that it seemed only natural for her to begin talking to him. They chatted steadily together in low tones on some subject that was evidently engrossing to them both, which left Beuvron to Magdelon. This pleased the latter very much: no one, she thought, could possibly be ill at ease with him.

She even dared to patronize the Marquis slightly on one or two points, and tried out her version of a few of her sister's airs and graces with telling effect.

There was not time, however, for much conversation, for with a flourish of trumpets the lights were extinguished, and a hush fell over the hall as Maître Boësset, the royal superintendent of music and conductor of the orchestra known as the *King's Twenty-Four Fiddles*, appeared, bowed low before his sovereign, and gave the signal to begin the overture.

For the next two hours Magdelon was in fairyland. It had been so long since she had seen a ballet that everything about it seemed marvellous to her eyes. She was incapable of passing critical judgements as her companions did, all three of whom voted the *Pleasures of Town and Country* tiresome old stuff. All Benserade's ballets, they complained, were the same. There were always the same stupid gods and goddesses, the same rows of jigging monkeys and dwarfs, and grotesque monsters with pasteboard heads; the insipid, inevitable rustic interludes, during which mock-Greek shepherds and shepherdesses sang of love.

'It was much better last year,' pronounced Cateau decidedly, stifling a yawn; and she deigned to applaud only once, at the entry of Pan and his nymphs, which was led by the young King himself.

Louis, whom Magdelon recalled as a half-grown, gawky boy, was now a handsome, rather hard-looking young man of seventeen. He appeared as regally self-possessed as a monarch of forty, and performed the steps allotted to him with much grace and assurance.

Magdelon noticed that his partner was frequently a roly-poly dark girl, with small, snapping black eyes and absurdly self-important airs, who Beuvron told her was Cardinal Mazarin's niece, Olympe de Mancini.

'A certain person's madly in love with her,' added Cateau, in an undertone. 'You can imagine how the Queen feels about it. They're looking desperately for a husband for the little upstart, of course. I don't know who'll take her — perhaps *your* friend, Chevalier, of whom we were just speaking?'

'Candale?' said Saint-Evremond, raising his eyebrows. 'Hardly, my dear. He's refused a whole line of the Cardinal's nieces.'

Magdelon knew they were speaking of the King's cousin, the Duc de Candale, generally considered the most brilliant parti at court. She had never met the Duke, as during the years of her residence in Paris he had been almost always away, commanding an army in

Spain or Guienne; but she had heard — what young woman had
not? — glowing accounts of his beauty, his riches, his martial prowess, and, most of all, of the trail of broken hearts he left behind him
at the end of each season. Meditating on these, she had sighed often
in secret — again like many another girl — and said to herself more
than once: 'Ah, if *I* could just try my hand . . .'

The Chevalier, as the friend of this illustrious hero, became immediately of vastly greater importance in her eyes. She gave him a
melting glance, beseeching him mutely to pursue a subject so deeply
interesting to her; but as he seemed reluctant to understand, she
remarked to Beuvron:

'I've not seen the Duke. But I've been told he is a most gallant
young man. Will you point him out to me, please, if he comes here
tonight?'

To her surprise, Beuvron turned suddenly sulky, and snapped out:
'He's no friend of *mine!* Ask your sister!'

'Gallant as he is, he must at length choose a wife,' declared Cateau,
paying no heed to Beuvron's displeasure. 'And I've a fancy I should
like to try my skill at picking a bride for His Highness.'

She smiled at her sister as she said this, and Magdelon thought:
'Heavens! Has she guessed . . . ? Does she think . . . ? Oh, how
wonderful it would be if . . .'

Cateau continued, as it appeared, with intention:

'Will you not bring him to call on me? He is so great a friend of
yours, I am sure he will do anything to please you.'

'Nay, by no means so great a friend as he used to be,' said Saint-
Evremond. 'He has a string of gayer, more youthful intimates now.
That young man is as fickle with his friends as a mistress with her
lovers.'

'But you still see him every day, don't you?' Cateau persisted.
'What simpler, then, than for you to suggest that there is someone
you know who would be highly honoured to make his acquaintance ——'

'Madam! Madam! I beg you to desist! Do you not realize half
the ladies in Paris have made me the same request? How could I
comply with so many?'

'I don't ask you to comply with many. With one only — with
mine! Dear, *dear* Chevalier, to please *me —!*'

'Madam, so say they all. And were I to do so, how should I face
the charmer who, as everyone knows, has for five years and more held
his affections in her keeping?'

'You mean —?'

Saint-Evremond made no reply, but lifted his hand and pointed
smilingly to a pretty, small woman in blue, who was seated, demurely
composed, by herself directly across the hall from their party.

'Madame de Saint-Loup?'

'Madame de Saint-Loup.'

'He *still* cares for that little bourgeoise? I don't believe you! I think better of his taste than that!'

'Nay, madam, she is an amiable creature, I assure you. You must not speak so scornfully of one who is your equal neither in birth nor in beauty. I have known Madame de Saint-Loup for years; she has many most agreeable qualities. True, she is an exacting mistress, and demands what is perhaps a fanatical adherence to the niceties of the tender passion; but is that not all the more proof of the power of her own attachment? She has loved my young friend devotedly for a very long time — for longer, in fact, than I, who personally place little faith in an emotion that everyone talks of, but few have experienced, could have supposed possible. She has sacrificed everything for him: her husband's love, her friends' esteem, honour itself. Can you blame her if she clings with ardour to the one central support of her life, without which she would now be desolate indeed?'

'Saint-Evremond,' said Cateau crossly, 'you talk like a child! Don't you see what a fool she is? That the easiest way to lose a lover is to show him he means all the world to you? No: the Saint-Loup is an obstinate ninny — she deserves to be left! And I've an idea — only an idea, mind you — that she very soon will be.'

She flashed another look charged with meaning at Magdelon, who coloured self-consciously and tried not to show she had guessed its import.

'So young — so fair — and so uncharitable!' the Chevalier was beginning, in a rallying manner — when Beuvron, who had been listening to the conversation with smouldering irritation, suddenly rose and bowed stiffly to the ladies.

'Madam, there's no bearing this any longer,' he said, in a choked voice. 'I beg you and your sister will excuse me.'

And that was the last they saw of him that evening.

'Well!' exclaimed Magdelon, in amazement, after he had gone. 'What on earth was the matter with *him?*'

But Cateau put her finger to her lips and whispered: 'Hush! I was only teasing him. I'll explain to you later. . . . The ballet's beginning again. I wish you'd look at the Mancini as one of the Graces: she's like a Christmas sausage tied up in ribbons!'

After the ballet there was an interval before the ball began, during which the actors changed their costumes and light refreshments were served.

'Come!' said Cateau to her sister. 'We'll go make our bow to the Queen before the crush gets too thick.'

A line was already forming, marshalled by Anne's equerry and various gentlemen-in-waiting; but Cateau had no intention of waiting to take her turn, like everybody else. She pushed her way through the ranks with a deprecating smile and a series of charming 'I beg your pardon's,' which almost succeeded in making the people displaced feel that she was conferring a favour upon them; and presently the sisters were curtsying low before their sovereign.

Her Majesty gave Cateau a rather pinched smile — evidently the incident of last year's ballet costume still rankled in her memory — and bestowed a more cordial one on Magdelon, against whom she could know nothing as yet.

'So you are back in Paris, mademoiselle,' she said affably to the latter. 'It is a pleasure to see you at the Louvre.'

Magdelon thanked her as well as she was able, and added a few words in praise of the ballet and of His Majesty's skill as a dancer, which the Queen received with a complacent smile, as her due.

Cateau stood still and said nothing at all. Magdelon gathered that the Queen was annoyed by this silence, feeling it to be an unspoken criticism. However, she did not betray her annoyance, but turned to the Countess, with a shade more warmth in her manner, and said: 'Madam, you must be sure to show your sister the new apartments.'

'I intend to, Your Majesty,' replied Cateau, unabashed by Anne's glacial attitude.

She curtsied again, with an exquisite politeness that still somehow managed to convey her supreme indifference to the Queen's disapprobation, and led Magdelon away to begin their tour of inspection.

Accompanied by the complaisant Chevalier, they made a leisurely round of the palace, which was a gloomy enough old building, representing the taste of earlier centuries, though lavishly done over since the royal family's return from the country.

For someone who, as she said, came rarely to court and, moreover, made no pretensions to being a connoisseur, Cateau displayed a remarkable knowledge of the disposition and decoration of the various rooms. She was able to point out the best pictures and the handsomest pieces of furniture, and seemed to know exactly where they came from and how much they had cost.

The only object for which she herself appeared to show any enthusiasm was, curiously enough, a small leather bellows with a frame of ebony inlaid with silver, which hung by the fireplace in the Queen's cabinet, a room where Anne and her ladies were wont to play cards in the evenings.

This, Cateau told them, had been a present to the Queen from her sister-in-law, Madam Royale of Savoy: she, Cateau, had looked all over Paris for one like it, but in vain.

She dropped to her knees, like a child, in front of the fire, and blew on the flame; the leather of which the bellows was made was strongly impregnated with frangipani, which scented the air when it was blown. Magdelon thought it a pretty toy, but she was amused at the extravagant pleasure Cateau seemed to take in it.

When they returned to the Hall of Apollo the ball had already begun, opened by the King with the little English princess Henriette. Monsieur, the King's brother, partnered Mademoiselle de Longue-ville, a plain, gimlet-eyed young woman, quite twice his age and size; and the Comte de Saint-Aignan, First Gentleman of the Bed-chamber, led out Madame de Bade, the only Princess of the Blood young enough to appear on the floor.

As soon as the royal courante was over dancing became general. The Queen and her ladies settled themselves in a balcony at one end of the room, from which they could view the scene undisturbed; and the maids-of-honour, released from their duties, fluttered off to join the revellers.

Several prospective partners approached Cateau and Magdelon. The latter, with her sister's permission, tripped away with Bussy-Rabutin; but the former refused all offers, saying that she felt too tired to dance. She stood at the entrance to the ballroom, at the top of a short flight of steps, scanning the crowd and chatting with Saint-Evremond, who did not dance at all.

Magdelon noticed that Madame de Saint-Loup was standing at the foot of the same flight of steps, still alone, but quite obviously waiting for someone. At close range, she was by no means so pretty as she had looked from a distance, nor so young as Magdelon had supposed her to be. There were little petulant lines round her mouth, and her eyes, which were very much made up, looked strained and unhappy.

During the first sarabande a sudden commotion arose at the far end of the hall — buzzing voices, and some peals of loud, rather forced laughter. Then a little troop of courtiers in full dress burst in, and made their way towards the royal balcony through the maze of dancers.

Magdelon saw that the Comte de Moret was amongst them. But the centre of the group was a very tall, brilliantly handsome young man, with blond curls as long as Cateau's own, and a spectacular figure that seemed to make every other male in the room look squat and insignificant.

This personage appeared to have an excellent opinion of himself. He swaggered theatrically across the floor, brushing aside with an impatient hand any couples luckless enough to find themselves in his path. As he bowed to the Queen Magdelon remarked that the breast of his coat was ablaze with orders.

'Now we'll have some fun!' whispered Bussy in her ear. 'That's Candale, you know. The Saint-Loup's been waiting for him all eve-ning. Watch him put her through her paces! Poor monkey! She'd jump through a hoop if he told her to.'

Magdelon paused for a moment in the stately, swaying figures of the dance, to observe the little scene.

It was true, what Bussy had said: as soon as Madame de Saint-Loup caught sight of the Duke she ceased her anxious survey of the room and stood pluming herself, consciously smiling, at the foot of the steps, as if feeling that her trials were over.

Meanwhile, Candale, having made his obeisance before the throne, approached his mistress without any show of haste. Indeed, he seemed, if anything, to have slowed down his pace just a trifle.

Madame de Saint-Loup smiled ecstatically and held out her hand. But, to everyone's surprise, the Duke passed her by with a cold, silent inclination of his head, mounted the steps, and bowed low before Cateau, who was standing, pale and glittering, at the top. He said a few words in a low tone to Saint-Evremond, who replied, equally inaudibly, to the crowd's frank dismay. And then Cateau, without saying anything at all, gave her hand to the newcomer, and together they descended the stairs and sailed away to the proud, parading measures of the sarabande, like two statues of gold set in motion, stiff, unsmiling, and superb.

Chapter VI

THE MORNING AFTER THE BALL THE BELLS OF SAINT-ROCH DID NOT
wake Magdelon, but when Quinette at last succeeded in rousing her
they were ringing loudly

'The Countess's compliments,' said the solemn Quinette, 'and she
hopes you have slept well, and will join her at breakfast directly.
The Countess is going to Mass this morning.'

'Oh!' said Magdelon, blinking drowsily. 'Very well, Quinette:
say that I'll go with her.'

It was even harder to get out of bed today than it had been yesterday: her eyelids felt glued together, and all her senses were relaxed, dulled by an agreeable languor.   But she was glad they were
going to church. It was high time, really.... Old Mahaut had been
right: Paris was a wicked city.... 'And oh, dear,' thought Magdelon, with remorse, as the veils of sleep slowly lifted from her brain,
'I must be a wicked girl, for I forgot all about saying my prayers
last night!'

This was dreadful: would God ever forgive her?

She dressed as fast as she could, while the bells went on ringing
accusingly, and murmured a hasty but heartfelt appeal to her patron
saint Magdelaine to intercede for her privately, the first time a good
opportunity should be offered.

In Cateau's dressing-room a bright little fire was burning, as usual.
Breakfast was laid on the small table in front of it — but for two
only. Where was Monsieur de Beuvron?

Cateau, wearing a dove-grey satin gown trimmed with fur to
match and a long veil over her golden curls that made her look like
a lovely Madonna, kissed her sister in an absent-minded manner and
forgot to ask her how she was.

'Darling,' she said, 'I thought, if you didn't mind, we'd go to early
Mass this morning, for a change. If we wait for the late one, that
tiresome Montmorency is sure to drop in and want to come with
us — she's no coach of her own! And I can't pray in company, can
you?'

Cateau appeared for some reason to be in a great hurry this morning. She ate almost nothing, rushed through her interviews with the
servants, scarcely glanced at the pile of notes Brossard, the Swiss,
brought in.

'I'm going out this morning,' she said to Brossard. 'I can see no one, unless it's important. Who's waiting below?'

'Your glove-seller, madam, and two journalists, and a man to see about designing the new coach ——'

'Send them all away! Tomorrow will do as well.'

'Yes, madam. But will madam not see Monsieur de Beuvron —?'

'Monsieur de Beuvron? Is *he* there, too?'

'Yes, madam. He has been waiting in the antechamber for more than an hour. I asked him to go up, but he said he would not, without your permission.'

Cateau stamped her foot.

'The insolence of the man!' she said. 'Tell him to go at once. D'you understand? Tell him not to come back any more, until he's sent for — see?'

'Yes, madam,' replied Brossard, looking startled.

He bowed and departed, and Cateau turned to her sister.

'My dear, are you ready? — Then let's be off!'

At the door the Countess's own pretty little gilt carriage, drawn by a pair of yellow Spanish ponies, was waiting for them. The ladies got in, attended by Lindor and Quinette and Quentine. As they drove away Magdelon spied Beuvron's coach trundling sadly in the opposite direction: she wondered if Cateau, too, had seen it.

It was a glorious winter's day, brilliantly clear, with a bright sun and a cutting wind that raced round corners, blowing the snow from the ground up into the air in glittering puffs of diamond-dust.

Magdelon was surprised to find that Saint-Roch was not their destination. She mentioned the fact to her sister, who explained that, for all it was so near, Saint-Roch was not their parish church: their end of the rue Neuvre-Saint-Augustin belonged to the parish of Saint-Eustache.

To Saint-Eustache, accordingly, they went, down in the bustling market quarter, where the air, even in winter, smelt faintly of fish and cabbages.

By the time they arrived the church was full, and services had already begun. Cateau slipped to her knees at once and began to pray, with folded hands and eyes upturned devoutly.

Magdelon, next to her sister, kneeled and tried to pray, too. But she found her mind wandering away from her devotions. Presently her eyes started wandering as well; she stared with lively mundane curiosity at the occupants of the neighboring benches.

Saint-Eustache was a fashionable church, in spite of its proximity to the markets; many nobles and rich financiers lived in the parish. Magdelon recognized a number of her acquaintances. There were Monsieur de Bonnelle and his stout, pop-eyed wife; the latter, who had doubtless been up half the night at the card-tables, was telling her beads with mathematical exactness, as if attempting to devise a new 'system.'

Next to them were the Senneterres, La Ferté's father and step-mother. The Marquis de Senneterre, the Queen's friend and trusted adviser, was a little dried-up match of a man, who looked as brittle as glass, as though his first fall would dash him to pieces. He was so old that no one could remember when he had been born; perhaps he himself was no longer sure. But there was life still in his bright, beady eyes; he carried his tiny figure as erect as a soldier's, and was bravely arrayed in maroon velvet, with a starched ruff round his pipestem neck as the only reminder that his gallant days had been spent at the court of Henry IV. Moreover, there was his bride of less than a year — a sandy, doll-faced young woman, who looked as if she had no will of her own (probably, with such a husband and step-son, it would be just as well if she *hadn't*) — to prove that the Senneterres were hard to kill.

The Maréchal was not with his family when Cateau and Magdelon first arrived, but he came in shortly afterwards and sat down beside them, looking rather subdued.

During the sermon he remained motionless, his black bull's eyes fixed immovably on a point just above and behind the altar, all his intense physical energy not so much held in leash for the moment as actually cut off, like that of a hibernating animal.

Magdelon did not want to look at him; she told herself that she *would not* look at him . . . yet her glance strayed back again and again. . . . What was he thinking of? Was he thinking at all? Or was his mind as dormant as his huge, lifeless body?

Magdelon herself was afraid she was thinking of almost anything rather than the elegantly empty periods of the Abbé de Roquette, who was one of the preachers most in vogue at present, and there-fore sure of a good congregation, no matter what platitudes he chose to deliver. But was *anyone* really listening to the Abbé? The well-bred, worldly faces in the surrounding pews showed no traces of emotion: their owners were there, not for conviction's, but for cus-tom's sake. . . . Yes, Paris was indeed a wicked city! And Magdelon was becoming more and more sure she was as wicked as anyone in it. She had been at her sister's less than two days, and already it seemed to her that she had never lived anywhere else . . . worse still, that she did not *want* to live anywhere else. La Louppe, her own home, ap-peared as shadowy as a dream; Maman — her own mother — Aunt de Marville, old Mahaut, and the rest were like characters she had read about in a book, receding ever further into the background of her mind. (She loved them still, but it was becoming hourly harder to remember them.) And the foreground was now occupied by a host of more compelling figures: Cateau, in her golden dress on the bed, laughing and tossing her head; Madame de Choisy, under her top-knot of feathers, performing archly mysterious rites of coquetry with her fan; Brother Louis, holding his eyeglass on its silken cord and saying to Magdelon, in his kindly, fussy way: 'Exquisite! Exquisite!'; Monsieur de Beuvron, with his handsome head and his courteous manner, and the wounded look in his grave dark eyes. . . . But most vivid of all in the mass, though confused in her recollection as individuals, were the scores of young men she had met. Men . . . men . . . men everywhere, bowing, and smiling, and paying her compliments. . . . Ah, she had really forgotten, in those quiet years in the country, how exciting men were! Surely no life could be more satisfying than Cateau's, with a beautiful house, a noble husband, and a dozen gallants at her beck and call, to send her flowers and verses, sing serenades at her window, and whisper pretty speeches in her ear!

Magdelon meant to live precisely the same sort of life herself when she was married. . . . Married! Yes! She would be married soon. That was what she was here for, really; that was why Maman had sent her to Paris, because in the country there were no suitable partis looking for wives; while in town, under Cateau's astute direction, the possibilities were endless. It was strange to think that there had been a time — not so long ago, either — when she had supposed matrimony to be the supreme disaster, and had pitied Cateau from the bottom of her heart, as an unwilling sacrifice laid on its altar. In those days both girls had been certain that men were great, rough creatures, good for nothing but drinking and brawling and marching off to war to get themselves killed as soon as possible. It was all right, it was rather amusing, to dance with them and even flirt with them, in a coy, correct way. But as for anything further, as for responding seriously to their advances . . . oh, impossible!

Heavens, thought Magdelon, how naïve she had been! Why, men were delightful, thrilling, the only reason for living! She saw now, clearly, what it was she had been wanting lately, in those torturing moments when she felt choked with vague emotions, undefined longings, for which there seemed to be no outlet. . . . It was a husband she wanted! Only — how to choose amongst so many? Magdelon was sure she would be happy with almost anyone. . . . 'Magdelaine d'Angennes de la Louppe, Comtesse de Moret,' she said to herself experimentally. Yes; it sounded quite well. . . . 'Magdelaine d'Angennes de la Louppe, Princesse de Marsillac. . . .' Even better, maybe? Bussy was married, of course; so, alas! was Monsieur de Beuvron. But Souvré? Gramont? Manicamp? . . . Or had Cateau, perhaps, already chosen her fate? Did she —? Was it —? Could it be —?

Magdelon did not dare put her thought into words, but, as if in answer to her unspoken wish, when she fell to her knees for the final

benediction, there, directly across the aisle from the sisters, kneeled
the Duc de Candale. Dressed all in black, his blond head bent
reverently, his hands clasped in pious preoccupation — but as Magdelon, rosy with confusion, peeped at him through her fingers he
turned quickly and gave her an expressive glance of his keen cornflower-blue eyes. . . . Jesus! What eyes he had!

Magdelon nudged her sister, and whispered: 'Look! Cateau!
The Duke! He's there. . . .'

Cateau, however, would not look. She whispered back, quite
crossly: 'What if he is? Why shouldn't he be? He lives just across
the street.'

True enough: so he did. The Hôtel d'Epernon, which belonged to
his father, the Duc d'Epernon, was hard by, in the rue Plâtrière.
But then, knowing that, had Cateau come to church this morning
on purpose? Had she planned a meeting secretly for the two young
people's benefit? It seemed quite likely that she had.

Magdelon had been greatly disappointed, the night before, not to
have had the Duke presented to her at the Louvre. But she realized
now that that might have looked as if they were trying to force his
hand. Cateau had known better than to risk too much at too early
a stage of the game; she had, as usual, been the cleverer of the two.
Only . . . only . . . could it really be true that she, little, inexperienced
Magdelon de la Louppe, had attracted the notice of this marvellous
creature, this glittering demi-god, with eyes that pierced one's soul
to its depths? . . . Ah, if it were so! If it were so! . . . See! He was
smiling again . . .

Cateau pinched her sister's arm sharply.

'Magdelon! Where are your eyes? Control yourself, child!'

Magdelon, with a guilty blush, looked down, and folded her hands
in ardent prayer. . . . 'O Holy Virgin, Blessed Mother of God,'
she prayed, 'forgive me my sins, which are many and grievous,·and
make me worthy of this great happiness that may be in store for me!
. . . O Louis-Charles-Gaston de Nogaret de la Vallette, Duke of Foix
and of Candale' — for she had known his names and titles all by
heart for months — 'I love you!'

As soon as the service was ended the midday chimes began to ring.

Candale got up and strolled towards the door, with that nonchalance of demeanour Magdelon had so often observed in Cateau.
'Here I am,' it seemed to mean: 'take a good look at me, if you like!
I don't mind, in the least; I'm used to it; that's what I was born for,
really!'

Magdelon took full advantage of the opportunity offered, and was
rewarded by a much closer view of his face than she had hitherto enjoyed. It was almost incredibly handsome — 'the face of an angel!'
she said to herself, ecstatically — its regularity of feature marred
only by the unusual width of the mouth, accentuated by the thin

pencilling of the moustache that spanned his upper lip. But his teeth were peculiarly white and even, which gave his smile a most attractive brilliance; and he smiled a great deal, for he appeared to be very good-tempered, and was constantly laughing and joking with the group of young satellites that accompanied him everywhere.

Magdelon tried her best to hang back in the procession, in order to arrive at the door at the same time as this absorbing small party; but Cateau, annoyingly, seemed bent on getting away with uncalled-for dispatch.

On the steps outside the church something out of the ordinary was happening. Lackeys in livery were swearing and pushing each other roughly back and forth. One man even knocked another man down. There were cries of indignation at this from the supporters of the second man, and an ugly muttering arose from the crowd.

The ladies hesitated inside the door, uncertain whether it were safe to proceed.

'Stop here a moment, please,' said Monsieur de Bonnelle, who as a councillor of parliament assumed an air of authority in the crisis. 'I'll see what the trouble is.'

'It's those wretched stable-boys of La Ferté's,' said a man who was standing near Magdelon and Cateau. 'They tried to get the Maréchal's carriage in line ahead of the Duke's. A pack of cut-throats, that's what they are! And their master's the worst of the lot!'

Magdelon, craning eagerly forward, perceived that the man was right: she recognized the blue-and-silver coats of Candale's retinue, the scarlet worn by La Ferté-Senneterre's. The Maréchal was in the midst of his unmannerly crew, standing there on the top step, making no attempt to quiet the disturbance — on the contrary, adding to the din by roaring, in his deep bass voice: 'Hit him again, Robert! Hit him again! Go to it, lads!'

Magdelon felt she positively hated him.

At this point the Duke and his friends arrived on the scene.

Several people at once started explaining to him excitedly what the matter was.

He did not seem to be at all angry or upset, but listened calmly, smiling a little and stroking his pencilled moustache.

When the whole story had been told he arched his eyebrows and laughed.

'So,' said he, in a light, rather husky voice — Magdelon realized that it was the first time she had heard it — 'Neighbour Henri's getting out of hand again, is he? Let me speak to him.'

'My Lord,' said the Comte de Moret hastily, 'he's beneath your notice. Allow us to deal with the dog as he deserves.'

'No, no!' replied Candale, still smiling. 'Then we *should* have some trouble, my friend. I can manage this by myself.'

He strode forward across the threshold, although the shouting and pushing on the steps had now redoubled in violence, and, laying his hand on the Maréchal's shoulder, said a few words to him in a low tone.

No one could hear what they were, but their effect was immediate: La Ferté cringed before them, like a naughty small boy caught by his parent in an act of overt disobedience. He called off his men at once, with a sheepish imitation of his former blustering manner, and would have kissed the Duke's hand; but Candale shook the Maréchal's heartily instead and said, quite loudly: 'No hard feelings, eh, old chap?'

It was most disappointing: the quarrel had apparently ended as abruptly as it had begun.

Cateau turned to Magdelon and said quickly: 'Come with me!'

She made her way through the crowd, now streaming out on the steps and into the street, and peered this way and that, in search of her carriage.

While they were in church the sun had gone in, and it was snowing again. The wind had dropped, so that the flakes fell straight down: the square before Saint-Eustache was already white with them. Grey stones — white snow — and Cateau on the steps, pale and fair in her dove-coloured dress, with the long floating veil on her head, looked like the Winter Queen herself.

Candale came up to her at once and swept off his big plumed hat.

'Madam, good morning. I did not hope to have the pleasure of seeing you again so soon. What can I do for you? Are you looking for your coachman?'

'The stupid fellow!' said Cateau. 'I can't think where he is.'

'Why, but, Cateau——' Magdelon was beginning, for she had seen François drive his yellow ponies twice past the church while they were still inside: it was obvious that he would be round once more directly.

Cateau did not listen. She said instead, in her drawling, fine lady's voice: 'My Lord, my sister Magdelaine.'

Magdelon's heart turned over within her. She gave the Duke her hand; the young man kissed it, smiled at her, and said: 'I thought it must be she, you look so much alike. Ladies, will you not do me the honour of letting me drive you home?'

Magdelon's heart turned over again: ah, thrice-clever Cateau! No doubt she had planned this all along!

But Cateau seemed suddenly to have forgotten her part.

'My Lord,' she said, 'it is most kind of you, but I've my women with me, and a page as well — I fear we'd crowd your carriage.'

'Not at all,' said Candale. 'I've always room for ladies. Moret shall foot it, if necessary.'

Cateau still protested that she could not think of inconveniencing him. Then she looked about, and saw that Quentine and Quinette were waiting behind her, but that Lindor had vanished in the crowd. Nobody seemed to know where he had gone. It was most annoying.

The maids were sent off at once to find him, and Cateau begged her sister to accompany them.

'Poor silly fools, both!' she said, right in front of Quentine and Quinette. 'They'll be less than no help, if you're not there to tell 'em what to do.'

Magdelon felt she had no choice but to obey. It was scarcely bearable to leave at this juncture; but afterwards she reflected that Cateau had been right, as she invariably was: there were a few words to be said — delicate though they were — that could be said with propriety only in her own absence.

And, after all, she was gone not much more than a minute, for Lindor was discovered just inside the church, dutifully waiting for his young mistresses, whom he had somehow suffered to elude him in the press about the door.

When Magdelon returned with the servants she saw that the Olonnes' carriage had come. François, no doubt by the Duke's orders, had contrived to draw it up in front of Candale's own magnificent coach, which stood empty, blocking a whole line of vehicles, whose owners were impatiently waiting to be allowed to drive on.

Cateau was inside her carriage, leaning forward a trifle, holding out her hand and smiling; and Candale, heedless of the confusion he was causing, stood before her, hatless, his bent blond head covered with snowflakes.

'Madam, I would give my life ——' he was saying as Magdelon came up.

Cateau laughed.

'That's a good deal more than is necessary,' she said. 'No: what I ask as a pledge is a much smaller thing, as you know.'

'You shall have it tomorrow! That I swear! Moret shall fetch it at once. But can I be sure ——'

'Here is my sister,' said Cateau. 'And Lindor as well. Good-bye, my Lord. You keep your part of the bargain — and I'll keep mine.'

As they drove away she laughed again, to herself, but refused to explain the cause of her mirth. Nor did she glance back even once at the hatless young man in the whirling snow. Magdelon did, however — and the look she surprised on his face roused her, once and for all, from her rose-coloured dream of the last few hours. For, inexperienced as she was, she knew very well what that look was intended to convey: it was the look a man gives a woman with whom he is violently and incontrollably in love.

And it was not meant for her.

Chapter VII

IT WAS TWO DAYS LATER THAT THE DUC DE CANDALE MADE HIS FIRST appearance at the house of the Comte and Comtesse d'Olonne.

He walked into the white-and-gold saloon late one stormy afternoon, contrary to his custom quite alone save for six lackeys, who stood behind him on the threshold in an azure velvet semicircle, like a jewel-box encasing the rare diamond in its centre. In the doorway he paused, stroking his moustache and surveying the company with his cornflower-coloured eyes, while small electric shocks of excitement radiated through the room. Then, catching sight of the other golden head on the bed in the alcove, he started towards it slowly, deflected in his course for a moment only, halfway across the floor, by the greeting of his host.

'This is indeed an honour, my Lord,' said Olonne, bowing respectfully.

The Count was not easily impressed by names or titles. In fact, he made rather a point of not being. But it was undeniable that Monsieur de Candale was the most important visitor they had ever had: a duke of the royal house of France — for his late mother had been a natural daughter of the old king, Henry IV; Knight of the Order of the Holy Ghost; governor in his own right of the province of Auvergne as well as, jointly with his father, the Duc d'Epernon, of Burgundy; Colonel-General of the French Infantry; Commander of the King's army in Catalonia . . . holder of so many insignia of distinction that the mind was staggered by the effort to retain them. . . .What wonder Olonne was much pleased that this fabulous princeling had decided to pay them a call? No doubt he had seen and admired the Countess the other night at the Louvre. Who could have helped admiring her as she had looked on that occasion, in her stiff embroidered metallic gown? . . . Olonne was sure he had the handsomest wife in France. She was a credit to him anywhere — a bit flighty at times, perhaps, but, on the whole, a good-natured, high-principled young woman. If she had not been, neither her looks nor her dowry would have tempted him. As it was, though, if only she'd give him an heir — about which business she seemed unaccountably slow — he'd have no fault whatever to find with her.

Meanwhile, here was His Highness about to lay a proper, though quite unexpected, tribute at her feet and, in so doing, departing from his well-known custom of never calling on commoners. It was all most delightful, highly gratifying, indeed. . . . The Count screwed up his eyes and rubbed his hands together, to express his satisfaction, and hurried off to the dining-room to speak to the butler about a special brand of champagne. There were still a few bottles, he thought, of that Auvilé '49. . . . .

Magdelon was standing in the alcove by her sister's bed. So were Madame de Montmorency and Madame de Choisy. The latter, being a famous hostess herself, was not able to drop in every day, as she would have liked, but had managed to run over this afternoon for an hour to discuss a supper-party she was giving for Madame d'Olonne. (Madame de Montglas had been there, too, a moment before, but she had vanished upstairs in response to a mysterious summons from Bussy. . . . 'Poor thing! If it weren't for me . . . Yes, the yellow cabinet . . . I never ask what they do,' murmured Cateau, forgetting, as she often did, that there was an unmarried girl in the room. Madame de Choisy shook her plumed head mournfully and agreed that 'some people's husbands were very hard,' while Magdelon dropped her eyes and pretended she had not heard.)

The four women watched Candale's approach in silence, their chatter hushed, as if by common consent. Magdelon had by this time quite got over her disappointment concerning the Duke. After all, she had hoped for so short a time, and even then she had known in her heart that such a splendid destiny could never be meant for her. She could not, however, repress a flutter of emotion as the Duke mounted the step leading to the alcove and saluted the ladies. His manners, she thought, were perfect — a pretty blend of courtliness and gaiety: she could scarcely believe the Chevalier de Saint-Evremond was serious in maintaining that Candale had not long ago been an awkward, impetuous boy; that his grace of address was due altogether to the tactful schooling he'd received at the hands of Madame de Saint-Loup.

Now he was bowing low before Cateau and smiling; but he had himself well in hand today; no trace of the melting look Magdelon had surprised in his eyes remained to betray his plight to curious onlookers.

He said, casually, to his hostess:

'Madam, I've kept my part of the bargain. Here, if I mistake not, is what you asked for.'

He whipped out from under his lace-trimmed coat a package of an irregular shape, and dropped it into Cateau's lap, adding:

'With Moret's compliments — and your humble servant's.'

Cateau unwrapped the parcel — her fingers, Magdelon noticed, were trembling a little — and displayed a miniature leather bellows of sweet-scented Italian leather set in a silver-and-ebony frame.

'Why,' cried Magdelon, amazed, 'that's the bellows that belongs to the Queen!'

'A copy, mademoiselle,' said Candale, 'and a very fair one, I believe. Our good friend Moret was charged with the task of showing the original to a clever workman I know on the Pont Rouge — and here, within twenty-four hours, is the result. Madam, does it please you?'

Cateau drew a long breath; her eyes were shining.

'It pleases me very much. I am deeply grateful to you and to Monsieur de Moret. Will you convey him for me my most humble thanks?'

'With pleasure, madam.'

He bent again over her hand; and Magdelon, shamelessly eavesdropping to the best of her ability, heard him whisper before he looked up:

'And for me, what?'

'For you?' said Cateau, not at all in a whisper. 'Let me see: what can we do for you? I have it: Madame de Choisy shall ask you to her supper tonight. Are you free, my Lord?'

'I wasn't,' replied Candale, 'but I am — now.'

'And you, madam,' continued Cateau, 'I need hardly ask whether there's room at your hospitable board for one more gentleman?'

Madame de Choisy, who had been listening to their dialogue with an exaggerated air of roguish complicity, emitted a sort of whistling gasp.

'My Lord! — If you would deign — my poor house would be too greatly honoured ——'

'Madam, you are only too kind,' said Candale, smiling. 'I accept your gracious invitation with pleasure. As for you, madam,' turning back to Cateau, 'my coach and my company will be at your service this evening, and at any other time you may care to make use of them. Dare I hope ——'

'My Lord, you overpower me with attentions.' Cateau was determined not to be outdone in gallantry. 'My sister and I should be only too happy . . .'

She raised her voice and clapped her hands as she addressed the company at large.

'Come, everyone, and see what His Highness has brought me!'

There was immediately a crowd about the bed, admiring, exclaiming, all striving to handle the marvel at once — though Magdelon could not help thinking that they really did not care what they were looking at, and would have made just as much fuss over a pin or a handful of straw, if their hostess had asked it.

As for herself, she felt uneasily that the conversation she had overheard meant more than it had seemed to mean. She could not for

the life of her have told what it was that made her uncomfortable:
she was conscious only of two faces standing out in the little group,
for Cateau and the Duke were both radiant with a satisfaction far
exceeding its apparent cause . . . no; of *three*, really: in the midst of
the commotion she became aware of Madame de Montmorency,
surveying the scene from a little distance, a crooked smile on her
pale, ugly lips.

Madame de Choisy's party that night was a great success. Madame de Choisy's parties were always great successes. Like most
spoilt middle-aged women, she was at her best in her own house.
Sometimes, as if suddenly recalling that she had a reputation for
originality to keep up, she would disconcert a roomful of guests by
sweeping down on them with the cry, 'There are too many people
here! Which one of you is to go?' and an occasional visitor had been
known to be put out of countenance, on entering her drawing-room,
by his hostess's cocking her head to one side and exclaiming: 'Jesus,
sir! If I make no mistake, you were here just last week!' . . . But, on
the whole, her tact was as unfailing as her enjoyment of her own
hospitality. She knew everyone in the Queen's set, as well as a good
many others outside it, and mixed them all up with a cheerful disregard of ages, stations, and temperaments, rather like an adventurous apothecary.

The results were frequently amusing. Her small, dark, crowded
apartment rang with merriment till late in the night: no one ever
seemed to want to go home from Madame de Choisy's, and the most
unlikely combinations of persons managed to get on there as nowhere else.

This evening she was in especially high spirits, having captured a
genuine royal duke to serve as centrepiece to her table. She had also
the Comtesse d'Olonne and the Duchesse de Roquelaure — the latter a pale, languid nymph, Cateau's chief rival — the two most admired beauties of the moment: Ménage, the scholar; Benserade, the
poet; Madame de Nouveau, a pretty, talkative bourgeoise with a
great deal of money, and her sister, the Maréchale de Castelnau;
besides half a dozen of the best-looking and most popular young-
men-about-court.

Magdelon had a very good time, as she always did when she went
out with Cateau. It was thrilling to be driven to the party in Candale's state coach, a tremendous silver carriage lined with sapphire-
blue satin, manned by a retinue of lackeys in uniforms to match,
and escorted by so many postilions bearing lighted torches that they
seemed, as they clattered along, like a great comet trailing tails of
fire through the icy streets.

Magdelon sat quite still in the coach, breathless with a sense of
their importance.

Everyone at Madame de Choisy's greeted her gallantly, as if they were really glad to see her; Madame de Nouveau, who was reckoned the best-dressed woman in the 'town crowd' (as distinct from the court), asked her who had done her hair and where she had had her gown made; and all the young men were extremely devoted.

As usual, she was unable to make up her mind which one she preferred, and so followed the politic course of smiling alluringly at everybody.

After supper more guests arrived, and the inevitable card-tables were set up. However, it was not necessary to play at the Choisys', if one preferred other forms of diversion. A large group in one of the smaller saloons went on chatting during the whole evening; in another, Ménage read some of his new Italian poems to a select audience. (Italian was having a vogue just now on account of the popularity of the Cardinal's nieces, the Mancini sisters; Magdelon told herself that, really, she must set about learning it.)

Later, Maître Boësset, the King's music master, came in and played delightfully on the clavichord, accompanying Madame de Montglas, who had some renown as an amateur soprano, in his own latest airs, while the devoted Bussy turned the pages, and the lovers exchanged languishing glances under cover of the music.

Magdelon enjoyed herself so thoroughly that it was not till the very end of the evening that she noticed that it had been an hour or more since she had seen Cateau.

As the ladies were donning their cloaks Magdelon suddenly realized she did not even know how she was to get home. She fancied that the other women in the room were nodding and whispering amongst themselves about her plight; she felt the Montmorency's contemptuous glance upon her, and inwardly quailed.

Fortunately, at this uncomfortable juncture Cateau reappeared, looking strangely perturbed. She carried her head very high: there was an unwonted flush on her cheek, a glint in her eye, as if she were excited, or angry, or both.

She paid no attention to the others, but came straight to her sister and said: 'Are you ready to leave?'

'Yes, dear, whenever you are. Where's the Duke?'

Cateau lifted her chin.

'I'm sure I don't know — and I care less. What does it matter?' Magdelon looked surprised.

'Why, nothing — only I thought — as we came with him ——'

'That doesn't follow at all. Why should he drive us anywhere? Haven't I seen enough of him for one evening?'

'But then who ——'

Cateau gave a sigh of exasperation, and almost snatched her cape from the maid.

'My carriage is waiting below. You can come with me or not, as you choose.'

She swept out, without another word to anyone.

Magdelon, unpleasantly conscious of the smiles and meaning looks that passed between the remaining guests, hesitated a moment, and then followed her sister, making a halfhearted and wholly unsuccessful attempt to copy the latter's superbly theatrical exit.

The next day it snowed again: Paris, it seemed, had not known so stormy a winter in years. But Cateau rose early and dressed, as was her custom. She was sitting for her portrait to Monsieur Beaubrun, the younger, who was painting her as Minerva, in robes of flowing white silk and a gold helmet studded with deep purple ostrich plumes, against an imaginary background of ruined temples and sinister mauve mountains. To beguile the tedium of the long hours of posing she sent for Magdelon to come to the drawing-room and read them the latest instalment of Mademoiselle de Scudéry's *Clélie.*

The reading, however, had hardly got under way when the door opened and the Comte d'Olonne came in.

Magdelon looked up with a smile, which faded uncertainly as she perceived that, for the first time since she had known him, there was no answering smile on her brother-in-law's face.

'Good morning, sir,' said Cateau, not relaxing for an instant her pose, left foot behind her, right arm held up, the fingers slightly parted in an attitude of studied grace. 'Up so early! To what do we owe the honour . . .?'

The Count, who was in street costume and carried his hat in his hand — Magdelon saw that there was snow on it — clicked across the polished floor in his very high heels and halted before the dais where his wife was standing. Magdelon noticed that his mouth was drawn down at the corners in a petulant pout; his slits of eyes were sunk deep in his pink doll's cheeks.

He peered at the portrait on the easel and seemed on the point of saying something about it. Monsieur Beaubrun, in fact, was so sure that his patron meant to pay him a compliment that he laid aside his brush and stood, consciously smiling, to receive it. But after a moment's uncomfortable silence the Count dropped his eyeglass and said abruptly: 'I've just come from the Louvre.'

'Indeed!' said Cateau. 'And how is Her Majesty this morning?'

'I did not see her, madam. She was in bed and, I was told by her ladies, most unwell. All the court's in a dither over the theft of something that the Queen was particularly attached to — no less an object than the bellows of sweet-scented leather that hung in the crimson cabinet, and was a present from Madame Royale of Savoy. Someone must have picked it up yesterday at the lever and got it

out of the palace under cover of his cloak, for Her Majesty used it
herself only the night before last, according to Madame de Noailles
— and this morning, when the fire was lighted after breakfast, it was
found to be gone.'

'Why, how strange!' exclaimed Magdelon. 'That's the very bellows Monsieur de Candale had copied for you, sister! I wonder if he
knows anything about it.'

She glanced across the room to the hearth, beside which, on a
handsome wrought-iron rack, hung the Duke's gift. Lindor had been
teasing the flames with it scarce five minutes before.

'That's impossible,' said Cateau, very calmly. 'How could he
know?'

'Is the Queen much upset, my brother?' asked Magdelon.

'Very much upset,' said Olonne. 'She has been suffering from the
vapours ever since the loss was reported. Madame de Noailles and
Madame de Motteville have been in constant attendance at her bed-
side, and old Beauvais, her chambermaid, told me herself that she
swooned dead away when the news was broken, and that they'd had
to burn half a basket of feathers under her nose before she'd come to.
Fortunately, her suspense could not have lasted long, for before the
morning was over the thief was discovered.'

'The thief was discovered!' cried Magdelon. 'Impossible! Who
was it, then?'

The Count made no answer; but Magdelon, following the direction of his eyes, encountered Cateau's. Cateau, who was still posing
for Monsieur de Beaubrun, simpered prettily as she murmured, in
her cool little voice: 'I know nothing about it. How should I? It's
no concern of mine.'

'Of course it's not!' said Magdelon warmly. 'She asked the Duke
to have the bellows copied for her, and the Duke said he would,
and got the Comte de Moret to attend to the matter. That's all
there's to it, as far as she is concerned. If anything happened to the
original through Moret's carelessness or the dishonesty of one of his
servants, that can surely have nothing to do with Cateau.'

She paused, rosy and a little breathless after making the longest
speech she had yet dared address to her brother-in-law. Olonne
smiled for the first time since he had come into the room — but it
was, Magdelon thought, a rather nasty smile — and put his finger
in his mouth, like a baby.

'No?' he said meditatively. 'No? Your loyalty, dear sister, does
credit rather to your heart than to your understanding. Unhappily
for your theory — which I myself was at first tempted to accept —
our friend Moret was invited last night to a supper-party. At this
supper-party a barrel of wine was opened — what it was, my in-
formant was unable to say: half the young fellows at court don't

know or care what they're guzzling — the tradition of how to drink like a gentleman is vanishing faster than yesterday's snows!... At any rate, Moret had more than his share, and as the evening wore on he told, as a joke, the story of how Candale had persuaded him to steal the Queen's bellows as a present for the Comtesse d'Olonne.'

'Oh, but that couldn't be true! Cateau has only the copy.'

'You think so, my sister? You really believe that such workmanship could be duplicated within twenty-four hours?'

He walked to the fireplace and picked up the toy as he spoke, running his hand with a collector's appraising touch over the delicate lines of the silver inlay.

'Well, then,' said Magdelon, 'if it *is* the original, Cateau doesn't know it. You *know* she doesn't. Anyone could tell *she's* innocent.'

'Perhaps. I hope so, indeed. I am waiting for her to tell me herself that she is.'

There was an edgy silence, during which the only sounds in the room were the roar of the fire in the grate and the soft beating of snowflakes against the windows; it was broken at last by little Beaubrun, who dropped his palette and began to scrabble his brushes together, crimson with confusion.

'Excuse me, sir — with your permission, I'll return another time. Excuse me, madam — tomorrow at ten, if it suits madam's convenience? I have now another appointment I must fill.'

'Don't go, my friend,' said Cateau.

These were the first words she had uttered since her initial disclaimer: she spoke them slowly, evenly, as if considering each one.

'Your tact is most amiable, sir, but I assure you I have not the least objection to your remaining in the room. Pray, if you will, let us continue with the sitting.'

'Oh, Cateau,' cried Magdelon, almost in tears, 'tell Brother Louis he's wrong! Tell him there's a stupid mistake! You know you haven't the bellows that belongs to the Queen.'

'And if I did tell him,' said Cateau, still more slowly, 'do you suppose he'd believe me? No, child; it's much better to say nothing at all.'

'Much better, indeed, madam. Your friends who were here yesterday when the Duke came to call have already said quite as much as was necessary. The whole town has heard that you admired the bellows extravagantly and expressed a desire for it; that Monsieur de Candale, for reasons best known to you and himself, chose to gratify your desire; that he took advantage of his power and position to force Moret, a reckless young man, though not naturally a dishonest one, to do what he himself had neither the courage nor the effrontery to do; that today, thanks to your criminal folly, the Louvre is in an uproar. All I hope, my dear, is that your satisfaction with your performance is as complete as mine is in reflecting on the good fortune I enjoy in possessing so prudent and dutiful a wife.'

The Count's voice was no more excited than Cateau's; he spoke on an expressionless level, twirling his hat in his short, soft fingers and glancing obliquely from the fair young woman on the dais to the dark young woman in front of the fire, and then back again. It was really his lack of emotion that most alarmed Magdelon; she felt that his anger must be all the greater for remaining unexpressed. It seemed unnatural for him to be distraught by so trifling a cause: Cateau had been foolish, certainly, and perhaps a little rash, but nothing worse. The Duke and Moret were the real culprits. There was some mystery here.

Magdelon waited a minute, to see if Cateau were going to say something. As the latter stayed scornfully silent, it seemed best to proceed, with all possible caution, to try to patch up the quarrel:

'My brother, you know Cateau is guiltless. You *must* know it. But if there were anything she could do to mend matters, I'm sure she'd be only too willing to help. Wouldn't you, Cateau, dear?'

'This much she can do,' said Olonne. 'This much I insist upon her doing. She can return the bellows *at once* to its rightful owner, with a note reading thus: "Madam, I humbly beg your pardon for having received, though quite unwittingly, goods stolen from your possession. A pedlar sold me this bellows yesterday; today I find it was filched from your cabinet in the Louvre, and so return it, with deep apologies for having caused you, without my knowledge, even a moment's displeasure. I remain Your Majesty's most obedient servant, Catherine-Henriette d'Angennes de la Louppe, Comtesse d'Olonne." '

Cateau's face blanched under her crown of purple plumes.

'And if I refuse to do this?' she said haughtily.

'Madam, you will not refuse.'

'Why should I tell her what we all know to be a lie?'

'Because the truth, in this instance, is too shocking to be related.'

'I won't do it! I won't!'

Cateau, who all during the preceding scene had remained serenely poised on the dais, suddenly jumped down from it and switched across the room in a rustle of silken draperies. Seizing the bellows, which her husband had deposited on a table by one of the windows, she turned to face him defiantly.

'It's mine. I tell you, it's mine! You can't make me give it up. Try to make me do it. I dare you to try!'

For answer, Olonne without haste transferred his hat from his right hand to his left, and with the palm of the former struck his wife smartly in the face. The mark of his fingers remained faintly imprinted in red across the pure pallor of her cheek.

Cateau stood staring at him in a daze, while the mark deepened and spread a little. Poor Beaubrun, in a fright, dropped his brushes with a clatter, and fell to his knees to pick them up. Magdelon, horrified, started forward to her sister's aid; but Cateau waved her magnificently away.... Magdelon began to cry from sheer nervousness. Oh, this was awful! No one had ever dared do such a thing to Cateau; no one had ever so humbled her pride. How would she revenge herself? What would happen now?

To Magdelon's amazement, Cateau said nothing. She gazed at her husband with an expression of almost incredibly concentrated insolence while her lips moved slightly, but no words came out. Then she picked up her skirts and walked deliberately towards the door, which Monsieur Beaubrun hurried to hold open for her; gave the obsequious little man the pale gleam of a smile; and glided out with her plumed helmet only slightly askew.

It was Magdelon who wrung her hands, as soon as the door was shut, and exclaimed, in a tone of anguished conviction:

'Oh, what have you done? *What have you done?* Brother Louis, she will never forgive you.'

MAGDELON RAN UPSTAIRS TO HER SISTER'S DRESSING-ROOM, BUT found no one there. She then tapped timidly on the door to the bedchamber. After a short pause a muffled voice from within called out: 'Who is it? What do you want? Go away, for Heaven's sake!'

But Magdelon opened the door just the same, and entered.

Cateau was lying on the great canopied bed in the alcove facing the window, supporting herself on one elbow, with her chin in her hand. She still wore the gold helmet with its topknot of purple plumes; beneath it her eyes looked almost purple, too, dark and sparkling with anger. She was not crying, as Magdelon had feared. ... Magdelon was, though, a little. She felt frightened and oppressed by a sense that something terrible had happened. She could not have put into words her feeling that nobody ought to dare treat Cateau as Brother Louis had done, but all her life she had known it was true: you could not bully Cateau. It was useless, even dangerous to try. You might coax her easily enough; a little well-timed flattery, a tactful phrase or two, worked wonders; but at the slightest hint of coercion something hard and coldly determined arose in her nature, that neither force nor cunning could conquer.

Maman had known this well enough, in the old days at La Louppe, likewise all the servants at the castle, and her playmates at the convent in Caen; even the nuns, after a few disastrous experiments with the usual disciplinary methods, had rather insincerely concluded that 'Catherine-Henriette was a little original,' and might safely be left to achieve a state of grace in her own peculiar way.

Magdelon had supposed that Brother Louis, in the course of three years' married life, must have learned it, too; it was unsettling to discover how mistaken she had been.

'Anything may happen now,' she said to herself uneasily. 'Anything at all. Oh, dear!'

She approached the bed on tiptoe, clasping and unclasping her hands as she wondered what to say.

Cateau lay as quiet as if she were still posing for Monsieur Beaubrun, her chin still resting on her hand, her gaze fixed on the swarm of snowflakes outside the window, whirling hither and thither like busy white flies. In spite of the extreme relaxation of her attitude her eyes were mutinous and fiery: all her vitality seemed centred in her eyes.

Magdelon slipped to her knees at the edge of the bed.

'Cateau,' she said, 'I'm so sorry, dear. If there's anything I can do . . .'

Cateau laid her unoccupied hand on her sister's shoulder.

'I know you are, darling. But what is there to be done?'

'Why, I don't know, exactly — but couldn't I perhaps help explain things to Brother Louis? He acted dreadfully, of course; he had no right in the world to say what he said or do what he did — but truly, dear, I'm sure it was because he didn't understand.'

'And what,' asked Cateau, 'do you think there is he doesn't understand?'

'Why, but, Cateau, you *know* — about the bellows! If I were to go to him now and tell him that he'd made a mistake — that you hadn't the least idea that Monsieur de Candale had stolen it from the Louvre . . .'

Cateau turned her enormous eyes on Magdelon, still without moving her head.

'What would be the good,' she said clearly, 'when he knows as well as you and I do that it's simply not true?'

It was Magdelon's turn now to stare.

'What do you mean — "not true"?'

Cateau went on stroking her sister's shoulder.

'Well, well!' she said. 'Poor child! I see I shall have to explain things to you in words of one syllable. Listen to this, then: I knew all about the bellows from the very beginning, d'you see? I asked Candale to steal it for me, that day after Mass at Saint-Eustache. He promised he would. If only he'd done it himself, as I bade him, there'd have been no trouble at all. But no, he thought he knew better — men are such obstinate fools! He said he hadn't called at the Louvre for a month — it would cause too much comment — that Moret, who's attached to the Cardinal's suite, was the man for the job. And Moret did it — but he had to get drunk the very next night and let the cat out of the bag. It's too bad, that's what it is! All that bother for nothing! For now I'm afraid there's nothing for it but to send it back to the Queen, as Olonne told me to, and pretend I had no idea where it came from. Not that she'll ever believe me — horrid suspicious old hag!'

Magdelon's eyes were round with surprise.

'But why, sister, *why* . . . What made you . . .'

'Oh, why? Why does one do anything? How can I tell? To tease Olonne, perhaps.'

'He's very angry,' said Magdelon, shaking her head. 'But I'm sure in the end he'll forgive you.'

'I'm sure of it, too. I wish sometimes I weren't. If only he cared what I did! If only he'd really *see* me just once!...'

'He's very angry,' repeated Magdelon solemnly. 'But I don't know why. It can't be only the bellows. He doesn't give *that* for the court or anyone in it. There must be something more. Cateau, there *must* be. Darling, won't you tell me what's the matter? I love you so much... I do so want to help.... What's gone wrong between you and Brother Louis?'

Cateau lifted the plumed helmet from her golden curls and laid it beside her on the counterpane.

'It's so heavy,' she murmured, with a plaintive look, as if Magdelon were somehow to blame for its weight. Then she smoothed her hair, and fiddled with the ribbons of her bodice, and drummed with her fingers on the bedpost, all the while staring out the window at the snow, before she was able to bring herself to speak.

When at length there was nothing left to do, she turned to Magdelon and said demurely: 'Candale is in love with me.'

'Yes,' said Magdelon, 'I know.'

'He's been in love with me for months. Even before we met he was. He made up his mind to be while he was still with the army in Spain, he said, though he'd seen me only once, driving in the Cours la Reine.'

Magdelon swallowed hard, almost choked by a sudden wave of emotion. She dropped her eyes, blushed bright red, and finally managed to mumble: 'Are you in love with him, too?'

'What a silly question! Naturally I'm not!'

'Oh, but ——' Magdelon's cheeks were still flushed, while her voice had sunk to a whisper — 'how can you help...? I mean...'

'Why should I be? Why, in Heaven's name? A vain, spoilt boy like that, who imagines he's only to smile to have every woman in France at his feet, begging him to notice her! Why should I sue for his favour, that can have any man at court I choose? Yes, and that's what I said to him, too, the other night at the Choisys'. I told him quite plainly I was not interested. The conceit of the creature! He simply refused to believe I wasn't the sort of woman who'd stoop to be unfaithful, just for the glory of snatching a prize that everybody else is after. Oh, but I'll show him I'm in earnest! I'll show him a woman's honour means more to her than any pair of long-lashed blue eyes — though he were twenty times a duke!'

'Dear me, yes, there's Brother Louis!' said Magdelon, much abashed to think she had forgotten him. 'There's your husband, isn't there? You couldn't deceive *him*.'

'My husband?' cried Cateau. 'Who said anything about my husband?'

'Why, but Cateau ——'

'I never mentioned Olonne. When I said I wouldn't be faithless, I meant to Beuvron, of couse!'

'Monsieur de Beuvron! But Cateau, you told me he wasn't... that you never...'

Cateau glanced away for a moment, and grew faintly pink.

'Oh, well, my dear, what could I say? You'd just come from the country... it didn't seem at the time that I ought.... But, after all, you're not a child. You're old enough to have some ideas about life. Naturally I supposed that you guessed...'

Magdelon gazed at Cateau and slowly shook her head, while two large tears, that had been waiting to fall, rolled down her cheeks and splashed onto the wide lace collar of her dress. As she wiped them away she thought how wicked she must have grown to be.... Only a week ago this revelation would have shocked her beyond speech, but now, although she could not say she approved, it seemed to her quite natural that Cateau should have had a lover all the time.

There was, however, an interval of acute embarrassment to be got over as gracefully as possible. Cateau, apparently, was as well aware of this as Magdelon herself, for she kept her eyes averted and talked a good deal more than was necessary in order to state her case.

'My dear, if you were married, you'd understand. When you've a husband of your own you'll begin to see.... Life is sometimes very difficult.... It's not altogether my fault... in the circumstances.... If you knew the things I've had to put up with.... Oh, why did Maman make me marry Olonne?'

'But, Cateau, you chose him yourself, didn't you?'

'What if I did? I was only eighteen, a mere baby, too young to know my own mind. And then the war came... all that excitement ... the glamour of a uniform.... Maman should have known better. She should have saved me from myself. Then all this mess needn't have happened. Other girls' mothers make matches for their daughters. But we've had no one to help us, no one.... Magdelon, you've seen for yourself what he is. You know very well no woman on earth could possibly live with Olonne, unless there were someone ... Why, there are days on end when I simply don't exist for him, when he forgets all about me — or, what's worse, when he doesn't quite forget, but looks at me as though I were part of the drawing-room furniture, just something to be painted and gilded and covered with taffeta and stuck in the middle of the room, to be stared at and admired without using. He's inhuman, he's a kind of vegetable.... I swear to you, it's not blood that runs in his veins, but green apple juice! And that rabble around him, they're no better than he is. There's not one among 'em that's man enough to care for a woman.

All they think about from one day's end to the next is their spleens
and their stomachs ... what's digestive and what's not! ... the best
way to serve truffles or bake a lark pie! Hateful selfish beasts! I
could scream when I think ... How do you suppose I'd have been
able to go on living if I hadn't found someone else to love and protect me — who'd be on my side and keep me from dying from boredom and neglect? And can you blame me if I was grateful enough
to give him in return all I had to give, what nobody else wanted —
nobody? After all, *I'm* a human being; I'm not made of stone.'

But Magdelon thought that Cateau looked as if she were; that
what she resembled more than anything else was a beautiful statue,
stretched out on the bed in her white silken robes, with her golden
hair streaming over the pillows and her face quite cold and remote,
in spite of her torrent of words.

'Poor Beuvron!' Cateau continued, rather as if she were talking
to herself. 'He's an honest man, and a very kind one. I don't regret for a moment what I've done ... Only now ...'

'Yes, now?'

'Oh, why did I have to marry Olonne? Why? Why? If I could
be free ...'

'Free? But, Cateau, what for? Isn't Monsieur de Beuvron married, too?'

'Yes — yes — but his wife's a poor sickly wretch. She's not long
for this world. And if he weren't single, there'd be others who are.'

'Cateau, what others? You don't mean ...'

'And what if I did?'

Cateau looked Magdelon straight in the eye, but a warm wave of
colour, all the more becoming because it was so rare, suddenly
flooded her cheeks.

'But, sister, you said that you hated *him*.' (Magdelon could not
bring herself to pronounce the magic name, but it vibrated unspoken in the silence between them.)

'So I did. So I do — I do hate him. But how can I tell what might
have happened if we'd met three years ago? Or even now if ... Ah,
I've no luck in my life! Everything comes to me too late to be any
good. I'm finished — done for — at twenty-two! And Olonne will
live forever, just to spite me.'

She leaned back against her pillows and shut her eyes, as if her
future were too distasteful to bear looking at.

Magdelon got up from the floor and sat on the foot of the bed,
clasping her hands round her knees. She did not know what to say
next. It was all such a puzzle.... What did Cateau really want?
She had spoken first of her love for Beuvron, but now it seemed that
the *other* ... Magdelon, who had little enough knowledge of the way
marriages were arranged, still could not help feeling that, even if

Cateau were free, the Duke would be out of the question. He was such an important young man — almost royal — and so rich that he'd already refused half the heiresses in Europe. How, then, could one hope...?

Cateau opened her eyes again, and patted Magdelon's hand.

'Darling, don't heed what I've been saying. I'm half out of my mind this morning with the vapours, to say nothing of the stupid fuss with Olonne. I'll pay him out for it yet — see if I don't!'

'But, sister,' protested Magdelon, 'how can you? After all, he's your *husband*.'

'Husbands,' said Cateau smartly — she was smiling now — 'don't matter any more than anyone else. Not so much as most people. At least, in Paris they don't. Besides, they're always head over heels in love with some awful actress or other. All the men I know seem to be.'

'Is Brother Louis?' asked Magdelon, ready by this time to credit almost any enormity.

'No,' replied Cateau. 'But then, he's not really a man: he's an animated menu!'

She gave a sudden high little hoot and began to laugh. Magdelon laughed, also, although she was not quite sure what she was laughing at. The bed-curtains shook with their mirth; even the white snow-flies outside the window flew faster than before, as if sharing the joke; and when Quentine came in presently, with an armful of ribbons and laces to stow away in the wardrobe, she smiled to find both her young mistresses so merry.

THE MORNING AFTER THE QUARREL THE COMTE D'OLONNE FELL ILL. He awoke very early in great pain, with a touch of fever; his right foot was so swollen that he could not bear to put it to the floor.

'A cold,' said Olonne. 'It's a cold I have caught being out in the snow yesterday.'

And he rang angrily for his valet, and ordered a litre of Beaune — a wine he never touched when in his usual health — to be warmed to room temperature.

But as time went on he began to feel so much worse, in spite of the Beaune, that Doctor Patin was sent for; and Doctor Patin, driving over after midday dinner, crusty and formidable in his long wig and black robe and big feathered hat, pronounced the malady a sharp attack of gout. Wines of all sorts were banished from the sufferer's bill-of-fare; a regimen of slops inaugurated; purges and bleedings prescribed; and a frightening list of remedies sent in from the apothecary's, to be administered in case the patient failed to respond to the treatment promptly.

Cateau's behaviour in these trying circumstances was, Magdelon thought, exemplary. She stayed in the sick-room most of the morning, attired in a penitential steel-grey serge, with almost no lace on the sleeves; rubbed thousand-flowers-water on her husband's forehead and some strong-smelling liniment on his foot. She also postponed her sitting with Monsieur Beaubrun and dismissed callers with a curt 'The Countess is not receiving today.'

Most significant of all, she made a copy in her own writing of the note Olonne had composed to the Queen and dispatched it, together with the bellows, in Lindor's care to the Louvre.

Magdelon, who had hung about the house all day, depressed and nervous, with nothing to do, was surprised when her sister sent for her, late in the afternoon, to come to the Count's bedchamber.

It was the first time she had been in her brother-in-law's apartments, which were at the back of the house on the first storey, across the hall from the white-and-gold saloon.

The room she entered was nearly in darkness, with only the flames of the fire to cheer it. The curtains had not yet been drawn, but the evening light was pallid and lifeless; through the tall windows one had a glimpse of the Butte Saint-Roch with its windmills, looming gaunt and lonely through the grey-blue dusk.

Brother Louis was in bed, propped up by a great many pillows. His face was very pink, but he did not look so cross as Magdelon had expected. In his frilled white nightshirt, with a peaked cap perched on his uncombed blond hair, he reminded her of a pig — a pretty one, to be sure, but still a pig — dressed up like a baby.

Cateau, in an armchair by the fire, was stitching at a piece of tapestry. As she sewed, the firelight glinted on the rings she was wearing, and struck vagrant sparks from her golden curls.

She did not raise her eyes as her sister came in, but Brother Louis did. He lifted one finger straight up in the air, with a schoolmaster's gesture, and said abruptly: 'What day of the month is it?'

'Why, I'm not quite sure,' replied Magdelon. 'Is it the eighth of February?'

'It's the ninth,' said Cateau. 'Lent begins the sixteenth.'

'Exactly,' said Brother Louis. 'Just so. Lent begins the six-teenth. There's but one week left of the carnival. One more week before the lights go out and the music stops and the weary season of repentance begins. Ladies, these are not nights for spending quietly in the chimney-corner. Paris is full of gay young folk in search of amusement: why don't you join them?'

'Why, but, my brother, you are ailing. How could we dream ——'

'Nay, that's no excuse. I should have to be far more ill than I am before I'd consider asking you to forgo an evening's entertainment on my account. And for that matter, my dears, you know very well that, even if I were well, no persuasions on earth could induce me to quit my hearth and run about town all night long dressed like a monkey. But why shouldn't you go, if you care to? The fiddles are tuning up; the masks are assembling in the Cours Saint-Antoine. It would give me great pleasure to know that you two were amongst them.'

Magdelon glanced at her sister, intending to follow her lead, and wondering how the latter would take her sudden release from duty; but Cateau did not even look up from her tapestrywork.

'Sir,' said Cateau, sewing busily, 'it's a matter of perfect indifference to me whether I join the maskers or not. To be quite frank with you, I'd as soon remain where I am.'

'Madam, your kindness of heart does you infinite credit. But I refuse to accept such a sacrifice.'

'It's no sacrifice, I assure you. I've been at other carnivals in my time. And I dare say I'll see still more of 'em before I die. What's one more or less ——'

'Nay, my dear, I insist, I *insist* on your going!'

'And I say, I'd far rather not. I don't want to go out tonight.'

'But why, my love, why? It's not like you to lag ――'

'I've already told you, *I don't want to go.* Is that not enough for you?'

'If not for your own sake, then for your sister's. *You* may have seen all the carnivals you wish, but our poor little Magdelaine has been buried alive in the country for nearly three years. Surely we owe her some compensation. Dear child, it's your duty...'

'Oh, please, Brother Louis,' cried Magdelon, 'don't think of me! I don't care ――'

'Ah, but you do,' interrupted Olonne; 'and it's right that you should, at your age. And so does my Catherine-Henriette, though she's loath to confess it. Be off with you! Quick! There's not a moment to lose. And if you should find in your dressing-room two costumes of Chinese ladies of high degree, complete with jewelled headdresses and embroidered satin slippers, I hope you may consent to accept them, with my most devoted compliments... that is, of course, my dears, provided that they fit!'

'Brother Louis, how kind you are!' exclaimed Magdelon happily, jumping for joy. (It was a very small jump, but Magdelon was ashamed of it, and immediately drew herself up with dignity, hoping that Cateau had not noticed.)

Cateau said nothing. She got up and folded her tapestry; then approached the bed, and gave her husband her hand with her usual dazzling but meaningless smile.

Olonne pressed her fingers to his lips and smiled, too.

'I've only one request to make of you, madam,' he said, 'and that is, that when you are dressed you and Sister Magdelaine will deign to honour me with a private inspection of the two most charming maskers in Paris tonight. Good luck attend you! Now ring the bell for that fool of a Crispin: it's time for me to take another of Patin's foul messes.'

He smiled again: after Cateau and Magdelon had left him the latter remembered his curious smile — not vague, like his wife's, but charged with good-tempered malice, and something else rather less pleasant, that Magdelon felt, though she could not name it.

An hour later, twin glittering figures in gold-embroidered robes and high flowered crowns, their eyes shining through masks of black velvet, met on the stairs and clasped hands in convulsive excitement.

'Darling!' said Magdelon. 'You look lovely!'

'And so,' said Cateau, 'do *you*, darling. I'd never have known you.'

'Nor I you,' said Magdelon. 'Oh, isn't this fun?'

Crispin, the Count's valet, having conveyed outside his master's door the whispered intelligence that the patient was sleeping, there was nothing further to keep them.

François was waiting at the door with the carriage, which was

decorated for the occasion with loops and bows of scarlet bunting.
It was a fine moonlight night, cold but dry; the air seemed tingling
with life, pricked here and there with tiny dancing diamonds of
snow.

The streets were already full of coaches, all making in the same
general direction. By the time they had reached the rue Saint-
Antoine the crowds had grown even greater, so that it was difficult
for François to manage the horses. Once outside the city gates,
however, they turned into a wide park-like promenade, bordered
by rows of clipped limes, the Cours Saint-Antoine, society's winter
rendezvous (which served the same purpose as the Cours la Reine,
at the other end of the town, in summer).

Here there were many more carriages, tricked out like their own
in bright-coloured bunting, driving slowly back and forth, in the
very shadow of the great grim Bastille, which looked silver-grey and
slightly unreal in the rays of the moon.

But there was nothing grim about the carloads of maskers in
fancy dress, who laughed and sang snatches of song and called out
gay greetings, as their coaches passed and repassed one another in
the fantastic parade.

Magdelon lay back against the satin cushions and drew a long
breath of delight. She watched the lines of bare lime trees, the
flaring torches of the postilions, slip past her; heard the hard-packed
snow squeak under the wheels of the coaches, as if in a dream.
There was something hypnotic in this endless procession, lacking
both head and tail and quite purposeless: it might very well go on
forever.... 'And I'm here, I am part of it.... *Who am I? Magdelaine d'Angennes*.... I'm here in Paris, at night, in the Cours Saint-
Antoine, with the maskers ... oh, lovely! ...'

She was roused from her reverie by Cateau, who was pinching her
arm and laughing.... 'Look, dear, we've found friends already!' ...
There abreast of their carriage was another, filled with young men
dressed as pilgrims; among them Magdelon recognized Bussy and
the Marquis de Manicamp, who were bowing and smiling to the
Chinese princesses.

After some preliminary compliments the pilgrims accepted
Cateau's invitation to dismiss their coach and transfer themselves
to the ladies' — and from then on there was no time for dreaming.

The party made a few more turns in the avenue, stopping at a
pastrycook's booth, strung with red-and-silver lanterns, to buy
cakes and candied fruits and a bottle of sweet, strong liqueur known
as rossolis; then, this pleasure soon palling, it was decided to return
to the town, where the balls would now be well under way.

Cateau and Magdelon, squealing with laughter, led their pilgrims
first to the Chancellor Séguier's, in the rue de Grenelle, where the

Chancellor's younger daughter, the Duchesse de Sully, was holding a rout. Here they picked up Madame de Montglas and Madame de Montmorency, who were dressed as peasants from the Bresse, wearing broad-brimmed straw hats with streamers and bright orange aprons, and accompanied by a number of men, including Beuvron.

Magdelon, self-consciously aware of her new knowledge of his relations with her sister, watched their greeting, breathless with an emotion half sympathy, half pure embarrassment. Surely these two, of all people in the world, could not look upon each other with everyday eyes! They could not meet as most men and women did, could not bow and laugh and talk, as if nothing... Beuvron kissed Cateau's hand and said: 'Madam, good evening.' Cateau did not even bother to speak. But she gave him her most amiable 'society' smile, and stood up with him for a branle; and for the rest of the evening he remained attached to their party.

It was at the Séguiers' that Magdelon lost one of her earrings and fell in love with the Marquis de Manicamp.

They then swept on to the Bonnelles', where the young King and his troop, disguised as shepherds and shepherdesses, had just arrived. Everyone knew who they were, but pretended not to know: that was carnival etiquette.

Olympe de Mancini, looking plumper than one would have believed possible in her tight-laced bodice, seemed to be the most popular of the shepherdesses, though Monsieur, the King's brother, who was a shepherdess also, pouted and preened himself and flirted quite openly with the handsome Comte de Guiche. Guiche, apparently, was rather bored by these royal advances, for he deserted Monsieur as soon as he could, much to Magdelon's dismay, for her cavalier Manicamp.

Magdelon, however, had a very good time at the Bonnelles'. The entertainment was even more sumptuous than at the Séguiers': Scaramouche was there with his actors from the Petit Bourbon; some trained Barbary apes in court costume danced a pretty ballet called *The Loves of Adonis*; and a magnificent supper was served.

Magdelon lost her other earring at the Bonnelles' and fell in love with the Chevalier de Gramont.

The next port-of-call was a rich bourgeois family that lived hard by in the rue des Poulies. No one seemed to have any idea who they were, but that made no difference: it was great fun to swagger past the protesting Swiss at the door; to swarm upstairs, laughing shrilly, in a body to the ballroom where fires were blazing and fiddles squeaking, and the master and mistress of the house, absurdly overdressed, for all the world like royalties in a pack of cards — poor wretches! of course, they knew no better — bobbed up and down, overcome with delight and confusion, at these noble visitors from another planet.

The ordinary rules of polite behaviour were strangely relaxed on such occasions. You spoke to your hosts or not, as you liked; you ate their food, drank their wines; danced a courante or a gavotte with their daughters, if they happened to be pretty enough to merit your favours; then, all of a sudden, at a signal from the leader, with a swoop and a shriek the intruders would be off to seek other diversions.

Young men at court had always done this, more or less; what was new nowadays was that they brought their women with them.

Cateau and Magdelon found a number of friends at the house in the rue des Poulies. Some gypsy dancers were telling miraculous fortunes, and Ninon de Lenclos, brown as a gypsy herself, came in all alone, dressed as a Magyar queen in superb fur-trimmed robes of purple-and-red. At this point a good many of the more interesting men temporarily deserted their partners, as Ninon must have known they would do. (These included Bussy, who had just quarrelled with Madame de Montglas and, being Bussy, felt an irrepressible urge to call attention to the fact.)

Ninon sat on the other side of the room from the 'respectable' ladies, laughing and waving her fan. Most of the women there, including Cateau and poor, silly Cécile de Montglas, glared at her through their masks; but Magdelon did not follow their example. She was interested in the courtesan, whom she had often heard of, but never before beheld at close range, and regarded her critically. ... Ninon's appearance was a trifle disappointing: she was said to be thirty-five — 'Oh, forty, dear, if a day!' Madame de Montmorency whispered in Magdelon's ear — and when she removed her mask, as she presently did, she looked all her age. But her sidelong smile Magdelon thought fascinating, likewise her impudent, heart-shaped face; and the way in which she used her eyes and fan betrayed a careless consciousness of power.

At the bourgeois ball they ran into the Duc de Candale and his suite, including Moret, garbed as Oriental potentates in turbans and full velvet trousers embroidered with precious stones. It was the first time Magdelon had seen her sister's two lovers together: she noticed at once that they bowed to each other stiffly. Shortly after his arrival Cateau was seen to signal to the Duke with her fan: they disappeared together for several minutes, and when Cateau came back, looking flushed and a little out of sorts, she was alone.

Magdelon did not have leisure just then to speculate on the meaning of this incident, for one of the gypsy fortune-tellers had stolen her bracelet of brilliants; and by the time she tired of looking for it she found she had fallen in love with the Comte de Moret.

It was late when they came out of the house in the rue des Poulies: Magdelon was beginning to feel very sleepy. Her heart sank when

Cateau proposed that before going home they should call at the Senneterres', where there was said to be 'something going on.'

'Oh, dear,' said Magdelon, 'don't let's go there! Do you really want to?'

She remembered now that she had never spoken to Cateau of her encounter with the 'bull-man' on the bridge, the day of her arrival in Paris. She could not have said why this was; she had always intended to tell her about it, and, indeed, had begun the recital more than once; but somehow the words would not come. She had, of course, often seen the Hôtel de Senneterre, where the bull-man lived, in her drives round the quarter, and as often had shivered at sight of its forbidding grey walls. Known as 'Great Senneterre,' it was the largest private house in town and decidedly the gloomiest. Tales were told of its interior splendours: of the chapel as large as a church, decorated with baroque painted stucco in the Italian style; of the rows of reception rooms culminating in the celebrated Gallery of Aminta, with frescoes after Tasso; of the gardens, with their grottoes and mazes and spouting fountains, and rows of orange trees the size of oaks; of the high-vaulted mews where eighty horses could be stabled at once. Few people had been privileged to inspect these marvels of late years: the Marquis had grown old and, it was whispered, exceedingly mean; and La Ferté, his son, was a widower now and often away with the army or at Nancy, the seat of his government; so that the rumour that they were entertaining to-night was greeted with cheers.

Beuvron, who alone knew of Magdelon's aversion to the Maréchal, tried to discourage Cateau's suggestion, but in vain: into the coaches they piled pell-mell, whooping with glee, and clattered off through the silent streets, livid now in the melancholy light of the winter dawn.

As Cateau had promised, Great Senneterre was prepared to receive them. The heavy outer gates stood ajar, and the huge building, usually dark and deserted, twinkled extravagantly with candlelight from every window.

As they entered the door the air seemed heavy with smoke and sweat, to say nothing of liquor fumes; and once fairly inside they found the grand staircase seething with a mob of drunken servants. Valets and porters, their uniforms torn and dishevelled, were swilling tankards of ale and sporting with a flock of frowsy maids, who screamed loudly at stated intervals with the peahen-like mirthlessness characteristic of their sex and class. One of the Maréchal's lackeys had a wench cornered in an angle of the banisters: he was pressing her back as hard as he could against the marble rail, tearing her bodice open with one hand, while the other dangled a hunk of sausage just out of her reach. The girl was making strenuous efforts

to seize the sausage with her teeth, but none to free herself from his
clutches. . . . In the other angle of the stairs another lackey was
vomiting vigorously, surrounded by a circle of jeering companions.

It took some determination to force a passage through this unsavoury mob to the upper regions.

At first sight the Gallery of Aminta appeared to be uninhabited,
in curious contrast to the scene of coarse revelry below. At one end
of the enormous room stood a long supper-table, looking as thoroughly devastated as though the Maréchal's army had looted it.
A great joint of beef and two glacé hams had been ruthlessly
slashed to the bone, several pheasants reduced to mere skeletons;
the wine-bottles, too, were quite empty; only a faint smudge of
carmine in some of the glasses proved that there once had been
Burgundy in them. The damask cloth was fouled and greasy; a line
of yellow-green trickled sluggishly across it from a smashed decanter
of some sticky liqueur to fall drop by drop, with slow hopelessness,
to the floor. Even the candles guttering low in their sconces looked
wan and dejected, as if the good had gone out of them.

At the other end of the room the remaining guests were grouped
about the gigantic chimney-piece, beneath which the dregs of what
had once been a roaring fire fitfully smouldered. Now and then the
remnant of a log would spurt up into a momentary semblance of life,
only to subside into ashes. The guests, like the logs, were nearly
spent. They lay in rows on benches and divans, half asleep, too
tipsy to get up and go home, not quite tipsy enough to have stopped
trying to act as though they weren't tipsy. The men were mostly
young officers from various regiments; the best of the women were
actresses from the Marais or the Théâtre de la Bourgogne — Magdelon recognized several of them — pretty, gaudily dressed little
creatures, with beaded eyelashes and splotches of paint on their
cheeks. One old harridan, with a face like a parrot's and a black
lace mantilla, was huddled as close to the fire as she could get, holding her claw-like hands, which were dreadfully deformed by rheumatism, to the sulky embers and muttering to herself, over and over,
something that sounded like 'Holy-Catherine-night-such-as-this!'

The entrance of Cateau's company of maskers, who, though some
of them were far from sober, still were in perfect control of their
limbs, brought fresh vitality into the torpid gathering. A wave of
languid motion swept round the circle: arms were stretched, hair
put to rights; those who were able — as well as several who were
not — attempted to struggle to their feet; one very fat little girl,
wearing a headdress of white furry rabbit's ears, squeaked in a
piercing treble: 'God save us, the gentry are here!'

Presently the Maréchal heaved himself up out of the chair whose
high back had concealed him till now. Unlike most of the merry-

makers he was neither masked nor in costume, and, though his face
was flushed and his step not quite steady, he seemed in full possession of his forces.

'Welcome, friends! Welcome, ladies and gentlemen! Heartily
welcome!' he bellowed benevolently. 'The Marquis, my father, I
fear has retired, but I'm here to do the honours in his place as well as
I'm able. I'm much afraid there's nothing more to eat, and not a
drop left to drink in the house — Jesus! What a stingy old codger
he is! Ah, when he dies — if he ever does — things will be different
at Great Senneterre! Come warm yourselves by the fire, though
that's nearly out, too, and if there's a stick of wood left in the cellar
to replenish it with, I'll break my best sword into bits and swallow
'em whole. . . . But welcome, good friends, none the less!'

He passed his hand over his thick curly black hair and beard in a
gesture of comic bewilderment, and laughed disarmingly. It was a
little boy's laugh, Magdelon thought; much as she disliked him, she
could not help feeling for a moment that he looked like a little boy,
too, caught unawares in some mischievous act, as he stood there
blinking at the newcomers with a sort of sleepy, shamefaced good-
humour, begging them mutely to overlook the ambiguities of the
situation as well as his involuntary shortcomings as host. . . . How
odd to see the bull-man suddenly as a child! Magdelon almost
laughed aloud at the conceit . . . but the next instant she was sobered
and silent, shrinking back amongst her companions as La Ferté
lumbered forward to salute the ladies, who stood huddled together,
their gaiety quenched, uncertain how to act.

Even Cateau's bright assurance had deserted her. She turned to
Beuvron and said, in a low voice: 'Oh, this is no fun! Hadn't we
better leave?'

'Leave? Not a bit of it!' cried the Maréchal. 'On the contrary, I
beg you will make yourselves quite at home. Lacking a feast to
regale you with, I still can provide music for a dance. What, ho!
Jacquino, there! Jean! Robert! Give us a tune, I say!'

A group of musicians in a small gallery aloft overlooking the
banquet-hall — who had no doubt been drowsing at their posts —
were roused by their master's shouts and burst promptly into a
branle.

'Music? Oh, Lord, deliver me!' squeaked the fat girl in the white
rabbit's ears.

Cateau, with an impatient shrug, prepared to lead her friends
downstairs — but the Maréchal was too quick for her. His rolling
black eyes had spied Magdelon — all the more surely for her frantic
efforts to remain unobserved — and he snatched her by the hand and
led her forth against her will.

'My beauty of the Pont Neuf!' he exclaimed. 'At last we meet

again! Will you be my partner, mademoiselle? That much you can't
refuse me tonight.'

He bowed grotesquely and wheeled about, as if ready to begin
dancing; then, unexpectedly, changed his mind, swept Magdelon's
trembling figure into his arms, tore off her mask with his big, greedy
fingers, and planted a resounding kiss on her mouth.

Beuvron started at once to the rescue, but he was forestalled by
Bussy, who was standing nearer to the couple. The latter neatly
drew Magdelon away with one hand and, with the other, gave La
Ferté a push — by no means a hard one, but sufficient to send him
sprawling full-length on the floor.

'You drunken lout!' said Bussy, in a high, unnatural voice he
must have assumed in an attempt to preserve his incognito. 'Let
that teach you a lesson, to leave well-conducted young ladies alone!'

He turned with a magnificent gesture, gave the half-fainting
Magdelon his arm, and escorted her from the room, followed in silence by the rest of the maskers.

They made their way down the grand staircase, swarming with
rowdies, and out into the street. It was morning now: the sun's
flame-red disk was pushing up slowly through a thick blanket of fog.
The revellers were stumbling with fatigue; Magdelon, all but unconscious, still quaking with fright. But, tired as she was, she gave
her saviour a grateful smile as he helped her into the coach.

For the last time that night Magdelon had fallen in love.

Chapter X

WHEN MAGDELON OPENED HER EYES, THE DAY AFTER THE MASQUER-
ADE, it was already afternoon. She had slept heavily but uneasily
through a series of troubling dreams in which rows of men's faces,
half recognized but still strange to her, flashed through her brain.
It took her a long time to dispel the illusion of their reality, and even
afterwards a feeling of restless foreboding remained.

In Cateau's dressing-room she was surprised to find Monsieur de
Beuvron with her sister. It was the first time he had come to the
house in nearly a week.

Cateau, who seemed never to tire like other people, presented her
usual serenely benign appearance, notwithstanding the feverish
dissipations of the evening before; but Beuvron looked haggard and
miserable.

Magdelon, now that she knew he and Cateau were lovers, could
no longer see them save in that relation. It was humiliating, even
painful — but there was no help for it: when they were together
she had only one thought, and that a shocking one.

It seemed to her excited imagination that Beuvron must be thinking the same thing: he had tortured eyes and an air of almost physical suffering, as if he were there in spite of himself — as if he hated
the chains that bound him to Cateau's side, though powerless to
break them. Passion, then, could degrade as well as uplift, and
lovers in real life, unlike the heroes in the romances of Scudéry,
were not always happy even when they had what they wanted. . . .
'Oh, poor thing!' thought Magdelon, who felt that there could be
little now not revealed to her about human emotions. 'I know why
you're here!'

There were so many things to be said that one could not say that
by comparison the few things one could say appeared strained and
false; it was a relief when Lindor trotted upstairs to announce that
the Comte de Bussy was below and desired to pay his respects to the
ladies.

At the sound of his name Magdelon started guiltily: her heart
turned over within her, and she began to blush. (Oh, had Cateau
seen . . .?)

Bussy made a smilingly self-possessed entrance. He was much

too clever to show his hand directly. His ostensible errand was to inquire how the Countess and her sister did, and whether the latter were suffering from shock after her misadventure last night at the Hôtel de Senneterre. This led to a string of compliments from the ladies on his chivalrous behaviour, which Bussy accepted with modest composure.... Not at all ... not at all.... Any gentleman must have acted the same in the circumstances. What La Ferté deserved was a thorough horsewhipping. These upstart commoners, with but one generation between them and the soil whence they sprang ... But was Mademoiselle de la Louppe certain the accident had left no ill effects? That was all that mattered to Bussy.

'Tell me you are well, my dear young lady,' he said earnestly, 'and we'll forget the whole thing as though it had never been.'

Magdelon, who had meant to own to languor at least and perhaps an incipient case of the vapours, also, forgot her intention when his eyes smiled at hers, and blurted out instead: 'I'm quite all right, sir, as well as ever I was in my life.'

'Then *everything*'s all right,' said Bussy easily.

He turned the talk tactfully into other channels, and began making plans for their diversion during the last few days of the carnival. There was, alas! so little time left. What would the ladies like best to do this evening? How about the new comedy at the Bourgogne? Or an excursion to the Fair of Saint-Germain?

'I don't know,' said Cateau doubtfully, though Magdelon's sparkling eyes had already assured him that anything *he* suggested ... 'Olonne's still far from well. We must see what the doctor says.'

Bussy overruled her objections with graceful insistence, declaring that his good friend the Count could not possibly dream of depriving his wife and sister-in-law of the smallest pleasure.... 'No! No!' said Bussy, shaking his head. 'I know him far too well to think *that*. Of all gallant gentlemen, madam ...'

He stayed ten minutes longer, chatting pleasantly on indifferent subjects. Most of his words were addressed to Cateau, but his glances were for Magdelon; when he left he bowed over the latter's hand with a meaning smile and a whispered compliment that left her trembling with delicious agitation.

For the next few days Bussy had everything his way.

Later, Cateau reproached herself greatly for this. She felt she should have foreseen the peril. But there were several good reasons why she did not. For one thing, Olonne went on being ill, and if Cateau danced all night and slept all morning, it seemed clearly her duty to spend most of her afternoons at her husband's bedside. For another, clever as she was about running her own affairs of the heart, she seemed, like many attractive women, to be extraordinarily blind to other people's.

Of course, as Cateau said afterwards, the whole thing was really Madame de Montglas' fault. One could hardly blame Magdelon, who was too young and too little experienced to know what was happening to her until too late to prevent it. As for Bussy, who was neither especially young nor in the least inexperienced — being nearer forty than thirty, with two Mesdames de Bussy to his credit, to say nothing of numerous more casual adventures — he was a man, after all; and men nowadays were out for everything they could get. (Oh for the stately chivalry, naïve though it sometimes seemed now, of the court of Louis XIII!) But the affair could not even have *begun*, according to Cateau, if Cécile de Montglas had not been the stupidest woman in the world....

She had always been that, poor wretch! Neither her birth (she had been one of the Touraine Chevernys), nor her riches (she was an only child), nor even her looks (she was a striking brunette) had kept her from making a mess of her life. Her family and fortune had won her a noble and good-tempered husband, but her dullness had cost them their position at court, while her husband's was responsible for losing a great part of their money in foolish investments. Now, at seven-and-thirty, her beauty was beginning to go. Moreover, a succession of disastrous emotional entanglements had not taught her the first thing about managing men. She made all the moves that most women make; she was shy, seductive, elusive, and bold, by turns — but her gestures were invariably ill-timed. She advanced where she ought to have retreated, and waxed wilfully haughty when the most unschooled coquette should have seen that only abject submission could save the day. In short, her tactlessness became proverbial.

As a result, her career of gallantry was a tragic one. After twelve years of marriage she had succeeded in estranging her husband without retaining a single lover save Bussy, who was as skilful as she was the reverse. He must, however, most people said, have been truly fond of her; for, though they quarrelled continually and were always parting 'forever,' they had never, so far, failed to turn up again in each other's company next week, or next month, or even next year.

It was too bad that, at this particular moment, they were not speaking. Madame de Montglas, in a fit of pique over their latest misunderstanding, had shut herself up at home to sulk, and ordered her Swiss to forbid Monsieur de Bussy the door.

All this Cateau explained to her sister, cleverly and logically, but not, unluckily, soon enough to do any good.

Even if she had done so a week earlier, Magdelon might not have believed her.

During the last days of the carnival Magdelon found it hard to

believe in a good many things. There were, for example, the two
Mesdames de Bussy, one of whom was safely dead, the other, almost as safely, in Burgundy. Of course, she knew perfectly well that
Bussy had no intention of divorcing his wife; that he was merely
amusing himself; that the shower of letters and verses and tender,
provocative looks meant only that he had been bored, and she was
young and pretty — and Lent had not yet quite begun.

Magdelon told herself, at least twice a day, that *she* was not
serious, either — naturally she was not! — and that the minute she
felt in danger of getting too deeply involved, it would be simple to
stop the whole business.

Meanwhile, it made the carnival twice as amusing to have a
cavalier all to oneself. Without being willing to admit it, Magdelon
had felt inferior to her sister in this respect: now at last she was
Cateau's equal; she, too, had a lover.

Bussy called every day at the Hôtel d'Olonne with devoted
punctuality; sent Mademoiselle de la Louppe pretty, arch notes and
little presents wrapped in pretty, arch sonnets — for, although a
soldier by profession, he was no mean poet; it was whispered that he
aspired to membership in the Academy. He was also her constant
companion on drives and at dinners, and took part in their nightly
masquerades, which continued throughout the week.

Everybody agreed it had been the gayest carnival season in
years. Paris went mad in its search for diversion: all barriers seemed
to be down; music never stopped playing, nor wine, flowing; nobody
went to bed before dawn; and more than once bands of roisterers
were caught whooping their way through the streets by pious folk
setting forth to early Mass.

Before the week was up the matter became a public scandal.
Preachers thundered from their pulpits daily denunciations of the
maskers' excesses, which, of course, only lent them additional
piquancy. Older courtiers shook their heads, even those who were
hoary enough to recall the days of Henri IV, the 'Green Gallant,'
and his turbulent crew of ruffians. As for Queen Anne, she was
thoroughly shocked; when she was told, as she presently was by
some malevolent meddler, that the Comtesse d'Olonne and her
sister were the leading spirits in the wildest group of young revellers,
she pinched her full Bourbon lips together till they resembled a ripe
red cherry, and raised her sandy eyebrows alarmingly, and remarked: 'I am not surprised to hear it.'

As a matter of fact, since the unfortunate affair of the bellows,
both the Count and his wife had been out of favour at court, and the
latter had lately been given to understand by Madame de Senecé,
the Queen's elderly lady-in-waiting, that it would be as well for her
to stay away from the Louvre until further notice. Cateau had

tossed her head airily and replied: 'Very well, madam. As Her Majesty wishes. It makes no difference whatever to *me*.'

Nor did it. The only result of Anne's edict was to plunge Cateau and Magdelon more furiously than ever into the pleasures of the town, which fell in perfectly with Bussy's designs.

On Shrove Tuesday the long string of gaieties was approaching its climax.

Bussy called on the ladies after dinner, as usual, to ask them to drive with him in a handsome coach (borrowed for the occasion from one of his friends) as far as Vincennes. Cateau, as it happened, was not at home; she had gone out to comb the shops for a yard of some special gold lace, which was needed to trim the skirt of the costume she intended wearing that night, and had taken Lindor and Quentine with her. Quinette, however, was available to serve as duenna for Magdelon, who promptly accepted the invitation: she was in a fever of excitement at the prospect of being alone — or as good as alone, since Quinette hardly counted — for the first time with her lover.

The drive was a great success. They met the King and his court out hunting near the castle, and followed the hounds through the grey leafless forest till the sun began setting and the winter air grew too sharp for comfort.

On the way back they stopped at a house in the Faubourg Saint-Antoine (borrowed from another friend: Bussy had no home of his own in Paris), where the *King's Twenty-Four Fiddles* were playing. Here a dainty feast was spread in the banquet-hall in readiness for their coming. As Magdelon entered the room a shower of artificial rose-leaves fell on her head; a fountain in the centre of the table started spouting, which caused a concealed organ to wheeze out a tune; and three pretty girls dressed as sea-nymphs appeared in a grotto made of shells and sang a song in honour of Mademoiselle de la Louppe.

The air was Baptiste's new gavotte, but the words were by Bussy himself.

'*To Time's cold, cruel sway*,' sang the sea-nymphs, in high, thin, sweet voices,

> ' *Your own coldness exposes*
> *Your charms.... Fickle its way,*
> *Changing all life discloses.*
> *Beauty lasts but a day;*
> *So, alas! do the roses.*'

It was a gay little refrain in a sprightly minor key; the sea-nymphs sang it through twice, repeating the last lines several times with coy emphasis, while Magdelon stood in the doorway, blushing self-consciously.... But when they had finished she straightened up, smiling with new assurance. She was the queen of the fête. Bussy, she knew, had designed it especially for her; it was what was known in society as a 'gift,' and a most gallant one, indeed. Convention decreed that she should not admit her knowledge in public, but she gave her admirer a charming smile and led off the dance with her slim hand in his, her head very high and her cheeks very pink.

Not even the presence of some of Bussy's older women friends — Madame de Montmorency among them — could spoil her enjoyment. They were, of course, friends of Madame de Montglas, also; they surveyed Magdelon with critical eyes, showing their teeth in grudging, perfunctory smiles — but miraculously it did not seem to matter. Magdelon, who an hour before would have cringed beneath their hostile scrutiny, now only felt her sense of triumph sharpened by disapproval.

'Poor things!' she thought tolerantly. 'How they wish they were in my place!'

When the party was over Bussy drove Magdelon home. Cateau, it appeared, had not yet returned from her shopping excursion, but Bussy begged permission to come in all the same for a minute: he had the music of the new gavotte in his pocket, and since he had learned that Magdelon played the lute nothing would satisfy him but to hear his song sung by her.

The Grand Saloon they found dark and empty, but a lackey told them that a fire had been laid in the yellow cabinet, which was the Countess's small upstairs sitting-room.

Bussy and Magdelon sat on a couch in front of the fire. The damask curtains had been drawn; only two tapers were lighted in a silver candelabrum that stood on Cateau's writing-table. They looked at each other tenderly in the flickering candlelight, and smiled, as if at some secret nobody else could guess; and then Bussy unfolded his music, and Magdelon took up her lute, and struck a chord or two, and began to sing, quite softly:

> 'To Time's cold, cruel sway
> Your own coldness exposes ...'

It was very dark, and their heads were very close together. Presently their hands were close together, too: Magdelon stopped playing the lute, Bussy's music slid to the floor; they stared wide-eyed at one another, with flushed faces, smiling a little still, but their smiles no longer had meaning. There was something in the room with them, Magdelon felt, as surely as if someone had opened the door to let it in — but what could it be? ... 'Oh, no! ... no!'

In a sudden panic she tried to rise, but her knees seemed to have turned to water. It was strange: although her whole body was quivering with emotion, it was perfectly passive; she could not control it any more.

Bussy clasped his hands round her waist and pulled her down gently beside him on the couch. Before she realized what was happening to her she was in his arms, his lips tight on hers, their bodies pressed hard together.

Magdelon's heart was pounding; the blood sang in her ears; but she could not speak or cry out for help. That was not *her* voice, surely, that went on whimpering over and over, like a fretful child: 'No, no ... please don't!'

The next moment the door was quickly pushed open — no mistake about it this time — and in walked Cateau, Cateau in a brown velvet street dress, enveloped in furs, her eyes big and staring and devoid of expression.

For several seconds no one spoke. Cateau was pulling off her red Russia-leather gloves with a kind of finicking deliberation. Bussy, who at her entrance had given one wordless gasp of annoyance and dismay, bent to the floor to pick up the lute and the scattered sheets of music; his face was flushed, but no more so than a few minutes earlier; he did not look nearly so much embarrassed as Magdelon thought he ought.

Magdelon herself was overwhelmed with confusion. She began lacing her bodice as best she was able with trembling fingers, but knew not what to say nor where to turn for shelter.

'Cateau,' she bleated, still in that queer whining voice not in the least like her own, 'Cateau ... dear ...'

Cateau laid down her gloves on the writing-table and crossed the room slowly to the fireplace; her face was puckered up, as if she might be going to cry.

Suddenly, however, she turned on Bussy, her eyes blazing with indignation.

'Leave the room, sir, at once! Get out of my house! And don't you dare show your nose in it again as long as you live, or I'll have my Swiss flog you to death. D'you understand?'

After this spirited introduction she launched immediately into a wrathful tirade, during the course of which Magdelon learned more about men in general, and about Bussy in particular, than she had supposed, in her innocence, there could be to know. Cateau's voice was harsh and toneless; it went on heaping insult upon insult until she literally had no breath left with which to continue.

Bussy made no effort to defend himself. When he saw that she had finished, he got up, laughing softly, made the ladies a mocking bow, and went out without a word, shutting the door carefully behind him.

After he had gone Magdelon buried her face despairingly in the cushions, and began crying in earnest.

'Oh, Cateau, dear, I'm so terribly ashamed! What can I do? I didn't know . . . I'd no idea . . .'

Cateau sat down on the couch and put both arms about her sister. She did not attempt to say anything, but sat quite still, stroking the latter's shoulder, until the first violence of the storm had spent itself.

At last Magdelon lifted her tear-stained face and quavered: 'Dearest, are you angry?'

'Angry?' said Cateau. 'Yes, of course I am, awfully angry. But not with you, child. With myself. I've been blind and neglectful. If I hadn't been, this could never have happened. It's entirely my fault. But oh, Magdelon, something will have to be done — right away!'

'Sister,' whispered Magdelon, 'what do you mean? Must I be married? Is that it? Oh, will anyone *want* to marry me, after this?'

Cateau made no reply. She was gazing with narrowed eyes into the fire; her beautiful face looked sterner than Magdelon had ever seen it.

Magdelon, feeling that perhaps it was better not to say anything more for the present, leaned back with a sigh of mingled remorse and relief, content to wait until Cateau chose to speak. It seemed safe to leave the solution of the problem in her sister's capable hands. All her life Magdelon had been sure — and never surer than now — that Cateau would always know best.

Chapter XI

WHEN THE TIME CAME TO DRESS THAT EVENING, MAGDELON TOLD
Cateau she would rather not go out. She had worried herself into
a state not far from hysteria; she felt, and said, over and over, that
she had so disgraced the name of La Louppe that she could never
show her face in public again. What was it Cousin de Rambouillet
had said, that night at the castle, on their way to Paris? The words
came back to her now with painful clearness, as they had been
spoken in the old lady's grave and measured tones: 'A well brought-
up girl who is proud of her family, and wishes her family to be
proud of her, will hold her virtue — nay, even the report of her
virtue — above rubies.' . . . Alas! And was *this* the way she had
kept the promise made, with the eager confidence of ignorance,
to the titular head of the tribe of Angennes? . . . Oh, and if Maman
were to hear what her daughter had done! . . . Magdelon began crying again, and clung to her sister, and protested that she would
sooner die than go to the fair. What if Bussy should be there?

'What, indeed?' said Cateau vigorously. 'I can't see that it
makes the slightest difference to us. You'll have to see him some-
time or other, you know. But I'm much mistaken if that young
man dares to trouble you any further, after what I said to him this
afternoon. Child, you're exaggerating the importance of a trifling
accident — for it's no more than that. Lent's beginning tomorrow,
when you can stay home and mope as much as you please. But
tonight you're coming with Beuvron and me to the fair — d'you
see? If you don't come, you'll only make people think that what's
happened is a thousand times worse than it is. Now pull yourself
together, for goodness' sake! Give me a smile — hold up your
head — look everyone straight in the eye! . . . That's better already.
I'll tell you what you need: Quentine!' — clapping her hands —
'My jewel-box, please! And be quick about it!'

The little maid came running, and before Magdelon had realized
what Cateau intended to do, the latter had opened the gilt casket
that held her treasures, selected a string from amongst them, and
clasped something long and shining round her sister's neck.

'There, child!' said Cateau, with satisfaction. 'My second-best
pearls — you may wear them till tomorrow, if you like. Now,
doesn't that make you feel very much better?'

'Oh, Cateau, dear, thank you!' cried Magdelon, who knew that Cateau particularly disliked lending anything she owned. 'But do you really think you ought...? In that awful crowd.... If anything were to happen...'

'Nonsense!' said Cateau, with her usual air of infallibility. 'Nothing can possibly happen if you look where you're going and take care not to get separated from the rest of us. Besides, they're of no special value — an old string of Aunt de Marville's, she gave me on my eighteenth birthday. I dare say, when you're married, you'll have a dozen necklaces far handsomer than this.'

'When I'm married!' echoed Magdelon disconsolately. 'But I may never be!'

'Nonsense!' said Cateau again, tossing her head. 'Why, you could have a husband tomorrow, if you wanted òne! You don't suppose I've given no thought to your affairs, little innocent, all these weeks? What else did Maman... I mean, it's not been for lack of an offer — but I wouldn't consider nine out of ten of those callow courtiers. Conceited monkeys! And, after all, there was plenty of time. At least, that's what I felt. Perhaps I've been wrong. But oh, Magdelon' — with a sudden softening — 'my dear, you're single so short a time, and married forever! And after you're married all the fun is ended.'

Magdelon, who had sincerely supposed that then it had only begun, thought it wiser to conceal her opinion. She glanced shyly at Cateau, and smiling at last, though traces of tears were still on her cheeks, ventured to say, greatly daring:

'Sister, tell me... is there someone *now?*'

But Cateau looked at her watch and gave a small shriek, crying out that it was past seven, Beuvron would be there in a quarter of an hour, and neither she nor Magdelon had even begun to get dressed. And no hints, however broad, nor pleadings, however wistful, produced any more definite response than a reiterated 'Darling, I simply don't know.... Only trust me, and you'll see soon enough.'

In spite of Cateau's second-best pearls it was a pale and subdued Magdelon who, a few minutes later, followed her sister downstairs, where Beuvron was waiting. Luckily, the party this evening was rather large, so that her being somewhat out of spirits was less liable to be noticed. Madame de Choisy, beplumed and bejewelled, was already fretting impatiently in the coach, with the young Prince de Marsillac and his uncle Sillery; and after leaving the Hôtel d'Olonne they stopped, before crossing the river, to pick up the Duc de Roquelaure and his wife.

Most of the rest of the time it took to reach their destination was occupied by an exchange of languid courtesies between Cateau and the Duchess, who, as rival beauties and queens of fashion, could not bear each other and therefore 'my-dear'd' each other punctiliously.

Madame de Roquelaure was a fascinating young woman, with masses of chestnut ringlets and appealing violet eyes, so fragile that she looked, Magdelon always thought, as though she would come apart, like a doll, unless handled with care. She was said to be on bad terms with her ugly old rascal of a husband, and to be dying by inches of a secret passion for the Marquis de Vardes (Moret's brother); but as she confided in no one, and treated friends and enemies alike with listless disdain — the merest 'good morning, sir' or 'good night, madam' seeming sometimes to call for an effort beyond her forces — it was hard to judge the truth of this report.

Nobody remarked on Magdelon's wan appearance except Madame de Choisy, who leaned forward, as they were alighting from the coach at the entrance to the fair, to tap the young girl's cheek with her bony finger and exclaim with odious archness: 'Where are the roses gone tonight? Late hours — late hours, my beauty!'

The Fair of Saint-Germain, which was held in a big barn-like structure in a square near the church of Saint-Sulpice (where Cateau had been married: Magdelon remembered that she had not seen it since), lasted for several months every winter and could not be considered a novelty to Parisians. It was, however, especially popular during carnival time. Booths displaying all kinds of merchandise — silks and linens and laces, furniture, leather-work, jewelry (both real and the false sparklers manufactured at the Temple) — did a brisk business from early morning till late at night; and in the afternoon and evening some small sweet-shops were open as well as several buffets, where wines and liqueurs were served. There were various lotteries and games of chance, such as the great grey gander, round whose unwilling neck a company of merry-makers were perennially trying to drop a brass hoop — though a spice-cake was the only reward —; a puppet show, and also a real theatre, where the Italian comedians danced tarantellas and gave farces with music.

Tonight, being Shrove Tuesday, the crowds were denser and more unruly than usual. Cateau, warning her sister to beware of pickpockets and to keep as close as possible to her side, gave her hand to Monsieur de Beuvron and led the way into the huge building, where they were at once engulfed by a screaming mob. Bourgeois and merchants, pages and priests, soldiers and lackeys made up the greater part of it. Here and there a group of nobles detached themselves from the common herd, easily distinguished by their dress and the fact that their ladies were masked. . . . Magdelon, craning nervously in this direction and that, spied Monsieur, the King's brother, and the young Comte de Guiche, with a party of pretty painted boys, buying cakes at one of the pastry-cooks'. Farther on, Ninon de Lenclos and her accepted lover, the Marquis de Villarceaux, were considering panels of Brussels lace; the Duchesse de Roquelaure, so languorous that she scarcely deigned to open her lips, was haggling *in a whisper* with a vendor of rare Oriental carpets, while her husband, like a true Gascon, ogled the vendor's plump young wife.... But, search as she would, Magdelon saw no sign of the miscreant Bussy.

When she had established this to her own satisfaction she relaxed, with a sigh, and almost contentedly followed Cateau, who was picking a path across the greasy, littered floor to the corner where the glove merchants held sway (gloves being the Countess's greatest weakness).

But this evening even her favourite scented Russia-leather gauntlets failed to hold Cateau's attention. Strangely restless, she drifted from booth to booth, buying a flask of perfume here, a few yards of rose-coloured ribbon there; nibbling one bite of a cake, the rest of which she immediately tossed to a beggar; sipping a cordial, but laying the glass down before she had drunk more than a third of its contents. They watched a troop of trained dogs jumping through hoops; marvelled at a tiny bird carved out of solid gold, with diamonds for eyes, which when wound up flapped its wings and stretched its throat and sang most musically; listened awhile to the Italian comedians, who were performing a lovely play about Arlecchino and his Colombina.... But Cateau hardly looked at anything. She was forever glancing back over her shoulder, as if in quest of someone. Finally, when they had almost completed their circuit of the booths and had paused in front of the puppet theatre, where Punch and his wife were enacting a domestic drama, she caught up her skirts and hurried off through the crowd, whispering hastily to Magdelon: 'Wait here for me.'

Beuvron, who could not make up his mind which sister to squire, hovered distractedly between the two for a few moments, and soon succeeded in losing them both.

Magdelon did not realize at once that she had been deserted. The marionettes were very amusing: she decided that Punch, with his humped back and huge nose and droll, leering eyes, looked exactly like Monsieur de Roquelaure. She wondered if Madame de Roquelaure thought so, too.... Presently, forgetful of her surroundings, she was chuckling as merrily as a child, the long, clear notes of her laughter echoing high under the rafters.

What brought her to herself at last was an accident. In her eagerness to see the play from a nearer point of vantage she must have pressed too close to the railing that divided the puppet booth from the main part of the floor. Before she had quite taken in what was happening, her necklace had caught on an iron spike in the railing, the chain had burst, and Cateau's second-best pearls went skipping and rolling all over the place.

With an exclamation of dismay Magdelon clutched at her throat, but too late to save more than half the beads: the rest were already scattered far and wide.

'Oh, dear!' cried Magdelon, in an agony of dismay. 'What shall I do? What will Cateau say?'

She dropped to her knees in the slimy sawdust that covered the ground, and began wildly groping for the pearls, assisted by some pages and stable-boys, who fell to work with suspicious speed and appeared to be pocketing the lion's share of what they picked up.

In her utter confusion she scarcely felt a light touch on her arm, and looked up in amazement when she heard a familiar voice saying: 'Mademoiselle, will you allow me...?'

The Duc de Candale, smiling and self-confident, gave her his hand and helped her to her feet. He did not say another word, but, still smiling, clapped his hands smartly together. As if by magic, his six lackeys in blue velvet sprang forth from the crowd, dispersed the rapacious stable-boys with a few well-aimed slaps and kicks, gathered up the remaining pearls, and presented them to their master, who thereupon handed them to Magdelon with a little bow.

'Oh, my Lord!' gasped Magdelon. 'How can I thank you? I thought... I shouldn't have dared... Those are my sister's pearls ... Oh, dear me!'

Candale turned aside courteously to permit the young lady to recover her self-possession. He did not speak to her for a minute or two; but when Magdelon, having stored the pearls in her purse, wiped her flushed face, and smoothed her ruffled locks, dropped him a curtsy with a renewed murmur of thanks and made as if to withdraw, he put out his hand to detain her.

'Mademoiselle, are you alone?'

'I ... why,' stammered Magdelon, 'my sister was here, just a moment ago. I don't know where...'

'You must let me remain with you, then, until such time as I can restore you to her company. The Fair of Saint-Germain is no place for a young lady without escort, on this night of all nights. Moreover, if you will, you can do me a very great favour.'

'Why, my Lord, anything in my power, of course,' said Magdelon, much embarrassed, but even more curious; for she could not imagine how she could be useful to the all-powerful Duc de Candale.

'Grant me ten minutes of your time, mademoiselle. That is all I ask. There is something I must say to you.'

'But surely,' said Magdelon, more and more embarrassed, 'there can be nothing that I ...'

'Mademoiselle, I *must* speak with you,' declared Candale, his light, husky voice tense with feeling. '*Please!* You do not know how unhappy I have been. I have not slept for many nights. Only you can help me.'

Magdelon gave him a timid smile and said, quite simply: 'My Lord, I give you leave to say what you will. Only I really can't think . . .'

'No, mademoiselle. I know. Only wait. . . . But we cannot talk here.'

This was perfectly true. Even as they stood by the railing in front of the puppet booth they were continually jostled this way and that by a shifting stream of people; and, in order to make themselves heard above the babble of voices, they were forced to pitch their own so high that they were only just not shouting at each other.

Magdelon shook her head and shrugged her shoulders helplessly; but the Duke said at once: 'Will you follow me? I've my coach waiting at the door. We can drive about the Faubourg and talk as we go. . . . Oh, you need not hesitate, mademoiselle. You will be perfectly safe with me.'

Magdelon smiled, not so timidly as before, and looked him straight in the eyes.

'My Lord,' she said, 'I am certain of that. It's only that I fear my sister will miss me; she'll have no idea where I've gone.'

'Then come,' urged Candale; 'come quickly, so that we may be back before she's had time to wonder where you are. Ah, please, mademoiselle. . . . Just ten minutes, out of your life. . . . It's the one favour I shall ever ask of you. My whole happiness is at stake.'

Magdelon looked at the young man again. It was true, he *was* deathly pale, as if indeed he had been sleepless for a very long time. Moreover, save for his lackeys, he was quite alone. The mirthful troop of sycophants who followed him everywhere, as the king of their miniature court, had all deserted him tonight . . . no doubt by his orders. . . . Still, dressed in black, with his drawn face and his great, suffering blue eyes, he was a romantic and pathetic figure. And Magdelon, who might possibly, after her recent misadventure, have been proof against the first quality, was all the more vulnerable to the appeal of the second. Feeling that she herself that day had plumbed the depths of human shame and sorrow, she could not find it in her heart to refuse him the pity of which she also had stood so sorely in need.

She did not say anything more, merely gave him a quick nod of assent. The Duke stepped forward to wrap her cloak more closely about her shoulders. Magdelon, her heart beating fast, let him take her hand and lead her away from the pushing people with their discordant voices, out into the cold, calm emptiness of the February night.

Afterwards, she could never be sure where they had driven. She had a vague recollection of rows and rows of dark houses and silent, snow-bound streets. She thought, too, that they must have crossed the river several times, for she had more than once been conscious of water gleaming blackly beneath them. But she had no exact remembrance of anything — no, not even of the Duke's splendid silver coach, with its smart trappings and cushions of sapphire-blue. The clattering hoofs of the horses of the postilions riding beside them reached her ears faintly, as if from an immense distance. In the flaring light of the torches they carried only one object stood forth: Candale's face, pale and purely outlined against the surrounding void.

Having achieved his purpose in carrying her off, he was apparently in no hurry to press his advantage. Magdelon, peeping demurely through her mask, thought from his demeanour that, if anyone else had been sitting beside her, she would have supposed he was too shy to speak.

As if in reply to her thought the Duke turned to her presently and remarked, with engaging frankness: 'Mademoiselle, this is a new experience for me. I have not been tête-à-tête with a young girl for more years than I care to count — since I was less than your age, perhaps. Truly, I know not how to begin.'

He was silent for another moment, and when he spoke again, though addressing his companion, it seemed as if he were really talking to himself.

'Mademoiselle, you behold in me the most miserable of men.'

'You, my Lord? Is it possible? Surely you have everything that ——'

'Everything — and nothing! All my life I have been alone. My poor mother died when I was born — or so shortly afterwards that she left not the faintest shadow in my memory — hounded to death, it's been said, by my father. My father is an upright man, mademoiselle, and a splendid soldier; but I'll not deny he is haughty and unapproachable. This I, who know him as no one else can, attribute largely to the bitter fact that his career has been a crushing disappointment to him. With his great talents for war he's been passed by, again and again, in favour of lesser men, who've known better how to please the powers at court. He has done his best to bend his proud spirit to please, too — but an evil fate has seen to it that all his efforts should not avail him. . . . He married, as I dare say you know, for his second wife, Cardinal Richelieu's cousin, Mademoiselle du Cambout de Coislin — and within a few years of the marriage the Cardinal died, leaving him with an amiable but portionless simpleton on his hands, and nothing to show for his pains. She's given him no children. My sister and I are his only heirs — and she, whom I loved like a second mother, broke his heart and mine six years ago by becoming a Carmelite nun. But of that grief I cannot even now trust myself to speak. . . . I was brought up to be a soldier, like my father. I took to the sword naturally enough; it seemed to me that the path to glory lay clear before me, since I had had the luck to attract the attention of Cardinal Mazarin, who — why should I not confess it? — was as mad about me as a man about his mistress. He kept fawning on me, saying over and over that there was nothing I might not aspire to, with his influence to back me. . . . I guessed well enough what he wanted: I was to marry one of his precious nieces, in return for being made general in the army of my cousin, the little King. . . . Soft! thought I. We'll wait first and see what he's willing to do. For the civil wars were just breaking out, and every good man's sword was needed. There were many enough in the family who broke away then into open rebellion: my cousins, the Condés, Mademoiselle and her father Orléans, at their head. . . . I was loyal for five long years. I fought in the foremost rank whenever they sent me; took orders as meekly as a lamb from Turenne and that ruffian La Ferté. In the end, they were glad to be able to count on me. I finished the war in Guienne single-handed, and signed the treaty of peace myself with the Frondeurs of Bordeaux. And then, as a recompense for my loyalty, I was sent to Spain to the paltry Catalonian campaign, where nobody cares who wins the battles, under Conti, my younger cousin, who'd been head of the rebel army I whipped. . . . Yes, and to cap the climax, *he* was given to wife the little Martinozzi, the only one of the Cardinal's nieces I'd ever considered for a moment — while *I* was told that, as a consolation prize, I might take my pick of the black Mancini brood! . . . Ah, mademoiselle, since that day I've given up hope as surely as my father has! I've gone on fighting because that's my trade, I know no other. But I realize now I'll never achieve my ambition. I'm finished — done for — at twenty-eight! My life is ended — and I've never really lived!'

As Candale brought his monologue to a dramatic close with a sweep of his arm, Magdelon was vividly reminded of the scene Cateau had made in her bedroom, the day her husband had slapped her. His eyes were sparkling now as her eyes had sparkled then, with a visionary light born of luxurious indulgence in self-pity. Why, even some of their words were the same. . . . Like Cateau, the Duke was honestly suffering — Magdelon was sure of it — but, again like Cateau, his expression of that suffering afforded him exquisite relief: nay, more, it was an artistic histrionic performance that gave the actor no less pleasure because he felt every line he spoke.

'My Lord,' said Magdelon, after a suitable interval, 'I am very sorry for you — I am, really and truly! Some day, I feel certain . . . You are still young, after all . . .'

She floundered, unable to make up her mind how to proceed, and in her anxiety clasped her hands tightly together.

Candale patted her shoulder and smiled, and said — as men, according to Cateau, always did —: 'I don't know why I am telling you all this.'

But it was evident why, even to Magdelon's simplicity. As she could think of nothing to say in return, she smiled back at him — which seemed to answer the purpose.

'You are sympathetic, mademoiselle; one feels you have a heart.'

Yes, thought Magdelon, unluckily for me, I have! And, because I have, I can be sorry even for you, sir, who are as handsome as a god and have half a million francs a year to spend and every woman in France in love with you. . . . For if you don't know you are happy, you can be as miserable as a beggar, in spite of all your riches!

Feeling positive that these reflections would not seem consoling to their subject, Magdelon went on smiling in silence at the blond young man at her side, and nodding her head encouragingly.

Candale, as if he had somehow contrived to guess her thoughts, threw himself into another graceful attitude (again Magdelon was reminded of Cateau recumbent on her bed of gold, while the snow came down outside the window), and continued: 'You will say, I know' — Magdelon would not have dreamed of doing so, but she lacked the courage to say even *that* — 'that I have much to be thankful for in my private life. I am young, I am strong; my fortune is ample for my needs, though by no means so large as it's supposed to be; some women have thought me not uncomely. . . . Forgive me, mademoiselle, if I admit what no gentleman should. But I am "Handsome Candale," the King of the Fops, whether I will or no. If I order a hat, or a new pair of riding-boots, all the gallants in Paris will have duplicates within twenty-four hours. If I adjust my laces and ribbons a hair's-breadth to one side, every collar in town is askew the next day, and a new mode à la Candale has been launched. My gloves, my scents, my very waistcoat-buttons are slavishly copied wherever I go. And I — *I* — have sunk to this! — to be a pretty plaything, a perfumed toy, a frivolous nonentity! I, who might have made my cousin a better general than Turenne and Condé in one, had I been given their opportunities to prove my worth!'

Magdelon remained speechless before this impassioned outburst. She was beginning to be bewildered and to wonder why she had left the fair to go driving about Paris on a cold February night with this melodramatic young man. All the same, as she had said, she felt exceedingly sorry for him; for, with all his bombast, there was a note of sincerity underlying everything he said. . . . Magdelon did not think it possible that he would have made another Condé or Turenne, or even a La Ferté; but it was doubtless true he was a talented soldier, whose talents and loyalty had received shabby treatment at the hands of the Cardinal, notoriously kinder to his enemies (because he feared them) than to his friends. She remembered having heard it recently said that Mazarin was still very fond of the Duke, and that the latter might yet win all he desired if he could be persuaded to marry a Mancini.

But this, obviously, was not for her to say.

Candale again appeared to have read her mind — for such an introspective young man, he was remarkably intuitive as well (or was it merely that his train of thoughts and hers were naturally following parallel courses?) — for he burst out at once with great vehemence: 'And I will never marry one of those cursed nieces! Never, never, never! Mazarin knows it, too. He knows what I think of his scarecrows. I've seen what came of my father's abasing himself to accept old Richelieu's poor relation. Moreover, mademoiselle, what has long been repugnant to me has now become forever impossible.'

'Impossible, my Lord?'

'Alas, how shall I put it to you? I am not accustomed to talking with young maidens!'

'I think,' said Magdelon, 'you will find, my Lord, that there is little beyond my comprehension. I, too,' she added, with a gentle sigh, 'have lived.'

'You, my dear child? You are on the very threshold of life, a rosebud still scarcely unfurled!'

Magdelon sighed once more, thinking how shocked Candale would be if he could know of the tragic experience she had passed through, the scars of which she felt she must bear on her soul forever.

'Yet your voice is kind,' the Duke went on pensively, 'and I dare swear your eyes would be, too, were I privileged to see them.'

There was a question in his tone, which Magdelon answered by raising her hand and slipping off her mask. She faced him then, in the flickering torchlight, as pale almost as he, her eyes large and liquid and, as Candale had predicted, full of soft, heart-warming emotion.

He seized her hand and kissed it, crying passionately: 'Child, you are an angel! I can no longer keep my secret from you. I am madly in love with your sister.'

Magdelon kept her eyes fixed on his.

'Yes,' she said, 'I know, my Lord. I guessed it a long time ago.'

'That does not surprise me, mademoiselle. The torments that have racked me are painted plain across my brow, for all the world to see. I've never known what it was to be in love before. Oh, mademoiselle, have pity on me! Since I first saw your sister I have had one thought alone in my heart. I cannot eat, I cannot sleep! I think always of her, only of her! Alas, what shall I do? At first she treated me with kindness. She smiled on me, let me press her hand and offer her my life's devotion in exchange for a look — one little look! But now she smiles no longer. Worse than that, I am forbidden her very presence. Her doors are barred to me. What have I done, that it should come to this? I am not conscious of guilt. *What have I done?* And what can I do, to be restored to her good graces? Only tell me that, mademoiselle, and I shall be your debtor forever. What does the Countess want, that I may give her? Speak, for the love of Heaven — for without her I faint, I die!'

'My Lord,' said Magdelon doubtfully, when this flood of words, so artfully chosen that only the Duke's distraught manner convinced her that he meant them, had subsided, 'I hardly know ... I hardly dare say what I think.'

'Speak, mademoiselle! Speak, I implore you!'

'My sister is a married woman, sir, and a virtuous one. It would be unseemly for her to receive such ardent addresses under her husband's roof.'

'But she receives them from Beuvron!' cried Candale, with bitterness, touching at once the heart of the matter. 'Beuvron may pay court to her when he chooses. Yes — and that rabble that hang round Olonne — that gang of card-sharpers and freethinkers and worse.... Forgive me, mademoiselle, for referring in such terms to your brother-in-law's friends, but, after all, their reputation is too well known at court. All are received except me, who have most right to be there, for no one cares for her as I do. How can this be?'

Magdelon had no reply ready. She was extremely embarrassed by the turn the conversation had taken, knowing only too well that Candale, with the swift intuition of a lover, had hit upon the truth. Cateau was Beuvron's mistress; Beuvron had plainly shown his jealousy of the Duke; no doubt, in order to quiet the former's suspicions, she had treated the latter with a coldness more than half feigned.

'My Lord,' said Magdelon, 'what shall I say? Monsieur de Beuvron is a very old friend, a native of our own province of Normandy. My sister and I have known his family since we were children. It is only natural that he should stand in the house on an intimate footing. And as for my brother-in-law's friends, whoever they are, it is my sister's duty to make them welcome.'

'Yes,' cried Candale; 'but why am *I* not made welcome, too? Why am I — only I — banished to the outside darkness? I ask no more than the rest — just to be allowed to call each day, to pay my respects as the others do. Why am I alone shut out?'

'I do not know,' said Magdelon frankly. 'My Lord, I really do not.'

And, indeed, she was sure that she herself would be incapable of refusing this golden princeling anything he desired. How Cateau had found the strength ...

'I've done nothing to offend her? You are positive? That wretched affair of the bellows, now ... Moret's been banished for a month for his stupid bungling there....'

'Oh, no, my Lord,' said Magdelon, shaking her head. 'Cateau's forgotten that long ago.'

'Then what——'

'There's nothing. Truly, there's nothing.'

'Then will you intercede for me, like the angel you are? Oh, mademoiselle, on my knees I beg you...'

On his knees he was, having slipped from the cushions of the carriage in a pose that only Candale's innate grace and assurance could have saved from the ridiculous.

'Oh, my Lord!' exclaimed Magdelon tremulously. 'Please.... If there's anything I can do...'

'There is! There is! You are the one person close to your sister's heart. That I know: has she not told me herself? If *you* cannot persuade her to see me, all will indeed be lost. But I have faith in you, mademoiselle, faith in your sagacity and your gentle spirit. You will help me, and, with your help, I cannot fail. Say you will help me! Say it! Say it!'

'I will help you,' Magdelon whispered, as Candale covered her hand with kisses. 'I will do all I can. My Lord, I promise. Only now ... please ... I must go back to the fair. What will my sister think?'

As she drew her hand away a sudden illumination flashed over her: she knew now why Cateau would not see the Duke: even Cateau, who was afraid of no one, was afraid of him. She *must* be. Even Cateau, thought Magdelon dizzily, could never say no for long to Monsieur de Candale.

It was quite late when they got back to the fair. Most of the people had gone home. As Magdelon had feared, Cateau had missed her some time ago; had looked for her everywhere, fretfully at first, then frantically. She was standing at the entrance to the booths when Candale and Magdelon drove up in the blue-and-silver coach. The six lackeys in azure velvet sprang to earth and took their places, three on each side of the door, as Candale got out and helped Magdelon to alight. He kissed her hand and bowed low before her.

He bowed, also, with no less ceremony, to Cateau; but Cateau, who was standing stiff and angry in her white swansdown cloak, her eyes as hard as the diamonds in her hair, pretended not to see him.

'Miserable child!' she cried. 'Where on earth have you been? I've been half out of my mind for the last three hours.'

That was an exaggeration, of course: Magdelon knew she could not have been gone more than one, at the most. But it seemed better to attempt no defence.

On the way home in Monsieur de Beuvron's carriage Cateau was crosser than ever. Magdelon had never seen her so angry. Fortunately, Madame de Choisy and the Roquelaures had left by themselves, some minutes earlier, so that there was only Beuvron to overhear what she said — and Beuvron was used to counterfeiting deafness and dumbness whenever it was required of him.

'Really, Magdelon, this is too much!' scolded Cateau. 'Can't I turn my back on you for five minutes without your getting into mischief? You're not fit to be trusted out of my sight. After what happened this afternoon, too! ... You're a bad girl, that's what you are, and I've half a mind to send you packing back to Maman in the country, first thing tomorrow morning!'

There was much more in this strain, delivered in a harsh, breathless voice that was quite new to Magdelon. Tears gathered in the latter's eyes as she listened; once or twice she tried timorously to interrupt, to offer a faltering explanation of her innocent intentions; but Cateau would not heed her.

'And to think,' said Cateau, 'on this night, of all nights, when it was of the utmost importance that you should be on your good behaviour! When proposals have been made for your hand of such a nature that only an idiot like yourself would not be on her knees, thanking her stars that she has such a sister as I to look out for her interests!'

'But, Cateau, dear, I didn't know. . . . *What* proposals?'

'What kind of figure do you suppose *I* cut,' demanded Cateau, 'when your bridegroom appeared to seek an introduction — and I had to tell him I hadn't the least idea where you were? If he withdraws his offer tomorrow, it'd be no more than you deserve.'

'But, Cateau, *what bridegroom?*' sobbed Magdelon, in despair. 'I've not heard a word. You wouldn't tell me today. You know you wouldn't. Who wants to marry me? *Who?*'

Cateau threw her a withering glance as the coach drew up in front of the Hôtel d'Olonne.

'Goose!' she said. 'Don't pretend you don't know, after all that's gone on! Don't stand there, looking me straight in the eye, and tell me you haven't the faintest idea that, this time next month, you'll be married to the Maréchal de la Ferté!'

Chapter XII

IT DID NOT TAKE MAGDELON LONG TO REALIZE WHAT THE MATTER was with Cateau.

In fact, they had hardly had time to get upstairs to the dressing-room before the latter collapsed in her sister's arms, weeping stormily.

'Darling, forgive me!' she cried, between sobs. 'You know you don't have to marry anyone you don't want to. You know I said it just to plague you. You know that, don't you, dear? Oh, how could I speak to you so? I'm sure you've done nothing wrong. It's just that — oh, Magdelon! If you only knew!'

She wept again, even harder than before; while Magdelon, feeling that their rôles had been strangely reversed — for surely she ought to be the comforted, not the comforter? — dismissed the round-eyed and wondering Quentine and Quinette. She said to herself that she knew very well what had upset Cateau: it was the fact that she, Magdelon, had gone driving with Candale, no more, no less.

Of course, Cateau was not going to admit this; her pride would prevent it. Nor did Magdelon expect her to do so. It was enough for Magdelon to be sure that Cateau was not really angry; that her fit of temper had been due to an attack of nerves, which she could not control. ... 'And indeed, indeed,' thought Magdelon, as she embraced Cateau warmly and implored her not to say any more about it, 'I don't blame her in the least for wanting him all to her-self; in her place, I should feel exactly the same!'

So both sisters cried a great deal and exchanged a great many kisses — penitent, on Cateau's part; loving and forgiving, on Magdelon's — ; and by the time they were ready to separate for the night they had drawn closer together than ever before in their lives.

Magdelon duly delivered the Duke's message and, as she had promised, begged Cateau to forgive him, if he had offended her, and to grant him an interview.

Cateau listened, with a faint smile on her lips, and said, when Magdelon had finished, that she would 'see about it.'

But nothing more was said about marriages.

Next morning, however, Magdelon awoke feeling that something terrible had happened. For several minutes she lay still, unable to recollect what it was. Then all of a sudden she sprang out of bed and ran barefoot, in her nightgown, with her hair falling loosely over her shoulders and her eyes big with fright, into Cateau's room.

'Cateau!' she cried. 'It's not true, is it? You said it last night just to tease me, didn't you?'

Cateau, who was also just awake, was lying propped up on her pillows looking pale and interestingly fatigued. She had begun to sip a cup of bouillon that Quentine had brought her. Before replying, she handed the cup back to Quentine, wiped her mouth on her napkin, and made a little face, as if the bouillon were not very good, after all.

'What's not true?' she said. 'What did I say to tease you?'

'Why, but, Cateau, you *know!* you know what you said! Must I marry the Maréchal ——'

'Oh,' said Cateau calmly, 'you mean *that!* ' — as though Magdelon could possibly have meant anything else! 'Well, dear, that's for you to decide, isn't it?'

'But he doesn't want to marry me!' wailed Magdelon, aghast. 'How can he? He's scarcely ever seen me in his life. And when he did ... Oh, the horrible creature! The hateful, horrible monster! Why, he's old enough to be my grandfather!'

She flung herself on her knees at the foot of the bed. A black pit of horror had opened beneath her feet, and, as she slid into it, she said to herself, most unreasonably, that she had known all along it would come to this.

Cateau put her head to one side, rather like a bird, as she considered her sister's prostrate figure, which was racked with sobs and trembling from head to foot.

'Water!' she said to Quentine. 'And brandy. Quick, you fool! And burn some feathers — all the feathers you can find.'

As soon as the maid had left the room, Cateau leaned forward and put her hand on Magdelon's shoulder.

'There!' she said soothingly. 'Now we're alone, dear, let's talk it over sensibly. I did mean what I said last night about the Maréchal, though I had no business to spring a surprise on you, and I shouldn't have done it if I hadn't been foolishly overwrought at losing you at the fair. But I meant, also, every word when I told you that you needn't marry anyone you don't want to. That's true, Magdelon. Neither Maman nor I should dream of forcing you into making a hasty decision, or one that is distasteful to you. All I want to do is what she would do if she were here, and that is, point out some of the obvious advantages in the match, which I'm sure you'll see for yourself when you come to think about it.'

'Advantages!' sobbed Magdelon, burying her face still more deeply in the bed. 'I don't care how many advantages he has. I hate him! I hate him!'

But even as she said this, and wept, and shuddered, and refused to be consoled, two thoughts occurred to her. The first was that, no matter how she felt and no matter what she did, in the end she would have to give in. Because, of course, if the Maréchal wanted to marry her, it would be almost impossible to resist him. What private persuasion had not the power to effect, the pressure of public opinion might drive her into doing. No girl in her senses could refuse to become Madame the Maréchale de la Ferté-Senneterre. . . . O God, save me! Won't You save me? . . .

The second thought — which was not actually a thought, but rather something beneath it, on the plane of instinctive, unreasoning emotion — was that she did not really *want* to be saved. . . . Perhaps what she now fled from was what she might come to desire most of all. Who could say? . . . She remembered the old fairy-tale Mahaut used to tell them about the princess who wedded an ogre, and how the latter was thereupon changed into the romantic prince of her dreams. . . .

It was very puzzling. Magdelon could not even try to understand it. But a little later, when she had collected herself sufficiently to talk it over 'sensibly,' as Cateau suggested, she could see that there was much to be said, even on the surface, in favour of the marriage. La Ferté was the eldest son of the family, heir to the vast estates and fortune of the Senneterres. True, his father was still living, which was a pity; but if La Ferté was no longer in his first youth — an undeniable fact — the Marquis de Senneterre was so incredibly antique that he could not possibly last many years more. Nor was his young wife likely, in the circumstances, to produce inopportune rival offspring. . . . As for La Ferté himself, he was that rarest and happiest of combinations, a childless widower.

Cateau had no need to enlarge on his brilliant career as a soldier, since it was familiar in all its details to every school-child in France. He was one of the two ranking generals in the King's army — sharing his supreme position only with the mighty Turenne. He had been, for four years now, a maréchal of France. And it was simply a question of time, everyone knew, before he was granted a dukedom for his services to the Crown. As governor of the important province of Lorraine, he lorded it in his castle at Nancy with all the pomp and assurance of an absolute monarch. In short, looked at from any conceivable point of view, there was nothing one could object to in La Ferté. . . . Old? Well, if you called fifty-five old. . . . He didn't, Cateau thought, look within ten years of his age and, in his brutal, rather dashing way, he was one of the handsomest men at court . . . not even a bore, like so many professional soldiers — Turenne himself, for instance —: he had a ready wit and a gay and spacious personality. Moreover, had Magdelon any idea (it had been a complete surprise to Cateau) that the Maréchal had fallen in love with her at first sight? So, strange as it might seem, was the case: since the day of their first accidental meeting on the Pont Neuf he had cherished, it appeared, one resolve, which was to find out the name of the pale, beautiful young lady with the black curls; to be introduced to her as soon as he had found out her name; to propose to her as soon as he had been introduced to her; and, as soon after that as he possibly could, to make her his wife.

'I call it a tremendous compliment, really,' said Cateau. 'He made inquiries for weeks without any success. It wasn't till the other night, when we went to the Hôtel de Senneterre by chance — d'you remember? — that he found you again. And then there wasn't an opportunity to say anything because ... Oh, well,' added Cateau hastily, as she recollected that that particular evening was not one to dwell upon at this moment, 'that's neither here nor there, dear. No one's accountable for what goes on during carnival time. But as soon as he was able, next day, he sent me a very proper letter of apology, asking me for your hand quite formally. He'd have written to Maman, too, he said — he used to know her, by the way, years ago before she was married: isn't it odd? she's never mentioned him to us — only he hadn't her address. I gave it to him, of course. ... There, dear: that's absolutely all that's happened, up to now. I wrote to Maman myself directly, and I expect a reply from her any day. I've made the Maréchal no definite answer. I shan't say a word to him — not one single word — till you give me leave to do so, and tell me what I'm to say.'

Magdelon did not speak for a moment; then she raised her luminous dark eyes to her sister's face.

'Cateau, dear, what ought I to do? What would *you* do, if you were me?'

'Why,' said Cateau, returning the look with perfect candour, 'if I were you, I'd marry him. He'll give you money, power, position — everything a woman could wish for — and I'm quite sure he'll make you an excellent husband, besides. He loves you, Magdelon.'

'Yes,' said Magdelon; 'but *I* don't love *him*.'

'Oh, well, dear, that's not half so important, is it? Husbands must love their wives, or their wives are quite miserable. But it's by no means necessary for wives to love their husbands. In fact, on the whole,' said Cateau, with a judicial air, 'it's probably a good deal safer for them not even to try. If they can respect them — which is a deal more than some of 'em do — that's all the creatures deserve.'

'Did you love Brother Louis?' asked Magdelon solemnly.

'I thought I did,' said Cateau — 'and see what a mess it landed me in!'

'Did you respect him?'

'I thought I did. But you know quite well now that nobody could.'

'But at least you *began* by thinking so — before you were married, I mean. I neither love nor respect the Maréchal, *now*. And I never, never can!'

'Never's too much to say, child. How can you tell? You might end by doing both.'

'But,' cried Magdelon, once more in tears, 'how can I be *happy*, Cateau?'

For answer, Cateau bent over to lift her sister's quivering chin and pressed an affectionate kiss on her cheek.

'Do you want to know what I really think, little Magdelon?' she said — and there was a note of earnest sincerity in her voice that was all the more convincing to Magdelon because she so seldom had heard it. 'This is it: I think you'd be happy with almost anyone. I think you're a naturally happy person. And I think anyone lucky enough to live with you couldn't help being happy, too.... Pho, child! Out of my sight! Take those damned feathers away!' (This last to Quentine, who, after hanging about in the hall outside the door as long as she dared, had at length made a false hurried entrance with the tray of restoratives.)

Magdelon straightened up and dabbed her eyes with the lace on the sleeve of her nightgown; as usual, she did not know what she had done with her handkerchief.

'Very well, then,' she said, swallowing hard, with an earnestness that matched Cateau's own. 'If *you* think I'd better take him, sister, I'll — take him. And I promise you now I won't cry any more.'

Nor did she. Indeed, had she felt like it, she could hardly have found time; for the following two months turned out to be the busiest she had ever known.

It was fortunate, as Cateau remarked, that Lent had begun, as otherwise they could never have managed to get through all the necessary business before the wedding.

The first thing that happened was that Maman and Aunt de Marville rushed to Paris, with such headlong haste that it seemed as though they must have been shot from a gun all the way from La Louppe. (Later, Magdelon discovered that they had actually been with the Daughters of Holy Mary at Chaillot for several days, deeming it more delicate to wait for the final word from Cateau before making their official appearance.) They were accompanied by Aunt de Marville's maid, the pig-faced Célie, and by two startled half-grown girls, whom Madame de la Louppe referred to, superbly, as 'my women,' although the eldest of them could not have been more than thirteen; but old Mahaut, much to Magdelon's secret relief, had been prevented from coming by a slightly sprained ankle, on which her rheumatism had 'set in.'

Maman was delirious with joy at the unexpected realization of her brightest hopes, which had confirmed, once and for all — that, Cateau confided to Magdelon, seemed the sole cloud on the horizon — her belief in other-worldly guidance, as relayed through Father Denis. Such crying as went on in the family circle fell to her share: she was in tears a good part of the time — but they were happy tears. She often declared, with an arch April smile, that nobody could know what a pang it cost her to part with her baby, but that her one comfort was the certainty of the glorious future awaiting the bride of the greatest general in France.

'My little Magdelon a maréchale! My little Magdelon a duchess!' moaned Maman, twenty times a day.

Whereupon Aunt de Marville, with a scrupulous regard for the truth, invariably rejoined: 'My dear Marie, La Ferté's not a duke yet.'

'No, dear,' said Madame de la Louppe. 'But everyone says he might as well be.'

The endearing thing about Maman was that, for all her raptures, she did not care a pin whether her little Magdelon were going to be a duchess or a draper. What charmed her was simply the fact that romance was in the air; that a marriage was going to take place. To tell the truth, she paid no attention to the practical aspects of the affair.

It remained for Olonne — now convalescent from his attack of gout — and his wife, with the assistance of Aunt de Marville and Cousin Hector de Montausier (Cousin Julie's husband), to see to the details of the settlement.

Maman was with difficulty restrained from stripping herself to the bone, in order to show the Senneterres how deeply she appreciated the honour of the alliance. As it was, Magdelon was given a handsome dowry, larger than Cateau's had been: she was also to inherit the castle and estate of La Louppe after her mother's death.

Much to Cateau's annoyance old Senneterre, rich as he was, showed no similar disposition to liberality. But as Olonne, whose conduct throughout the tortuous negotiations had been surprisingly businesslike, observed to his wife in private: 'My dear, he's eighty-one. It can't be more than a year or two, at most...' Moreover, the Maréchal already possessed an ample income of his own, a generous portion of which he was apparently more than willing — 'But not a word of this to Papa!' said La Ferté, a reflective finger pressed to the side of his nose — to bestow on his future wife.

The marriage contract, entailing interminable bickerings with lawyers about questions of phrasing and fierce disputes over comparatively paltry sums, was the least of Magdelon's concerns.

In fact, as the bride, she was supposed to remain more or less in ignorance of the whole business.

There were, however, a number of obligations she could not hope to escape so easily.

Letters, for instance. Etiquette demanded that Madame de la Louppe should write to her relatives, even the most distant, including in-laws (some of whom Cateau and Magdelon had never heard of), as well as to all her friends and acquaintances, to inform them of the betrothal of her second daughter, Magdelaine d'Angennes, to Henri II, Seigneur de Senneterre, Marquis de la Ferté, Maréchal of France, and governor of His Majesty's province of Lorraine. As Maman herself was far too feverish to hold a pen in hand, and Cateau's spelling was considered inadequate to the dignity of the occasion, most of these notes had to be composed by Magdelon, in her mother's name. Less than a week after they had been sent out, replies began to pour in, containing showers of conventional compliments to the Baronne de la Louppe and her daughters. These compliments had to be acknowledged by return compliments. Thus, in many cases, endless unnecessary correspondences were set in motion, neither party to which cared to be the first to let drop, though both (thought Magdelon wearily, as another post-day from the provinces approached) must secretly be dying to do so.

Then — as if this were not punishment enough — it was further decreed that friends and relatives of either of the families concerned, living in Paris or anywhere near it, should don their best clothes and pay visits of state to the Hôtel d'Olonne, where Maman and Aunt de Marville, Cateau and Magdelon, in *their* best clothes, sat to receive them.

Most of these visits were extremely tedious. Magdelon grew very tired of being told what a lucky girl she was and being kissed on both cheeks by disagreeable old women with antique headdresses and bristling moustaches, who usually turned out to be Cousin This from Rouen or Cousin That from Coulommiers.

The one call that really gave anyone pleasure was the Rambouillet family's. They appeared one afternoon, as in duty bound, in full force save for Cousin de Rambouillet herself, whose age and infirmities excused her from venturing from home on any pretext. But Cousin Julie was there, positively yellow with bile and dismay, and her husband, Cousin Hector, a dour and argumentative gentleman; likewise little Mademoiselle de Montausier, who sucked her thumb in silence the whole time, and two of Cousin Julie's sisters, Claire-Diane, the abbess of Yerres, a difficult, unapproachable old maid; and Mademoiselle de Rambouillet, the carrot-haired Clarisse. Clarisse, it seemed, was also engaged ('At last!' as everyone immediately exclaimed) to the Comte de Grignan, a Provençal nobleman of small fortune, who was said to be the ugliest man in France.

There was, of course, no comparing this bridegroom with such an altogether exceptional match as the Maréchal. Cousin Julie's persistent attempts to do so were firmly nipped by Cateau and Aunt de Marville; while, although she said nothing, Maman's outbursts of slightly hysterical laughter underscoring each of their 'points' was perhaps even harder for the Rambouillet ladies to bear.

Foiled in this unamiable purpose, Cousin Julie fell back upon the rather obvious expedient of casting broad hints about the Senneterres' family history and financial solvency.

'Estates in Auvergne,' she said. 'Well and good, my dears. They may be there. Mind you, I don't say they're not. But who has seen them?'... And, 'I remember La Ferté's aunt, old Mademoiselle de Senneterre, quite well. You must have known her, too, Cousin de la Louppe?... Oh, she died long before *your* day, Catherine-Henriette! A most disreputable old person! Well, she'd been maid-of-honour to Catherine de Médicis — one of the "Flying Squadron," they called them — and we all know what *that* must have meant. As for the way she and her brother Senneterre worked the old Comtesse de Soissons for money, I've many a time heard my mother say they could have been jailed for it.... Dear, dear, but we mustn't rake up ancient scandals *now*, must we?'

'Weak; decidedly weak!' whispered Cateau to Aunt de Marville, as Maman went off into another gale of uncontrollable mirth.

Meanwhile, Clarisse, who squinted so badly that one could only guess which way she intended to look, was saying spitefully to Magdelon: 'How can you marry that horrid great bear? I wonder you're not afraid, cousin: they say he murdered his poor first wife!' To which Magdelon tossed her head and replied: 'I like him very much indeed. I'd rather marry a bear any day than a baboon!'

Altogether, it was a delicious afternoon.

However, each of these visits had to be returned; and long before Maman and Aunt de Marville reached the end of their list, which they had subdivided systematically by parishes, Magdelon was faint with boredom and had quite run out of prettily appropriate rejoinders to the congratulations of the army of old women with bristling moustaches.

The worst ordeal of all was the ceremonious call that the whole family, including Olonne — whom Cateau had induced to accompany them that day — made at the Hôtel de Senneterre. Magdelon found herself tongue-tied in the presence of the old Marquis. His bird-like hops and clucks kept her in a state of perpetual apprehension; and when he took her by the chin with his brittle, little, old hand and squeaked in his brittle, little, old voice: 'How's the beauty today? Hey? Hey? Dreaming of her bridal night, I'll be bound!'

and then exploded into a series of cackling senile chuckles — which did not in the least disguise the fact that his piercing eyes were studying her astutely all the time — Magdelon could have sunk through the floor.

Her one consolation was that, on this particular afternoon, the Maréchal was absent, having received a sudden summons to a cabinet council at the Palais Mazarin.

It was a relief when Madame de Senneterre, the Marquis's sandy, doll-faced wife — who looked as if she were quite as terrified of the old man as Magdelon could possibly be — asked the ladies uncertainly if they would care to inspect the house.

In spite of herself, Magdelon could not help being enormously impressed by the number and grandeur of the state apartments they were shown through in rapid succession, though she was too ill at ease to pay much attention to the details of the sculpture by Thibaud Poissant and the overpowering array of frescoes and painted ceilings by Perrier, Mignard, Nicholas Loir, and other famous artists. (Madame de Senneterre reeled off their names and identified their several achievements with the lack-lustre glibness of a professional guide.) Moreover, notwithstanding its oppressive magnificence, she thought the mansion gloomy and tasteless compared to Cateau's elegant modern house. And the sole picture that succeeded in rousing more than a flicker of interest was a portrait of the first Maréchale de la Ferté — who had died only a year ago — a pretty, laughing little baggage dressed as Diana, carrying a bow, and with a silver crescent in her hair, which was arranged in the tight sausage-shaped curls fashionable in the early reign of Louis XIII.

Maman, too, seemed soon to have had enough of the Senneterres' domestic splendours; her eye began to rove, though she went on politely ejaculating: 'My dear! What a divine mantel!' or (when they were being taken through the garden): 'Fancy! Forty orange trees in a row!'

It remained for Cateau and Aunt de Marville, whose curiosity was insatiable, to open all cupboard doors not actually locked; make quick mental inventories of the contents of each linen-chest; and — when their hostess was not looking — scratch with inquiring finger-nails the frames of the long line of gilt mirrors in the Grand Saloon, to see if the gold leaf were real.

When Magdelon was not busy either reading letters or writing them, paying or receiving visits, these two energetic women took her in hand and provided her trousseau.

Here Cateau, especially, was in her element. Magdelon had imagined, in her innocence, that, as she had just been given a handsome wardrobe for her Paris visit, no more new clothes could be needed for the present.

But Cateau soon exposed the naïveté of this supposition: she was determined that her sister should outshine any bride at court during the last decade, herself included. Accordingly, she spent money right and left — Maman's money, to be sure; but Maman objected to nothing, these days. Magdelon stood patiently for many hours each day, while Quinette and Quentine and various dressmakers' assistants, their mouths full of pins, kneeled before her, and Cateau and Aunt de Marville engaged in critical conferences with the dressmakers themselves. Gowns for morning, afternoon, and evening wear were contrived in feverish haste: gold-and-silver embroidered robes of state for court; velvet riding-habits for hunting parties at the castle of La Ferté; travelling dresses, robes-de-chambre, mountains of linen, petticoats by the score, all edged with lace; plumed hats, gloves, handkerchiefs, silk stockings, shoes and slippers of leather and satin . . . such an extravagant profusion that at length the bride began to wonder if there were enough days in the year to display so much finery.

Cateau's only worry had to do with the wedding-dress itself, for there was great uncertainty concerning the choice of the place where the ceremony was to be held.

La Ferté at first had inclined to be married in their parish church of Saint-Eustache — which called, according to Cateau, for a conventional white satin robe, with a long train and plumes. . . . 'Perfect!' said Maman. 'A smart town wedding, with all the court in attendance. Just what I myself should choose for my darling!' . . . On further reflection, the Maréchal decided that perhaps it might be better to wait until he went to Nancy, where they could be married in martial style at the head of his troops. . . . 'Something a trifle more cavalier, then,' said Cateau. 'Velvet, I think, don't you, Maman, instead of satin? — and perhaps heavy gold embroidery on the skirt and train rather than lace; it looks better from a distance.' Maman only babbled: 'Lovely! Lovely! My dear La Ferté, you are a true prince at heart!'

Still, on thinking the matter over a little longer, the Maréchal felt that Nancy would not do either, as his duties might keep him in Paris another two or three months, and it was unthinkable for the wedding to be postponed to such a distant date. 'I'm in far too great a hurry to claim my bride!' he shouted, with a huge, jolly laugh; and Maman tittered improperly. . . . What, he added, would Madame de la Louppe say to a quiet country wedding — very small, of course; attended only by members of the two families and their most intimate friends — at La Chevrette, a hunting-lodge he owned in the immediate neighbourhood of Paris? . . . 'No train at all, then,' mused Cateau regretfully; while Maman, who was resolved to find everything her future son-in-law said or did absolutely charming, threw up her hands in ecstasy and declared that nothing could be more appropriate to her modest little violet, who was a country girl herself, than rustic nuptials, 'quite, quite away from everything but baby lambs and apple blossoms and ... and all that sort of thing. April,' said Maman, who had had plenty of involuntary experience in that line, 'is, after all, one of the very few months in the year when I really can bear to be in the country.'

Echoes of the momentous discussion appeared in the newspapers, whose society scribes knew perfectly well that this was to be *the* wedding of the season.

In the end, La Chevrette and the quiet country wedding won out, and April twenty-fifth was appointed as the day, thus allowing the couple a month's stay in Paris before the Maréchal would have to rejoin the army for the summer campaign in Flanders.

Presents began to pour in: there was a solid silver table-service from the young King, a gold wine-cooler from the Queen Mother, who also sent her portrait in miniature, set in an oval frame of lapis lazuli studded with sapphires and diamonds. Cardinal Mazarin, saving as usual — not to use a less complimentary term — bestowed on the couple a picture from his private collection, a somewhat inferior Madonna that might or might not be a Perugino. There were costly gifts from everybody the La Louppes or the Senneterres knew, as well as a good number from people they didn't know at all.

La Ferté gave his bride a gorgeous string of pearls.

The day she received it remained afterwards fixed in Magdelon's memory, for it was the first and only time that she and her fiancé were alone together.

It was, naturally, not considered fitting for a young girl to see much of her betrothed during her engagement. ... 'Time enough for that *later*,' Maman observed, with a leer, whenever the Maréchal complained, as he frequently did, that he was never permitted to talk with his bride. But, to tell the truth, what with letters and visits and fittings, Magdelon had not a moment to spare.

Doubtless it was better so, she thought — when she found time even to think, which was seldom.

However, one afternoon about a week before the wedding, it happened that Magdelon and her stepmother-in-law-to-be were strolling in the latter's garden. Madame de Senneterre was called away by a message to the house, but Magdelon continued her walk by herself along the gravel path, which was moist and glistening from a recent shower.

It was a warm spring day, with puffs of white cloud in a pale turquoise sky; the sun was hot enough to have brought most of the trees and shrubs into full leaf. The big fountain in the centre of the garden had been set to playing only that morning. Magdelon was standing beside it, watching some energetic sparrows taking a bath in the spray of the spouting tritons and dolphins, when she heard a step on the gravel behind her.

Thinking it must be Madame de Senneterre, she looked round with a smile, which faded rapidly, and then died away altogether, as she beheld her bridegroom.

La Ferté had the wit not to refer to her sudden change of manner. He chatted with Magdelon for a few minutes about the weather — was it not unusually warm for so early in the year? — and the garden, in which some improvements were to be made: had Mademoiselle de la Louppe seen the new statues from Rome, and the plans for the terrace, which the Marquis his father had just received from his architect, Monsieur Lefèvre of Orléans?

Magdelon strove to answer intelligently, which she managed only by keeping her eyes away from the Maréchal's face.

Presently La Ferté took a leather case out of his pocket, opened it, and produced the pearls, handing them to Magdelon with studied carelessness.

Magdelon stared at them blankly: it was the most beautiful necklace she had ever seen.

'Oh, thank you, sir,' she said. 'Thank you very much: they are lovely.'

There, somehow, she stuck, unable to get out another word, though she knew she had not said half enough in praise of her gift.

'Mademoiselle,' said La Ferté suddenly, 'you do not need to thank me.'

'Oh, sir, but I ——'

'All the gratitude should be where it is, on *my* side, child. These toys are but a poor expression of my obligation to you for doing me the infinite honour of taking my name.'

'Oh, sir,' said Magdelon — and then again she halted, powerless to finish her sentence.

'Child,' said La Ferté, in a gentler tone than Magdelon had ever heard him use, 'I wish only that I might share my happiness with you. I fear you are not willingly disposed to link your life with that of a man old enough to be your father. Aye, and with a rough old soldier, too, a hardened campaigner, who'd been years in the army before you were born. . . . No, don't deny it, mademoiselle. I know well how you feel; it is natural. I want to say just this — perhaps it may help you a little to hear it — I love you, mademoiselle. I have loved you since the first moment I saw you. If I was not able to prove my attachment either then, or the second time our paths crossed, that night during the carnival, it was because,' said La Ferté, with unexpected frankness, 'on both those occasions I was drunk. I'm no confirmed sot, mademoiselle, as anyone who's known me can tell you; but soldiers do drink a good deal sometimes, you know. All I'd like you to realize is that I'm sorry for my behaviour in the past, I hope to do better in the future — and I promise to love you and care for you all the days of my life.'

'Thank you, sir,' said Magdelon, touched by this handsome avowal.

She did not know what else to say; so she gave him her hand gravely, and together they paced the path in silence for a little, to the accompaniment of the splash of the fountain and the twittering of the sparrows.

La Ferté did not speak again until they had reached the chapel, at the far end of the garden. There he paused, looked straight at her, and said: 'Mademoiselle, I should like to pray to God that He may bless our union, and give you one half the joy with me I know will be mine with you. Will you come, my dear?'

'Yes,' replied Magdelon, 'with all my heart, sir.'

There were tears in her eyes, as there had been often before when she thought of her approaching marriage. But for the first time they were not for herself.

That night La Ferté flew into a passion with Robert, his head valet, over some household accounts, and flogged within an inch of their lives two of his lackeys, who had been caught using the horses without leave.

And then, before anyone realized it, it was the twenty-fifth of April.

It had snowed, unluckily, on the twenty-fourth — only a freakish spring flurry, which melted almost as soon as it fell — but it meant that the roads, none too good at best after the winter storms, would be muddy and in places all but impassable.

Maman and her daughters, Brother Louis, Aunt de Marville, as well as La Ferté and his family, had driven out to La Chevrette through the snow on the previous night, so that all might be in readiness for the wedding, which was to take place at high noon in the small village church at the gates of the castle.

After the ceremony, to which only a few intimate friends had been invited, there was to be a breakfast at the house provided at Maman's expense; and, after that, the newly married pair were to drive back to Paris to take possession of the grand suite of state apartments prepared for them at the Hôtel de Senneterre.

Magdelon felt she would rather have gone almost anywhere else; but this was a matter in which she had no choice. It was a bride's chief duty to lie enthroned on her bed of state, the day after her wedding, at home to all the world who cared to view her in her unfamiliar rôle of dignity as wife and mistress of her husband's house.

It was cold when they arrived at La Chevrette, a small Gothic hunting-lodge with very few comforts on the edge of the vast forest of Montmorency. And cold it remained, cheerlessly, penetratingly so, even though so many fires had been lighted that the old Marquis, whose wood was being burned, was in a perpetual twitter of indignation. (Cateau declared she had caught him, when he thought no one was looking, pouring water on the flames.)

It was colder still in the chapel, which smelled of wax candles and stale incense and that indefinable mustiness characteristic of a building long shut-up and unused.

Magdelon, kneeling before the altar, shivered in her white satin gown and thought wistfully of the heavy velvet train Cateau had decreed unsuitable to the country.

She was too nearly frozen to think clearly of anything else. Certainly the fact that she was actually being married to the bull-man did not seem half so important as she had supposed. She did not even turn to look at him during the ceremony; she felt rather than saw him kneeling by her side; heard, as if it were something that had nothing to do with her, his voice rasping out the responses, gruff with emotion.

The vicar from Saint-Eustache, who was marrying them, had a bad cold; his nose was inflamed, and he sniffled continually.... Magdelon was vaguely conscious of Maman in one of the front pews, because she had seen her when she came in. Maman was crying softly, and her nose was as pink as if *she* had a bad cold, too. Aunt de Marville was standing next to her, her whole face scarlet with joy and excitement. And Magdelon knew, though she could not see them, that Cousin Julie and Cousin Hector de Montausier were also there; they had brought Clarisse with them, but had left Marie-Julie at home, which was a mercy.... Madame de Choisy was on the other side of Maman, with Monsieur de Beuvron and his wife, who seldom appeared in public together, and the Bonnelles, and one or two others.

Magdelon, however, paid no attention to any of these people, which was perfectly proper in her present situation. She looked round only once — and that was to smile at Cateau. Cateau was placed a little apart from the rest, resplendent in cloth of gold and sparkling with jewels. She smiled back at Magdelon, with a bright resolution that did more than anything else to sustain the latter's courage.

Presently, a good deal sooner than one had expected — could he have omitted part of the service? — the vicar pronounced the final benediction, and blew his nose violently. It was over. Magdelon was the Maréchale de la Ferté. Why, getting married was nothing at all!...

As she rose to her feet, feeling slightly stiff after having kneeled for so long, she saw that someone else had come into the little church. Cateau was no longer alone. Another figure in gold stood next her, as proud and glittering as her own. And this second figure was smiling at Magdelon no less kindly than Cateau had done. Why had no one said that Monsieur de Candale was coming to the wedding? ...

When everyone present had signed the parish register the company pressed out of the church into the road, where carriages were waiting to convey them up the avenue to the castle for the wedding-breakfast. Maman was embracing the new Maréchale, with a rain of crystal, charmingly becoming tears. The guests crowded round, smiling, exclaiming, congratulating. Magdelon held out her hand to Monsieur de Candale, saying: 'No, really, Your Highness, what a lovely surprise!' ...

And it was at this moment that something extraordinary happened. A man on horseback, in the crimson uniform of the Cardinal's messengers, came galloping along the road. He reined in his mount as soon as he caught sight of the little crowd of gaily dressed people streaming out of the church; fell rather than jumped from the saddle; and hurried to Magdelon's husband.

'My Lord!' he cried. 'A dispatch for you from His Eminence!'

Even before La Ferté tore it open with blunt, impatient fingers Magdelon was sure that the dispatch carried bad news; it was not surprising to hear that hostilities were threatening along the Alsatian frontier; a sedition was feared in His Majesty's troops; in short, much as the Cardinal regretted being obliged to ask such a favour at so inopportune a time, there seemed to be nothing to be done except beg the Maréchal to tear himself away from his fair young bride and leave post-haste for Nancy.

La Ferté did his duty speedily, dispensing with vain lamentations. He called for his coach and horses to be ready within an hour. Robert was sent on the run to the castle with orders to unpack his master's court clothes and pack his uniforms and military regalia instead. Meanwhile, the festivities were to proceed precisely as planned — the Maréchal implored that no one would consider leaving for a moment — except that they would, unfortunately, have to take place unadorned by the two principal figures. ... Yes, *two* figures: they had heard him correctly. Naturally, that line about tearing himself away from his fair young bride was a bit of the Cardinal's polite rhetoric, nothing more. Equally naturally, the Maréchale would accompany her husband to Nancy.

There was a general outcry at this, every older lady present being anxious to register a violent protest against such a barbarous flouting of time-honoured conventions. But La Ferté refused good-

humouredly to listen to reason. What did it matter, he roared, with
his usual rumbling laugh, if they *didn't* go to Paris till later? The
formal bedding of the newly married couple, the visits of ceremony
to the bride — pah! What were they, after all, but a chance for a
lot of tattling women to crack unseemly jokes and poke about other
people's houses, where they weren't wanted? Damned good idea,
said the Maréchal, if you asked *him*, to get out of all that!

Aunt de Marville, almost fainting with horror and shock, exchanged a helpless glance with Madame de Choisy, who waggled
her feathered head disapprovingly and murmured through her
teeth that she had never, never thought to see the day.... Cousin
Julie wavered, obviously torn between her desire to wait to see
what further enormities the Maréchal might be guilty of and her
inclination to rush straight home and report the present scandal to
her mother. Even Cateau, although she said nothing, felt that a
wedding was hardly a wedding if there were to be no visits afterwards. Only Maman, true to her conviction that La Ferté must
always know best, valiantly upheld her son-in-law's departure from
tradition: 'My dear, you are perfectly right. Duty ought to come
first. What's etiquette worth,' demanded Maman, with an heroic
air worthy of one of Corneille's heroines, 'in this hour of national
crisis? And, of course, my little Magdelon will go, too. A soldier's
wife ... Her place henceforth is at your side. Why, you *want* to go,
little Magdelon, do you not?'

'Why,' said Magdelon, who had stood aloof during the rapid development of the drama, 'I — yes, certainly, Maman.'

Somewhat to her surprise, she discovered she was speaking the
truth. In many ways she knew she would prefer to go directly to
Nancy. It would save so much trouble and confusion....

Nevertheless, when in less than an hour they were really off, she
felt bewildered and shaken. La Ferté, seething with impatience,
had cut the wedding feast, or at least his share of it and his wife's,
as short as he decently dared. Healths were gulped rather than
drunk, speeches rattled through with what Cousin Julie later told
her mother was 'sacrilegious speed.' Without quite knowing how
she had got there Magdelon found herself in the coach with her
husband, leaning out of the window and waving back up the avenue
of budding poplars to the little group of familiar faces on the castle
steps. It was bitterly cold: flakes of snow were falling from an iron-
grey sky, and the wind chilled her fingers that held a fluttering
handkerchief. Still she leaned as far out as she dared and went on
waving until a bend in the road cut off her view. Her last smile and
wave had been for Cateau.

As she settled herself decorously against the scarlet velvet cushions of La Ferté's state chariot Magdelon saw, to her dismay, that

she was crying a little. She stole a glance at her husband, to see if he had noticed.... If he had, he gave no sign of it in words: he was sitting bolt-upright in his seat, staring straight ahead with that wooden, lifeless look that had so struck Magdelon that day (it seemed years ago, now) at Mass at Saint-Eustache.

Presently, however, without turning, he stretched out a big, horny hand and grasped one of hers. His touch was warm and friendly, and Magdelon was glad of it. It was odd.... She could see herself and her husband, quite clearly, advancing through life hand in hand, as they were now, and growing ever fonder each of the other... 'more and more,' thought Magdelon, her mind reverting to the simile that had first occurred to her, 'like the princess and the ogre in Mahaut's fairy-tale!'...

The prospect no longer alarmed her. Still she could not help crying a little more. She kept thinking of Cateau's words about marriage — 'All the fun is ended!' — and then of Cateau's face during the wedding, smiling enigmatically but victoriously, as if, no matter what she said, she meant just the opposite. And there was Candale beside her to prove it. 'Oh, dear,' sighed Magdelon. 'I wish I knew ... how I wish I knew!'...

But whatever it was she wished she knew she did not express, even to herself, as the coach went on swaying and jolting over the rough country road through the cold, capricious, quickly melting April snow.

BOOK TWO

CATEAU
(June, 1657 — August, 1659)

Chapter I

GILETTE DE FIESQUE WAS LATE AGAIN.

Cateau, glancing impatiently for the twentieth time out of the drawing-room window in search of the carriage that obstinately refused to appear, told herself she had known it would be so. Of course it would... today, of all days, when it was of the utmost importance that they should reach the Cours la Reine promptly at five o'clock. Five o'clock... and it was already ten minutes to five. There was no excuse for such flagrant unpunctuality either. The hour of their meeting had been definitely settled the night before, at Madame de Montglas' concert. Not content with this oral assurance alone, Cateau had dispatched a note by Lindor early that morning to confirm the engagement, begging Gilette to be dressed and ready to leave her door at four o'clock sharp. And she herself had given the order to François, to make sure that he understood he was to fetch the Comtesse de Fiesque from her house in the rue des Tournelles with the new English ponies and the new summer coach (the one with the pretty glass windows), and to be back at the Hôtel d'Olonne, *with the Countess inside the coach*, not a minute later than half-past four. The rue des Tournelles, where Gilette lived, in the Marais quarter, was a long way from the rue Neuve-Saint-Augustin. Still, such a delay was unpardonable. The minx knew perfectly well how much it meant to Cateau to be on time today. If she were not the most consistently scatter-brained creature living, this vexing slip could never have happened.

But that, unfortunately, was exactly what she was. Cateau, looking out of the window for the twenty-first time, wondered now, as she had often before in the last five months, what on earth had induced her to choose society's celebrated spoilt child, Gilonne-Marie-Julie d'Harcourt — wife to Condé's henchman, Charles-Léon de Fiesque, but better known in Précieuse circles as 'Queen Gilette' — for her best friend.

Cateau did not approve of best friends. At least, not if they were women.

Cateau thought women a waste of time — silly, chattering magpies, who cared for nothing but clothes and lovers!... Of course, she did not include Magdelon in this sweeping denunciation of their sex. If her sister had been settled in Paris, Cateau would not have wanted another confidante. But alas! for the last two years since her marriage Magdelon had been away most of the time, either at Nancy or at the Maréchal's principal country house, the castle of La Ferté-Saint-Aubin near Orléans. And even when she was in town, as she had been lately for a number of weeks, she was too much occupied with her new duties — which comprised, in addition to her husband and his houses and their official appearances at court, her baby, six-months-old Henri — to be able to spend many hours with Cateau.

It was a pity; for, though no one could possibly take her place, it was just then that, for the first time in her life, Cateau had begun to feel the need of someone to talk to. Isabelle de Montmorency was too sharp, and Cécile de Montglas too stupid, to be of any use. And it was at this juncture, towards the end of January, that the Comtesse de Fiesque had suddenly reappeared in Paris, after four years' exile in the country.

There was quite a little flurry at court over Madame de Fiesque's return. She was somehow one of the people who counted. It was hard to tell precisely why. She was by no means a beauty, although often acclaimed as one. Nor was she especially cultured, though for years she had been accustomed to receive extravagant homage on that score as well. She was not even young any more: her fortieth birthday was not very far off, and she was the mother of five children — four daughters, worse luck! and a son. (The son was supposed to be somewhere at boarding-school; the eldest daughter, heir to the estate of Gilette's first husband, the Marquis de Pinnes, was already married; the other three girls, who had no dowries, were scattered casually about the country in various convents. Cateau had sometimes a suspicion that their mother was not perfectly sure *which one was where....*) Worst of all, the Countess's financial situation was most precarious. The Comte de Fiesque (really Fieschi), like all Italians a born intriguer, with the reputation for choosing the wrong side in every conspiracy, was one of the few rebels of the civil war to remain unpardoned. He had followed his chief, the Prince de Condé, out of the country, and was still fighting somewhere in Spain. One could say what one liked about loyalty to one's leader, but the fact was, he was a traitor to the Crown, no less; and his wife was in no position to expect help from the court. It had been all very well in the turbulent days of the Fronde, when Gilette had played at being a political hostess, and pranced about Paris in helmet and shield on a battle-charger, and called herself a Maréchale-de-camp in the army of the Princes. (What fun it had been!) But the fun was all over; Gilette had quarrelled with her patroness, Mademoiselle de Montpensier, which was surely a foolish thing to have done, and had been practically thrown out of the castle of Saint-Fargeau. People wondered quite openly what she would do now. . . .

Gilette herself, however, refused either to wonder or worry. She arrived one day, unexpectedly, at the house in the rue des Tournelles that had been vacant so long, with a troop of servants (goodness knew how their wages were paid!) and a great many boxes. Rumours flew round of a secret reconciliation with the Queen and the Cardinal, said to have been brought about by Madame de Fiesque's powerful friend, the Abbé Fouquet, who was Mazarin's most trusted confidential agent. Gilette neither confirmed the rumours, nor denied them. But her gay little triangular face was seen at all the assemblies of a particularly busy carnival season; her shrill terrier's laugh dominated every group in which she found herself. And her group, in spite of her age — which, to tell the truth, no one could have suspected — soon resolved itself into the youngest and smartest and most dissipated set of courtiers in town — into Cateau's own circle, in fact.

Cateau, who as a young girl had known Madame de Fiesque fairly well at Mademoiselle's little court at the Tuileries, but had thought of her then as someone much too old to be intimate with, soon found, to her surprise, that they were now precisely the same age. As a matter of fact, Cateau often felt she was the elder of the two. Her sparkling blue eyes met Gilette's mocking, wide-open hazel ones in quick mutual recognition — and, after that, once and for all, they were friends.

In the strange new need for companionship that had come upon Cateau since the rapid development of emotional complications in her life, Gilette seemed to suit her as no one else, save Magdelon, could have done. Gilette never bothered, never scolded, never asked indiscreet questions, never ventured to speculate unkindly — as the Montmorency was far too apt to do — as to 'how all this would end, my dear.' Gilette was tactful and unanalytical, brightly determined to see everything in the best possible light. Gilette, in fact, but for her fatal disregard of the clock, would have been the ideal companion. . . . But oh, where was she now? How could she fail, on this day of all days?

Cateau, drumming on the window pane with nervous fingers, peered out once more — for the fiftieth time by now, surely! — and at last beheld François and the new English ponies turning the corner of the rue de Richelieu. She had seen them do that so often in her mind's eye that, when they were actually there, she could not at first quite believe it, but stood a moment longer in front of the window, beating her fingers on the glass and stupidly staring.

Then, all of a sudden, she came to life. Picking up her full turquoise taffeta skirts, she ran to the stairs, and skimmed down them
so fast that Quentine and Quinette, who were waiting at their
foot to attend her, were almost bowled over in her impetuous rush;
and Brossard had barely time to get to the door in time to open
it for his mistress.

'The Cours la Reine! Drive as fast as you can!' cried Cateau
imperiously to François.

She was in so great a hurry that she forgot she had meant to
enter the carriage with a flounce, in order to make her displeasure
clear to the tardy Gilette. Gilette, however, aware of her fault,
turned to greet her friend with a placative smile.

'My dear ... how too tiresome of me ... I know: don't tell me
how late it is! But this time it wasn't my fault, really. Madame
Cornuel came to call just as I was getting ready to leave — and
you know the things she'd say if I told her I had to go out, and
couldn't offer to take her! By now I'd not have a shred of reputation left the length and breadth of the Marais!'

Cateau made no reply: she smiled a little, in an absent-minded
manner, to show that she was not seriously angry; but her thoughts
were wholly bent on one all-consuming object: would they get
to the Cours in time, and, if so, would Mérille be there with news
of his master?

Gilette, who no doubt could guess what was passing in Cateau's
mind, then said, with unwonted hesitation: 'My dear, I hardly
think, do you, that the Duke will be able to come today?'

'Why not?' said Cateau loudly. 'He promised me he would.'

'I know,' said Gilette. 'And he will, of course, if he can: I'm sure
of that. But don't forget he's been banished for a week — a whole
week. Madame Cornuel was telling me just now that Mazarin and
the Queen are really displeased with him: they say this quarrel
between his father Epernon and the Duc de Vendôme was all of
Candale's making.'

'That's a lie!' said Cateau. 'But even if it were true, what was
it to make such a fuss about? — a silly question of precedence,
that's all.'

'Yes, I know, dear,' said Gilette sagely, 'but there's just the
trouble: the Cardinal says Candale is always being involved in
those sorts of things. It's only a few weeks ago he was mixed up in
that dreadful street-brawl with the Montrevels — and the poor
Chevalier de Montrevel lost his life in that.'

'What if he did?' cried Cateau. 'It wasn't Candale's fault.'

'I didn't say it was,' said Gilette mildly. (One had evidently to
be very careful with Cateau this afternoon: Gilette could imagine
how her friend's eyes were flashing behind their mask of black

velvet.) 'But there it is, dear: innocent as he was, he got into a mess all the same — just as he's got into one now, on his father's account. It's too bad — but there it is! And the court is taking it seriously this time. I hear that from everyone — not only from Madame Cornuel, who no doubt is a great gossip, but the Abbé Fouquet was talking about it only last night at Cécile de Montglas' . . . and you know how close he is to the Cardinal. . . .'

'I don't care. I don't care. It can't be important.'

'I didn't say it was,' repeated Gilette, still more pacifically. 'I dare say it will all blow over in no time. And now that he's leaving to command the army in Spain, it'll give everybody a chance to forget before he comes back in the autumn. Only, since he *has* been exiled for a week, it would be the height of imprudence for him to show himself now, of all times, and in the Cours, of all places, where the whole world meets every afternoon. And if he should be mad enough to come, dear, which I personally very much doubt, do you think it's wise for you to be seen together in public?'

Cateau stared in amazement.

'Why not, for Heaven's sake? It wouldn't be the first time!'

'All the more reason, then, to commence being careful,' said Gilette, with an emphatic nod. She began looking unutterable things: 'Oh, my dear, I've been through this so often, myself — and I've seen my friends through so many affairs! Be warned by me: I know — *I know* — this is the time to go slowly! People are starting to say dreadful things about you. . . .'

'What if they are?' Cateau tossed her head. 'Haven't they always . . . ever since I was married . . . and before, even? It makes no difference to me.'

'Oh, my child, but it *must!* And you've been — you must admit — frightfully reckless lately. Now, dear, I'm going to be quite, quite serious, whether you like it or not, and give you a little lecture, which I fear you richly deserve. Will you listen to me?'

'Oh, very well.'

Cateau sighed and sat back in her seat, twisting her gloved hands together in a fit of nervous abstraction. Anything, *anything*, to help pass the time. . . . The traffic in the long, busy rue Saint-Honoré was worse than usual today: their coach was merely crawling along. . . . Oh, would they never get there?

Madame de Fiesque assumed an air of preternatural wisdom and held up her dainty hand — scarcely larger than a child's —as she prepared to tick off Cateau's sins. Anyone who did not know her — but then Cateau did, very well — would have supposed her as discreetly judicious as a sibyl. As it was, it was easy to guess that what one was about to hear was simply an echo of Gilette's half-hour with the venomous Cornuel creature. That was all Gilette was:

an echo. She could repeat precisely what she had heard, with as much impassioned conviction as if it were an original opinion instead of merely a parrot-like copy. Cateau had known her to change her ideas a score of times on a single subject in the course of an afternoon. Everything depended on whom she had been listening to last. One could not help speculating occasionally as to whether Gilette actually had any mind of her own.

Whether *she* had or not, it soon became evident that Madame Cornuel possessed quite enough for two, and that the latter's numerous spies had left no recent move of the Comtesse d'Olonne's unobserved.

'In the first place, my dear, you two went together last week to Berny, to Monsieur de Lyonne's party for the King. Everyone saw you, coming in arm-in-arm, just like a married couple. Where was Olonne?'

'Oh, you know he'll never go to those stupid official receptions. I'd not have been able to get there myself,' said Cateau, 'if Candale hadn't offered to take me.'

'Very well — but you needn't have marched in an hour late before the whole court, both of you dressed so richly that the King and Queen looked like nothing beside you. Anyone would have thought the party was given for you instead of for them. That sort of thing is bound to cause talk.'

Cateau made a face.

'I can't help it, can I, if we know how to dress, and they don't?' she said languidly.

'Secondly' — Gilette was being strictly categorical — 'Sunday night, at the Portuguese Ambassador's fireworks on the river, you and Candale were together again in a front-row bench, where everybody could see you — your husband nowhere in sight ... or am I wrong, dear? Was he concealed in the crowd?'

'You know very well he was not.' Cateau's voice was still silken and listless. 'But what difference ——'

'There, as I say, child, you were, for all the world to behold — and if they didn't have an eyeful that evening, it wasn't *your* fault! What possessed you to get yourself up like that poor crazy Queen of Sweden? — or, rather, I should say, like a man, for her toilets are always extravagantly cavalier. That military jacket and the black toque with plumes — I'll not deny they were very becoming. ... Still, in the circumstances, something slightly less striking ...'

'Why,' said Cateau, with simplicity, 'what would be the good of going out, if one weren't to be looked at?'

'Thirdly,' said Gilette impressively, 'your impromptu boating-party on the Seine, two nights ago, in Monsieur de Bonnelle's new yacht: don't you suppose all the tattle-tales in town have been gabbling their heads off about that ever since? I heard nothing else mentioned at Cécile's.'

'I'm sorry people are so dull they can't find anything more exciting to talk about. Why, there was nothing to that, absolutely nothing at all. I simply went to look at the boat, at Monsieur de Bonnelle's own invitation, as all his friends have been doing since he bought it. I'd no idea Candale was coming, or La Feuillade either, for that matter. Besides, I wasn't alone with them: the little Roquelaure was with me the whole time, and the Comtesse de Soissons, too. You can ask them if they weren't.'

'I shouldn't ask Olympe de Soissons anything about it, dear, if I were you. It'd have been a great deal better for all concerned if you'd left *her* at home, where she belonged. Never trust an Italian. (I ought to know: I married one!) Why, she's been telling everyone all over Paris that you met your gallants on board by appointment — that the sailors were bribed to take you to Saint-Cloud — and that the midnight supper you had there was served by your orders. Whether it's true or not — and I dare say it's not: we all know what a tongue the Soissons has! — there's no doubt she's made the most of the scandal to the Queen. And Roquelaure boxed his wife's ears when she got home at dawn, before all his servants.'

Cateau tapped on the glass of the front window of the coach, to make François look round.

'Hurry! Hurry!' she called out fretfully. 'I've never known you to take such centuries. For Heaven's sake, whip up the horses! I'll tell the Count his new English bargains are worthless.'

Then she turned back to Gilette.

'All that you say may be true,' she murmured, as if it did not make the least difference to her. 'I'll not deny a good deal . . . but these are trifles.'

'Trifles, perhaps — but not to be overlooked, just the same. And what's not a trifle is the way you and the Duke have been meeting openly everywhere for months. A rendezvous, my dear — that's something everybody understands — but it must be kept secret. That's the whole point of an affair: discretion — *discretion!*' cried Gilette, who had never been discreet in her life, but felt convinced for the moment that she was a pattern of prudence. 'No one objects to a woman's having a dozen lovers, if she likes — as long as she's willing to save her face by pretending *not* to be having them. But you and Candale: ah, my dear! You're seen everywhere together, not only in public, in the Cours, at the play, but at all sorts of houses, besides: Charlotte de Bonnelle's, old Choisy's — I don't know where not! And one can't be in the room with you five minutes without realizing how things stand between you. Such smiles! Such glances! Such colour as flames in your cheeks!

My dear, old campaigner that I am, I tell you frankly I've never seen anything like it. The other evening in my own drawing-room, I didn't know where to look! One would suppose you were actually proud to have people see ——'

'And so I am — proud!' exclaimed Cateau, coming at last to life, her face suddenly as pink as it had been ivory-pale before. 'I am proud of having the finest gentleman in France in love with me. And he's just as proud of having me in love with him. So there! We don't care who knows it. As for other people, it doesn't matter a pin what they think: hateful, lying, jealous.... But they can't touch us. This is what we've waited for, all of our lives — and now that we've found it nothing on earth can separate us.'

'And your husband?' said Gilette softly. 'What does Olonne say to that, my dear?'

But Cateau was not to be influenced thus:

'Who cares what *he* says about anything? Besides, you know what he's like: he lets me do exactly as I please, always. After that fuss about the yacht he did tell me not to ask Candale to the house. But what do I care — when there are all the other houses?'

'Catherine-Henriette!' sighed her friend. 'You are incorrigible! I give you up. I'll not say another word. Only this: don't tell me, later, I didn't warn you. You've made yourself the scandal of all Paris. Why, only this morning on the Pont Neuf I heard a horrid little boy singing some verses about "the beautiful Countess and her golden-haired gallant"! Naturally, I stopped the carriage, to see if I could buy a copy of them to bring you, but they were all sold already! And, my dear, when they start writing jingles on the Pont Neuf, you know what that means! Oh, Catherine-Henriette, if everyone wanted to help you, it wouldn't be easy — and you know very well they don't! People like you and Candale have always more enemies than friends. The world's a jealous place. So do, *do* beware....'

But now Gilette perceived that there was really no use in saying anything more; for François had arrived at the Cours at last. Bowling through the gilded wrought-iron gates that guarded the entrance, they were swept suddenly into a scene of animated gaiety.

It was a fine summer afternoon. The wide promenade was bordered on either side by double rows of tall elms in their feathery new June dresses: to the left, through the trees, gleamed the river; to the right, lay the green wilds of the Champs Elysées. Two solid lines of carriages, one coming, one going, rolled in stately procession along the avenue. They were laden with groups of ladies in *their* new June dresses, who were busy looking for friends amongst the crowd of cavaliers on horseback that filled the space between the two lines. As the cavaliers were equally busy looking for ladies, and frequently stopped to salute them — and as, furthermore, what little room was left was taken by vendors of liqueurs and sweetmeats, who dashed about under the wheels of the carriages, plying their trade with bright disregard for the safety of life and limb — it was natural that the traffic should be a good deal impeded. In fact, the horses were seldom able to proceed at even a sluggish trot, but as no one was in a hurry, it did not greatly matter.

As soon as the Olonnes' coach had taken its place in the slowly moving stream Madame de Fiesque gave a few self-conscious pats to the clusters of ash-brown curls under her plumed primrose-yellow bonnet, smoothed the folds of her gown, and began to bow and smile graciously to various people she knew.... Ah, how good it was to be back in Paris once more! In the dreary years of her exile at Mademoiselle's poky provincial court, Gilette had missed nothing so much as the promenades in the Cours; she had thought of them often with passionate regret: for twenty-five years, more or less, she had been one of their chief ornaments. And how delightful it seemed now to find herself here once again, just as if she had never been away! Better still, it was no small satisfaction, at an age when most of her contemporaries were on the shelf, to be able to demonstrate firmly that she was still to be reckoned with in the gay younger set. For, in spite of malicious gossip, Cateau remained the leader of that; to be seen with her placed a public seal on one's title to smartness.

So Gilette went on smiling and bowing, keeping up meanwhile a running commentary on her passing acquaintances: 'My dear, there's the Comtesse de Soissons, with little Villeroy: they say that's quite, quite definite.... Charlotte de Roquelaure in a black toque just like yours: did you give her permission to copy it?... The Comte de Guiche — how do you do? How do you *do?* — with the Sully girl and her mother. I hear that's to be a match. Poor little thing, I don't envy her, do you? He's as volatile as a butterfly, and the less said about morals... Besides, she's only thirteen, and naturally hasn't the least idea... I was thirteen myself, when I married Piennes.... My dear, the shock to the nerves!... How do you do?... It's Madame de Saint-Loup, Catherine-Henriette. You'd better turn the other way. My dear, she looks a million! They say she's never got over losing Candale, and spends all her time washing beggars' feet in the charity hospitals.... If it's true, then what is she doing here with Monsieur de Sillery, who doesn't waste efforts on women who — my dear Sillery, good afternoon!'...

Cateau paid no attention to this tinkling rivulet, which went happily on in spite of her studied neglect. (The caustic Madame Cornuel had once dubbed Gilette the 'word-mill.') Cateau sat rigid in her seat, pale and anxious, straining her eyes to catch sight of a familiar face. She scarcely took the trouble to acknowledge the numerous greetings she received in their triumphal progress up the avenue. Certainly she could not be bothered to smile and scream as Gilette was doing: a cold, preoccupied nod was the best Madame d'Olonne had to give this afternoon. Twice only did she rouse herself from her trance — the first time in order to wave to Magdelon, who was driving with her stepmother-in-law and little Henri in the Senneterres' big golden coach, drawn by the Maréchal's six coal-black horses with scarlet plumes on their heads. The second time, she leaned forward, without haste, to bestow a brilliant smile on the luckless Madame de Saint-Loup. That, of course, was a point of honour not to be omitted on any account. But as soon as her carriage and her rival's had passed each other the smile faded out as if it had never been there, and she resumed her tense, waiting air.... Where was he? Oh, where could he be? Had they got there too late, after all? True, it was already long past five ... but Candale had said, between five and six he would come, or else send word.... Between five and six....

Now they had reached the great circle midway up the Cours and were driving round it preparatory to turning back. Cateau leaned forward once more, but this time very quickly indeed.

'There! There! Stop a moment, François: it's Mérille!'

A square-faced, intelligent-looking man on horseback, wearing the Duke's blue-and-silver livery, hastened towards Madame d'Olonne's carriage, dismounted, and kissed the hand hurriedly thrust through the window.

'Madam, I'd begun to fear you weren't here. I've looked everywhere for the last half-hour ——'

'Yes! Yes!' exclaimed Cateau impatiently. 'Never mind about that now. Where's your master? Is he coming?'

'Madam, he is. He waits at the end of the avenue, by the far gate. But just a minute ...'

Cateau hardly listened to what Mérille was saying. On receiving the news she had longed for a wave of colour flowed into her pallid cheeks: she became a different creature from the lifeless beauty of five minutes ago.

'Thank Heaven! Not too late, after all! Drive on, François!'

'Madam! Madam!' called out Mérille, spurring on his horse in order to keep abreast of the coach. 'His Highness bids me tell you that he can stay for a moment only ... that the utmost caution will be necessary. He is in Paris against the King's orders, as you know, and hopes to leave tonight for Spain. Therefore, if he were to be seen ...'

'Yes, yes, Mérille, I know! I understand perfectly. I will be careful. Thank you a thousand times.... Good-bye, and good luck to you!...The far gate, François, as fast as you can get there!'

The upper part of the Cours, beyond the great circle, was not nearly so crowded as the lower part had been, so that their progress was more rapid than before. The English ponies trotted along so briskly that Gilette had scarcely time to change her face between greetings, and, much to her annoyance, found she had bestowed on the Bishop of Le Mans, whom she hated, the tail-end of a smile she had meant exclusively for her particular friend, the Chevalier de Gramont.

But Cateau, conscious only of her absorbing purpose, was deaf to prayers to moderate their speed.

At the end of the Cours la Reine the avenue was shut off by a pair of iron gates exactly like those by which they had entered. Beyond them stretched an expanse of open, partly wooded country, with nothing between it and the huge wild forest of Boulogne save the village of Chaillot.

As the Olonnes' carriage came to a halt a blond young man in the uniform of an infantry officer — scarlet and blue, white and gold, and glittering with orders — stepped out from behind a clump of trees and held up his hand.

Gilette, with a gasp, gave the blond young man her best smile, and then sank back tactfully on the cushions in order to leave the lovers as much privacy as possible.

Cateau, however, who had been half beside herself with nervous impatience all afternoon, seemed to have recovered her customary command of her forces.

She smiled, too, at Monsieur de Candale, but serenely; the hand she gave him did not tremble as it had in the grasp of Mérille; and her voice when she spoke sounded calm, almost lazy.

'Well,' said Cateau, 'I see you managed it, after all.'

Candale shrugged his shoulders.

'By the skin of my teeth. I've no right to be here. The old boy's really angry this time, you know; I doubt if he'd give me a niece if I got down on my knees and begged for one!'

'You're leaving tonight?'

'Yes. At seven. By carriage as far as Epernon — and then on horseback to the frontier. The sooner I can get to Spain, the better. Moret is joining me in an hour. We spent last night at Prudhomme's bathhouse on the river; none of Mazarin's spies were likely to look for me there.'

'You ran a great risk,' said Cateau.

The Duke smiled cheerily.

'Perhaps — but I had to get back to Paris just once before going away for the whole summer, you know. I said good-bye to my sister at the Carmelites', and called on my stepmother this morning.

That accounted for two of my errands in the city. The third . . .
Madam, I think you must guess what the third one was, and why
I wasn't willing to leave until I'd performed it.'

Cateau did not listen very carefully; her thoughts appeared to
have been following a course of their own.

'Where are you going now?' she asked, still in that cool, tranquil
voice, as if it did not really matter very much.

'To Chaillot — in a minute or two, I'm afraid. Moret is meeting
me there with my servants and the carriages.'

'And how will you go?'

'Through the wood. On horseback.'

'Oh! Your horse is here, too?'

'Yes.' Candale nodded towards the tangle of shrubbery behind
the iron gate. 'I ought to be off directly. There's nothing for me
to go back for — now.'

'And if I asked you,' said Cateau deliberately, 'before you left,
to ride beside my carriage in the Cours — as you've done so many
many times before . . .'

Gilette, who had kept her face studiously averted during this
brief dialogue, gave a shriek.

'My dear, you're mad! What are you thinking of? If he were
to be seen, it would be fatal — *fatal!*'

'The court's in Compiègne this week,' said Cateau.

'Even so, they'd hear about it soon enough. You know quite
well they would.'

'Well, by the time they've heard, and long before they could *do*
anything, he'll be gone,' said Cateau; 'so what difference can it
make?'

'But, my dear,' moaned Gilette, 'the Cours, of all places! . . .
where everyone in the world . . .'

Cateau raised her eyebrows and looked at Candale. Candale
looked back at Cateau, without saying anything for a moment;
but his eyes began to kindle with dangerous excitement. Then,
'It's a bargain, madam,' said Candale, 'if you will do me the
honour of unmasking while I accompany you.'

He clapped his hands and whistled; immediately a groom led
the Duke's big tawny battle-charger — which was almost as well
known as its owner — out from behind the trees. Candale swung
himself into the saddle, swept his plumed hat off his golden
curls in a splendid salute to the ladies, and wheeled about just
as François whipped up the ponies, the quaking groom trotting after
them on foot.

In this fashion they rode the whole length of the Cours la Reine.

Gilette, shrinking back in the coach and giggling hysterically,
tilted her bonnet over her eyes and hoped she would not be recog-

nized: it was too bad that she had been so liberal with her greetings, only a few minutes earlier.

Cateau, on the other hand, sat up very straight with her head very high, flushed and smiling, bowing affably to everyone they met.

And Candale, a superbly conspicuous figure, rode unconcernedly at her side, bowing also, when occasion demanded it, with his courtly and faintly exaggerated grace.

Ripples of interest and curiosity passed through the crowd at their appearance, ripples that rolled on in ever increasing circles till at length they assumed the proportions of waves; for Candale's decree of banishment was generally known — and that he had chosen to brave it now, of all times, and with the Comtesse d'Olonne, of all people, could not fail to create a sensation.

Both Cateau and Candale were intensely aware of this sensation, which provided them with the sort of dramatic excitement on which they depended in order to live. They betrayed, however, no outward signs of self-consciousness, playing their parts with a charming nonchalance far too natural to be convincing to one, at least, of their audience: the Italian comedians, thought Gilette wrathfully, could not have done better.

Nor did they betray their feelings towards each other directly, although, as always when they were together, sparks of mutual magnetism seemed to make the air electric between them.

When at last they got to the end of the avenue and passed through the gilded iron gates into Paris again, by the Porte de la Conférence, just opposite Renard's restaurant with its terrace overlooking the Tuileries and the river, Madame de Fiesque heaved a sigh of relief. Thank God, it was over! — and perhaps no one of importance had seen them? After all, the court *was* at Compiègne, so the chances were better than even . . .

'If nothing terrible happens,' thought Gilette, 'I'll burn a candle to the Virgin tonight at Saint Paul's. . . . Holy Mother, what an escape!'

Cateau looked at Candale, Candale at Cateau, once more. They had done it! But what next? Surely this could not be the end?

With quick decision Cateau rapped on the window of the coach. 'Stop here!' she said to François. 'I'm going to take a walk in the park. Gilette, darling, I'd meant to give you an ice at Renard's — but you don't mind, do you? My man will drive you home or anywhere else you prefer.'

And before Gilette had any idea what she intended to do, Cateau was out of the carriage, and Candale had sprung from his horse and tossed the bridle to the breathless groom with a hasty 'Wait here for me!' — and together, hand in hand, the lovers had vanished amongst the trees of the Tuileries Gardens.

IT WAS COOL IN THE SHADE OF THE BEECH GROVE, AND VERY SOLEMN and still. The late afternoon sun filtering through the branches turned the transparent young leaves a luminous greenish-gold, as if they themselves were part of the light. There were no sounds at all except the occasional call of some unseen bird, the rustle of Cateau's taffeta skirt, and the clank of her companion's spurs and of his sword that swung in its scabbard at his side.

They walked, still hand in hand, without speaking. Cateau was afraid to say anything, for fear of upsetting the delicate balance of the accord that existed between them, oddly enough, only when they were silent, or actually making love to each other. It was strange, she thought, that it should be so; strange that two people, who cared for each other more than for anyone else in the world, could not be happy unless they were mute, or else straining and sobbing in each other's arms.

What was strangest of all was that, realizing this — as they had now had two years to do — they should still be unable to resist running to court temptation and embarking on one of the forbidden subjects whenever they found themselves alone together.

All subjects, really, seemed forbidden to Cateau and Candale. . . . Oh, the precious moments they had wasted in arid, useless scenes of jealousy! Oh, the many, many times Cateau had accused the Duke of planning to marry one of the Mancinis! — though she knew perfectly well that he had no intention of doing so —; of still carrying on his affair with Madame de Saint-Loup, or of starting a new one with some provincial siren he met on his annual travels! To each of these charges Candale could oppose a countercharge no less violent: How did the Countess amuse herself every summer whilst her lover was in Spain? What tales had he heard concerning Paget, the rich banker, who was said to have called on Madame d'Olonne daily last year, and to have sent her twenty bushels of flowers when she fell ill of the smallpox? Better far for her to have died than to lay herself open to such ugly rumours! *Paget*, of all people — a base commoner — not even a gentleman! Pah! One could scarcely believe it.

At this, Cateau would raise her eyebrows, shrug her shoulders, and murmur tantalizingly: 'Well, my dear, you shouldn't stay away

so long. What do you expect a woman to do, when every decent
fellow she knows has gone to the army?'... Very well, then, retorted Candale — but it was the same story when he was at home:
how about Beuvron, madam — and Boisdauphin — Manicamp —
and the Chevalier de Gramont — and a dozen others he might mention?

This sort of thing could go on indefinitely, and frequently did,
neither of them being willing to admit what both secretly knew was
the truth: which was simply that they were accomplished professional flirts, and could no more help exercising their physical fas-
cinations on all available targets than a peacock can help spreading
its tail.

When they were not quarrelling about love there were a great
many other things they could quarrel about. They were jealous, not
only of each other's amorous exploits, but also of each other's social
conquests: of their respective clothes, and jewels, and coiffures, and
coaches, and gambling debts, and general reputations as leaders of
fashion. Here, again, it was their very likeness that was the cause of
their disunion. Not for nothing did they resemble each other so
closely that they might have been taken for brother and sister; so
that when they embraced there was always a nameless sense of
yearning towards an unattainable object. (It was like Narcissus
trying to kiss his own reflection in the pool.) Perhaps an instinctive
feeling for their decorative value as a pair had drawn them together
in the first place. But each wanted to be the dominating member of
the pair. Cateau suffered actual pain if anyone else — her lover included — attracted more attention in public than herself. She would
not say so, of course. Candale suffered quite as much, in his way, if
he felt that *he* was not the centre, even momentarily, of his not inconsiderable universe. Naturally, *he* would not say so either.

So they went on spinning bright, interminable monologues, cataloguing their achievements for the other's discomfiture, singing their
own praises unweariedly, with matchless variety and resource, until
— like as not — they came to blows, and then to tears, and then to
kisses, and then — ah, but for such a brief moment! — to peace.

That, apparently, thought Cateau, with despair, was what love
was.

Today, however, she was resolved not to quarrel about anything,
not to stray for an instant onto dangerous ground, no matter what
the provocation. Candale was going away, and, as always when that
was the case, she was filled with tenderness for her lover and a virtuous inclination to be and to do in his absence only what he would
have her.

They walked farther and farther in under the trees. Swish-swish
went Cateau's skirt, and Candale's sword and spurs went on jan-

gling in time with his long, even stride. While Cateau was considering gingerly what might be the safest opening the silence was
abruptly broken by the Duke, who turned to her with a sunny
smile and remarked, out of a clear sky: 'Jesus! What a stingy old
miser my father is!'

'Come, now,' said Cateau to herself. 'This *can't* lead to trouble!'
Aloud she said: 'Is he, my dear?'

'He wouldn't give me a cent,' said Candale, 'to prepare for the
campaign. Not one cent. It's the same story, year after year. He's
always got some paltry excuse. This time he pretends he's too poor
because he's just bought the Hôtel de Chevreuse for two hundred
thousand francs... if you can believe he gave such a price for that
old firetrap! Personally, I doubt it. I've had the Devil's own time
scraping up enough cash to get off. If my stepmother hadn't come
across with twelve thousand crowns at the last minute, I couldn't
have made it. I don't know what happens to my income. There's
never a thing left over at the end of the year. Of course, Forcade,
my steward, is a rascal. So's Budon, the maître-d'hôtel. Between
the two of them I'm robbed right and left. If I had any sense at all,
I'd give them both the sack tomorrow.'

'I never have anything left over, either,' said Cateau reflectively.
'And *I* can't think why.'

'Oh, well, my dear, with a woman it's different. She's not expected
to use her income for anything except pin-money.'

'That's not always the case; at least, it's not so with me. I pay
my share of the household expenses regularly, every month. Where
would Olonne be, if I didn't? Our food bills alone... Oh, he knew
what he was doing when he married me! I don't say I was an heiress,
but I was given a very good settlement as settlements go, and my
husband's always had the disposition of the income of my dowry.'

'Well, dear, it's good of you to be so generous — but you needn't
do it, unless you like to. Look at *me*, though, and the household *I've*
got to maintain on my own, year in, year out, with no outside help!
I've a steward — two secretaries — treasurer — maître-d'hôtel —
three valets-de-garde-robe — six valets-de-pied — besides another
valet in charge of the pages.... Yes, and there are the pages themselves, a score of 'em, and eight gentlemen-in-waiting, and ten
house officers in the pantry and kitchen, and as many more in the
stables, to say nothing of all the under-servants and the separate
establishments I have to keep in the country, in my governments of
Auvergne and Burgundy. Good Lord! I must feed over a thousand
people!'

Cateau nodded her head, but not as if she were listening. 'Yes,
my dear,' she said. 'But think of *us*: Olonne and I keep an enormous
staff — of course, nothing like so large as yours, we're not princes;
but then, we haven't a princely income. Still, there are twenty or

twenty-five in the house in town, in addition to the people at our places in Poitou and Normandy. And then there are my clothes: you can't compare a man's wardrobe to a woman's. Why, I often have to spend a thousand francs a week just on incidentals, not to mention my frocks!'

'So must I; I spend *twice* that much, sometimes,' retorted Candale firmly. 'Even three times. I have to dress just as well as you do, my dear. And after I've got all my regular clothes there are the uniforms of my various regiments. Dear Heaven! I can't go on wearing the same ones, can I, year after year? — no matter what Papa says! And think what it costs to keep me in horses...!'

They continued thus amiably disputing for a quarter of an hour, comparing sundry items of their personal expenses. Both kept their tempers admirably; on the other hand, neither would give ground. At the end of this time it had been clearly established: (1) that Cateau spent more money a year than any other woman in Paris; (2) that Candale spent more than any man; (3) that any man spent more than any woman; and (4) that any woman spent more, *in proportion to what she had*, than any man.

'But, darling,' said the Duke suddenly, 'I'm going away today. I shan't see you again for months, perhaps for almost a year. Can't we find something better to talk about than petty finance?'

'Certainly,' replied Cateau, with a radiant smile. 'We'll talk about anything you like, my dear. I never care to discuss money matters, anyhow. I'm sure I can't think how we began.'

'I believe, dear love, it was what you said about dowries ——'

'I? My dear, how ridiculous! Why, now that I come to remember, *you* started the whole thing by telling me what a hard time you'd had raising twelve thousand crowns for your campaign expenses.'

'I was not aware of it. Still, does it very much matter ——'

'It doesn't matter in the least. Only I don't like being accused of something I'm perfectly innocent of.'

'Who's accusing you, madam? As far as I know ——'

'You were; you know you were. It's not fair, really... But oh, my dear, we're quarrelling — and we mustn't — not today! How shall I ever be able to live without you?'

'You'll write to me by every post?'

'Faithfully, faithfully!' cried Cateau heroically, for her lover's sake willing even to conquer her lifelong aversion to pen-and-ink. 'And *you'll* write to *me?*'

'You know that I will, my beloved — every day, with my heart's blood! And I'll think of you every minute of every day, no matter where I am or what I am doing.'

'So shall I think of you.'

'And you'll promise me, dear, not to see that villain Paget any more? — not to accept any of his presents or presumptuous invitations to his house in the country?'

'But, sir, I told you months ago I wouldn't. Don't you believe me?'

'My darling, of course I do! You know, don't you? — you *must* know by now that I trust you anywhere or with anyone! It's only that Paris is full of evil-minded talebearers who've nothing better to do than try to sling mud on the most spotless reputations. And you will admit, my love, you've been ... well, a little careless; we'll say no more ... now and then, in the past.'

'I know I have,' said Cateau honestly. 'I don't care *that* what people think of me, as long as you and I ——'

'I know you don't. Nor should I, if it weren't that your happiness and well-being were supremely important to me. But I do beg you, for the sake of my peace of mind, if not for your own, to run no unnecessary risks this summer.... You'll not see Beuvron again, either, will you?'

'My dear, I've told you a hundred times ——'

'I know — I know! I've no right to doubt your precious word. It's only because I love you so much ...'

'If you loved me as much as you say you do,' said Cateau, with a touch of crispness, 'I should think you might be willing to trust me. I've said I won't see anyone you don't want me to see — and I won't. But it hurts my pride to have you doubt my good faith. I rely implicitly on yours: you've promised you won't go near that horrible Madame de la Baume when you're in Lyon, and I am sure I believe you. I *must* believe you, or I'd not be able to stand it. What do you think my life is, all those months while you're away with your army? It's all very well for a man, who's got battles to fight and soldiers to order about and take care of. But what can *I* do, left all alone, with no one to talk to but Olonne, and nothing to keep me from going quite mad when I start to think ... Ah, if you weren't selfish — but then all men are — you'd not want to deny me the few little innocent pleasures that come my way! I don't ask *you* to deny *yourself* anything.'

'Why, but, my dear, you've told me a thousand times if I so much as bowed to Madame de la Baume, all would be over between us! Come, now, be reasonable ——'

'So I did. So I do. But that's entirely different. You know yourself it is. I said "innocent pleasures." And that hag of a La Baume is a terrible woman — why, even her own husband won't live with her!'

'And I suppose Monsieur Paget is perfectly harmless — a filthy little toad with his nose in every dirty deal in the city! Yes, and whose reputation with women of a certain class smells to heaven!

To think you'd permit that sort of trash to enter your door; much less kiss your hand and send you posies and pay you boorish compliments by the yard! Women are all alike: they don't care who praises them, as long as they are praised!'

'What a lie!' exclaimed Cateau. 'Men are far vainer than any woman could be. At least, some men are — and you're the vainest of the lot! How else did the Saint-Loup manage to hold you for six years, except by flattering you till you began to think you were a god on a marble pedestal? Ah, don't I know it? Poor, misguided wretch, how my heart bleeds for her — deliberately stooping to drag herself in the dust as long as she'd any hope of keeping you! But could you be faithful, even to that tragic, loving soul? No! Not you — nor any man!'

'Well, madam, since it was for your sake I left her, I might have expected a little gratitude on your part for the sacrifice ——'

'Sacrifice! Pooh! You were tired of her, that's all. So you left her. And you'll leave me, too, when you're tired of me, in the very same way. Don't think I don't know it! All the love I've given you — all the loyalty — are worth nothing in the balance ——'

'Madam! Madam! I beg you to stop. Don't you love me any more?'

'No! No! No!' Cateau was crying now as she walked, and wringing her hands. 'No more than you really love me! How can I love you, when I know that the minute you've left me you'll go back to that monster?'

'What monster?'

'Oh, Saint-Loup, or La Baume, or that hideous wall-eyed little Castellane woman in Avignon — or any one of a dozen others! What difference does it make which one it is? They're all in love with you. Only, don't flatter yourself that I've no idea what you're doing, when you're off in the army with your horrid rough soldiers — what all men do, no matter what they promise the women at home they pretend to care for!'

'"Pretend to care for!" How dare you say I don't love you more than life itself! Madam, this is unworthy of you — when all that I am, and all that I have, have been laid at your feet for two years and more. But for you, I might have married one of the Cardinal's nieces. But for you, I might today be holding one of the principal posts at court and commanding the army in Flanders, instead of tamely submitting to being packed off every year to run the Catalonian campaign, which no one else thinks important enough to bother about.'

'The idea! The very idea! Reproaching *me* for your own lack of ambition — for it's that, and nothing else, that keeps you down! In your heart you must know it. There are a hundred ways of get-

ting the Cardinal to give you what you want without basely com-
plying with his demands. You're lazy, sir — that's what's the matter with you! You enjoy nursing a grievance, and blaming me for
the pass your own indolence and folly have led you to. Or am I
wrong? Are you really regretting the smug little dumpling Olympe,
now that she's married to the Comte de Soissons? Are you so ser-
vile a courtier that you must love all whom your master loves? —
and we know his strange weakness for those plump Italian pullets!
If that's what ails you, never mind, my dear; there are plenty more
of 'em in the henhouse, being fattened for market. Olympe may be
gone, and Laure, too — but there's Marie, and Hortense, and I
don't know how many others coming along after them. Take your
pick, sir, take your pick — and I'll dance at your wedding with the
merriest heart in the world!'

'Damn it all!' shouted Candale. 'I suppose that's what you would
like. Yes, of course, that's what you'd have me do, isn't it? I can
see it, plain as day — sell myself and my title for the Cardinal's
gold, and marry a chit I could neither love nor respect — while you
sat back in your lover's arms and laughed at me! Just for that, I
won't do it — see? I won't give you the satisfaction. Not while that
rat Paget's above ground! Because...'

Cateau and Candale then rehearsed their scene, *da capo*, innumerable times, until both of them were weeping hysterically and completely exhausted.

When there was no longer anything left they could say, they
stopped talking, without any special reason, as suddenly as they had
begun, and faced each other desperately in the wavering lime-green
light under the beeches. They had now walked so far into the wood
that they could not walk any farther; the path ended in a blind alley depressingly symbolic of their emotional predicament. So they
stood there, because there was nothing else to do, the tall yellow-
haired soldier in his glittering uniform and the slim yellow-haired
young woman in the turquoise taffeta dress, haggard and miserable,
their eyes strained to catch a glimpse of the happiness they both
firmly believed in, though neither of them had ever experienced it.

The next minute they had fallen into each other's arms in a violent
embrace.

Once again it was quite still, except for the birds, in the Tuileries
Gardens.

It was an hour or more before the Duke managed to tear himself from his sobbing mistress, and rode away to the war on his
tawny charger. Cateau got herself home, she knew not how. It
seemed to her that she would die; that it was impossible for her to
support life for the next seven months without her lover. Yet, in

the midst of her grief, she was haunted by two minor regrets, which, unimportant as they were, she felt certain would tease her every day until they met again. She wished very much she had been able to make it clear to Candale that it was *he* who had started that paltry conversation about money. She also wished, even more strongly, that when he had launched into his extravagant tirade to the effect that all he was and all he had were laid at her feet, she had remembered to remind him of the cross of emeralds he had refused to buy her, cheap as it was, last year at the Fair of Saint-Germain.

CATALONIA BEING A GOOD DEAL FARTHER OFF THAN FLANDERS, IT was another week before the main part of the army, under Turenne and La Ferté-Senneterre, had to leave Paris for the summer campaign.

It was a gay week, too. The streets were full of flags and marching men; the air resounded with cheerful military music; and there were a great many farewell parties for the officers.

In the end — although at first she had protested that she could not think of it, that it was useless to ask her — Cateau went to most of the parties. After locking herself in her room for a whole day and night and crying until she thought her heart would break, she suddenly emerged, looking much the same as usual; bought two new dresses and three new hats; and gave a very smart evening reception for her sister and brother-in-law.

She would not have admitted it for worlds, but she was experiencing, as always after Candale left her, a definite feeling of relief. Not that she loved him less ... certainly not: she'd tied up all his letters with rose-pink ribbons, and gazed at them, with streaming eyes, and at his portrait in miniature, which she kept in a gold locket, every night for half an hour by the clock. But love, Cateau found, was an exhausting emotion. She had never loved anyone before; she hoped, quite frankly, she would never love anyone again. How could people pretend that what they called a great passion was the height of human bliss? There were compensations, it was true — moments so thrilling that even to recall them afterwards made you close your eyes and catch your breath — but most of the time love was anything but agreeable. It turned you, quite against your will, into someone entirely different from your ordinary self: you said things you didn't mean and did things you didn't want to, and heard yourself saying and saw yourself doing these things with the queer, helpless detachment of a third person. In short, you became, for as long as you and your lover were together, an altogether irresponsible being.

But — and this, thought Cateau, was perhaps even stranger than the effects of love itself — as soon as you had said good-bye to each other, for even a very short time, you could change back to your

old personality ... your *real* personality. (Or was the other the real
one? Who was to say?) The moment Candale had ridden away to
Spain — or no, not quite the *moment:* she had cried, after all, for
twenty-four hours, but say twenty-*six* hours afterwards — she was
once more able to laugh and talk and flirt and order people about,
just as she always did, without the slightest sense of strain. She
might miss the Duke so keenly that the pain was as sharp as a knife
in her heart whenever she thought of him — but she could not think
of him all the time. Indeed, there were days when she was really too
busy to think of him at all.

At first, as in other years, this had troubled her conscience a little.
She had felt faithless, even though she knew she was not interested
in anybody else; she had reproached herself for instability of character and lack of constancy to grief. But after a while it occurred to
her that, very likely, Candale was feeling just the same as she did:
maybe being in love as violently as they were used up certain parts
of the emotions, which would grow again in time, but only after lying
fallow for a period, during which it was wiser, and surely much
pleasanter, to have no emotions whatever.

So Cateau wiped her eyes and, with a gentle sigh, put away the
letters tied with rose-pink ribbons and shut the gold locket, and then
rang for Quinette and Quentine to do her hair and polish her nails
with that new Italian pomade. ... Yes, there was no doubt about it,
it was restful to feel that you belonged to yourself, even temporarily.

Both the new dresses were highly successful. So were two of the
hats. (The third hat, one of Cateau's rare failures, she very kindly
presented to Gilette.) Moreover, she was beginning to entertain the
first faint stirrings of that indefinable restlessness experience had
taught her meant that it was time for her to have her portrait
painted again. ... Would Mignard ...? or perhaps Petitot? ... At
her own party for the La Fertés Madame d'Olonne looked so beautiful, chatted so gaily with her guests, so willingly went to the clavichord, after supper, to sing a new song composed for her by Maître
Boësset (she had a pretty, piping soprano, though her sense of
rhythm was slightly defective), and, altogether, seemed in such
spirits that people began to whisper that, perhaps, there was nothing to those dreadful stories after all. ...

Unfortunately, at the end of the week the army left the city —
and in the army went every Frenchman young enough and strong
enough to handle sword and musket.

Paris, overnight, became a desert. The brilliant, tinny march
tunes died away, flags fluttered no longer in the June breeze, the
streets ceased to echo to the tramp of marching feet. Everyone had
gone except the women and children and invalids, and a few grey-
beards like Magdelon's father-in-law, the old Marquis de Senne-

terre. And they would be leaving soon, too, for their country estates. Ever since Cateau could remember life had been like this,
the year divided into two nearly equal parts, the lively winter season and the dull, apparently endless summer, when the men were
away at the war. It was not always, of course, the same war. But
intervals between hostilities were so brief and infrequent that even
the oldest beldame at court could not recall a time when France had
not been fighting *someone*. If no enemy were to be found outside its
frontiers, there were invariably civil disturbances brewing at home.
Men asked for nothing better, certainly. War was man's natural
profession, a glorious opportunity — the only one there was for the
nobility — to make a name for oneself abroad and a place of distinction for one's family at home. The women, too, got used eventually to this odd way of living, as year succeeded year and peace
seemed just as far away as ever. They jammed every bit of fun and
dissipation they could into the tragically short winter weeks, and
accepted with resignation the long, empty months of the summer —
months spent with their children on their immense country estates,
looking after the crops and the tenants with the help of their stewards, doing a little desultory reading and a great deal of needlework in the evenings, and exchanging polite, gossipy letters with
female relatives and friends in similar situations to their own. Except for those hours of terrible suspense after every battle, when
they waited, half dead with anxiety, to scan the lists of the casualties in the *Gazette de France*, life was a kind of pleasant, interminable
waking-dream.

Yes, they would all be leaving soon. Cécile de Montglas, whose
husband was already in Flanders, was taking her children to Cheverny, her parents' beautiful castle in Touraine. Isabelle de Montmorency, whose places were all mortgaged or in an uninhabitable
state of disrepair, was going to Bagnolet to visit her friend, the Duchesse de Nemours. Madame de Roquelaure, who had been seriously
ill and was said to be still in a delicate state, talked of taking the
cure at Vichy, as soon as she should be strong enough to support the
fatigues of the journey. Even Madame de Choisy, that most urban
of creatures, had business to attend to in Normandy, and had announced her intention of stopping on the way back to Paris for a
series of baths at Forges. ('So good for the joints, dear; and I shall
be halfway to Flanders, so that I'll get all the news from the army
days before anyone else!') And Magdelon, who, Cateau felt, had
only just come to town, was on the point of retiring once more to
the rural solitude of La Ferté-Saint-Aubin, with her little son and
an imposing train of servants.

The day before she left she brought young Henri to say good-bye
to his aunt.

Cateau was alone in the yellow cabinet, feeling unusually out of sorts. She sprang up with a cry of delight when Madame the Maréchale de la Ferté was announced.

Magdelon, having dismissed her attendants at the door with as convincing a copy of Cateau's regal carelessness as she was able to produce, came upstairs to find her sister, accompanied only by the baby and the baby's nurse.

She paused on the threshold a moment to compose herself, smiling shyly, and hoping no one had seen that she had run, from sheer excess of high spirits, halfway up the last flight of steps. Magdelon was slightly plumper now than she had been before her marriage, but the rounded lines were most becoming; and her little air of guileless diffidence, which unkind critics might have called awkward in Mademoiselle de la Louppe, seemed merely a charming modesty in Madame de la Ferté-Senneterre.

'Darling!' she said to Cateau. 'How are you?'

Cateau embraced her sister warmly, and made a great fuss over her small nephew, although, to tell the truth, she rather disliked babies.

Young Henri, at six months, was a rosy-cheeked cherub, with curls as dark as his mother's and round black eyes that surveyed the world with the calm assurance that their possessor was the most important person in it. When Cateau remarked on this to his parent, Magdelon snatched her son from the arms of his nurse and covered his face with kisses.

'So he is, the precious!' she cried. 'Oh, Cateau, it's such *fun* to have a baby! You don't know how sweet they can be, until you have one of your own — much more satisfactory than a dog or a bird or any kind of pet! They're real people in little. If only you could see more of them . . . My dear, why don't you come to La Ferté with me? I should so love to have you. It's a huge house, really: there'd be room for you and Brother Louis and as many of your staff as you cared to bring with you — and my papa-in-law and his wife are never there!'

'That would be an inducement, certainly,' drawled Cateau. 'But no — no —— It's sweet of you, dear; but, to be quite frank, I simply can't bear the country! Neither can Olonne; often I think it's the one bond between us. We'll manage to get along in Paris somehow or other.'

'Oh,' said Magdelon, as they took their places on the sofa together, with their arms round one another, 'I do so hate to leave you! I feel we've seen nothing at all of each other since I've been here.'

'I know,' said Cateau. 'I feel that, too, little sister. But it's not altogether my fault. This time it's been you who've been busy rather than I.'

'It's a job being Madame the Maréchale,' said Magdelon. 'And I'm afraid, often, I'm dreadfully inefficient at it. There are dozens of times when I wish I could have you near me to ask your advice. So many servants to order about, for instance ... It's hard for me to think up enough tasks for them to do to keep them busy — and I simply can't get used to sitting still and ringing for things when I want 'em! I'm always disgracing La Ferté by jumping up in the middle of parties to wait on myself! And Madame de Senneterre's no help at all; she told me once she was scared to death of her own Swiss. Poor thing! ... I call her Mother Anne now, you know.'

'Do you, indeed?' said Cateau thoughtfully. 'I can't say I'd care to, myself ... Still, I suppose, in your position ... Watch out, girl! He nearly had the lacquer box that time!' (This to Henri's nurse, a rather dull-witted peasant from Montmorency, who was so much impressed at actually being in the same room with the celebrated Madame d'Olonne that she could do nothing but gape at the beautiful Countess.)

'No, dear; but, after all, we're so nearly the same age that we had to think of something. She's really very kind,' said Magdelon apologetically, 'and I've grown quite fond of her. But she's so terribly frightened of her husband that she never dares open her mouth when he's with her — and he's with her practically all the time!'

'I don't blame him,' said Cateau. 'If I were eighty-three, and had a wife not five-and-twenty ——'

'He's mean to her, too,' Magdelon went on. 'Whenever she does anything that displeases him he starts calling her names. You know, her father and mother weren't married — poor girl! As if that were her fault! ...'

'Which gives him a beautiful name to start off with,' said Cateau. 'Boo! The horrid old man! Why won't he die and leave you his money?'

'Oh, well, I oughtn't to complain, really; he's been very good to me. And — isn't it fortunate? — we don't have to see much of him: our apartments at the Hôtel de Senneterre are quite separate, thank Heavens — kitchens and all! *They* live on rusty lettuce and scraps of meat I wouldn't feed to a dog! ... Then, as I say, they *never* come to the country.'

'Speaking of kitchens reminds me,' said Cateau. 'Will you stay to dinner with Olonne and me?'

Magdelon looked wistful.

'I wish I could, dear — but I promised La Ferté I'd go to midday Mass at Saint-Eustache and burn a candle to Our Lady for his success in the campaign. You know, he feels he *must* make up this summer for last year's disaster at Valenciennes. And we're off first thing in the morning, worse luck. ... Darling, I *can't* say good-bye to you!'

Magdelon began to cry and clung to Cateau, who hugged her hard and cried, too, though keeping a watchful eye meanwhile on little Henri, who was far too much interested for his aunt's peace of mind in the bric-a-brac on the marble-topped console.

'Little Magdelon!' she said. 'I love you! I'll write to you — yes, I *will!* See if I don't, this time, just to surprise you! Tell me, child, before you go: are you happy?'

Magdelon gave her sister a look of perfect candour.

'Why, but, darling, *of course!*' she said.

'That's all right, then,' said Cateau. 'Mind he doesn't kick the stair-rail, nurse!'

The two young women kissed each other a great many times, and cried some more; and then Magdelon left the room with the nurse and the baby, and assembled her maids and her lackeys and little pages, and the whole troop swept off in the big gilt coach drawn by the prancing black horses; while Cateau, misty-eyed, stood in the window of the yellow cabinet and blew kisses until they had turned the corner of the rue de Richelieu and were lost to sight.

It was strange: they loved each other as much as ever — more, perhaps, even than before—; still they were no longer so close as they had been. There were so many things, thought Cateau, you could not say to people unless you saw them every day; and she realized what separated her from Magdelon was that they'd both been living through emotions lately neither could share with the other. But, 'She's happy,' said Cateau proudly. 'That's a lot to be thankful for. I *knew* she would be; I'm never wrong about things like that.'

And Magdelon, driving away half drowned in tears in her splendid carriage, was thinking that the one dark cloud in an otherwise radiant sky was her feeling that Cateau was not so contented as she herself was. . . . Poor Cateau! Poor darling! She was more beautiful than ever, but rather pale and thin and sad-looking. Poor Cateau! Of course, one could not say it, but *she* ought to have a baby, too . . . then perhaps she would not mind about Brother Louis so much.

Magdelon herself was a great believer in babies. She hoped devoutly she would have at least a dozen of them before she had finished providing the Senneterres with heirs to the dukedom that could not be very many more years on its way. Babies were so warm and soft and comforting . . . 'Angel!' cried Magdelon to little Henri, who had gone to sleep at last in his nurse's arms, worn out by excitement. . . . Not that *she* needed to be comforted for anything in particular, for she was happy — she had told her sister the simple truth — very happy indeed. She felt more and more like the heroine of old Mahaut's fairy-tale; and when in this mood was wont to recite to herself dreamily sentences like 'The palace door opened, and out walked a beautiful black-haired princess dressed all in white velvet and rubies, who distributed smiles to her faithful subjects' — or, 'A slim, fascinating young brunette, in a charming robe of dead-leaf satin trimmed with tourmalines, gave her hand to her awkward but devoted squire and leaped, lightly and gracefully, into her coach. . . .'

There seemed to be nothing left to wish for, except that life should go on as it was forever. She had everything in the world she wanted; for La Ferté, rough as he was to everyone else, treated his young wife with tender affection. He was so immensely proud of his 'infant Maréchale,' as he called her, that he could deny her nothing. Sometimes, to test him, she had expressed purposely freakish desires, such as a wish to own a troop of dancing dwarfs from Morocco or twenty trained snow-white wolfhounds, to draw her light pony-cart in the country. It made no difference what she asked for: her will was law to La Ferté-Senneterre.

Magdelon felt she would have been ingratitude itself not to love him as much as she could in return for all he had done for her. She did love him, a very great deal — perhaps more as a child might its father than with a wife's love for her husband (although — and this was another thing she had not been able to say to Cateau — she did not at all object to what were vaguely referred to as one's 'marital duties.' . . . In fact, after her first moment of terrified surprise was over, she could even have wished . . .)

But, most of all, she looked up to the Maréchal as a brave soldier and hero, the saviour of his country. When the papers were full of his praises, as they frequently were — for La Ferté was proverbially lucky in the field — no one was more pleased than his wife. She had several times attended the pompous *Te Deum* services which were held at Notre Dame to celebrate each of his victories against the Spaniards. As the organ pealed forth in the huge candle-lighted cathedral, and hundreds of voices rose in a reverent shout of triumph, the 'infant Maréchale,' kneeling piously in her place of honour next the court, felt her heart swell with pride and devotion. At those times, there was not in all France a more blissful creature than Magdelaine de la Ferté.

At midday dinner the Comte and Comtesse d'Olonne sat down alone together for the first time in months. They faced each other, bored yet not unfriendly, across the table, with its glittering array of silver and china and rare Venetian glass. The meal was, as always, a procession of costly delicacies perfectly prepared. There was an unobvious and indescribable soup, salmon from the Rhine, a brace of partridges smuggled in out of season from the mountains of Auvergne, a crisp and tempting salad, figs from Provence stewed in cream . . . and a bottle of the golden wine of Ay, chilled to exactly the right temperature, stood in the cooler at the Count's elbow. But there was no one to help them enjoy it.

'I *told* Camille I wanted a trout!' Olonne exclaimed, in a pet, as the salmon was presented to his critical eye; and when it was the partridges' turn to appear he glanced tragically at his Countess and said that he *had* hoped he was going to have ortolans — though even ortolans... 'What we really need, madam, is some new kind of animal to eat.'

'I know,' said Cateau, sympathetic for once, as she nibbled languidly a very small morsel of Brie. '*I'm* tired of everything, too. Isn't summer a bore? My dear, would you care to go to Bourbon later, perhaps, in the season? You know Doctor Patin thought the baths might be good for your foot.'

Olonne frankly shuddered.

'Good God, madam! Would you condemn me to death by slow torture? Bourbon would be worse than Paris — much. In fact, if there's anything in the world I detest, it's a cure.'

'Oh, so do I,' agreed Cateau. 'As a matter of fact, I'm not keen to go anywhere. I only thought, if *you* thought you ought to try it, I'd be perfectly willing to come along. It's so dull to be in that sort of hole by oneself.'

Her husband gave her a softened look.

'That's kind of you, my dear.'

'Not at all, sir. After all, I am your wife. It's no more than my duty...'

Cateau tactfully left the end of her sentence hanging in mid-air; and Olonne, still more tactfully, failed to make the obvious retort. Cateau knew what he was thinking, however, and was grateful to him for his forbearance; so, in her turn, she surveyed her spouse amiably, and dinner continued with more sprightliness than before.

That was the way it always was, Cateau reflected, with her and Olonne: they forgot all about each other for weeks, for months, sometimes for a whole season at a time, while both of them led perfectly independent lives; then suddenly, when there was no one else there and nothing else to do, they rediscovered one another with a kind of mild surprise. Only ennui, it appeared, had the power to unite them. The Count, of course, seldom left his own house, and his small circle of intimates seldom left theirs save to come to his. They were, moreover, too exclusively wrapped up in the pleasures of the table (both dining and gaming) to pay much attention to personal gossip. Still Cateau supposed it was hardly possible that some of the rumours that had been flying round Paris about her and Candale had not reached her husband's ears. He had never mentioned them, but that was no proof he had not heard them.... After the escapade on the yacht he had told her not to ask the Duke to their daily receptions for a week or two — just that, nothing more —; and Cateau had naturally not cared to pursue the subject.

There now, however, they sat, to all appearances in perfect con-
cord: the Count pouting a little (but not at Cateau) as he told her of
his trying negotiations with the court concerning the succession to
his father's title of Seneschal of Poitou — Cateau smiling vaguely as
she played with her cheese and made pellets of her bread and wondered whether she had better have the second coach relined next
autumn. . . .

It was unaccountable to her that Olonne, who had never shown the
slightest interest in or capacity for business affairs and, as a rule, interviewed his steward every other month for an hour, should suddenly have taken it into his head he wanted to be Seneschal, now
that his father, having held the position for years, was resigning it
owing to old age and ill health. To be a petty official of a quiet remote province — what did it mean, after all, in these days of a
strong central government? Cateau imagined that he would not
even have thought of it had he not heard that the Duc de Roquelaure, whose estates were in the same part of the country, was intriguing to get the post. Since then Olonne had spent every minute
when he was not eating or sleeping or playing cards in writing a
series of important letters to Cardinal Mazarin, who seemed disposed to haggle with both gentlemen in his usual ignoble tradesman's
fashion.

These various iniquitous plots, and the wily means he had devised
to circumvent them, were all the theme of Olonne's discourse —
emphasized by many a click of the tongue and jerk of the head and
his odd, inevitable gesture of raising a didactic forefinger — while
Cateau nodded, her beautiful mask as inscrutable as ever, and said:
'I see, my dear' and 'Of course, you must' and 'What a very good
idea!'

It was in the midst of this harmonious domestic scene — just as
they had got to the final disposition of Roquelaure's pretensions and
the candied fruits — that the Comtesse de Fiesque was announced.

Gilette made a fussy, rustling entrance, preceded by one of
Olonne's very tall lackeys and followed by her own very small page,
Jeannot, who was bearing her train. ('He's only six, my dear —
fancy that!' she was wont to remark to people who did not know her
very well. 'I get him cheap because the poor little mouse is so
young. . . .' But Jeannot's face was as ageless as that of the Sphinx;
he had been with the Countess for years; and was popularly supposed to have a wife and four children somewhere in the suburbs.)

Cateau's mask came to life at sight of her friend; and if Olonne
were less pleased than his wife at the new arrival, that could not be
observed in the correct courtliness of his greeting, nor in the hospitable insistence with which he pressed Madame de Fiesque to call for
whatever she liked, from a sugared violet to a whole roast suckling

pig.... 'Only do, my dear madam, say at once what it shall be!'

Gilette squeaked, and said she never, never ate between meals, thank you very much just the same, sir . . . and then, during the following ten minutes, she deftly disposed of a whole plateful of pastries, eyed askance by Cateau, who did not grudge her the tidbits, but did envy her her ability to eat what she liked without adding an ounce to her weight.

'Madam,' said Olonne to their guest, 'I suppose that you, too, are on the point of departing to the country for the summer? Where do you expect to spend the holidays this year?'

Gilette squeaked once more.

'Right here in Paris!' she said. 'My good man, I've had enough of the country, these past four years, to last me the rest of my life. No, no; God willing, I never expect to leave the city again!'

'But your particular friends must have left: the Chevalier de Gramont, Abbé Fouquet . . . how can I hope to keep track of them all? Surely so gallant a beauty as Queen Gilette,' said Olonne, with a little bow, 'could never submit to sitting alone of an evening, with no squires attending her alcove to whisper pretty speeches in her ear.'

'Well, of course,' said Gilette airily, 'the men one *really* likes *are* all out of town. Do you know, though, as I grow older, I seem to become more broad-minded! And say what you will, society's not nearly so exclusive as it used to be before the war. *Look* at some of the people who get received at court nowadays! My good mother, who was lady-in-waiting to Marie de Médicis, would turn in her grave . . . But I must say some of them are very nice, really. Take the Bullion-Bonnelles, for instance. Of course, *she* was a Prie, and as well born as anyone — but *who* were the Bullions? Nobody knows — still Bonnelle's father was finance minister, and he himself is a decent little fellow, and it's no disgrace these days to be a member of parliament. It's an amusing house to go to: I always say that nobody mixes her worlds more successfully than dear Charlotte!'

Cateau's expression had brightened considerably during this speech. Of course, there were the Bonnelles; she had forgotten all about them; *they* weren't army people, were they? — really, the only members of the court set who weren't, except Chancellor Séguier and his wife, who were too old to count.

'But, my dear,' said Cateau, 'surely Charlotte is going away, too? She's always at Vichy for a month — and they've an enormous place somewhere near Rambouillet, I think.'

'Well, this year, they're not opening it,' said Gilette. 'At least, not for the present. Charlotte feels just as we do about life in the country — and, besides, as she says, it's such an economy not to have to run that big house. She's sending her three boys to one of their farms with a tutor, and she and Bonnelle are staying on here till the first of August, anyhow. Oh, and that reminds me, Catherine-Henriette. I've just come from dining with Charlotte now, and she told me to tell you that she is giving a supper-party tonight — just a tiny, informal affair, quite on the spur of the moment — and she hopes very much that you are free, and will come.'

Cateau laughed.

'Yes,' she said, 'I am free. But ...'

Gilette rolled her hazel eyes at the Count and fluttered her thick black eyelashes, which curled charmingly, though not naturally. (Only Cateau had had the secret confided to her that it took their possessor twenty minutes' patience with a pin, every morning.)

'I fear, sir, it would be useless to inquire if *you* ——'

'Quite useless,' replied Olonne, smiling pleasantly. 'I consider Bonnelle's chef the worst in Paris. I remember a ragoût of ox-tongues I had there once.... No, my dear madam, I shall stop at home comfortably, have a bite to eat in my room by the fire, and play a hand or two at piquet with my valet ... failing more illustrious company.'

Gilette put her head to one side, and went on fluttering her eye-lashes.

'How wise you are!' she exclaimed. 'How much I envy you! Dear me, that's precisely what I should like to do myself, if only I hadn't promised Charlotte.... But there it is: I *have* promised — and I hope you won't mind my borrowing your sweet little wife for the evening? If I turned up without her, the Bonnelles would never forgive me.'

Olonne inclined his head.

'Madame d'Olonne knows she is at liberty to accept whatever invitations she pleases. I constrain her in nothing.'

'Oh, but how *wise* you are!' cried Gilette again. 'No wonder dear Catherine-Henriette is devoted to you! Ah, if only more husbands could be persuaded to follow your example! I've been a slave to both of mine — one after the other — positively, a slave! Poor Piennes never let me out of his sight, and as for Fiesque, he is so jealous that, even when I am right by his side, he won't allow me to speak to another man. The tortures,' said Gilette, 'he must be undergoing this very minute, on my account, away off in Spain!... Well, child, then it's agreed? Will you stop for me about ten? I'll be ready and wait-ing this time, without fail!'

She dropped a butterfly kiss on her friend's cheek, and linked arms with her as they rose to leave the dining-room, slightly in advance of Olonne, who had lingered behind to say a word to one of the footmen.

In the hall Gilette assumed an air of extreme mystery, and laid her finger on her lips.

'Thank goodness, *that's* settled!' she said. 'My dear ... I suppose you know.... *He* will be there!'

THE BONNELLES' TINY, INFORMAL PARTY CONSISTED, AS USUAL, OF not less than seventy-five guests.

The dashing military note contributed by the younger members of the nobility was, of course, entirely absent this evening; but there were, as Gilette had said there would be, plenty of men. Monsieur de Bonnelle, as a councillor of parliament, counted a great many friends in upper bourgeois circles — fellow-councillors, lawyers, judges, and bankers, who together made up the rich and powerful world centring about the courts of the Palais. These were useful people to be on good terms with, in case one needed a loan or had a lawsuit pending — and, after all, almost everybody one knew spent their lives trying to borrow money and suing, or being sued by, their friends and relations.

Not all of these influential gentlemen were old, either. There was, for example, Jeannin de Castille, who, although he had been treasurer of the Savings-Bank for more than ten years, was a young man still in his early thirties, whose chief desire was to be taken for a courtier. He was handsome enough to play the part quite convincingly, with thick chestnut hair that was naturally curly and big, slightly bovine blue eyes. His nose and mouth were good, but a trifle flat, so that he looked better seen full-face than in profile.

Jeannin de Castille dressed exceedingly well. In the winter-time, when the town overflowed with warrior-nobles, he remained somewhat in seclusion, attending strictly to business, in which he was highly successful, and venturing forth into general society as seldom as most of his colleagues did. But every June, as soon as the troops had marched off to war, he emerged from his chrysalis in all the shining splendour of his new summer wardrobe, gave a number of expensive and very well-staged supper-parties, and devoted himself assiduously to whatever disconsolate ladies of fashion were left behind in the capital.

The ladies of fashion found Monsieur Jeannin indispensable in more ways than one: he could turn a sonnet or strum a serenade on the lute with as much grace as the most practised cavalier at court; and, unlike the cavaliers, he was both affluent and openhanded, seeming eager to pay for his privileges (just as a few illnatured rivals maintained that he paid for the sonnets).

The Comtesse de Fiesque, who was perennially hard up, had been saved from utter ruin time and again by Jeannin de Castille. She made no secret of her indebtedness: why should she have been ashamed of it? In return, he had asked for so little — simply to drive with her in the Cours twice a week, and to be seen occasionally at her evening receptions. Truly, an admirably modest as well as an invaluable young man!... It was only very lately that, with downcast eyes and troubled mien, he had been emboldened to suggest, if Queen Gilette were really so grateful for his trifling services as she had often and loudly professed herself to be — but pray, madam, never mention them again! — there was one very small favour he would be rash enough to crave....

Cateau and Gilette arrived fashionably late at the Bonnelles', and were immediately surrounded by a crowd of admirers.

Cateau was wearing her best new pink satin evening dress and all her diamonds: she was so pleased to be at a party again that she was less disposed than usual to be critical of the entertainment offered her. It was like a return to life and health, after a serious illness, to find herself once more in the midst of gay talk and laughter and admiring glances.

On the threshold of the room she paused for a moment, less to look over the guests than to give the guests time to look at her. And how reassuring, how comfortable to the heart, was this sudden turning of the mass of men's faces in her direction! How promptly she responded to the warmth of their collective approval, as a flower responds to the sun! Oh, what should she do when the time came at last, as she supposed it must, even to her, when the faces failed to turn? Death itself, thought Cateau, could not be more awful. But, at twenty-five, that time still seemed a very long way off, so far, in fact, that it was impossible to believe in it.... Meanwhile, she was one of the three most beautiful women in France... and it was generally agreed (Cateau felt rightly) that her two chief rivals, the Duchesse de Roquelaure and dear little Magdelon, lovely as they were, were not quite in a class with Madame d'Olonne.

She assumed her accustomed bright, inexpressive smile and sailed slowly forward, distributing greetings here and there, whose studied languor bore no resemblance to the lively sense of enjoyment that prompted them. As she advanced she became aware that her beauty and charm, which really needed no external aids to produce their effect, had nevertheless acquired an additional glamour through her semi-public connection with the Duc de Candale. Everyone knew that he was her lover; it added the final touch of romance to the figure of the most beautiful woman in France to be told that she was the mistress of the handsomest man.

Cateau was determined to be very, very careful tonight. She

had not forgotten her promise to the Duke; she had every intention of being faithful to it. Monsieur de Beuvron was in Flanders, like everyone else who counted, so that the problem of what to do about him had not to be faced just yet. (As Gilette's first cousin and a very old friend of her own, Cateau felt that he could not be altogether ignored; but she had the whole summer in which to work out a compromise.)

She bowed with icy hauteur to Monsieur Paget, who had been hurrying through the crowd to accost her with an oily and calculating smile. . . . That, of course, was something that ought never to have happened. She could not understand now how she had ever . . . Thank Heaven, Candale had not learned the whole truth about that disgraceful episode! Nobody knew it except Quentine and Quinette, and they'd been well paid to keep their mouths shut. . . . In a way, really, it had all been Candale's fault. If he had not been so fatally fond of gambling, she would not have played so much herself; for cards, on the whole, did not interest her. Certainly, until they had begun playing together, she had never in her life lost sums so appalling that she could not possibly hope to repay them from her own resources. Olonne, naturally, would not give her a penny; and if Candale had refused to help her financially, over and over, with a most unprincely stinginess, what, after all, could he expect her to do?

Just the same, she could not bear, now, to look back on that terrible week when she had come within an ace of being Monsieur Paget's mistress. Since then, she had so firmly dismissed the whole business from her mind that it was almost as though it had never taken place. One could think things away if one were strong-minded enough — and were careful never to put them in writing. . . .

So Cateau, full of good resolves for her future conduct, gave poor Paget, who had undoubtedly meant everything for the best, the tips of her fingers to kiss, and passed on to the centre of the room, where her hostess was waiting to greet her.

Madame de Bonnelle, of course, was already at cards: it spoke much for the genuineness of her affection for the Comtesse d'Olonne that she actually looked away from the table for a second or two, turned round in her seat, and gave her friend a smile and a kiss and an almost completely focussed look.

'Dear child!' she exclaimed. 'I'm delighted you've come. Monsieur de Nouveau shall move over at once and give you his place. We're just about to start a new hand.'

'Oh, no, thank you, dear,' said Cateau, still sustained by the strength of her virtuous inclination. 'I'm not playing this evening — at least, not for a while. There's your good man I've not yet spoken to. He and I will have a little chat together by the fire.'

Madame de Bonnelle looked surprised.

'Very well, dear; as you like. I'm sure Bonnelle will be enchanted,' she said carelessly.

Her mind reverted at once to the game, but she still went on smiling amiably at her guest; for after all, though it was odd of Catherine-Henriette not to want to play — and so unlike her, too — simply to have her in the room made all the difference in the world in the quality of one's party.

Cateau smiled back at Madame de Bonnelle, because she liked her as well as she could like any woman except Magdelon, and because Madame de Bonnelle had been very useful to her all winter: the lovers had met at her house by appointment, times without number — and as far as one could tell, Charlotte had never 'said anything.'

It was, unfortunately, exceedingly difficult to keep away from the gaming-tables tonight. Cateau sat for a while with her host; but Monsieur de Bonnelle was not at best an amusing companion, and this evening he appeared unusually distrait. At length he rose and excused himself, saying that he had to consult the butler about some details of the service at supper.

Cateau, left alone, posed picturesquely in front of the fire — but this diversion soon palled, since she lacked an audience: everybody was too deeply absorbed in reversi to observe her. Moreover, she saw that Monsieur Paget, who had been prowling round the room uneasily for some minutes while she and Bonnelle were chatting together, longing to approach them, but not daring to, now showed symptoms of wanting to engage her in conversation.

'Tiresome man!' thought Cateau. 'Can't he see he's not wanted?'

She rose hastily and beckoned to the Maréchale de la Mothe, who was apparently the only other guest not playing cards at the moment. (And everybody knew quite well why: the Maréchale, who was Madame de Bonnelle's younger sister, was too stupid to manage even the simplest sort of game. Besides, she was in mourning, having lost her husband only a few months ago; so that, even if she had not been stupid, it would have been considered unbecoming of her to show signs of interest in so worldly a pastime.)

'Shall we make a tour of the picture gallery?' suggested Cateau, with a bewitching smile. (What a pity it was to waste it on another woman!) 'I am longing to have a glimpse of those delicious new Poussins dear Charlotte has just had sent up from Rome.'

'Certainly, madam,' replied the Maréchale, with a lugubrious sigh. 'I should be charmed to show them to you.'

Madame de la Mothe was even less lively company than her brother-in-law. Cateau had not seen her, though of course she had called at her house, since the latter's recent bereavement; and now, as they strolled through the hall, the Maréchale began loudly lamenting her position as a portionless widow with three unmarried daughters 'mouldering,' as she expressed it, on her hands.

'But surely, madam, they must be very young yet?' murmured Cateau, as she adjusted her lorgnette for a closer inspection of the famous Poussins.

'Françoise, the eldest, is seven years old,' said their mother, with a groan; 'Charlotte, my sister's godchild, is not quite six; and poor little Gabrielle, my ewe lamb, is but three and a half. Ah, madam, when I consider their plight, robbed at such tender ages of the best father in the world, I can scarce restrain my tears! I should, I know, not attempt to appear in public, bowed to earth as I am by such heavy woe — but I dare not stop at home! No sooner do I find myself alone than I start to think — and that Doctor Patin has strictly forbidden me to do. Nothing, he said, could possibly be more dangerous to a person in my condition than to make such an effort. My dear sister has been sympathy itself: "Come to me, Louise," she says, night after night, "if you feel you can bear it to see a few people; you know you are always welcome." And so, for the children's sake, I try to master my grief, though were it not for them, a cell at the Carmelites' — yes, madam, it's the best of the lot. My brother-in-law gave Monsieur Poussin four thousand francs for that alone. Is it not an exquisite thing? Oh, dear me!...'

'Exquisite,' said Cateau stonily. 'A truly ravishing creation. And now show me...'

They made a detailed tour of the entire collection, most of which was already quite as familiar to Cateau as to her guide; while Madame de la Mothe interspersed her remarks on the various pictures (which had a certain interest, as she seemed to know exactly what dear Noël and Charlotte had paid for everything) with harrowing accounts of the late Maréchal's ultimate moments and a minute description of little Gabrielle's last attack of colic.

This was not in the least what Cateau had come to the Bonnelles' party for; and when at length they bent their steps once more towards the Gallery of Ulysses she hoped they might find that the game was over and supper about to be served.

'Supper will be fun,' said Cateau to herself. 'I mean to enjoy myself at supper.'

Unluckily, the guests were still hard at reversi; no one even noticed the return of Madame d'Olonne and her plaintive attendant dove except Gilette, who jumped up from her seat and tripped over to them.

'My dear,' said Gilette to Cateau, paying no attention to the Maréchale de la Mothe, 'where *have* you been? I've looked for you everywhere. Come sit near us, child; there's plenty of room between me and Monsieur Jeannin.'

'I'm not playing this evening,' said Cateau, obstinately repeating her formula. 'Really, I'd rather not.'

Gilette stared, and batted her lashes more furiously than ever.

'Very well; as you like,' she said, just as Madame de Bonnelle had done. 'But look on at the game, anyway, won't you? We've been pining for your company. I forget, dear — have you and Monsieur Jeannin met each other?'

'I've not yet had the honour of being presented to the Comtesse d'Olonne,' said Jeannin de Castille, in his rich and faintly caressing voice. 'But I cannot say that she is unknown to me. All Paris admires her as its undisputed queen: am I not, therefore, as a good Parisian, already enrolled on the list of Her Majesty's faithful subjects? Madam, your humble servant!'

'Sir, I thank you,' said Cateau, in an expressionless voice.

She acknowledged his really creditable low bow with a graceful curtsy. Also, she smiled just a little — which she had not meant to do. For all his meticulous formality, Jeannin de Castille was like a little boy playing at being a courtier; and his obvious delight in his own success Cateau found both naïve and touching. More-over, she knew that he admired her very much — nay, more, was already in love with her. (Had not Gilette said so a thousand times during the last week?) Cateau meant to be prudence itself; she would not give him the slightest cause for hope. On the other hand, one must amuse oneself — and the Duke had not forbidden her to speak to the treasurer of the Savings-Bank (though, of course, Cateau knew he would do so as soon as he'd heard about Jeannin's passion: very likely, next year, she'd not be able even to bow to this most presentable young man).

That being the case, it seemed wise to take advantage of the present opportunity.

Cateau sat down next to Gilette in the seat Monsieur Jeannin had eagerly abandoned to her. He himself stood respectfully just behind her chair, which gave him a rather poor view of the table, but an excellent one of Cateau's splendid white neck and shoulders under the rippling golden curls. Also, fortunately, it enabled him to present his charming full face rather than his slightly amorphous profile to the lady's gaze, when she deigned to turn in his direction.

She had not intended to play herself, merely to watch the others play. This intention she kept to, for a long while. However, it seemed rather silly to sit there like a dummy, hand after hand, tak-ing up space someone else might have been glad to occupy. Pre-sently Monsieur Jeannin whispered: 'Take my cards, madam, this time, will you not? I feel it will bring me good luck.' And so, before she realized what she was doing, she was in the midst of the game.

She won, too. She had felt she was going to win because, for once, it did not make very much difference to her whether she did or not; and, sure enough, by the time supper was announced she was the richer by several hundred francs.

Cateau had not intended, either, to say very much to Monsieur Jeannin. During the whole of the evening she scarcely looked at him, and all that they talked about was the progress of the game.

Once, when she found herself temporarily out of funds, the low, caressing voice behind her murmured: 'Madam, let me be your banker. It would be the highest honour I could aspire to.'

Another time, when she dropped her fan, the young man stooped quickly to pick it up for her, with as polished an air as if he had been His Highness Louis-Charles-Gaston de Nogaret de la Vallette, Duke of Foix and of Candale, himself, instead of only Jeannin, the banker. He gave it back to Cateau without a word, and she thanked him briefly, but with one of her most agreeable smiles, which acquired perhaps an additional radiance from the fact that Madame de Nouveau, Jeannin's official mistress, was seated directly across the table.

This was all that passed between them until the end of the party, after supper, when Cateau rose to take leave of her hosts, and Jeannin respectfully requested that he might have the pleasure of seeing her and Madame de Fiesque to their coach.

'May I call on you some afternoon, madam?' he asked, in a perfectly noncommittal tone.

And Cateau, equally noncommittal, smiled impersonally, and said that she was generally at home after four o'clock.

She did not say a word to Gilette about Monsieur Jeannin, as they drove to the Hôtel de Fiesque in the rue des Tournelles.

Her face, however, looked unusually thoughtful; when she got home at last she paused, on the way up to her room, outside her husband's apartments on the first floor. There was a faint light showing under the door, and after a second's hesitation Cateau turned the handle softly and went in.

The Count was sitting propped up in bed by a great many pillows. He wore one of his peaked tasselled white nightcaps, and was slowly sipping a cup of some kind of herb tea and, even more slowly, reading the *Essays* of Montaigne (which he had promised his friend Saint-Evremond he would surely get through during the summer).

As the glittering figure of his wife trailed into the bedroom Olonne raised his sandy eyebrows in mild surprise.

'Well, my dear, and how was it? Was the ragoût as shocking as I said?'

'Yes — no — I don't know,' replied Cateau. 'Really, I didn't eat anything to speak of. Olonne' — fixing her husband with her large, light eyes, which, as usual at the end of an evening's diversion, were larger and lighter than ever from sheer fatigue — 'I've changed my mind about Bourbon. I should like, if you don't mind, to go there directly. Directly, d'you hear? Tomorrow, if we can manage to get our things ready in time — or, at any rate, no later than the first of next week.'

Olonne laid down his book, with the fingers of one hand placed between the pages to mark his place (for if once one lost one's way in those confounded rigmaroles, there was no hope of finding it again) — but went on sipping the herb tea.

'My dear child,' he remarked, 'I thought you said today that you didn't want to go to Bourbon at all.'

'Yes, I know — but I've changed my mind, I tell you.'

'Oh,' said Olonne, 'you've changed your mind. Well... well... what a pity this was not thought of before! Because, madam, directly after you left me this evening, I received a message from the Cardinal concerning the seneschalate of Poitou. It appears now that my chances are excellent of being appointed to the post. Only — worse luck! — I shall be forced to make a trip to the country very soon to arrange the details of the transaction. At once, in fact. To tell the truth, I am leaving for Poitiers at nine o'clock tomorrow morning. It is too bad, my dear, that I shall require the big coach and all the horses, as otherwise you might have gone to Bourbon while I ——'

'Sir,' said Cateau, 'may I go to Poitiers with you?'

At this, Olonne looked even more surprised than before; he not only put aside Montaigne altogether, but abandoned the cup of herb tea as well.

'Madam,' he said ceremoniously, 'your offer is amiability itself. I hardly know how to refuse it. And still, much as it pains me to deprive myself of so many hours of the most charming company in the world, I fear I must be firm and say no. It will be a hard trip, Catherine-Henriette. I shall have to travel as fast as I am able — at night, too, if need be — and whilst I am in Poitiers I shall be very much occupied with all sorts of tiresome business, and should have no time to entertain you. . . . No, no, my love; you shall go to Poitou with me one day, but in state as the Seneschal's lady, when you and I will attend some provincial assemblies given in our honour and laugh ourselves sick at the rustic gentilities of our worthy vassals. Meanwhile, I think it is better for you to wait here in Paris until my return, which will be as speedy as I can possibly make it, that I promise you. Then, at our leisure, if you are still of the same mind regarding our journey, we can proceed to the baths of Bourbon together. Together, my dear. Quite alone, by our two selves! A delicious prospect, is it not?'

His voice remained smooth and uninflected, so that there was no way of telling if he were being ironical.

Cateau stood there a minute longer at the foot of the bed, sparkling and solitary in her pink satin gown and diamonds by the pale light of the one lonely candle.

She twisted her hands together, unable to make up her mind whether to say anything further or not.

Then, suddenly, with a smothered exclamation, she turned on her heel and almost ran from the room.

'Good-night, my love; pleasant dreams!' Olonne called after his wife, as, with tranquil deliberation, he returned to Montaigne and the herb tea.

But the door had already slammed behind her.

Chapter V

THERE ARE CERTAIN PENALTIES ONE HAS TO PAY FOR BEING AN important or celebrated person. One of the chief of them is that it is almost impossible ever to be allowed to be quite alone.

The Duc de Candale, who was both very important and exceedingly celebrated, had never since he was born, thirty years before, been left entirely by himself. As a rule, this did not affect his spirits in the least. Quite the contrary: being a charming and sociable young man, he was at his best in a crowd, provided he were the centre of it.

But on his way back from Spain he suffered a sudden revulsion of feeling, for the first time he could remember, when he was met at Narbonne, not far from the border, by a deputation of one hundred noblemen from his own province of Auvergne.

The noblemen were most courteous and deferential. They explained at once, with profuse apologies for interrupting him on his journey, that they had come because the Duc d'Epernon, Candale's father, had sent them. Brigands infested the lonely regions through which he would have to pass on his homeward way; moreover, there were rumours about that the Marquis de Montrevel, who was still half mad with rage and grief at the death of his only son in that unfortunate street brawl last year — as if Candale had been to blame for *that!* — had sent a troop of hired assassins to lie in wait for His Highness in the stony wilderness of the lower Rhone Valley.

Candale smiled, and thanked the gentlemen from Auvergne; and declared that he would be glad of their company, because he was a naturally polite young man, who could not say anything disobliging as long as people treated him with what he considered proper respect. But, inwardly, he cursed his father's confounded officiousness.

It was really rotten bad luck: here it was already the middle of January; he had just succeeded in planting his army in their winter quarters at Perpignan near the Spanish frontier, and had been hoping to get back to Paris as quickly as possible, travelling on horseback, accompanied only by Mérille and two of his lackeys, while the rest of his suite followed with the coaches and luggage at a more leisurely pace. He could have made the trip in a week.

But now, with a cavalcade one hundred strong swarming about him, and the round of entertaining at each of the overnight halts that their presence entailed, he would be lucky if he got home within a fortnight. . . . 'It'll cost me a pretty penny, too!' grumbled the Duke to himself, thinking with irritation of all the meals and bottles of wine he would have to pay for. What on earth could Papa have been thinking of? Or, perhaps, was this his idea of a joke? . . . But, actually, it was neither the delay nor the unavoidable expense that annoyed him most; it was the realization that he could not be alone when he needed solitude.

For once in his life, Candale was in a bad humour. Everything seemed to have gone wrong this year. For one thing, the campaign had been a flat failure. After dragging along dully for months, the Duke had at length grown impatient at the series of half-hearted, indecisive skirmishes and had staked everything on a cavalry engagement at Campredon, in which his men had been soundly whipped by the Spaniards under General Mortarre.

It was his first real defeat in years. He smarted still to recall the surprise and dismay he had felt when he beheld the new wholly unlooked-for detachment of the enemy's troops riding down the defile from the top of the pass to put his own army to flight. He had relived that moment of acute discomfiture far too many times since for his own peace of mind; it had haunted his dreams nightly with discouraging persistence. Even now, though he had days ago quitted Catalonia for France, he had only to close his eyes on the flat, swampy fields round Narbonne for the arid red rocks of Campredon to reappear in a trice, with the horrid clarity of a nightmare vision. . . . Good God! There they were again, as plain as day! And there came the Spanish horsemen, in their dusty jerkins, one by one, riding with slow, assured insolence. Was there no way of blotting them out? Would he have to go on seeing them for the rest of his days?

Candale spurred his tawny charger ahead, to try to put some space between himself and the good gentlemen from Auvergne; but the latter, interpreting his increase of pace as a desire to get on a bit faster towards Béziers, where they were to spend the night, came clattering after him in a cloud, just like the thoughts from which there was no escape.

The young man groaned aloud and clapped his hand to his forehead.

'Is Your Highness indisposed?' inquired one of the leaders of the deputation, with respectful solicitude.

'Yes — no — I don't know — oh, I have a slight headache,' replied Candale, not altogether truthfully. 'You would oblige me, my good Saint-Alyre, by letting me ride by myself for a while. I think that a little fresh air and repose . . .'

'Certainly, Your Highness; as Your Highness commands,' said Monsieur de Saint-Alyre — and the cavalcade fell back once more, full of conscientious sympathy.

After that, Candale felt forced to clap his hand to his forehead several more times, and groan anew each time, to lend an air of verisimilitude to his complaint. But as a matter of fact, though he was tired and unhappy, his head had never been clearer, nor had his thoughts ever come faster than now.... Those rocks... the red rocks of Campredon...

In order to take his mind off war, he tried to think instead about love, which was the only other subject, barring money and his own wardrobe, that ever was able to occupy him for more than a few minutes at a time.

There was Cateau — his own dearly beloved mistress! Just to say her name called up a vision of smiling blond beauty that had been with him, day and night, for many months past. Her last letter to him, which had reached him at Perpignan, lay on his heart at that very moment; he had no need to find it in order to recall what it said, for he had long ago memorized every word it contained.

> My dearest [it began]:
> They say here that you have been beaten: perhaps it is only a false report your enemies are spreading, but perhaps it is true. Dear God, in this uncertainty, I beg You only for my lover's life, and abandon the army to You! Yes — and not only the army, but the country, the whole world, even....
> Since getting this news, without being told anything in particular about you, I make twenty calls a day. I start talking about the war everywhere I go, to see if I can learn anything that will console me. I hear on every hand that you've been beaten — but no more than that. I don't dare ask what has become of you — not that I mind showing I love you — I'm far too frightened to care about appearances now — but I fear to learn more than I want to know.
> That's how things are with me, and will be till the next post-day — if I've the strength to live until then! What makes my anxiety twice as hard to bear is that you've promised me so often to send me a letter if anything out of the ordinary should happen that I take it very ill, this time, to have had not one word.

Darling Cateau! Her letter was exactly like her, in its adorable mixture of pride and formality and deep, true feeling. And Candale knew, because he knew her so well, what an effort it cost her to write at all, even to someone she loved: only a very strong, sincere passion could have prompted her to do it so regularly. He had heard from her every week for the last seven months; he had written to her every week, also. What was even more remarkable, this time both the lovers had kept their letters singularly free from reproaches. For once in their lives, they had been content to trust each other. . . . Well, but *of course* Cateau ought to trust him! She knew perfectly well that her gallant was exiled to the most desolate corner of one of the most God-forsaken lands on earth. In Catalonia he was surrounded by nothing more exciting than flocks of stupid brown Spanish goats and the peasants, equally brown and stupid, that guarded them. Candale, on the other hand, had had every reason for jealous suspicions; he took great credit to himself, on the whole, for refusing to harbour them. Not a post-day had passed since last June without his receiving damaging reports of his mistress from various relatives. Of course, one knew what relatives were. . . . Papa, especially — poor Papa! — had written, over and over again, to say that Madame d'Olonne was being seen everywhere with Jeannin de Castille. (Jeannin! One of Candale's best friends, from whom he had borrowed many a neat little sum in the days before he had come of age and into his property.) That was a pathetically transparent manoeuvre; Papa had been against the liaison from the first, naturally enough, because he wanted his son to marry one of the Cardinal's rich nieces. Candale understood; he was even rather sorry, in a detached way, for his father. But after what he and Cateau had promised each other, he wouldn't believe . . . *couldn't* believe . . . !

He had just mentioned the matter, casually, in one of his letters to his beloved; and she had replied, quite as casually, that she was glad he *had* mentioned it; that of *course* there was nothing whatever in the rumour. She had been to a dull rustic fête with Jeannin *and his wife*, and, in return, had thought it her duty to ask him to one of her routine pay-back dinner-parties. (Madame Jeannin had been ill with an attack of tertian fever, and was thus prevented from accepting the invitation.) Aside from these two occasions, Cateau and the treasurer of the Savings-Bank had scarcely even met in public.

Poor Papa! . . . Candale hugged his letter to his breast and thought rapturously of the supreme moment awaiting them in Paris, when he and Cateau found each other again. Ah, but, at this rate, it seemed likely that they would never reach Paris at all! Or, if they did, that Candale would arrive both bankrupt and completely worn out. That was a nice way to start the carnival season, wasn't it?

The Duke ground his strong white teeth in a fury — and then displayed them in an amiable smile (Lord! What it was to be always on parade!) as Monsieur de Saint-Alyre drew up alongside to ask with anxiety whether His Highness's head felt better.

'Eh — oh — much better, thank you, old fellow,' replied the Duke, as graciously as if he had not forgotten he had ever said that there was anything the matter with it.

Béziers... Montpellier... Nîmes.... The next three days passed in a blur of boredom and fatigue. The Duke's one hundred gentlemen never left their liege-lord for an hour. By day, they cantered along the dusty highway, beaten upon by the fierce sun of Provence and battered by its chill, searching winds, laughing, joking, disputing, shouting bawdy inanities back and forth to one another up and down the line till Candale's head, in sober truth, nearly split from the noise. And, every night, there was a feast in the citadel: the rich, greasy dishes of the Midi abounded, its coarse red wines flowed like fountains — toasts were drunk — songs sung — and regiments of city fathers and various petty provincial officials appeared to do homage to His Highness and deliver harangues in his praise by the yard.

'Oh, Mérille, what torture this is!' sighed the Duke to his valet, as he sat in front of the glass on the third evening having his golden curls brushed and scented, just as Cateau was probably doing at the same moment in front of *her* glass, many miles away in Paris. 'I could murder my father for inflicting these well-meaning churls upon me.'

'Your Highness will no doubt be able to escape from them, at least temporarily, at Avignon,' suggested Mérille, with a discreet smile. 'If I mistake not, on the occasion of Your Highness's last visit, the papal palace was found to be too draughty for Your Highness's comfort, and Madame the Marquise de Castellane very kindly offered to put us up in her own house.'

Candale bit his lip.

'I do not intend, this time, to see Madame de Castellane at all,' he said.

'Oh, but, Your Highness ——'

'That will do, Mérille. There are reasons for this, into which I don't care to go at present. You will see to it that the Marquise is told that I am busy — ill — dead — what you will, as long as I am not allowed to be pestered by her attentions. All women are bores, except one. Now tell me frankly: would you wear a blue ribbon or a scarlet one with this coat?'

As the days dragged by Candale found himself looking forward to Avignon with keen anticipation, even though he had made up his mind not to accept Madame de Castellane's hospitality. For at Avignon he would have letters from Paris. That alone was enough to make his heart beat faster and his spirits rise triumphantly above their present vexations. Another dear note from Cateau, breathing love and devotion, and no longer clouded by her worries for his safety, as long ago she must have received the letter he had sent her from Spain, saying that all was well.

He could scarcely restrain his impatience during the final few miles of the journey, and when at length they came within sight of the walls and towers of the famous city on the Rhone, and beheld an unusually large party of officials, headed by the mayor himself, advancing from the gate to meet them, Monsieur de Candale kept his temper better than most of his henchmen.

At Avignon the bise was blowing more strongly than ever, but the Duke was determinedly cheerful. Even the undeniable draughtiness of the papal palace, perched high on its rock overlooking the river and the serried roofs of the town, could not quench his enthusiasm. He ordered fires lighted in each of the huge, damp stone rooms, and said, with a brilliant smile, that he would be very comfortable indeed, thank you so much.

The mayor and his attendants smiled back at His Highness and rubbed their hands together and said to themselves that, really, no one was so affable as Monsieur de Candale. . . . This opinion they still held ten minutes later, after the Duke, continuing to smile charmingly, had cut the speeches of ceremony scandalously short, and gently but irresistibly pushed the speakers, one after another, out of his chamber.

Alone at last, he flung his hat into one corner, his sword and riding-whip into another, and called out to Mérille: 'Well, now for the post! What have you for me?'

Having seized the pile of letters the valet handed to him, and run through them hastily until he found the one he was looking for, it was Mérille's turn to be ejected from the room, with a friendly shove.

'Not even *you* can be with me when I read this,' said the Duc de Candale, with his most charming smile of all.

Half an hour later, when Mérille ventured to tap on the door, to see if His Highness were ready for dinner, he found his master lying on the bed fully dressed, even to his heavy Russia-leather riding-boots and spurs. The sheets of the letters were scattered all over the floor.

The Duke did not look up as his man entered. He lay where he was, with his face turned to the wall, not saying a word.

Mérille said nothing, either. It was not his place to speak; moreover, he, too, had had letters from Paris, which had given him a fairly good notion of the news in his master's that had proved so disturbing.

Silently he began picking up the litter of papers. There were a great many of them, covered by a great many different handwritings.

Mérille had been with the Duke too long not to recognize most of the handwritings. There was a letter from the Comte de Moret, Candale's best friend, who had preceded his patron to Paris; also one from the Chevalier de Saint-Evremond, and from the young Duke's stepmother, Madame d'Epernon, and his sister, the religious Anne-Marie de Jésus of the Great Carmelites convent.

The Comtesse d'Olonne's big, black, awkward scrawl was, strangely, not amongst them.

Mérille glanced sharply about the room, last of all at the fireplace, where a blaze had been lighted.... Were there some charred, tell-tale fragments on the edge of the hearth? Better not look too closely, perhaps; there are limits to the privileges of even the most confidential valets.

Outside, the hot, cruel sun shone, and the cold, cruel bise blew — and the air was yellow with flying dust over the river and the helpless huddle of houses at the foot of the hill.

Inside, it was very still. There was no noise but the crackling of the fire, and the twittering of some sparrows that made their nests in the eaves of the palace roof, and ... but no; that could not be a faint sound of sobbing, surely? ... Mérille was certain it could not, for there was no one in the room except the Duke and himself. His own heart might be heavy with sympathy for his young master, but his eyes were quite dry — and as for His Highness, it was beyond the bounds of possibility that the Colonel-General of the infantry forces of the army of His Majesty Louis XIV should be guilty of the unmanly weakness of tears.

So after he had finished tidying the room Mérille stood at attention, with a blank look on his broad, blunt face, waiting patiently until his master chose to recognize his existence.

It seemed a long time before the Duke turned round and raised his head from the pillow.

'Mérille?'

'Your Highness...'

Mérille stood up even straighter than before, but he was careful not to look at what his master was doing with that lace-edged silk handkerchief (one of the dozen his stepmother had given him, with the crest of the Epernons embroidered in silver thread).

'Has any message come for me?'

'Only from the Marquise de Castellane, Your Highness.'

'Oh ... And what did she want?'

'She offered Your Highness the use of her house, as we knew she was going to do. I sent word to Madame the Marquise that Your Highness was exceedingly grateful to her for her kindness, but had decided this time not to trespass upon it. I took the liberty of hinting that Your Highness was slightly indisposed, and thought it best

to remain in seclusion and at rest for the very few hours that Your
Highness expected to sojourn in Avignon.'

'Oh ... thank you, Mérille.'

'Not at all, Your Highness.'

'But one moment ... Mérille, I may be in Avignon for a week, or
perhaps even longer. I don't know. I can't tell yet. My plans have
suddenly changed. I think, under the circumstances, you had better
send a lackey at once to Madame de Castellane, to say that I was
asleep when her message came, but that now that I am awake I feel
very much better and shall be glad, if her gracious offer be still open,
to take advantage of it. And stay ... Mérille ... Say, also, that if
the Marquise should be free this evening, it would give me the
greatest possible pleasure to entertain her and her friends at supper
at the papal palace.... Now, where the devil did I put the address
of those gypsy dancers who amused us so much at the ball when we
were here last spring?'

Chapter VI

THE DUC DE CANDALE STAYED IN AVIGNON ALMOST A WEEK.   HE DID
not, after all, move from the palace to Madame de Castellane's
house. However, the Marquise and he were constantly together, at
dinner, at supper, at play, on various excursions into the country,
which they made whenever the weather permitted and the attractions of the provincial carnival proved a trifle stale. They went to
Tarascon and the Grotte de Thouzon and the Fountain of Vaucluse.
At Vaucluse Madame de Castellane quoted Petrarch's sonnets (she
knew three of them by heart), and glanced tenderly at her companion, who, unfortunately, did not remember who Petrarch was,
and, when told his romantic story, obtusely could not see any resemblance between Laura and the piquant, over-eager little woman
at his side.

Each morning when he awoke the Duke said to himself that he
would leave for Paris that day. But for some reason it was difficult
to do it. What made it especially hard was that Mérille was no
longer there. His master had sent him on ahead, the day after their
arrival in Avignon, bearing a note to the Comtesse d'Olonne breaking off their relations, and charged with secret instructions to procure a great deal of information concerning her affair with Jeannin
de Castille, which none of the Duke's correspondents had seen fit to
supply.

Without Mérille, Candale was helpless; the machinery of life
appeared to defeat him.

He might, perhaps, have spent the rest of the winter in the south
if another letter from Cateau had not come in the midst of his uncertainty and despair. It was not, of course, an answer to his, which
she had not had time to receive when she wrote: it was like her last
letter, and the one before that — like all her letters, in fact — a
charming, inconclusive scrawl, saying very little, but saying that
little prettily. At the end, Cateau hoped that her lover, whilst in
Avignon, was not seeing too much of the Marquise de Castellane.

When Candale read that, the veins stood out on his forehead. He
clenched his hands; then, suddenly, rolled the letter into a ball, cast
it on the floor, and deliberately stamped on it.

After that, he rang for the valet who had temporarily replaced

Mérille — a white-faced boy who looked and acted rather like a
disconcerted rabbit — and shouted in a voice much louder than
usual: 'Colin, we leave for Paris tomorrow!'

'Yes, Your Highness,' replied the rabbit, with a terrified gasp,
scuttling from the room on legs that were just able to carry him.

That evening Madame de Castellane gave a farewell moonlight
picnic for the Duke at Villeneuve on the Rhone. It was a delightful
affair: the shrubbery at the river's edge was strung with gay-
coloured lanterns; fireworks were set off after supper; an invisible
string orchestra played discreetly in an adjacent thicket; and there
was a new dancer from Italy, a bold, black-eyed wench, who performed acrobatic tarantellas till she was quite out of breath and fell,
panting and triumphant, at the feet of the guest-of-honour.

Monsieur de Candale raised her courteously from the ground and
pressed a purse containing some gold-pieces into her hand.   (There
were not so many of them as he would have liked to have given her,
but his trip home was proving a damnably costly business — besides, when one came to think of it, the purse in itself was a dainty
trinket, worth a number of francs.)

'Thank you, child,' he said kindly, thinking how young she looked
and how fresh compared to his hostess and her friends, the other
local beauties, who were painted and powdered within an inch of
their lives. (Provincial belles invariably overdid their effects.)

The moon shone brightly all evening, but the wind was rather
chilly. Either the wind, or the dampness of the bosquet where supper
was served, must have affected the Duke, for when he woke up the
next morning he found he had taken cold.

He felt dull and feverish; his chest pained him vaguely; and his
throat was exceedingly sore.

His first thought was to cancel his plans for departure. Then it
occurred to him that it might be really less tiring to go ahead. After
drinking some hot broth and a strong dose of brandy, he began to
feel better; the mists cleared away from his brain — and, after all,
it was a fine sunny day.

'Maybe the air will do me good,' said Monsieur de Candale.

So he bade good-bye to the city fathers, sent a posy with a cordial
note to the disconsolate Madame de Castellane, and trotted smartly
astride his tawny charger over the bridge of Avignon and out of the
town, on the first lap of his long journey north.

The hundred gentlemen from Auvergne trotted along with him,
as usual — but Candale no longer paid any attention to them.

The sun-warmed air did do his head good: he soon felt much more
like himself. With the return of his forces, however, came also a
sharp realization of his grief, the grief he had kept at bay for a week
by stoutly refusing to give himself time to think. Now, alas! there

was nothing further he could do to protect himself: the cup had to be drained to its dregs. . . . Cateau had betrayed him. All these months he had been living in a false paradise, thinking of her and imagining, in his simplicity, that she must be thinking of him, because she had said she was. God! What a fool he had been! What a fool! *What a fool!* . . . And the worst of his folly was that he had refused to take warning time and again. Papa's letters had told him the truth, but, like an obstinate ass, he had chosen not to heed them.

Even now, if Candale had not had confirmation of his dishonour from others outside the family, he could scarcely have brought himself to believe that for six months and more Cateau had been brazenly lying — that as long ago as last June she had been the mistress of Jeannin. Yet how could he longer doubt it, when Moret, the best friend he had in the world, had written him that the affair was the talk of all Paris? And not only Moret, but Saint-Evremond, and La Feuillade . . . nay, every one of his friends at court had added his word to the chorus of condemnation! It was almost as though they had conspired to bring his air-castle tumbling in ruins round his feet. 'The talk of all Paris' . . . When had Cateau not been just that, in spite of his anxious entreaties and her solemn promises to mend her conduct? . . . Candale did not suppose for a moment that she was in love with Jeannin. How could she be? . . . No, the story was more sordid: she had been bored and lonely, unable to exist for even a few weeks without masculine admiration. There was a question of money, also: she had needed a certain sum in a hurry to settle a gambling debt, and had no doubt applied to her husband in vain. Jeannin had obliged her, as he had many another lady of fashion; she, in her turn, had repaid him as many another had done.

So, for lack of a few hundred louis or so, their happiness had been destroyed. . . . 'And why in God's name did she not come to me?' cried Candale, in his bitterness of spirit quite forgetting the numerous occasions on which she *had* come to him — and for one reason or another (all perfectly convincing at the time) it had not been convenient to help her. Once or twice he had found the sum necessary to clean up her score, and these times he recalled now, very clearly: the others had passed from his memory, so that, in sober truth, he could say he had always been ready to do his part.

Well, but it was useless to think of that any more. The deed was done; nothing on earth could undo it. He had broken with Cateau for good; the letter he had written her from Avignon could have left no doubt in her mind of his decision. He would never see her again. But of course, never as long as they lived! . . . Then was it not odd that just at this moment she should appear to him, more plainly than at any time since they had parted last June in the Tuileries Gardens? He had not even to shut his eyes to be able to see her; she haunted his vision as ceaselessly as the red rocks of Campredon had done, a week earlier. . . . There she was, there she would be, he feared, to the end of his life — not weeping, as when he left her, but tranquil and smiling, as she usually was — even laughing a little, as if the spectacle of his agony faintly amused her. Oh, God, was there *nothing* that could efface . . . ?

Monsieur de Candale drew his cloak more closely about his shoulders, and shuddered, although the sun was beating full upon him.

'Saint-Alyre, let us stop at Orange,' he said — though Orange lay only ten miles ahead, and they had meant to get on at least as far as Montélimar before the first night. 'I feel far from well.'

The next three days seemed absolutely endless. They were like one very long day, with no definite points to mark the merging of one into another; and the nights were worse than the days. Candale's cold grew so troublesome that he could hardly sleep at all. The moment he lay down alone in the dark Cateau appeared to him, laughing and gay, to disturb his feverish dreams as she did his waking hours.

The Duke's gentlemen urged him every morning to give up his trip, to rest, for a day or two at any rate, until he felt stronger; but the Duke shook his head and replied that he would not think of it. Obstinately he called for his riding-boots and a bottle of brandy, and tumbled shivering out of bed. Lord! How cold he was! Even the sun could not warm him now. . . . But one had to admit that it was a very temperate sort of sun indeed: bright as it looked, there was no virtue in its rays; it was as dazzling and unsympathetic as Cateau's perennial smile. No one had ever known such a hard winter in the south of France. Nothing was blooming; even the grass looked sere and brittle; not a bird sang in the scrubby stunted trees lining the banks of the river; the water froze hard every night in the puddles in the road, and in the ewers that were placed in their bedrooms at the small country inns they frequented. Orange . . . Montélimar . . . Valence. . . .

At Valence they were received by the Bishop, a fussy, hot-tempered, ambitious little man, whom Candale had known years ago as the Abbé de Cosnac, the tutor of his boyhood friend and later rival-in-arms, the Prince de Conti.

Candale and Cosnac had never got on especially well: the latter had been jealous, for his pupil's sake, of the former's looks and charm and effortless skill at putting himself forward.

How long ago it seemed now! Directly after the Fronde Conti had married Mademoiselle de Martinozzi, the Cardinal's niece. Since then, he and Candale had made one or two Catalonian campaigns together, but Conti seemed to have lost his martial fervour: he soon retired with his wife from the court: they had a baby every year, and were said to have grown extremely devout, and to pray all the time when they were not having babies.

As for the Abbé, he had been metamorphosed overnight, to everyone's surprise, into the Bishop of Valence.

Monsieur de Cosnac received the young Duke and his suite with due ceremony, and served them a magnificent banquet, which Candale, unhappily, was barely able to taste.

He had a pleasant chat, however, with his host, and was amused, in spite of his physical discomfort, to observe how eager the little man was to efface any unfavourable impression that might have lingered in the Duke's memory, and to establish friendly relations between them.

Cosnac was close to the court, or one section of it — and that not the least important: if he thought it worth his while to propitiate Monsieur de Candale, the latter's position must have improved during his absence. (Who could hope to fathom the devious policies of His Eminence, Cardinal Mazarin?) So that when he got back to Paris, there might be something left to look forward to, after all. . . . Ah! But what did that matter now? What did *anything* matter?

Candale coughed half the night and slept for a few minutes only, despite a stiff dose of opium.

In the morning he was unable to touch his breakfast, but sat shivering harder than ever by the fire, while the rabbit-faced valet drew on his master's boots, and the Bishop, hovering uneasily in the background, twisted his hands together and besought his guest to remain another night. His Highness was not fit to travel . . . in this appalling weather, too. . . . Surely twenty-four hours more or less could not seriously upset his plans . . .

'No, thank you, my friend,' said the Duke politely. 'It is most kind of you, really — but I must get on to Lyon. I'll never be able to have any peace until I can get rid of my escort — and my good Auvergnats have promised to quit me there.'

'At least, Your Highness, will you not accept the loan of my carriage?' begged Monsieur de Cosnac, who was actually frightened by the Duke's heavy, red-rimmed eyes and spiritless air. 'You are in no condition to ride horseback today — truly, I fear you are not!'

This offer Candale decided to take, less because he was afraid to ride than because he was impatient to arrive in Lyon as soon as possible. And for that he had another reason besides the one he had already given the Bishop: at Lyon he expected to find Mérille once more.

Although he would not admit it, even to himself, Candale had still a faint hope that the terrible news he had heard might not be true. When he saw Mérille he would know, once and for all. Mérille he trusted as another self. If Mérille told him that Cateau was false, then indeed the world would come to an end.

The relief of not having to make the effort to sit upright in the saddle was so great that the Duke actually dozed a good part of the way to Vienne in the Bishop's carriage.

Even when he opened his eyes he did not return to full consciousness, but lay languidly on the cushions, half asleep, half awake, and comfortable for the first time since leaving Avignon.

He could see Cateau as clearly as ever, but only when he purposely thought of her; she was no longer in the foreground of his mind.

As he lay there in a semi-stupor he began to recall the past so vividly that it was almost as though he were reliving a great part of his life. It was not the immediate past that returned to him. The Spanish campaigns, the last three stormy years of his love for Cateau — even poor Diane de Saint-Loup, with her painted eyes and her petulant mouth and her cuckoo-cry of 'If-you-cared-for-me-as-I-care-for-you' — receded like shadows into the distance. He went back instead to his childhood days at the castle of Cadillac, near Bordeaux, in the flat, green, vine-covered country he still loved better than any other. He saw himself and his sister as they had been then, two fair, blue-eyed children, much alike in appearance, but already differing widely in character; for Christine was as grave and reflective at ten as her brother, three years her junior, was the reverse. Yet what happy times they had had together! They had meant everything in the world to each other; Christine, especially, had been mother and sister in one to little Gaston, who had never known his own mother.

Papa, at that time, had hardly figured at all in their lives. He was nearly always away, at the wars or with the court in Paris. It was Grandpapa, the old first Duc d'Epernon, the famous ex-mignon of King Henri III, who haunted their youthful imaginations as a fearsome, yet not unkindly, spectre from the still recent past. Candale remembered very plainly his grandfather's sharp-pointed beard and the round starched white ruff that appeared to divide his head from his body, as if they had belonged to two different persons. He had a keen recollection of the old Duke's stately bows and splendid demeanour in public — last souvenir of the court of the Valois — as well as of the tones of his voice, querulous but impressive, with his old-fashioned pronunciation and a sprinkling of citations from Latin and Greek, which Grandpapa had been proud to display as a token that, in *his* day, gentlemen had been scholars, too.

It was Grandpapa who taught the children their catechism — and slapped their hands smartly when they missed an answer — but it was Grandpapa, also, who gave them their ponies; and, later, when Gaston was a little older, bought him a pack of staghounds and sent him out hunting, early every frosty autumn morning, through the dense beech woods of the Epernon estates.

Later still, in the perilous period when the family had got into trouble with Cardinal Richelieu and Papa had been forced to flee to England for safety, it was Grandpapa who continued their mainstay in evil times as in good. Even at the very end of his life, held in a kind of semi-voluntary imprisonment at the castle of Loches, the proud patriarch of nearly ninety had gathered his little flock of descendants and dependents about him and exhorted them not to fear for the future. (It was only a pity he could not have lived to prove the truth of his words.)

Candale would never forget the day the old Duke died — the black-draped castle, the tolling bells, the fantastically formal procession that set out on the long journey from Touraine to Cadillac to bury their militant leader in state — himself, a lad of fifteen, as chief mourner riding behind the funeral chariot. He had been proud then of his new dignity as heir to the title, yet sad to think that the old days were over forever.

In his mind he divided his life into two sections: the first one had been closed abruptly by Grandpapa's death. Within a few months Richelieu and King Louis XIII followed the rebel Duke to the tomb, Papa hastened back from England to receive a full pardon and his father's estate; and, after that, Candale and Christine had lived most of the time in Paris with the new Duc and Duchesse d'Epernon. They were children no longer. Loving each other as dearly as ever, the press of events separated them inevitably. Christine had grown into a young lady almost overnight, still grave and reflective, and oddly impervious to the admiration her wealth and beauty commanded at court.

Candale thought afterwards it should have been obvious from the first that she was destined to become a nun. Her gentle, unimaginative piety, her total lack of worldly ambition, were surely better suited to the cloister than to the frivolous society of the early days of the Regency. It had not needed the death of the equally gentle and pious Chevalier de Fiesque — Gilette's brother-in-law, the only man she had ever loved, who had been killed at the siege of Mardick — to turn her thoughts seriously to the religious life. . . . Papa, of course, had never forgiven her. He had simply not been able to understand it: his only daughter, one of the greatest heiresses in France, who might have had half the princes in Europe to choose from, beginning with Prince Casimir, heir to the throne of Poland, himself! . . .

As for Candale, he had never got over it, either — but he had divined and sympathized with the motives that prompted her act. Although he missed her cruelly at times, he knew she was still there in the background, still loving them all as much as ever, like a lovely saint on earth, in the world but no longer of it.

He went to see her at the Carmelites' as often as he could, whenever the busy, brilliant rush of his days gave him a few minutes' respite from his duties that were pleasures and pleasures that seemed often to be duties as well.

Sister Anne-Marie de Jésus had saved him, over and over, by her earnest advice and her prayers, from the follies inseparable from his age. Yet, love him and watch over him as tenderly as she might, she could not be by his side any more as she used to be.

As he looked back on his crowded, spectacular youth, outwardly so impressive, but (as he now felt it to have been) so poor and mean within, Candale saw it as a long road with a great many turnings — all of them wrong, none fatal in itself, but each one leading him farther and farther into a labyrinth, from which there appeared to be no way of extricating himself.

He had had everything — yet he had nothing. He had tried to please everyone — yet, in the end, he had succeeded in pleasing no one, not even himself. That was all he was sure of now. But, for the life of him, he could not tell where he had made his first false step. That, and each succeeding one, had been taken without his knowing it; he had not been aware even of the necessity for making a choice until it was already too late to go back. . . . Ah, Christine, if *you* hadn't left me! . . .

There she was now, gazing at him seriously but sweetly, as she always did. . . . And then Christine suddenly changed into Cateau. . . . Cateau . . . Christine. . . . He could scarcely tell which one was which. . . . Lord, forgive me! That was blasphemy, surely, to confound the best of women with the worst!

But so it was, and so it remained, their faces appearing and disappearing, melting imperceptibly one into the other, until they became indistinguishable . . . and at length the Duke laid back his head and shut his eyes, and fell asleep once more.

At Vienne the Comte de Moret was waiting for them, having ridden posthaste all the way from Paris to greet his master. That was the sort of gesture people often made for Candale; he had the gift of inspiring a fanatical loyalty in his subordinates, without having to lift a finger for them in return. (Though, if he were sure it was not going to cost him too much, he was always glad to oblige when he could.) But it was as Saint-Evremond had said, years ago: his friends vied for his favour as fiercely as a group of rival lovers for their mistress's smiles.

Moret was shocked to find the Duke looking so ill. Like everyone else, he begged His Highness to go to bed at once, and to stay there till he should feel able to continue the journey without risk to his health.

Candale, however, still shook his head. He was barely able to speak above a whisper; the blood was pounding in his face, over his cheekbones, up under his eyes, and ringing in his ears like the waves of the sea; but he said resolutely that he must get on the next day to Lyon. At Lyon he would, if necessary, rest for a few days. There were decent doctors in Lyon, who would know what to do for his cold — for that was all it was, just a common cold he had caught, nothing more.

'Too many late parties in Avignon!' said the Duke, with a smile and a feeble attempt at sketching one of his old dashing gestures. 'What a gay little rogue the Castellane is! Come and sup with me at my lodgings, dear boy, and I'll tell you a tale of our merrymakings that will make your old Paris carnival look washed-out by comparison. And there's something else I must say to you. . . .'

But when Moret duly appeared at the door the Duke was already in bed and asleep, and they had no conversation that night about Madame de Castellane or anything else.

He slept again the following day most of the way between Vienne and Lyon, while Moret sat beside him in the Bishop's coach and guarded him tenderly.

At Lyon the Duke and most of his suite were to put up at the house of the Baron de Saint-Maurice-Perrachon, an old friend of his father's.

The Baron was waiting to receive his guest on the steps of the mansion, surrounded by the members of his household and his servants, amongst the latter of whom was Mérille.

Candale was all but unconscious; he had to be helped out of the carriage, and walked very slowly up the steps, leaning heavily on Moret's arm. He had no voice left to return his host's compliments; for the moment he had even forgotten what it was he wanted to say to Mérille, and why, only that morning, it had seemed so desperately important to get on to Lyon as fast as possible in order to find him.

At present it was enough to know that he was there — good old Mérille! the most faithful friend he had ever had.

Moret exchanged a worried look with the Duke's valet.

'I fear His Highness is far from well,' he said, in a low tone. 'He should be put to bed at once. And send for a doctor directly. If I'm needed at any time during the night, don't hesitate to call me. I shall lodge in the next street with my cousin La Forest.'

The Comte de Moret was a most conscientious young man. He went away from the Hôtel de Saint-Maurice, a few minutes later, his hawk-like features sharper than ever with anxiety; before retiring that night he called at the Baron's twice, to inquire how His Highness did, and received word that the Duke was resting quite comfortably; he had drunk some hot soup and a little wine, and after a long talk with his valet had gone to sleep peacefully in his chair by the fire.

Even after getting this reassuring message Moret felt that it would be wiser not to undress, in case he should be needed, after all. So he lay down fully clothed on the bed, leaving the door of his room ajar, and telling his cousin not to be alarmed if he should hear a knock at the front door during the night.

He must have had a premonition that something was going to happen; for, sure enough, at two o'clock in the morning, there *was* a knock at the front door, and there in the street, with a lantern in his hand, stood the rabbit-faced valet, crying out that His Highness was raving in delirium and refused point-blank to go to bed: Monsieur Mérille had done everything he could think of to force him to be reasonable, but in vain.

Moret said: 'I'll come at once!' He hustled into his greatcoat, for a wet, driving snow was pelting the streets, and followed the rabbit-faced valet to the house of the Baron, which was quite dark, save for the lights in the windows of the state guest-chamber.

The Duc de Candale, dressed in one of his best black velvet and silver court costumes, was sitting by the fire. His cheeks were very pink and his eyes were very blue; in the glow of the embers his long golden curls gleamed as brightly as flames.

In spite of his alarm, which was extreme, Moret could not help thinking that his friend had never looked better.

Mérille, who had been flitting like a restless ghost about the room, hastened forward.

'Sir, I am thankful you've come. His Highness will not hear of going to bed. Perhaps *you* . . .'

The Duke turned his bright blue eyes full on the new arrival, and smiled amiably.

'Bed! What nonsense! We're going out hunting directly, aren't we, old chap? I want to be back again with the kill before Grandpapa is awake, to surprise him. Are the dogs ready?'

'Certainly, Your Highness. Whenever they're needed,' replied Moret promptly. 'But it's rather too early to leave yet, you know; it's still dark outside. Meanwhile, as there's some time to wait before we go, why won't Your Highness rest for a bit and try to get a little sleep? You had a hard day yesterday.'

Candale looked at the young man with a curious pert expression in his eyes.

'I believe you're like everyone else, and think that I'm ill.'

'No, Your Highness, certainly not; only do, please, come to bed!'

'I'm not ill at all. As a matter of fact, I never felt better in my life. Why shouldn't I feel well? I've every reason to. I've not a worry in the world. That business about the Olonne, you know. I thought you'd be glad to hear that it doesn't matter at all, any more. I sent Mérille to Paris, after your letter came, because I had to be sure. Damn it all! a man can't be fooled all his life by a woman, can he? There's not one of 'em worth it — not one! D'you hear? Remember that, my dear, when your time comes to suffer. . . . At first, I own I was fairly cut up. I wrote the lady a pretty sharp letter, and told Mérille to deliver it and to find out what he could. Mérille's a sly fellow — devilish sly — aren't you, Mérille? Well, it was just as you said, a matter of money. Gaming debts — the old story! Poor Catherine-Henriette! She didn't dare tell her fool of a husband. Ah. why didn't she come to me, *to me*, who'd have done anything on earth to help her? But no: she said never a word — and Jeannin was waiting, like a snake in the grass, as he's done often enough before. The dirty rascal! If he were a gentleman, my seconds would be on their way to him now. As it is, there's nothing for it but to have him horsewhipped by my lackeys. Poor Catherine-Henriette! It's quite over. There's nothing more to be done. I cried like a baby — didn't I, Mérille? But I'm not going to cry any more. I've promised Mérille I won't, and I always tell him the truth — don't I, my friend?'

'Yes, Your Highness. But will Your Highness not go to bed? It's nearly three o'clock.'

'Bed? Nonsense! I'm going out hunting, I tell you. Monsieur de Moret's going with me. And we'll have a glass of wine together before we go, to drink a toast to Madame d'Olonne and her gallant Jeannin — and the other fair ladies of Paris! Quick, Mérille, there's a good fellow! See what the poor old Baron has got in his cellar worth drawing the cork from in honour of my Patient Griselda!'

When Mérille returned, ten minutes later, with a bottle of Burgundy on a tray, he found that his master had fainted. Moret had managed to carry him over to the bed — no mean feat, as Candale, for all his slenderness, was six feet tall and as hard as iron.

The Duke lay flat on his back, breathing heavily, his eyes shut, his cheeks still pink in spite of his swoon, his blond curls streaming in disorder across the pillow.

'Send for a doctor at once,' said Moret quickly. 'And take this wine away; it's brandy we want.'

'Yes, sir,' said Mérille; and then he added, in a whisper — although there was no need for words between these two men who both loved their master —: 'You understand, sir, about Madame d'Olonne — I tried not to tell him tonight. I tried my best — but he would have it . . .'

'Yes, yes, Mérille — I know! Now look sharp! There's no time to lose.'

Time, however, seemed no longer to have any meaning for Monsieur de Candale.

When he opened his eyes again, shortly afterwards, to find Mérille bending over him, he felt he had been lying there for hours, or even days, and might well continue to do so for the rest of his life.

The fire had been replenished and was blazing briskly; but, in spite of that, the room appeared gloomy. It was a very large room, with a very high ceiling, full of flickering shadows; the few monumental pieces of furniture it contained loomed mysteriously in distant corners, looking larger than life-size, as furniture always does in a place that is dark and unfamiliar.

People seemed to be coming and going, even more mysteriously — Moret, Mérille, the rabbit-faced valet — then the Baron, his host, in a nightshirt and flowered silk dressing-gown — and a strange man in black with a big feathered hat, who kept shaking his head and muttering something only partly intelligible about fluxions, and then going off into Latin, as poor Grandpapa used to do. (Was that not the doctor?)

After a while the Abbé de Roquette was there, too. (How on earth had he arrived, and from where?)

Candale, who had known him many years and liked him, was pleased to see the Abbé. He tried to smile at him and say his name — but his voice annoyingly refused to work; when he moved his lips no sound came out.

The man in black with the big feathered hat put his hand on Candale's shoulder and said: 'Don't try to talk, Your Highness.'

Candale moved his head impatiently; he disliked being touched by strangers.

It hurt him to move. His chest hurt, as if knives were sticking into it. But as long as he remained quiet he was not too uncomfortable. His cough did not trouble him nearly so much as it had done during the day, and the blood no longer pounded unpleasantly up over his cheekbones.

He could see Cateau again, too. She was actually in the room with him this time, standing beside the fire, dressed in the sparkling gold dress she had been wearing the first time they had danced the sarabande together at the ball at the Louvre. (Where had she kept it, all these years?) Candale loved that dress; he had always had a great feeling of sentiment for it. He wanted to tell her now to go on wearing it, for his sake. But when he tried to speak, once more his voice failed — and it seemed to him that Cateau moved a little farther away in the shadows.

This distressed him very much — for he wanted her to come nearer instead. Why wouldn't she come straight up to the head of the bed, and let him take her hand, and tell her what he was longing to say?

Candale knew he ought to be angry with her, though for the time being he could not recall why. Dimly he felt that the trouble between them had been a mistake; it was really quite unnecessary for them to quarrel. Surely Cateau would understand that now, and would be willing to make a fresh start. See, she was smiling, she was evidently in one of her angelic good-tempers. And so was he — why, so was he! ... Perhaps they would be at peace together as they had never been at peace, if only he could tell her what he wanted to tell her!

At the moment Candale could not think what it was, could not remember the word that would make everything clear, once and for all, between them. It was most irritating — confound his stupid head! Why in Heaven's name must it feel weak and giddy now, of all times?

If only Cateau would come closer, Candale was sure he would be able to remember the word. He *must* remember it; it seemed to him the most important thing in the world that it should be spoken now, this minute, before she should vanish from the room and never know ... and never know ...

Then, all of a sudden, it did not matter any more: Cateau's face was lost in the blur of all the other faces; the crackling of the fire rose to a roar in his ears; the golden head nodded gently on the pillow — and Monsieur de Candale, with a smile on his lips, fell asleep.

Chapter VII

DURING THE REST OF THE LAST WEEK IN JANUARY THE UNUSUAL COLD continued to hold France in its merciless grip. The whole country froze as hard as a stone; violent storms lashed the coastline all the way from Flanders to the Spanish border; while snow fell so heavily and persistently that many communities were temporarily isolated, and the post-wagons were unable to make their way through the ever increasing drifts.

In fact, letters from the south were so much delayed that the news of the death of the Duc de Candale reached Paris only a few hours after the report of his serious illness.

Cateau was just going out when the first word came. She had been out all day, every day, since the Duke's letter from Avignon had arrived, striving unsuccessfully to escape from her pain and remorse by ceaseless physical activity. That letter had frightened her terribly: knowing herself to be guilty, she could not parry this blow from her lover; his tone of cold, still anger struck fear into her very bones, and she knew not where to turn for comfort.

Magdelon was away with her husband in Nancy, where they were spending the holidays; Olonne, who would at least have been someone to talk to, had gone for a week to Poitiers on business connected with the seneschalate; and though Gilette was at hand, she was of little use in a crisis. Gilette could do nothing but look flurried and murmur helplessly: 'Dear me, Catherine-Henriette, who'd have thought . . . ?'

Cateau would have prayed, if she had believed in prayer. But her haphazard upbringing and the scorn engendered by the spectacle of Maman's religious vagaries, combined with six years of constant companionship with the Count's freethinking circle, had reduced God, for Madame d'Olonne, to the rank of one of her more casual acquaintances, whom she called on occasionally because custom demanded it, but paid very little attention to, between calls.

There remained nothing for it but to rush about Paris to every stupid party she was asked to attend — there were a good many of them in these first days of the carnival — and laugh and chatter and hold her head high, as if nothing had happened, though her mouth was dry with anguish and little waves of terror and dismay flowed up and down her spine whenever she was left to her own devices for even a moment.

The note from the Comte de Moret, announcing the illness of the Duke, was handed to Cateau just as she was stepping into her carriage to drive to the theatre with Saint-Evremond.

It was a bitterly cold afternoon, so cold that the snow refused to fall any more; but Cateau, muffled to the ears in soft grey fur, paused on the doorsill to open her letter.

'You'll forgive me, my friend?' she murmured to Saint-Evremond, who, watching her smilingly, thought that it would be hard indeed not to be willing to forgive her almost anything, as she stood there in her fluffy fur cloak, her lovely face rosy from the cold under its bonnet of nodding grey ostrich plumes.

She read the note at a glance, but gave no sign that its contents had disturbed her, save that her breath, freezing into vapour as it rose in the air, came short and fast for a few seconds. Then she crumpled the sheet of paper, stuffed it into her muff, and drove off to the Hôtel de Bourgogne with Saint-Evremond without saying a word about what had been in it.

In the carriage she realized — though she was ashamed to admit it — that she felt secretly relieved by the news from Lyon. It was as if she had received a reprieve from death just as the headsman's axe was about to descend on her shrinking neck.... Poor Candale! Poor darling! But perhaps it was all for the best: if he were laid up for a week or two, he would have time to recover from the first force of his rage against his faithless mistress. By the time he was able to return to Paris he might well have come round to viewing the matter in a more philosophical light and to realizing that Cateau had been false to the letter of their agreement rather than to the spirit. That was how Cateau herself looked at it. She still loved Candale, and only Candale; the other affair had been a mere passing peccadillo, such as men themselves were guilty of, over and over, and thought nothing more about afterwards. Cateau could not help thinking that, if Candale had wanted to insure himself against the possibility of such misadventures, he should have been wise enough not to leave her — at least, not for so long.... Seven months... Why, seven months were a small eternity! If it was not good for man to be alone, neither was it good for woman. She had been idle, and lonely, and unhappy — and Jeannin had been amazingly kind.

Naturally, she had never meant things to go as far as they had. She had been surprised, even extremely shocked, to find that Jeannin expected to be repaid just as Paget had done, and in the same way. She had struggled vigorously for many weeks; she had waxed haughty and beseeching, remote and capricious, by turns — but all to no purpose. Jeannin was not to be dismissed as Paget had been; he continued, respectfully but assiduously, to claim his rights; in the end, his insistence and the forces of youth and propinquity had got the best of her scruples.

Cateau knew she had been wrong; she knew it was a sin; she fully intended to confess to her lover the very moment he came home. She would be perfectly sincere, perfectly repentant, abject even, if necessary — and she was confident of her power to win his forgiveness, especially if, as she strongly suspected, *he* had something to confess to her as well. (Those letters all winter had been really too good to be true.)

So Cateau sat smiling in the coach beside Saint-Evremond, and said to herself: 'A week or two, at the most ... but not more....'

The play they saw that afternoon, *Astiniax*, was something clumsy and Greek in five overstuffed acts. The tailpiece likewise, in which the comedian Floridor starred, was neither novel nor particularly amusing. But Cateau was in a mood to be diverted: she laughed heartily whenever there was anything to laugh at — even sometimes when there was not. All the time, of course, she was miserable as well, and kept reproaching herself for her levity and wondering how poor dear Candale was getting on, away off in Lyon. Moret's letter had been vague and unsatisfactory: 'a fluxion on the chest' might mean much or little: how on earth was she to learn more details? Moret, she knew, had not been especially friendly to her since the affair with Jeannin, and it was out of the question to appeal to Candale's own family, for neither the Duc nor the Duchesse d'Epernon even spoke to her in the street. ... Ah, where should she turn? And how could she keep from praying perversely: 'Let him be ill for a while — but not too ill — and then come back to me, and let everything be as it was before ...'?

In the midst of this distracted reverie she was recalled to herself by becoming suddenly conscious of Saint-Evremond's quizzical eye upon her. She gave a nervous, not-quite-natural laugh, and observed, with a toss of her head: 'Decidedly, the Beauchâteau has grown too stout to be endured as a heroine!'

When she got back to the house Brossard announced that the Comtesse de Fiesque was upstairs in the yellow cabinet, waiting to see her.

A queer sick throb clutched Cateau's heart as she heard this; and when she saw her friend there was no need of words to tell her what had happened.

'He's dead,' said Cateau at once, in a whisper.

Gilette nodded without speaking. Her poor little face was strained out of all semblance to its natural gaiety; she could not express what she felt, and so she expressed nothing: the staring hazel eyes were perfectly blank.

'Dead,' repeated Cateau, in a very small voice. 'Yes, of course. I knew he was going to die all along, didn't you, Gilette?'

'No,' said Gilette. 'No, I can't say I did. I'd hoped that our

thoughts... our prayers... Oh, Catherine-Henriette, he was so
young to die! He had so much to live for!' She burst into loud
sobs and fell, weeping, onto the couch in front of the fire.

Cateau sat down beside her. Her knees had begun to tremble so
hard that she could not have stood up any longer; she felt too
stunned to cry, as Gilette was doing.

'How did you hear...?' she asked, after a minute.

'Moret came to see me after dinner today,' replied Gilette, between sobs. 'He arrived from Lyon this morning, and had just been
at the Hôtel d'Epernon to break the news to the Duke. They said
there was no hope from the first. Oh, Catherine-Henriette, think of
his poor family! his poor father! I always hated the old man myself,' added Gilette, in parenthesis, 'but one can't help pitying him
now. What will he do? The duchy will be extinct, you know, at his
death. How he must regret that Candale didn't marry and — oh,
my dear, forgive me! I didn't think...'

'That's all right,' said Cateau. 'It doesn't make any difference.
Nothing makes any difference now.'

She sat quite quietly beside Gilette on the couch; she was still
wearing her hat with the nodding grey ostrich plumes, and had forgotten even to draw off her gloves.

Presently she said: 'Was there no message for me?' Her lover
could not have left her forever without a word of forgiveness, to tell
her that, after all, at the end he had thought of her, to whom for
three years all his thoughts had been devoted.

Gilette shook her head and went on sobbing.

'No message,' said Cateau. 'Oh, but that can't be! There *must*
have been. You always get things wrong, Gilette — you know you
do! Send for Moret and see what he's got to say. Send at once —
d'you hear?'

'But dearest, you forget, I've seen him already.... I asked him
myself about you ... and he said there was no word at all. I suppose
the poor fellow was unconscious... how could he have said anything
to anyone then? And perhaps it's for the best, when you think...
Oh, Catherine-Henriette, don't look at me like that! *Don't*, for pity's
sake! I can't stand it! Go ahead, dear, and cry if you want to; it
will do you good — truly, it will!'

'I don't feel like crying,' said Cateau slowly. 'I don't feel anything, really. You had better go, Gilette, if there's nothing more you
can tell me.'

'Darling, I can't leave you! What are friends for? At a time like
this ——'

'Please go,' said Cateau. 'Please, Gilette. I'd rather be alone.'

'Oh, but, dearest ——'

'*I mean it,*' said Cateau.

She raised the weeping Gilette from the couch and conducted her firmly to the door of the yellow cabinet.

After her friend had gone, protesting volubly all the way down the stairs, Cateau went to her own room, drew the curtains tight shut, and called for her women to undress her. Then she dismissed Quinette and Quentine and retired to her bed, where she remained for the next twenty-four hours without eating or sleeping, silently, tearlessly contemplating the portrait of her lover by the light of a solitary candle.

She saw no one but her servants, having sent word to Brossard to say that she was positively not at home — a timely precaution; for every friend and relation she had in the city made haste to call on Madame d'Olonne, indecently anxious to learn 'how she was taking it.'

Paris, in general, had been overwhelmed by the news. The court was in deep mourning, not only officially, but also because the King and the Queen Mother and their whole circle were genuinely stricken by their loss. It seemed impossible to believe that the Duc de Candale was dead — Candale, the leader of fashion, for ten years the pattern of the perfect courtier, the darling of the alcoves, the hero of the smartest and gayest set in France! Every feminine friend he had had — from the youngest and prettiest of the maids-of-honour to the half-blind and grizzled old Beauvais, the Queen's waiting-woman — was dissolved in tears at the thought that she would see him no more. As the Chevalier de Saint-Evremond wrote shortly afterwards, in a clever, rather heartless little portrait of the lamented young man: 'All women felt they had loved him, and a common tenderness soon produced a general grief. Those whom he had formerly loved recalled their old feelings and imagined that they were losing again what they had already lost long ago. Several to whom he had been indifferent flattered themselves that he might not always have remained so. . . . There were some who regretted him from pure vanity, and others, quite unknown to him, insinuated themselves with the truly afflicted in a communion of tears, to make themselves a merit of gallantry; but his true mistress rendered herself illustrious by the excess of her grief! She would have been fortunate,' Saint-Evremond added sententiously — and it was months before Cateau forgave him — 'if she had never consoled herself.'

Saint-Evremond, as a matter of fact, knew nothing of what she was feeling. He could imagine what he liked — indeed, he imagined a very great deal: the week was not up before a poem from his hand, a touchingly pretty elegy on the death of the young Duke (in which the Comtesse d'Olonne was represented as pouring out her heart in charming hexameters), was making the rounds of the salons with great success.

But how could he, or any man, guess what Cateau thought as she lay on her bed in the deserted, candlelit room, hour after hour, with Candale's portrait before her dry eyes? How could he, or any man, penetrate and analyze the indescribable mixture of shame and remorse that racked the pale figure lying cold and motionless, deaf alike to the prayers of her women and to her friends' importunities?

To do Cateau justice, she did not care in the least what was said of her; she was as indifferent now as she had always been to public opinion. It was merely a lucky accident that the one thing she wanted to do was the one thing people could admire her for doing. She had achieved dignity in her sorrow by keeping it to herself. For once the bitter, evil tongues were silenced; one heard on every side the liveliest expressions of commiseration for the lovely Countess; it was said, again and again — her loss somehow lending a kind of respectability to her emotion — that she must really have loved the Duke very much. . . .

For nearly a week Cateau steadily refused to see anyone except Gilette de Fiesque, who called every morning for a brief quarter of an hour, to kiss her cheek and weep afresh, and beg Catherine-Henriette to weep, too.

One day, however, when the two women were alone together, Mérille was announced. Gilette, with unusual tact, made a move to depart; but Cateau detained her with a gesture.

'There's no reason, my dear, why you shouldn't stay,' she said.

Nor was there. Mérille remained in the room less than five minutes, and confined his remarks to the minimum necessary to discharge the errand that had brought him. This was to return to Madame d'Olonne the letters she had written the Duke during the last three years, which the young man had carefully preserved in a silver casket, together with portraits in miniature, scraps of ribbon, faded roses, and other paraphernalia dear to a lover's heart.

Mérille, who was dressed all in black, and whose broad, honest face was stony with grief, handed the casket with its key to Cateau, saying simply: 'This is your property, madam. The Duke requested me on his death-bed to return it to you.'

Cateau bowed her head, and after a moment turned the key in the lock and opened the casket. As soon as she saw what was in it she felt no further desire to explore its contents; it was Gilette who could not restrain herself from peering and prying and moaning softly at the wealth of tender souvenirs it held.

'Catherine-Henriette, do look! There's the lace scarf you lost at the Queen of Sweden's supper — and a buckle off the little red shoes you wore two winters ago. . . . Poor boy! Poor dear fellow! Fancy his keeping them all this time! Ah, my dear, that's what I call a grand passion! . . . And see here — what's this? . . .'

Cateau paid no more attention to Gilette than she generally did. She looked Mérille straight in the eye and said:

'Is this all you have for me?'

'All, madam.'

'Was there no letter — no last word? Did your master not think of me before ... before ...?'

'Madam,' replied Mérille coldly, 'I know not what His Highness was thinking in that dread hour. He was delirious, all but unconscious, for two days before he died. Let us hope that his mind was with God, as I pray that his soul may be now. If the Countess has nothing further to say to me, may I beg her leave to retire?'

He kissed the hand Cateau held out to him, and hastily left the room.

As soon as he had gone Cateau sprang up impetuously from the bed, showing the first signs of life since the fatal news had arrived, five days ago.

'Gilette,' she said, 'I'll go mad if I lie here any longer: I must see someone!'

'Yes, dear,' said Gilette, looking doubtful, 'but *whom?*'

'You see how it is — you see how they avoid me — the lot of 'em — as if I had the plague! There's not one of 'em been near me but that wretch of a valet — and look how he treated me!'

'Why, Catherine-Henriette,' said Gilette, who could sometimes be very stupid, 'I don't think he said anything he shouldn't!'

'Ah, that's not it! Can't you understand? It's what he *didn't* say — Oh, no, it's not fair! It's too cruel! I can't stand it! I've got to see someone who'll tell me ...'

'You might call at the Hôtel d'Epernon,' suggested Gilette, after a moment's reflection. 'I can't very well go with you, because Mademoiselle is doing the honours — you know she was Candale's first cousin — and she's strictly forbidden me to appear anywhere that she is. Not,' Gilette added, 'that I let that stop me for a minute, if there's a party I want to go to. But say what you will, a call of condolence isn't quite the same thing as a ball. If *you'd* like to go, though ...'

Cateau shuddered. 'No, no — not there!'

The thought of the great black-draped halls, the shrouded windows, the hushed voices, the stately ceremonial curtsies — all the family drawn up in a solemn semicircle, with Mademoiselle de Montpensier, their royal cousin (who was in her element on such occasions), at its head — struck a chill to her heart. Besides, she could glean no information she sought there — if indeed she even managed to be admitted? For it was quite possible that Monsieur d'Epernon had given orders to have his son's mistress turned away at the door.... Cateau was frankly afraid of the old Duke.

When Gilette left her she was still undecided what to do. Finally, however, she remembered Candale's sister Christine. She had not seen the former Mademoiselle d'Epernon for almost ten years; she had never actually met her. When Christine quitted the court in the early days of the Fronde Cateau had been a very young girl who spent most of her time in the country and had not yet been officially presented to Paris society. But she recalled having caught a glimpse of the Princess at a ball at the Tuileries; the fair, sweet face and gentle manners had made a particular impression on young Mademoiselle de la Louppe that, although long forgotten, emerged once more into the foreground of her mind as a pale beacon of hope.

Cateau dressed in a whirlwind of haste, sent for her carriage, and drove muffled in furs through the icy streets across the river to the Great Carmelites in the rue du Faubourg-Saint-Jacques.

If it had been cold in Paris, it was colder in the country. A nipping wind swept between the high walls that divided the cloister gardens from the Val de Grâce on the other side of the street. It was so sharp that Cateau gasped for breath as she got out of the carriage and rang the bell at the porter's lodge. The bells of Notre Dame des Champs, the convent's own church, just behind the lodge, were dismally tolling, thereby disturbing the flock of pigeons that had been huddled for warmth in the shelter of its tower. . . . Perhaps a service was in progress, and no visitors could be admitted? . . . No matter: *anything* now to get out of the wind. . . .

But it was almost as freezing within the lodge as outside in the street.

The chill, stale air of the little parlour smelled of incense; the whitewashed walls were as comfortless as a prison, and were quite bare save for a portrait of an elderly nun holding a crucifix, which Cateau recognized as that of Mother Madeleine de Saint-Joseph, the late foundress of the Paris house.

She shivered, and pulled her furs more tightly about her throat.

'I want to see Mademoiselle d'Epernon,' she said peremptorily to the portress, a stout, rosy-faced woman in the habit of a lay sister, who came waddling out of an inner cubbyhole to answer the bell.

The portress stared at her blankly, and made no reply.

Cateau grew impatient.

'Mademoiselle d'Epernon, the Duke's daughter,' she said loudly. 'Do you not understand? Tell her I should like to see her at once, please, if it is possible; it's very important. Tell her the Comtesse d'Olonne is waiting.'

The portress still continued to stare.

'Mademoiselle d'Epernon ceased to exist nine years ago,' she said at length. 'We know no one here by that name. If the Countess would care to speak with Sister Anne-Marie de Jésus, that is a different story.'

Cateau coloured and bit her lip in annoyance. How stupid of her to have forgotten Mademoiselle d'Epernon's name in religion! Of course, she had not really forgotten; only in her agitation and haste she had spoken without thinking.

The portress, noting her confusion and impressed, in spite of herself, by Cateau's beauty and the lavish good taste of her costume, said more kindly: 'I think you have come at a very good time. Our sister is at present in the garden, attending the novices during their hour of recreation. If you will follow me, I shall be glad to show you where she is. Only' — she paused, hesitating a little — 'it is perhaps too cold for you, madam, outside? Would you prefer to wait here, while I take the word to Sister Anne-Marie?'

'No, no,' quickly replied Cateau, only too thankful to be able to make her escape from the lifeless little parlour and the unsympathetic painted eyes of the Reverend Mother Madeleine de Saint-Joseph. 'The garden will do quite well; I've a very warm cloak.'

The portress unlocked a small side door in the lodge and led the way through it into the gardens of the Great Carmelites.

Cateau, following her, was struck by the vast extent of the property they were entering. No private citizen of Paris possessed such a large estate at the very gates of the city. There were acres of flower and vegetable beds, orchards and vineyards and neat miniature meadows, which last were grazed in summer by the convent cows: it was a whole little kingdom walled away from the outside world. A long brick walk bisected diagonally the part of the grounds they were now traversing; it was bordered by rows of gaunt grey elms, whose last traces of leaves, still clinging here and there in thin shabby bunches, only added to their air of desolation.

At the far end of the walk Cateau perceived the novices approaching, dressed all alike and sober enough in their dark brown gowns and cream-coloured cloaks — but at least something moving and breathing in the great frozen enclosure. They were chatting together decorously, but cheerfully; the sound of their voices, where nothing else sounded, was audible a long way off. As they drew nearer Cateau noticed that now and again one of the smaller, younger novices gave a little run and a jump, on account of the cold.

Cateau advanced along the brick walk under the elm trees to meet the band rather slowly, because she felt suddenly very shy.

The portress had already waddled ahead, officiously calling out: 'Sister Anne-Marie, here is a lady come to see you.'

A tall, thin figure, in no way distinguishable from the others save by her black veil, detached herself without haste from the group of white-veiled novices.

'Who wants me, my sister?'

The deep, firm voice was unfamiliar, but as Sister Anne-Marie looked up to examine her visitor Cateau caught her breath: the eyes that gazed calmly into hers were Candale's own. The lids were pink and swollen, the eyes themselves dimmed by much weeping — but there was no mistaking that peculiarly intense shade of cornflower-blue.

A wave of embarrassment swept over Cateau: she could not think what she was doing here, nor how she was going to explain her errand satisfactorily to Sister Anne-Marie.

'It's the Comtesse d'Olonne,' said the portress, who had evidently taken more heed of the caller than she had appeared to be doing at the time. 'She wishes to speak to you on a matter of the utmost importance.'

Having thus discharged her duty, the portress returned to the lodge — albeit reluctantly, with many a pause and lingering look over her shoulder. (How annoying it was not to be able to stay and hear what the beautiful Countess was going to say!)

The novices, too, were whispering and fluttering in the background, as they eyed the newcomer from the great world with lively curiosity.

Sister Anne-Marie was obviously aware of this movement amongst her charges, for she clapped her hands smartly together and said in a most determined way: 'Children, continue your walk at once. Two by two, just as usual. Sister Ignacia, I leave you in command. I shall rejoin you in a minute or two.'

She then waited deliberately until the procession had moved out of earshot before saying to Cateau: 'Madam, what can I do for you?'

'You don't know me,' began Cateau impulsively, 'but I know who you are very well, mademoiselle.'

'Mademoiselle no longer,' said the nun, in a tone of gentle rebuke. 'Anne-Marie de Jésus now, please, madam, your sister in Christ.'

'Forgive me, of course, I know,' stammered Cateau, who could not take her gaze from the cornflower-blue eyes so like (and yet unlike) another pair she had known. 'Please forgive me, also, my sister, for intruding on you, especially at this time, when you must be in deepest mourning for the death of your brother. The Duke was a very dear friend of mine.... I don't know whether you knew...'

'My brother had a great many friends,' said Sister Anne-Marie remotely. 'You must pardon me, madam, but I did not quite hear your name; I am a little deaf since a bad cold I had two winters ago. You are...?'

'Madame d'Olonne — the Comtesse d'Olonne,' said Cateau. 'Perhaps that means nothing to you....'

'Ah, but it does,' said Sister Anne-Marie, though still remotely.

'Your husband, I think, must be one of the La Trémouilles? Yes, just so. Oh, I have not lived out of the world so long that I have forgotten my genealogies! But... I don't quite see.... You were a friend of my brother's, you say?'

She continued to survey her caller as if she had no idea what the latter wanted; her manner was kindly, yet impersonal, as of one who had ministered to much woe and could supply prompt consolation on a businesslike basis.

Cateau decided to plunge recklessly ahead — there was really nothing else to be done!

'Yes, a very particular friend. I was terribly shocked to hear of his death. I — I should like to tell you, as his sister, how deeply I sympathize with you in your loss, and to ask, if it is not impertinent in me to do so, for some details concerning his end. I know nothing — nothing beyond the mere fact that he *is* dead! And I've no one to turn to.... Oh, my sister, is it asking too much ...?'

The tall woman in brown hesitated for an instant, while an almost imperceptible shadow passed across her face. She was evidently making up her mind about something. Cateau could have sworn at that moment that the nun knew what she had been to Candale — that Sister Anne-Marie was the mistress of all the details of their miserable story, and had no doubt assisted at the conclaves of the Epernon family, who had striven so long and vainly to break up the fatal liaison.

But it was too late now to retreat. Besides, whatever the austere Carmelite might have thought of her in the past, there was no longer, alas! any reason for harbouring resentment against an unhappy abandoned creature.

That this was the conclusion Sister Anne-Marie de Jésus had come to was made manifest in her next speech, the first she had spoken in which there could be detected a note of recognition of Cateau as a human being.

'It is good of you to sympathize with us in our sorrow,' said Sister Anne-Marie. 'Come, madam, shall we not walk a little? I see you are shivering. It is, of course, a heavy blow to our family; my father, I fear, at his age and with his infirmities, will never recover from it. Since you knew my brother, you knew also, I dare say, how much he meant to us all. I am afraid I can tell you very little about his end. He caught cold at Avignon, and grew steadily worse through his persistence in continuing his journey in unfavourable weather. At Lyon he was forced to take to his bed with a fluxion on his lungs and a high fever.... The doctors did all they could — his friends naturally summoned the best available help — but it was already too late to save him.'

'Yes — yes!' cried Cateau anxiously. 'I know all that — but can you tell me — was he conscious at the last? Who was with him? What did he say? Was there no word . . .? Oh, my sister, forgive me — but I must know — I cannot rest till I do. . . .'

'Ah, *there* I can give you a good deal more information,' said Sister Anne-Marie. 'My dear brother, I am thankful to say, was fully conscious for several hours before he died. He had with him the Archbishop of Lyon, and the Abbé de Roquette, who was his own confessor as well as a very old family friend. Happily he was able to make a general confession in form and to receive absolution from the Archbishop and the accustomed last sacraments of the church. The Abbé has written me a beautiful letter on the subject; I shall be glad to show it you, since you are good enough to be interested. He has also written a funeral oration, which my father and I think a truly excellent work; it is to be delivered next month in solemn session in the cathedral at Dijon before the officers and clergy of the late Duke's governments. The Abbé has taken for his text this verse of the Sixty-Second Psalm: "Also unto Thee, O Lord, belongeth mercy: For Thou renderest to every man according to his work." By a blessed dispensation of Providence, dear madam, it was given to my brother to repent of the sins of his past life before he was taken from us. He had the strength to turn aside from worldly vanities and renounce them boldly, clinging firmly at the last to the holy cross alone. Thanks to this, I do not despair of his salvation. I feel he will be called to dwell with Jesus Christ, our Lord and dear Redeemer, in eternal glory, after, of course, having duly expiated his sins, as all of us must in the life to come. I pray for the repose of his soul, madam, every day; so must everyone do who loved him on earth. May I dare to ask you for your prayers as well? It is the only service we can render him now.'

Sister Anne-Marie's face was white and drawn from suffering and sleepless nights, and her eyes filled with tears as she finished speaking; but there was a look of serenity in their depths, a calm certainty in her matter-of-fact voice that convinced Cateau it would be useless to attempt to explain. She wanted to cry out: 'But you and I are thinking of different persons! You talk of a cold, resigned penitent on his death-bed — and I, of my darling lover, with his laughing blue eyes and yellow curls, and all the dear sweetness that was mine — *mine*, I tell you, and no one else's! Surely he could not have forgotten me and the delights that we shared, even when he was dying!'

But there were things she could not say to the pale, self-assured woman at her side. The eager, crowding words died away on her lips, choked into silence by Sister Anne-Marie's invincible assumption that there was nothing more to be said.

The nun conducted her visitor back to the door of the portress's lodge. When she bade her good-bye she smiled slightly, showing a gap in the front of her rather wide mouth where two teeth were missing.

'Come again, madam, whenever you like; you will always be welcome in our house. I promise to send you a copy of the funeral oration as soon as it has been printed.'

Cateau thanked Sister Anne-Marie faintly and murmured an incoherent farewell.

Then she stepped into her carriage and drove away, feeling more wretched than before she had come to the Great Carmelites.

Chapter VIII

THE MARÉCHAL DE LA FERTÉ AND HIS WIFE RETURNED TO PARIS from Nancy towards the end of the first week in February. It was a difficult trip of several days across the snow-blanketed plains of Champagne and the Brie; they had to stop many times to change horses, for the beasts tired quickly fighting the wintry blasts; and Magdelon was relieved when at last, at the close of the third day, they turned into the familiar rue Neuve-des-Petits-Champs and drew up in front of the Hôtel de Senneterre.

The sun had just set; the big pile stood out black and threatening against the pale evening sky; only a few lights showed here and there on the sombre expanse of stone. Yet Magdelon was glad to be at home once more: the gloomy old house *was* home to her now. It had no secrets from her any longer; she knew what lay behind each tall, staring window; and the tapers, gleaming from the wing where her own apartments lay, winked like friendly beacons through the frosty plum-coloured dusk.

There was a moment's wait before footmen came running, torches in hand, to open the door. The horses pawed and pranced with impatience on the snowy cobbles, their flanks dark and steaming with sweat. The Maréchal, too, was fuming at the delay. But Magdelon, though she was eager to see little Henri, who had not been taken to Nancy on account of a slight cold, laid her hand gently on her husband's arm and gave him a radiant smile.

The next minute she was out of the coach and into the house, flying up the great stone stairs to the nursery, still in her cloak and fur tippet. Snatching her son from his cradle, where he was tranquilly sleeping, she covered his face with kisses: his cheeks were as rosy from sleep as hers from the cold air outside.

'Angel!' cried Magdelon. 'How could I have left you for as long as a fortnight? I'll never, never again.... Hélène, how is he? Has he quite recovered?'

'Oh, quite, my Lady,' replied the smiling nurse. 'He's not even so much as sneezed for nearly a week.'

Magdelon fell to kissing Henri again, because she was so pleased to hear that he was well; and while she was doing so the door opened and Madame de la Louppe came in.

'If you ask *my* opinion, dear,' said Maman, without preliminaries — just as if she had been seeing her daughter every day for the last six months — 'that child is being killed by kindness. Such a nonsensical régime I never-in-my-born-days...! Doctor Patin must be mad; I told him so, quite frankly. All those pills and tonics! Why, when you and Cateau were young, children were left to themselves — and a great deal better they were for it, too! "Keep your back straight and hold up your head," I used to say to you every day — d'you remember? A kiss night and morning, and a stiff dose of brandy in case of chills — and any normal baby will bloom like a rose. Oh, my dear...'

Maman was off, full sail, into one of her florid, interminable monologues; while Magdelon, smiling, with her head to one side, twisted Henri's crisp black ringlets round her finger and tried to look as if she were listening intelligently to what her parent was saying.

She was not in the least surprised to find her mother in the house; and she could truthfully say she was glad to see her, although it was not perhaps an especially convenient time to have a guest. La Ferté was so busy.... Poor La Ferté! What would he say when he knew...? Maman was Magdelon's relative; but it was the Maréchal's fault that they had been so often descended upon in this way. Shortly after the wedding he had written, in an unwisely expansive moment, that of course Madame de la Louppe must consider the Hôtel de Senneterre a second home. It was the sort of thing one often said to relations, without expecting them to take it seriously. Certainly La Ferté had not supposed that his mother-in-law would look on it as more than a graceful compliment. But the next week Maman had appeared in her shabby carriage, with her very old coachman and her very young maids, as well as an indefinite number of boxes, and announced gaily that she had come to stop.

She was with them for a month, that time; and the following winter she had come for two months.

After that, she turned up every year, sometimes twice a year, and made herself thoroughly comfortable in the large, handsome suite of rooms she managed successfully, in a playful manner, to claim as her own.

She was perfectly frank about the money it saved her; she was even franker in expressing her preference for her elder daughter's gayer, more amusing establishment. Cateau kept a much better cook and a good deal more company. But then, Cateau had never asked her mother to visit her. On the whole, the Hôtel de Senneterre did very well. It was an excellent address in the quarter, the Maréchal made a genial host (when not out of temper), and dear little Magdelon was most amenable to suggestions — which Cateau had never been. Besides, old Senneterre and his wife were absorbing neighbours: Maman spied upon their ill-assorted ménage with tireless enthusiasm and, strange to say, had succeeded in becoming exceedingly popular with both husband and wife.

There was much to relate, this time, concerning their most recent quarrel: the Marquis, it seemed, had thrown a chamberpot (fortunately empty) at 'Mother Anne's' head, but (still more fortunately) had missed, since when the poor lady had kept to her bed, overcome by nervous shock. In fact, the Senneterres proved such an inexhaustible subject that it was not until the middle of dinner that Maman remembered to tell her daughter and son-in-law about the Duc de Candale.

'And oh, yes, my dears,' she remarked, quite casually, with her mouth full of stewed ortolan, 'I knew there was something I'd forgotten to say: that young man of Cateau's — he's died!'

'*What* young man?' cried Magdelon. 'You don't mean her husband, surely?'

'No — no — certainly not — on the contrary! That good-looking blond creature — that handsome fellow with the well-turned calf! I really never,' declared Maman, 'came across a young man with a better-turned calf! Poor thing — poor dear wretch! You know the one I mean — Cateau's been mad about him these three years past. . . . Was he not a duke, or something of the sort? It seems to me . . .'

'Not *Candale?*' exclaimed Magdelon.

'Yes, yes — that's the name — that's the one I mean,' said Maman; and she went on to narrate, with as many harrowing details as she could recollect or, in default of memory, invent, the tale of the Duke's tragic end, while Magdelon listened with a shocked and incredulous face.

Like everybody else, she found it difficult to believe that Monsieur de Candale was dead.

'And the worst of it is,' concluded Maman, brandishing her fork expressively, 'that Cateau is behaving like an idiot. She's shut herself up in her room and refused to see anyone — anyone at all, even *me*, her own mother! Did you ever hear anything so unnatural? I had my name sent in twice, to make sure, because of course I thought there must be some mistake — but no: back came the word, the Countess is not receiving today. Can you imagine . . .? On top of that, I tried to argue with her brute of a Swiss — but he was as obstinate as a mule! "My orders is, madam, no one's to get in," he said to me, over and over. Well! It wasn't even of any use to bribe him. I tried that, too — naturally, as a last resort; he just kept the money, and nothing came of it. But it's so silly of

Cateau to act that way. If her husband weren't out of town, she wouldn't dare.... And nobody'll think any the better of her for it, you know. If the boy's dead, he's dead, and no power on earth can bring him back. As a matter of fact, though,' added Maman, as an afterthought, 'I've heard of a marvellous woman on the Pont Marie who can put one in connection with the spirit world at a moment's notice. Of course, she's rather expensive — a hundred francs for a half-hour's interview — but Cateau needn't consider that — and they say she's achieved some really remarkable results. The Maréchale de la Mothe's been going to her for a month, and I hear she's quite made over: she talks to her husband every day, and tells everyone he's twice as kind to her as he was when he was alive! That's the sort of thing Cateau ought to try, to take her out of herself. Yes, and if I could see her, I'd tell her so, too.... None of this morbid moping round the house for *me!*'

'Oh, poor Cateau!' said Magdelon softly: there were tears in her dark eyes. She thought of Henri asleep upstairs in his cradle, and told herself how much more fortunate she was than her sister. 'Oh, I must go to her at once! Sir, you'll permit me to leave you?'

La Ferté had been silent during the whole of dinner. He had been sitting slumped down in his chair, his chin sunk on his chest, while he tore his meat to pieces with his fingers — he never used cutlery when it was possible to do without it — and tossed an occasional scrap to the pair of spaniels on the hearth. (The Maréchal had a great many pet dogs, all of them, curiously, of small breeds.)

Now he looked up with a scowl and said gruffly: 'Your sister, madam, is a most unhappy woman. She's been openly false to her marriage vows, and Providence has seen fit to punish her for it. I've no objection to your calling on her in private, after a suitable interval — it's natural you should want to do so — but I must insist that in public you avoid any association with the Comtesse d'Olonne for some time to come.'

'Oh, but, sir, my own sister,' began Magdelon warmly — though Maman was making warning signals to her daughter across the table.

La Ferté spat on the floor and shouted: 'Zounds, madam, is it my fault?' — exactly as if Magdelon had been Robert, the valet. 'Sister or not, she's a loose woman, and I won't have my wife seen with a trollop — d'you understand? It's a damned shame! Candale was one of the best fellows in the service, and she was the death of him, as surely as we're sitting here at this table.'

'My daughter a trollop!' screamed Maman, rolling up her eyes and dropping her fork with a clatter. 'Sir, do you realize what you're saying?'

'Perfectly, madam — and I dare say I could mention where she found her example, too, if I were minded to do it!' retorted the Maréchal testily — and then they were off, as they frequently were, into one of their spectacular scenes, in which La Ferté's blunt wit and savage thrusts were matched by Maman's theatrical emotionalism and dizzy blows in every direction, only a tithe of which landed, those few, however, deriving a certain telling effect from their very wild aimlessness.

Here were opponents worthy of each other's mettle: they understood the game thoroughly, in the same way, and bore each other no rancour afterwards. Very likely, half an hour later, they would be peacefully playing piquet by the fire.

Just the same, it was a pity that there had to be a quarrel at all on their first night at home. Magdelon, sitting round-eyed and demure between her husband and her mother, decided prudently that it would be better not to say anything more for the present about Cateau. It could only add fuel to the flame, and that the latter was already burning dangerously high was proved by the fact that La Ferté had spoken angrily to his wife before a third person for the first time since their marriage.

Dissimulation was not easy for Magdelon. It was natural for her to say at once what lay nearest her heart; she could be silent only when she was afraid to speak.

The next day the Maréchal woke up in a particularly pleasant humour. He spent the whole morning, in his dressing-gown, in his wife's apartments, frolicking with young Henri and the spaniels. He assisted, also, at Magdelon's singing lesson with the renowned Abbé de Bacilly, who was teaching her some of the latest airs of Lambert: he twitted both professor and pupil unmercifully; but when the Abbé had bowed himself out, he took Magdelon on his knee, and pinched her cheeks, and called her his linnet, and gave her an embroidered silk purse with a gold-piece in it.

After dinner he had to go to the Louvre for a conference with the Cardinal and Chancellor Séguier. Maman, who had sat up half the night playing cards with her women and the Maréchal's pages, retired to her room for a nap. Nevertheless, Magdelon felt distinctly guilty as she commanded her coach: she crept out of the house like a conspirator; not even a handsome red-feathered hat could restore her confidence; and her voice shook strangely as she murmured to the coachman: 'The Hôtel de la Mothe-Houdancourt.'

An hour later, armed with much mysterious information procured from the widowed Maréchale, she hurried furtively into her carriage once more, glancing fearfully from left to right to see whether she were observed, and gave the order to drive to her sister's house.

It never occurred to Magdelon that Cateau might refuse to see her. She did not even ask Brossard's permission to enter; and when the porter saw who it was his brow cleared and he announced directly that Madame the Maréchale would find the Countess upstairs in the latter's dressing-room.

Cateau was seated in front of her dressing-table, gazing vacantly into the glass. She had lately taken to passing hours of her time in this position, doing nothing, even thinking as little as possible.

Magdelon was frightened when she caught sight of her face. Cateau was not able to summon a smile. She allowed herself to be kissed, but did not offer a salute in return; her eyes were unnaturally staring; and her hand when Magdelon pressed it felt cold and dead. She made, too, no more than a perfunctory response to the latter's eager greetings.

Magdelon, however, full of her new resolve, refused to be discouraged by a listless welcome. She said very little about Candale. For one thing, she had not been in her sister's confidence concerning that affair. It was, of course, impossible to ignore it entirely. 'I know how sad you must feel, just now,' said Magdelon, glancing obliquely at Cateau to see how the opening would be received. 'I quite understand your not wanting to go out. People can be so odious, can't they? I thought, though, perhaps you'd let me take you for a drive this afternoon? It's a beautiful day; the sun's almost warm; and I've a dozen errands to do, after being so long in the country.'

'Oh, very well,' replied Cateau, without enthusiasm. 'I'd as soon go with you as not; it doesn't matter what I do.'

This was certainly not a promising beginning. But at least Cateau could be induced to leave the house, which was the principal point to be gained.

Magdelon, congratulating herself on her tact, said nothing more about the purpose of the drive until they were actually in the carriage, bowling along in the winter sunshine towards the river. Even then, she introduced the subject of the soothsayer casually, as if it were of no particular importance. It seemed that there was a woman called La Trianon, who lived on the Pont Marie and was said to be marvellous at telling fortunes. Everybody was going to her. She had been sent for by the court more than once to amuse the Queen and her ladies, and had told them all most remarkable things. . . . La Trianon was an adept at palmistry and crystal-gazing, and had also been known to supply efficacious love potions to young ladies who were not yet assured of their gallants' affections. It was wonderful, really, what she was able to do in that line — take the case of Mademoiselle de Fouilloux, for instance, and the Marquis d'Alluye . . .

Magdelon went on to describe several striking examples of the
seeress's powers, without, however, mentioning the chief of the lady's
abilities, that which had especially endeared her to the Maréchale
de la Mothe.

'Of course it's all nonsense, I know,' she concluded gaily. 'I
dare say there's not a word of truth in these reports. After all, look
at Maman and her spooks! Still I thought it might be amusing to
hear what she'd tell us. What do you say, darling? I've got her
address from Louise de la Mothe: shall we run down to the Pont
Marie and call on the creature?'

Cateau raised her eyebrows and frowned; it was the first sign of
feeling she had given since her sister had seen her.

'Oh, my dear,' she said, 'that sort of thing is so awfully silly,
don't you think? I'm not in the least credulous, are you? I mean,
really, it's all very well as a pastime for children — but we're grown
women, we're married, we're done for — what on earth can there
be for us to find out? Everything's happened already that's going
to happen to you and me.'

Having thus expressed her opinion of fortune-tellers in general,
Cateau said no more. She remained silent and scornful during the
rest of the drive. Magdelon was afraid that she might refuse to
leave the carriage. But when they reached the entrance to the
bridge and the driver had been bidden to halt, Cateau made no
audible protest and followed her sister meekly.

'I believe it will be best for us to walk from here,' whispered
Magdelon. 'I don't want them to see our coach in front of the
house. We'll be incognito, of course — that's so much more fun,
don't you think? You be Madame Dupont, and I — I'll be Madame
— Madame Leroy. What fun! Now come quickly, dear, before we
run into anyone we know!'

The house of La Trianon was a tall, narrow one in the middle of
the Pont Marie. Like most of the others on the bridge, it was old,
a crazy half-timbered structure with a pair of tourelles sprouting
like horns at each end of its high-pitched roof, and chimneys
dilapidated and sadly askew.

It looked, in short, precisely like the kind of house a sorceress
ought to have. Inside, however, it had been modernized and bore
a banal resemblance to the dwellings of most Parisian bourgeois.

'Madame Dupont' and 'Madame Leroy' were ushered by a
melancholy manservant in conventional livery and a slightly moth-
eaten wig through a series of small tapestry-hung antechambers —
which smelled as if they had not been aired out for years — into a
larger apartment at the back of the house. This was filled with a
haphazard collection of gilt drawing-room furniture; an immense
oak cabinet standing in one corner, which was surmounted by a

stuffed owl with yellow glass eyes and menacing outspread wings, was the only unusual piece in the room.

Here they were abandoned by the melancholy manservant, who announced in a hoarse voice that 'Madam' would be with them shortly.

Cateau and Magdelon sat side by side, holding hands, on a hard gold sofa upholstered in worn Chinese-blue silk.

The room was very still after they had been left alone in it: they could hear nothing but the soft, steady wash of the river, flowing below them round the heavy stone piles on which the bridge was built. Now and then a small block of ice would break away with a creak and a groan from the frozen mass in the middle of the Seine and bump into the piles before setting forth on its journey down-stream.

There was nothing in the least alarming, so far, about La Tria-non's establishment, but Magdelon could not help recalling, with a shiver, as she sat there tightly clasping her sister's hand, the stories she had heard in her childhood from the servants at La Louppe about magic and those who practised it. Maman had always been frankly interested in the subject; there had been an old woman in the village whom she had frequently visited and who had been re-ported to possess 'second sight.' This old woman was supposed to have been seen several times flying about the churchyard after dark. Ugly rumours spread through the parish about the curious disappearance of various unwanted children amongst the peasantry: in the end, the old woman was accused of being a witch, and it had taken all Maman's powers of persuasion, as well as the impregnable protection of the castle walls, to save the wretched hag's life.... Magdelon was quite sure she did not really believe in such things, any more than Cateau did. Still there was an awful fascination about the very idea of the 'black arts'.... And this woman, this La Trianon, now ... Could one be certain she was not a criminal? How easy it would be to dispose of a body in a house so conveniently placed over a swift-running river!... Ah, had they been foolish to venture here?

The door opened, and 'Madam' came in.

La Trianon was a stout middle-aged woman, with masses of blond hair that looked false and lifeless like a doll's, a round face, very flushed (it was so heavily powdered that it appeared almost purple), and bulging grey eyes, which seemed unable to focus properly. She was dressed in a handsome green quilted taffeta gown with a too tightly laced bodice that creaked a little when she walked, and wore a number of sparkling rings on her pudgy fingers.

She entered the room almost running, breathing heavily — no

doubt on account of the bodice — and then stopped short, to peer
nearsightedly at her visitors.

'Madame Leroy?' she said, in a resonant voice, whose dragging
Picard accent was belied by her native briskness of manner. 'I
have the powder you were asking for. It comes rather high —
rather high, I'm afraid — that couldn't be helped, you know. I did
my best for you, but some of the herbs were hard to get hold of.
I don't know what's got into my people lately. A good powder of
succession used to be a very simple matter, but since the war everything's doubled in price.'

'I beg your pardon,' said Magdelon shyly. 'I think there must
be some mistake. Perhaps you are thinking of another Madame
Leroy? I — I've never been here before. I — I'm from Lyon; my
husband is a merchant in the silk trade. And this is my sister,
Madame Dupont.'

'Tut, tut!' said La Trianon, raising her bushy black eyebrows
(which did not look as if they could belong to the possessor of the
flaxen doll's hair) and pursing her full red lips. 'I am at fault, then.
Excuse me, ladies — no offence meant. I see so many people, you
know — just in the way of business — that it's hard for me sometimes to keep their names straight. I ought to have a secretary,
that I ought! And then my eyesight's not what it used to be —
dear, no! I'm shut up in my laboratory so many hours at a time,
I'm blind as a bat in the daylight. Well, ladies, what can I do for
you? Do you need a good headache remedy, or a pill 'gainst the
vapours? Or how about one of my longevity syrups? I've perfected
an admirable one in the last fortnight, that's guaranteed to add not
less than thirty years to the span of your natural life. I spent
weeks evolving it from an original recipe I had from an English
alchemist who lived last winter in Paris, and worked under me for
some months. An interesting man, by the way! — though most of
his formulas turned out quite valueless: this was the only real
success in the lot. The syrup is perfectly safe; even a child can take
it! The old Dean of Westminster used it for years, and died only
the other day at the age of one hundred and sixty-six. Positive fact,
I assure you! ... But that's not, I surmise, what you ladies are after?
You wouldn't be interested either in my complexion balm? ... No,
of course not; I can see that quite clearly, blind as I am. . . . A love
philtre, perhaps? I've two excellent brands that have proved successful in the most obstinate cases. . . . Or even . . . well . . .'

La Trianon lowered her voice mysteriously and paused to examine her patrons with a bright clinical interest, as if to say: 'Anything within reason, my dears . . .'

Magdelon, after waiting a moment to see if Cateau were going
to say something, stammered, blushing: 'Oh, we — we just wanted
to have our fortunes told.'

'Ah?' said La Trianon, looking a trifle disappointed. 'Of course.
A very simple matter indeed. How would you prefer to have it
done — cards, crystals, or palms, if you please?'

'Why — we hadn't thought... I don't really know. Which
would you advise?'

'Well, madam, it all depends. On general principles, if no especial
help is required, I always say, try the cards first. They're interesting
and informative, and one often gets hold of surprising little facts
that prove extraordinarily helpful. At the same time they're safe,
couldn't alarm the most sensitive mind. The crystal, now, is more
on the spiritual side. I can't undertake *that* without a certain
amount of preparation — and for the best results there's no denying
the sitting ought to take place after dark. But for a truly scientific
summing-up of character, there's nothing to be compared to a reading of the palm. Lips may lie — and faces, too — but hands can*not*.
They tell the whole truth. If you've the courage to listen to that,
why, I've no hesitation in recommending you to have your palms
read at once, without bothering with any little preliminaries. It's
all one to me, ladies: my fee is the same in any case — one hundred
francs, payable in advance.'

Magdelon paused, glancing once more at Cateau, as if waiting
for her to take the lead; but Cateau averted her eyes and obstinately
refused to speak.

'We'll have our palms read, then,' Magdelon said, as firmly as
possible. 'Sister, would you like to begin?'

Cateau shook her head. 'No,' she said. 'Have your fortune
told, dear, if you care to. I don't want in the least to hear...'

La Trianon, who from the first had been markedly more aware of
Madame Dupont than of Madame Leroy, fixed her bulging eyes on
Cateau and nodded her head several times.

'Ah, I see how it is,' she said cheerfully. 'Madam, I take it, is
incredulous. That I could tell from the moment I entered the room.
Perhaps madam would prefer to leave before I begin the reading?'

'Oh, no,' said Cateau, shrugging her shoulders. 'I'll stay and
hear what you have to say to my sister. It may amuse me, at any
rate.'

'But you cannot believe — is that it? Yes, I thought so. Very
sad, very sad. Never mind, my dear: maybe I'll be able to convince
you of my powers in spite of yourself. Some seeresses object to an
hostile influence in the room — they say it obstructs the spiritual
forces that flow through the atmosphere — but to me it's a matter
of absolute indifference. Very well, then, madam' — to Magdelon.
'Let us begin at once, if you're ready. Will you seat yourself in
this chair, whilst I take my place here on the opposite side of the
table? — so! Now lay both your hands flat, palms up, if you please,

and remain quite still, so that I may concentrate on the problem before me.'

Magdelon, laughing a little and blushing even more rosily than before, complied with La Trianon's request. Before sitting down she produced her purse and laid the prescribed fee in gold-pieces on the table. La Trianon paid no attention to the money. At least, she refrained from pocketing or even touching it; but Cateau thought that the protruding eyes managed to add up the sum, all the same.

The seeress's guesses, if guesses they were, fell astonishingly close to the mark. She dwelled upon Madame Leroy's kindness and candour, love of pleasure and innate simplicity, all of which, she asserted, were strongly indicated in the lines of the young lady's palm. 'But then,' said Cateau to herself, 'it's there in her face, for anyone to read!' From these fundamentals La Trianon passed into the realm of pure speculation.... Magdelon was married to a man many years older than herself, who had many years yet to live. But other men also would love her — a great many other men! 'And you, too, madam, will love many times. You will love as often as you are loved. It is a heart all affection and passion, that feels an imperative need to give everything it has to give, again and again.... Yes, there's no doubt of that.'

'Dear me!' murmured Magdelon, looking more embarrassed than ever. 'Are you sure...? I don't really know...'

'But I do,' said La Trianon calmly. 'It's all here, madam, quite clear before me.'

She went on to expand her theme, weaving a tapestry with threads so gay and diverse that she might have been telling a tale out of one of Mademoiselle de Scudéry's romances; while Magdelon listened with parted lips, smiling like a child, half amused, half convinced, in spite of her reason, that these marvellous adventures were going to come true.

A ray of late afternoon sunshine slanted through the window over the river, falling full across the smiling face — but Magdelon did not heed it. She was enraptured, lost in a fairy kingdom of which she herself was the queen.... Poor little girl! Of course, she could not really place any faith in such balderdash; no grown woman could. Cateau, listening impatiently, while she tapped a restive foot on the floor, thought how silly it was, and yet could not help admiring La Trianon's astuteness in inventing precisely the sorts of details most likely to appeal to Magdelon's naïve, undeveloped imagination.

'... and you will have six children, three boys and three girls — and you will live to a ripe old age,' concluded La Trianon brightly, straightening up in her chair at last and pushing the untidy hemp-

like blond curls out of her eyes with a gesture calculated to express
an unwilling return to the prosaic world about her.

'How perfectly lovely!' exclaimed Magdelon. 'Shall I, really?
How can you tell?'

'It's indicated in your palm very plainly, madam,' said La Trianon, with a touch of severity. 'Your life-line is of an exceptional
length.'

'But how old shall I be exactly when I die? Can you tell that?
I've always wondered...'

'How old? No, I can't say, to a year or two. Four score, maybe —
maybe more. It depends on other influences still to be determined.
All I can tell you with certainty now is that you will have a long
life — very long — but not so long as you would wish.'

'Not so long as I would wish! What do you mean? Why——'

'That's *all* I can say,' said La Trianon, with finality.

There was a minute of absolute silence. Magdelon sat looking
down at her hands in bewilderment; nothing was heard but the slow
swish-swash of the river beneath them and the creaking complaint
of the ice. Then Cateau rose without warning from the gold-and-
blue sofa and approached the table deliberately, fixing the seeress
with challenging eyes.

'You pretend to know the future, don't you?' she said.

La Trianon's purple cheeks flushed darkly through the thick
layers of powder.

'Madam, I pretend nothing. I *do* know it.'

'Very well, then,' said Cateau insolently, drawing off her gloves.
'If that's the case, how long shall *I* live? Tell me that, if you will.'

La Trianon smiled. 'Has madam changed her mind? Will she
follow her sister's example and have her fortune read?'

'No, no,' said Cateau. 'I don't care to listen to nonsense. Besides, it's too late — my day's over — there's nothing you could
say that would interest me, except this: I've some slight curiosity
to learn the probable span of my life.... Here, look, if you want
to....'

Abruptly she thrust out her slim white hands, so like Magdelon's
in both size and shape that only a palmist could have told them
apart.

La Trianon seized them eagerly and held them to the light, displaying far more interest than she had done over Madame Leroy's.

'Now *that's* what I call a truly repaying pair of palms!' she exclaimed, with a note of genuine excitement in her loud voice. 'My
dear, the possibilities are unlimited — absolutely unlimited! Do
sit down and let me see——'

'I want to hear only one thing,' said Cateau stonily. 'Shall I
live to be old? Quick! Tell me...'

'Old? I should say so! My dear, you'll outlive your whole generation. There's practically no end to that life-line of yours. I'd
not be surprised if you reached the century-mark!'

Cateau tried to snatch her hands away, but La Trianon held
them firmly in her plump grasp.

'Your life will be as long as you wish,' continued the latter, speaking fast in order to get in all she wanted to say. 'Even longer,
perhaps. Yes, I can see that distinctly. But, dear madam, what a
curious fate! Here's a long life, and a prosperous one — even
longer and more prosperous than your sister's! Here are lovers by
the score, all helplessly under your sway.... But — can it be? —
you love none of them in return. Fie! What a cold heart it is!...
No, wait a minute: I see I have made a mistake. You do love
once in your life — or, rather, I should say, you *have* loved once;
for, unfortunately, the affair appears to be finished. Yes, that's it:
you have been parted most cruelly, either through death or another
kind of separation almost as final; for I don't see you meeting again
this side of the grave. Ah, madam, my dear, I fear your friend's no
longer in this world! Alas! But he's thinking of you still, wherever
he is. Yes, he's thinking of you, and he wants to speak to you.
There's a message he has to deliver, an important message.... Only
wait, and I'll try to get it for you. Yes, he says himself it's very
important. Please, madam, don't take your hand away — don't,
I beg of you! How can you expect me to hear ——'

Cateau, pale as wax, wrenched herself free and ran to the door.

'I won't have any more!' she said. 'I won't, I tell you! It's all
nonsense. Come, Magdelon, we've wasted too much time here already.'

Magdelon, looking frightened and remorseful, rose hastily to
follow her sister. As she went out she had a final glimpse of La
Trianon still sitting beside the table, breathing heavily, a strange
half-smile on her thick red lips.

The two young women scarcely exchanged a word on their way
home. When they arrived at the Hôtel d'Olonne Brossard handed
his mistress a note: it was a line from the Count, announcing his
return from Poitiers on the following day.

Chapter IX

OLONNE DID NOT ARRIVE IN PARIS UNTIL RATHER LATE IN THE evening.

Cateau, who had no way of finding out when to expect him, spent an uneasy day of suspense, listening for the fateful sound of wheels in the quiet street. Too restless to settle to anything, she paced the floor of her rooms for hours on end.

Like many frivolous and wilful people, she had reached what seemed to her an impasse in her life: there was nothing to be done save retreat, with as much caution as possible, and attempt to start out in an entirely new direction. But who was there to advise her which way to turn? . . . For the first time since she had married him the figure of her husband had assumed serious significance in her eyes. How was she to tell him what she would have to tell him? And what would he do when he had heard all she had to say? — for Cateau had decided, after thinking the matter over for days, that the best way to begin would be to make a full confession of sin. It was her duty to confess, she said to herself, thrusting into the bottom drawer of her mind the unhappy conviction that, if Olonne did not hear of her plight from her own lips, he undoubtedly would from someone else's.

Everything considered, Cateau hoped that it might not be too late to save the situation. If she were not interfered with — if she could see him before any of her enemies had a chance to do so — she felt fairly confident of her power to present the case in the light most favourable to herself. No one, however, could answer for Olonne's reactions. He had never betrayed his jealousy openly — but then, Cateau had never admitted anything up to now. She had deceived him, it was true, for years; but Olonne had often seemed to be pushing her, half against her will, into the way of temptation; and he at all times had acted as if he had wanted to be deceived, as if it were immaterial to him how she behaved, as long as he were left to pursue his peculiar ideas of pleasure in peace. Determinedly he had evaded, over and over again, every opportunity for making a scene. They had quarrelled, of course, often enough, like most husbands and wives — even indulging in occasional face-slapping and hair-pulling (there was that time at the Baths of Bourbon last summer, when they had come to blows over her gambling debts) — but it had always been for some trivial cause.

Here at last was an issue that could not be evaded, that demanded to be dealt with at once in decisive fashion. . . . Ah, what would he do? What would he do? Would he storm and scold, as he sometimes did over nothing at all? — or assert his manhood by beating his wife with his own bare hands? Perhaps he would lock her up in her chamber and feed her on bread and water. He might even go to the length of exiling her temporarily to one of his country estates. However he chose to act, no one would blame him, for a husband's right over his wife in these circumstances was absolute. His duty, too, was clear: he must avenge his honour, and speedily. Candale was dead, beyond reach of vengeance. Therefore, nothing remained but to discipline the erring woman.

Cateau told herself she was resolved to meet unflinchingly whatever fate was in store for her. She supposed it was right that she should be made to suffer. To tell the truth, she really *wanted* to suffer. It seemed to her that, if the penance imposed were heavy enough, it might assuage the grief still gnawing at her heart.

By the time night had fallen — darkly and stormily, with a sharp wind that rattled the windows and raced through the streets and blew the snow from the branches of the bent elms and plane trees in the garden — Cateau had succeeded in working herself up into an appropriately melodramatic mood.

The Count had not got back in time for dinner, so she countermanded the meal and ordered a late supper to be prepared instead. Then she repaired to her dressing-room and made an elaborate toilet. She donned a robe of simple black velvet, unrelieved save by a cross of pearls on a plain gold chain gleaming softly against a bosom only a little less white. Her hair she pulled back into a severe classic knot, unfashionable but becoming to her regular features, and vividly reminiscent of a portrait she had once seen of Mary Stuart on her way to execution.

Thus attired, there was nothing to be done but await, with what patience and self-control she could muster, the return of her lord.

It was shortly before midnight when the Count's carriage rolled up to the door. Cateau descended the stairs slowly, with great dignity, followed by Quentine and Quinette, who were vaguely excited, though they did not know why.

The three women met Olonne in the entrance hall. Cateau motioned to her maids to remain in the background and, advancing to the centre of the room, sank to the floor in a stately curtsy.

Olonne bowed and smiled with his customary politeness and said: 'That you, my dear?' (Though who else could it possibly be?) He was, however, so busily engaged in superintending the disposal of his luggage that he neglected to give his hand to his wife to help her rise, so that Cateau was obliged to get up unaided, which she did with the suspicion of a flounce.

The Count appeared unaware of the unfavourable effect of this small omission. He stamped his feet several times, to make sure that he was carrying no snow into the house on his boots — for the rug in the hall was Persian and priceless — and remarked good-humouredly: 'My God, what a trip! I'm as tired as a dog. I hope, my dear, you've some supper prepared?'

Camille, the maître-d'hôtel, who had been standing respectfully beside Quinette and Quentine, waiting for an opportunity to greet his master, hurried forward with a deferential smile and began reciting the menu.

'Salmon — and a leg of lamb — excellent, my good Camille, excellent! Let it be served directly. I'm starved to death after a fortnight in the wilderness. Shocking food in Poitou — positively shocking! Nothing to be had anywhere but ragoûts, which are death to a delicate stomach like mine, as you know — and I wasn't able to turn up a single bottle of Ay or Auvilé, the whole time I was away! What do you say to that? Oh, I've suffered, I can tell you! Shall we proceed to the table at once? Madam, you'll give me the pleasure of your company, I hope?'

Olonne led his wife to the dining-room, which was blazing with candles as if for a feast. Cateau, too full of what she intended to say to offer any objection, took her place across the board from the Count and sat there, brooding and preoccupied, while a bountiful meal was served. She herself ate almost nothing, but her abstinence could cause no comment, for it was her invariable custom to diet rigorously.

Nor did Olonne seem to be so hungry as he had declared. Although he helped himself liberally to the contents of each dish that was passed, he ate only a small portion of what was on his plate; presently he waved away the sweet and pushed his chair back from the table, as if the thought of more food were distasteful.

All during supper he had kept up a stream of remarks, detached bits of information concerning his trip and the various trials arising from his duties as Seneschal of Poitou. So-and-so was a stupid ass. ... Somebody-else was a crook and a rogue of the deepest dye. ... What's-his-name had made a devil of a mess with last year's tax reports. These and other similar items, each in itself depressing, Olonne delivered in his usual cheerful staccato style, as if they had been the best news imaginable. He remained, too, deliberately unconscious of Cateau's unresponsive silence until Camille had brought the nuts and raisins and a platter of sweetmeats and had set decanters of rare old liqueurs in front of his master. ... There were rossolis and ratafia and some especially prized fenouillettes from the Isle of Ré.

But finally, as soon as he had made certain that they were alone, the Count glanced at the rigid figure in black on the other side of the table, and remarked unexpectedly: 'My dear, you look pale. Have you been ill?'

It had come, then. Merciful Heavens, what should she say?.... Cateau had spent a good part of the day preparing a diverse selection of introductions to her admission of guilt, but now that the time had arrived to speak she could call none of them to mind. She felt frightened and confused; tears started to her eyes; she remembered only the sorrow that had been caused by her irreparable loss.

'Oh, sir,' faltered Cateau, 'I am a most unhappy woman! I have sinned — and I have been punished for it.'

Olonne's reception of this avowal was disappointingly noncommittal. He neither changed colour, nor averted his eyes, but began cracking the pile of nuts in the dish before him with the single-minded industry of a squirrel, laying the kernels as he extracted them in an orderly row.

As he did not choose to speak, Cateau continued, after a moment: 'My husband, I must ask your pardon for what I have done. Have you heard that the Duc de Candale is dead?'

Olonne nodded, still without speaking, and went on cracking nuts busily, as if that were the most important business in life.

'It has broken my heart,' said Cateau, tears now streaming down her face. 'Sir, I cared for him very much. And he cared for me. We were lovers. For three years I have had no thought for anyone save him. It was wrong — I knew that — but I could not help myself. My feeling for him was stronger than my sense of duty to you. Oh, sir, forgive me, if you can — and know that I truly repent of my fault!'

She had meant, at this point, to fling herself at her husband's feet and clasp his knees in a graceful gesture of submission. But, now that she had said what she wanted to say, she seemed incapable of physical action. She sat where she was, quite still in her high-backed chair, while the tears coursed unchecked down her cheeks — the first tears she had shed since Candale's death.

Olonne's indifferent expression did not change; yet Cateau was sure, from the way in which he fiddled with the nut-kernels, arranging and rearranging them in little patterns on the polished surface of the table, that he was cruelly embarrassed. When at last he spoke his voice sounded toneless and remote.

'I am glad that you have told me this,' he said quietly. 'I have known it for a very long time, naturally — but you were right to tell me. That's as it should be — the only thing that *is* so in this miserable business.'

Cateau bit her lip and made a valiant attempt to keep from sobbing aloud.

'Sir, you knew . . .?'

'Madam, how could I help knowing what all the world did? I trusted you too far. I have been partly to blame for what has happened.'

Cateau covered her face with her hands. Whatever she had expected from Olonne, it had not been this. Whatever he had been in the past, there had been nothing in his conduct to lead her to suppose he would be reasonable now, magnanimous even. His magnanimity put her at a terrible disadvantage; broke down her defences, made her weak when she most needed to be strong; worst of all, it reduced her to hysterical weeping, which was something she had never been forced to before. In all their life together Cateau had not once let her husband see her cry. It seemed to her that she must regain control of her nerves, even at the cost of provoking his anger.

'Yes!' she cried out. 'You have been very much to blame. You never loved me as you ought to have done — never — *never!* I have been lonely — you'll never know *how* lonely! Do you wonder that I turned to others for the affection that was denied me at home? that I gave someone else what *you* never asked for?'

This sounded so well that, greatly encouraged, Cateau proceeded to compose variations on her principal theme, painting a picture of neglected merit and long-suffering virtue so plausible that, as she talked, she began to believe it herself. She traced her tribulations from the early days of her marriage, when Olonne, as she said, had 'abandoned' her for the army, to the present, freely acknowledging and blaming herself for her guilty connection with Candale, but mentioning neither Beuvron nor Paget nor even Jeannin de Castille. She did this only partly on purpose, for these last endless grief-stricken weeks had almost succeeded in convincing her that there had been only one man in her life. The others no longer counted; therefore, it was as if they had never existed. . . . By the time Cateau had finished her speech — which appeared more and more like an accusation instead of a plea and in which, carried away by the force of her own eloquence, she had said a good deal more than she meant to say — she had very nearly recovered her poise. Moreover, she could see that her words had had the desired effect on Olonne. The little man was no longer apathetic; his face had grown flushed; sparks flashed from his blue slits of eyes; and the hand that was holding his wineglass grew white from the strength of his grasp round its stem. As soon as she had ceased — which was not until she could think of nothing more to say — he brought his other hand, tightly clenched, down on the table so hard that the rows of nut-kernels bounced off it and went skipping all over the floor.

'Zounds, madam! Lies — all lies!' shouted Olonne. 'I wonder you've the face to sit there and brazen 'em out. Besides, even if they were the truth — which I deny — they don't excuse you. Damme if they do! A man has a right to believe in his wife — he has a right to trust in her virtue — if she's a decent woman instead of a hussy! Oh, my father was right: he warned me before I married you what would happen. He knew what you were long before I did. He begged me not to make such a mistake — but I was blind — *blind!* I was determined to have you, no matter what came of it. By Heaven, when I think . . .!'

Here Olonne, in his turn, embarked on a fiery tirade against women in general, and his erring wife in particular, delivered in a choked and snarling voice, while his eyes wandered everywhere in the room except towards Cateau's face. It was almost as though he were talking to himself. . . .

Cateau did not move. She sat with bowed head and quivering lips, scarcely even hearing his insults, and repeating over and over, as if it were a charm: 'Sir, I loved him. . . . I loved him too well. . . .' And indeed it seemed to her that she had never known until that moment how much her love had meant to her.

When the Count had exhausted alike his breath and his vocabulary he stopped talking suddenly in the middle of a phrase, like a run-down mechanical toy.

There was a painful pause. Then Cateau rose from the table and kneeled at his feet, as she had intended doing all along.

'All that you say of me is true,' she said, with simple nobility. 'I admit it. I have been a wicked woman. Deal with me as you will; nothing you do can abase me lower than I am now in my own estimation.'

She remained kneeling for several minutes, waiting to hear her sentence delivered. As she did so she felt the first faint stirring of pity for Olonne. She had not listened to his string of profane reproaches, but she was glad that he had been capable of them, since they proved he was not so completely indifferent to her as she often had feared. It had been right for him to express his feelings as he had; now it would not have seemed amiss to her if he had struck her in his wrath, or dragged her round the room by her hair. That was his privilege as an injured husband. Anything — even physical violence — would be better than this unnatural silence.

As it continued unbroken Cateau ventured to steal a look at him: his face was still very much flushed, beaded with sweat, and he was panting slightly, as if he had been running a race. But even as she watched him he appeared to be slowly returning to normal. When at length he spoke his voice was not hoarse nor angry any more; it had resumed its characteristic unaccented monotone.

'That's enough of that,' said Olonne. 'I'll not refer to it again.'

'Oh, sir,' said Cateau, who was still on her knees, 'what are you going to do? Am I not to be punished?'

'Do? What should I do? How can I fight a duel against a dead man? As for punishing you, madam, I fancy you've been punished enough already. You have forfeited my esteem, but you are still my wife — and in future, as long as you remain conscious of the duties implicit in that position, you may be assured of the protection of my house and name. Only mind: if there is a recurrence of your false and scandalous behaviour, I shall be the first to hear of it — the first, d'you see? — and you must be prepared to accept the consequences of your act. I'm not quite the fool you take me for. I may not dog your footsteps like a paid spy — but I've my own methods of finding out what I want to know.'

Cateau got up from the floor, once more resentful that she should be forced to do so without her husband's assistance. The great scene was over — and she felt somehow that it had been robbed of its climax. Was it perhaps because, though they both had been angry and had spoken their minds, they had not been angry at the same time? Whatever the reason, something vital had been lacking — but there was something yet to be said, if she could find the words to say it. She fixed her luminous eyes, still wet with tears, on her husband's face.

'I pledge you my word, sir,' she said, 'that I shall be prudence itself. I have been, I own, greatly at fault. But indeed, indeed, it would never have happened, believe me, if you had continued to love me as you did when we were first married! Oh, if you knew how I've hated living alone . . .!'

'Alone, madam? I don't know what you mean. I've my manner of living: you've yours. What's pleasure to you spells boredom to me — and t'other way round. Why must we be eternally chained to each other, like galley slaves, just because we are man and wife? No, no, girl: you go your way, and let me go mine — and if you've the wit to comport yourself as you should, you'll find me lacking in neither appreciation nor sympathy. Now let's have no more of this disagreeable business. I trust I'll not have to refer to it again. It's very late — time we were both abed. Come, madam, I'll attend you to your chamber.'

Olonne rose and, blowing out all the candles on the table but one, seized it in his left hand and gave his right to his wife — and together the Comte and Comtesse d'Olonne quitted the dining-hall and ascended the curving stairs.

Outside his wife's apartment Olonne bowed low over her hand, and kissed it formally, as if nothing untoward had occurred between them.

'Madam, I wish you a very good night.'

Cateau threw him one last desperate look, in which were mingled pity and contempt and a mute, imperative appeal for something he had too often withheld from her — but as she did so she realized that it was already too late. The moment that might have brought them a new understanding was past — and everything was as it had been before. She could no longer even try to find the word she had been frantically seeking all evening, the word that, only a few minutes earlier, had seemed to promise a solution to their problem.

Slowly she turned and entered her bedroom.

FOR THE FIRST TIME IN YEARS MADAME D'OLONNE TOOK NO PART IN the carnival. An infected foot, which had troubled her, off and on, all winter, served as an excellent pretext for eschewing the gaieties of the season. She saw no one for several days but the doctor and her maids, not even her husband, who sent Crispin, his valet, each morning to knock on the Countess's door to inquire how his mistress did, but otherwise left her to her own devices.

At first Cateau could not stem the flood of her tears. They had been dammed up so long that, when at last they were able to force their way to the surface, there seemed to be no means of stopping them. She cried and cried, until her face was red and her eyelids discoloured and all her handkerchiefs were used up and no more tears would come. She cried so hard and persistently that, finally, she forgot what she was crying for: her grief appeared to have become an end in itself.

But once the tempest was spent she realized it had been a good thing. Gone was the icy clutch of pain that had held her heart in a vice. She felt tired and languid and agreeably void of emotions; it was a comfort to reflect that everything had happened to her that *could* happen: henceforth there would be no cause for either hope or fear.

Nor, on the whole, had her beauty suffered. She called for her handglass one morning and gazed long and curiously at the reflection therein, with as much objective interest as if it were a stranger's. Her face was startlingly pale and remote, like the face in an old portrait-drawing; but affliction had not altered the pure perfection of its outlines: her hair was no duller, her eyes, for all the tears they'd shed, were no less blue than ever.

Marvelling that this could be so, Cateau wisely resolved, then and there, to lock her sorrow away in her breast as for so many years she had locked the Duke's picture in her jewel-casket. The best part of her life was over, she told herself; to the end of her days she would mourn poor Candale and grieve for what was lost — but still, one had to go on living.

Sighing gently, she handed the looking-glass to Quentine and said, with a faint smile, that she would like a cup of beef-tea....

Yes, thank you, she really felt a good deal better today; she intended, unless Doctor Patin forbade it, being carried into her sitting-room after dinner to spend the afternoon on the couch by the fire.

After that, signs of improvement were numerous. It was still some time before the foot was entirely healed, but meanwhile the Countess began to look and act very much more like her old self. Although she declined to preside over her husband's receptions, she ordered an elaborate new afternoon gown of turquoise satin and Valenciennes lace and, thus splendidly attired, was at home to a few privileged callers in the yellow cabinet.

The first to be admitted was Madame de Fiesque, whose devotion had not wavered through the weeks of her exile, and who was delighted to run in to sit with her friend whenever the dissipations of the carnival permitted. From Gilette Cateau heard the latest news of the court, which lost nothing in its transmission through this lively narrator. There were many matters of importance to be discussed: to begin with, the première of the King's new ballet, *Alcidiane*, in which the airs by the young composer Lully (known to society as 'Baptiste') had been much admired. Then there was the extraordinary behaviour of the Queen of Sweden, who had appeared uninvited at a private ball — dressed in her usual outlandish fashion, half male, half female — and sent the company into fits of laughter by her uncouth style of dancing. And there were odd bits of gossip about various personages of the day: the social ambitions of the stout, vulgar Maréchale de l'Hôpital . . . the interest of Monsieur, the King's brother, in Miss Gordon, the Queen's Scotch maid-of-honour . . . could it be that the young Prince might forsake his pretty boy companions for a woman at last? . . . and the former's quarrel, on that account, with his belligerent Cousin de Montpensier. . . .

On such subjects Gilette was invariably informative and amusing.

By degrees other people managed to slip away from Olonne's drawing-room to spend a few minutes upstairs with his charming wife. Mesdames de Montglas and de Montmorency appeared together, frankly curious to observe how poor dear Catherine-Henriette had stood her ordeal. If, however, they had come to spy, they stayed to applaud and to envy their friend her unfailing attraction, which was all the more seductive for a hint of fragility.

Magdelon was there, also, as often as she could be without attracting her husband's attention, though she tried to choose hours when she would not find too many other visitors, being still as shy as in her girlhood of anything resembling cleverness.

There was no doubt that Cateau's circle was very witty and almost frighteningly advanced in its views.

The Marquis de Sillery and his nephew, the Prince de Marsillac, were amongst her most assiduous courtiers. Sillery was an old friend, and in his rôle of mentor to the Prince (whose father La Rochefoucauld was a martyr to gout and misogyny and had not gone out in years) was charmed to be able to introduce the young man on an intimate footing at the house of the reigning queen of fashion. Another uncle-and-nephew combination frequently to be seen in the yellow cabinet were the Chevalier de Gramont and the Comte de Guiche, who were both enrolled on the list of Gilette's official adorers, but whom that lady had treated so casually that it was no wonder they had begun to grow restive under her sway. And Saint-Evremond, whom Cateau scolded severely for what she called his 'betrayal' of her in his now celebrated elegy, sometimes came, too.

As time went on even Beuvron was added to the group. Cateau had decided, after much consideration and the insistent pleading of his Cousin de Fiesque, that it might be as well to allow him to resume his former place in the household. After all, she had been fond of him as a friend many years before he had been her lover; Olonne liked him as well as she did and had never, thanks to Beuvron's tact and discretion, suspected the true state of affairs, so that there was actually less risk involved in receiving him than in creating a situation by forbidding him the door.

The one person whom she steadily refused to see was, not unnaturally, Jeannin de Castille. She had felt she owed it to Candale's memory ... It was incomprehensible to her that Jeannin could not view things as she did. In the midst of her illness the treasurer of the Savings-Bank had sent her what Cateau considered, in the circumstances, an offensively impertinent note. She had thought, at first, of replying to it in kind, but sagely reflected, later, that she had never written to him even once during their brief, accidental liaison, and that, as long as he did not possess a single line from her hand, he would be powerless to harm her. She therefore sealed the letter up again and returned it to its author as unread, and when Jeannin called at the Hôtel d'Olonne, shortly afterwards, he was informed by Brossard that the Countess was not at home.

On the last day of the carnival Magdelon drove over late in the afternoon to ask her sister's opinion of the costume she was going to wear at the masquerade. The weather was dismal; night was already closing in, although it was only four o'clock. For some reason, however, Cateau had ordered the heavy yellow brocade curtains left undrawn, so that the wintry court with its bare trees and, beyond it, the windmills on the Butte Saint-Roch were dimly visible. Everything — trees, windmills, the roof of the wing on the other side of the court — was thickly covered with snow, which looked soft and insecure, as if on the point of sliding to the ground. (There had been a slight thaw earlier in the day.) Inside, though the candles had not yet been lighted, the room was cheerful with firelight and gay with the voices of the Countess's guests.

Magdelon noticed with relief that the gathering was smaller than usual, owing no doubt to the distractions of the carnival.

Gilette de Fiesque, garbed as a pilgrim, with a wide-brimmed hat and a tall ebony staff, was revolving complacently in front of a long mirror, while she explained at the top of her voice that she was waiting for her cousin Beuvron to call for her: they were planning to begin the evening with a drive to Vincennes — would that not be too, too exciting? — stopping on the way back at Chancellor Séguier's, where a large company was expected. But there were so many balls, tonight... the Sullys', the Montglas', the Bullion-Bonnelles' — one could not really remember them all.

Sillery and the Chevalier de Gramont were playing piquet at a small table in front of the fire: the former's clever fox-face was crinkled with laughter, which did not prevent him from keeping a watchful eye on his nephew Marsillac, who sat on a stool at the feet of their hostess.... Poor Marsillac! It did not take a clairvoyant to tell what was the matter with him. His solemn silence, his undeviating stare, the candid blush on the smooth young cheeks were sufficient proofs of his sentimental predicament.

The Comte de Guiche, who had lately shown symptoms of developing into Marsillac's rival, had placed his chair as near to the other's as possible. He, too, was looking at the Countess, but there was no distress in his gaze — admiration, yes; but it appeared to be directed towards his own charms quite as much as towards those of the lady. At barely twenty Guiche was already a bridegroom of two weeks' standing. His bride, however — poor little thirteen-year-old Mademoiselle de Sully — could claim but a small part of his time and attentions. Flirt smiled at the world from the Count's big dark eyes; his wealth of gay ribbons, the too-glossy sheen of his scented curls, betrayed the dandy; while an assured poise of manner underlined his social competence and overweening self-satisfaction. Only his voice — a flute-like falsetto, with such an agreeable way of saying malicious things that it almost succeeded in removing their sting — seemed scarcely manly enough to sustain the dignity of the eldest son and heir of the great Gramont family.

Cateau, between her two gallants, but sublimely unconscious of them both, lay almost full-length on her couch in a picturesque pose, one foot peeping coquettishly out of a swirl of laces, her golden head flung back in characteristic abandon. Her laugh, loud and jarring, contrived, as always, to dominate the surrounding babble of voices, and brought Magdelon to a halt on the threshold with an uneasy realization of how many weeks it had been since she had heard it. Magdelon was a little hesitant, anyhow, about making her entrance. She hung back as long as she could, though she felt she really looked very well in her pretty Greek costume, which was copied after that of the heroine in the new play *Astiniax:* her curls were piled high and bound with a silver fillet; she carried a spear and shield of silver, also.

The Chevalier de Gramont, facing the door, was the first to catch sight of the new arrival. He clapped his hands and cried gaily: 'Bravo! Here's Diana herself! Welcome to our midst, divine goddess!'

His nasal buffoon's voice caused a general laugh, which gave Magdelon the courage to come in. She curtsied shyly to the gentlemen, who rose and bowed in return, Marsillac hastening with comic anxiety to recover his post by Madame d'Olonne's couch before Guiche could pre-empt it.

'Dear madam, you've come just in time to advise us,' said the Marquis de Sillery, who had sat down again, as soon as Magdelon was seated, to finish his hand at piquet with Gramont. 'We've been desperate trying to make up our minds what to do this evening. It's Shrove Tuesday, as you know: tomorrow Lent will be upon us, the season of sackcloth and ashes. (Pic, Chevalier; that adds thirty points to my score.) Doesn't it seem a pity to waste it indoors? Unfortunately, Madame d'Olonne cannot be persuaded to smile on our projects. Perhaps *you,* dear Maréchale, may succeed where we've failed, and induce her to reconsider her cruel decision.'

'Oh, but ——' began Magdelon; and then she stopped, not knowing how to express her opinion. She had been about to say that this did not seem to her an appropriate moment for Cateau to make her re-entry into society; surely it would be wiser to wait until after Easter and be seen first at some stodgy reception at the Louvre?

Cateau quite possibly was thinking the same thing, for she shook her shining head and said positively: 'No, sir, I will not go out tonight. But because I remain at home there's no reason why the rest of you should miss your pleasure.'

There was a chorus of protest at this. Marsillac, greatly daring, ventured to say, with a tender look: 'Madam, where you are not, pleasure vanishes!' — after which he blushed scarlet and choked, while Sillery snapped his fingers and clucked with annoyance over his nephew's awkward manner of paying a compliment, and Guiche snickered shamelessly at his rival's discomfiture. ('Dear boy — *so* sincere!' he whispered behind his hand to Gilette. 'What a pity he's not on bowing terms with the Graces!')

'Nonsense!' said Cateau, not even bothering to smile at the

Prince (a very bad sign!). 'You've got along quite well without me up to now.'

'Oh, but darling!' screamed Gilette, pirouetting about so that the folds of her smart crimson taffeta cape took the air. 'This is different! It's the last night, you know, the very last one of all! We'll be simply miserable if you don't come.'

'You can disguise yourself so that no one will recognize you,' added Sillery. '(Repic, Chevalier; that's sixty points more.) Why not all be pilgrims together?'

'Fie, Marquis!' snapped Gramont, slapping down his cards in a pet. (What was the use in cheating so cleverly if your opponent contrived to win, after all?) 'How dare you suggest the eclipse of a beauty the whole world adores? If Madame d'Olonne will trust herself to *me*, I'll undertake to devise a costume that will serve as a suitable frame for the most famous charms in France. Rely on me, madam; I'll not disappoint you.'

'Yes, uncle,' said Guiche, in his coolly ambiguous accents, 'that is all very well; but time presses, does it not? If we are going to mask ourselves, it is high time we were setting about it. And no one, so far, has made any definite proposals as to what we shall be. *I* certainly don't intend to waste the opportunity! This, you might say, is my wedding masquerade, though I'm bereft of my partner — dear Marguerite has by now, I trust, been safely tucked up in bed by her nurse!... and I am determined to do something splendid for our hostess's sake.'

Cateau looked about the circle of eager faces and smiled indulgently.

'Children, you're all very kind,' she said; 'but my mind is made up: tonight the Comtesse d'Olonne remains at home.'

In the middle of fresh expostulations a knock was heard at the door, which opened, disclosing the Comte d'Olonne.

Everyone stopped talking immediately. It was his first appearance in the yellow cabinet; most of Cateau's friends knew that there had been some trouble between her and her husband; but none of them, not even Magdelon or Gilette, realized that the couple had met but once since Candale's death.

Olonne entered the room stiffly self-conscious, with his neat, clicking steps; he saluted the men and bent in turn over each lady's hand — his wife's first of all. Magdelon remarked as he did so that his cheeks seemed puffy and unusually pink and his eyes had a fixed look, as if he had been drinking heavily. His utterance, however, was as fussily precise as always.

'Well, well, ladies and gentlemen, what have we here? 'Tis almost five o'clock, time for the masks to be assembling in the Cours Saint-Antoine. Why are you not on your way thither? I've sent my own guests packing a good hour ago. Madam, my sister, I perceive that *you* are on the point of joining the revels: what a ravishing costume! Quite in keeping with the Greek spirit! And you, too, madam' — turning to Gilette — 'never, I swear, have I set eyes on so gallant a pilgrim! Let your fellow wayfarer, whoever he may be, beware lest some wandering swain abduct his fair charmer in the thick of the crowd. But as for the rest — now, really, I am ashamed of you all! What, no masks? No piquant disguises? My dear Catherine-Henriette, is this *your* fault? Have you deliberately chosen to hold your friends in subjection to your peevish whims? Nay, this must not be!'

'Sir,' said Cateau tranquilly, 'I have done my best to persuade them to go. There's no reason on earth why they shouldn't.'

'Save, I surmise, that they will not leave you, and you have doubtless refused to accompany them,' said her husband. 'But, my love, why should you not make one of the troop? You've lain abed long enough; already you've missed far too much of the fun.'

'Sir, I dare not,' said Cateau, frowning a little. 'My foot is still but just healed. How could I trust my strength to bear ——'

Olonne swept this objection aside.

'Madam, if you prefer, you need not walk a step. There are courtiers aplenty at your service — I speak, I dare say, for all of you gentlemen — to see that your feet do not once touch the ground. Why, I'll do more than promise their aid: I'll join the maskers myself this evening! What do you say to that? To please you, I'll conquer the aversion of a lifetime and brave the mob in the streets of this noisiest of all cities on Shrove Tuesday night. Will you deny that's a gallant offer?'

Cateau frowned again, but not at Olonne: she had not, her sister perceived, yet faced him directly.

'I could not think of troubling you, sir ——' began Cateau.

'Trouble? Why, nonsense! It would be a pleasure and a privilege, I assure you. With you by my side, my dear, I'll renew my youth.'

'But we've no costumes prepared. It would be impossible on that account, sir, even if my health permitted me to leave the house. Really, you don't know what you're saying . . .'

Olonne rubbed his pudgy pink palms together and cackled delightedly.

'I've thought of that, too. Now confess that I'm cleverer than you ever imagined! This morning, when I made up my mind to go masking tonight, I said to myself: "We shall have to do something quite out of the common." Yes, dash me! I knew your aversion to ordinary dominos: your charms and your taste, my dear madam, were a real challenge to my powers of invention. 'Twould not be sufficient to trick you out in velvets and jewels, as if for a ball at court, for your own beauty puts such banal adornments to shame. No: what I wanted was something quite new and original, and so daring that it would be sure to make this masquerade of ours an event never to be forgotten. I pondered and pondered, for hours in vain. But at last I hit upon what I was seeking. Crispin, bring in the costumes I've designed for the Countess's party.'

The valet, who had evidently been waiting in the hall just outside the door, now made his appearance carrying a big brown bundle, which he deposited on a table before disappearing as silently as he had appeared.

For a few moments nobody spoke. In the dim light it was almost impossible to make out what was in the bundle. Then Magdelon, who stood nearest the table, gave a gasp as she saw that it was made up of a number of monks' and nuns' robes, the drab corded habits with peaked hoods worn by the order of Capuchins.

The Count held one of them up for the company's inspection.

'Neat and simple — not at first sight especially striking to the eye,' he declared. 'But I can assure you, ladies and gentlemen, that all who go with me tonight will be famous throughout Paris by tomorrow morning. Now, who's bold enough to try his luck in this mad adventure?'

Still nobody spoke for an appreciable time. Then suddenly, as if a spell had been broken, everyone started talking at once; a mounting storm of excitement and curiosity was let loose in the yellow cabinet. Madame d'Olonne's guests appeared to be vying with one another to see who would be the first to try on one of the deliciously daring costumes. The Chevalier de Gramont, seasoned intriguer that he was, almost came to blows with Monsieur de Sillery, who, though the eldest person present, seemed even more eager to be a ringleader in the mischief; the latter proposed, to end their dispute, that he and his friend should add the further confusion of sex to their disguises by donning the nuns' robes instead of the monks'. (He was, however, just prudent enough to forbid his nephew to join the party, although poor Marsillac pleaded with tears in his eyes.... 'Oh, please, my uncle, only this once!...') The Comte de Guiche, who as a married man was free from his relative's jurisdiction, and was charmed to discover this unlooked-for opportunity to steal a march on his rival, had already slipped into one of the gowns while the others were arguing. Now he was twittering with glee and pluming himself as he demanded if he did not look 'too fascinating for *words*, my dear.'... Gilette loudly lamented that she and her Cousin de Beuvron could not cast in their lots with the band, since they must soon be off to the Hôtel Séguier.... Only Magdelon was at all scandalized by Olonne's proposal. Surely Cateau and Brother Louis would never really dare....

Cateau, heedless both of her sister's shocked eyes and of the hubbub about her, sat aloof, not committing herself one way or the other. Privately she thought the whole thing rather silly. But, after all, did it make any difference to her what happened now? Her life was finished. If Olonne had taken it into his head to play the fool, why should she not do so, too? Perhaps it might help her to keep from thinking too much. Besides, what a relief it would be to escape for one whole evening from Marsillac's burning glances! That unfortunate youth's behaviour had lately become extremely annoying. She could tell well enough, tongue-tied as he was, what he wanted; and if she had not guessed, Sillery's odious insinuations would have made it quite clear.... Bah! The young calf! She'd have none of him. She was through with *that* sort of thing forever.

So Cateau jumped up without warning and said: 'I'll go!' and then stood still to allow her husband and Sillery to dress her. Soon she was chatting and laughing as gaily as anyone in the room; by the time they were ready to leave her spirits had apparently risen so high that she had resumed her old position of leadership in the company. But just before they streamed downstairs to the waiting coaches she called for a glass of wine: when Crispin had fetched it she drank it hastily, and called for another, and drank that, too. She felt, all of a sudden, terrifyingly cold; it seemed to her that, no matter what she did, she could never manage to get warm again.

Chapter XI

THE COMTE D'OLONNE HAD BEEN PERFECTLY RIGHT WHEN HE PROM-
ised that all who took part in his masquerade would be famous
within twenty-four hours. The 'Shrove Tuesday Scandal,' as it
was spoken of for years afterwards, had the town in a turmoil
even before the evening was over.

Of course, the conspirators had realized from the start that it
was a risky business. That had been part of the fun. And, as things
turned out, it had almost been worth it. What a merry time they
had had, whirling about through the slush and snow of the streets,
in the pallid light of a waning March moon! How amusing it had
been to run in at this house and that, to toss down a glass of wine
and romp through a few dances, while hosts and guests stared
aghast — and then flit away with shrill laughter and mocking
salutes before they could be unmasked and identified! The Sullys
were appalled at the sudden invasion of their ballroom by the brown-
hooded troop; the Montglas were terrified; Madame de Bonnelle,
whose party was the gayest of all the carnival routs, fainted dead
away, while her husband crossed himself at sight of the impious
crew and vowed to forswear champagne and claret during Lent —
he really preferred Burgundy — for surely these must be appari-
tions from the spirit world? ... His theory would have gained
wider credence had not one of the monks, brushing past Monsieur
de Turenne on the great staircase, placed a hand momentarily in
the Maréchal's horny grasp — a hand made of living flesh, slim,
white, and graceful. And later in the evening the same monk had
been surprised deep in a flirtation with Monsieur, the Duc d'Anjou
— which caused such an outburst of shocked whispers that the
King himself had been forced to interrupt the dialogue and drag
his protesting young brother away, leaving the ambiguous monk
dissolved in fits of mundane and obviously feminine laughter.

So they were not ghosts, after all. Everywhere the maskers were
buzzing excitedly: 'Have you seen the Capuchins? My dear, did
you *ever* ...? Have you the *least* idea ...?'

For several days the queries received no authoritative answer.
Then, all of a sudden, everyone seemed to have heard the names
of the guilty parties. Nobody, apparently, was able to say for

certain who had betrayed them. It could not have been Magdelon
or the Prince de Marsillac, both of whom had close relatives impli-
cated in the affair. Gilette de Fiesque, the only other person who
had actually seen them dress, swore volubly, with her hand on her
heart, that she had not breathed a word — but *naturally* she had
not!... And none of the Olonnes' servants had been in the secret,
with the exception of the ever-reliable Crispin. Really, it was a
mystery how the rumour had started.

However it happened, the fact remained that the week was not
out before the particulars of the masquerade were common gossip
in every drawing-room from the Place Royale to the remotest
corner of the Faubourg Saint-Germain.

The commotion it caused in ecclesiastical circles was astounding.
With the beginning of Lent it had become fashionable to go to
church a great deal — and here, under the clergy's collective noses,
was an ideal subject for a sermon on the iniquitous tendencies of
the day. Every preacher in Paris fulminated against this wicked
travesty of religion; the whole order of Capuchins, especially,
was up in arms, and sent daily deputations to complain to Cardinal
Mazarin. Worse than all, the Queen Mother and her set of court
bigots joined with vigour in the crusade.

With age, Anne had grown increasingly pious. She spent many
hours every day praying in her oratory, reading dull devotional
books in Latin and Spanish, and driving about with her train of
elderly dowagers from convent to convent, where she indulged in
long, soul-satisfying, confidential talks with various popular
prioresses.

This powerful cabal threw up its hands in horror at the sacrilege
committed. After talking the matter over with her confessor the
Queen decided to speak to the King about it. She had never thought
well of Madame d'Olonne since the incident of the immodest ballet
costume; in addition, the affair of the stolen bellows, three years
ago, had fanned smouldering disapproval into flaming resentment,
so that she was gloomily pleased to observe that her blackest suspicions about that young woman had been amply confirmed....
'The Olonne is a creature devoid of honour and conscience,' declared Her Majesty, with a steely glint in her pale grey eyes; and
the group of timeworn scarecrows surrounding her nodded their
heads and made ticking sounds with their tongues to express complete agreement with their sovereign.

The young King, at twenty no Puritan, had nevertheless been
brought up in a strict observance of the outward forms of religion.
Like nearly everybody else, he had been sincerely shocked by the
masquerade, so that his mother had little difficulty in arousing his
anger against the culprits. Divers suitable punitive measures were

discussed in turn. There was talk of imposing heavy fines on the ringleaders ... of exile ... at one moment, even of petitioning the Pope to pronounce a sentence of excommunication. While these dread possibilities were being debated most of the maskers thought it tactful to disappear temporarily. The Chevalier de Gramont sailed very suddenly to England 'for business reasons.' Sillery retired to his brother-in-law's castle of La Rochefoucauld near Angers; and the young Comte de Guiche recalled opportunely that his family's estates in Béarn, many miles to the south on the Spanish frontier, really required a thorough inspection.

Only the Olonnes, who had most to fear, refused to fly before the gathering storm. The Count, inert by nature, had never paid any attention to what happened at court; in the past, indeed, he had often seemed to take a positive pleasure in braving its disapprobation. His life had been laid out according to his own highly personal tastes, and was lived quite as if the Louvre had not existed. As for the Countess, she applauded Olonne's independence of spirit; it was the one quality he possessed that she truly admired; and husband and wife had never been so close as during these dangerous days. It even occurred to Cateau that perhaps he had organized the masquerade on purpose to show the world they were still a united couple, in spite of reports to the contrary. As long as she could persuade herself that this might be so she felt kindly disposed towards the strange little man she had married. For a brief moment they actually appeared to be hovering on the verge of a real understanding, such as they had not had since the days of their courtship. What if, after all, *this* were what had been needed to bring them together? Cateau held her breath, incredulous yet hopeful.

Unluckily, Lent could not last forever. The preachers grew tired of preaching; the people, of being perennially scolded for other folks' sins; even the Queen and her friends, having slaked their thirst for vengeance in profitless talk, turned to newer pastimes — and gradually the great 'Shrove Tuesday Scandal' was forgotten. The Olonnes were forbidden to come to court for six weeks after Easter, which, as they had frequently gone a year without setting foot in the palace, could not be considered a crushing punishment.

With the removal of the imminent peril the pair's sense of solidarity vanished almost overnight. Olonne returned to his guests and his gaming, while Cateau had no choice but to solace herself with the callow admiration of Monsieur de Marsillac, the sole diversion that offered itself for the moment.

The Prince was still fatuously in love with her. Cateau found him, alas! no less dull than before; she would probably never have changed her mind about him, had he not unexpectedly acquired a new lustre by becoming engaged to his cousin Madamoiselle de la

Rocheguyon, the granddaughter and heiress of the old Duc de Liancourt. The match was an excellent one for the impoverished Marsillac, whose father had ruined the family fortune in the civil wars: the fiancée was young, pretty, and exceedingly rich; it was a disappointment to the gossips not to be able to say a word against it.

But the mere fact of the young man's now being the acknowledged property of someone else gave him a piquant attraction for the world-weary Madame d'Olonne. What his uncle's campaign of thinly veiled hints and his own weeks of silent, ardent devotion had been powerless to accomplish, came about in a trice, at a time when he had quite given up believing in the possibility of his good fortune.

Cateau took him as a lover partly out of boredom, partly out of indignation at her husband's neglect of her, but mostly out of a spirit of bravado. People said she was a 'terrible woman': very well, then, she'd give them something to talk about! With calculated carelessness she insisted on advertising the liaison by appearing in public everywhere with Marsillac: he was her constant companion in the Cours, at the play, and on various small excursions to the country which the beginning of spring had made possible. Not even his official betrothal, and the pompous ceremony of the signing of the marriage contract — an act almost as binding as the wedding itself — could keep the bemused young man from following his mistress with the unreasoning fidelity of a pet spaniel.

His family were outspokenly annoyed by his actions. What they had eagerly sought, only a few weeks ago, as the finishing touch to an oddly belated sentimental education, had now become unsuitable, if not something very much worse. Old women tittered and whispered behind their fans when the lovers entered a drawing-room, and her 'best friends,' Mesdames de Montglas and Montmorency at the top of the list, looked askance at the Olonne and wondered openly 'how her husband put up with it'.... But Cateau paid no heed to her detractors. She carried her blond head triumphantly high — having invented a new way of dressing it that was immensely becoming — ordered half a dozen alluring silk gowns, and went out driving in the park every afternoon in the English coach, while Marsillac rode his bay mare at her side, as securely attached as though held to the carriage by invisible cords. (Ah, what was the use in remembering another rider, and other springs, *now?*...) Let the old hags talk their tongues tired! Even her worst enemies continued asking her to their best parties, because they knew, if they left her out, that none of the attractive men would come.

Apparently, judging by Cateau's crowded engagement calendar, no one was nearly so shocked by a simple case of adultery as they had been by the carnival masquerade.

No: the difficulties of the situation came not from without, but from within. Since she had accepted Marsillac as her lover, it became a matter of pride with her to hold him well in hand; and as the weeks passed Cateau began to find him hard to manage. Marsillac loved her as violently as ever; possession had not yet had time to dull the edge of his passion; but unfortunately it had sharpened his sluggish wits. He became frantically jealous; it took all the tact and skill at her command to steer a safe course through the turbulent rapids of his adolescent emotions.

Cateau succeeded in doing so, and also in contriving to have her own way most of the time in spite of everything — but there was no denying that it was tiring, and perhaps more trouble than it was worth. In fact, the whole spring had been spoiled by several mishaps, all trivial enough, but adding up to a sum total of surprising proportions. The stupid fuss over the masquerade and Marsillac's trying tempers were only two in a string of annoyances. For instance, Quinette suddenly took it into her head, at Easter, to marry one of the Count's footmen and leave her mistress's service; and when Cateau remonstrated with her, and asked her why she wanted to resign such an excellent post, the silly girl only blushed and hung her head and faltered that if you please, madam, she was in love. . . . In love! What utter nonsense! Cateau, in a pet, had slapped Quinette's face as hard as she could; then burst into tears, begged her little maid's pardon contritely, and pressed a purse with fifty gold louis in it into her hand as a marriage portion. ('But what was the *matter* with me, to behave so, over nothing at all?')

Then, the week after that, out of a clear sky, Olonne decided to bring suit against his brother-in-law, the Maréchal de la Ferté, over some question of property settlement. The sum involved was ridiculously small; the Count spent more in a month on solicitors' fees than he could hope to gain even if he won the case, which was doubtful. He was doing it, Cateau was sure, just to make himself disagreeable: haunting the courts of the Palais de Justice, engaging in lengthy but inconclusive conferences with his steward and secretaries, and receiving a perpetual stream of lawyers and lawyers' clerks and laden messengers, that sped daily back and forth between the Cité and the house in the rue Neuve-Saint-Augustin.

Both Cateau and Magdelon thought the whole business too foolish, but they were helpless to remedy matters, as neither had any real influence over her husband. Whatever the outcome might be, their principal irritation was due to the impossibility of appearing in public together while the men of their families were engaged in litigation. Not that they would have cared much what people might say — but Olonne and La Ferté had strictly forbidden it; and a husband who was powerless to prevent his wife from breaking her marriage vows had full authority to stop her from seeing her own sister. It was absurd as well as maddening — but what could one do?

The two young women wrote to each other constantly; and Cateau sent her nephew Henri a handsome gold mug on the occasion of his christening, which took place with much magnificence at the church of Saint-Eustache towards the middle of June, shortly after the Maréchal had left for Flanders to command the army. Magdelon wrote back to acknowledge the gift, saying that the baby had behaved extraordinarily well. So had the godpapa, old Monsieur de Senneterre, who might easily have proved a problem. On the contrary, Maman, who had insisted on standing as godmother — there had seemed to be no way of avoiding it, as she had delayed her departure for the country a fortnight on purpose to witness the ceremony — had been 'terrible'.... Cateau could imagine that; she longed for a good gossip with Magdelon. How infuriating it was not to be able to rush to her at once!... for her letters, though better than nothing, were as awkward and inexpressive as they had always been.... Ah, men ... *men!* The trouble they made in this world...!

Cateau tossed her head as this thought ran through her mind. Young Marsillac, sitting at her feet in his accustomed post by the couch in the yellow cabinet, looked up to ask anxiously: 'Darling, what's the matter? What are you thinking of?' — and remained only partly appeased when she stroked his hand and murmured, quite truly: 'My dear, it's nothing you'd care to hear.'

She had had scant patience lately to deal with his thundercloud moods, so that it was a relief to be able to say, as she detected signs of a possible tempest brewing, that she had made plans for the evening for them both: they were expected at a concert at the Choisy's.

Madame de Choisy, who in her usual rôle of social barometer had held aloof from the Olonnes all winter — no doubt with the object of waiting to see how badly they were going to be disciplined by the court — had recently made friendly overtures, which Cateau was disposed to accept. Why bear a grudge, after all, when it was a question of finding amusement? — and the Choisy's house was always delightful to go to, especially now that she had moved to the other side of the river and occupied a charming apartment in the Luxembourg Palace.

On their way to the party Cateau and Marsillac stopped to pick up Monsieur de Vineuil and his lady-love, Margot Cornuel, two of their newer friends. Vineuil was the Duc de la Rochefoucauld's secretary and an amateur literary man, a pleasant little fellow with a nervously placative smile and an air of just not noting down your epigrams on his cuff for future delivery as his own. And Margot Cornuel, who was the stepdaughter of old Madame Cornuel, the witty bourgeoise of the Marais quarter, was as bright as her redoubtable relative and a good deal better-tempered; she was a laughing, lively girl with saucy violet eyes and not too many scruples. Of course, neither she nor Vineuil was quite . . . But then standards were much less rigid since the war, and Cateau was beginning to find it convenient to cultivate people who had not known one long enough to know all about one. Besides, Margot was intimate with the La Rochefoucaulds, and this intimacy served Marsillac in good stead; for now he and his mistress were able to meet when they liked at the Cornuels'.

Madame de Choisy's party was in full blast by the time they arrived. It was the last assembly of the season before the final detachments of the army left for Flanders; the big, light, handsome rooms were gay with the scarlet and gold of the officers' uniforms. As the evening was unusually balmy, even for June, the tall windows at the back of the house had been left ajar, to permit the guests to wander out into the gardens; the clipped lime allées were bathed in warm moonlight and a-tinkle with high, happy laughter that mingled with the crystal splash of the fountain in the great basin behind the palace.

The Choisy greeted the newcomers with shrill screams of pleasure, but also with a rapidly glazing eye: there were too many people present for anyone to arrest her attention more than momentarily.

Cateau, moving slowly towards the centre of the room, felt rather than saw Marsillac stiffen defensively at her side. She could not imagine what the matter was, being constitutionally insensitive to atmospheres other than that created by her own personality: and Marsillac only muttered something unintelligible through his teeth when she asked him to explain. However, she was enlightened by Margot Cornuel, whose round rolling eyes saw at times even more than they were intended to see: the latter had hardly entered the house before she halted, hunched up her shoulders with the air of a fastidious cat drawing back before water, and ejaculated, not at all in a whisper: 'Humph! She's collected every sodomite in Paris!'

This, of course, like most of the things Margot Cornuel said, was a gross exaggeration. Nevertheless, Cateau, following the direction of her friend's glances, spied the smartly dressed Abbé de Boisrobert, rouged and bepatched in spite of his age, coquetting in a corner with the hostess's son, the fragile young François de Choisy, who was frankly wearing a woman's wig and long diamond earrings. Next to them, a pale, saturnine youth, the Duc de Nevers, paid assiduous court to the Marquis de Manicamp with his curious

flat features and feline grace. There were a number of other exotic
couples scattered here and there amongst the company, but the
king of the little troop, who received the lion's share of their languishing looks, whilst remaining himself elusive and unattachable,
was the Comte de Guiche.

The discovery gave Cateau a merely momentary shock. She had
not seen the young man since his return from Béarn, and she had
never thought much about his morals, one way or the other; it was
a matter of indifference to her what people did when she was not
with them, as long as her own life was not affected by it. So now
when the Count, catching sight of her, at once ceased his dragonfly
flittings and hovered over her hand with a smile and a tender salu-
tation — all the more tender by reason of Marsillac's glowering
presence! — she smiled back with bland affability and, as the music
was about to begin, allowed him to find her a seat.

Guiche stood for several minutes leaning over the back of her
chair in an attitude of flattering devotion, while Cateau presented
her familiar smiling mask to the room. When he was called away
by an agitated signal from his hostess, Margot Cornuel, who was
not musical, hitched her stool up into the vacant place and enlivened the progress of a somewhat cloying instrumental trio by
pouring into her friend's ear a lengthy whispered account of what
she called contemptuously 'the old hen's new campaign.'

It appeared, according to Mademoiselle Cornuel, that Madame
de Choisy, whose ruling passion throughout her life had been to
play a part of consequence at court, had lately observed her position
slipping. She, who had once been a prime favourite with both the
Queen and the Cardinal, had grown steadily less popular as they
all three grew older: her looks had long ceased to be an attraction,
but, what was more serious, her perennial giddiness seemed sadly
out of key with Anne's pious preoccupations. His Majesty, too,
found her ornate last-reign style of wit forced and out-of-date;
there was, therefore, no one else in the royal family on whom she
could concentrate but the King's brother, Monsieur, the Duc
d'Anjou. The way to *his* heart had been easy to find: at eighteen
that important young man was a child still, caring for nothing but
bonbons and trinkets and pretty clothes. He would spend hours
before a glass adorning his smart little person, or devising coiffures
and toilettes for his mother's maids-of-honour; but it was well
known that his real inclinations were not towards the opposite sex.
... There, also, Madame de Choisy had not scrupled to pander to
the peculiar tastes of her new hero.

'Things have got to such a pass,' declared Margot, 'that the
Queen's forbidden him even to speak to Guiche — so what does the
old harridan do but contrive a series of secret interviews for Mon-

sieur and his perfumed pet — as if Guiche were some singing girl from the Italian theatre! Oh, my dear, the things I could tell you ...!'

Cateau stopped smiling long enough to yawn delicately behind her fan. She was not particularly impressed by what Margot was saying. After all, what difference did it make if a few highly specialized individuals could take no interest in one's charms — when there were all the other men who not only could but did? So: 'Does it matter?' said Cateau languidly.

'Well, dear,' replied the astute Margot, 'only in this way, of course, that it's made a minority party at court, just as in the time of the old Monsieur, the King's uncle. All very well, if one cares to go in for that kind of thing — but I should think, shouldn't you? that the Choisy was old enough now to have given it up. She's sure to get her fingers scorched for her pains sooner or later, and as far as I'm concerned I'd like to see it happen sooner — vain, interfering old parrot! ... My dear madam, what a treat you have given us! I vow, Lambert never played more divinely!'

This last was addressed to their hostess, who had hardly been able to wait for the music to stop to start weaving her tortuous way amongst her guests, pausing now and again to glean as many compliments as possible on the success of the entertainment.

Cateau stayed at the party till late, and enjoyed herself very much in spite of Margot Cornuel's scathing remarks. Certainly there was no lack of impressionable young men to pay her extravagant homage, Guiche markedly foremost amongst them: it was diverting to flirt with him, just to see Marsillac frown and set his long, obstinate jaw with unconcealed jealousy.

Here Cateau went perhaps a little further than she had meant to do, in her amusement at the comedy her gallants afforded her. All the while she was strolling in the garden, laughing and waving her fan, she was faintly aware of a feathered head nodding benignantly from a distance; and when at last she sought her hostess to bid her good-night, Madame de Choisy's restless eyes became unglazed for the first time that evening, and she embraced her young friend with such enthusiasm that her crown of jewelled aigrettes sagged over one ear as she shrieked: 'Darling, it's been too sweet having you with us! Mind you come again very soon!'

During the following fortnight Cateau did, in fact, return a number of times. If it had not been for Madame de Choisy, the last half of June would have proved extraordinarily tedious; for Paris was, as usual, bereft of its men, who had all marched off to wage their annual campaign against the Prince de Condé and his Spanish allies on the Flemish coast.

The first news to filter back from the army was most gratifying.

Dunkirk was besieged by the French, and taken in short order. The Battle of the Dunes was another great triumph: in speedy succession Bergues, Furnes, and Dixmude fell before the victorious forces of Turenne, while the Maréchal de la Ferté began to advance with fresh troops, prepared to attack Gravelines, the most important citadel in Flanders.

The Prince de Marsillac had left to follow the latter, after a tender farewell scene with his mistress. The usually stolid and inarticulate youth shed a great many tears, tore his hair, and protested that he lived only for the moment of his return.... 'Ah, madam, have pity...!' Cateau did not weep. She patted his head and said that she would miss him very much — and yes, she would write to him every week — and no, she would not dine with anybody else.... 'My dear, how can you think...?' Smiling gravely, she performed her part in their final dialogue with a light but convincing touch. But all the time she was doing it, it seemed to her a heartless mockery, a mere burlesque version of the agonized partings of other Junes, when her lover rode southward to Spain instead of northward to the marshy flats of Flanders.

Besides, how ridiculous of Marsillac to exact these solemn pledges of fidelity, when there was obviously no one in sight worthy of exciting his suspicions! Poor, stupid fellow!... Paris was duller and emptier this year than it had ever been. Even the epicene young men had fluttered away like a flock of twittering, bright-coloured birds, with the fascinating Comte de Guiche at their head. (He had since received a slight but painful wound in the hand at the siege of Dunkirk, an accident that provoked lively expressions of dismay amongst his admirers of both sexes.)

Magdelon and little Henri were leaving for La Ferté-Saint-Aubin. The former had been somewhat out of health: she had had a miscarriage in May, and the doctors had ordered her to take the waters at Forges, later on in the summer. As always, of course, she begged her sister to accompany her, and — also as always — Cateau smiled noncommittally and said she would 'think about it.'

There was no reason now why she should not go, as Olonne's suit had been suddenly settled out of court — it had taken the personal intervention of the Cardinal to bring about an amicable solution — no reason, except that Cateau still cherished a stubborn aversion to life in the country.

So Magdelon, too, drove away with her son and her servants and her long train of wagons laden with clothes and furniture and provisions, and Cateau was left quite alone. There was no one to see and nothing to do; she would have had a very poor time of it indeed, but for Madame de Choisy.

As a matter of fact, Cateau soon found she was getting into the habit of calling on her old friend almost every afternoon. The Choisy was excellent company, as full of gossipy tidbits as the warm June nights were of stars: moreover, if there were any interesting bulletins from Flanders or travellers of note passing through Paris, they were to be found at the Luxembourg, which, as the residence of Mademoiselle de Montpensier, the King's cousin, in the King's absence was the nearest approach to the Louvre.

One day when the Comtesse d'Olonne had herself announced as usual, she was obliged to wait several minutes in the antechamber before being received. The house seemed pervaded by an unaccustomed air of excitement: maids were giggling together in the hall, notes being carried on trays to mysterious destinations by breathless lackeys; and although the door to it was tight shut, Madame de Choisy's private cabinet was obviously the centre whence the stir emanated — there was a great crackling of paper to be heard as well as the sound of voices raised in husky, purposeful whispers.

Cateau was just about to leave word that she would call again another day when the door to the cabinet flew open as sharply as though it were part of a mechanical clock and Madame de Choisy appeared on the threshold, dressed — although it was still early in the afternoon — in her best plum-coloured satin and decked with some rich strings of rubies Cateau had never seen before. As soon as the old lady perceived her visitor she pursed up her withered lips, tapping them archly with a folded fan, and with her other hand beckoned to Cateau with a gesture that somehow suggested a procuress in politics.

'Dearest!' cried Madame de Choisy, in a sibilant *sotto voce*. 'You've come just in time. *Who* do you think has ridden all the way from Calais to see us?'

Cateau could not imagine, nor did it greatly matter, in her present desert of boredom, as long as it was a man. Her mind explored a dozen possibilities with rapidity; she was, however, surprised and a little disappointed when she was ushered into the cabinet to find the Marquis de Manicamp seated in a big carved oak chair by the open window.

The Marquis was not in uniform, but was wearing ordinary travelling clothes, which were dusty and rather dishevelled, and a pair of high riding-boots with spurs. When he saw Madame d'Olonne he jumped up and bowed with alacrity, although he looked white and spent from the fatigue of the journey.

Cateau had never liked 'Little Manicamp,' as he was called, very much; his indifference to her beauty seemed a discordant note in the universal chorus of praise it inspired. He was Guiche's intimate friend, but possessed not a tithe of Guiche's charm; Cateau knew him to be oblique in his methods and suspected that he might easily be dangerous as well.

But she gave him her fingers with a graceful inclination of her head and the refulgent smile that had become with the years almost automatic: it was less a question now of impressing others than of holding untarnished her luminous impression of herself.

The young Marquis handed her politely to a chair next his own, and Madame de Choisy, with an air of comic self-importance, resumed the seat she had evidently just quitted behind her massive gilt writing-table.

Madame de Choisy's writing-table was a kind of cross section of her private life. It was invariably a litter of household accounts and half-written notes, bits of string and sealing-wax, partly woven tapestries, little books she meant to read some day when she had time for it, and sheaves of letters from various persons of international importance, such as the Queen of Poland and His Holiness the Pope, with whom she kept up an indefatigable correspondence. There was nothing the Choisy more dearly loved to do than flutter the sheaves alluringly as she chatted with a friend, pausing now and then to read an extract aloud and implying with considerable skill that what she allowed one to hear was a mere bowdlerized sample of what they contained, and that secrets of world-shaking significance lay embedded in the unshared pages.

Cateau, therefore, supposing that this time would prove to be no exception to her hostess's rule, composed herself in a pretty listening attitude and assumed a complaisant half-smile, though she was not really sure where Poland was and cared less, and could not for the life of her have told who was Pope.

But today Madame de Choisy appeared to have matters of even greater moment on her mind. She rolled her black eyes at each of her callers in turn, and hemmed and ha'd a number of times before beginning in a gusty stage whisper: 'My dear, I hardly know how to tell you.... This is an affair of the utmost delicacy, where a hasty word may work incalculable harm. Dear sir, perhaps *you* will be amiable enough to assist me in this emergency? After all, it was you who brought me the news; the story is yours to relate rather than mine.'

Manicamp's cool green eyes sparkled with suppressed animation, but otherwise he showed no emotion as he replied smoothly: 'Certainly, dear friend, as you wish' — and then, turning to Cateau, continued: 'Madam, I am in truth the bearer of grave tidings. You are doubtless unaware that His Majesty, our gracious Sire Louis XIV, lies desperately ill at Calais — nay, more, that at this very moment he may be at the point of death?'

Cateau exclaimed in amazement: 'Impossible, sir!'

Ah, pursued Manicamp, he, too, had thought so when the report had first reached him. It had seemed incredible that a young man of twenty, abounding in life and vigour, could be struck down in the very flower of his age. Yet so, he assured them, it was. The King had followed the army unscathed through the whole first part of the campaign; he had attended the siege of Dunkirk in person and also assisted at the various successful engagements that followed. Then suddenly — no one knew how it had happened — he had fallen ill of a fever, the day after the victorious Battle of the Dunes. Even the most skilled physicians were at a loss to account for the malady. Some thought he might have eaten tainted food, or exposed himself too long to the rays of the torrid June sun. Others were of the opinion that the situation of the camp at Mardick, where the officers were installed, was unhealthy — that flat, treeless green plain, surrounded by so much stagnant water.... Whatever the reason, he had apparently been unwell for several days before he was willing to admit his condition; and he had no sooner been put to bed than the illness took a frightening turn for the worse.... A deadly lassitude overcame him, accompanied by complete loss of appetite and a very high fever. He had then been transported to Calais, where the court was. Naturally, everything was being done that could be done. The doctors had tried every known remedy, including the fashionable antimony, to alleviate his distress — but so far in vain. The Queen Mother, poor woman! was frantic; she had not closed an eye for many nights. The Cardinal and all his immediate circle were in despair.... News of His Majesty's condition had been kept secret as long as possible, for fear of alarming the country needlessly; but now that his life was actually in danger concealment was no longer deemed advisable. Prayers were to be offered in all the churches of the land ... special litanies ordered at the cathedral of Notre Dame.... Manicamp had ridden post-haste from Flanders to report to the King's cousin, Mademoiselle de Montpensier, at the Luxembourg. He had just come now from an audience with the Princess, and had stopped for a word with his dear Madame de Choisy before retiring to sleep off his fatigue, for he had had a note to deliver into her own hands, a message of the highest importance from the Comte de Guiche....

'You understand, dear, of course,' put in Madame de Choisy, 'what this means to me. God forbid that our beloved sovereign should be snatched from his devoted subjects in the very dawn of his reign! But if such should be the will of Providence — and we must be prepared now for any eventuality — you realize that our dear Duc d'Anjou, our sweet little treasure, Monsieur, will succeed to the throne. Precious angel! I am sure nothing could be further from his thoughts at this time than ambition or worldly schemes for

the future — but we, who love him, must plan for him. All must
be made ready in advance to inaugurate the reign of His Majesty
Philippe VII.'

Here the old lady straightened her back and sketched the movement of standing at attention, as if the happy event she was antici-
pating had already come to pass. There was a short silence, during
which Cateau's face no doubt expressed bewilderment as to what
she had to do with all this; for presently Madame de Choisy went on,
with a touch of roguishness in her manner: 'My dear, it is clear to
me that much — I might say, *everything* — depends on surrounding
our adorable prince with the right sort of people. He must have
friends — devoted friends — devoted *women* friends, shall I add,
to make my meaning plainer? Oh, I know you will say that he has
me, and therefore who else is necessary? True, true, my love — but
alas! I am already too old to play the part in his life I might have
played, twenty years ago. No, no, don't deny it! I feel it is
so. Ah, when I glance in my mirror and think...! Watch over
him tenderly, counsel him wisely as I may, there is yet need of another sort of influence in his life, of some fresh young face to capture
that roving fancy and anchor those volatile affections. Our dear
Monsieur has never yet engaged in a serious gallantry: fancy that!
Naturally it is highly desirable that he should begin his emotional
life under the most favourable auspices — that he should, if possible,
be spared the heartaches and often fatal mistakes due to youth and
inexperience. Young men unfortunately are seldom prudent in
affairs of the heart. They are far too liable to rush ahead blindly —
to attach themselves without reflection to the first pretty face that
captures their fancy. How much cleverer, then, to confide the selection of one's *innamorata* to a third party — to some disinterested,
intelligent woman of the world — in short, dear, why not confess it?
— to *me!* I am very proud and happy to tell you that I have been
honoured with His Royal Highness's confidence for many months; he
has spoken to me freely of his hopes and fears; and now that apparently he is to be called to fill the first position in France, I feel deeply
impelled to assume the responsibility of choosing his confidante, the
friend of his bosom. As I cast about in my mind for a young person
qualified to occupy the post your name occurred to me at once, dear
child. You are young — but not too young! Made wise by experience — but not battered by it: oh, thrice-fortunate combination!
And you are universally recognized as the most beautiful woman in
Paris. Moreover, my dear — and this seems to me particularly important — you have never been identified with the King's set....
Those ill-bred, flighty maids-of-honour, for instance, I'd not consider
for a moment! No: when Philippe reigns I intend to encourage quite
a different atmosphere at court. There has been lacking there lately,

I regret to say, a tone of elegance, of easy civility, such as I remember so well, in my younger days, at the house of your cousin, the illustrious Arthénice — dear, wonderful Madame de Rambouillet herself! Ah, when I look back and contrast the company at those unforgettable receptions in the Blue Room with what's to be found in our salons nowadays... but that's neither here nor there, dear! Take my cherished Monsieur in hand, sweet friend. Mould him with skilful fingers, as only *you* can do. Lead him gently forward in the path of grace and duty on a chain of roses — and he will emerge from your schooling, I dare swear, the perfect and accomplished gentleman whom we who love him all long passionately to see.'

Cateau burst out laughing — she could not help it — at the close of this remarkable oration.

'But, my dear madam,' she said, 'what you ask is impossible — quite impossible... or don't you know...? His Royal Highness has no interest in women.'

Little Manicamp shot her a malevolent look from his cold, watchful cat's eyes, but said nothing. Madame de Choisy, on the other hand, bridled and blushed: such uncompromising candour of speech had been surely unknown at the court of the illustrious Arthénice!

'Ahem, my dear!' she said. 'Ahem! It is, unluckily, quite true that the dear Duke has not in the past entertained serious designs on the fair sex — but for his seeming coldness only his youth and natural timidity are responsible, I assure you. And our trusty friend Manicamp asserts that he and his ally, the Comte de Guiche, are resolved to see to it that Monsieur embarks on a career of honourable gallantry directly the court returns from Calais. Is it not so, sir? Have you not in your hands this minute a letter from the Count, in which he suggests the very alliance I've been proposing to Madame d'Olonne?'

'Madam, it is so,' said Manicamp. 'He writes me from the camp at Mardyck himself, in spite of the pain caused by the wound in his hand, to say that an attachment to the Countess is the very end we all most heartily desire to reach. As you know, his word is law, or something like it, to His Royal Highness, the Duc d'Anjou. Can you then doubt the success of our project? — especially as Guiche writes me that he has already observed definite signs of a dawning interest in you on the Duke's part, which he will of course make it his duty to foster. Madam, how can you refuse to lend us your aid? It is a glorious mission you are called upon to perform.'

After Little Manicamp had finished speaking he sat quite composed, only his baffling green eyes, darting unquietly from the old woman to the young one, and then back again, betraying his inner agitation.

No one said anything for a moment or two, and nothing moved in the room except the breeze blowing in from the garden, fresh and fragrant with the scent of roses and newly cut grass. It stirred the gold fringe on the stiff brocade curtains in the half-open window and ruffled the little curls, almost equally golden, on Cateau's white forehead. In the distance the fountain was splashing in the great basin and, still farther away, a pair of doves called to each other, lost somewhere in the dense green groves of the park of the Luxembourg.

How still it was! thought Cateau. How still and peaceful! One might think oneself miles away in the country, instead of just outside the gates of noisy, crowded Paris. She smiled vaguely at nothing in particular, while she made up her mind what she was going to say. . . .

It was not easy. Ever since one could remember the Choisy had been the centre of an elaborate system of diplomatic spider-webs, the threads of which she manipulated with amazing dexterity, considering that she possessed the two cardinal feminine weaknesses, garrulousness and susceptibility to flattery. But where did she, Cateau, fit into these subtle, shifting patterns? By what conceivable combination of circumstances had she suddenly become necessary to Madame de Choisy? . . . Naturally it would not do to take the report of Monsieur's nascent infatuation too seriously. Cateau had encountered the youth times without number at parties at court, on which occasions he had treated her with slightly timorous politeness, stood up with her once or twice in a ceremonial branle — that was all. She had not been piqued by his indifference, since she had seen that he was equally indifferent to every woman. (To be sure, there was the episode of their brief encounter at the Shrove Tuesday masquerade, when she had been dressed as a Capuchin monk — but ought that even to be counted? Cateau was not perfectly sure that he hadn't taken her for a man, all the time!) Monsieur seemed to her a flighty, unformed child, totally unimportant in the political scheme as he was in the world of gallantry. He had had no apparent chance of succeeding his much more robust elder brother, and he lacked both the personality and the talents to provide a rallying point for intriguers against the throne, who had swarmed about his uncle Gaston, the Duc d'Orléans, in the reign of *his* brother, the late king.

But now everything was changed. If Louis were really going to die, Philippe would be king — there was no help for it; and there would be no limit to his power or to the power of those who were clever enough to get into his good graces before his accession. As far as that went, Cateau did not care for power, herself. She was too lazy to exert herself, too uninformed and too apathetic to want to meddle in the affairs of the nation. Besides, that sort of thing was definitely dated. The antiquated wire-pullers of the Fronde had had no successors.

On the other hand, it was well to remember she had been in disgrace at court since the tiresome to-do over the carnival masquerade. There was nothing that vixenish prude of an Anne had not thought of, to try to get her into trouble: she had spoken in the nastiest possible way to the King and the Cardinal, made every effort to have her exiled, betrayed her personal animosity so plainly that, as long as she lived, Madame d'Olonne could never be sure of her footing again. How droll, therefore, it would be . . .

As Cateau's musings reached this point she turned for the first time since she had entered the room to face Little Manicamp and, in so doing, caught sight of herself in the tall glass on the wall of Madame de Choisy's cabinet. Inquiringly and with a kind of impersonal appreciation she gazed at the charming image reflected therein — at the long, supple lines of her figure in a becoming gown of lime-green taffeta and lace — the translucent pallor of her ivory skin — the proud poise of her little head with its cascade of shining curls mantling her splendidly sculptured shoulders. There was not, assuredly, in all Paris, perhaps not in the world — but then, Paris *was* the world, really! — another beauty to be compared to hers. And it was Cateau's sincere conviction that no one could resist its spell when she wished to exert it. Why, but of course. . . . Men had told her so for years, and time had abundantly confirmed the truth of their assertions. What if chance had actually chosen her to be the instrument of Fate — to encompass the miracle of inflaming the heart of this cold, coy princeling, who had seemed, until now, incapable of ardour?

Cateau smiled once more, no longer vaguely, but with definite intention, and blew a little kiss to the reflection in the mirror.

Madame de Choisy, who needed no answer in words, sprang to her feet and bustled forward, exclaiming: 'Ah, my love, I knew I could count on you! Now, sir, let us write a letter at once to our dear wounded friend in Mardyck. . . .'

Chapter XII

DURING THE FOLLOWING WEEK CATEAU AND MADAME DE CHOISY
continued to meet every day. They walked together along the sun-
flecked paths and through the cool and solemn bosquets of the vast
Luxembourg gardens, while fountains splashed and pigeons cooed
and the old lady, with many a meaning nod and. wink, began in-
structing her pupil in the subtleties of the absorbing rôle of King's
Favourite.

Cateau did not say much in return; she contented herself with
listening politely, her head characteristically bent to one side and a
small quizzical smile playing about her lips. No matter what she
was told, she could not manage to take the Choisy's schemes very
seriously, although she pretended to do so. It was easy to see why
she had been chosen for the leading part in this bustling comedy of
intrigue: her beauty had little to do with it, her family connection
with the illustrious Arthénice even less. It was simply the fact that
she was known to be devoid of political ambition that had caused
the conspirators to turn their eyes in her direction. Working
through her, as an aimless and docile catspaw, doubtless each of
them hoped to arrive at some hidden personal goal. . . . Well, that
was all right, too; she had no objection to their making as many
plans as they liked. And it was true that she had no desire to
meddle, even in the most private manner, with public affairs. But,
thought Cateau, as she strolled and smiled and idly twirled the
stem of a fresh-plucked rose in her fingers, once she had attained the
power these crafty campaigners intended to make her a present of,
she might use it as she willed: not one of them would be able to stop
her.

As time passed she realized that she had become the centre of a
well-defined and highly organized plot, of which Madame de
Choisy and Manicamp, though the prime movers, were by no
means the only important links. Notes by the dozen flew back and
forth between the Luxembourg and Calais, where the King was.
The Comte de Guiche wrote constantly to advise and encourage his
friends at home; he was still laid up at the camp in Mardick, suffering with a fever caused by his wound. Bit by bit the seditious pattern fell into shape with surprising speed. . . . The day Louis received

the last sacraments — it was felt now that only a miracle could save his life — Cateau even heard that it had been arranged for Monsieur to flee to Boulogne, a stronghold commanded by the Marquis de Villequier, who was a member of the cabal, and thence to issue decrees dissolving the ministry and appointing new officers to all the leading government posts, directly the breath had left his brother's body.

Really, things were beginning to grow tremendously exciting. . . .

However, when Cateau appeared at the Luxembourg the next afternoon for her daily promenade she found all in a state of confusion. Madame de Choisy herself was out; but from the servants she learned that a change for the better had taken place in the King's condition. No one could tell how it had happened — whether the latest dose of antimony, which the doctors persisted in administering, had at length taken effect, or whether the happy result had been brought about by some new medicine desperately resorted to by his frantic physicians. Whatever the cause, the King's health was decidedly improved. . . . The following day, his fever had gone and his pulse was much steadier and, the day after that, he was pronounced entirely out of danger.

'God be praised for His mercies!' ejaculated Madame de Choisy devoutly, with a glassy look in her eye.

She had just returned from a hasty visit to Little Manicamp, who lived on the other side of the river; and the spectacle of the rejoicing crowds milling about on the Pont Neuf — laughing, weeping, embracing one another — had somewhat unnerved her. But, 'The dear King!' she said . . . and 'No one, my love, could possibly be more thankful than I!' . . . and 'I hope I know my duty as a loyal subject of Louis XIV. . . .'

As the day wore on the glassy look in her eye became more noticeable, and her nervousness increased to such a degree that she could not sit still, but paced the floor of her drawing-room continually, pausing now and then to give Cateau a mechanical smile and to murmur: 'Dear me, I must have an attack of the vapours coming on! Remind me, child, to send for the doctor to purge me tomorrow.'

Cateau could guess well enough what the matter was: Madame de Choisy was undoubtedly remembering the avalanche of notes that had sped in and out of her cabinet in the last fortnight. . . . Ah, who knew where they had ultimately come to rest, or what mischief they might even now be working against her? . . . Cateau was sorry for Madame de Choisy, but she could not help thinking her a sadly silly woman. As for herself, her own conscience was clear: she had neither said nor done anything that could possibly implicate her in the abortive schemes of the cabal. Throughout the hazardous business she had kept true to her principle of putting nothing on paper; she had not written a word to a living soul.... If only the Choisy had taken pattern by her example! Poor misguided creature!...

Cateau went away shortly afterwards, congratulating herself on her cleverness. She had certainly nothing to do with this mess. Nobody could shift even the shadow of blame onto her gracefully guiltless shoulders. (Then why, she wondered, did she, too, feel an indefinable restlessness that caused her to drive at top speed all the way to Vincennes and back before going home, and to spend the evening feverishly picking over the contents of her wardrobe chests?)

The following morning, when she called at the Luxembourg she was told that Madame de Choisy was ill in bed and could receive no one. And later in the day Cateau heard in the Cours that the old lady had suddenly packed up her things and left Paris with Mademoiselle de Montpensier, who was going to take the cure at Forges.

That same afternoon a letter came from Magdelôn, who had also just arrived at the little watering-place in Normandy, and wrote to say she did hope so much that her sister would join her there.

Cateau read the letter through twice, with a pensive expression in her large light eyes, while across the court she could hear the voices of workmen calling cheerily to one another as they tacked up bunting to decorate the streets in honour of the *Te Deum* services for the King's recovery.

Early next morning the Comtesse d'Olonne and her suite, in the best English coach, drove out of the Porte Saint-Honoré on the first stage of their journey to Normandy....

When they reached their destination, shortly after sunset on the evening of the third day after quitting Paris, the village square of Forges was quite deserted. Although it was not yet perfectly dark, all the inhabitants seemed to have gone to bed: not a light showed in the twin rows of neat brick-and-timber houses bordering the square; one small lantern flickered feebly as it swung over the door of the village church.

François reined in his horses and sent a groom to inquire at the Capuchin monastery next the church where the Maréchale de la Ferté-Senneterre lived. (There was, unfortunately, no inn worthy of the name at Forges; if one wanted to take the cure in comfort, it was necessary to hire a house and provide one's own furniture and staff of servants, as Magdelon had done.)

Cateau meanwhile sat stiffly on the back seat of the coach, tapping her fingers on the window beside her, and trying to control her temper as she waited for the groom to return. The country had already begun to depress her spirits. She detested the darkness and the silence.... How horribly quiet it was!... A dog howled once in the distance, and then stopped, its voice serving only to underscore the unnatural stillness. . . . Cateau shivered. She had been feeling out of sorts anyhow since leaving home. The journey from Paris had been longer than she had expected, and exceedingly stupid, with nothing but her own rather gloomy thoughts to occupy her. Besides, François had been obstinate about stopping to ask for directions towards the end, so that they had twice lost their way in the dense hilly forests near Rouen. And Pernelle, the new maid — Quinette's successor — had proved the worst sort of incompetent ninny. (Cateau had gathered, from the incessant idiotic questions with which the girl pestered Quentine, that she had never left Paris before: she should not — so much was sure — leave it again at the Comtesse d'Olonne's expense!)

It was a good thing that they had not much farther to go, for Magdelon's house was found to be one of the high brick-and-timber buildings directly on the square. Servants came running with torches in response to their knocks; candles were lighted in one of the upstairs windows; and presently Magdelon herself, wearing a velvet dressing-gown and a frilled nightcap over her tumbled curls, flung back the blinds and thrust out her head to cry joyfully: 'Darling, what a lovely surprise! Who'd have thought you could get here so soon?'

It was too late that night to do more than snatch a bite of supper before falling into bed. Cateau was so tired that she slept even more soundly than usual. It seemed only a few minutes afterwards that she was roused by a loud ringing of bells in the square, followed by a shuffling of feet and a creaking of boards overhead. (What on earth was the matter? Could the house be on fire?)

Cateau turned over angrily in bed and tried to go to sleep again, but without success; for the shuffling and creaking continued.

After a few minutes she rang in a pet for Quentine, who came tripping into the bedchamber fully dressed, with an odiously wide-awake smile, and announced to her mistress that it was time to go to the spring to take the waters.

'What nonsense!' exclaimed Cateau. 'It can't be more than the middle of the night.'

'It's six o'clock, madam; the Maréchale told me to call you.'

In drifted Magdelon, also fully dressed, with a fur pelisse pulled over her handsome dead-leaf brocade street gown and all her maids in attendance. (She'd four of them now, which was pure swank, Cateau felt, considering that she had not yet been made a duchess.)

'Darling,' said Magdelon, 'I know it must seem a frightful hour, but it's the custom here; you won't mind it so much once you've got into the swing of things. Be sure to wrap up warmly; the air's fresh at this time of the day, and the water we drink is like ice!'

Cateau dressed wrathfully, shivering and protesting that she had not the slightest intention of taking the cure — why should she, indeed, when there was nothing she had to be cured of? — and followed her sister out into the square, which by this time was crowded.

The early morning sun was shining rosily, but dew still lay thick on the grass-plots and shrubberies of the Capuchins' garden adjoining the springs, which was the favourite promenade at Forges. In spite of the dampness and the painful eccentricity of the hour the little knot of people about the stone fountains (there were three of these, dubbed the Royale, the Reinette, and the Cardinale) were chatting and laughing merrily. There were merchants and lawyers from Rouen amongst them, sprightly abbés and portly priests; here and there a rheumatic old knight or nobleman from the provinces (all the young able-bodied ones were away at the war) — and, of course, a discouraging number of women.

As soon as Magdelon approached she was surrounded by a group of her special admirers — it had not taken her long, Cateau saw, to make friends. But then, her husband was one of the greatest generals in France — why, at this moment he was in charge of the siege of Gravelines, which many people thought might well prove the decisive victory of the war with Spain. So it was only natural...

Magdelon smiled and nodded pleasantly to everyone, and presented the lawyers and merchants from Rouen and their incredible strings of female relations to her sister. The good bourgeois bowed politely, but without particular enthusiasm; it was easy to see that they reckoned a countess from Paris, whom they had never heard of — charming though she might be — of infinitely less importance than the young wife of their national hero. Some of the women even stared rather rudely at Cateau's hair (no doubt the 'new' coiffure had not yet reached Rouen); and one or two of them whispered to each other what were probably uncomplimentary comments concerning it.

This was distinctly irritating.

Moreover, the water, which tasted strongly of iron, was excessively nasty; Cateau was not long in making up her mind that this would be her last as well as first visit to the springs.

After they had each drunk three or four glassfuls, there seemed to be no real reason for remaining outdoors any longer. There was, nevertheless, a feeling of vague anticipation in the air; the crowd appeared to be waiting for something; and when Cateau inquired tartly whether it might not be possible now to go back to breakfast, Magdelon looked rather shocked and replied: 'Oh, no, dear, we can't — Mademoiselle's not here yet.'

Almost as she spoke the front door of the largest house in the square was flung open, and a little procession streamed out upon the cobbles. It was led by a pair of small pages in the livery of the

Montpensier family — one of whom was whistling silently, his lips pursed up with an indescribably impudent expression, much to his companion's amusement. They were carrying a varied selection of shawls and rugs, and were followed by six maids-of-honour, who looked sleepy and cross; then came Segrais, Mademoiselle's secretary, a blond good-humoured Norman, and Mademoiselle de Vandy, the Princess's chief lady-in-waiting, a pale, ascetic little creature with a pinched and anxious mouth (she was generally reckoned the greatest prude at court, and the gayer young men took an especial delight in saying things just to shock her).

Finally Mademoiselle herself made her appearance, wearing a sable-trimmed bonnet and a long woolen scarf wound round her throat over a morning gown of green serge. Under the sable-trimmed bonnet her pronounced Bourbon countenance, whose most striking features were the massive aquiline nose and the full bee-stung red mouth, had the slightly sheeplike naïveté that had marked it since girlhood. She strutted slowly across the square with what Segrais doubtless had told her was the port of a goddess, holding aloft a small parasol and chirruping to two slender greyhound bitches that walked sedately beside her, as if aware of their dignified position as bodyguards to the first Princess of the Blood.

Directly Mademoiselle reached the fountains the whole company bowed low before her; all the ladies present curtsied to the ground, regardless of the rather slimy stones upon which they were standing. Mademoiselle acknowledged the salutations affably: she curtsied in return, and then made a tour of the little circle, stopping before each member of it to utter one of the small civilities that are royalty's chief conversational stock-in-trade. She inquired kindly after this one's gout, that one's attack of vertigo, hardly pausing long enough in her course, however, to take heed of the replies she received.

When she got to the sisters La Louppe, at the end of the line, she greeted Magdelon with emphatic cordiality — 'Dear Maréchale, good morning — and how is the spleen today?' — but extended her hand to Cateau woodenly without a word.

Cateau and Magdelon curtsied again and murmured: 'Good day, Your Royal Highness.'

The former felt ill at ease with Mademoiselle, of whom she had seen little since the end of the Fronde. There were reasons enough for that. . . . Mademoiselle had spent five years in exile at Saint-Fargeau, and when at last she came back to court, just a year ago, she appeared astonishingly to have turned into an old maid — her yellow hair fast greying at thirty; her tastes and manners definitely pre-war. (It was hard to imagine now that she had ever galloped in full armour about the streets of Paris, scaled the walls of Orléans to capture it single-handed, and in person turned the cannons of the

Bastille on the King's troops at the famous battle of Saint-Antoine.)
... Oh, Mademoiselle had learned her lesson well!... She had become prudent, not to say precious, and in deference to her Aunt
Anne's well-known prejudices had allied herself with the most con-
servative elements in society.

So now she barely recognized Cateau's curtsy and greeting, and
was obviously going to pass on with no further remark, had not
Magdelon impulsively burst forth: 'Your Royal Highness, may I be
permitted to bring my sister to your reception this afternoon?'

Mademoiselle smiled, but not very much; her teeth were by no
means her best feature, and she somehow contrived to contract her
full lips as she parted them.

'Certainly, Maréchale ... any favour *you* ask ...'

She inclined her head, even more woodenly than she had given
her hand, to the Countess, and then proceeded to the fountain,
where Segrais was already holding a silver goblet of water to proffer
with a neat couplet about 'morning dew for the dawn's own fair
deity,' which he had scribbled on his wide linen cuff while dressing.

The lawyers and merchants from Rouen and their wives heard
what had passed between the Princess and the sisters; they were
standing so close that they could not have helped hearing, even if
they had not been frankly straining their ears. What Mademoiselle
said and, more important still, her manner of saying it had set the
tone in regard to Madame d'Olonne at Forges: she was to be tolerated civilly, but neither flattered nor shown any special attentions.
The worthy Rouennais might know nothing of the Countess — but
they did not need to know anything: here Mademoiselle's word
was law.

Cateau shrugged her shoulders impatiently, and attempted to
restore her shaken serenity by pretending not to recognize little
Mademoiselle de Vandy, who had just given her a faintly flustered
bow. (If the mistress had no time for her, then *she'd* have no time for
the mistress's maid!)

'How disgusting this water is!' she said, frowning, to Magdelon.
'No, dear, not another glass on any account! Do, for Heaven's sake,
let's go in to breakfast!'

The rest of Cateau's first day at Forges proved equally disappointing. The water, she found, was not only unpleasant in itself,
but also left one feeling bloated and distinctly chilly for some hours
afterwards. Then, one was supposed to walk off its effects by a
brisk constitutional in the Capuchins' garden — and Cateau did
not care for walking. That made no difference, though: in Forges
one did what the others did. Round and round on the gravelled
paths went the whole crew of cure-seekers — and round and round,
also, arm-in-arm, went Cateau and Magdelon, till the former felt

as faint from the heat of the summer sunshine as before she had felt cold on account of the water she had drunk.

After hearing Mass in the village church people returned to their houses to dress for dinner; and after dinner all the ladies and gentlemen of quality called at Mademoiselle's to pay their respects.

The reception, Cateau thought, was even duller than the Princess's 'days' at the Luxembourg. Segrais read several of his poems — there was a very long one about Minerva, generally understood to refer to his mistress, that was unbelievably boring — and recited a few impromptu quatrains in compliment to various ladies present, which were no better, but at least not so long. When that diversion began to pall, Mademoiselle, smiling smugly, proposed to give her friends a surprise and, as a special favour, read aloud a selection of literary 'portraits' she had composed of herself and members of her intimate circle. This form of writing had lately become the rage in Paris drawing-rooms; it was so simple, really, that almost anyone could do it. You described complacently, in the first person, and with great detail, the exact size, shape, and colour of your eyes, lips, hair, teeth, throat, arms, bosom, and hips — the hip was as far as it was usually thought proper to go — together with a breathless recital of your perfections of character. Here there was strangely less variety to be found: every lady with any pretensions to fashion was apparently gentle and generous, modest and sweet, invincibly hostile to any form of constraint, and unfalteringly faithful to her friends. A few social leaders, less skilled or less confident than the rest, had commissioned their more self-assured acquaintances to come to their rescue. . . . 'Segrais has promised to do me next week,' Magdelon whispered to her sister. 'At least, he's *almost* sure he'll be able to — but if he can't find time for it, he said he'd get Monsieur de Bouillon to help.'

Cateau tossed her head and said nothing. Secretly she thought the whole business was silly, though it would not do to say so here. . . . Perhaps, considering everything, it might be politic to pretend to join in. She could not write herself, but she had plenty of friends who could — and if she were going to have her portrait done, she would take care to entrust the task to an expert. (There was Vineuil, and her dear Chevalier de Saint-Evremond. . . .)

'" . . . I am the most grateful person in the world,"' gabbled Mademoiselle, in a high, unnatural voice. '"I am naturally sober, and eating bores me; it's even a bore for me to watch people who enjoy it too much."' She paused to stuff a candied rose-leaf into her mouth before continuing: '" . . . I am not an intriguer; I like to know what's going on in the world rather in order to avoid it than to get mixed up in it. I have a fine memory and do not lack judgment. I must hope that, if others judge me, it be not by the events of my life, for it has been so unlucky up to now, compared to what it ought to have been, that my friends' reflection might not be favourable to me. But assuredly, to do myself justice, it can be said that I've lacked good conduct less than Dame Fortune's lacked judgement, since if she had had it, she would doubtless have treated me better.''

Mademoiselle shut up her copy-book with a bang, and the guests burst into polite screams of 'Charming!' 'Ravishing!' and 'Furiously gallant, Your Royal Highness!' The Princess accepted their praise with a sidelong smirk, as no more than her due; Cateau, however, who had caught Segrais' eye several times in the course of the reading, fancied that she detected the conscious blush of authorship. . . . But of course! The new game was no trick at all, if you had a writer for your secretary. . . .

The intellectual part of the entertainment being concluded, servants began to pass liqueurs about and trays of little sweet cakes; and the ladies fluttered and chattered like a colony of magpies round their hostess. They paid her extravagant compliments on her literary prowess and retailed bits of stale provincial gossip — which could not be too stale or too provincial to interest Mademoiselle, who sat on a kind of throne in the middle of the hot pink assembly-room, devouring rose-leaves and violets preserved in sugar and laughing her loud, childlike, undiscriminating laugh at everything that was said.

Magdelon, too, came in for her share of attentions as the spouse of the future conqueror of Gravelines. Of course, the Maréchal had not yet captured the town, but it was certainly a mere question of days, perhaps only of hours, before he would do so. The victor of Landrecies and Montmédy and a score of other celebrated battles had justly come to be deemed invincible. And his pretty young wife smiled and blushed and acknowledged the gallant speeches addressed to her with so much modesty that no one could envy her her prominence.

Cateau had almost made up her mind to slip from the room unobserved — something she had never yet done in her life — when Mademoiselle called for the card-tables to be brought, and the ladies were formed into sets for hoca and reversi. Just as the game was beginning Madame de Choisy scuttled into the room and dropped a breathless curtsy to the Princess. Cateau had been wondering where she was, but the old lady explained that she had had to walk all the way from her house, the sedan-chair she had contracted for having failed to arrive. ('I asked her to stop here, of course,' Cateau heard Mademoiselle whisper to Magdelon, 'but she said my pages made so much noise that they kept her from sleeping. She's taken a cottage all by herself in the middle of a field at the very end of the village — I can't think what for!')

As soon as the Choisy caught sight of Madame d'Olonne she bridled and blinked. The two exchanged cool, unsmiling curtsies, and shortly afterwards found themselves placed opposite each other at one of the tables of reversi.

During the course of the game, which was rendered rather tepid by the fact that their hostess, though a most inexpert player, as royalty could not be allowed to lose, Madame de Choisy did not once address Cateau directly. On the other hand, she let no opportunity slip to launch small oblique darts across the board.... 'Well, I declare! If the Countess hasn't stolen *all* of the hearts!' she would ejaculate genially. 'Nothing unusual in *that*, I dare say!' — or 'What? Has Madame d'Olonne no diamonds left? La, who'd have thought it could come to such a pass, with the generous friends we all know she's got!'

Each time she delivered herself of one of these heavy-handed gibes she hunched up her scrawny shoulders and bridled and blinked again. Mademoiselle, from her armchair at the head of the table, remarked the Choisy's behaviour at first with a droll look of bewilderment; she glanced inquiringly at both ladies until mincing little Mademoiselle de Vandy, who was leaning over the back of her mistress's chair, whispered something in the Princess's ear; whereupon Mademoiselle nodded her head and said: 'Oh, I see!' in a loud voice.

Cateau succeeded in curbing her temper till the end of the game. But she felt relieved when Mademoiselle's majordomo appeared on the threshold to announce that Her Royal Highness's carriage was waiting below, and Mademoiselle rose without ceremony, casting down the cards, to which she had given but scant attention. The ladies rose, too, in a flurry of ribbons and laces; and Cateau made her perfunctory obeisance and sped away from the assembly-room, without even waiting for Magdelon, to avoid the humiliation of seeing herself omitted from the list of guests chosen to make up the party in the Princess's coach.

As she rustled indignantly downstairs she muttered to herself: 'I'll not go back *there* in a hurry!'

But of course she did go back, over and over, in the ensuing fortnight, and that for the best of reasons: there was nowhere else to go.

With time Mademoiselle relented towards her former favourite, and her manner became less disapproving — she was, after all, a kind-hearted woman; and besides, possessed that penchant for the society of the lively and frivolous so frequently observed amongst the blamelessly sedate.

Madame de Choisy, too, after the first difficult encounter, behaved with her usual courtesy towards Cateau, though she certainly did not seek her company, and indeed remained apart from all the Princess's circle. She never, for instance, came to the springs as the others did, but drank the waters at home, protesting that the morning air was bad for her teeth — which, as she had scarce three whole ones left in her head, was obviously absurd. Most of the day she stayed by herself in the little cottage in the field, writing and receiving a great many letters; and when she did appear in public she assumed an air of overdone innocence that deceived nobody. Although she continued to asseverate that she was not in the least nervous — why, in Heaven's name, should she be? She had done nothing wrong! — the news that trickled through from Paris was hardly reassuring on this score. One by one the conspirators in the plot had been discovered and sent into exile; the week was not up before a special messenger arrived at the cottage, after a conference with whom Madame de Choisy packed hurriedly and disappeared overnight, in a tumble-down hired coach, with a number of mysterious parcels rumoured to contain the files of her secret correspondence (which no doubt she intended to burn on the way). And, a few days later, it came out that she had been sent by the Cardinal to one of her husband's houses near Caen.

During the second week of Cateau's cure Margot Cornuel and a troop of her gay young friends came to join the Paris contingent at Forges, so that the afternoon receptions at Mademoiselle's were a good deal less poky than before.

Cateau was especially glad to see Margot because — though she would not have admitted it for worlds — she and Magdelon were not getting on together so well as usual.

Neither sister would have believed it possible, if an actual experience had not convinced them that it is not easy for two married women to live under the same roof, no matter how much they may love each other.

It was the first time they had shared a house for more than three years, since the winter of Magdelon's wedding, in fact. In those days Magdelon had been a little girl, eager and humble and in all ways subservient to her brilliant and self-assured elder sister. She had thought Cateau wonderful — as, indeed, everyone did; but it was Magdelon's thinking so that had contributed most to Cateau's tranquil belief in her own infallibility.

Now, though that admiration was perhaps stronger than ever, their respective rôles were reversed. As the Maréchale de la Ferté-Senneterre Magdelon's position in society was a great deal more solid than the Comtesse d'Olonne's had ever been. The La Fertés were increasingly powerful at court: as the Maréchal's military prowess became more and more generally recognized and relied upon, his wife's social value naturally rose in direct ratio to it. Not that Magdelon betrayed an overawareness of this — on the contrary, she was as simple and unpretentious as ever. But other people deferred to her continually, whether she wished it or not. She was constantly being singled out for preferment — pushed first through doors, served first at table, placed on the right hand of Mademoiselle when they went driving through the forest in the huge state coach of the Montpensiers.

And then, too, Magdelon was a married woman, the mistress of three splendid houses: Great Senneterre, the castle of La Ferté-Saint-Aubin, and the governor's palace at Nancy, to say nothing of a score of lesser dwellings scattered over the countryside. In spite of her innate timidity, she had grown used to running her places to suit herself; and she was plainly less receptive to hints from her sister than she had been in the early days of her duties. When Cateau advised her to alter the pattern of the footmen's breeches, or asked why on earth she let her mushrooms be broiled in butter instead of having them cooked in that delicious new way with red wine and truffles, Magdelon was very apt now to lift her chin with gentle defiance and reply quite firmly that the footmen's breeches were very well as they were, thank you, and she *liked* her mushrooms cooked in the *old* way best.

Even here in Forges, where their housekeeping arrangements were of the simplest, there were plenty of opportunities for friction. For example, in the beginning Magdelon had generously given her sister the best apartment on the first storey of the brick-and-timber house, confining her own far more numerous suite to the smaller rooms on the second storey. That was all very well — but Cateau liked to lie late abed in the morning and sleep as long as she could, being exhausted by the strenuous Paris season; while Magdelon, although lazier by nature, was following the cure, and therefore rose daily at half-past five. No matter how quietly she tried to dress, she and her maids could not help making a certain amount of noise. After Cateau had several times complained of the racket with asperity Magdelon good-naturedly offered to exchange rooms with her sister — and Cateau then felt that the minx must have had her eye on the *piano nobile* all along and taken these questionable means of acquiring it. The noises continued, too, even after they had moved, though not quite so penetrating as before.

Their servants did not get on well with one another, either. . . .

All in all, it had been a most unsatisfactory holiday.

The climax to Cateau's vexations came about two weeks after her arrival. Mademoiselle had issued invitations one evening for a dinner-party she intended giving the following day in honour of the Abbess of Jouarre, who had just come to the springs and, as the daughter of the famous Duchesse de Chevreuse, was too well connected not to have a fuss made about her. (Indeed, after a fortnight in Forges, almost any new face...) Magdelon was asked to the dinner; Cateau was not. The next morning, as soon as the latter realized that she had been slighted on purpose, she gave vent to her feelings in an attack of hysterics, crying, and screaming, throwing herself about until Magdelon became frightened and threatened to send for the doctor. Cateau said not to do that upon any account; she would feel much worse if he came. Magdelon said that of course *she* intended to refuse Mademoiselle's invitation for herself. Cateau said that she forbade her to do so. Magdelon said that she would tell Mademoiselle de Vandy to speak to the Princess about it. Cateau said that, if Magdelon dared even think of such a thing, she would fling herself out of the window directly. Magdelon thereupon burst into tears and said: 'Darling, what *do* you want me to do, then?' And Cateau said: 'Nothing at all!' — and began weeping afresh.

In the end, Magdelon went off to Mass with her maids, leaving her sister still fretting on the couch in her bedroom.

Directly she was deprived of an audience, however, Cateau came to herself with amazing swiftness. Ten minutes later, dressed in a ruffled white dress with a tiny white parasol to protect her from the glare, Madame d'Olonne sallied forth into the street and surveyed the empty prospect with undisguised boredom.

The square, with its trim, prim clipped trees and trim, prim brick-and-timber houses, dozed in the flat, unimaginative light of a warm July morning. The entire population of Forges had been jammed into the diminutive stone village church, whence a measured droning of voices betokened that Mass was in progress. It was too hot for even a dog to be stirring. But at the far end of the square the feathery elms and green bosquets of the Capuchins' garden promised a cool and inviting refuge.

Hoisting her parasol, Cateau tripped across the cobbles, her train held high by little Lindor (who was not so little now as he used to be, alas! One would soon be forced to find his successor), Quentine and Pernelle following their mistress at a respectful distance. Idly she wandered along the pleasant paths in search of a suitable nook till she came to a dark pool fed by trickles from an overflow of the water in the springs. Beside the pool there was a summer-house, with a dilapidated thatched roof that looked damp and earwiggy. Inside the summerhouse there was a bench, the only one to be found in this part of the garden. Cateau seated herself on the bench and motioned to the servants to leave her.... Lindor skipped off at once into the shrubberies, but Pernelle and Quentine lingered by the pool, where dragonflies flitted tirelessly in the hot, still sunlight and great splendid white water-lilies floated on the calm surface.

The girls were kneeling at the water's edge, rolling up their sleeves and stretching out their arms in an attempt to pluck some of the lilies without getting their dresses wet: their silly, parrot-like cries were borne back on the heavy air to where Cateau sat in the summerhouse in her ruffled white gown, a rose tucked in her bodice and another bound in the fillet that circled her gleaming curls. . . . What a pity there was no man in the garden to admire the exquisite picture she made! That was the whole trouble with Forges, really: there was nobody, nobody at all, to pay one compliments, gaze meaningly into one's eyes, elbow his fellows purposefully aside in his frank determination to sit next one at dinner or at the card-tables in Mademoiselle's stuffy pink drawing-room. . . . Ah, truly, life in Paris spoiled one permanently for the charms of a less so-phisticated existence! Cateau felt now she could scarcely breathe in this lazy, impersonal atmosphere. Worst of all, there was no-body here to distract her from the unprofitable company of her own thoughts.

For the first time in her life she had time — far, far more than she wished — to take stock of the perils of the situation into which she seemed to have drifted. The prospect was appalling! Cateau was plaintively confident of the innocence of her intentions — yet somehow she had so mismanaged her life that people had begun to talk about her in an alarmingly horrible way. She could tell that well enough from the scathing remarks dropped now and again by Mademoiselle (who since her own disgrace had become peculiarly sensitive to signs of social eclipse in others) and by the rigid touch-me-not attitude adopted by that idiotic white mouse of a Vandy woman. But the matter went deeper. Cateau was beginning to be afraid that she was not only calumniated in court circles — had this been all, it would have been nothing new! — but that when she went home she would have other more serious problems to face. Margot Cornuel had told her frankly, only yesterday, that before she left Paris the rhymesters of the Pont Neuf had started circulating all sorts of odious libels about the Comtesse d'Olonne. Hateful creatures! Where on earth, she wondered, did they contrive to pick up their mixture of damaging facts and highly spiced misin-formation? No matter what one did to keep them off the scent, they appeared to hear everything that went on in the alcoves, sooner or later. Cateau knew women who tried to propitiate journalists by sending them Christmas puddings and bottles of wine and even substantial money presents, from time to time, to make sure that their names would be used only in flattering connections. But she herself had never done this. She thought too much of the value of money. Besides, such craven tactics were no more successful than they deserved to be, for the serpents were apt to turn and strike without warning, whenever one's enemies paid them a trifle more handsomely than one did oneself.

Cateau was too proud to ask what the rhymes were about — but Margot had hinted unutterable things — had rolled her saucer-round violet eyes with insufficiently disguised delight and indicated that there were 'all kinds of atrocities, dearest!' ... Obviously her detractors had some knowledge of her most private history. The Candale liaison had been raked up again, and the Shrove Tuesday masquerade, not to mention her affair with young Marsillac and the more recent ambiguous dealings with Madame de Choisy and Little Manicamp. ... Ah, people were too vile! Cateau had never done anyone harm — why must she be singled out to bear the brunt of so many venomous attacks?

It was no comfort to reflect that Gilette de Fiesque had warned her against precisely this. Gilette had foreseen the danger; had implored her, again and again, to be careful — and Cateau had sincerely supposed, after Candale's death, that she had been so ... well, very nearly all of the time. ... How *dared* they? Oh, if Candale were alive, he'd have had those wretches flogged to death publicly for their filthy insinuations! But she had no one left to protect her — no one in all the world!

With the conviction of her pathetic defencelessness two bright tears gathered slowly in the corners of her eyes, poised themselves for an instant on the dark fringe of her lashes, and then rolled symmetrically down the pale ivory cheeks. Yes, she was truly alone ... worse off, with Olonne for a husband, than if she were not married at all. As for that dolt of a Marsillac, and the brilliant but undependable Guiche ... well ...

After fumbling a little in her pocket Cateau produced two letters that had arrived in the post-bag from Calais only that morning — one from each of her alcovists. The Comte sent her an amusing, gossipy bulletin from the court, full of satirical tidbits such as the Queen Mother's tantrum over the King's affair with Marie Mancini, and Mazarin's paltry resolve to skimp on sickbed expenses, even when his sovereign was lying at death's door. ...

As for our own plans, madam, let us say that they are postponed, but by no means discarded. Our dear little Monsieur, young as he is, seems to be developing an overmastering desire to attach himself in a worthy quarter. To be frank with you, I've done all I can to make him resolve to be your gallant when we return to Paris. He's anxious enough for it, but unfortunately he's mortally afraid of the old woman. My brightest hope, however, at present, lies in a new project of the latter. It is Her Majesty's thought that her poppet is in need of distraction, and as she will be kept here indefinitely by her duty to the King, she has conceived the notion of sending Monsieur in charge of the Abbé Fouquet — in whom, as you know, her trust is unbounded — on a journey to Forges. They are to travel without suite in strict incognito. Should this project come to pass — and I have every reason to believe that it will — it would offer the liveliest opportunities to you, dear madam, who are, I am well aware, as resourceful in invention as you are deft in demeanour. I have told Monsieur that you are by no means disinclined to listen to his suit. All he wants is a little tactful encouragement — and that, I feel, I may safely leave in your hands. The Abbé Fouquet, naturally, has no inkling of our hopes. It seemed to me wiser not to take him into our confidence, in view of his strong attachment to Mazarin and the Queen. But you yourself, madam, will best know how to deal with the gentleman. . . .

There was more in this bantering strain, as well as a concluding line in which the gay Count did not scruple to hint that, if in spite of his skilful manoeuvring their scheme finally fell through, he could still suggest a delightful alternative as a means of consoling themselves . . .

Cateau's lip curled as she read this, and she turned with relief to Marsillac's note, which was written from camp in front of Gravelines.

Madam, my love [the Prince scrawled, in his round, childish hand], I am, thank God, very well at this present, as I hope my letter may find you, too. I miss you very much, my dear friend; do you miss me? Our siege continues very fine, to the general satisfaction. Yesterday the enemies made a sortie from the citadel, but were repulsed with small losses on both sides. I regret to say that amongst our officers who fell was the poor Comte de Moret; he was a particular friend of mine, and I think of yours, too, madam? Your brother-in-law, the Maréchal de la Ferté, hopes to capture Gravelines by the first of August. If he be correct, I think it will not be long till the close of the campaign, for there are not many towns in Flanders left in the hands of the Spaniards. Would this were so, madam, my love, for I miss you furiously and am counting the hours until we can be together again. Do not, I beg you, dine with a gentleman whilst you are at Forges. . . .

Trusting that the waters of the celebrated spring were doing her good, and sending her all his love and duty, Marsillac remained her most humble and obedient servant.

Cateau crumpled the two notes into balls, made as if to cast them from her into the shrubbery — and then suddenly stuffed them back into her pocket once more. Not that she felt the slightest softening of the heart towards either of the writers: quite possibly she might break with them both on her return to Paris. What were they, after all? — a milksop and a butterfly! — (Oh, for a real man! Someone to stand by her through thick and thin and ward off the insults of the mob! Someone, above everything, whom she could look up to and respect, as she had never yet respected any man!) At the same time they were the best she had to boast of just now, and she could not afford to dismiss them unless she were sure of something very much better. Of course, if it were true what Guiche said, that Monsieur was really coming to Forges... Cateau's eyes became dreamy as she envisaged the possibilities of that long-delayed meeting. Although the Duc d'Anjou's political importance had dwindled since his brother's reprieve from death, he could never in future be considered a cipher; for what had once happened might happen again; it had been demonstrated clearly that even Louis the Well-Beloved was mortal. Socially, it went without saying, there was everything still to be gained from the connection. Cateau had to admit she yearned to try her hand on the elusive young man. What a triumph would be hers if she succeeded in making the conquest no woman had yet made! The chances were that she could achieve the impossible, if anyone could. Guiche had confidence, it was evident, in her powers; and Cateau had confidence in Guiche — if not in his loyalty or devotion, certainly in the shrewdness of his judgement. What if Madame de Choisy's prediction were fated to come true at the eleventh hour in this unexpected fashion? Oh, and what if...

But the bells were ringing in the village. Mass must be over now. Cateau rose deliberately, shook herself, and stepped out of the dank depths of the summerhouse into the hot sunshine on the path. She then clapped her hands to summon Lindor and the maids, and started back through the garden towards the church. If she could get there before the congregation had dispersed, it would be possible to mingle with the crowd and create the impression that she, too, had attended the service. In her present plight such impressions might not be without value.

As she reached the square a carriage dashed past her, a big grey one trimmed with gold and drawn by four lively roan horses. It came to a halt in front of the house next to Mademoiselle's; from it alighted two men: the first, a rather tall fellow in an abbé's dress, surmounted by a cape of vaguely military cut and a big plumed hat, turned to give his hand to the second, a smart little person in scarlet velvet with a great many curls and a great many ribbons. Even at this distance their identity was unmistakable. Cateau smiled at their characteristic occupations — the smart little person being busy setting to rights his curls and his ribbons, while his companion, who was thickset as well as tall, with a decided chin and an air of restless vitality (as though he were longing to be resolute with people, if only he could make up his mind whom to begin on!), stood poised on the steps of the house, sweeping the prospect with a vigilant eye. His glance travelled round the square till it fell on the arresting picture of Madame d'Olonne in her frilly white gown, Lindor bearing her train, the smiling Pernelle and Quentine, their arms full of water-lilies, bringing up the rear.

The man swept off his hat with a flourish that seemed strangely unecclesiastical, and then hastened over to bow before her.

'Why, Countess,' he exclaimed, 'who would have thought to find you here?'

Cateau curtsied, and negligently gave him her hand to kiss. She had known Basile Fouquet slightly for years, but it had never occurred to her that he could be important to her, one way or the other.

Of course, he was one of the most powerful men in France — a brother of the finance minister, and the Cardinal's trusted secret agent, much feared and respected. Scorning as vulgar all public display, the Abbé Fouquet was content to work his will by subtle underground means: many were the tales of his incredible, inescapable spy system — and Cateau had been told most of these by Gilette de Fiesque, who, though his friend, was just as much afraid of him as anybody else.

Cateau, therefore, had long ago made up her mind that it was best to have nothing to do with this dangerous gentleman; the resolve had been easy to keep, since he went out very little in general society, and, besides, was supposed to be madly in love with the widowed Duchesse de Châtillon. (If he had the bad taste to admire that coarse-featured brunette, why, then, what would be the use . . .?)

Today, however, his appearance, and that of the smart little person, seemed the direct answer to prayer. What could possibly suit her plans better than to be discovered conversing with such illustrious company when her friends came out from Mass? Moreover, Cateau fancied she had spied, in the forthright glance of Fouquet's clouded blue eyes, a dawning admiration — almost, one might say, a positive intention. . . . Yes, there it was again; she could not be mistaken. This, instead of upsetting her, was exactly what she had hoped might happen. A flirtation with the Abbé would serve as an excellent smoke-screen to cover the initial operations of her campaign for Monsieur. That the latter was already expecting a siege, and would welcome it, was made manifest by the haste with which he fluttered up to greet the beautiful Countess, and by the series of killing smiles he was sending in her direction. ... 'Nay, madam, and how are *you?* I vow, I've never seen you looking so handsome! And I've dozens of messages — positively, *dozens* — to give you from a *very* dear friend of yours and mine in the army. ...'

But Cateau intended to be careful. It would not do to rush the citadel, however eager it seemed to be to capitulate! No, indeed! That was where, she felt sure, all other women had made their mistakes. It was best, with a shy creature like Monsieur — how like a field-mouse he looked, to be sure, with his long nose and beady, almond-shaped eyes! — to proceed with infinite caution, step by step, trusting to intuition and the inspiration of the moment to guide her.

Therefore, she took pains to appear unaware of the youth's evident desire to establish intimate relations between them. Smiling languorously, she adjusted her parasol to an angle that shielded her not at all from the sun, but allowed its rays to gild her curls most becomingly as she chatted for a moment or two on indifferent matters. Had His Royal Highness and Monsieur Fouquet come for the cure? Really — how delightful that was! What an addition to their afternoon assemblies! (Evening parties, alas! there were none, since the rule of Forges prescribed bed for everyone at nine o'clock sharp. Tiresome, was it not? But what could one do but submit?) The gentlemen would find many friends already installed for the season. And Monsieur's cousin Mademoiselle de Montpensier was here. ... Oh, yes! Hadn't they heard? The Princess paid a visit faithfully every summer; the waters were said to have done her weak chest untold good. But no doubt they would be waiting upon her presently. There was to be a state dinner, she believed. ... No, unfortunately, *she'd* not been bidden to it.

The ladies came trooping now out of church in their best morning gowns and bonnets, Mademoiselle and her eternal satellite Vandy the nucleus of the group. As soon as they perceived the newcomers all with one accord rushed with cries of joy to surround them: Monsieur was the most popular (because the most approachable) of the royal family, and there was not a woman at court, old or young, beautiful or ugly, married or single, who did not hope to get something out of Monsieur the Abbé and who did not feel that, where others had failed, *she* could surely succeed, if only she were not interrupted!

Mademoiselle herself, who in her early days had held herself proudly aloof from the Cardinal's creatures, now truckled shamelessly to anyone she thought had the slightest influence in responsible quarters, and therefore almost skipped forward in her eagerness to have her bony hand kissed by the Abbé. She paid more attention to him than to her little cousin, who, to tell the truth, repelled her embrace with an affected shriek and explained, pouting, that no one was to take the *least* notice of *him*, as he was in Forges in *strictest* incognito.

'La! Coz, it's never you!' exclaimed Mademoiselle. 'How did you leave my aunt and his poor dear Majesty at Calais? *And* Monsieur Fouquet! Dear me! I was saying to Vandy only this morning before Mass: "Now, *whom* do you think I dreamed of last night? And whom would you like to see turn up in Forges in time to come to my party today?" Mind you, we neither of us had the faintest idea that you were on your way hither, but the poor girl answered at once — as how else could she do, when we all remember that you were the life of every little assembly last season — "Why, the Abbé Fouquet, *of course!*" And there you are, like Jupiter wafted on a storm-cloud! Well, this is a delightful surprise! Come, sir, you must promise to attend me at dinner. You, too, coz, of course, if your impenetrable anonymity will permit it. (Nay, then, I know you not — 'twas the light in my eyes deceived me and made me think I saw my cousin Anjou approaching.) I am offering a collation to the dear Abbess of Jouarre, who joined our ranks yesterday. Such a rare, pious soul — so unlike her poor mother! Between you and me, I have sometimes thought — but here she comes, to add her prayers to mine — and no doubt *they've* a far better right to be heard! Now don't disappoint us!'

Fouquet thanked Her Royal Highness most humbly for the honour she did him. His companion, he was sure, would be charmed to accept the invitation, but he himself, in spite of measureless gratitude, would, alas! be unable to profit by her distinguished hospitality. His travelling clothes were in no condition to be worn in the Princess's presence — they'd but just arrived by coach from Calais — 'And besides,' said Monsieur the Abbé, glancing about him with the complacence of a man who knew that his word was law to every woman he met, 'I fancy I understood that the Comtesse d'Olonne had been good enough to reserve me a place at her board. Correct me, dear madam, if I have made a mistake, I beg of you.'

Cateau smiled and said nothing — there was nothing, really, she needed to say.

'Oh,' said Mademoiselle, with a gulp, but no perceptible pause to indicate that this was a perfectly new idea to her, 'but *of course* the Countess is dining with *me!* Aren't you, my dear? Didn't you know that my invitation to your sister included you? Fie, Maréchale, this misunderstanding must be *your* fault! It's not too late, though, I trust, to set matters right? For I'll not take no for an answer, you see.'

Cateau smiled again, and dropped a curtsy, and murmured that Her Royal Highness was very kind — but she feared to intrude...

'Nonsense!' cried Mademoiselle, with an awkward attempt at sprightliness; two spots of red were glowing high on her prominent cheekbones. 'We've known each other far too long, dear child, for it to be necessary to stand on ceremony. Till half-past noon, then, my friends, at the Hôtel de Montpensier *pro tem.!*'

She neighed loudly at her own little joke — all the ladies genteelly echoing her amusement — waved her hand to the still pouting Anjou, and moved on across the square with a step she seldom could remember to slacken to the point of stateliness.

Fouquet glanced at Cateau and bared his strong white teeth — it could scarcely be called a smile.

'Our fate, then, it seems, is decided, madam,' he said. 'May we escort you and the Maréchale to your lodgings, before seeking our own to make what repairs to our toilet are possible in the brief moments at our disposal?'

'You are too kind, sir,' replied Cateau. 'But it's not at all necessary; we live here in the square, you know.'

'Capital!' exclaimed the Abbé, showing his teeth again. 'So we're to be neighbours! I shall do myself the honour of waiting on you, madam, with your permission, this very evening. Come, Your Royal Highness; it's time we retired to prepare for your cousin's dinner-party.'

And he strode off with a look over his shoulder that caused Cateau to catch her breath, and that would have been wholly welcome, if only she had not been conscious that Monsieur was looking at her, too.

She and the young Prince exchanged salutations once more; the latter gave Madame d'Olonne another of his killing glances, and as he took his hand to kiss it, pressed a folded scrap of paper into her palm.

Then, with a flirt of his ribbons and a shrill giggle, he fluttered off after the Abbé; while Cateau unfolded the paper and read: *Madam, I must see you alone tonight on a matter of the utmost importance.*

This time it was Magdelon who was looking at her queerly.

Chapter XIII

CATEAU OPENED THE FRONT DOOR OF THE HOUSE FROM THE INSIDE, slipped through, and shut it behind her as softly as possible. Then she stood for a minute on the steps surveying the square, which was wrapped in a sombre hush. It was late, well past midnight; everyone in Forges had gone to bed. No candle showed in any of the buildings.... The moon was not shining either, but the air was so clear that the stars gave a great deal of light; the sky behind them was pussy-grey rather than black.

The place was empty except for the soldiers on guard before the entrance to Mademoiselle's lodgings. There were two of them wearing helmets, and with muskets over their shoulders. It was so still that Cateau could hear the clank of their armour and the rattle of their swords in their scabbards as they tramped to and fro. She waited, watching the pair until she was sure that their backs were turned, before skimming across the cobbles to take shelter in the Capuchins' garden.

Here under the trees she breathed a sigh of relief, feeling safe from discovery. And even if someone chanced to spy her, she would never be recognized in her linen wimple and flowing white skirt. Cateau chuckled merrily and congratulated herself, not for the first time that evening, on her cleverness in devising the ideal means for safeguarding her rendezvous with Monsieur.... It had come to her unexpectedly in the middle of Mademoiselle's stupid dinner-party, suggested no doubt by the sight of the chief female guest of honour seated primly on the right of their hostess. Madame de Jouarre was a dark insignificant scrap of a woman, as withered as a walnut-shell in spite of her youth.... Cateau eyed her compassionately.... What a pity it was that nuns could not wear rouge! That dead white stuff gave the Abbess's skin the hue of an unripe vegetable marrow. It was too bad.... The Bernardines' habit was lovely in itself. One could not help thinking how becoming it would be to one's own fair pallor.... From this it was but a step to the project of trying it on. Nothing would be easier, when Madame de Jouarre went to Vespers, than to whisper a word to Quentine. The girl was ready for anything. Besides, she was a friend of the Abbess's servants, so that a little gold would be all that was necessary....

Then, suddenly, Cateau saw the whole plan in a flash. Hadn't Monsieur admired her extravagantly last winter at the Shrove Tuesday masquerade, in the drab corded gown of a Capuchin monk? How much more attractive he'd be sure to find her in this exquisite costume of virginal white! It would be original, daring — dangerous, of course, in the extreme, if she were fool enough to be caught — but there was no need of that. She would take her measures too well. And instinct told her it was just such a bold stratagem that would be most likely to capture the callow imagination of the little Duke. Monsieur was young enough and mischievous enough to be certain to prize a touch of wilful audacity....

Yes, it was perfect! Cateau could have clapped her hands in glee there where she sat at the foot (what an insult!) of Mademoiselle's dinner-table. Her eyes began to sparkle with excitement; she smiled brilliantly across the board at Anjou, who had been striving (she knew without looking) to attract her attention all during the meal.

When they rose he wriggled his way through the press of courtiers and approached her with an inquiring glance and an eager 'Well, madam? Have you nothing for me?'

Cateau shook her head, laughing. But as the youth turned aside with a petulant pout and toss of his curls she murmured very low and rapidly, behind her fan: '*Tonight at twelve in the Capuchins' garden....*'

And then at the last moment, when every detail of her scheme had been laid, it had almost been spoilt by the Abbé Fouquet.

He had appeared punctually after supper, as he had said he would, to wait upon the Comtesse d'Olonne and her sister. That was all right; that was most flattering, to be sure; Cateau only hoped Mademoiselle and her ladies could see the gentleman's lackeys waiting outside her own door.

But Monsieur Fouquet's idea of a social call was strangely expansive.

After an hour's polite chit-chat Cateau, in desperation, had begun doing everything she could think of, short of being openly rude, to get rid of her gallant. She yawned delicately behind her fan; she left sentences unfinished, as though from sheer fatigue; she declared her head ached — that she felt the vapours coming on — even (as a last resort) that the fish dish at Mademoiselle's banquet did not seem to have agreed with her.

The Abbé professed the utmost solicitude concerning Madame d'Olonne's indisposition. He made bold to recommend Queen-of-Hungary water for her head, and dispatched a lackey to fetch a flask of it from his rooms. As for the fish, he admitted that he himself had had doubts of its freshness. Perhaps it were wise for them

all to abstain from the fountain for a day or two, until they were
sure they had recovered from any possible ill-effects. ...

In the end, it was Magdelon who, unwittingly, succeeded in relieving them of their importunate visitor. She had certainly not
meant to do it; she had followed the conversation as best she was
able, dropping a word here and there whenever she could think of
anything to say. But, after all, she had been up, poor dear, since
five o'clock that morning: the lateness of the hour, the torpor
induced by the Princess's excellent dinner, combined with a general
state of relaxed nerves owing to her regular life and an ample supply
of fresh air to send her nodding to sleep, before she knew it, in her
highbacked, uncomfortable chair.

Then, indeed, the Abbé broke into profuse apologies: how had
he had the temerity thus shockingly to outstay his welcome?
Would the ladies be so kind as to forgive him, and allow him to
return to resume their amenities another day at a more auspicious
time?

The ladies could and would forgive — though Magdelon, blushing rosily, protested vainly that the fault was hers alone — and
their parting was both cordial and stately. Once again as Fouquet
bent over her hand Cateau was conscious of the compelling fervour
of his blue gaze — it moved her more than she liked to confess,
although she would have been at a loss to say why. Assuredly his
last words were trite enough: 'Till tomorrow, my dear friends,
allow me to wish you, despite dietary indiscretions, a very good
night!'

The sisters kissed and took leave of each other — luckily Magdelon was too weary to want to stay up and talk, as she usually did
— and then Cateau skipped up to her own apartment, where
Quentine was waiting with the wimple and habit of Madame the
Abbess of Jouarre. After that, there remained only to wait until
one was positive that the household below were all fast asleep. ...

How quiet it was under the trees! How quiet, and how dark!
(It was cool, too, in the dew-drenched tangle of shrubbery, but
Madame de Jouarre's gown, being made of thick serge, kept her
perfectly warm.) Cateau had supposed she would feel afraid,
alone at night in the Capuchins' garden; but she was not afraid.
It was as if she had been turned into somebody else; nothing could
hurt her as long as she clung to her disguise.

Her heart beat high with pleasurable excitement. Thank goodness! something had happened at last to pull her out of her morass
of dullness and discouragement. For weeks she had been sinking
in deeper and deeper, well aware of the ruin ahead, but helpless to
save herself from it. But now suddenly life was again charged with
all manner of amusing possibilities. And *she* was changed, also. ...

The bored, drifting creature was gone; she felt on her mettle, keen to seize her new opportunity and use it to the full. The spice of real danger only made the game better worth playing. A misstep now would be fatal. But she would not make a misstep. . . .

How quiet it was under the trees! Crickets were chirping industriously, but theirs was the only sound to be heard. The topmost branches of the great elms and beeches, stirring faintly, were so far above her head that their languid motion was noiseless. . . .

The bell in the church tower chimed the half-hour. Cateau was late for her rendezvous. Would he be out of temper because she had kept him waiting? But perhaps he, too, had not found it easy to slip away from home at the appointed time. The lad was so young — not quite eighteen — that he was still under more or less strict surveillance. It was fortunate for their plans that here at Forges he was without his usual suite — and the Abbé Fouquet was surely ill adapted to the rôle of nursemaid to an adventurous stripling! Cateau wondered what Monsieur wanted to tell her. After all, though, did it matter much? What was important was that they should meet alone, after dark, under picturesque circumstances. The rest, Cateau thought, the further charting of their sentimental relations, could safely be left to take care of itself.

Unconsciously she turned towards the summerhouse by the pool where the water-lilies grew. They had not agreed on a meeting place — there hadn't been time for that at Mademoiselle's party — but the garden was small: sooner or later they must find one another.

Cateau picked up her heavy dragging skirts and trailed through a series of bosquets, along the same path she had followed that very morning with downcast heart. How different things looked to her now!

When she emerged finally into the clearing beside the lily-pool the absence of shade made everything seem much lighter. Even without a moon the scene was bathed in a pale grey radiance. There was more air here, too. A soft breeze rustled through the tall rushes by the waterside, where frogs were harshly croaking. Cateau could not see the summerhouse, but she knew well enough where it was. Probably Monsieur would be waiting inside.

But as she picked up her skirts once more and prepared to circle the pool she saw with a shock that she was not alone. Someone had got there before her. Not Monsieur — it was no man at all, but another woman, a young girl, bent, very likely, on an errand similar to her own.

The young girl was seated by the water's edge on a large rounded rock; she was so still that it was no wonder Cateau had not at once perceived her. She was slender and dark, with long waving hair, and was wearing a dress of some gauzy material that gleamed like dew-spangled cobwebs in the grey starlight. Her face was turned so that Cateau could not see it. ... There was something unreal about her, as if she had risen out of the pool like a naiad and might, at a word, dive from her rock and disappear in the darkling waters. Presently she plucked a ring from her finger and began to play with it, tossing it up and catching it again just in time to save it from falling into the pool. And this seemed an unnatural thing to do. ...

With a shiver Cateau crossed herself. But the next moment she was smiling at her own fear: there was nothing queer anyhow about the ring — that must be valuable — a thick circlet of gold studded with jewels. And only real diamonds could glitter so brightly in such a dim light. Almost involuntarily she stretched out a warning hand. ... 'Oh, please! Do take care! ...' At the same instant the ring slipped through the naiad's figers and dropped with a soft plop into the water. Uttering a cry of alarm, the mysterious figure on the rock wheeled round, and Cateau beheld the startled black eyes and long, suspicious rodent's nose of His Royal Highness, Philippe d'Orléans, Duc d'Anjou.

For a breathless moment Monsieur went on staring. He was shaking with fright, far more seriously upset than she. 'Are — are you — a ghost?' he stammered, in a terrified whisper. And indeed Cateau might have passed for one, in her white dress and long flowing wimple, with her pale face and light, widened eyes.

The next minute he recognized the Countess and burst into a delighted chuckle.

'Madam — it's *you!* 'Pon my word, what a turn you did give me! I vow, I'd never have known you. Nay, but I know where you got it, though — 'tis the habit of our guileless friend the Abbess, is it not? ... I thought so! Dear madam, how deliciously naughty of you! As you see, I, too, am in disguise; it was the only way I could be sure of keeping our tryst. How do you like my frock? I had it made in Calais from some stuff imported from England. My dear, you'd never believe what it cost — ten crowns a yard — isn't that shocking? But I simply couldn't resist it. I laid in a fine store of linens, also. Those English goods are not to be beat. I find them superior even to the best from the Flemish looms. Do you know, it would almost be worth your while, whilst you're here, to run up to Calais to look at the shops for yourself. But what's amiss, madam? You seem so silent. Why do you not speak to me?'

Cateau had opened her mouth several times, but, strangely, no words would come. At last she managed to mutter stupidly: 'The ring — Your Royal Highness — the ring — it fell into the water!'

It was all she could think of, at the moment. For some ridiculous reason she seemed to be much upset by its loss.

Monsieur laughed merrily.

'Never mind that trumpery toy! It belonged to my Grandmother de Médicis — I couldn't bear the old thing!'

'But the Queen will be wroth when she hears ——'

Monsieur only laughed the harder, throwing back his head and opening his round red-cherry mouth so wide that all his pointed teeth showed.

'Well, of course — poor Maman! She's always in a pother, no matter what I do. Just fancy how angry she'd be if she could see the two of us now! If the Queen ever hears of our meeting, dear madam — but why *should* she hear? There are no witnesses in the wood to betray us. Come, dear friend, sit down, I pray, on the rock here beside me — there's plenty of room — nay, no ceremony, I *insist!* The occasion is quite unofficial.... There! That's better! Oh, how charming this is! I can't tell you how much I've been looking forward to it, ever since I heard that our trip to Forges was in the air. The Comte de Guiche had told me, you see, that you were here, but I thought it best to say nothing of it to Maman or the Abbé. Fouquet has a nose like a rat for other people's private concerns, and Maman is very suspicious, you know, and easily shocked. Somehow or other you've managed to get into her black books. I know what that means! I'm in them myself a good half of the time. Poor dear Maman is frightfully religious — she's never got over the scandal you made last carnival dressed as a Capuchin. ... Dear me! If she were to behold you this minute, I believe she would burst with rage — positively burst! He! He! It's *too* good — really, you know ...!'

Monsieur stuffed a lace handkerchief between his lips to stifle the gale of mirth that threatened to burst out of bounds. He laughed like a child — clear, high peals that rang through the silence of the little garden and caused Cateau to shudder with apprehension. What if anyone were to hear ...?

'I beg Your Royal Highness will say nothing of this masquerade,' she said, a trifle stiffly. 'It was very imprudent, I realize — the misguided impulse of a moment — I can't think now how I ever ——'

'My dear friend, please don't worry! Your secret is safe with me. I'll not whisper it to a soul!'

The Duke leaned forward and patted her cheek in a friendly manner.

'And indeed, Countess, you're quite ravishing as a Bernardine. If Madame de Jouarre were to see you, she'd be sick with envy, I vow. Poor wretch! White's horribly trying to her skin. Why do

nuns have such dreadful complexions? Now *yours* is perfection.
How on earth do you keep it so fair in summer? I burn to a crisp,
whatever I do. I've tried everything, simply everything — rose
balm — thousand-flowers water — nothing does the least bit of
good.... But, my dear, you're so quiet tonight. What's the matter?
Are you afraid of me? Please don't be! I've hoped so much we
might be particular friends. Our beloved Guiche has told me,
over and over, how well we should suit each other, and I am sure
he is right. He always is. I have no women friends, you know.
The Queen's so desperately jealous. The only ladies I'm permitted
to see familiarly are her maids-of-honour — and of all the malapert,
spiteful — well! we'll not go into *that*, or I'd never have done!
But Guiche promised me you'd be different. He admires you tremendously himself — oh, tremendously, I assure you! In fact, I've
often been quite jealous, far more than I am of his wife, poor
silly thing.... Why, do you know ... But that's not at all what I
meant to say. La, how I do run on, to be sure! My brother Louis
says I'm the worst chatterbox at court, and sometimes I'm afraid
he's right. We can't all be like Louis, can we? It's fortunate, in a
way, he and I are so different. I've often thought, if Maman hadn't
brought me up as she did ... But still you say nothing, madam?
I declare, it's most disappointing, after all the trouble I've taken,
to find you as dumb as a stone. And Guiche always says you're so
vastly diverting — he's made me rock with laughter, time and
again, with accounts of his mirthful interviews with you. Have I
offended, without my knowledge? Nay, tell me — there must be
something sadly amiss....'

Cateau shook her head.

'No, Your Royal Highness. Nothing's amiss. You've not offended
me.'

And, in truth, he had not. How could she be angry with this
blithe, confiding little creature, who chattered so gaily, totally
unaware that he was giving himself disastrously away with every
word he spoke, every gesture he made? No! The person she really
was irritated with was herself. Why had she been so stupid as to
take Guiche's idea seriously? What had kept her from dismissing
it in the very beginning, when the Choisy first proposed her tinsel
plot? ... The whole business was plainly absurd! Monsieur was
not *a man* at all — he was a chatty, cheerful little girl, perfectly at
ease with a woman once he was persuaded she wanted nothing he
could not give her. Cateau could quite believe that, under the
Count's sedulous coaching, he was prepared to be her friend, on his
own terms. Much might be gained by accepting his offer in the
spirit with which it was made. *Monsieur's Friend* — just that,
nothing more — would always be a person of importance at court.

Cateau, however, had no mind to play the part. She shrank with instinctive repulsion from its bloodless intricacies. Then why in God's name was she here, risking an already shaky reputation for — *what?* Ah, what a fool she had been!

But here was Monsieur, smiling and patting her cheek once more, as he offered her almond drops from a small crystal box. 'Dear me! I'd almost forgotten. . . . Mademoiselle gave them to me this afternoon — you know, she's fearfully fond of sweets. I think they're rather good, don't you?'

Well, there was nothing for it now. Biting her lips to keep from screaming with senseless laughter, Cateau accepted an almond drop. Monsieur took one, too: they munched them solemnly, side by side on the rock in the starlight, while the frogs in the lily-pool went on croaking ironical comments.

It was Monsieur who heard it first. He sat up straight, pushed his mop of curls out of his eyes, and lifted his hand.

'Was that a footstep?'

Cateau thought not. The frogs croaked so loudly, how was it possible . . .? She went on munching her almond drop. But Monsieur's sharp ears were still alert.

'Hark! There it is again! I'm sure someone's coming.'

This time Cateau agreed with him. A heavy tread sounded on the gravel, quite far away, but coming rapidly nearer. And presently they heard a voice that doubtless belonged to the tread, carolling lustily in a resonant, slightly nasal baritone:

> *'Since to charming Phyllis*
> *I gave my heart away,*
> *Sometimes I am cheerless,*
> *Sometimes I am gay!'*

Yes, it was only too obvious: both step and voice were headed towards them. Where could they hide? In the summerhouse? But they'd never be able to reach it in time . . .

> *'Thus my love and life are flowing,*
> *And I know not where I'm going.'*

Apparently, however, in spite of his words, the singer knew only too well. He came out from under the trees just as Cateau sprang up, gathered her skirts together, and made ready to flee. But quick as she was, Monsieur was quicker. He slid off the rock into the grass, picked himself up with incredible speed, and screaming shrilly rushed off into the wood, without a thought to spare for his companion.

Cateau was left alone by the lily-pool, tall and white in her stolen robes, to face the Abbé Fouquet, who had evidently chosen

to round off his evening with a midnight stroll in the fresh air of
the Capuchins' garden. It was too late to think of running away.
Besides, how could she run in this damned dress? No, she must
stay and make the best of a bad business. Perhaps the Abbé had
not recognized her. It was very dark, even here in the clearing.
With shaking fingers Cateau loosened the folds of her wimple, and
tried to draw it across her face, though even as she did so she realized
it was useless. For of course that wretched Monsieur, with his curls
and his screams, had already given the whole show away.

Fouquet's first words made it clear that he had grasped the unsavoury situation only too well.

'Countess, this is unworthy of you! To dismiss me from your
rooms like a troublesome child, and then steal off to a secret tryst
in the park! And if you had a mind to meet a lover, surely you
might have found a man more to your purpose than the Duc
d'Anjou! I am surprised at your want of judgement, madam, to
say no worse.'

Cateau wrung her hands, unable to answer. She had never in all
her life felt so completely at a loss. There was nothing she could
say that would not make her look like a fool. But she was no
coward: all was not lost as long as the Abbé had not identified her
costume.

'Sir,' said Cateau at last, very gently, 'you are mistaken. I did
not come hither to meet a lover.'

She drew her veil still closer and began walking down the path
as slowly as she could, so that the fellow should not suppose she
was trying to elude him.

Fouquet fell into step beside her.

'Ha, madam!' — he gave a bark of dry laughter — 'I can well
believe you there. If Monsieur were man enough to plan such
sport, I'd think better of him than I do. It was a foolish lark, no
more — that I could swear to. But 'tis ill done, madam, all the
same, and most imprudent, in your present circumstances. If the
Queen were to get wind of it ——'

'Sir, I beg you, if you have any regard for our friendship, to say
nothing of this to Her Majesty. It's as you say, a childish escapade
— yet I have many powerful enemies at court, who are eager to
seize any pretext to blacken my name. And the Queen, as you
know, is only too willing to listen.'

Cateau threw a pleading note into her voice that had served her
well, often enough, in the past. Whether Fouquet were susceptible
to it, she could not tell, but she must hope for the best.

Just then, as it happened, they reached the summerhouse where
she had sat so long that morning. It was empty; the door was ajar;
but a beam of light fell through it from a lantern above a rustic

shrine on the wall. The shrine was very small, and the beam was very feeble, but Fouquet gave a gasp as he saw Cateau's dress.

'What — in Heaven's name, Countess — you're garbed as a Bernardine — why, 'tis Madame de Jouarre's habit you're wearing! By'r Lady! Is there no shame in you?'

Cateau gave a moan, and attempted to glide past him into the shrubbery. But it was useless: she felt her wrist held in a grasp of iron. The next moment the Abbé had dragged her into the summer-house and flung her to the ground.

'Godless woman! When will you learn not to make a mock of religion? Lord! If I'd not seen with my own eyes, I'd never believe. . . . Is *nothing* sacred to you?'

Cateau, cowering on the turf in a corner, saw that his eyes were blazing with indignation — and more, with genuine horror. The man was honestly shocked by what she had done. Here was a turn of events she had scarcely looked to find — she had forgotten, as most people did, that the Abbé Fouquet belonged to the church.

'Hussy! Vile pagan!'

The names fell thick and fast, tripping over his tongue as they struggled to beat one another out. He had hold of her now, and was shaking her as a parent shakes a refractory child, but so hard that her breath was broken and the blood roared in her ears. With a powerful wrench of one hand (still shaking her with the other) he tore at her wimple; the stuff gave way and ripped full across, releasing her hair in a golden shower. And still he continued to shake. 'You trollop! You Jezebel!' . . .

Cateau was painfully conscious of his nearness. She could smell the strong musky scent he affected, watch the cords in his neck throb with the vehemence of his rage. In the midst of her fright she was reminded suddenly of a lion she had seen once in the King's menagerie at the Tuileries, panting and whining as it fought with its mate. Oh, it was awful! awful! In the whole of her life no one had ever treated her so; no man she had known had dared raise his hand . . . She was so taken aback that she forgot to be angry; amazement had robbed her of both feeling and motion. . . . 'Help! Help! Who wlll save me?' Her voice was dry, querulous, un-meaning.

After a while the shaking became rhythmic, almost mechanical. Cateau, on her knees, peered up fearfully at her assailant and saw that the blaze in his eyes was burnt out — or, rather, had been re-placed by a fire of different origin. ('Save me! Who will save . . . ?')

But she caught her breath again, this time with surprise and relief, as the Abbé Fouquet loosed his hold long enough to quench the light in the lantern and bar the summerhouse door. So, after all, she would save herself, in a way she had never expected!

Chapter XIV

MAGDELON BADE HER HUSBAND GOOD-BYE VERY DUTIFULLY AT THE
door of the Hôtel de Senneterre. She held up her face like a child to
be kissed, and lifted little Henri high in her arms, so that his father
might kiss him, too. Then she hurried upstairs to the Gallery of
Aminta and waved from one of the tall windows at the front of the
house. The window was open, as the March day was unusually
mild; she leaned out and went on smiling and waving as long as the
Maréchal's great state coach was in sight.

When at last it lurched round the corner and disappeared she
stopped waving mechanically, though her face still held the faint
impress of her parting smile; gave a strangled sob, and ran out of the
gallery down the hall that led to her own apartments. But it was not
until she was safe in her bedroom, with the door locked and the key
to it in her pocket, that she flung herself down on a couch and wept
as if her heart were breaking.

Magdelon had always cried a good deal — the easy and copious
tears of childhood — but she could generally control them at will.
This time, however, it was different; indeed, she seemed powerless to
stop, although she told herself that she *must* do so — that she was
being ridiculous — that most wives, sooner or later, were forced to
face what she was facing — and that, no matter what she felt, it was
wrong to give way to her grief. . . . No, it would never do! She would
have to be sensible and think of her health, or — if even that thought
could not stem the tide of her overflowing emotions — then of the
health of the child she expected to bear in June — of Henri's little
brother-to-be. (For of course the new baby would be a boy; she was
certain of that. How could it fail . . .with all the Masses she'd had
said at Saint-Eustache for a 'special intention'?)

Still the salt stinging tears kept on coming, in spite of her valiant
resolve to suppress them. They appeared to well up of their own
accord, as if their will were stronger than hers. Nor did they cease
till she had actually none left to shed.

Finally Magdelon sat up on the couch — her face flushed, her
eyes unbecomingly swollen — and said to herself almost fiercely:
'Come, now, you *know* you are being a fool! What on earth have you
to cry for?'

It was hard to answer that question. It would not be because her husband was leaving her, for he did that every year when he went to the war. Each spring since their marriage he had marched off to Flanders at the head of his troops — drums beating, flags flying — while Magdelon buried herself alive in her dull old castle in the country, and missed him, and prayed God on her knees twice a day every day to keep him safe from the Spanish bullets. That was bad enough, certainly — a featureless, empty half-life — and it grew harder to bear year by year, all the worse because she refused to admit how bad it was, even to herself.

But this trip was quite another matter. La Ferté was not yet bound for the army, merely driving to Nancy on a private mission for the Cardinal, to be away for a month at most. And Magdelon had always gone with him to Nancy — *always!* If they had not to stay there too long at a time, she enjoyed those excursions immensely. Her memory was crowded with tender souvenirs of the grim old ducal palace she had entered first as a bride. Besides, she thought it great fun to play the part of governor's lady at the numerous assemblies held in her honour by the good people of Lorraine. Madame de la Ferté was exceedingly popular with the local nobility; in fact, they liked her so much that she had often been able to be of service to the Maréchal, whom nobody liked at all. (It was too bad about that.... Magdelon knew he was stingy sometimes, and incredibly grasping about taxes; but the antipathy was an old one, dating back twenty years to the time of the wars with the Duke Charles IV, when La Ferté had had to be strong and high-handed in the King's service.)

Now, for the first time, she was left alone in Paris, where she had never been alone; shorn of all her gaiety and consequence; shoved unceremoniously into her own chimney-corner and told to 'sit and spin' till her master chose to return and recognize her existence once more. It was unfair! It was almost past bearing! Yet what could she have done to prevent it? She had begged and begged to be taken along — but La Ferté had simply stopped her mouth with a kiss and not even answered her entreaties — as if she'd been a naughty spoilt child! (That was the trouble with being thirty-odd years younger than one's husband.) Magdelon knew he was right when he insisted it would be best for her to stop at home — though that did nothing to allay her irritation! Nancy *was* a long way off, and the roads were sure to be shockingly bad, especially at this time of year, when winter storms and snow had worked their will on them for months. No doubt it was true what he said, that it would be the worst thing in the world for her health, and for that of the baby to come, to be jolted about in a coach for three days on those roads. Obviously she would be far better off in Paris, where her own doctors were within call, and friends and relatives could be summoned in case of need. And, as he had reminded her gently, it would be only for a few weeks — and then he'd be back again for at least a fortnight before setting out for Flanders...if he went to Flanders at all, this year. (There was talk of peace at long last, of a secret treaty with Spain; and La Ferté, who was close to the Cardinal, very likely knew more than he cared to admit.)

Just the same, Magdelon could not help being angry and indignant, with a strange unreasoning sense of injustice burning in her breast, and another feeling even stranger and less reasonable, that caused her to yearn to show her independence of her husband by doing immediately whatever she thought he would least like her to do. (But what, *what on earth* could it be?...when there was nothing, really, he'd ever forbidden her?...)

Moreover, though she honestly struggled against it, she could not prevent a dark suspicion from entering her mind. She told herself that she was being absurd. . . . Surely her physical condition must be the cause of this. But there it stuck, like a stationary cloud obscuring the sun of her confidence in her lord: had La Ferté perhaps private reasons for preferring to journey to Nancy alone?

Naturally he had led his own life there in the past, feasting his miniature court on wine and song and story like a Troubadour king of the Middle Ages. That was what he had been, and still was, in Lorraine — a king in his own right — nor had he always, his young wife feared, refrained from sharing the prerogatives of the throne. Magdelon had her own lurid ideas on this subject, gleaned from servants who had spent their lives in the La Fertés' household and whose impressible resentment towards a new mistress had taken the form of half-whispered hints about the vanished charms of the 'old days.' ... It became clear that her predecessor, the first Maréchale, an invalid most of her life, had never budged from Paris — and that La Ferté, whose behaviour at home was exemplary, had more than made up for it by enjoying a riotous existence in camp, and, especially, in his own particular fortress, the ducal palace at Nancy. There were piquant tales concerning the crowded list of frail enchantresses who had graced the governor's house, from the all-but-legendary beauty Marion de Lorme — dead and buried these many years, poor wretch! — to sirens of more recent vintage. . . . Oh, there was no doubt about it: La Ferté had drained his cup to the lees! That it was empty now, as far as romantic adventures went, and that the Maréchal did not regret it, had been manifest to the world when he married pretty Magdelaine d'Angennes de la Louppe and started a dynasty to inherit the Senneterres' fabulous fortune.

Magdelon had supposed it had been manifest to her, too. But now, unfortunately, she was no longer so sure. This hastily arranged

trip to Nancy, this pointed exclusion from his plans of his desolate
wife, might mean nothing at all. On the other hand, it might mean
a very great deal. . . . Magdelon had no mind to play the innocuous
rôle of an old man's darling, a prattling child to be petted and
played with when it suited his fancy — then conveniently forgotten
the moment grave issues were at stake. Yet lately she had begun to
suspect that that was precisely what she was, for La Ferté. Yes —
in spite of her serious efforts to be an adult wife worthy of her husband's confidence as well as love, after four years of marriage she
was still the 'infant Maréchale.'

'Oh, I'll not stand it!' cried Magdelon aloud, beating the pillows
despairingly with her fists. 'I've tried my best — he knows I have!
— and I've been useful to him, too, whether he'll admit it or not.
There was the time he had that quarrel with the Chancellor — and I
made it up between them . . . and the dinner I gave for the Bishop
last summer in Lunéville. . . . Everyone said the new taxes could
never have been voted without that! So it's not that I don't — that
I can't — then *what?* . . . Oh, there must be a woman in it somewhere! That's why he won't take me with him. Oh, what shall
I do?'

She might perhaps, tired as she was, have begun crying once more,
from sheer inability to decide how else to express her sense of frustra-
tion, had not the door to her inner cabinet softly opened and Madame de la Louppe slipped into the room. (Magdelon had not remembered in time that the inner cabinet connected with the best
guest-chamber, and she had completely forgotten that the latter was
occupied by her mother, who had arrived only the night before for
one of her periodical visits. . . . 'A little wardrobe-freshener,' Maman
called it this time. 'One gets so tiresomely dowdy, my dear, living
all by oneself in the country.')

When she beheld her daughter's flushed face and prostrate form
Madame de la Louppe hastened forward with an expression of startled concern.

'My child!' she exclaimed. 'You've not . . . it hasn't. . . . You
don't mean to tell me the *baby* . . .'

Magdelon shook her head, almost smiling, in spite of her distress.

'Oh, Maman, you know it's not . . . it couldn't be! The time's not
till June, and this is only the first week in March. Have you forgotten what the doctor said?'

Maman sat down heavily on a corner of the couch and fanned herself with her handkerchief.

'Dear heart, what a turn you gave me! I know what Patin said
as well as you do — but doctors are fools! There's not one of 'em has
the instinct in these matters of a *mother!* . . . Well, love, I suppose
then you're moping because your husband has left you. Poor fellow!

I had every intention of saying good-bye to him myself, but I over-slept after dinner, and that idiot of a Jeanneton forgot to call me in time. I must say, Magdelon, I sympathize with you deeply. In your delicate situation who knows what the strain of a long separa-tion...? and Lorraine's a desert at this time of year. I'm sure there's nothing amiss that La Ferté couldn't set right with a diplo-matic exchange of notes. When in doubt what to do, I always say, wait a few days, and then settle everything by letter. That's been my invariable rule throughout life — and you'd be surprised, dear, how often you find that, if you wait long enough, it's really not neces-sary to do *anything at all!* But men, of course, are impatient, and your good man — God save him from harm! — is no exception to the general run. There he goes, stamping off at full speed, without even waiting to see whether the matter is serious or not! Just when I've come to stop with you, too! I make no complaint, child — no complaint whatever, mind you — but I declare it's hardly compli-mentary to *me.*'

'Oh, Maman, you know he had no choice; you know the Cardinal asked him to go,' said Magdelon, who found herself unexpectedly defending her husband.

Maman put her head to one side with a sapient smirk — it looked, Magdelon thought, like a caricature of one of Cateau's prettiest poses — and lowered her voice portentously.

'Well, dear, naturally, that's what he *said* — and I dare say it may be true. Very likely it is. At the same time, while he's away transacting all this vital business for His Eminence, I see no reason — do you? — why you and I should not amuse ourselves here as best we can. You're looking sweeter than ever, and in your condi-tion, as long as you feel able to make the effort, I consider it posi-tively beneficial to go about and see people as often as possible. Nothing's so dangerous as staying at home and being sorry for one-self. I ought to know: I had to do it often enough when I was your age, for lack of somewhere to go!... Thank Heaven, your complex-ion's not altered! And really, now that skirts are so full, I don't see how anyone could tell — though even if they could, I've heard men maintain there was something seductive in a certain sort of curve — if you follow me? I remember, love — though I say it who shouldn't — what the Cardinal de Richelieu said to me the winter I was carry-ing Catherine-Henriette. Lord have mercy on his sins! *He* had an eye for a charming woman to the day of his death.... But that's neither here nor there. What I meant to tell you is that your sister has just written me a note — or, rather, her husband's secretary has (the sloven's too lazy to hold a pen in her fingers!) — to say that she's receiving this afternoon. Just a tiny assembly in the yellow cabinet, to celebrate the first reading of her portrait by Monsieur de

Saint-Evremond. I know it will be deliciously clever, and a truly distinguished occasion.... Now, dear, what have you to wear?'

'Oh, but ——' said Magdelon, objecting from force of habit — and then it occurred to her that this was exactly the opportunity she had been looking for, to assert her liberty from marital obligations: there was nothing, she well knew, her husband would be more likely to disapprove with violence than a call on Cateau.

So she smiled up at her mother, and said she thought that the cramoisie satin would do very well — and would Maman order the carriage? (Perhaps there might be time, later on, to snatch a moment's private conversation with her sister: no balm could be more healing to her present soreness of spirit than Cateau's brusque, realistic approach to the problems of life, which often, after she had dealt with them, appeared as unsubstantial as air.)

On their way through the windy March dusk to the Hôtel d'Olonne Magdelon recalled the first time she had driven there with Aunt de Marville (over four years ago now — it seemed centuries!). The quarter had changed a good deal since those days: the rue Neuve-Saint-Augustin, then considered almost rustically remote, had lately begun to look more built up; some of the great walled gardens had disappeared, giving place to rows of new houses; and there was talk of pulling down the old mills on the Butte Saint-Roch and razing the hill to make room for additional streets.

When Brossard admitted them and Magdelon heard as she stepped into the hall the same warm buzz of voices drifting downstairs to greet her, she had a swift, startlingly vivid vision of the trembling young figure, standing eager and unnoticed on the threshold of the future, that cold January day. But the future had become the past. ... Here, too, there were changes that gave unmistakable evidence of it. The gold-and-white drawing-room, where the Olonnes had been wont to receive all elegant Paris, was sacred now to strictly masculine gatherings. The Count and his friends still met there daily to play cards and perform their fantastic Lucullan rites — there was, in fact, a very special party taking place today, Brossard told them, as they tiptoed half fearfully past the doors: a smart little dinner to celebrate the inauguration of a new vineyard in Champagne, which the Gourmets' Club had just bought. (The club was another innovation, consisting exclusively of three members: Olonne, Boisdauphin, and Saint-Evremond, who doubtless would slip away to join his comrades as soon as the reading was over.) But ever since her return from Forges, six months ago, Madame d'Olonne had been 'at home' on the second storey in the more intimate refuge of the yellow cabinet; the gold-and-white drawing-room knew her no more.

No franker indication of the rapidly widening rift between husband and wife could have been shown than this pointed division of their social interests. Cateau was still under the Count's roof, officially still the mistress of his house; but in their daily lives the separation seemed to be absolute.

By the time that Magdelon and Madame de la Louppe had arrived, the yellow cabinet was already quite full. The ladies made their way through the crowd to the alcove where Cateau was receiving, with the Prince de Marsillac on one side of the great golden couch and the young Comte de Guiche on the other. At her feet lay her latest acquisition, a small lemon-coloured spaniel named Mouche (the gift of Guiche, who declared it exactly matched his mistress's hair); curled up in a tranquil crescent, like a dog carved in stone on a tomb, it watched the guests with limpid, unresentful eyes.

Cateau herself was looking beautiful in a new dress of stiff white brocade sewn all over with brilliants; she was wearing her diamonds and carried a small spangled fan, with which she beat the air as she tossed her head and laughed her queer noisy laugh and flirted impartially with her two gallants. She bestowed a languishing smile apiece on her mother and sister — exactly as if she had never seen them before — and greeted them in the high drawling mew she was accustomed to employ in public.

'Ah, my dears, you've come just in time!' she exclaimed. 'The Chevalier is about to read us the famous "portrait" — or no, I forget: he calls *his* creation a "character." Is not that appallingly affected? I tell him, too, it strikes fear to my heart — for *I've* no character to lose!'

'It may be, madam, you'll gain one instead,' suggested Guiche consolingly; while the Chevalier added in his quiet voice — which, nevertheless, always seemed to Magdelon to be making fun of them all — : 'My dear child, one must at least strive for originality when attempting to describe the "great original" of our century.'

Cateau laughed again, brassily; and so, after a moment, did Magdelon, though she was not sure why she was laughing.

There were so many people in the room that it was not easy for the newcomers to find seats. Magdelon and Madame de la Louppe glanced inquiringly this way and that, and were still uncertain whither to turn when Monsieur de Beuvron appeared, bowing gravely before them, and suggested that he had some chairs to offer them next the window.

Magdelon smiled at the dark, dignified young man, and gave him her hand; she had always liked Beuvron best of all Cateau's friends: it was a pleasure to see him again.

No sooner had the ladies seated themselves with a rustle of silk and a flutter of ribbons than Cateau rapped smartly on the bedpost to silence the expectant hum of conversation, and the Chevalier rose to begin the reading. He held his manuscript quite close to his eyes, because, though it was rather dark in the yellow cabinet, his hostess had refused to have candles brought(preferring the subdued glow of the firelight that burnished her curls and her glittering gown, while cleverly leaving her feminine guests in semi-obscurity).

'"I doubt if I shall be more fortunate in drawing your character than our artists in painting your portrait, in which task I may say that the best of them have lost their reputation,"' read Saint-Evremond smoothly. '"Up to now we have not beheld beauties so perfect as not to be forced to seek to acquire certain graces on canvas or to rid themselves of certain defects. You alone, madam, are above the arts that have power to flatter and embellish; they have never worked upon you save unhappily, nor without injuring you and robbing a faultless person of as many advantages as they are wont to bestow on those who are not without flaw.

'"If you are scarcely indebted to painters, you are even less so to the splendour of your attire. You owe nothing there either to other people's skill or to your own industry, and may tranquilly resign yourself to Nature for the pains she has taken in your behalf. Since negligence is seldom wise, I should not counsel others to trust in that sort of providence. In fact, most women are agreeable only on account of the charms they manufacture; whatever they don to adorn themselves hides a defect; whatever *you* discard of your finery gives you back some grace, and it is as much your interest to return to the natural self as it is theirs to escape from it."'

The Chevalier paused for an instant to clear his throat, and as he did so there were subdued murmurs of 'Charming! Charming!' from the feminine part of his audience; while Cateau, whose habitual restlessness remained in abeyance for as long as she felt that people were admiring her, fell into an exquisitely classic attitude of reverie — chin in hand, eyes dreamy and deliberately faraway.

Saint-Evremond, well pleased by the effect of the introduction, proceeded with his string of complimentary phrases. . . . The Countess's eyes outshone the sun, her complexion was fairer than flowerpetals . . . the delicacy of her features . . . the marble purity of her neck and bosom . . . '"Madam, only appear amongst all these portraits and characters, and you will eclipse every possible likeness of your beauty. . . ."'

Magdelon, her attention wavering slightly, let her eyes wander round the circle of faces in the yellow cabinet, to see how Cateau's friends were reacting to this complaisant recital of her perfections. Magdelon herself thought it very pretty, but she had a depressed feeling, which frequently assailed her when people were being clever, that she had not a notion *how* clever they were. (Maman, too, although swooning in ecstasies, had probably stopped listening long ago, and was merely inhaling incense with vicarious pride.) The

Abbé de Boisrobert liked it, of course — but then, he was a writer by trade and could appreciate Saint-Evremond's wit. So did the Chevalier de Gramont and Madame de Fiesque, who had come to the party together. (Poor Gilette! Her husband had died in Spain the preceding November, but though she had dutifully gone into mourning for him, her little face under the black widow's bandeau wore an expression of constant surprise, as if she still could not bring herself to believe that *this* had happened to *her*.) ... Margot Cornuel, also, exhibited a tolerant simper for once instead of her usual sarcastic air; but her lover Vimeuil, whose portrait of Madame d'Olonne had been last week's sensation in society, was quite naturally seething with professional jealousy. Jealousy of another kind was betrayed on the candid, clumsy features of the young Prince de Marsillac (now a bridegroom of four months' standing), who was glowering at Cateau and the Comte de Guiche, in spite of his uncle Sillery's warning eyebrows. And Little Manicamp's unwinking green gaze, fixed steadily on the same spectacular couple, assuredly boded no good to his hostess.

However, it was that inseparable pair of companions Cécile de Montglas and Isabelle de Montmorency whose demeanour most disturbed Magdelon's peace of mind. They were seated together directly in front of Madame de la Louppe, and from where she was sitting Magdelon had an unobstructed view of the series of acidulated smiles they exchanged at diminishing intervals during the reading. It was perhaps to be expected that the ladies should find it hard to relish Monsieur de Saint-Evremond's gallant tribute to their friend, since it was well known that Cécile's portrait, by the illustrious hand of Mademoiselle de Montpensier herself, had contained as many unpalatable truths as the Princess's pen-pictures of others invariably did — while no one as yet had been found bold enough to be willing to venture on Isabelle's! ... But as the minutes passed Magdelon realized there was more than passive displeasure here; a suggestion of sulphurous malevolence pervaded their looks and their whispered asides. Even Maman had begun to notice that something was wrong. She leaned forward, frankly eavesdropping, while Isabelle in a hoarse but audible undertone poured into Cécile's ear a shocking little story concerning one of Cateau's rendezvous with the Comte de Guiche. Cécile rolled her eyes in return, and both young women clucked and cackled and made scurrilous references to a 'modern Messalina' and 'Three-lovers-all-at-once-dear' and 'What-the-Abbé-Fouquet-will-say-when-he-hears...' that were too pointed to be ignored. Magdelon assumed her iciest manner, and Maman drew herself up and said 'Ahem!' very loudly, which produced the desired effect of silencing the scandalmongers.

But even after the whispering had stopped, Magdelon could not help worrying about what they said. It prevented her from concentrating on Saint-Evremond's delicate analysis of her sister's moral qualities, though Maman went on nodding her head triumphantly and glancing with intention towards Cécile and Isabelle while the Chevalier continued: "'As for your conduct, it is both blameless and agreeable, but since you may slight the small formalities that are real trials in life, you must fear the opinion of fools and the anger of those whom your merit has made hostile to you.

'"Women, who are your declared enemies, are constrained to admit a thousand advantages you have received from Nature. But there are times when we men are obliged to confess that you could take better care of them than you do, and that you don't make of them what others might. I shall conclude with your caprices, of which you yourself draw such an amusing picture. They are trying to those who suffer from them, of course. But, for my part, I find something piquant there, and I see that the more men complain of your temper, the more they are engaged by your person.... People annoy you easily without meaning to, and the hope of pleasing you has even ended more than once in the misfortune of displeasing.

'"Believe me, a man must be very lucky to find you in a favourable moment, and very clever if he can contrive to seize it. This much I can truly say after having examined you, that naught is so sad as loving you, but naught so difficult as to keep from doing so...."'

'Ahem!' said Maman again. *'Ahem!'*

But Magdelon was not listening any more. She felt sick and frightened; her thoughts revolved endlessly on a new and sinister theme.... Had Cateau really three lovers at once? It seemed hardly credible ... and yet Magdelon had to admit she knew very little of what had been happening lately to the Olonnes. She could see, of course, what the world saw, that the Count and his wife were separated in everything but name, and that Cateau appeared to have cast prudence to the winds and to take a defiant pleasure in receiving her throng of gallants under her husband's very nose. She had come back from Forges with Fouquet her acknowledged lover (which had temporarily restored her social prestige); but she had not therefore broken with Marsillac, as one might have expected her to do: on the contrary, that bemused young man paid court to her more assiduously than ever, and during the carnival season just past he had been her constant escort on the wildest of masquerade parties. (That much Magdelon was sure of, since the maskers had several times dressed at the Hôtel de Senneterre, to avoid Brother Louis' disapproving eye.)

Guiche, too, had been madly devoted all winter. There had been tales enough current about that affair.... People said that the handsome stripling had forsworn all his pretty boy companions for sake of the Comtesse d'Olonne — that the Duc d'Anjou and Little Manicamp were in despair. And everyone had heard how the dashing young Count had suddenly left the court at Lyon last autumn and rushed back to Paris to keep an engagement to attend a certain lady to Mass at the Church of the Minims in the Place Royale. Ugly rumours started circulating in the alcoves, and the rhymesters of the Pont Neuf — who, after all, only echoed their betters — had become so libellous that the Maréchal had forbidden his wife to read them.

Even here, in Cateau's own drawing-room, hostile female elements had contrived to creep in that were no less to be feared because simple jealousy was their motive power. And Magdelon felt an obscure difference in the attitude of the male guests towards their hostess: Cateau might be admired as much as ever, but she was no longer respected. Though she bore herself as proudly as before, and held her golden head high with all the old nonchalant serenity, it seemed to Magdelon's excited imagination that a sword hung over her sister; she saw Cateau menaced all the more surely because Cateau insisted on remaining unconscious of danger.

The reading was at length drawing to a close. Magdelon, who had heard scarcely a word of it, glanced up with a startled blush as the Chevalier embarked on what was obviously his concluding paragraph:

"'It remains only for me to speak of my boldness in picking out your faults; I have not been able to restrain myself from doing so, as otherwise I should have been sinning against the rules of the composition of a character, whose success consists in distinguishing good from bad qualities. In any case, I am far more to be pitied than you. You have merely to suffer their recital for a quarter of an hour, whilst I have been forced to pass whole nights discovering them. It was the first difficulty of that nature I ever encountered, and in token of your extraordinary merit, dear madam, I beg you to inscribe in capital letters the following legend: *He found my praises natural and easy; my dispraises gave him a vast deal of trouble.*'"

The Chevalier laid down the sheets of his manuscript with a satisfied half-smile: he knew he was brilliant and that there was no one else who could have composed so witty and penetrating a trifle as this *Character of Madame the Comtesse d'Olonne....* Cateau smiled, also, a little vaingloriously, as she had every right to do; for if it was clever of Saint-Evremond to have written the piece, it was still cleverer of her to have coaxed him into doing what he would not have done for any other woman in Paris. This sketch from the hand of an acknowledged master had quite eclipsed the scores of insipid amateur 'portraits' with which the salons had been flooded since

Mademoiselle made them the fashion. As a matter of fact, she honestly preferred Vineuil's less deft but more fulsome flatteries; the Chevalier had really been rather cruel to her; but it would not do to take him to task for it, because he was a genius. Everyone thought so. Had not Guiche told her a hundred times that Monsieur de Saint-Evremond was a master of French prose, the only modern worthy of being ranked with Rabelais and Montaigne? And Guiche should know what he was talking about, if anybody did, for he had his nose buried in books all day long: worse still, he thought that Cateau ought to read, too!... Cateau had done her amiable best to please him, and had actually gone so far as to buy a volume of translations of the Greek philosophers; but it was uphill work. She would perhaps not have persisted if she had not still smarted when she recalled her lover's shout of laughter at her confusing Don Quixote with the new Spanish ambassador....

But never mind that now: her literary party was being a huge success. Servants brought lighted candelabra into the room to add to the gaiety of the scene, and were beginning to pass liqueurs and sweetmeats about on trays. Meanwhile Cateau had only to go on laughing and tossing her head as she accepted the stream of compliments lavished alike on author and subject, to show that *she* could be literary, too.

Maman and Magdelon pressed forward to join the vociferous group round the Chevalier and his model.

'Matchless, my love, simply matchless! A veritable gem of the first water!' declared Madame de la Louppe, who had dozed during the first half of the reading and made faces at Cécile and Isabelle during the second. 'Dear Chevalier, Raphaël could not have done better. But if you're not careful, this little flaxen head will become sadly turned, I fear!'

'Why, Maman,' said Cateau, 'you can't have been listening! He's been abusing me like a thief! I vow, I ought to be dreadfully angry with him — ought I not, Chevalier?'

'Madam,' said Saint-Evremond, 'you know what I've written of you — and I stand firmly by what I have written: "People annoy you easily without meaning to, and the hope of pleasing you has even ended more than once in the misfortune of displeasing."'

'Isn't he wicked?' cried Cateau; and Maman tapped him reprovingly on the shoulder with her folded fan.

'Naughty man!' said Maman. 'Don't you dare make a character of *me!*'

Saint-Evremond bowed.

'Impossible, madam — I should lose my own vainly in the attempt!'

Madame de Fiesque came skipping up with Gramont in tow.

'Delicious, darling!' she fluted, batting her eyelashes madly.
'Never was anything more furiously successful! Poor Mademoiselle
will not dare try her hand again, I'll be bound! Sir, my most humble
compliments. . . . I've some verses at home — oh, the merest dilet-
tante scribblings, I assure you! — on which I've half a mind to implore you to cast a critical eye, when you've some leisure to give me.
Is it asking too great a favour, I wonder? Perhaps a little afternoon
during Lent — with only a tiny gathering of truly sympathetic
souls — and if we begged our prettiest, would you be kind enough to
read us a few of your sonnets as well?' (How like Gilette, to rush in
and try to make social capital out of someone else's bright idea!)
'And here's Monsieur de Gramont, who's positively pining to express his enthusiasm to you, himself. "The new Voiture," he calls
you already! But come, sirs, we women must leave you to savour
the pleasures of pure intellect; our poor conversational powers are
no match, alas, we know only too well, for such sparkling repartee as
yours!'

Under cover of the slight flurry caused by the approach of the
Abbé de Boisrobert and Little Manicamp, Gilette managed to lean
forward and whisper in Cateau's ear — but not so low that Magdelon failed to catch it — : 'My dear, I must speak to you privately,
at once! Something *dreadful* has happened!'

Cateau nodded, without changing colour or showing the least sign
of surprise or dismay — and went on chatting with Maman and the
Abbé de Boisrobert. It was Magdelon who flushed and dropped her
eyes in confusion. The vague feeling of apprehension that had oppressed her all afternoon suddenly sharpened: she was convinced now
it had been only too well justified. 'Something dreadful has happened' — yes; but what could it be? Gilette's staring eyes under her
black widow's bandeau gave no clue to the mystery, for her face remained as null from innate lack of character as Cateau's did from an
obstinately cultivated indolence.

There was nothing to do except wait until everybody else had gone
home.

This seemed to Magdelon to take a very long time, though it was
actually not more than half an hour. Madame de la Suze, the poet-
ess, was receiving that same afternoon at her house in the Marais,
quite at the other end of town; and although her party would be a
tepid contrast to Cateau's gay little gathering, most people felt they
ought to look in for a moment, because Madame de la Suze was 'one
of the Châtillons' and a granddaughter of old Admiral de Coligny.
Besides, the Count's dinner was just getting under way downstairs;
for some time the epicures of the company — which included, first
and foremost, Saint-Evremond himself — had been distracted by the
knowledge that divers subtly extravagant dishes were being pre-

pared for their approval below. One by one, therefore, they pressed their hostess's hand to their lips (soon to be consecrated to pleasures of a different nature) and made their adieux, till presently there was nobody left in the yellow cabinet except Madame de la Louppe and her daughters, Gilette de Fiesque, and her cousin Beuvron. (Magdelon saw that Guiche and Marsillac had wanted to be allowed to stay, too; neither would give ground to the other; but Cateau ended the matter by smilingly dismissing them both. The two rivals exchanged scowls at the door, and then stamped through it simultaneously, leaving Magdelon with an odd feeling, based on nothing at all, that they would never come back. . . .)

Maman, after surveying the scene through her lorgnette, bestowed a gracious glance of secret complicity upon the pair she conceived to be lovers (it was like her to have forgotten that the Beuvron affair was ancient history!), and was about to draw Magdelon with her out of the room; but Cateau raised a detaining hand and said placidly: 'Don't go, Maman,' while Gilette burst out: 'Madam, for Heaven's sake, stop, and give us the benefit of your advice! Your daughter is in a terrible situation!'

Surprised, and not a little flattered (it was so long since anyone had asked her advice about anything), Madame de la Louppe made a gesture of acquiescence, seated herself in a high-backed carved walnut chair by the fire, and looked up with an air of intelligent expectancy that would have deceived anybody who knew her less well than her children. Magdelon, shivering, drew unconsciously nearer her sister, as if to protect her from the threatening blow. She could not think what to say. Cateau, who had not moved from her place on the golden couch, remained silent likewise, but not, apparently, from fear; she had taken the supine spaniel Mouche into her lap, and began caressing its lemon-yellow curls, perhaps as a means of soothing her nerves (she was not naturally fond of animals). But at the same time she lifted her eyebrows and smiled her eternal unmeaning smile, as if everything were exactly as usual in the small world she ruled as queen.

It was Beuvron who, turning away from the window whither he had withdrawn with his customary tact, now approached the mother of his former mistress and said, very gently: 'My dear lady, we must all do what we can to help Madame d'Olonne. She will have need, I fear, of our combined good offices in her present dilemma. It may be we can avert the consequences of her imprudence, and the whole affair blow over and prove nothing serious.'

'Nothing serious!' exclaimed Gilette, who had begun to run back and forth on the hearth, like a fowl trying to find its way out of a pen, and to wring her hands distractedly. 'What *would* you call serious, then? You know what the Abbé Fouquet has done!'

Cateau's idol-like impassivity did not desert her; she went on stroking Mouche, as though nothing else mattered; but Magdelon turned pale at mention of that dread name, and even Maman said: 'Oh, Catherine-Henriette, haven't you broken with him *yet?*'

'And what,' said Cateau quietly, 'has the Abbé Fouquet to do with *me?*'

'Ah, my dear, my dear, don't tell me you haven't heard he's betrayed you to the Cardinal and the Queen! (I had it direct from my cousin here, who's just come from court.) It seems that the wretch has accused you of all kinds of horrors. He's told the Queen everything — *everything!* — about your affairs with Marsillac and Guiche — and shown them letters to prove it!'

'Letters!' said Cateau. 'I don't know what you mean. I've written letters to nobody.'

'Of course she hasn't!' cried Maman, with spirit. 'Why, the poor darling scarcely knows how to put pen to paper! They must be forgeries. Speak up, Cateau, and defend yourself. Tell Madame de Fiesque she doesn't know what she's talking about!'

'Oh,' wailed Gilette, 'I only wish I didn't! I didn't say the letters were yours. As a matter of fact, they weren't written *by* you, but *to* you, by those two wretched boys.'

'Letters to me from Guiche and Marsillac! How absurd! How could they have got into the hands of the Abbé Fouquet?'

'I haven't the least idea,' replied Gilette. 'Don't look at me like that: I've nothing to do with it all. Oh, I don't know what was in them — I don't even want to know — Thank Heaven, this is one mess I've kept clear of! All I can tell you is that the Queen and the Cardinal have read them and are furiously angry. But that's the least of our worries, isn't it, cousin?' She turned to Beuvron. 'Tell them the rest — what you heard at the Louvre this morning — how the Abbé has exposed his own relations with Catherine-Henriette — every detail! — and worse — how she threw herself at his head last summer at Forges, and went after not only Fouquet, but Monsieur, the Duc d'Anjou, too! Yes, and how — but go on, cousin — it's your story, not mine — they'll believe *you* if they won't believe me, for all the world knows you've never lied in your life. Oh, Catherine-Henriette, I *told* you Fouquet was dangerous! I warned you in the very beginning to have nothing to do with a man like that. And now see what's happened because you wouldn't take my advice!'

'Cousin de Fiesque, calm yourself, I pray!' said Beuvron, as Gilette, looking more than ever like a distracted little black bird, showed signs of going off into an attack of hysteria. Maman shook an admonishing finger at the Marquis and murmured, not particularly helpfully: 'Young man, young man, be careful what you say: remember a lady's reputation is at stake!'

Beuvron had spoken in his habitual calm, well-bred voice. Magde-

lon thought no one could have told he was labouring under an unusual strain if it had not been that somehow he could not bring himself to look at Cateau. Though he addressed her, his dark, deep-set
eyes remained fixed on Maman's vacuous face.

'Dear madam,' he said, 'forgive me if I speak of matters that
must be even more painful to you than they are to me. It is long, too
long, since I have been privileged to call you friend; yet I have never
forgotten my early attachment to you, which will last, I dare say,
as long as my life. For the sake of that attachment and what it has
meant to me all through the years, I feel I should be lacking in
chivalry if I failed to warn you of the dreadful pass you have come to,
whether you know it or not.

'What truth lies in Fouquet's charges, I neither know nor care to
know. But it is my duty to tell you that, as my Cousin de Fiesque
has said, he has shown Her Majesty letters addressed to you by
various young men, and in so doing has attempted to blacken your
character generally. How these letters came into his possession —
whether through your carelessness or the writers' — I cannot say.
They may even, as your mother suggests, have been forged by his
spies for his own base purposes. But that is the least of his treachery.
He has declared that last summer, with Madame de Choisy and
others, you entered into a conspiracy against the throne, whose object was to place you at court in the rôle of mistress to Monsieur, the
King's brother. When Monsieur appeared at Forges you even contrived, in pursuit of your design, to meet him in secret at midnight
in the Capuchins' garden. Fouquet asserts you were both in disguise
— you, in particular, in the garb of a Bernardine nun, having filched
the habit of Madame the Abbess of Jouarre — and that when you
were discovered by him, you bought his silence at a price I dare not
mention.

'Madam, these are grave accusations indeed. For your own sake,
let us hope that the Abbé is lying — he has done so often enough before; there is nothing, I fancy, he would not stoop to in order to gain
his vile ends. Monsieur Fouquet and I have never been friends. I
owe my information solely to the fact that I was at the Louvre today
just after his interview with Her Majesty and heard a full account of
it from old Beauvais, the Queen's waiting-woman.

'What steps, if any, are to be taken against you, I am unable to
say. We must pray that Her Majesty may rest content with her assurance that your schemes came to naught and that you are no
longer in a position to pursue them. But, my poor friend, do be careful in future, I entreat you! By all you hold sacred — by your faith
in Heaven above — by your affection for the family who cherish you
— even, perhaps, by the fondness once felt for a man who will never
cease loving you while there's breath in his body — let me implore . . .'

Beuvron's voice broke; he turned away for a moment, to hide the pain in his eyes.

Cateau deposited Mouche on a cushion (where the spaniel at once resumed its carved-stone attitude) and rose slowly to face the Marquis without flinching. She had succeeded marvellously, Magdelon thought, in keeping her temper during this trying scene, evidently realizing that cool serenity was the only weapon that could avail her now.

'I tell you, there's not a word of truth in all this,' Cateau said steadily. 'Don't believe me if you had rather not. It's all one to me. But I burned my letters from Guiche and Marsillac weeks ago. As for the so-called conspiracy, the whole story is a barefaced invention of the Abbé Fouquet's — no more and no less.'

She spoke with a simple nobility of manner that convinced her sister that she must be lying. . . . Alas! And five years ago Magdelon would have thought just the opposite. 'Oh, the things one learns about life!' said Magdelon to herself. She moved still closer to Cateau; she felt ill and horribly frightened. . . . But Beuvron had not finished yet. He went on speaking, in a queer, dead voice as if against his will, as if the words were dragged out of him by his conscience.

'Ah, madam, do you know what the truth is? Have you ever known? Woe that I should have to speak thus! Yet your actions for years could have led me to no other conclusion. Ever since I first loved you I've had to watch you coquetting with this man and that, unable to let a single prize slip through your fingers because it flattered your vanity to have us all at your feet. Yes — and because you felt each of us might be put to some purpose. What you wanted *me* for, God alone knows! Fouquet's uses were plainer. And I suppose even young calves like Guiche and Marsillac . . . Ah, madam, madam, to think that all your beauty, all your talents, should have come to *this!* I pity you from the bottom of my heart for what may well lie before you — and I pity myself, too, for having been such a fool. Shame, madam, shame on us both! On you for sinning so ignobly — on me for loving so unworthy an object! I'd give my right hand if I could save you from the consequences of your recklessness and folly. Yet I can do nothing. That must be my worst punishment in time to come — to remember to my dying day that my love was useless when disaster came!'

Cateau stood unshaken and immovable before the blast, a faint chilling smile on her lips. Beuvron bowed over her hand, and then left the room without another word. Maman and Gilette burst into tears on general principles, because they really could not think what else to do. But it was Magdelon who brought the painful scene to an end by crumpling up on the floor in a scarlet satin heap, having fainted dead away.

FOR SOME MINUTES THEREAFTER ALL WAS CONFUSION IN THE YELLOW cabinet. Mouche abandoned his tomb-like torpor and rushed about in circles barking loudly, until forcibly ejected from the room. Cateau sank with a cry to her knees, expressing all the emotion over her sister's plight that her own had failed to call forth. Burnt feathers and brandy were sent for; servants ran uselessly to and fro; the sufferer was placed on Cateau's own couch, with her head in Cateau's gleaming white brocade lap; while Cateau herself, pale and anxious, bathed her temples with thousand-flowers-water, Gilette called constantly for cold applications to the feet, and Maman as constantly kept exclaiming: 'Oh, hot, dear — hot, by all means! And not the feet — the pit of the stomach! Though really, with the poor lamb in her present condition, I'm not sure *where* the *pit ...*'

It was Monsieur de Beuvron who saved the situation — Beuvron, whom everyone had forgotten, as everyone always did, but who proved to be still in the house; when the footmen carried Magdelon downstairs there were his lackeys waiting in the hall, his coach-and-four stationed in the street, and the Marquis himself solicitously inquiring if he might be granted the favour of taking the Maréchale home.

'Sir, you are our saviour!' cried Maman hysterically; and indeed that was not overstating the case; for not only did this kindest of men convey both ladies to their house as speedily as possible, but as soon as Magdelon had been handed over to the care of her own servants, he sent his carriage to fetch Doctor Patin and the midwife, and insisted on remaining on call for several hours in a freezing cold marble antechamber at Great Senneterre, until he received word that Madame de la Ferté was resting comfortably and her physician did not fear any imminent danger.

He called, too, in person every day for more than a week, to inquire how the patient was doing; sent hampers of fruit and flowers, with most polite notes; and was altogether thoughtfulness itself, though it was several days before Magdelon was well enough to appreciate how much he had done for her.

She fell exceedingly ill of a fever, which was succeeded by a period of great prostration. However, by exercising extreme care and keep-

ing her absolutely quiet in bed for as long as there was any possibility
of an accident, Doctor Patin was able to prevent a miscarriage; and
by Magdelon's own wish no word of her illness was dispatched to the
ducal palace in Nancy. (The Maréchal had written to his wife that
unlooked-for developments in the political situation would keep
him away from Paris for some months to come.)

In the end, youth and a naturally strong constitution being on
her side, it was not long before she was sitting up in a fur-trimmed
dressing-gown, looking little and lonely under the stiff cut-velvet
canopy of her monumental bed amid the vast gilded wilderness of
the state drawing-room at Great Senneterre.

Then at last Monsieur de Beuvron was permitted to see her. He
tiptoed into the room, his face solemn and sympathetic over an armful of posies from his own garden; and Magdelon, who was sipping
beef-tea with a pensive air, smiled when she saw him and leaned
forward, so that her black curls tumbled across the front of her rose
satin gown edged with sable, and looked so charming that Beuvron
wondered why he had been stupid enough to let a lapse occur in his
friendly relations with Madame d'Olonne's little sister.

He could stay that day only a very few minutes, during which he
found they had not a great deal to say to each other. The remembrance of his former connection with Cateau, which could not help
being uppermost in his own mind, was, he supposed, uppermost in
hers, also: neither of them cared to recall, though they could scarcely
forget, the incidents leading up to Magdelon's collapse in the yellow
cabinet. But the pauses in their conversation were comfortably
ones, filled with a kind of unspoken harmony; when Beuvron took
his leave he said: 'Madam, may I come again?' — and Magdelon
replied: 'Soon, I hope, sir' — and both were left with a cheering
glow round their hearts and smiles that persisted, even when there
was nobody to see them.

After that, the Marquis called every day, as before; only now his
visits, instead of being restricted to a conventional quarter-of-an-
hour in the marble antechamber with the obliquely coy Madame de
la Louppe, were sometimes lengthened to include the whole afternoon. As Magdelon regained her strength she was allowed to walk
in the garden, to take advantage of the pleasant warmth of the sun
during this mildest of Marches; and Beuvron was often her companion there. Together they strolled along the maze of neatly gravelled
paths, watched the sparrows splash in the fountain with the spouting tritons and dolphins, and counted the colonies of tulips, scarlet
and yellow and white, that formed gay geometrical patterns under
the budding elms. (Most of these were rarities of fabulous price
brought back by the Maréchal from his Flemish campaigns: Magdelon recited their names with shy seriousness to her friend, proud of

her horticultural knowledge: Beautiful Dawn, King's Favourite,
Pride of Haarlem....) Soft grey clouds drifted high in a melting
blue sky; a gentle breeze dissipated the clinging mists left over from
winter, ruffled the curls of the strollers, brought a touch of rose to
Magdelon's ivory cheeks; and every day the green curtain above
them spread wider and deeper and grew more murmurous with the
songs of birds.

It was the earliest spring, and the loveliest, Magdelon could remember.

Sometimes, of course, it rained; and then their meetings took
place in the Gallery of Aminta, where a fire was laid beneath the
huge hooded chimney-piece with its sculptured stone coat-of-arms of
the Senneterres. On such afternoons Beuvron was apt to read aloud
selections from a volume of Voiture's poems or perhaps a chapter
out of one of the endless romances of the prolific Scudéry (for Magdelon's taste in literature had remained curiously childlike); while
the ladies, stitching at their equally endless tapestrywork, would
glance up from time to time to marvel at the ingenious adventures
of the hapless Clélie or Mandane, and little Henri played about
amongst the rushes on the hearth with his father's spaniels, which
were friendlier, if less aristocratic, than the exquisite Mouche.

These days passed as quickly as any the Marquis and Magdelon
spent together; it was always a surprise to the latter when the footmen appeared to draw the curtains and light the candles, and she
saw that it had grown dark outside while all was so cheerful within.

So the agreeably innocent idyll continued till April brought the
trees to full leaf in clouds of misty green and turned the walled garden at Great Senneterre into a blaze of colour. Then, one day,
Beuvron did not come. Magdelon, pacing the flower-bordered paths
expectantly in the full sunshine of early afternoon, was handed, instead, a letter that told her his wife was ill. After that, silence until
the end of the week, when a second letter came saying that Madame
de Beuvron was dead.

The news was a tremendous shock. At first Magdelon could
hardly believe it. It seemed impossible that anyone so young *could*
die. She had known the dead woman very slightly. During the
whole of the time the Marquis had been devoted to Cateau, Magdelon recalled having seen his wife twice only: once, at her own wedding to La Ferté; and again, at the Fair of Saint-Germain with her
two little sons. (They had been standing in front of the booth where
the wonderful golden bird was singing, each little fellow clinging to
one of his mother's hands.... Magdelon had had a dim impression
of china-blue eyes, elaborately frizzed dun hair, and a total effect of
colourless commonplace good looks; but she remembered quite
clearly the lady's impatience when the children begged to be allowed

to listen a little longer, the petulant determination with which she had said: 'No, no; there's no time left, I tell you!' and dragged them protesting away.) Beuvron seldom spoke of his wife to his friends; people thought of her as dull and rather devout, and as caring as little for general society as society in general cared for her.

Now, with terrifying suddenness, she was gone, blotted out as though she had never been: nothing was left of her, nothing even to show she had lived save the two little boys, who were still so young that they would soon forget her — and Magdelon's memory of the querulous voice crying: 'No, no; there's no time...,' which would endure, she felt, as long as she lived, since time indeed had stopped for her who'd said it.

It was dreadful to think of — dreadful!... Magdelon shed a few vaguely frightened tears, and prayed God to forgive her for having been so neglectful of Madame de Beuvron. She had a special Mass said in the oratory of the Hôtel de Senneterre by the priests of Saint-Eustache for the repose of the soul of her friend's wife (taking care to send word first to her miserly father-in-law that she intended to pay for the candles herself). She called, also, promptly on the various members of the Le Tellier family (Madame de Beuvron had been born a Le Tellier); but she did not happen to encounter Beuvron in any of the black-draped drawing-rooms she visited. And her note of condolence to the widower — couched in the politely empty phrases custom prescribed in these cases — was acknowledged in no less formal a manner.

Magdelon's walks in the garden were lonelier now than they had been before her new friendship began. But the first wet afternoon became a sort of slow torture, for Maman's high, breathless gabbling was a poor substitute for Monsieur de Beuvron's mellifluous tones (which had seemed to bring the characters of the novel to life as he read); and when the book was laid aside Madame de Senneterre came to see them, and sat toasting her toes in front of the fire and retailing musty bits of gossip until Magdelon felt ready to scream. ... Poor Mother Anne! Her idea of being amusing consisted in cataloguing ladies of her acquaintance who had come to untimely ends. Madame de Beuvron had been thirty-one at the time of her death — just six years older than Magdelon was now — but Madame de Mercoeur, Mazarin's niece, and the poor little Duchesse de Roquelaure (who had faded out of life a year ago out of sheer inability to maintain an interest in it) had been much younger.... Of course, *they'd* been expecting babies.... Magdelon, feeling her unborn son move, looked at Maman, whose childbearing days were long past, and at Mother Anne, who had never been able to have a baby at all, and wondered how long she could stand it.

After Mother Anne left them Magdelon mounted to her chamber

and sat down at the inlaid writing-table that stood in the central window, from which there was a view of the feathered green elms in the garden below. It was early evening; the rain had stopped, and the sun was just setting over the chimneys in a patch of saffron sky. Every raindrop that clung to the leaves of the trees caught a tiny reflection of its mellow last rays. The air blowing softly through the open window was fresh with the smell of wet earth and growing things; it was filled, too, with bird songs and with the chorus of bells ringing for Vespers in the numerous churches of the neighbourhood. There was the big slow boom of Saint-Eustache, the busy tinkle of the monastery bell at the Little Fathers, near at hand; and, more in the distance, the varied notes of the Chapel of Saint Mary of Egypt, Saint Oportune, Saint-Leu-and-Saint-Gilles, Saint-Jacques-de-l'Hôpital, Saint-Nicolas-des-Champs.... Farthest of all, very faintly and sweetly came the chimes of Saint-Thomas-du-Louvre and Saint-Germain-l'Auxerrois, over by the river.

Magdelon knew and loved each one. She listened, leaning her elbows on the table and cupping her chin in her hands, while the bells went on pealing and the sun slowly sank; when it had quite disappeared — as if that were some signal agreed upon — she lighted a candle on the table, picked up a quill-pen with a brave scarlet feather, and wrote very fast, without stopping even once, the only letter of her life that did not cost her a pang:

> Sir — Will you come to see me tomorrow? Or, if not tomorrow, as soon thereafter as may be convenient to you? I must apologize for intruding upon your privacy at this time, when sad cares oppress you and you are doubtless in heavy affliction and distress of mind; but there is something I must say to you.
>
> Hoping that God may keep you in His holy care, and that He may bring you the consolation none on earth can offer, I beg you to believe me, sir,
> Your very humble and affectionate friend,
> The Maréchale de la Ferté

The next day the sun was shining again and Magdelon was walking in the garden, as usual, when Monsieur de Beuvron was announced.

He came towards her, bareheaded under the elms; his face was pale, and graver even than its wont; his dress all a sombre black.

When Magdelon beheld him, the fine phrases she had intended to speak took wing from her mind, like the flock of sparrows fluttering over the garden wall. She gave a little cry, and stretched out both hands without a word.... It was Beuvron who murmured, as he stooped to kiss them: 'Madam, *I* have been lonely, too.'

After he had gone, at the end of the afternoon, Magdelon remembered that she had never told him any of the things she had meant to tell him. Nor — come to think of it — had he asked her what it was she had wanted to say. But did that matter — since there were all the other days ahead when they could be together?

During these weeks the sisters had seen almost nothing of each other. Cateau, haunted by the vision of Magdelon's bloodless face with its staring, horrified eyes on the floor of the yellow cabinet, called at the house every day while the latter was really ill; and later, when the invalid was strong enough to bear it, the two young women had one long and affecting interview.

Cateau cried copiously — a luxury she rarely permitted herself — and made a clean breast of her chain of misdeeds of the last six months, omitting nothing from the first interview with Little Manicamp and Madame de Choisy to the masquerade in the Capuchins' garden.... 'But indeed, indeed, darling, I meant no harm! Things just seemed to happen one after another, without my knowing how to prevent them. I can't think now how I ever ... Oh, that loathsome Abbé! Gilette was right about him from the first. Why wouldn't I listen? Men are all alike, Magdelon; there's no trusting the best of 'em!'

Magdelon cried, too; kissed her sister many times; dried her tears on a corner of Cateau's handkerchief (her own having mysteriously disappeared, as always); and said that she understood perfectly — though she was far from sure that she did —; the fuss would undoubtedly blow over soon; Cateau must on no account worry....

In the end Cateau went away somewhat comforted, feeling that very likely Magdelon was right and it *would* blow over. She then drove to the Palais and ordered a set of extremely expensive Flemish lace dresses for the new baby.

What she had said was precisely the truth: she could not see where she had been so glaringly at fault. Granted that a woman had a right to engage in a career of gallantry — and nine tenths of the women she knew did so, without half so much justification for it as herself — what had she done that others had not? Of course, there was that wretched affair of the Bernardine's dress ... Magdelon, Cateau could see, had been more shocked by that than by everything else put together — and Cateau herself was shocked sometimes when she remembered ... But, after all, it had been only an accident, an unlucky accident. Was *she* to blame if ...? And ruling that out, what else was she guilty of? Why, almost nothing! ... God knew, she was no conspirator! And certainly the gossips who attributed three simultaneous love affairs to Madame d'Olonne had accused her of sins she had not dreamed of committing.... Well, naturally, she had been forced to accept Fouquet's attentions while

Marsillac was still with the army in Flanders. She had not felt it fair to the poor boy to break the bad news to him while he was doing his duty so bravely. But directly he came home she had told him quite plainly that everything would have to be over between them. Was it *her* fault if the Prince had refused to recognize his dismissal, and had hung round the house forlornly all winter, looking so dejected (in spite of his poor little abandoned bride) that, in the end, Cateau had not had the heart to refuse him a few smiles and stolen kisses?... But nothing more! The business had gone no further than that, no matter what horrors people might assert she was guilty of.

As for the Abbé Fouquet, she had not, to be sure, been in love with him any more than he had been in love with her. There had not been even the pretence of a sentimental attachment between them. They had embarked on the liaison clear-eyed and disillusioned, impelled by the least romantic of motives: Fouquet, to attempt to cure himself of his unhappy passion for Madame de Châtillon; and Cateau, at first because she had thought it the best means of saving an awkward situation, and, later, because she had hoped the connection might serve to bolster up her crumbling social position. It seemed to her that both had got what they wanted out of the prosaic compact. The Abbé, an ambitious commoner, had very much enjoyed boasting that the most beautiful titled woman in France was his mistress; and Cateau had found, on returning from Forges, that her enemies were not nearly so nasty about her as they had been the preceding spring. She had stumbled upon a most efficacious, if rather unusual, means of recovering her lost respectability.

The affair with Guiche, she admitted, had been a mistake from start to finish. She saw that clearly, now that it was too late to undo what was done. Probably she would never have encouraged his advances if Fouquet had not been sent by Cardinal Mazarin after the holidays to England, where he had stayed for more than two months. Cateau had been painfully bored with no man to squire her about — and then, there was no use in denying that Fouquet was at best an awkward lover, harsh and impetuous, boorish and self-seeking. Whereas the Comte de Guiche, whatever one might think of his morals, was perhaps the most charming young man at court. There was not a woman of her acquaintance who would not gladly have yielded to him; of all the Countess's conquests none was more generally envied. (And was it not delicious to be able to snap one's fingers at the epicene cabal? — in particular, to pay Monsieur back, in the only way he'd understand, for his flouting of her last summer at Forges?)

Oh, yes! Cateau felt she could find excuses for her conduct, even

there. Where she had been blind was in supposing that the Abbé
would overlook what she had done in his absence. She still was convinced she was right, theoretically. Since there had been no semblance of love between them, why need there be any jealousy either?
Why were they not both free as air at all times when they were not
actually occupied with each other? Cateau was sure she would not
have minded if Fouquet had had a dozen mistresses in London. . . .

Unfortunately, she had miscalculated the strength of the masculine sense of ownership that follows physical possession.

When Fouquet came back from his trip their relations were resumed as if nothing had happened to interrupt them. He was far too
clever to betray his knowledge of his mistress's infidelity. On the
contrary, smiling and dissembling, he had set to work in secret, like
the despicable spy he was, to destroy his young rivals and Cateau as
well. . . .

The stratagem of the letters had been subtle indeed — too subtle
by half for the two young men who walked unsuspecting, one after
the other, into the snare that had been laid for them. Cateau could
not understand, for the life of her, why there had been so much talk
about those few silly scrawls. She wished now, with all her heart,
that she really *had* burned them as she pretended she had. She had
kept them simply because it was the custom to keep billets-doux;
they had seemed of so little importance that she had been just as
willing to give Guiche's notes to Marsillac as to give Marsillac's
notes to Guiche. It seemed a trifling concession to settle a jealous
dispute and place both her gallants on the same footing. How could
she have guessed that Fouquet had put them up to it, planned the
whole thing from the start, in order to get them all into his power?
. . . Naturally, if she had had the least suspicion of his slimy schemes,
she would *never* . . . But really, *really* there was nothing in either correspondence to have churned up such a sea of trouble! The Abbé
himself must have seen that was so, else he would never have proceeded to further, more fatal exposures, even risking his standing
with the Queen by revealing his own share in the scene in the Capuchins' garden. . . .

Cateau felt she could never forgive him for that. In the midst of
her fright for the future, which was extreme, she realized that what
angered her most was the fact that it was the one man she had
favoured for interested reasons who had compassed her downfall.

As the spring days lengthened, it became unpleasantly obvious
that the Comtesse d'Olonne was ruined.

True, in spite of her fears, no official steps were taken against her
at court. But the uproar caused by her misconduct grew louder and
louder till its reverberations were audible from one end of the kingdom to the other.

The pamphleteers of the Pont Neuf waxed busier than ever, with such quantities of fascinating new material at their disposition; scarcely a day passed that some unmentionable infamy in the way of a scurrilous verse or scrap of imaginary dialogue was not brought to her notice by Gilette de Fiesque, whose idea of being helpful in this crisis was limited to rushing to show her friend each fresh evidence of disaster.

Cateau's name was pointedly excluded from the lists of guests for the various festivities that occupied the court after Easter. She was not asked to the King's hunting-party at Vincennes, nor to Monsieur's supper-and-fireworks at Saint-Cloud. And Monsieur de Lyonne, her old friend, the new Secretary of State, left her out of his magnificent fête at Berny (an exact duplicate of the famous one he had given two years ago, where Candale and she had been undisputed king and queen). Cateau felt particularly badly at being ignored by Monsieur de Lyonne, because his party had a kind of official character, being given for Pimentel, the Spanish envoy, and intended as a celebration of the armistice that had just been declared between Paris and Madrid.

This was in the first week in May. Several days later Madame d'Olonne was hissed by some rowdies in the pit as she entered her box at the Hôtel de Bourgogne.

They were very small hisses, and the disturbance was soon calmed; but she was so much shaken that she left the playhouse at once and drove home in tears, striving in vain to control her twitching fingers and tremulous lips.

Oh, what was going to happen? Who would save her? She had no one left but Gilette — and even Gilette's friendship had lately shown signs of the increasing strain to which it had long been subjected. Why, it was only yesterday that the transparent fool had pretended to have a cold, as an excuse not to drive in the Cours — and not an hour later Cateau had spied her, looking perfectly well and very pretty in a brand-new gown, on the back bench of the Comtesse de Soissons' coach! So it would not do to count too much on Gilette. . . . What was worse, Cateau had not one man friend in the world. Neither Guiche nor Marsillac had come near her in weeks (the toads!); and when Fouquet called (oh, the impudence of the creature!) she had sent word to Brossard to say that Madame d'Olonne was not at home to Monsieur the Abbé, then or on any future occasion.

So there was no one — no one at all! She had never in her life felt so hopelessly alone. Even that debatable solace, the company of her husband, was denied her; for a number of weeks now Olonne had been closeted in his own apartments with Maître Prideau, his steward, and his lawyers, and refused to emerge to dine with his wife.

(Some tiresome business to do with the seneschalate of Poitou, without doubt.)

Cateau was at her wits' end what to do. She could not sit at home in the yellow cabinet, her hands folded in philosophical resignation, waiting for the callers who never came. She had lived in a crowd for so long that she was almost literally unable to support life without it. To console herself, therefore, for her cruel isolation, she launched into an orgy of spending — ordered two new carriages and a sedan-chair, elaborately gilded and lined with rare velvets from Venice; a set of Flemish tapestries of fabulous value; some solid silver furniture for her dressing-room; and commissioned Monsieur Mignard to paint her six panels for her bedchamber, a series of life-sized scenes illustrating the story of Rinaldo and Armida. She laid out, also, vast sums on her personal adornment, buying dress upon dress for parties to which she had not been invited; hats, gloves, feathers, laces, and jewels in incredible profusion. For she had come to the conclusion that she must have been falling off lately in her looks. . . . Yes, of course, that was it; that would explain everything. She was no longer so young as she had been; twenty-six was a dangerous age. Anxiously she consulted her mirror, begged Quentine not to spare her the truth, squandered a small fortune on ointments and powders and elixirs of youth that were sold in the booths of the Palais and the Temple. . . .

She went on spending right and left, until there was no money left in her purse — and when that happened she had only to apply to Maître Prideau, her husband's steward, in order to have the golden hoard renewed. This occurred, however, so often that spring that the old man, who looked like a grudging owl (only *he* slept all night and was wise in the daytime!), blinked disapprovingly at his mistress, and grumbled at length that, really, he couldn't imagine what the Countess had done with the *last* twenty thousand francs. . . . Cateau had been obliged to scream and stamp her foot more than once, and threaten to report him to the Count, before he could be induced to comply with her wishes.

In June the Peace of the Pyrenees was announced between France and Spain, amidst wild rejoicings of the populace. At the same time it became known that King Louis was to wed his cousin, the Infanta Maria Teresa, and would soon start south with his court on a triumphal tour of the country, which was to end at the Spanish border, where he would receive his bride from the hands of her father, King Philip IV.

As soon as the news became public, society was thrown into a turmoil, like a hive of bees at swarming time. Only in this case it was a new queen's coming, not an old queen's going, that caused the excitement. The arrival of Maria Teresa would create scores of new posts to be intrigued for. Gentlemen-in-waiting would have to be appointed, and ladies-in-waiting; equerries and grooms; bailiffs and stewards; chaplains and almoners; secretaries and women-of-the-bedchamber. Not since the marriage of Anne of Austria and the late King Louis XIII, five-and-forty years ago, had it been necessary to form a complete royal household almost, as it were, overnight. The whole court suffered an attack of the strange fever, Ambition. Every cabinet minister and officer of the crown — indeed, every servant, from butlers and cooks down to lackeys and scullions — anybody, in short, no matter how humble, who was supposed to have an avenue of approach to the King and the Cardinal — was begged or bribed to use his influence on behalf of less happily situated acquaintances.

Paris was divided into two camps: those fortunate ones who were going south with the King, and those others who might as well consider themselves dead and buried because they were not able to go. The former group bustled about self-importantly, making preparations for the journey. Coaches were relined and regilded, lackeys tricked out in new liveries, while their masters commanded whole trousseaux, as though *they*, too, were going off to get married on the Spanish frontier.

Cateau's young lovers had been amongst the first to depart. Marsillac, whose favour with the King had suddenly become strongly apparent (he was said to be His Majesty's preferred partner at cards every day at the Comtesse de Soissons'), was sure of a place in the new household; and the Comte de Guiche, as the son of the Maréchal de Gramont, governor of the border province of Béarn, had been chosen to accompany his father to Madrid with the official embassy to demand the hand of the Infanta.

The whole world — or, at least, all of it that Cateau knew — had been caught in the vortex; the undignified scramble for preferment was on; and in its passionate preoccupation with the young monarch and his future bride Cateau felt dimly that a new era was beginning for society, in which, alas! there would be no room for her.

Towards the end of June Cardinal Mazarin left for Saint-Jean-de-Luz, to meet the Spanish Minister, Don Luis Haro; while the King and the Queen Mother were at Fontainebleau, which became the rallying-point for the courtiers who were planning to accompany their sovereigns.

For the first time in years France was at peace — but Paris was as empty as ever it had been during war....

Magdelon's baby was born the first week in July, one very warm night in the midst of a terrific thunderstorm. Strange to say, she had an unusually hard labour, much more painful and protracted than it had been with young Henri. Cateau and Maman were up the whole night with Doctor Patin and the midwives, fearful to leave her bedside for even a moment; the grey light of dawn was trickling through cracks between the drawn curtains, and sparrows were starting to twitter in the drenched ivy outside the windows, before a faint cry was heard in the huge canopied bed at Great Senneterre, and the head midwife lifted a red, anxious face beaded with sweat to ejaculate: 'God be praised, ladies — a fine healthy boy!'

The word was passed quickly to the hall, where the long train of the La Fertés' servants had been standing for hours in the stifling semi-darkness, whispering, praying, sometimes giggling hysterically without meaning to, as they listened to their young mistress's screams; and before the sun was up a courier on horseback trotted out of the Porte de Vincennes, to carry the Maréchal in Nancy the joyful news that his second son Louis was born. (It was very odd — but as Cateau stood chatting with her brother-in-law's chief equerry she fancied that a figure in a dark cloak at the very end of the line, who had been waiting apparently for news with the others, but who vanished unaccountably the moment she appeared, was familiar to her. If she had not known that such a suspicion was ridiculous, she would have sworn she had recognized Monsieur de Beuvron.)

The summer dragged on, growing warmer and duller. Everyone had left town except the Olonnes — and, of course, Magdelon, who was slow to recover her forces after her difficult confinement, though Doctor Patin had urged an early removal to La Ferté-Saint-Aubin, where the fresh country air would be sure to prove beneficial after the sticky uncomfortable heat of Paris. . . . It was the hottest August people could remember in years, and one of the most disagreeable. Almost every day brief torrential thundershowers poured over the city, drowning the gardens and parks and transforming the unpaved streets into a noisome mass of well-nigh impassable mud, without relieving the temperature.

The river had never fallen so low before; the fountains in the Tuileries and the Luxembourg had ceased playing, while their basins, half-filled with stagnant rain-water, began to be covered with thick green scum. In the crowded tangle of narrow streets in the older and poorer parts of Paris the suffering was acute. No one went abroad who could possibly manage to remain within doors, but the sun beat down so relentlessly that the houses were nearly as warm as the streets; even at night the baked stones retained much of their heat; and only an occasional whiff of cooler air, scented with garlic and cheese and the strong red wine affected by concierges and Swiss porters, lingered in the little passageways leading from the front doors of some of the great hôtels to their inner courts. Flowers stopped blooming, birds stopped singing — and Maman, for once tired of Paris, drove home to La Louppe, her shabby carriage piled high with the bargains she had secured in the aftermath of the recent shopping stampede.

But Magdelon still refused to stir, protesting that she was very well where she was, really, and would infinitely rather await at Great Senneterre the Maréchal's return (which could not now be much longer delayed).

As for the Olonnes, they stayed at home because there was nowhere else for them to go. The Count spent more and more time shut up in his rooms with Maître Prideau and the lawyers; he was hardly ever visible, even at mealtimes; with the departure of the court his circle had dwindled so sadly that the afternoon receptions and even the dinners of the Gourmets' Club had been discontinued temporarily.

Cateau would have gone away if she could have thought of a place to go. But she could not — and in any case, she might well have been incapable of giving the necessary orders to pack up her clothes and make ready to leave. She felt like an automaton, moving as if in a dream. She felt, also, that some disaster was impending, some avalanche that must sweep her away to instant perdition, but whose implacable course she was powerless to avoid, since she knew not where the danger lay. These forebodings were peculiarly liable to overtake her at night, when she tossed sleeplessly on her bed of gold in her lonely and airless chamber, or sat at the window, gazing dry-eyed and wretched at the sparkling, inaccessible stars that mocked her desolation.

In the morning she awoke from uneasy slumbers, expecting the worst to have happened; when the day passed without untoward incident she was relieved and mildly surprised. But, of course, things could not go on like this much longer. Today ... or tomorrow, maybe ... or, if not then, the day after that, the axe would fall.

Chapter XVI

CATEAU CAME IN RATHER LATE FROM A SHOPPING EXCURSION, ONE particularly hot and humid afternoon, to find Quentine in tears. It was the climax to a thoroughly tiresome day. The streets had been scorching under a pitiless August sun; François, the coachman, who was beginning to grow a little deaf, had twice misunderstood his mistress's orders and taken wrong turnings; and the Maison Gautier, Madame d'Olonne's favourite purveyors of dress materials, had stupidly sold the Princess Palatine a piece of special gold-and-silver brocade they had promised to save for *her* (a shabby trick unredeemed by their candid avowal that the Princess had needed it for the train of the gown she intended to wear to His Majesty's wedding).

This last mishap had put Cateau in a petulant mood. She entered her dressing-room frowning, quite prepared to give both her women an uncomfortable quarter-of-an-hour. But the sight of the sobbing Quentine at once altered her plans. Quentine was a good little creature. She'd served Cateau faithfully for years, without making a single indiscreet or impertinent remark. (No doubt she'd been paid to be wise. . . . Still, by whatever means they'd been achieved, the results were the same. And there was, it was generally admitted, not a cleverer hairdresser in all Paris.)

Cateau, therefore, stroked the girl's shoulder and questioned her kindly. It appeared that Quentine had had a quarrel with Crispin, the Count's valet, which had ended in her declaring she would report his insolence to her mistress; whereupon Crispin had laughed in her face and observed that that could do her small good, since the Countess would not be there very much longer. . . . 'She's to be packed off to the country, the hussy, to repent of her sins. . . . Yes! By God! And if Master's got his wits about him, he'll pack *you* off, too — as precious a pair of trollops as ever I hope to lay eyes on!'

Thus, in tear-choked accents, Quentine reported the sentiments of Crispin, valet-in-chief to Monsieur the Comte d'Olonne.

'And oh, madam,' cried Quentine, 'I'm afraid he knows only too well what he's talking about! Naturally, I wouldn't give him the satisfaction of thinking I believed what he said. But the lawyers have been closeted with the master since early this morning — all four of 'em! — and Malet, the secretary, told me at dinner he'd had orders to write the bailiff at the castle of Olonne to make everything ready for our arrival.'

A small involuntary shiver ran over Cateau as she listened to Quentine. She knew quite as much as she wanted to about the castle of Olonne, having once passed a fortnight in it with her husband shortly after their marriage. (Had it been the winter of '53 or '54? At all events, not long after the close of the civil war.) Olonne had gone there on a reluctant tour of inspection of his various estates, to estimate the amount of damage done to them during the Fronde; and even now Cateau retained a nightmare memory of the angular, forbidding, more-than-half-ruined old house set among the desolate sand-dunes of the Poitevin coast. Miles of salt marshes and bare open heath, here and there a grove of scrubby dwarf pines — but not a hill in sight to relieve the monotony of the landscape or to break the force of the wind sweeping constantly in from the sea.... How could she ever forget the dreariest two weeks of her life spent in that gloomy setting, with no one for company save the crude fisher-folk of the almost uninhabited region and the grey gulls crying plaintively in the mist? ... The castle of Olonne! Why, that would be terrible! That would be the end of everything — worse even than the convent to which in less hopeful moments she had already consigned herself; for in a convent there would at least have been the sisters to talk to. At Olonne there would be nobody — *nobody!* — not even Quentine, Cateau thought: it was really too much to expect the girl to leave Paris and all her friends to follow her mistress into an exile that would certainly last for weeks — probably for months — possibly even for years. Who could tell? ... This much, however, Cateau knew: a husband's power over his wife's person was unlimited. If he chose to murder her, no one would object.

Ah, but there was no time now for weakness or vain lamentation! She must be stronger than ever before. It would not do to let Quentine suspect what she was feeling.

Hastily she comforted the tearful girl as best she was able. 'There! There! You goose! Why, what a fuss over nothing! Where's your handkerchief? Here — take mine, if you like. I dare say there's not a word of truth in what Crispin told you. I dare say he was lying on purpose to tease you. But even if he were not lying, why should we cry? What's a month in the country to *us*. And anyhow, if you'd rather stop here, you know I could always arrange it for you. It's not at all necessary for you to come with me.'

Quentine dried her tears, and kissed the Countess's hand, and affirmed that she would rather die than desert so noble an em-

ployer, even if it meant spending the rest of her life in prison —
which, if sincere, was undeniably handsome, since Cateau knew for
a fact that half a dozen of her friends would be overjoyed to engage
the skilful Quentine any day at the latter's own figure.

The maid also offered to fetch Crispin at once, so that her mistress
might interrogate him; but Cateau refused, saying she preferred to
go straight to her husband.

If the worst had indeed befallen her, she had no wish to learn
her fate from servants.

The Count she found in his bedroom unpacking a box of ornaments he had just received from the Orient. He was sitting in his
shirtsleeves cross-legged on the floor, squinting anxiously as he
lifted each delicate bit of china or crystal out of the bales of damp
brown spicy-smelling cloth in which they had made the long and
hazardous journey, dusted it with a fine linen handkerchief, and
handed it (scarcely breathing the while) to Crispin, who placed
each treasure gingerly on the top shelf of the best walnut cabinet.

'Take care of the mutton-fat snuffbox,' he was saying as Cateau
came in. 'It's an exquisite piece, worth five times its weight in gold,
I wager. Old Vanel knew what he was about when he sent me that.
On the whole, Crispin, an excellent shipment in excellent condition,
should you not say, my good fellow?'

'Excellent, indeed, sir,' replied Crispin, who was standing behind
his master, between the latter and the open door, and therefore was
the first to perceive Madame d'Olonne. 'But here is the Countess,
sir — begging your pardon ——'

'Begging my pardon, eh? That *would* be a novelty!' remarked
Olonne dryly.

He did not get up from the floor, but moved his head sideways —
stiffly, as if it were worked by machinery — and pursed up his lips.
(Could he be about to whistle?)

'Good afternoon, madam. Will you forgive my not rising? I am,
as you may observe, in a somewhat perilous situation. I beg you,
also, to overlook the informality of my attire; the unusual heat of
the day is my excuse. Great Heavens! What a summer we are
having! But you, my love, would appear to be impervious to the
ravages caused by our climate, since I infer, from your bonnet and
the parasol you are carrying, that you have either just returned
from a promenade in the Cours or are on your way thither. If the
latter should be the case, pray do not let me detain you. I regret
only that I may not have the pleasure of offering you my company
as escort — but the heat, dear friend, the heat has quite overset me!
I am capable of nothing. I did not touch a morsel of solid food at
dinner — did I, Crispin? In fact, all I've eaten since morning has
been a slice of chilled melon and a very few peaches from the garden

of the Temple, which the Commander de Souvré was good enough to send over with his compliments. They were admirable, I assure you — far better, alas! than any we've been able to raise on our own premises. I can *not* understand it! The soil of Paris is said to be everywhere of a similar consistency — and Heaven knows, we spare no pains in its cultivation! But every year it's the same story. Why, would you believe — ah, madam, please pardon my running on like this, without asking you what I may do for you, or even having the gallantry to procure you a chair! The temperature must have affected my brain. Crispin, a chair at once for the Countess!'

Cateau, who had been standing poised as if for flight in the doorway, eying her husband dubiously, now entered the room with a rustle of silk, but refused the stool Crispin placed before her.

'I will not sit,' said Cateau, in her clear, composed voice, 'but I should like to speak with you *alone*.'

'Madam, I am entirely at your service,' replied Olonne. 'Leave us, Crispin. You may return, if you will, in a quarter of an hour — or shall we say, twenty minutes? Yes: at half after five, exactly, I shall have need of your good offices once more.'

The valet bowed and left the room — not without a backward glance that seemed to Cateau just to skirt the edge of a malicious smile: Crispin, she knew, had always hated her — and the Count turned to his wife with a look of inquiry so guileless that it could not possibly have been spontaneous.

'Well, madam, you wished...?'

Cateau surveyed the little man at her feet — who did not appear so far, it had to be confessed, a very formidable adversary — with dispassionate attention; then, changing her mind suddenly, she trailed across the shining, slippery parquet and seated herself on a chair in the middle of the room, just where a slanting ray of sunshine from the court touched the golden crown of her curls.

'Sir,' said Cateau gravely, 'it has come to my ears — never mind how — that I am to be exiled to Olonne. Can this be true? I could hardly believe ——'

'Madam, what nonsense is this! "Exile" is an ugly word, one which I have never used, nor shall permit others to use in my presence. I fear, my love, that you have been listening to idle tales from the servants' hall. No — no, dear child — the matter is quite otherwise. The fact is, some business affairs will require my presence in Poitou for a number of months to come. Annoying, is it not? — but unluckily necessary in my position of Seneschal of the province. Ah, why did I ever covet such a paltry distinction — but there! It's too late to speak of it now.... Well, then, I must be off to Poitiers next week, and I cannot feel I should be doing my duty by my wife, were I to leave you behind. Paris is a tropical furnace this year — the heat has been cruel — cruel!... Besides, I cannot bear to deprive myself on this journey of your company, a charm I've been privileged to savour all too rarely of late. So we'll be off on Monday for the country, if it suits your convenience to make ready so soon? . . .

'This thought, too, has occurred to me: Poitiers itself will be hideously dry and dusty in mid-August, and the Seneschal's house — which I believe, my dear, you have never seen? — would be a dreary hole in which to ensconce a lady of fashion from Paris. *I* must linger in the town to transact the King's business, but there is no reason why you should be penalized because your poor husband happens to be a petty government official. Therefore, I have decided to open our house at Olonne for the season; I have already given orders to that effect. I know the place is old and rather run-down — but the country is delightfully wild thereabouts, and the clean, cool sea air will soon bring the roses back into those pale cheeks. There you may rest in perfect peace and solitude, after the crowded and feverish diversions of the court. . . . Our nearest neighbour, if I remember correctly, is not less than eight or nine leagues away . . . and of course I shall join you as often as my duties as Seneschal will allow me. I fancy, madam, that as soon as you've settled down to the change in routine you will really enjoy the contrast to your present activities of living the life of a country gentlewoman.'

The Count picked up a small saucer of deep emerald-green jade, and blew on it lightly (it was too fragile, apparently, to support contact with so gross an object as the linen handkerchief) before smiling benevolently at his wife.

Cateau drew a long breath; her mouth felt dry with misery — and she moistened her lips before trusting herself to speak. . . . It had come, then, at last. This was the punishment, long overdue, for the sin of breaking the marriage bond; this was the score she had known all along she would sooner or later have to settle for the follies of her youth; this — whether Olonne were willing to say so or not — was Exile, the end of everything.

She stared, without really seeing it, at the bright white court in the bright white sunshine, and at the leaves, brown and withered before their time, drifting aimlessly down from the tall branches of the elms and the plane trees. (How many there were, and how softly they fell! No one cared... no one knew. . . .) At length she said quietly: 'I understand, sir. I am willing to go with you, of course. But "for a while," you say? Have you any idea how long that while is likely to last? I've business of my own to attend to here — certain measures to take ——'

'My dear, I only wish I knew,' replied Olonne, in his cheerful, fussy way. 'That's the worst of getting mixed up with the govern-

ment — one never can be sure how long anything will take. All
that stupid red tape!... However, this much I can promise you:
should my duties demand my continued presence in Poitiers throughout the coming winter, I shall make every effort to have the Seneschal's palace put in order, so that I may welcome you there as its
mistress. I think I shall be able to manage it — I am almost *sure*
I can. 'Twill be an expense I can ill afford — but perhaps we could
make shift with some of the furniture at Olonne — I don't like to
think of your spending the cold months all alone in that draughty
owl's nest.'

'But why should I stop there at all, without you?' asked Cateau.
'Why should I not return to Paris in the autumn and live here in
this house as I have lived since our marriage?'

She turned her blue eyes on him with an unspoken question in
their translucent depths. If she were to be condemned without hope
of appeal, at least she was determined to have the fruitless satisfaction of hearing why from her husband's own lips.

Olonne met her challenge with persistent good-humour.

'Dear friend, I shrink from telling you — but you force me to
face the issue squarely. I have had serious losses lately in my
estates: Prideau tells me that my income this year, and for some
years to come, will be sadly diminished. You can imagine how it
pains me to be obliged to consider such things — but there's no
help for it now. And, my dear, I must add — though it pains me
even worse to refer to it — that your personal expenditures have
been no inconsiderable item in the total sum of our liabilities. You
know — or perhaps you do not: why should you bother about such
prosaic details? — that I generally count on your revenues to take
care of the taxes on your properties in Normandy and the house in
Paris as well. Now Prideau informs me you've already spent your
income for the current year — worse, that a considerable portion
of next year's supply has been pledged in advance. I have never
sought to control the handling of your own fortune in any respect.
It has been a point of honour with me to leave your purse-strings at
your own disposal, feeling sure, as I did, that you would deem it
equally a point of honour to employ them only in ways I could
whole-heartedly approve. I have rejoiced in your well-deserved
reputation as the best-dressed and most elegant woman of fashion
at court. I have always admired your beautiful and tasteful toilets,
as well as the matchlessly gallant air with which you have worn
them — but my dear! my dear! It is time now to call a halt. Nay,
it *must* be done, and immediately, else ruin stares us blankly in
the face. And that I am assured you desire as little as I. I have
prepared, with Prideau's help, a detailed account of your dis-
bursements for the year 1658 alone — you will find it there on

my desk — with the bills for your purchases duly attached. I do not ask you, my love, to examine it too closely — the follies committed for last year's frocks make sorry reading — but if you will glance just once at the total figure they represent, I am certain you will realize, without further discussion, why I am being driven to this extremely unpleasant course. It is not of my own choosing, madam — but our alternatives are plain to see: it's the country for us, until further notice — or the Poor House.'

Cateau bowed her head, less in silent submission to her husband's will than because she simply could not think at the moment of anything disagreeable enough to say. She wanted, naturally, to be as disagreeable as possible, to give in with the least imaginable grace; for it went without saying that she would have to obey Olonne. All wives had to obey their husbands when husbands chose to exert their authority. It was Cateau's misfortune, rather than her fault, that she had been let do as she pleased for so long that she had almost forgotten her husband existed. She had never questioned his right to command. Even now, when the end of all things that made life pleasant appeared to have come, it was not so much her defeat she resented as the fact that Olonne had preferred to conquer her without battle. She longed to fight, to defend herself wildly, to answer accusations and fling out counter-accusations of her own, to scream and stamp and give vent to her feelings in the one way she knew — even if it meant confessing all her sins into the bargain. And here was Olonne purposely evading the issue, feinting, retreating, determined to cover up the danger-spots as though they simply weren't there!... Coward! Coward!... She saw now that he would never tax her with infidelity, never name her lovers openly to her face, so that she might toss them back into his teeth and cry brazenly: 'Yes — yes — it's true! And I'm glad I did it — glad, I tell you!'... He had not the manhood for that, though he must know what she'd done as well as she did. (Didn't all Paris know now, thanks to the rhymesters of the Pont Neuf?)... Coward! Coward! Unspeakable coward!

Cateau was trembling with fury she had no means to express. It seemed to her she had never hated her husband so violently as now; she would die unless she could think of some way of unleashing the passions that shook her. (But what, after all, was the use in screaming and making a scene? They'd done that too often before.)

She gave her enemy a level look, calm as a summer sky, her face only a little paler than usual, as she said: 'Very well, sir; it shall be as you wish. I'll give orders to my women at once. We'll be ready to start for Poitou on Monday.'

Then she rose and walked without haste towards the door, her taffeta skirts swishing softly behind her. Halfway she paused for a moment by the walnut cabinet, and with extreme deliberation stretched out her parasol and overturned the whole row of pretty fragile ornaments, bringing them down on the bare shiny floor in a welter of cracked china and splintering glass.

When Cateau got back to her room, still pale but otherwise quite composed, she found Magdelon waiting to see her — a fresh-faced, bright-eyed Magdelon, now completely restored to health and bubbling over with youthful enthusiasm and high spirits. The two had planned to drive to Vincennes together to take supper, the cool of the evening being the only time when it was pleasant to be abroad in the streets.

'Darling!' cried Magdelon, kissing her sister fondly. 'How are you? And how do you like my dress? It's brand-new; I fetched it from Maître Thomas only yesterday.'

'Very nice; very pretty,' answered Cateau absently, narrowing her eyes almost without being conscious of what she was doing. 'The waistband's a trifle high, though, don't you think? — and I hear lace on sleeves is going out.'

She dropped wearily into the chair before the looking-glass, and was about to ring for Quentine to arrange her hair when she was stopped by Magdelon, who begged for the privilege herself. 'It needs scarcely anything, dear; it's as smooth as silk, truly — only the ribbon wants retying, and that I can do as well as she. Besides, there's something I'd like to say to you.'

'Yes?' said Cateau. 'What is it, dear?'

But Magdelon only laughed in reply and stooped over her sister's chair, so that the two lovely heads were reflected side by side in the mirror's crystal depths. (What did that make one remember? ... a winter's night long ago, when they had been so happy because they had just found each other, after two years' separation — and now they were once more to be parted! But it would not do to think of that yet: Cateau felt only a passing wonder as she saw that their faces in the glass were still as young and as pretty as they had been then. How *could* they be — when so much had happened to them both?)

Magdelon went on laughing without saying why, and fiddling with the ribbon in Cateau's hair; but her efforts to fasten it in place were so clumsy that at length Cateau protested she would really rather tie it herself.

'Child, what's got into you tonight? You're different.... There's something about you I don't quite... Magdelon, tell me...'

Magdelon's image blushed a rosy red; she hung her head for a minute. Then, lifting it again, she grasped the back of the chair to give herself courage, and whispered: 'I meant you to know before, dear — but after all, it happened only yesterday! Oh, Cateau, I've

told nobody — nobody at all! What will you say when you hear?
I hardly dare ——'

Cateau stopped patting and poking her golden curls — which in
spite of her melancholy preoccupation she had been moulding swiftly
into shape with practised fingers — stopped staring at the reflection
of Magdelon before her, and wheeled about to face the real Magdelon behind: the real Magdelon, whose breathless laughter and
telltale blushes made the whole story plain without need of words.

'Child,' said Cateau quickly, 'I want the truth at once. It's
not . . . you haven't . . .'

'Darling!' said Magdelon. 'Yes! *I* have a lover, too.'

'Not . . . not . . .'

Magdelon nodded vigorously. 'Yes! It's Monsieur de Beuvron.
Oh, I *hope* you don't mind! — because of course I know that once
you and he — but that was long ago, wasn't it? And since then . . .
But I wouldn't have thought of him for a *moment* if I hadn't been
sure it was over between you — had been over for years. And then,
his poor wife's being dead made everything different, too. Oh,
I know it's wicked of me — but I couldn't help it! Poor La Ferté!
What will he say if he — I never, *never* meant — But he's been away
so dreadfully long, and I — Oh, Cateau, Cateau, why didn't you
tell me?'

'Tell you *what?*' said Cateau, in a very small, spent voice.

Magdelon clapped her hands together and began to dance excitedly about the room.

'But, darling, you *know* — you never said what fun it was to be
in love!'

BOOK THREE

YOUNG LOVERS
(*March, 1671 — June, 1672*)

Chapter I

IT WAS THE FOUNTAIN IN THE COURT THAT WOKE CATEAU. THE new gardener's boy, who did not know that the water was not to be allowed to play until it was certain the Countess had stopped sleeping, had set the works in motion: the discreet silver tinkle gradually made itself felt as a part of her dream; then grew more detached and insistent till, finally, Cateau opened her eyes and saw that morning had come.

She opened her eyes very wide because, as always, she was at once completely awake. But since it was still too soon to get up — this she could tell from the position of the square patch of pink sunlight that fell on the floor through the rose brocade curtains — she lay quietly staring at the ceiling, which was painted all over with very plump clouds and cupids almost as pink as the sun. As she lay she listened to the fountain and the sound of the gardener's rake on the gravel. She could hear, also — although her bedroom was at the back of the house — some noises from the front street: there was a chairmender's cry, and the rumble of wheels and clip-clop of horses' feet as a coach lumbered over the cobbles of the rue Villedo. That was because the house was small, much smaller than the Hôtel d'Olonne. There were only two reception rooms, one of them insignificant, and the dining-hall was scarcely more than a cupboard. However, the place was quite large enough for one person; Cateau had not hesitated when the agent had offered it to her. She liked the quarter, the big, smart, gay parish of Saint-Eustache where she had spent her whole married life; the rue Villedo, quiet and exclusive, was an excellent address; best of all, her new home was only a few steps from Magdelon's in the rue des Petits-Champs.

So she had signed the lease directly, and moved in the week after she received the final papers confirming her separation from Olonne — and there she had been ever since. Four . . . five . . . why, it was going on six years now since she had come to live in the rue Villedo! (How time flew, once one stopped being very young!) The decree from the court of the Châtelet, which its owner kept carefully locked in the secret drawer of the desk in her library, bore the date of the sixth of September, 1665 — and this morning was the thirteenth of March, 1671.... Cateau was sure of that because she had made an appointment with her lawyer, Maître Le Caron, to look over some papers connected with her properties in Normandy. He was coming at eleven, and she intended to be dressed and ready to receive him on the stroke of the clock — but it could not be anywhere near that....

No, it was early yet; the patch of pink sunlight had barely moved. Cateau relaxed once more on her pillows, and stretched with a cat's deliberate grace, as she thought how comfortable she was, and what a pretty room she had, and how delightful she found it to live alone and do what she pleased, all day long, every day. The house was hers, and all that was in it. (Most of its contents were priceless, too; she had had to buy everything on leaving her husband's bed and board, and she had spared no expense from the fine Flemish tapestries on the walls of the Grand Saloon to the smallest, most exquisite trifles in crystal and embossed silver adorning her dressing-room table.) She could get up when she liked, go to bed when she liked, see the people she wanted to (and none of those she *didn't* want to!) — and she was subject to no one's authority, exposed to no criticism save her own — in short, absolutely independent for the first time in her life.

Independence, thought Cateau, was an admirable thing. It made up for the storms and mistakes of her youth; for the dismal months of exile in Poitou; for the precarious years that followed her return to Paris, after eating her heart out by herself in the country as long as she could possibly stand it. She had refused, of course, from the very beginning, to go back to her husband's house, and had fled instead to her mother, who was a boarder at the Carmelites' convent — not the Great Carmelites outside the gates, but the new branch house in the rue Bouloi. That had not been amusing, either, but it was a thousand times better than living with Olonne; and besides, everyone told her it was the only thing to do. Women who had trouble with their husbands were invariably expected to retire to convents, sometimes — if the trouble could not be settled satisfactorily — for life, alas! For a time, indeed, it had looked as though Cateau might have to go on to the end of her days confined to her dove-like retreat, attending Mass with the nuns, conning the sermons of Nicole and Bourdaloue, and, by way of the wildest diversion, washing beggars' feet in the charity hospitals. (Repentant sinners had always to wash beggars' feet, whether they wished to or not, and whether or not the beggars wished to have their feet washed. Cateau would not soon forget, one day at the Hôtel-Dieu, looking up, sponge in hand, over the cot of one particularly loathsome specimen to find her old rival, Madame de Saint-Loup, holding the basin of water in readiness.)

Olonne had insisted, in the first place, on getting a separation of property from his wife; that is, he had himself made legally not responsible for her debts. But her personal freedom was another matter. Cateau had had to write letter after letter to the judges at the Châtelet, imploring, cajoling, even threatening by turns; she had used up reams of paper and quarts of ink and hours of her secretary's and the notary's time. It had been terribly trying and fearfully expensive. Cateau did not know what she would have done to cover the costs of the case if Aunt de Marville had not died, rather suddenly, in the midst of it, which caused Uncle de Marville's very considerable estate to revert to his nieces.

In the end, of course, she had got her way, as she had been certain she would. But because Olonne had been ugly and chosen to fight back, retreating step by step only as he was forced, it had taken her four years to get it. Four precious, irreplaceable years of her youth! ... Whenever she thought of what her husband had done to her, Cateau's eyes darkened with anger under implacable brows.

When he was no longer able to withhold her liberty by law he gave way with very bad grace. A divorce she couldn't have, merely a judicial separation; but that was nearly as good, since she was free to do anything she wanted except marry again — and catch her wanting *that*, after all she'd been through!... Cateau left the convent, hired the house in the rue Villedo, and said to herself: 'Now *at last* I am going to be happy....'

The chimes of Saint-Eustache — much nearer now than when she had lived at the Hôtel d'Olonne — were striking nine. Cateau stretched out her hand and shook the little silver bell that stood on the table by her bed, whereupon the door to the hall opened and Quentine, whose days of tripping were definitely over, came bustling in to greet her mistress.

'Good morning, Quentine,' said Cateau, with the smile she never failed to bestow on her faithful maid.

'Good morning, madam,' replied Quentine, sketching the curtsy she was now somewhat too stout to drop with ease. 'How did madam sleep?'

'Oh, well enough, thank you,' said Cateau, who had not opened an eye in nearly nine hours, but deemed it inelegant to confess it. 'What do you think of the weather?' (This bit of dialogue had been repeated daily between them for twenty years.)

Quentine, having drawn back the curtains of the Countess's bed, proceeded to do the same to the heavier draperies screening the window; she then screwed up her eyes and inspected the section of sky visible over the chimney-tops on the farther side of the court.

'The sun's very bright, madam,' she reported at length. 'But there's frost in the air still. And I don't trust that bank of clouds coming up from the south. You'd best wear your fur cape and take the winter coach to church.'

'Bother!' said Cateau amiably. 'What have I to do today?'

'Maître Le Caron is coming at eleven,' said Quentine.

'Bother!' said Cateau again. 'More tiresome business! Is there anything else?'

'The new gardener's to be interviewed, madam. I told him he might perhaps have five minutes as soon as madam had finished her breakfast. And La Martin will be here at ten sharp, to do madam's hair à la hurluberlu — it's the style all the ladies at court are wearing — you remember, you asked me yesterday to make an appointment for you.'

'Oh, yes, so I did — I'd quite forgotten,' said Cateau, most untruly; for she never got her engagements muddled except by design. 'What a bore! Dear, dear. . . . Is that all?'

'Yes, madam.'

Cateau smiled brilliantly, as if she were delighted to hear it. She sat on the edge of the bed, holding out her small white feet while Quentine, kneeling, pulled on her slippers. Then she stood up and held out her arms so that Quentine could draw round her body the long shining folds of the pink satin dressing-gown trimmed with Flanders lace. This was the hour she liked best in the day, the only one of the twenty-four when she was able to create the illusion that she was still a busy woman.

Cateau began to act. She had lived so long in the public eye that, no matter how small her audience was, or even if there were none, she could not keep from playing an appropriate part: it had been years, really, since she had made an unpremeditated gesture or an unrehearsed remark. She started to present with a good deal of skill, partly for her own amusement and partly because she could not help it, a series of living pictures, a whole row of miniature comedies of which she herself was the heroine.

There was, first of all, the Beauty at Breakfast. This play took place in the dressing-room, a charming oval apartment panelled and painted in the latest shade known as 'swooning blue.' The table was set in front of the fire, which was laid in the grate of one of the new and fashionable small marble mantelpieces (replacing the hooded monstrosities of the last reign). There was a gilt mechanical clock on the mantelpiece, a dainty shepherdess who struck the hours on the sun with her crook; but Cateau paid no heed to the clock: the first scene of the series was evidently meant to be played *adagio molto*.

Slowly and languidly she nibbled a roll, and sipped her coffee without enthusiasm, making a face as she did so (a stage face), for it was exceedingly bitter. Cateau detested coffee, but it had recently become the rage at court; all the ladies at Saint-Germain, from Queen Marie-Thérèse down, were beginning to drink it, so that there was no question of its ultimate triumph in the polite world of Paris. As she imbibed the draught in minute installments she wondered how long it would be before she commenced to enjoy it: chocolate had taken her nearly six weeks — and then her pains had proved to be vain, for its vogue had collapsed overnight, owing to the alleged injurious effect on the female complexion. (There were some, indeed, who asserted that it might be infinitely more dangerous still: it was rumoured that the Marquise de Coetlogon, of the well-known Breton family, had consumed so much of the sable beverage during her pregnancy that she had been brought to bed of a *coal-black child!* ...)

Coffee, say what one would, was safer.

Halfway through the Beauty at Breakfast the Beauty's Companion, Mademoiselle de Saint-Denis, rustled genteelly into the room, dropped a curtsy, seated herself in a straight-backed chair on the other side of the fireplace, and started to read bits of the weekly *Gazette* aloud to her mistress. She read in a high, mild monotone that sounded as if she were strangely surprised.... As a matter of fact, Mademoiselle de Saint-Denis had a right to sound surprised, for she had still not got over her astonishment at having achieved a post in the house of a lady of fashion. She was a recent acquisition and, in Cateau's opinion, an unnecessary one. Cateau had never had a duenna; she could see no reason why, at this time of her life ... It was Maman who had managed the whole thing; Maman who had insisted rather tiresomely that the position of a woman alone in Paris was distinctly perilous.... 'Consider, my love,' she had murmured, times without number, 'what people might say of you!' Cateau knew that what Maman really meant was 'what people *have* said'.... But she remained unreceptive to the idea, and only the fear that, if she did not engage a companion, she might wake one day to find Maman herself installed as a far more troublesome substitute, had induced her finally to comply with the request.

Mademoiselle de Saint-Denis had been a boarder at the Carmelites in the rue Bouloi, an orphan of twenty-seven, well born but poor, and touchingly grateful to the benefactress but for whose offer she might have found herself, like many another of her kind, obliged to adopt the religious life, though devoid of a vocation for it. She was docile, childlike, unimaginative, with doe-brown eyes as mild as her voice. Cateau found her useful, if occasionally exasperating through an invincible determination not to exasperate; and she had never been able to make up her mind whether Mademoiselle de Saint-Denis' inability to secure a husband was due to her lack of a dowry or of a chin.

There was little of interest in this week's *Gazette*.... Monsieur Cambert's new opera, *Pomona*, was to have its première on the nineteenth of March at the Jeu de Paume in the rue Mazarine. (Make a memorandum to engage a box for that night.) ... Mademoiselle de Montpensier had dismissed her secretary Segrais, who had been with her over twenty years. (Poor old maid! Since the King had forbidden her to marry that little rat of a Lauzun last January, her temper had become so uncertain that none of her staff felt secure.) ... Four of the Queen's maids-of-honour had been bitten by a dog in the park at Saint-Germain, and were being sent to Dieppe for a course of sea-baths by way of treatment.... The Maréchale de la Mothe-Houdancourt, governess to the royal children, was marrying her second daughter, Charlotte, to the young Duc de Ventadour. (That would make two tabourets in the family; it was only a year or so ago that the eldest girl, Françoise, had become the Duchesse d'Aumont. Some people were born lucky ... though Ventadour, to be sure, was as ugly and misshapen as a gnome, and Aumont so infirm that it took two canes to support him at the King's lever. But a duke was a duke!) ...

After breakfast was cleared away Cateau looked over her correspondence. This did not take long, as there was only one letter. She read it twice, half smiling, half frowning; made as if to tear it in two — and then suddenly slipped it into her pocket. There would be ample time to consider its contents later.... After that, she saw the new gardener for a moment, and as soon as he had been disposed of — Cateau had few ideas about flowers outside of a deep-seated conviction that roses were dear and violets didn't show enough for the money, so that It Had Better Be Bulbs — the curtain was rung up on the second comedy of the day, the Beauty at Her Looking-Glass. Quentine and Lucie, the assistant maid (who was Quentine's cousin), rubbed their mistress's arms with almond paste, anointed her face with virginal milk, and combed out the still luxuriant golden tresses in preparation for the professional ministrations of La Martin. Cateau, meanwhile, herself pencilled the delicate arches of her eyebrows, brushed her lashes conscientiously till they curled (a trick learned years ago from Gilette de Fiesque), and touched her cheeks with an almost imperceptible spot of rouge (which she rubbed off again a minute later). During these momentous operations she peered with awful anxiety at the gracious image in the glass, pursuing her daily — sometimes hourly — search for crow's-feet and incipient wrinkles.

So far, there were none to be found. At thirty-eight — an age at which most of her contemporaries were grandmothers — the Comtesse d'Olonne was still a beautiful young woman. Her outline was as slender and graceful as ever; her eyes were as blue, her curls

quite as yellow — or very nearly: Cateau had lately fancied that
they were losing something of their new-minted glitter and had
experimented, in spite of La Martin's vigorous protests, with various
blond powders, none of which, fortunately, had done any lasting
damage. Her complexion, too, had retained its pure ivory pallor,
so that even from as close a point of vantage as her own dressing-
table mirror Madame d'Olonne appeared to be the same white-and-
gold idol that had been the admiration of Paris for two decades.
Time had no power to harm her: it had stopped moving when she
had stopped feeling. Her beauty, it seemed, had received the final
glaze in the furnace of the emotions on the day she had learned of
Candale's death. Thenceforth she was doomed to remain as she
was — unless chipped by some careless hand — a museum piece
as authentic as any in her own collection of treasures.

At this point a lackey scratched on the door to announce that
La Martin was below, thereby precipitating the second act of the
Beauty at Her Looking-Glass.

The hairdresser, a brisk old woman with snow-white ringlets
and a face like a large withered apple, made a lively entrance, bag
in hand, out of which she produced several curling-tongs and an
ominous pair of shears, prepared immediately to turn the Countess's
head into the round curly cabbage that was sweeping court circles
in epidemic manner.

Cateau, of course, was no longer of the court, merely of the town;
but she had no mind to relinquish her reputation as a leader of
fashion. Moreover, La Martin's first words to her client settled
any lingering doubts concerning the wisdom of taking so revolutionary a step.

'Madam, I've come straight from the Hôtel de Sully. The
Duchess has had her hair cut this morning, likewise her sister-in-
law, Madame de Guiche. And I've a rendezvous with Madame de
Nevers at one o'clock, directly Mass is over.'

'Very well, then,' said Cateau grimly. 'You may proceed at
once.'

It would never do not to be the first to be seen in the Cours with
the new coiffure. As it was, it was risking a good deal to wait till
after church: she definitely discarded the idea she had been toying
with of hearing Father Bourdaloue's sermon at Saint Paul's in the
Marais; the rue Saint-Antoine was much too far away; Mass at the
Carmelites' in the rue Bouloi would do just as well, and would give
her half an hour's start on the ladies from the Hôtel de Sully.

There was one dreadful moment before La Martin's shears made
their first decisive stroke, but after that Cateau steeled herself not
to mind what was done to her; and the old lady's cries of rapture
at the success of her handiwork were most reassuring — even more

so, the frank admiration to be read in the eyes of the watching Quentine and Lucie.

'Madam is altogether ravishing,' declared La Martin enthusiastically, as soon as the last tendril in the bouquet of short curls had been crimped into shape at the correct angle; 'and, if I may say so, madam has a natural equipment that's a joy to work with. Now, the Comtesse de Guiche's hair is so fine and stringy that it simply won't stay in curl — and the Duchess's hasn't the least bit of life in it. Good hair enough *in its way*, madam, of course — but not at all what I call an interesting head.'

This was agreeable to hear; and a close scrutiny in the glass of the final effect convinced Cateau that, once again, luck was on her side: the new coiffure might have been made for her. The so-called bouquet of tight short ringlets all over her head, which might have transformed a less fortunate woman into a Medusa, took five years off her age: she could wear it secure in the knowledge that it was immensely becoming — and if, as time passed, she grew tired of it, it would always be possible to let it grow out again later on, when she went to the country.

Sustained, therefore, by the comforting consciousness that she was looking her best — so early in the day, too! — Cateau dismissed La Martin and turned her attention single-mindedly to her next rôle of the Beauty as a Businesswoman.

La Martin had no sooner been shown out the door than Maître Le Caron was shown in — a hatchet-faced little old man, whose twinkling black eyes appeared to have retired behind his spectacles, less in search of assistance to see any better than in the hope of concealing how much they already had seen.

Maître Le Caron was dressed in snuffy black serge trimmed with a number of jet beads and buckles no sharper than his eyes; he carried an immense bundle of papers under his arm; and blew his nose and said 'Hem!' and 'Haw!' and looked altogether so alarmingly intelligent that the average fine lady of fashion would have been at a loss how to match her wits with his.

Cateau, however, was not the average fine lady. Although she lamented frequently to her mother and sister how hard it was for a woman alone to manage her affairs, she betrayed no sign of incapacity to do so to her entire satisfaction. For this, oddly enough, she had her husband to thank. She had never got over the shock she received the day he told her her spending would have to stop. Before that, it had not occurred to her that one could come to the end of one's money: because she got full value for every franc, it seemed that the flow of gold ought to keep pace with her requirements. But during those long empty months in the country, when there was nothing to do but think, it had been borne in on her by degrees that money was very important, next to beauty itself; and that, like beauty, it could not be too well taken care of. Slowly, patiently, therefore, she had set to work to grow wise where she had been ignorant, convinced that if she herself did not husband her resources, no one else would do it for her. (Look at poor, silly Maman, robbed right and left by her rascally stewards, and condemned to pass her old age in a convent because she no longer had the means to keep up a suitable establishment!... And there was Magdelon, making ducks and drakes as fast as she was able of the noble inheritance of the La Ferté-Senneterres....)

Now, after nearly six years of financial independence, it was admitted by every lawyer within the precincts of the Palais that no man was keener in matters of business than the Comtesse d'Olonne. By skilful handling she had substantially increased the size of her principal, already enlarged through her legacy from the Marvilles. Her properties in Normandy were extensive and flourishing; she ran them herself, making a journey every summer to Caen, where she had taken a big, comfortable house on a lease for life, the better to attend to her affairs. While there she made it a point to get to know the various local dignitaries, such as President Foucault, the town overseer, whom she entertained at a series of smart little dinners; and, when free, night after night she buried her lovely blond head in the huge dry-as-dust volumes of Bereult's *Norman Laws* till there was no detail of legal procedure involved in the management of her estates she had not at her fingertips.

It was dull, perhaps — but it was exceedingly rewarding. Cateau was no miser. She still spent as much as she wanted; she bought everything handsome that caught her eye — and her eye caught a great deal — but there was no waste. And for every crown laid out two at least were stored in the bank.

This morning there was not much to be done: some farm-leases in the parish of Han had expired, and required renewing; a small sum of money realized on the sale of a wood in the parish of Canteloup had to be invested ... that was all. But, great or small, Cateau gave the questions her entire attention, knitting her beautiful brows as she examined the long parchment scrolls submitted to her inspection, and signing her name with a flourish at the bottom of each scroll only after she had made sure she knew what she was doing and that it was the best thing she could possibly do.

Maître Le Caron watched her appreciatively through his spectacles with his little twinkling eyes. When she had finished and handed the bundle of papers back to him with a smile, he leaped to his feet, clicked his heels together, and bowed profoundly, saying: 'Yours to command, dear lady!'

Cateau inclined her head affably in return, and made two separate social remarks — one about the weather, the other a polite inquiry concerning his health and that of his family — and then inclined her head again, as a signal that her caller might depart.

After that, she embarked on a whole new chain of picture-plays.

There was the Beauty in Her Sedan-Chair (since the rue Bouloi was too close for it to be necessary to order the horses put to the coach), and the Beauty at Prayer. Both of these were slightly spoiled by the mute, inoffensive presence of Mademoiselle de Saint-Denis, but only slightly: in the Carmelites' chapel Cateau kneeled a little apart, a soft grey veil masking the audacity of the new coiffure quite as effectually as her devotional pose concealed the fact that while the nuns prayed she was reciting her shopping-list.

A gusty spring shower having beaten up from the south (just as Quentine had predicted) while the ladies were in church, the drive in the Cours was reluctantly postponed, and Cateau and her companion took Madame de la Louppe back with them to the house in the rue Villedo....

The Beauty at Dinner with Her Maternal Parent was a rather dull play, and took a deal longer to act than the protagonist felt the lines were worth.

Maman, who had grown somewhat gaunter with the years and whose pale eyes were even more bulging, but who had otherwise changed remarkably little, ate an enormous meal, talking throughout it with her mouth full. Like most elderly ladies, she was uninterested in everything except herself and her own repertory of anecdotes. She had cried: 'Darling child, how well you look!' upon seeing Cateau, and embraced her emotionally; but she had not even noticed the new coiffure; nor did she ply her daughter with the conventional questions concerning the latter's health and pursuits.

Cateau supposed this omission was partly due to her mother's unexpressed but chronic irritation at not having been asked to join forces with her eldest child. Cateau knew that it would have been 'nice' of her to ask Maman to live with her — that it was almost her duty to insist on it — but really they had not got on together any too well in the days when they had been fellow-boarders at the Carmelites'.... It was much better, Cateau told Magdelon, when the matter was first brought up for discussion between them, for their mother to feel independent. As long as she wouldn't live at La Louppe any more and couldn't afford a house of her own in town, the Carmelites' in the rue Bouloi provided a nearly ideal solution of the problem of What to Do About Maman. It was smaller than the great parent-house outside the gates of Paris, and much cosier; it was also Queen Marie-Thérèse's favourite convent; she drove in from the country with her retinue of ladies to attend

Mass there at least twice a week; and the nuns were in consequence
a lively set, well up in court gossip.

This gossip Maman recounted at length during dinner, being full
of fascinating tidbits about Her Majesty's new Spanish dwarf,
who was said to be so tiny that he was kept in a bird-cage; and the
endless subterranean struggles between the King's two official
mistresses, Mademoiselle de la Vallière and the Marquise de
Montespan.

Although Cateau had not been to court for ten years, and Maman
not for twenty, they were both deeply interested in everything
connected with it. The court was the world, as it had never been
in the old days: what happened outside it seemed scarcely somehow to have happened at all.

They discussed, also, the various items in this week's *Gazette*,
turning them upside down and inside out till there was not a morsel
of meat left clinging to the not-too-abundant bones. But unluckily
the one matter about which they were most passionately concerned
could not even be mentioned between them, owing to the unconscious restraint imposed on their tongues by Mademoiselle de
Saint-Denis.

The lady companion sat at the end of the table between Madame
de la Louppe and her daughter, chewing her food into very small
fragments and bending her sleek, meek head politely first this way
and then that, as she ejaculated: 'Oh, dear me!' and 'Fancy that!'
and 'Who'd have thought it, madam!'

It was difficult to imagine what she would have done had Maman
and Cateau broached the subject of Magdelon's affair with the
young Duc de Longueville....

The rain stopped after dinner and the sun came out, so that it
was possible to go driving, after all. And Mademoiselle de Saint-
Denis, it was really most fortunate, felt an attack of the vapours
coming on.... Cateau, accordingly unaccompanied, took Maman
back to the convent.... There was then, alas! an awful moment
of indecision to be faced. Had she come prematurely to the end
of her picture-plays — with the day but half over?... What to do?
What to do? That was the question Cateau had to answer all too
often since she had begun to live by herself: as she could do whatever she liked, there was frequently nothing she felt like doing.

Being still in the neighbourhood of Saint-Eustache, she bade
her coachman drive to the Hôtel de Senneterre, on the off chance
that Magdelon might be at home. But it was no surprise to be told
by the Swiss at the door that Madame the Maréchale had gone
out in the carriage half an hour ago. (Cateau, smiling wryly, found
it easy enough to guess where.) Monsieur the Maréchal, however,
was at home as usual, the man added, if madam cared to wait while

he sent up to see if his master could receive her? .... 'No, no; please don't bother,' said Cateau hastily.

She and her brother-in-law had never been on especially cordial terms, and since gout had descended on La Ferté six years ago, cutting short his military career and confining him, off and on, to his bed, his temper had become something to shudder at. Not even the long looked-for dukedom, which had descended simultaneously with the gout, was able to sweeten the pill of idleness. He had, in fact, turned into the testy old invalid of fiction, shouting at his valets, abusing his doctors, his callers, the members of his family, anyone who dared approach him; liable, at an instant's notice, to hurl at their heads whatever lay nearest to hand.

It was only the week before that Cateau had successfully dodged an inkstand and a footstool upholstered in petit-point; she had no intention of repeating the experiment.

On second thoughts, nevertheless, she decided to run in for a minute to look at the children. The Beauty as an Aunt might not be so convincing a rôle as the Beauty as a Sister ... still, anything to help pass the time. ...

There were four young La Fertés: three boys: Henri, heir to the dukedom, at fourteen just out of school and madly impatient to join the army; Louis, aged twelve, still at the Collège de Clermont, the Jesuit Academy; and Jules, who was only six. There was also Cateau's goddaughter, nine-year-old Catherine-Henriette (known as Tinette for short).

Cateau was reasonably fond of her nephews and niece, particularly of the two elder boys, who were handsome and looked much alike, with dark curly hair, snapping black eyes, and rosy cheeks. Jules and Tinette were blond, plainer and quieter, but good little things in their way.

They came trooping into the Gallery of Aminta together, shepherded by Bonneville, the boys' tutor, and Madame Poussard, the smaller children's governess. Tinette dropped a painstaking curtsy: she was sniffing a little, Cateau noticed (being the sort of child who usually has a slight nose-cold). The elder lads kissed the Countess's hand and murmured: 'Good-day, my aunt,' in cheerful, confident voices that duplicated each other exactly. And little Jules, after some urging and a recurring tendency to retire behind Madame Poussard's brown taffeta skirts, recited a sonnet of Benserade's and two of La Fontaine's fables in a quick toneless treble.

Cateau smiled benevolently at the young people, though her eyes looked distrait, and distributed packets of dragées amongst them. Like all childless women, she had definite theories about bringing up children. She thought that the little La Fertés were outrageously spoiled by their mother: Magdelon's idea of being a parent consisted in loving her babies with blind partiality and popping a sweetmeat into their mouths whenever they opened them to roar.

Naturally they roared a great deal; and although when their father heard them he was apt to roar back and demand that the young devils be whipped immediately, no one ever saw to it that his orders were carried out.

Today was a holiday — Mid-Lent — which explained why Louis was at home with his brothers and sister instead of at school.

After putting them through the usual kindly elder relative's catechism, which took Cateau in imagination back to Cousin de Rambouillet's Blue Room in the days of her own childhood, their aunt felt that the boys seemed rather restive. On inquiry it developed that they had been on their way to the courtyard to play at racquets with their tutor, so they were excused from the drawing-room and made their adieux, kissing Cateau's hand once more and bowing ceremoniously. (Henri had a little trouble with his sword, a gift from Papa on his fourteenth birthday.)

Cateau kept Madame Poussard and Tinette with her a few minutes longer. She discovered by dint of oblique methods of questioning that 'Maman' had gone driving in the Cours la Reine with His Highness the Duc de Longueville, and therefore resolved to drive there herself. After all, she had not yet displayed her new coiffure in public. As she was not minded to go alone, Madame Poussard and her charge were pressed to accompany her.

The little girl, pale with delight, clapped her hands and cried out: 'Then may I wear my hat with the cherry ribbons?'

As soon as she had trotted away, hand-in-hand with her governess, to make ready for her treat, Cateau began acting the strangest of all her picture-plays. It was hard to hit upon just the name for it: an unsympathetic audience might have felt that the Beauty as a Busybody...

Madame d'Olonne made a comprehensive tour of the *piano nobile*, opening every door not actually locked. She inspected critically the new music-room, which Magdelon was having re-panelled in lacquer in the Chinese manner — monkeys dressed as mandarins in red, white, and gold — that was beginning to be the vogue. She felt the stuff in the thick brocade curtains of the windows of the Gallery of Aminta between an appraising thumb and finger. She poked about in odd corners to her heart's content and, finally, rang for the butler and interviewed most of her sister's servants, on the pretext that she had lost a paste bracelet the last time she had dined at the Hôtel de Senneterre.

Cateau was unendingly curious — she would have been the first to confess it — about the La Fertés' domestic arrangements. They kept a larger staff than anybody in Paris; in fact, it sometimes

appeared that neither the Maréchal nor his wife had a clear idea of
how many people were working for them or of what each one's
duties were supposed to consist. At the same time they were incredibly badly served, and were no doubt shamelessly pillaged without knowing it.

That seemed a shocking state of affairs to Cateau, though when
the Maréchal's father, the old Marquis de Senneterre, died a few
years ago, at the age of eighty-nine, she had been the first to maintain that the whole household would have to be reorganized. Magdelon being laid up just then (it was a week or two before Tinette's
birth), it had devolved on her sister — who, to be sure, had asked
nothing better — to lead the exploring party that set out armed
with mops, pails, scrubbing-brushes, bunches of keys, and even a
small but efficient hatchet, to discover what really *was* on the
premises of their new domain.

It was surprising to find that, with the exception of the wing already occupied by the La Fertés, Great Senneterre was very nearly
empty. The old Marquis, whose avarice had increased with age,
had sold a good part of his furniture, broken up more to avoid buying firewood, and discharged three fourths of his staff: a few furtive
lackeys and scullions lurked in the vast underground cellars, far
outnumbered by the colonies of mice that squeaked and scampered
in the mouldy walls.

'Heigh-ho! We'll change all that — we'll change *everything!*'
cried the Maréchal cheerfully, undismayed by the mould and the
mice.

Cateau had heard him say this, often enough, in the days of the
old Marquis's lifetime. But then it had been in a jovial aside;
whereas now it was trumpeted merrily forth in a voice loud enough
to rouse the dead. . . . Mother Anne, the Marquis's widow, moistened
her lips and glanced nervously over her shoulder, wondering whether
her late spouse, laid away behind a stone slab in the wall of the
Minims' Chapel at Chaillot, might not manage somehow to rise
into life again to rebuke his bumptious successor.

But nothing happened to La Ferté — and a great deal happened
to his house. Mother Anne's own apartments were left as they were,
at that lady's timid request. (She retired to a convent in the
provinces a year or two later, thus passing out of the family picture
for good.) But the rest of Great Senneterre was invaded by an
army of painters and sculptors and masons and upholsterers, who
did not stop work till the grand old pile had blossomed afresh in a
riot of silk and velvet, marble and gold-leaf, and frescoes in the
Italian style. Staircases were let into the walls; new reception-
rooms planned on an elaborate scale; rare oriental carpets spread
on the cold stone floors; and when the army retreated at last the

Hôtel de la Ferté-Senneterre, always the biggest, was now also the finest private house in Paris.

A second army then advanced on the scene, consisting of lackeys and valets and cooks and maidservants, pages and footmen and coachmen and ostlers; this army, unlike the first, did not retreat, but remained in possession, not only of the immense steamy nether regions, but, Cateau frequently feared, of the whole building.

Magdelon could not hold them in hand. She did not even try; nor did she pay much attention to Cateau's perennial suggestions and criticisms, though apparently unresentful of what most women would have considered gratuitous interference. Magdelon was far too busy being a fine lady to be able to keep house. The position of the Maréchale-Duchesse de la Ferté-Senneterre was as solidly brilliant as her sister's was the reverse; and what time the former was not nursing her husband in his bedchamber, or playing with her children in the garden, or flirting with her numerous gallants in the Gallery of Aminta, she spent trundling to and from Saint-Germain or Versailles, to attend some spectacular rout of His Most Christian Majesty Louis XIV.

'It must be a horrid nuisance having to rush out to the country so often,' Cateau would observe, with an acidulous smile. 'Thank Fortune, *I* don't have to budge from town any more! Now, *what* did you say the Montespan wore at the water-fête?'

But here Magdelon was apt to give her sister satisfaction as small as in domestic matters; it was more than likely that the Maréchale-Duchesse de la Ferté-Senneterre had passed the whole evening in the Grotto of Thetis sporting with her latest and most unsuitable young man.

Although the rain had stopped and the sun was shining, it was cold in the Cours la Reine. The unbudding elms stood in stiff grey rows, and the wind whistled in bad-tempered gusts through the bare branches, ruffling the ordered waves of Martin the coachman's periwig and setting each small metallic curl in the Countess's coiffure to bobbing gaily.

Deliberately Cateau arranged her pose for the last of her picture-plays, the Beauty on Parade. She sat perfectly straight in the middle of the back bench of the coach, her head high, her smile fixed and ambiguous. She wore no mask: masks, thought Cateau, were beginning to be rather old-fashioned.... Tinette, at her side, holding fast to her hat with the cherry-coloured ribbons, wondered whom Aunt d'Olonne was smiling at....

There were very few carriages in the Cours this afternoon, and of those few not more than half belonged to people one knew. That, of course, was only to be expected, since the King had moved his court from Paris to the country. It was said that he bore an unalterable grudge against his capital for the turbulent part it had played in the wars of rebellion in his youth. Whatever the reason, it was certain that he was seldom there any more; the Louvre was shut up and deserted at least eleven months of the year, and most of the nobles had grown accustomed to shuttling back and forth between their town houses and their master's various castles in the Ile de France.

Oh, there was Gilette de Fiesque, taking the air with Mademoiselle de Montpensier!... Cateau almost leaned forward to call out a greeting to her old friend before she remembered they were not on speaking terms. Since Gilette had made up her quarrel, some years ago, with her royal patroness and been reinstated in her post at the little court of the Luxembourg, she had become strangely staid. True to her rôle of echo, she faithfully followed Mademoiselle in all that lady's likes and dislikes — and Mademoiselle had by this time got to dislike nearly everybody. (Poor thing! How plain she looked, in that unbecoming shade of velvet! Had no one the courage to tell her she was too old to wear green?... As for Gilette, who was even older, she was simply absurd, with that topknot of feathers, for all the world like those worn in former days by Madame de Choisy — dead and gone now, like the rest of the dowagers of the late Queen Mother's time.)

Cousin Julie de Montausier was passing in a brightly painted chariot on the other side of the road — but there was even less point in attempting to speak to her.... Poor Julie! She was leaning back against her cushions, too exhausted to look at anyone, even at the little pug-dog curled up in her lap; and her face was as green as Mademoiselle's dress.... Poor Julie! Of what use were her wit and her tact and her grand connections now? What good did it do her for folk who saw her driving by to nudge one another and whisper: 'There goes the Duchesse de Montausier, the Queen's lady-in-waiting!' — when she was obviously dying?

Cousin Julie was not so old, either — not much more than sixty: her mother had lived until five years ago — but then Cousin de Rambouillet had spent *her* last days in dignified seclusion. Julie, on the contrary, after pretending most of her life that the court meant nothing to her, had unexpectedly picked up the best post in it.... Yes, and she'd had her cranky antique of a husband made a duke and the Dauphin's governor, and had run her own rheumatic old legs off in a series of shameful intrigues that did not bear mentioning. Hateful old hypocrite! Everybody knew she had been the King's go-between in the first stages of his affair with Madame de Montespan — so why did she take the trouble to purse up her lips and avert her eyes, while her coach and Cateau's rolled past each other, and act as if she and the Comtesse d'Olonne inhabited separate planets? (For it wasn't six months ago that the Marquis de Montespan, having discovered his wife's guilt, had told Julie plainly what he thought of her share in the business, since when she had gone into a rapid decline, fainting and shivering and seeing ghosts in broad daylight.)

'And I'm glad, I'm *glad* you're dying, you wicked old weasel!' exclaimed Cateau, under her breath; while Tinette, sniffing more than ever on account of the cold, marvelled that her aunt should look suddenly so cross at the old woman with the green face and the pug-dog lying in her lap.

The next minute Cateau was smiling once more, as the Sullys' carriage came into view with the Duchesse de Sully inside, and her sister-in-law, the Comtesse de Guiche. She was anxious to see how the coiffures La Martin had made them had turned out, and bowed pleasantly as the coaches drew abreast; for there was no denying that her own head was the most successful of the three. She was rewarded, however, by the blankest of stares. . . .

The same thing happened again, just before reaching the great circle, when she encountered Madame de Nouveau and the Maréchale de Castelnau; and yet again, beyond the circle, with the Duchesse de Nevers and the Comtesse de Soissons. The third cut was the most humiliating of all, as a basketful of ladies headed by the Présidente de Tambonneau (an ordinary upstart little bourgeoise) sailed by with their plebeian noses in the air.

Cateau's face flushed, but she kept her chin valiantly up. Even Madame Poussard, shortsighted as she was, could not help noticing that something was wrong; and Tinette tried to guess how Aunt d'Olonne managed to keep on smiling when there was nobody, really, who smiled back at her. . . .

She had little better luck with men than with women. The cavaliers riding in twos and threes in the space between the lines of coaches sometimes saluted the Countess, but none of them halted to speak to her, much less asked her permission to post beside her carriage, as they did with most of the ladies.

Her isolation was cruelly complete. Cateau asked herself, as she had often enough before, whether she would ever get used to it. It was silly to say she did not mind being sent to Coventry. Social position might be something to laugh at as long as one had it, but directly it was lost it had an unpleasant way of assuming its true proportions. It would have been vain, too, to pretend she did not know why she was being ignored. She was neither old, nor ugly, nor less amusing than she had always been. She had a smart house and a good cook and plenty of money to entertain with and dress herself better than any other woman in Paris. Even the damaging fact of her separation from her husband need not necessarily have proved fatal.... No: Cateau was only too sure what the matter was: it was not that her sins were worse than her friends', but the fact that they'd been *printed* that caused her downfall.

The pamphleteers had piled lie upon lie, in an odious effort to season their vulgar verses to the public taste. And then, just as she was beginning to live down their virulent attacks, Bussy-Rabutin's book, *The Amorous History of the Gauls*, was published in Holland — and everyone knew (if they hadn't known, the key would have told them) that its chief heroine was the Comtesse d'Olonne.... What a libel it was! What a caustic compilation of truth and fiction, all the more harmful because it was so cleverly written! Bussy was no hack pamphleteer; though venom dripped from his pen, his style remained sprightly and charming. He had sworn, years ago, to get even with Cateau; silently he had bided his time, only to pillory her the more surely at last. He knew just enough of her life to make his novel horribly plausible; her adventures with Beuvron, with Candale, with Fouquet and Guiche and Marsillac and the rest, were narrated convincingly, but with their motives left out or so perverted that a pretty, giddy, amiable woman was made to look like a monster of avarice and corruption.

It was small comfort to hear that the author of *The Amorous History* had been sent to the Bastille for his pains, and then exiled for life to his estates in Burgundy. The mischief was done: henceforth, for Parisians, Madame d'Olonne and the infamous Ardélise were one.

Her disgrace had been public; so must her penance be. But was it *never* to come to an end?

It was on the way back from the farther gate of the Cours that they finally found Magdelon.

'Look, dear!' cried Cateau encouragingly to Tinette, 'there's Maman!'

It would have been difficult to avoid seeing her, for the procession approaching them was a pompous one. The La Fertés' coach, like their house, was the largest in Paris: it had been newly gilded and upholstered in scarlet velvet embroidered in gold, and the plumed stallions that drew it were the Maréchal's best jet-black sextet. The coachman and footman were likewise stiff with gold tassels and trimming; four lackeys in livery trotted, two on each side, in time with the horses; and a pair of minute Moorish pages in turbans (Madame de Montespan had only one) stood guard on the steps, waiting to give their hands to their mistress, should she desire to alight.

Slowly the carriage bowled forward with stately mien. Cateau could see now the four comely maids — Magdelon had always the prettiest ones she could find — and Magdelon herself, swathed in scarlet velvet and sables with a bonnet of nodding feathers, seated on the back bench, like a winter version of Venus attended by an unusual number of graces. She was heavier than she had been twelve years ago — in fact, she would have seemed too stout save for her exceptional height, which enabled her to carry the surplus pounds gracefully. But her lovely face was as youthful as ever, round and fresh and singularly unlined: there were times indeed when she looked scarcely a day older than Tinette.

This was assuredly one of the times. Beneath the feathered bonnet Magdelon's brown eyes shone naïvely wondering, as if she still could not quite bring herself to believe that all this grandeur was really hers, and that it might not vanish on the stroke of a bell, like Cinderella's. It was her childish delight in her own good fortune that kept people from being jealous of Madame de la Ferté — that, and her patent inability to concentrate overlong on herself, which was at once her chief charm and her greatest weakness.

There was no trouble today in determining the current centre of her universe, for the limpid gaze was riveted adoringly, abjectly, and all the more shamefully because Magdelon was unconscious of shame, on the young man riding a lively white horse beside the coach.

The young man was short, but his lack of inches was only slightly apparent on horseback. He had blond hair, a good deal of it, a big aquiline nose — the badge of his family! — and an air of over-weening self-satisfaction. He, too, appeared fully as regardless of the crowd as his mistress — with this difference, that he realized the crowd could not afford to be regardless of him. Indeed, there was not a soul in the Cours la Reine who did not know that the young man was Charles-Paris d'Orléans, lately Comte de Saint-Paul, now Duc de Longueville; nephew to Monsieur the Prince de Condé; cousin to His Majesty Louis XIV; and the most important young noble in France.

When Cateau caught sight of this magnificent couple her face turned lead-white under the bobbing curls; all her pretty posing came to an end. For it was too late now for her to put up a pretence of being happy; it was painfully evident what was lacking in each of the picture-plays she'd been bravely presenting, one after an-other, ever since she had opened her eyes that morning in the room with the pink-painted ceiling: they needed a hero.

And although Cateau did not envy her sister her sable cloak, nor the coach-and-six, nor the prancing postilions, nor the four pretty maids — no, not even the two little black boys in their glittering turbans — she would have given ten years of her life to have a young man — any young man at all — to ride beside her carriage in the Cours.

AS SOON AS MAGDELON SAW CATEAU AND TINETTE SHE STOPPED looking at Monsieur de Longueville. Long before they were within hailing distance she began nodding and waving; when the carriages came abreast of one another she cried out to her coachman to halt, exclaimed with delight over the coiffure à la hurluberlu, and insisted on having her small daughter lifted up in a lackey's arms, so that she might kiss her.

This made a pretty tableau of maternal devotion for the edification of the young man on the lively white horse, though it might have been more to the point, Cateau thought, if Magdelon had wiped the little girl's nose! At the same time one had to give credit where it was due: it was highly probable that she would have acted the same, had there been nobody to observe her.

Cateau's changeless smile stiffened slightly as she made light conversation with her sister and the Duke. Ah, it was really almost more than she could bear to have them be sorry for her! She would infinitely have preferred it if they had passed her by superciliously, like everyone else in the Cours. But Magdelon *would* be kind. She wanted Cateau to go to the play with them.

'We're on our way now to the Marais to see *The Amorous Dupe. Do* come, dear; they say Rosimond is delicious! and it's quite... you know...'

But Cateau shook her bouquet of curls resolutely. 'No, thanks just the same, love — another time, perhaps.'

It was impossible not to see that Longueville was relieved by her refusal, although he added his protestations politely to those of his mistress.

Cateau made no objection when Tinette begged to be allowed to drive home with her mother. She went on smiling to the end, till she felt her face must crack from the strain — but directly the big golden coach had rolled away she collapsed against the cushions of her own smart little carriage, looking as limp as Cousin Julie, and shut her eyes, while two great tears gathered on her lashes and rolled unbidden down her cheeks.

She wanted to scream aloud in her misery. As that was obviously impossible, she tore her handkerchief to pieces instead, and then stuffed the pieces into the pocket of her dress (for the lace on the edge might be worth saving). In her pocket she found the letter she had placed there early that morning, and which she had not thought of once since. As her fingers closed on it a wave of new life seemed to flow through her body; she straightened up, tapped on the window to attract Martin's attention, and when he turned round called out in a sharp, shrill voice: 'Take me to the Hôtel de Bullion!'

There! She had done it, after all, the thing she had meant not to do if she could possibly help it. Desperation had driven her to fall back on the one anodyne she could always trust to assuage her pain. All the way to the rue Plâtrière she reproached herself for her weakness and muttered over and over, as if it were a kind of charm to ward off evil influences: 'I'll be good, I'll be good, I *swear* to be good! ... Oh, today you will *see* how good I can be!'

The Hôtel de Bullion was the only important house in Paris where the Comtesse d'Olonne was still welcome. Perhaps important was not the right word: although everyone went to the Bonnelles', no one was particularly proud to be seen there. It was a cheerful circle rather than a distinguished one; its hosts had been noted for years for their lavish, undiscriminating hospitality. After all, if you insist on running a permanent gambling resort, you cannot afford to be too critical of your guests. Provided one had ordinary good manners and reasonable powers of amusing, and were willing besides to pay one's own way, it was easy to secure the entrée to the Hôtel de Bullion.

Charlotte de Bonnelle had been fond of Cateau for twenty years. She was one of the few women at court who had stood by her friend through the whole of that wretched affair with Candale. They had somewhat lost sight of each other during the next few hectic years of the latter's gallant career and her subsequent exile in Poitou, but when at last Madame d'Olonne came back to Paris to live at the Carmelites', Charlotte's carriage was the first to stop at the door of the convent in the rue Bouloi, and Charlotte herself, in velvet and sables, had rushed into the cold little whitewashed parlour to embrace the penitent and exclaim in her unmodulated peahen tones: 'Poor darling! I'm *so* glad you're here! Now *when* are you coming to dinner?'

Cateau was touched, and tremendously grateful. It was not long before she had slipped back into her old habit of looking in at the Bonnelles' receptions three or four times a week; and if at first some of the older women guests shrugged their shoulders and stared blankly at that dreadful Madame d'Olonne, none of them quite dared to cut her under so respectable a roof as Councillor de Bonnelle's. If he and his wife chose to vouch for her socially, why, then ...

Besides, as time went on, a whole new generation began to grow
up that knew little and cared less about those old scandals of
Regency days. There were Noël's and Charlotte's three boys and
their first cousins, the three La Mothe-Houdancourt girls. The six
young people and their numerous friends fluttered and chattered
about the dark old house in the rue Plâtrière, forming a gay group
in which Cateau felt more at ease than with her own contemporaries.
These lusty youths and pretty, laughing maidens were too deeply
engrossed by their own affairs to remember that there had been
queer stories about one of their mothers' friends: they accepted
Cateau as they found her, a charming companion, with manners a
trifle more studied than they were used to at court, but sustained
by so definite an intention to please that it was impossible to resist
her. They had heard that she had been unhappily married and
lived separated from her husband; worst of all, that in spite of her
looks she was said to be nearly forty years old. (Poor thing! Who'd
have believed it? So her life must be as good as over. . . .)

Aside from that, they thought nothing at all about Madame
d'Olonne. And Cateau, after her many misfortunes, was only too
pleased to escape into an agreeable anonymity. She continued to
be grateful to Charlotte and to yearn for an opportunity to show
her gratitude. She was grateful to Noël, too, as long as she could be:
he had died in December, some four months before this particular
chilly March day, since when his widow had entertained, if possible,
more energetically than ever, on the principle that, if her late spouse
could return to earth, it would be the first thing he'd command her
to do.

Today Cateau paused in the doorway of the Gallery of Ulysses
before going in. It was earlier than usual; the card-tables were set
up, but play had not yet begun. She had fallen, it appeared, into
the midst of a purely family party.

Madame de Bonnelle and her sister, the Maréchale de la Mothe,
and their children made up the whole company. No doubt the approaching wedding of the latter's daughter Charlotte to the Duc de
Ventadour accounted for the little reunion, for Madame de la
Mothe, as governess to the royal children, and her daughter Gabrielle, who was maid-of-honour to Queen Marie-Thérèse, were generally kept by their duties at Saint-Germain.

The two widows sat together in the window, engaged on an
elaborate piece of tapestrywork destined, Cateau knew, to adorn
the drawing-room of the future Duchesse de Ventadour. Claude,
Marquis de Gallardon, the eldest of the Bonnelles, and Denis, the
youngest, were playing tric-trac; Noël, Marquis de Fervaques, the
middle boy, turned the pages for his cousin Charlotte, the bride,
who was at the clavichord strumming a minuet of Baptiste.

Charlotte was the beauty of the La Mothes, though the three girls bore a certain resemblance to one another. Françoise d'Aumont, the eldest, was a big, bovine young woman, so blond that her hair was all but white, and with features that had thickened to the point of inexpressiveness shortly after her marriage. She was sitting sewing in a corner by the fire, looking more massive than ever, for she expected an heir to the dukedom almost hourly.

Charlotte, known as Doudou, was a good deal less big and less blond. Her proportions were graceful, although Cateau had decided long ago that her head, like the heads of her sisters, was a shade too large for her body. Her hair was a lively yellow, touched by flecks of auburn; her eyes were round and grey and rather mournful; her chin, too, was round, and she had a sweet smile and a gentle disposition and was said to be so stupid that, at court, her mother wound her up every morning and set her in motion like a piece of clockwork.

Gabrielle, Mademoiselle de Toucy, the youngest of the sisters, had foxy-red ringlets (not naturally curly) and a somewhat pointed edition of the family profile. She was the smallest and plainest; it looked as though Nature — or could it have been her father, the late Maréchal? — had got tired when it came to her turn and run out of material; so that there was not quite enough of her to go round. However, she made what she had go a very long way: there was no doubt that she was the dominating member of the trio.

As Cateau prepared to make her entrance Gabrielle was pirouetting about the room, preening herself and tossing her curls to show off her coiffure à la hurluberlu, which she declared, in a penetrating soprano, to be the latest thing at court.... 'But I expect you've not seen it yet in town. Paris is always weeks behind Saint-Germain in the styles. Take a good look at it, dears, just the same — for mark my words, you'll be copying me sooner or later. Of course, it's not *everyone* who can wear it....'

'True enough, child,' said Cateau, rustling forward in her best blue taffeta afternoon gown. 'Now I wonder what you'll say when you see that I, too, have succumbed to the mode!'

She stood for a moment in the middle of the room, her head to one side, tall and slim, her long, elegant lines and exquisite composure a perfect contrast to the little maid-of-honour's stumpy figure and restless self-assertiveness. She said nothing more; nothing remained to be said; but jerk her head and flounce as she would, Mademoiselle de Toucy was made to look suddenly very common and strangely *thick through*.

She knew it, too. There was undisguised fury in the sidelong glance of her little olive-green rogue's eyes; for Gabrielle was the only one of the family who was not fond of Madame d'Olonne.

She alone held aloof from the flurry of welcome occasioned by the Countess's appearance. Madame de Bonnelle and the Maréchale dropped their tapestry with cries of delight. Gallardon brought a chair for the new arrival; young Denis, a footstool; Fervaques set the fire-screen to shield her from the warmth of the blaze; Doudou stopped playing and ran to kiss her dearest Cateau; and even Françoise d'Aumont relaxed her wooden immobility long enough to smile with a touch of malice and say: 'Truly, madam, Saint-Germain's quite cast into the shade by the rue Villedo. I'll warrant my sister is sorry she boasted too soon of her charms.'

Cateau had the wit to conceal her pleasure in her triumph. She turned the flow of compliments aside with a deprecating remark and offered a string of her own instead to the bride and her mother on the morrow's wedding.

'There'll not be a fairer duchess, I vow, in all Her Majesty's train,' said Cateau, pinching Doudou's soft cheek. 'I only wish I might peep through the palace windows the day she takes possession of her tabouret!'

'A tabouret's no such great wonder,' said Françoise d'Aumont, who had had one of her own for more than a year. 'Nasty, slippery things, I call them! I'd not dream of daring to sit on mine in my present condition of health.'

She bit off the end of the thread she'd been sewing and chewed it slowly, thus enhancing her likeness to a meditative cow.

'Nay, then, cousin, let poor Doudou get what amusement she can out of the honours of her new position!' cried Gallardon, who had a laughing way with him and more self-assurance than his brothers. 'For from what I've seen of her bridegroom 'tis all the joy she's likely to have in the bargain.'

'Well, if Villeroy hadn't been married already,' said Gabrielle, 'I suppose she'd have got Maman to give her to him, though he's no duke, nor likely to be one for years to come. There, now, Doudou! Have we surprised your secret? Only look how she's blushing!'

Doudou hung her head and glanced appealingly at her sisters, but she spoke not a word, being naturally silent.

The Maréchale frowned and shook her finger disapprovingly, but she stood too much in awe of Gabrielle's tongue to dare try to curb it. It was Madame de Bonnelle who remarked in her brusque, decided way: 'For my part, I find Ventadour perfectly delightful. Of course, he's not handsome — but why should you want a man to be handsome? He's rich and well born and utterly devoted to our Doudou, and I think she's an exceedingly lucky girl!'

Cateau then tactfully diverted the conversation by asking Doudou's mother a question concerning the cut of the wedding-dress made at staggering expense by Maître Thomas; and Gabrielle once more discovered that the wind had been taken out of her sails. She returned to the charge unabashed, however, as soon as she perceived a new opening; and presently was in command of the room again as she related the anecdote, slightly stale now to most of her audience, of the dog that had attacked her comrades, the Queen's maids-of-honour, in the park of the palace, and how she alone had escaped being bitten. *She* had seen from the first how it was with the animal; she had warned Rouvroy and that poor, silly Ludre to beware, and had told Théobon, the dog's owner, to summon a gardener to deal with the vicious brute. But would one of them listen to her? Not they! And look what had happened to them!...

From these sage reflections the Toucy passed on to a scathing summary of the various intrigues that were momentarily absorbing the scandalmongers at court.... Monsieur X had left his wife for a buxom milkmaid from Montmorency.... Madame Y had been surprised after sunset in the shrubberies with one of her footmen.... The Z's were said to be on the point of seeking a divorce, the sole consideration still deterring them being that both had so many sins to account for that neither quite dared to bring suit against the other....

Madame de la Mothe clucked and simpered, wagging her head as if to say: 'Dear me, how terrible! But isn't my Gabrielle clever?' — while Charlotte de Bonnelle, in spite of her widow's weeds not four months old, laughed her loud, cheery laugh at the most outrageous of her niece's tales. Life, thought Charlotte, is still too amusing for words....

'— and then, oh, yes, my loves, I'd nearly forgotten the best of all— about the poor, dear Duc de Longueville and that old woman who's so madly in love with him. They say she's three months gone with child already and is in a pother how she'll be able to explain it to her husband the Maréchal, since everyone knows they've not lain together these last five years. Isn't that killing? But I'd hate to stand in her shoes — for didn't La Ferté murder his first wife for much less? Aunt Charlotte, *you* told me ——'

Here, for a wonder, Gabrielle became conscious that her whole family was staring at her in open-mouthed horror. She checked herself in the middle of her sentence, blushed scarlet, and mumbled an awkward apology to Cateau.

'Forgive me, madam — I do assure you I'd *entirely* forgotten...'

'Very well, child,' said Cateau, in a matter-of-fact tone.

She had sat still during the other's spiteful monologue, only a slight narrowing of the eyes showing her inner agitation. Now she got up without haste, just as a lackey appeared at the door to announce the first of the afternoon's guests, and gave her hand to young Fervaques, who had been fidgetting beside her chair for some minutes, as if he were longing to intervene in her behalf, if only he had known how.

'I think,' Cateau continued quietly, 'I promised Monsieur de Fervaques, the last time I was here, that I would let him show me the garden. The trouble I've had with my planting, dear Charlotte, this year ...! And *your* bosquets are always delicious. Perhaps I may gather some hints from your good men below. Till later, then, ladies — and you, too, sirs!'

She swept the company a curtsy and left the room with her hand, which only the Marquis knew was trembling, lying lightly on her escort's arm.

In the hall the young man turned to face her, flushing hotly, and blurted out: 'Madam, I know not what to say to obtain your forgiveness! I — I could strangle that minx of a Toucy! Yes — and I'll do it, one of these days, if she continues so unruly of tongue! Those are fine manners she's picked up at the court of His Most Christian Majesty!'

Cateau smiled.

'Don't take it so hard, my friend — for you see that I don't,' she said. 'I admit Mademoiselle Gabrielle is not so ingratiating as her sisters — but then, consider her age! How young she is! Not more than seventeen, I fancy. And for all I know, it may be she spoke the truth about my poor Magdelon. I see so little now of her....'

'Whether it be true or not makes not the slightest difference,' declared Fervaques. 'It's her abominable rudeness in bringing the story up in your presence I can't overlook.... Pretending she'd forgotten that you and the Maréchale were sisters! Ah, I wish now I'd boxed her ears before the whole room!'

'Yes, I suppose she knew well enough of the relationship. But why talk any longer of so disagreeable a matter? See, I've forgotten it already! Now you must promise me that you will do so, too. There are other affairs to be discussed between us.... But, my dear, where on earth are you taking me?'

'Why,' stammered the young man, at the top of the grand staircase leading down to the entrance hall, 'to — to the garden! I thought you said ...'

Cateau burst out laughing: a musical peal of silver bells, carefully rehearsed, it had lately replaced the unrestrained mirth of her youth.

'Good Heavens! That's the *last* thing I meant you to do! You may take it as axiomatic, child, that I *never* under any circumstances wish to go outdoors. No, no ... I said that merely as an excuse to leave the room, partly on account of the Toucy, for my palm was itching to slap her pert little face — and partly because

'... Well, I'll tell you presently. Here: can we not have our chat in this corner quite by ourselves?'

She had suddenly stumbled upon the small antechamber behind the great gallery; it was the room where, years ago, she and Beuvron had had their first serious quarrel. Cateau had forgotten the details of the scene, though she retained a vague impression that something unpleasant had happened to her there, once upon a time. ...

However, the place might have been made for confidential interviews: dim and low-ceilinged, the walls hung with dark Gothic tapestries, a fire burning cosily on the hearth. Cateau seated herself on the long couch by the fire, trying not to be too conscious of the sardonic stare of the late finance minister, Claude de Bullion — tough old rascal! — fixed upon her and his grandson from the excellent portrait by Philippe de Champaigne adorning the over-mantel. Then she beckoned smilingly to her companion.

After a moment's hesitation the young man sat beside her, blushing furiously. Noël de Bullion was the handsomest of the three Bonnelle brothers. Like his cousin Doudou, he possessed the family's good traits in the highest degree: where Claude's features were a thought coarse and Denis's too small and waxy-neat, his own were bold enough to be manly and sufficiently well chiselled to attain distinction. He had a rather long, narrow face, with a mouth as soft and red as a girl's, and large grey-green eyes, appealing and melancholy in expression (there, again, like Doudou); he was tall, but stooped a little when he walked. Under the huge frizzed periwig fashion had clapped upon his unfortunate head Cateau knew that his own hair curled a crisp mahogany-brown; and in spite of this overwhelming adornment, his elaborately correct court costume, and the solemn efforts he made to live up to the dignity they imposed on their wearer, he looked a good deal younger than his twenty-six years.

Now he was gazing at her as a child might at his mother who had promised him a sweetmeat, but who he was not sure meant to keep her promise. Cateau was touched by the look, more than she had known she could be; it was so long since anyone had looked at her like that, from a completely personal angle, that she felt her crushed self-esteem rising magically under the steady pleading of those gentle grey-green eyes. At the same time she felt confused by the message she read in their depths, and uncertain how best to respond to it. ('I'll be good, I *swear* to be good! ...')

'You got my letter?' Fervaques began, in an eager whisper.

'Yes,' said Cateau; 'this morning. See, I have it here still.'

'I wrote it as soon as I knew — the very minute the King had settled that Sourches might make the sale. Nobody knows yet except you — not even my mother! I — I wanted you to be the first to hear the good news, because it was all your doing, you know. But for you I'd never have thought of daring so much. But for you I'd still be nothing but the younger son of an obscure councillor of parliament.'

'Instead of Governor and Lieutenant-General of His Majesty's provinces of Maine and Perche and the County of Laval,' said Cateau, smiling. 'How fine that sounds, to be sure! My dear, do you know, I believe I'm your vassal: all the barons of La Louppe were born in the Perche!'

'It was a job, I can tell you, to get the King to consent to it,' Fervaques went on, with kindling eyes. 'I don't believe he'd have ever said yes if Monsieur Le Tellier hadn't been one of the Marquis de Sourches' creditors: *he* persuaded him it would be the best thing for all concerned that the sale should go through. You see, my birth is against me. No one thinks anything of parliament any more. And the King's never seen me or my brothers: we haven't the luck of my Aunt de la Mothe and my cousins, who are attached to the court. In the end, His Majesty was most influenced by the fact that I'd already bought the charge of captain in the Queen's Light Horse Troop. There again, madam, my good fortune is due to you — for who else told me as long ago as last Christmas that the King was planning a war against the Low Countries, and that I'd better make sure in advance of a post in the royal forces?'

'Well, but you would have thought of it by yourself, surely, sooner or later. There's no chance for a man nowadays outside the army. As you say, parliament's finished. And what good is it to have had a rich father, if you can't spend a fair share of your heritage to launch yourself in the world? After all, your grandfather was finance minister under Richelieu: why shouldn't you be as good as he some day — or even better? My dear, I believe in your future.'

'I know you do!' cried the young man — there were tears of gratitude in his eyes. 'You're the only person in the world who does. My mother's kind enough to us all, but her heart is set on my brother Gallardon's career. She's treating with the government now to buy him the charge of first equerry of the Petty Stable. It's always been so: as long as Claude had what he wanted, the rest of us might whistle in vain for our supper.'

'And I tell you, my friend, that she's made a mistake,' said Cateau calmly. 'Madame de Bonnelle has been one of my best friends for more years than I care to count. No one could honour her more than I do — but the judgement of even the finest woman may sometimes be led astray. I am sure she will live to realize that she was wrong about her children. Gallardon's all very well — a pleasant young fellow — but it's you who can bring the Bullions back to the high position they had under the late King Louis XIII. Mark my words, Fervaques — I mean what I say!'

'Madam, how can I thank you? How can I ever hope to repay . . .?
Why should you be so good to me?'

Fervaques seized her hands ardently and covered them with
kisses; while Cateau, leaning back on the couch and shutting her
eyes, told herself firmly she must not forget for an instant that he
was young enough to be her son. . . . Well, not *quite*, for was she
not barely twelve years his senior? Still, they were divided by
much more than their difference in ages: the unbridgeable gulf of
what seemed like a lifetime of experience on her part yawned between them. She was old, *old*. . . . Naturally, therefore, her feelings
were purely maternal. Every woman had a certain amount of the
mother instinct; in her, who was childless, it had been thwarted
too long. That was all there was to it, of course! There was no
need for her to feel guilty. . . . Then why had her cheeks grown suddenly pink? Why did her breath, perfectly even a moment before,
start to come short and sharp in a series of gasps? And could that
be her heart beating under the lace ruffles of her bodice, hammering
at the walls of its prison like an animal striving to escape? ('I'll
be good — I'll be good!')

Gently she drew away her hands and laid one of them on the
shoulder of the young man beside her.

'My dear child,' said Cateau, in what she trusted was a convincingly parental tone, 'there's no need for such extravagant thanks.'

'Ah, but I *must* be extravagant! How else can I show . . .?
Madam — dear madam! — my life belongs to you. Take it, I
beg of you! It's a mean thing, I know — dull and insignificant —
but maybe in *your* keeping it will become something to be proud of.
Oh, if I thought that you cared as I do ——'

'No — please — you know you must not! These are things I
have forbidden you to say.'

'And why? Why? Am I a child, that may not be suffered to
speak? Or am I a man like other men, with feelings that must out,
if they are not to choke me? I love you, madam — nay, you *must*
hear me! I have loved you for months. All that I am, all that I
have, is yours for the taking. Here let me kneel and implore
you. . . .'

Cateau rose and stamped her foot smartly — for the door to the
hall was half open, and who knew who might be listening outside?

'No!' she said. '*No* — d'you hear me? It's not right. I'll not
have it! I am unworthy of such homage.'

'Who should be worthy, if *you* are not?' cried Fervaques, half
sobbing, his cheeks red as fire. (Would anyone have guessed so
bashful a creature . . . ? — But that was the way with timid people,
once they found courage to break through the barriers that pent
in their feelings.) There was no stopping the lad! He was babbling

on now: 'I know there have been bad things in your life — sad things — that people have been cruel — have misunderstood and maligned you. But *I* can see further than they. *I* can appraise your true worth. Madam, let *me* make amends for others' lack of wisdom and charity. Let *me* atone for the sins of my sex by caring for you and cherishing you always. Only so can I be happy, myself — only so can I live at peace! I am what you have made me. Take me *now* — or I'll sink back into the void from which you saved me!'

His face plainly showed, in its mixture of ardour and boyish desperation, that he meant what he said — that he was speaking the simple truth. Cateau had still sufficient detachment of mind to reflect that none of the Bullions was clever enough to invent anything else. However, she, too, was caught in a flurry of emotions, none the less agitating because they rested on the surface. She felt fear, confusion, gratitude, but, most of all, amazement that, after so many barren years, she could have come alive again. It was as though a spring, long dry, had suddenly begun to flow — or as though a tree, leafless through many seasons, had put forth young green leaves once more.... But alas! If she herself were astonished at what had happened to her, what would others say when they knew? How the gossips would laugh when they learned that the gallant career of the infamous Ardélise was about to unfold a new and unexpected chapter! She could imagine only too well the kind of bawdy remarks they would make.... No! It was impossible! How could she have thought for a moment...? That side of her life was ended forever. She ought not to have called at the Hôtel de Bullion today. She should have been wise long ago, foreseen what was surely on its way, and prevented the affair from coming to a head. (Best to stifle, if she could, the voice of her conscience, which went on droning insistently that she *had* foreseen the whole business and had deliberately sat back and waited....)

These thoughts flashed through Cateau's mind in less time than it takes to tell them, while she stood by the couch, her bosom rapidly rising and falling, her colour ebbing and flowing as she had not deemed it possible in a woman of eight-and-thirty.... To conceal her dismay she averted her head; Fervaques, interpreting this as a sign of displeasure, fell to his knees again and hid his face in the folds of her gown.

'Nay — now you are angry — now I've made you hate me!...'

What a baby he was! She would have patted his head, to console him — but there was no point in patting a periwig! (Cateau had a poignant fleeting memory of Candale's golden mane, dust in the tomb these many years.) As it was, she turned a laughing face towards the disconsolate young man.

'Nonsense, child, I'm not angry — only amused to see what a

position the governor of Maine, Perche, and the County of Laval has got himself into! Come, now, no more of this foolishness! Get up from the floor like a sensible man, dust yourself off — and then let us go back to the drawing-room and tell the good news of your appointment to your mother and her guests. If I mistake not, it will quite eclipse the excitement of Doudou's wedding. Nay, even the little Toucy's new coiffure,' added Cateau, with gentle irony, 'must, I fear, retire to the background for a few minutes at least.'

Fervaques rose as he was bidden and stood meekly before her. His arms hung limp at his sides; the light in his eyes had been quenched.

'Ah, what do I care for the governorship now,' he muttered sulkily, 'since you won't have me? It's but a parcel of petty official cares, scarce worth the fourteen thousand francs a year they'll bring me!'

'Nonsense!' said Cateau, a second time. 'It's an immense sum of money, and you are an extremely fortunate boy. Think of the hundreds of families at court who haven't a penny to spare for the heir to the title, much less for his younger brothers! Why, there's no limit to what you can do!'

'I could have done anything, madam — anything! But with *your* help only. Alone, I'll be nobody, just as I was before you met me.'

'Why, who said you'd be alone?'

'But I thought of course ——'

'You had no business to think anything of the kind. We'll be friends, just as we've always been.'

'And I may write to you as I've been used to do — and tell you all I think and hope and plan for — oh, madam ... !'

'You may write, of course,' said Cateau, 'whatever you like — except one thing.'

Fervaques' face fell once more.

'Ah — but I've only one thing to say!'

Cateau frowned.

'Too many men have told me that,' she said, with a sigh. 'And I thought it was agreed you were not to be like other men. But come, come! It's high time for us to find your mother.'

With this inconclusive answer Fervaques was forced to rest content. As he held the door open for her to pass through he looked at her adoringly. Cateau would not acknowledge the look, but she gave him her hand in the hall; and though he raised it to his lips, her frown did not return.

In the Gallery of Ulysses no one apparently had noticed their absence. The room was by now quite full, and gambling had begun. Madame de Bonnelle never delayed an unnecessary moment

once the proper complement of players had arrived. She was
tensely involved in a game of lansquenet, deaf and blind to all else
in the world, her eyes opaque and expressionless. It was droll to
observe the preoccupied stare that was the best she had to offer,
when the exigencies of the hostess obliged her to greet an advancing
or speed a retiring guest.

Not everyone in the company, however, was so wholly absorbed
by the business in hand. Cateau perceived that the Duc de Cade-
rousse, an ugly young man with a bony nose and legs as awkwardly
long as a grasshopper's, had established himself on a stool by the
fireplace next to the chair occupied by Madame d'Aumont. He was
leaning forward, his hands on his knees — as if to keep them from
flying off at a tangent — devouring her with his eyes. Cateau could
not hear what he was saying, but whatever it was, it had caused
the wooden statue to come to life: Françoise actually laughed once
or twice, and as she listened her paste-white face coloured high up
to her straight thick light eyebrows.... And in another corner the
Marquis de Villeroy, that accomplished young courtier known as
'Charming,' was pursuing — there was no other word for his peculiarly impudent brand of attentions — Doudou de la Mothe, who
by this time tomorrow would be the Duchesse de Ventadour.
Doudou, it was true, took care to repulse her admirer — but so
feebly that he seemed to be almost as much emboldened thereby
as if she were actually encouraging him. (Poor Doudou! How
pretty she was in her simple white gown, with a rose in her hair no
pinker than her cheeks, and a troubled look in the brooding grey
eyes! No wonder Villeroy... But someone really should tell her
that she ought not to thrust her forefinger into her mouth, like a
bashful young peasant.)

Cateau shrugged her shoulders: what were young people coming
to, she'd like to know? In *her* day the most audacious girls thought
it prudent to wait until they were properly married before per-
mitting themselves the luxury of a lover. She could still recall how
shocked she had been, the year she came out, by the flirtatious
proposals of that horrid old lecher, the Cardinal de Retz. And he,
she supposed, had not meant anything serious.... Whereas *now*...
But what could one expect at a court whose rightful queen was
ignominiously cast into the shade by the King's two brazen mistresses, one of whom was another man's legal wife — while the
other, though already the mother of two children, had never been
married to anybody?...

Cateau pursed up her lips in unconscious imitation of Cousin
Julie and began waving her fan to disguise her disapproval....
Gallardon approached her with an invitation to make up a set for
reversi with himself and Gabrielle de Toucy and the young Comte

de Fiesque (Gilette's son, who looked almost comically as his mother had done at his age). She stayed at the Hôtel de Bullion for another hour, laughing and talking and playing cards the whole of that time and exchanging scarcely another word with Fervaques. She joined in the exclamations of surprise and delight that greeted the halting announcement of his new appointment, precisely as if it were news to her as well as to everyone else. But Charlotte was not deceived by the careful assumption of innocence; she flashed her friend a glance of affectionate comprehension over the heads of the crowd; and when at length Cateau took her leave Madame de Bonnelle actually stopped playing long enough to plant two smacking kisses on each cheek and breathe ecstatically: 'My dear — my dear — you're the good angel of our house! Ah, don't deny it — *I know!*'

Cateau drove home that evening enveloped in a warm glow of self-satisfaction. She felt sincerely that, all things considered, she could not have handled the situation better. And it had not been easy to handle. . . . Perhaps it was not too much to say, as Charlotte had told her, that she was the Bullions' good angel. The rôle was a novel one: Cateau found it delightful to play; she was resolved to continue it until she had succeeded in making something creditable of her pupil. Poor young thing! He seemed to be the one human being who needed her — and surely her influence over him was as admirable as it was complete. How fortunate for a young man like Fervaques, on the threshold of his career, to have for his confidante a woman with sufficient experience of life to help him steer clear of its pitfalls! How much better a devotion like this than a vulgar liaison with some horrible actress, such as most youthful courtiers indulged in — or than an affair with one of the present generation of impudent, ill-bred girls of good family, like the Toucy, for instance, or even her sister Doudou, who was undoubtedly the best of the lot! . . . Cateau wondered how long she would be able to save her friend from some such unsavoury entanglement. Fervaques was a lad of high principles, she knew; but the examples he saw about him in camp, at court, even, alas! in his mother's own house, were not calculated to strengthen an attitude of uncompromising morality. And he was a man, and, like other men, could not be expected to live like a saint. . . .

Cateau had treasures of indulgence in reserve for masculine frailty, though, oddly enough, she was the first to condemn similar lapses of members of her own sex. That was because she herself was not subject to this particular weakness of the senses. True, she had had several lovers, but, save for Candale, none of them had been able to fire her emotions. It was enough that she had been able to fire *theirs:* what she had lived for had been the feeling of power over

men. As for the physical side of love, it hardly existed for her.
She was as cold temperamentally as Magdelon the reverse; she had
known that always about herself since her girlhood, and she had
been glad that it was so, deeming it gave her an advantage in the
game at which a woman was so often forced to play the losing hand.
That is, she had been glad till she found, to her cost, that not the
least of her troubles were caused by her fatal ability to kindle flames
she could neither share nor quench.

But now that time had ripened her judgement she could view
the problems of sex in their true proportions. She understood now,
as never before, the really useful part passion might play in the
relations between a man and a woman. Wisely controlled — of
course, by the woman, who must be old enough to know what she
was doing — it could add a comforting flavour of reality to the
most exalted kind of friendship, keep it from becoming bloodless
and desiccated, and lead in the end to the goal of every lonely
soul's ambition, an enduring sentimental attachment.

If she did not take Fervaques, it was obvious that someone else
very soon would — probably someone much less well fitted than
herself to lead him towards the summits she was determined he
should reach. Perhaps, therefore, strange as it might seem, it was
really her duty, as Charlotte's good angel . . .

To give Cateau credit, she came to no hasty decision in this
matter. She thought the thing over thoroughly for nearly a week —
there again clearly demonstrating the superior claims of maturity
over raw, impulsive youth. She reviewed the pros and cons with a
practised and disillusioned eye, balancing the almost inevitable
loss of Charlotte's friendship (for it would be too much to expect
Madame de Bonnelle to appreciate, at least for some time, the
disinterestedness of her motives) against the solid merits and undoubted attractions of beginning life anew as guide, philosopher,
and friend — and something more, as well — to the new governor
of the provinces of Maine and Perche and the County of Laval.

But when at last she sat down to her desk to write the note in
which she intended to convey, delicately yet unmistakably, that
Fervaques' future good fortune depended on his will, not hers, the
aspect of the affair that most struck her was that not once, in the
long series of deliberations leading to what she prayed might prove
an auspicious result for them both, had she considered the fact that
her lover was now master of an income of some eighty thousand
francs a year.

Chapter III

THE DAY AFTER DOUDOU'S WEDDING TO THE DUC DE VENTADOUR, Maman. who had attended the ceremony and the subsequent festivities at the Hôtel de la Mothe in fine fettle, fell ill with rheumatism. The poor woman really suffered a great deal: she had a series of chills, and her arms and legs were so swollen that she could not bear the least movement without groaning, even so much as was necessary to turn her over in bed.

The next night her fever ran so high that her mind wandered a little and she reverted to her old practice — long since abandoned at the earnest solicitation of her confessor and the nuns — of holding conversations with departed relatives. Her husband, a favourite younger brother, and Aunt and Uncle de Marville were invoked in turn, while the Superior of the Carmelites, who was a rather silly creature, easily alarmed and useless in an emergency, sent the convent porter to fetch the Comtesse d'Olonne, convinced that Madame de la Louppe could not last until morning.

Maman herself was of this opinion. In her more lucid intervals she started bestowing sundry scraps of jewelry as keepsakes on the frightened sisters who attended her, regardless of the vows that prohibited them from accepting anything in the way of worldly goods. But she waved away the grumpy priest, who had been hastily roused to confess her, with a magnificent gesture and a graciously confident 'My good man, I've nothing to tell you. If everybody I know had as little to trouble 'em on their consciences in this dread hour as I...'

Cateau arrived about an hour after midnight, in a towering rage — a fur cloak flung over her lace dressing-gown — and put a stop to the serio-comic business immediately.

'Nonsense, Maman, you're not going to die!' she said sourly to her prostrate parent. 'All you need is some good hot herb tea and another pair of blankets. I *told* you not to kneel in the draught at church while that chit was getting married yesterday — but you wouldn't pay any attention to me! *Now* you see who was right about that!'

She dismissed the grumpy priest and the flurried Superior (who was only too glad to relinquish the responsibility); brewed the herb tea herself in the convent refectory; and by the time she was ready to leave Madame de la Louppe was rid of her fever and had fallen asleep.

In the morning the patient was distinctly more comfortable, and a day or two later she was pronounced almost well. However, the swelling in her limbs persisted painfully, and Doctor Pecquet, who had become the family's physician since Doctor Patin was grown too old to continue his practice, recommended a cure at Vichy.

'Oh, sir, you want to kill me!' cried Maman, sitting up in bed swathed in shawls and imbibing a cup of beef bouillon. 'How could I venture so far from home in my precarious state of health?'

'Nay, madam,' objected Doctor Pecquet, 'it's precisely to remedy that state that I'm thinking of sending you . . .'

And Cateau clapped her hands and said: 'Splendid! The very thing, Maman! You remember how hard I tried to get you to go there with me last spring. If only you'd sometimes allow yourself to be guided by me. . . . But tell me, sir, would not the waters of Barèges be even more efficacious? Surely a warm southern climate, like that of the Pyrenees . . .'

Maman rolled a reproachful eye towards her daughter.

'Barèges!' she exclaimed. 'Worse and worse! I see what it is, dear — it's a conspiracy got up between you. I suppose you've grown tired of waiting for your inheritance. Ah, well, we all of us learn, sooner or later, what it means to outstay our welcome in this life! Don't worry, Cateau: I'll not be here to trouble you much longer. . . .'

'Maman! How absurd! You know perfectly well ——'

'I know one thing, child, and that is, what my income amounts to and what I can afford and what I *can't*, though you're always accusing me of having no system in my business affairs. System, indeed! I should like you to tell me who protected your property single-handed, when you and Magdelon were scarcely more than babes at the breast! God only knows the problems I faced, a young widow, alone in the world, not much more than a child myself, and beset by every temptation of the Devil — for I was considered a pretty woman in my day, a very pretty woman indeed, though I dare say you wouldn't remember that! But never once — no, not once: I can say it now, at seventy — did I falter in my duty, nor forget what I promised your poor dear Papa on his death-bed. And so these are my thanks. . . . I'm to be turned out of doors to die in the streets!'

'Maman,' said Cateau quietly, as soon as she could manage to get a word in edgewise, 'you know, of course, I mean to pay for your trip.'

'Oh, well, love, in *that* case perhaps ——'

'You may have the old winter coach and the chestnut pair I usually take to Caen. (You'll be back, I imagine, long before it's time for me to go to Normandy. And if you're not, it doesn't make any difference, for I've ordered some new carriage-horses from Ireland.) Pierre can drive you, and Jean be your footman. Yes, Maman, and besides — so that you shan't want for any comfort on your journey — I'll give you Mademoiselle de Saint-Denis for your companion!'

Afterwards, Cateau congratulated herself especially on this inspiration of the moment, for she had been wondering all week what to do with Mademoiselle de Saint-Denis. The idea of beginning her liaison with Fervaques while living under the same roof as that blameless virgin was somehow repugnant to her. What would the girl say when she knew . . .? And she would know at once, naturally. Cateau feared that those mild doe-brown eyes had already seen a good deal more than they were intended to see. Like all passive on-lookers at life, Mademoiselle de Saint-Denis was a matchless ob-server — and doubtless recorder as well — of the actions of others. It was more than likely that she could furnish, at a moment's notice, a complete catalogue of her mistress's deeds during the twelvemonth they had spent together. And now that there were to be misdeeds, also, Cateau had no mind to endure the patient vigilance a single unnecessary day.

Yet was it really a sin? Once Maman and her new attendant had been dispatched to Vichy Cateau gave herself to her young lover readily, almost gaily, with no sense of guilt. After all, whom were they injuring by their behaviour? Although technically still a mar-ried woman, she was no longer a wife; Fervaques, too, was as free as air. He had not even an old attachment to relinquish before entering the bonds of the new, like most young men of his age and class. . . . With amused surprise Cateau found that she was actually his first real mistress (barring a few tentative adolescent experiments that could scarcely be said to count). His first! And he was six-and-twenty. It seemed incredible. But he had whispered his secret shyly to her that night, as he lay sobbing with rapture in her arms — and it had only added to her feeling of almost maternal affection. . . . Ca-teau lay awake, long after her lover had fallen asleep, with his dark head pillowed on her breast. (Thank Heavens, it was not the fashion to wear one's periwig to bed!) His breath rose and fell as evenly as a child's; she felt his heart-beats, no longer pulsing wildly, but slow and steady like his breath — and her arms closed protectively around him. She felt old . . . but still grateful to the bottom of her heart for what he had given her. A strange tenderness, something none of the lovers of her youth had inspired, moved her almost to tears, and she vowed to do her best to cherish this young creature who trusted in her, and never to fail him in sympathy and devotion, whatever might befall.

Hour after hour her thoughts moved round in circles; she shifted her position again and again, for it was so many years since she had shared her couch with anyone that she had grown used to lie alone; and she heard the bells of Saint-Eustache chime two o'clock — then three — then four — before she, too, lost consciousness at last.

In the morning, when she woke to find him gone, she could not at first believe that he had really been there, and this though it was she herself who'd given him strict orders to depart before her servants were astir. Might it have been a dream . . .?

She yawned and stretched; the delicious fatigue invading her senses reassured her; and when at length she rallied sufficiently to shake the silver bell to summon Quentine, for once her matutinal languor was not assumed.

Quentine, it need hardly be said, was in high feather over the turn things had taken. She poked her head in the door this morning positively radiant; her manner was as discreetly merry as that of a soubrette in one of Molière's comedies. 'Now *at last* affairs are back on a proper footing,' it seemed to say, without the clumsy medium of words. 'My mistress is as good still as she ever was. No need any longer to hang our heads when we go driving in the Cours — *we've* got a gallant to post beside our carriage, too!'

From the width of her waiting-maid's smile Cateau deduced that Fervaques' tip had been twice as generous as it need have been. (Poor child! That was merely owing to his inexperience. Still, Cateau must remember to say a word to him on the subject later. There was no use in throwing money away — and besides, it would only spoil Quentine. As it was, the girl had far too good an opinion of herself.)

'Good morning, madam. I didn't know . . . I thought perhaps His Excellency the Governor . . .'

At this pompous phrase Cateau had a sudden vision of the sobbing boy with tumbled curls who had lain in her arms a few hours before, and suppressed a smile. Then she said severely: 'Quentine, I should like you to understand this, once and for all. As far as you know, no one's been here. No one whatever — d'you see?'

'Yes, madam, of course,' replied Quentine, slightly crestfallen, but still smiling. 'Naturally. I only thought ——'

'You may think what you choose as long as you keep your mouth shut,' said Cateau, compressing her lips and looking unaccountably prim. 'I dare say Monsieur de Fervaques has given you enough to ensure your silence. This is a matter I don't care to discuss with you or with anyone. Later, I don't say what may or may not happen — but for the present things are to continue exactly as they were before. Do you understand me?'

'Yes, madam.' Quentine looked rather frightened and dropped a curtsy in her confusion. 'Of course, madam.'

'Very well, then. I hope I shan't have to refer to this again. Now tell me, *what do you think of the weather?*'

Cateau could not tell why it was, but she felt that it was extremely important to keep her new relations with Fervaques a secret. It was very odd: she had not felt so in her younger days, with other lovers, when so much more had been at stake. Now she had nothing left to lose except Charlotte de Bonnelle's good graces and the impersonal friendship of the sisters at the convent in the rue Buloi, yet the thought of discovery was intolerable. Had she grown queer and old-maidish during the long years she had lived by herself? Or was it perhaps that she was unwilling to have people know she had taken so young a lover? (But then, look at Magdelon with her little Duke, scarce older than Henri, her eldest son!)

Whatever the reason, her reluctance to confess the liaison grew even stronger with time. She imposed rigorous rules of conduct upon Fervaques: he was not to call on her publicly more than twice a week, nor to ride beside her coach in the Cours oftener than every other afternoon. Moreover, when she was at his mother's house, he was to take care not to approach her too intimately, not to smile at her in the presence of others, and especially not to seek a private conversation, unless she should give him express leave to do so.

'Yes, madam, of course — whatever you wish — but why? *Why?* Are you ashamed of me?' Fervaques would demand of her when she repeated her injunctions, as she frequently did, with many a meaning look and tap of her folded fan on his knuckles, to impress their consequence on his youthful mind.

'You know that's not it,' Cateau was wont to make answer at such times, bending over to drop a kiss on his forehead, there where he lay at her feet. (She was generous enough with her endearments when there were no witnesses.) 'You know I am so proud of you there are no words to say what I feel. But don't you agree with me that our love seems twice as precious because it is hidden from everyone else?'

And Fervaques, clasping her slim white hand in his, kissed her fingers in ecstasy and assented passionately: what else, after all, was there for a gentleman to do?

So the weeks passed, and spring came, and the secret remained a secret.

Cateau confided in no one save Magdelon — and even that was an accident. The latter came to see her sister one afternoon when Fervaques was upstairs; Quentine was out, and Lucie stupidly admitted the Maréchale to the dressing-room without warning her mistress.

Magdelon, naturally, was enchanted by her discovery.

'Darling,' she cried, dewy-eyed, directly she and Cateau were alone — Fervaques' awkward and precipitate leavetaking would

have told an even stupider woman the truth, had there been nothing
else to reveal it — 'how happy I am! This is what I have prayed
might happen — now you won't be lonely any more!'

'Oh — lonely,' said Cateau, with a deprecating smile. 'There are
worse fates, perhaps.'

'Not for you or me,' said Magdelon, with conviction. 'We *need*
people. Oh, but it will all be too perfect! You must promise to visit
me at La Ferté this summer. It's so heavenly there in June when the
roses are in bloom, and we'll be quite undisturbed, just you and I and
the children — and of course Longueville and Monsieur de Fervaques, also — for I've given it out that I'm going to Forges for the
cure. There's nothing so satisfactory, is there, as a well-balanced
quartet?'

'A quartet? But surely the Maréchal . . .'

'Oh, well, of course *he* will be there, too. But he goes first to Bourbon to take the waters for his gout — that uses up nearly a month
— and then, when he is at home, he's almost always in bed, poor
dear! or else being carried in his sedan-chair to the farmyard or out
into the fields, so that he can abuse the men and tell them they're
doing everything wrong. Poor La Ferté! I only wish . . . Oh, Cateau'
— with a sudden look of fear — 'it's so horrible to grow old!'

'I don't ever mean to, myself,' said Cateau, with a new complacency. 'Age, my dear, is entirely a question of will-power.'

'But you'll come, won't you, dear? You haven't said yet that you
will,' Magdelon persisted.

Cateau kissed her sister.

'Yes, with pleasure.'

'And you'll get Fervaques to come, too?'

Here Cateau hesitated. It was all very well for Magdelon, who
was the mistress of a royal duke, to be sympathetic about her sister's
affair with a young son of the late Councillor de Bonnelle; but Cateau was not sure she cared to risk a comparison of their respective
gallants at close quarters. It was more than likely that the contrast
between them would serve only to crush the rising flower of her
hardly regained self-esteem. She could not, of course, admit this
without appearing in too petty and egotistical a light. Accordingly
she smiled instead and shook her head lightly as she murmured that
she thought it quite possible His Highness the Duc de Longueville
might object to meeting a junior cavalry officer in one of the regiments of his cousin the Queen on such an intimate footing. . . .

'Oh, my dear, he won't care in the least! He does whatever I say,
always. Besides, as long as *I'm* there, nothing else really matters to
him. And you forget — Fervaques is a governor now.'

'Well, so he is,' said Cateau tolerantly, 'though I confess he
doesn't yet look the part. I do want to bring him to see you some

day, for, come to think of it, you're to inherit La Louppe after Maman's death, and that's a part of the Perche, isn't it? It's just as well to be on good terms with officials. One never knows when they may be useful. . . .'

'Then you'll *both* come!' exclaimed Magdelon, radiant.

But Cateau only smiled and shook her head again and said she'd see about it.

As a matter of fact, she was exceedingly anxious this year to get out of Paris. It seemed to her that every wall in her house had eyes and ears; she longed to leave the too familiar background behind her and hug her secret to her heart in solitude and peace. In this softened mood she felt the country was just what she needed, though she had not forgotten the similar urge that had swept over her, two years ago, when she was recovering from a sharp attack of tertian fever. Perhaps her love for Fervaques was only another form of illness — and it, too, was passing. . . .

But privately she did not think so.

She stayed in town until the first week in May, when her lover left for Le Mans, the seat of his principal government. In spite of his urgent entreaties she refused to accompany him. However, in their farewell interview she promised, in order to soften his disappointment, to write to him every day: that was no longer a task, now that Quentine had learned to counterfeit her mistress's hand so cleverly. Cateau said nothing about Magdelon's invitation to the castle of La Ferté, deeming it best to wait and let future events shape themselves.

So the new governor of Maine and Perche and the County of Laval rode away in state with his train of horses and wagons and prancing postilions, while his mistress prepared to take her departure for Normandy a full month earlier than usual, much to her serving-women's disgust.

Cateau was precise in the performance of her business errands. Love might come, or love might go — but taxes went on falling due just the same, rents had to be collected and leases signed, even if a young man in Le Mans chewed his nails in despair and vowed that the skies would fall if his beloved stopped in Caen another twenty-four hours.

The Countess opened her pretty house in the suburbs as she always did, and gave her customary series of dinners to the local gentry, ending up with a very successful garden-party, whose attractions included a performance of *Tartuffe* by a troop of comedians from Rouen (they were only too glad to come for half-price in the dull summer season) and some beautiful fireworks imported from Paris. The polite world of Caen was enchanted by Madame d'Olonne. . . . When she finally left, after a stay of six weeks, she was several thousand francs richer than when she arrived, and her bailiffs agreed that the prospects for the harvest were most encouraging and that her affairs had never been in a more prosperous condition.

The journey to La Ferté was as long and dull as journeys in the country invariably were. The roads were exceedingly bad, and Cateau had no company save that of the dejected Quentine and Lucie, who were in a state of smouldering rebellion over the length of their absence from Paris. If *this* were what having a lover had done to their mistress! . . . And even granting that an exile might be temporarily necessary, why exchange Caen, which at least was a city of sorts, for the unrelieved rural seclusion of La Ferté, where there was no society worth mentioning? (that provided by the Maréchal's half-civilized grooms and farmers being beneath contempt from the viewpoint of supercilious town-bred damsels!)

Cateau remained markedly unconscious of the ill-temper of Quentine and Lucie. For once in her life, greatly to her own surprise, she seemed to be in a cheerful mood away from home. The roads might be rough, but the landscape they crossed was smooth and sweet and green. Let those silly sluts on the opposite bench frown as much as they liked, as long as the warm June sun went on smiling on the fruitful grain fields and flower-strewn hills! Even in the dense woods of oak and beech that occasionally varied their way, it managed to filter through the branches, making a cool lime-gold aisle for the coach to pass through.

Cateau found herself smiling, too, now and then, she did not know why, and humming casual scraps of tunes she had not thought of in years. She made it a point of honour not to stop at Le Mans, although it was so little out of her path that she could easily have done so without appearing to force the matter. But for the present she did not need to see Fervaques — she did not even *want* to see him, especially. It was enough to be comfortably sure that he was *there*. . . .

In her tranquil high spirits the days passed quickly, and the nights also. The latter she was obliged to spend, for lack of better accommodation, in small rustic inns by the wayside, where the hosts shared a smoky hall-and-kitchen-combined with their guests, and the solitary bedchamber above it that was put at the disposal of the Countess and her women was a dusty, airless garret the lowest scullion at the house in the rue Villedo would have scorned.

But Cateau continued to smile at everything and to make no objections, though it was her wont (Quentine told Lucie privately) to carp ceaselessly on a trip if the lodgings fell short of her exacting requirements. They had not brought their beds with them from Caen, as they ordinarily did when travelling, for the guest-suites at La Ferté were fully furnished; but there were clean sheets to spare in the Countess's trunk and a blanket or two, and, if necessary, 'We can

make our beds in the hay!' Madame d'Olonne declared, clapping
her hands and throwing back her head to laugh like a child. (Here
Quentine and Lucie exchanged a look of dismay: had their mistress
suddenly gone mad?)

They reached their destination late in the afternoon of the third
day after leaving Caen.

The castle of La Ferté-Saint-Aubin was a huge pile of rose-red
brick with stone trimmings, situated in a wood on the flat, marshy
plain of the Sologne about two leagues south of Orléans. Like most
such seats, it had been built at a good many different periods: the
main part of the house dated from the time of the Valois and had the
high peaked roofs and stately charm of the sixteenth century. Some
thirty years ago, however, the Maréchal had begun reconstructing
his residence according to the plans of the famous architect François
Mansart, who had modernized the original wherever he could and
added sundry outbuildings in the early Louis XIV style.

Cateau had always secretly thought it a dreary place. The neighbourhood seemed to her ugly; its flatness depressed her, bred as she
had been amongst verdant Norman hills; and the house itself was undeniably damp, standing beside the sluggish little river Cosson,
which crawled round it to provide the water for the moat and an unusually abundant summer crop of mosquitoes. Moreover, society in
the Orléannais was scarce and what there was, was dull.

She therefore took care not to visit Magdelon in the country more
than was absolutely necessary for the maintenance of amicable sis-
terly relations, preferring, if possible, to meet her at Forges or Vichy
in the season instead. Magdelon asked her, of course, to come every
year, and Cateau always said she would — and then, nine times out
of ten, wrote later to apologize — would her darling *ever* forgive her?
— but there was some stupid mix-up in her schedule . . .

They rolled over the drawbridge this evening past the two squat
red-brick lodges and the long green front lawn that was, as usual,
somewhat overgrown and weedy, and drew up at the handsome
stone entrance. Several flunkeys in untidy half-buttoned uniforms
hurried to meet them, colliding clumsily in their haste to open the
carriage door; and presently a sad-eyed butler, with soiled white
gloves and his wig on crooked, appeared, yawning — no need to inquire where *he'd* been! — to greet Madame d'Olonne and announce
that the Maréchale was, he believed, in the park with the children.

Cateau jumped out of the coach and nodded brightly.

'Good-day, Hippolyte,' she said. 'I'll go join my sister. No, don't
trouble to come with me; I know the way well. If you will be so good
as to take charge of my women . . .'

It took her longer to find Magdelon than she had thought. The
wood was damp and full of insects, and the path she followed was

rather tentative and twiggy. She was guided, however, by the sound of children's voices; and at length she emerged from the trees onto slightly higher ground, where there was a little field full of sunshine and singing larks. At the far end of the field some peasants were cutting hay, bending rhythmically with the precision of ballet-dancers as their scythes swished through the grass. But near at hand it still stood long and lush, starred with white daisies and blue corn-flowers and scarlet poppies in profusion. And on a knoll in the middle of the grass and the flowers, the sun and the lark-songs, sat Magdelon, surrounded by her family.

The Maréchale de la Ferté-Senneterre was wearing an old brown dress of some homespun material, put on anyhow; and she was hatless — her beautiful dark curls tumbling over her shoulders quite as loosely as her young sons'. She appeared to be very busy weaving a chain of field-flowers and nursing a chubby white puppy with one black ear, at the same time laughing and chatting with her children as merrily, Cateau thought, as if she were one of them. The late afternoon sun fell full on the rosy cheeks — but she did not care; little Jules and Tinette, repulsively grubby after their romp, clung to her skirts unchidden. Henri and Louis, who were playing tag with loud shrieks of delight about a small apple tree, ran into each other just as their aunt appeared, tripping over their mother's feet — and Magdelon only laughed, pushed the hair out of her eyes, and said: 'Careful, darlings, you nearly squashed Fido that time!'

Cateau took in her sister's appearance with horror, mingled with an unwilling admiration. It was like Magdelon to go to extremes: she was either the model fine lady at court, stiff with brocades and laden with jewels, painted and scented to the ultimate degree of perfection — or she simply let herself go, dressed like one of her own farmer's wives, and paid no heed to her hair and complexion. What was irritating was that she looked equally lovely either way; neglect did not seem to injure her beauty. As she sat there, windblown and sunburnt and laughing, in the midst of her babies and flowers, she might have posed for a picture of Ceres, the Goddess of Plenty herself.

Beside her, Cateau felt pallidly artificial in her pretty green travel-ling-dress and the feathered bonnet that allowed each yellow curl to escape so far — and no farther — over the graceful shoulders. True, she too was dressed for the country, but for a very different kind of country: the tame, trim park of her neat suburban house in Caen had no more in common with this sweet-scented, untidy meadow than the Parisian belle with the blooming mistress of La Ferté-Saint-Aubin.

For a moment Cateau stood on the edge of the wood, while the larks went on singing, the peasants mowing, and Magdelon and her children laughed and called out to one another. Then she started to pick her way gingerly through the long grass, taking care to poke with the point of her parasol well in advance of each step, for fear of snakes.

Magdelon heard the rustle of silken skirts and looked up with a cry of delight.

'Darling! It's you!' she said. 'How glad I am! Now our party is quite complete. Longueville got here last night, and it was only this morning that Monsieur de Fervaques arrived from Le Mans.'

As she sprang to her feet, still holding the white puppy with the black ear, but scattering the flowers in her lap far and wide, Cateau could not help seeing, from the full curves of her sister's figure, that the last detail was not missing in the picture of the Goddess of Plenty: so the Toucy's scandalous story was true, after all!

MAGDELON, WEARING A LOOSE LACY DRESSING-GOWN AND WITH HER black hair hanging in two long plaits down her back, came to Cateau's room that night as the latter was making ready for bed. It was very late: they had sat at table till well past midnight; the candles were guttering low in their sconces and the footmen, who were waiting to put them out, had begun to yawn prodigiously behind their hands, long before the quartet showed signs of breaking up.

But whatever the hour, Cateau's coucher was an elaborate process. Fervaques must restrain his impatience as best he could: she composed herself for twenty minutes by the clock, while Quentine brushed her curls and Lucie patted divers creams and powders and lotions on her arms and hands and face. She sat still, staring straight ahead, thinking even as little as possible; for one of her maids had once told her that wrinkles were encouraged by too active exercise of the brain before retiring.

Magdelon drifted restlessly about the big room, smoothing a cushion here, straightening a vase of flowers there, and obviously waiting until Cateau had sent her women away to unburden her mind.

So at length, with a sigh, the latter murmured: 'That will do, Lucie; good night. Good night, Quentine. I'll ring if I need you again' — and then turned to Magdelon with an arranged expression of bright interest. Magdelon was seated on the edge of the bed, twirling a rose she had plucked from one of the jars on the mantelpiece between her fingers; she was regarding the flower so intently that she seemed unable to look up to meet Cateau's questioning glance; but Cateau did not need to see her sister's face to know it was almost as red as the rose.

Magdelon was embarrassed. That was strange — for up to now she had sailed through the intricacies of the evening with far more serenity than any of her guests. She had been perfectly simple and unashamed about the whole thing, which was, of course, the only sensible way to behave. One could not help envying her her ease of manner, the innocence with which she appeared to maintain that there was nothing odd or improper in the fact of the four of them being there together — two middle-aged women (for one might as well face it: that was what they were!) with their young lovers, holding illicit rendezvous in the house of the husband of one of the women.

However one chose to look at it, it was not a savoury situation. The men, each in his way, proved that they realized that — Fervaques, by his frequent sober silences, in spite of an inner radiance that shone through them persistently; and the Duke, by an unaccustomed, well-nigh feverish loquacity. Cateau herself had felt less socially competent than usual, though she chatted gaily away with Monsieur de Longueville, discussing his trip to Flanders with the King to view the new fortifications, from which he had just returned, and His Majesty's hopes for a speedy and unequivocal victory in the forthcoming war with the Dutch. But while her tongue was delivering infallible judgements concerning the rival merits of commanders she had never seen and the impregnability of citadels she had never even heard of, she remained acutely conscious of what three at least of the company were trying to forget. . . . It was only their hostess whose eyes were guileless, Magdelon's laugh that rang out again and again over trifling jests, as clear and uncalculated as a child's.

Cateau had glanced at her sister admiringly, until her admiration faded as she perceived that Magdelon was acting naturally because she felt natural — she was as incapable of reflection as the child whose laughter her own evoked. This was followed by the inescapable comparison between their respective motives for taking such immature lovers: Cateau, quite frankly, preferring a young man who would be subservient to her and whom she could hope to mould. (Having failed to find a ready-made gallant to suit her tastes, she intended to make one to measure.) But Magdelon was irresistibly drawn to youth because she herself was still mentally adolescent.

This being so, why, then, had her happy aplomb deserted her? Why was she now half-crouched on the bed, with downcast looks and trembling lips, and a colour that ebbed and flowed while one watched it? Why did the hand that held the rose shake so pathetically when Cateau gave it a little pat? And why, at this modest sign of affection, did Magdelon suddenly cast pretences aside and fling herself sobbing into her sister's arms? . . .

It was some minutes before calm was fully restored. When she had finally checked her tears and put herself to rights once more, Magdelon looked up to say with a rueful smile: 'My dear, forgive me — this shan't happen again. I'm tired and overwrought tonight. And ever since dinner-time I've been feeling so horribly ill. . . . Oh, no, it's nothing serious. You know how it is in the first few months. . . . But you *don't* know, do you? I always forget, you've never had a child.'

So at last the secret was out! Cateau, in order to test her, pre-

tended on purpose to misunderstand and said, moistening her lips:
'Then you and La Ferté have hopes again? . . . I thought when I saw
you that it must be so — and yet it seemed hard to believe — in his
state of health. . . . Dear, I'm happy for you if *you're* happy about it
. . . but really, with four young ones already, and three of them
sons, perhaps it's not an unmixed blessing. Still, I suppose . . .'

Magdelon looked at Cateau steadily, though her cheeks burned
redder than ever.

'You needn't pretent to *me*,' she said. 'You know the baby's not
my husband's. It's Longueville's son I am carrying now. . . . It *will*
be a son. . . . I feel it will. . . .'

'Oh, but, my dear, how can you?' said Cateau. 'I mean — what
will people say?'

'I don't care — I don't care! Let them say what they like! They'll
have no proof. I am going to bear Longueville a son in December.'

This was terrible. Defiance Cateau had been prepared for, and
even a touch of hysterical bravado — but not this bright-eyed, tranquil obstinacy. . . . It was like a foolish hen-pheasant protecting her
nest, though the hunter's gun was already aimed at her head. Cateau almost wrung her hands in despair as she exclaimed: 'But your
husband, then! Have you thought of him? *He'll* know the truth,
whomever else you may trick. What will he do when he learns . . . ?
My dear, be warned in time. There are ways of avoiding this. Do,
do consider . . .'

'I *have* considered,' said Magdelon. 'But it's no use. Charles
wants his son, and he's a right to have him. And I want him, too,
just as much as he does. No, there's nothing to be done.'

She spoke still with that awful air of judicious decision, as though
she had reasoned the problem out by herself and come by a series of
carefully considered steps to its one possible solution. Cateau, who
knew Magdelon as well as Magdelon knew herself — if not better!
— was convinced that she had done nothing of the kind. Poor silly
girl! She was Maman all over again — her innate lack of wisdom
and incapacity for reflection masked by a gay glaze of trustful assurance that could deceive no one who loved her as Cateau did. Once
that small emotional outburst was over — which, after all, had been
due to purely physical causes — she would drift unerringly to perdition, without a single backward glance of misgiving. Cateau could
not bear to see it happen. She could not bear to let the frail, crazy
craft spin past her, headed straight for the dangerous rapids below,
and not at least stretch out a rescuing hand. Was it already too late
to save her? At any rate, she must *try*.

'My dear,' said Cateau, with all the patience she could muster, 'I
don't believe you realize what you're saying. Your husband will re-
pudiate you. If he chooses to cast you off into the street, there'll not

be a hand raised to stop him. And what can you do by yourself — alone, against the whole world, you, who have nothing except what he's given you?'

'But why need he know?'

Magdelon's eyes had not lost their annoying placidity. Cateau could have shaken her.

'Child — use your head! What else can he think...?'

'I mean — why need he know it's even been born? He's too old and too ill now to watch over me as he used to do. I can stay here in the country as long as I have to — and there's not a servant in the house I can't trust to be on my side.... Even Robert... now.... La Ferté's been hard on him once too often. Oh, we've talked it all over, Charles and I — there's no reason on earth why we can't go through with it! Of course, I can't keep the baby with me afterwards, which is a great pity. But Charles has thought of that — he's thought of everything, really, dear fellow! He's arranged for Clément to take care of me — you know, the accoucheur who goes to the Montespan when she and the King... It will cost two thousand francs, I'm afraid, but it's worth it. Then he's got a house ready in the Faubourg Saint-Germain, and Porlier, his secretary, who was his tutor when he was a boy, has promised to take charge of little Charles, too, when the time comes. Oh, you'll see — you'll see! It will be all right, dear — truly, I promise you! I can't refuse Longueville the one thing he's ever asked of me — what none of his other mistresses have been willing to do....'

'I should think not, indeed!' snapped Cateau. 'Naturally, they had more common sense. If he really considered you, he'd never suggest it. Oh, I'll say no more, since I see you've resolved to stake your whole future for the sake of a whim. Very well, then — go ahead, if there's no stopping you! Have your baby, if you must. Fool the world, if you will — and your husband into the bargain, if you're able to. God knows, I've no love for my brother-in-law! But don't forget, Magdelon, it's more than likely the whole story will come out, in the end. And then, what's to become of you? Have you and your precious Duke thought of that? What will you say to La Ferté if he finds out what you've done? — what you are?...'

'But, Cateau, dear,' said Magdelon, interrupting her sister in defiance of her custom, 'he *does* know what I am. Indeed, he's always known.'

'Then why...? How...?'

Cateau gave up the puzzle and shook her head in utter bewilderment. She had wondered for years how much the Maréchal guessed of his wife's way of living. It seemed incredible that he should not have had strong suspicions, to say the least, with Great Senneterre thronged from morning till night with the gayest, most gallant young courtiers in Paris. For alas! once Magdelon had broken her marriage vows she behaved very much worse than Cateau had ever done. She fell in love regularly every month, with the inevitable results, given her beauty and excitable temperament. Beuvron had been merely the vanguard of a long line of successful candidates for the affections of Madame de la Ferté. The naughty Comte de Gramont — the haughty Marquis d'Effiat — sly, unscrupulous Villarceaux (who had quarrelled with his mistress after a fortnight and shown her letters all round the court) — these were but a few of the names that everybody knew. Cateau herself could not begin to remember them all. But what was really extraordinary was that whilst Magdelon was parcelling out her favours breathlessly right and left with an almost ludicrous lack of calculation, she had gone on living with her husband on the best of terms, as far as anyone, even her sister, was able to tell. The old Maréchal, who shouted and stamped at all the rest of the world, still adored his wife — or appeared to adore her. But he was no fool. Must he not at times have doubted...?

'Magdelon,' said Cateau brusquely, facing her, 'just what do you mean? Have you confessed to your husband?'

'No. Oh, no.'

'Still, you say that he knows...'

'Yes,' said Magdelon, very low; 'he knows.'

Tears rose to her eyes, as they often did; she had not lost her childish habit of crying on the smallest pretext.

'Then why...? How...?' said Cateau again. 'No... I *don't* see...'

'My dear,' said Magdelon, brushing the drops away with the lace of her sleeve (another habit of childhood!), 'it's so simple, really. He knows about me — but he's so fond of me that he pretends he doesn't know. That's all. I found it out years ago when Gramont and I... Oh, I can recall it now as though it were yesterday! La Ferté had gone to court to a meeting at the war minister's, and Gramont was with me in the green cabinet... when suddenly my page rushed into the room — you remember Jacquinot, that horrid little boy with pimples I had to keep so long because his mother was the chef's mistress, and La Ferté said we'd never find another cook so good?... His sauces were marvellous, I must say, though I never could fancy his way with roast game.... But where was I, dear?'

'With Gramont,' said Cateau dryly, 'in the green cabinet.'

'Oh, yes, of course!... How silly of me!... Well, there we were, when Jacquinot burst in upon us, crying that the Maréchal's carriage was at the door, and the Maréchal himself was halfway upstairs at that very moment. Poor Gramont! You know what a coward he was. Off he dashed in his nightshirt with Jacquinot, leaving his clothes scattered all over the floor. My dear, I was nearly dead with

fright! I managed somehow to pick up his things, with my legs
trembling so I could scarcely stand.... It wasn't till after I'd got
back into bed that I saw I'd forgotten his wig — but it was too late
then to do anything about it — and there it lay on the table, as
plain as the nose on your face, when La Ferté marched in to see me.
I was so terrified I hadn't a word to say — but he kissed me just as if
nothing were wrong and sat by the bed for ten minutes — it seemed
centuries! — telling me about the meeting. I don't know now what
I said; naturally, I couldn't think of anything but that horrible wig!
— and finally La Ferté noticed it, too. How could he have helped it?
He shouted to his valet: "Take my peruque away directly! You
damned fool, to leave such an object in the Maréchale's room!" And
the valet said — he was a nasty new creature who'd taken a dislike
to me from the moment he came — I got rid of him the very next
day —: "My Lord, it isn't *your* peruque." But I shan't forget till
my dying hour the look the Maréchal gave him and the way he
roared out: "Damme! It *is* mine, I tell you! Take it away this instant, or I'll flog you till you won't be able to stand for a week!"...
So after that, I saw how it was. He knew quite well I was deceiving
him, but he couldn't bear to give me up. Oh, my dear, you needn't
think I wasn't touched! — that I didn't try to do better. I cried and
cried for days and days — and prayed, too.... But it wasn't any
use.... Oh, Cateau, you don't know how hard it's been sometimes!
You see, La Ferté's so old — so old — all *that* side of life was finished
for him before it even began for me. *You* married a young man....
Oh, I know he wasn't a good husband — not half so kind as mine —
but at least he was young when you were young: you must have
wanted the same things at the same time, in the beginning, anyhow.
It was different for me. All La Ferté asked for was a home and heirs
to inherit his fortune. Ah, I've tried to give him what he wanted, too
— I have, truly — and I do believe I've made him happy. Yes, I'm
sure I have. He's always better and more cheerful when we're together — though of course there've been times... But it's no good
going into that, is it? He loves me just as if I were one of his children
— and I — well, I've come to feel now that he's almost like a father to
me. You know I'm too young to remember Papa — I suppose *you*
can just do it — but I've always felt we'd have got on so well together. Maman says I'm like him in so many ways — sleeping late
in the morning, for instance, and liking my meat done to a turn, but
eggs almost raw.... Oh, darling, I'm wandering from the point again:
please forgive me — I hardly know what I'm saying tonight. What
I'm trying to tell you is this: I was twenty years old when I married.
I'm only thirty-six now. And you can't stop living because your husband has stopped. You know that's true. Oh, I'm a wicked woman!
But I can't help myself. And no one else can help me, either. I've

tried prayer. That didn't do any good. Nor confession. The priests
give you absolution, and impose their penances — and you tell them
you're sorry, you promise not to sin any more — and you mean it at
the time, of course.... But all the while you know perfectly well
inside that you'll do the same thing over again — maybe not with
the same man!... Oh, Cateau, Cateau! What can I do? I love
Charles so much — more than anyone I've ever loved before! I *can't*
give him up — and I can't deny him the child he wants as the pledge
of our love. Darling, do try to understand.... It's not as if *you*
hadn't been tempted, too....'

'No,' said Cateau slowly. 'No; it's not *that*.... There, there,
child! Don't cry any more, for pity's sake!'

But it was already too late: Magdelon had brought her flurried
monologue to a close with a renewed burst of weeping, which relieved
her overcharged feelings. At least so it seemed to Cateau, who began
stroking her sister's shoulder in a businesslike manner, but desisted
as it was gradually borne in upon her that she herself was the more
shaken of the two. To give herself time to recover her poise she rose
from her seat on the bed beside Magdelon and walked across to the
window, drawing the stiff brocade curtains aside and flinging open
the casement on the warm June night.... It was very still in the park
of the castle: a faint breeze sweet with the scent of new-mown hay
just stirred the tops of the beeches, and the frogs below in the moat
were loudly croaking. (There was no doubt about it, La Ferté-Saint-
Aubin was damp!)

Cateau felt perplexed by Magdelon's unforced display of emotions
to which she herself was a stranger. Never — not even in the reckless days of her youth — had she cared for anyone as Magdelon cared
for her little Duke. Never — not even for Candale, whom she had
loved as much as she could love any man — would she have risked
such security as she had by bearing a child out of wedlock. For that
matter, she had not wanted especially to bear one *in* it; it had been
no great disappointment to her to find that her union with Olonne
was sterile.... Olonne, on the other hand, had minded very much
indeed.... She recalled the little man's petulant grievance over his
growing conviction that he was not to have an heir. One spring, some
four or five years after their marriage, he had imported from the Orient some Japanese flowering cherry trees: exquisite, graceful little
things, they had been set out with due care against a wall in the sun-
niest corner of the garden, where they had done remarkably well,
becoming covered, as the season advanced, with a profusion of delicate pale pink blossoms. But the blossoms were not succeeded by
fruit; and Olonne, after his first fit of natural irritation had subsided,
had amused the Gourmets' Club by comparing the falsely promising
cherry trees to the deceptive bloom of his Countess.

This long-forgotten incident returned now to Cateau's mind; she could not help thinking that her life might have been very different if she had not been barren. But it was useless to speculate.... Her own problems seemed remote in the face of her sister's present need of succour and warm human comfort. For all the splendour of her outward existence, poor Magdelon was tragically alone....

So Cateau hugged Magdelon affectionately and patted her back, as she always did, and promised to help her in any way she could. (That, too, went without saying.)

Then the sisters kissed each other — their eyes solemn and staring in the wavering candlelight, despite the punctuality of their conventional smiles — and parted for the night, each to await the visit of her lover.

Chapter V

NEXT MORNING MAGDELON CAME DOWNSTAIRS LOOKING PRECISELY AS usual. Her face was round and rested, her smile brightly infectious, her temper, as ever, serene and accommodating. Nor did she vary by so much as a hairsbreadth from this agreeable ideal during the rest of the time her guests remained at La Ferté-Saint-Aubin. If she were feeling ill, she gave no sign of it. Cateau remembered that most of Magdelon's pregnancies had been easy; it was only Louis' birth that had cost her dear, for which unreasonable reason she loved her second son, if possible, even more passionately than her other children.

In the end, their hostess's persistent good-humour succeeded in galvanizing the whole party into something approaching her own refulgent high spirits.

Cateau never would have believed it possible, but that stolen fortnight turned out to be one of the pleasantest experiences of her life.

In the first place, the weather was really perfect, fine and warm, but not too warm; so that they were able to be outdoors a great deal of the time. There were walks in the terraced rose-garden beside the river, where dragonflies quivered and darted in the sunshine and willows bent to trail their branches in the slow-moving amber waters. There were drives through the deep bird-haunted beech woods surrounding the castle, and *al fresco* meals at various local points of interest, engineered by the Maréchale with so much artless enthusiasm that the most confirmed city-dweller could not have resisted its appeal. . . . 'We're just like the shepherds and shepherdesses in *Astrée*, aren't we?' said Magdelon happily.

Cateau, who had always supposed she detested the country, found herself, much to her own surprise, in a mood of mellow acquiescence. She slept well and ate well, laughed more than she had done in years, and hardly made up her face at all. She smelled the roses, watched the dragonflies, listened to the birds in the beeches; she kilted up her trailing silk skirts and strolled through the blossoming fields with Fervaques; she even asked herself more than once if it might not be a good idea, when she went back to Paris, to hire a small place not too far out of town — say at Saint-Germain or Vincennes — for an occasional refuge.

Of course, a good part of her enjoyment was due to its being shared. Fervaques was constantly with her; she found his companionship more satisfying than ever. His devotion was touching; apparently he had but one desire in the world, and that was to grant all *her* desires, if possible, even before she expressed them. This gratified her extremely — what woman would it *not* have gratified? — and the more he spoilt her, the more charming she was in return. Their eyes met scores of times a day in rapturous communion over many a small shared delight; they were forever asking each other the superfluous question, 'Are you happy? But tell me, my dear, are you *truly* happy?' just for the pleasure of exacting the inevitable answer. Moreover, the rare harmony of their relations was enhanced by their temporary removal from ordinary spheres of activity. No one knew where they were; no one could follow to break in on their idyll; so that afterwards, when Cateau looked back on the fortnight at La Ferté, it assumed in her eyes something of the quality of a belated honeymoon.

Once in her life, she told herself then, she had known what it was to love and be loved in peace.

Nor was her contentment shadowed, as she had feared, by the unavoidable comparison between her gallant and her sister's.

Reviewing the two young courtiers, if not quite dispassionately, at least with the perspicacity born of long experience of the breed, Cateau honestly felt that the advantage lay entirely with Fervaques. True, he was neither strikingly handsome nor alarmingly intelligent: with all his innate courtesy, he lacked, too, the pretty wit that enabled the other to turn a compliment on his mistress's eyes or her smile with an air of ease denoting assiduous imitation of the best available models. But he was a good young man, a kind young man; modest, yet manly, he bore himself in the company of his superior with exactly the right tone of self-confidence without fatuousness and deference without servility. (Behold what Cateau had already been able to accomplish with this pliable clay! Six months ago he would surely have stammered and blushed and fallen over his feet directly the Duke entered the room.)

As for Longueville, although as the days passed Cateau observed herself liking him better than she had at first supposed she could ever do, he by no means approximated her ideal of what a nobleman of his power and position ought to be. To begin with, while he had a handsome head, with the aquiline nose of the Bourbons and the keen blue eyes and ash-blond curls that recalled his mother, the Duchess Dowager (who had been the acknowledged beauty of her day), his figure was both short and puny. It appeared sometimes as though, if one were to strip him suddenly of his ribbons and laces, of his fine satin coat and his high Russia-leather boots, there would be little left of His Highness the Duc de Longueville save a small, peculiarly persistent draught.

His character, too, was contradictory and variable. At times he sat sullen for hours without speaking a word, passively hostile, managing somehow silently to convey his disdain for and total disagreement with the opinions of all other people in the room. Then again, he seemed bent on asserting his personality at any cost in whatever company he found himself: he laughed a great deal — a loud, ugly bray with no mirth in it — and contradicted everything that was said. When in this mood he ordered his servants about unmercifully — he had a great many servants, who, strangely enough, all adored him. He would also boast continually of his family, particularly of his uncle Condé, who was evidently his hero; make ill-timed references, in the worst possible taste, to his amorous exploits; and spin windily self-complacent monologues concerning various magnificent projects for the future. On one day, he was going to buy the charge of Colonel of the Swiss Guards for four hundred thousand francs from the Comte de Soissons; on another, it was as good as settled that he was to be Grand Master of the Artillery instead. Still later, it appeared that fabulous marriages were being arranged for him: Mademoiselle de Montpensier would become his bride and settle her huge estates on the Longuevilles — or the Queen of Poland had decided to divorce her husband and raise the Duke to the post of Prince Consort. . . . It was impossible to tell how much truth lay in these unguarded statements. The King, one had heard, was rumoured not to like his young relative — it was, alas! easy enough to see why — and therefore, in spite of the latter's bravery, which he had amply demonstrated in the Franche-Comté campaign and, later, in the unfortunate expedition to Candia, he had not yet found a place suited to his birth and undoubted ability as a soldier.

Cateau could not help being reminded sometimes of Longueville's cousin, her dear, dead lover Candale, who had been even more prominent and equally unlucky. Candale, she recalled, had had a similar preoccupation with his rank — only in his case it had taken the form of a regal splendour and serenity. He had not, at bottom, been in the least a more amiable person; but he had appeared to be so, because what was best in him showed most; while the reverse was true of young Longueville, who would often, one felt, have liked to be pleasant if he had known how to set about it. He was the unwilling prisoner of his ill-humour, as Candale had been of his good one.

Not unnaturally, this captious young man was at his best with women and children. The presence of another full-grown male, even so unassuming a specimen as Fervaques, was apt to put him on his dignity, ruffled up in quite uncalled-for battle array like an under-

sized gamecock. But he was generally courteous, not to say complimentary, to Cateau and Magdelon; and with the latter's children he
showed himself a delightful playfellow. He would recite verses or
tell fairy-tales by the hour to little Jules and Tinette; fence with the
older boys, and allow them to handle unchided his rare collection of
arms — muskets and rapiers and the cruel shining scimitars he had
brought back with him from Crete. Henri and Louis even invaded
the Duke's dressing-room in the morning while his valet was shaving
him, and sat side by side on the couch, wide-eyed in wonder at the
marvellous accounts of His Highness's adventures in such fantastic
corners of the world as Amsterdam and Vienna and the Grecian
Isles.

This pleasing state of affairs was brought to an end very suddenly,
one day a little over two weeks after Cateau's arrival at La Ferté-
Saint-Aubin.

It was an unusually warm afternoon; the ladies were seated at
their tapestry work in the shade of a clump of tall beeches on the
lawn in front of the castle. Fervaques, lying on the grass at their
feet, read aloud to them the new play by Racine that had been sent
to the Maréchale from Barbin's Library in Paris. In spite of the
breathless heat, however, Longueville was not able to sit still. He
had only that morning bought a string of ponies to replenish his
stables in Normandy; two of the gentlest and best-mannered beasts
had been selected for the momentous task of teaching the La Ferté
boys to ride bareback.

Laughing and hatless, his long yellow curls streaming over his
shoulders, the young Duke stood in the middle of the circular patch
of lawn encouraging his pupils, who squealed with excitement as
they raced round the drive, making innumerable well-meant if
clumsy attempts to follow his directions.

Cateau rather expected to see both her nephews plunge to the
ground on their heads at any moment, but Magdelon did not seem
in the least alarmed. She raised her eyes from her work now and
again, but only to beam benevolently on her lover and the two little
boys; no doubt she was thinking how happy Longueville would be
when he had a son of his own. . . .

Just as Louis, who, although the younger, was a good deal more
agile than his brother, had finally succeeded in circling the ring half
erect on his mount, and was shouting: 'Look, Maman! Look at *me!*'
there was a rumbling and a jingling and a big brown coach hove into
sight at the far end of the long straight avenue. It passed over the
bridge and through the lodge gates; then the six shaggy bay Per-
cherons that pulled it broke into a lumbering gallop, which brought
them up to the door of the castle in a cloud of dust, amidst the cracking of whips and the whooping of postilions.

Cateau glanced up in astonishment. She had often seen her brother-in-law driving in town, where his equipage was second to none at court in conventional magnificence; but it happened that this was the first time she had caught him off guard in the rôle of country gentleman. The heavy windowless carriage, with its enormous wheels and flapping side-curtains of Spanish leather, was like a page from the past. In just such a conveyance — perhaps in that very one — had the Maréchal ridden forth to war in the days of Louis XIII and Cardinal Richelieu. Then, as now, his coachmen and lackeys had worn leather jerkins and broad-brimmed plumed hats; his original band of followers, who had won their spurs at La Rochelle and later plundered the countryside guerilla-fashion in the famous campaign against the Duc de Lorraine, could not have been less prepossessing than the present crew. They were a swarthy, shifty-eyed lot, with long, unkempt black hair; several of the men wore gold hoops in their ears, and all had strident voices and uncouth manners.

Robert, the Maréchal's chief valet, a grizzled villain with a game leg — souvenir of the Battle of Rocroi in '43 — slipped with surprising nimbleness between the curtains of the coach and turned to help his master alight.

Cateau had not met La Ferté for several months; she was shocked by the change in his appearance. Since he had become a chronic sufferer from gout he had been forced to forgo the violent exercise that had once kept him in fine physical trim, despite his indiscretions at table. Now, although inactive, he had gone on eating as much as he liked of whatever he liked in defiance of the doctors' orders, with the result that he had put on some thirty pounds. For a time his splendid big frame and lordly mien had enabled him to carry off the excess weight; but in the end his whole body seemed to have softened, as old men's bodies often do. New creases appeared almost daily in his ravaged countenance, and as he had lately lost most of the lower row of his teeth (the upper row had gone years ago), his jaw looked greatly shrunken, a defect all the more obvious since he had shaved his beard and contented himself with a mere straggling tuft on his chin.

Gingerly now he stepped down from the high step of the carriage, leaning heavily on Robert and contorting his face in all manner of horrible grimaces, which would have been comic except that nothing the Maréchal did ever appeared so.

The little group on the lawn had risen to greet him. Fervaques, letting his book slide unheeded to the grass, stared openmouthed at his host. Magdelon was smiling calmly, evidently unembarrassed by this unlooked-for apparition. Longueville, too, Cateau thought, carried the situation off very well. He had clapped his hat on his yellow curls and hastened over to greet La Ferté with every indication of pleased surprise.

'Dear sir, how delightful!' exclaimed Monsieur de Longueville. 'We had not hoped to claim you from the charms of Bourbon for at least another week.'

The old man gave the young man a curious look, his thick lids drooping over the bold black eyes that alone of his features retained the fire of youth; then he bowed his head.

'This is an honour, my Lord,' he said, in a husky, metallic voice, like an echo of the clarion tones of the past. 'You are heartily welcome to La Ferté-Saint-Aubin. We meet all too seldom in Paris. But I must not complain. I know there's little enough nowadays at Great Senneterre to attract young people.'

Could he be speaking seriously? — or was his intention deliberately ironic? For there was Magdelon standing between her husband and her lover, and blushing as rosily as a girl....

Longueville, at all events, chose to ignore possible unfriendly implications. He returned the bow as he murmured smoothly: 'But, sir, it is always a pleasure to see you. I called at your house several times last spring before going to Flanders with the King, but I was always told that you were out. Did the Maréchale fail to deliver my messages? Fie, madam, I believe you must have played me false there!'

Magdelon smiled again and kissed her husband's hand, to hide the fact that she was blushing more than ever. La Ferté patted her head, as if she had been a child, with his other great hairy paw; and then Cateau rustled up smartly to bridge the difficult interval by presenting Fervaques, whom the Maréchal acknowledged with a hollow guffaw and a thump on his guest's startled back.

'I knew your father Bullion well, my boy,' he declared. 'Or no — that was your grandfather, wasn't it? In any case, a dirty, thieving old rascal, if ever I saw one! But he had a way with the ladies, had Bullion! Ha! I'll never forget what the Queen Mother said to Madame de Sault in that connection — but that's not to be repeated in present company. I hope you're as graceless a varlet, sir, as your late respected ancestor — God rest his soul! Now come along, come along! Zounds! But I've got a thirst to slake, after those cursed dusty roads! Shocking state they're in, to be sure! I don't know what the government's thinking of. In *my* day the soldiers cut 'em to pieces. But we've not had a war worth mentioning on French soil in more years than I care to count. Come along! Come along! Hippolyte, you dog, a flagon of Ay in the crimson cabinet — and look sharp about it!'

So the party passed into the house, Magdelon clinging to her husband's left arm, the Duc de Longueville, as befitted his rank, on the right of his host. Cateau and Fervaques followed the oddly assorted trio, while Henri and Louis, who adored their crusty old father, capered airily about in the rear.

Supper that night was served in the great hall for the first time since Cateau had come to La Ferté-Saint-Aubin. During her husband's absences from home, so frequent during the early years of their married life, Magdelon had grown accustomed to eat in a small antechamber opening off the state apartment, which was more intimate as well as more easily heated in cold weather.

The great hall was chilly even at midsummer, a vast room all gilt and marble and gaudy tapestries, lined with a double row of ancestral portraits. At least, that was what they were purported to be . . . nor did the stiffly smiling painted lips betray any secrets concerning their origin, though it had often occurred to Cateau, and even sometimes to Magdelon, that, really, they could not *all* be . . . since everyone knew that the Senneterres were so new that it was as much as the Maréchal could do to mention his grandfather's name. . . .

Supper itself was rich and abundant — far too abundant, thought Cateau, who would have preferred at least three fewer courses; she could not help worrying over the obvious waste in her sister's house. Indeed, she had once gone so far as to inquire severely of Magdelon what became of the left-overs, and had shaken her head in bleak disapproval when the latter replied, with an easy laugh: 'Bless you, my darling, there *aren't* any!'

It was a rather silent meal. The Maréchal, whose impressive bulk loomed larger than before, if possible, against its splendid, spacious background, sat in the centre of the long board, hunched up in his chair, with his chin sunk on his chest and an unfathomable look in his murky eyes. Beside him Monsieur de Longueville, brave in scarlet velvet, his bosom sparkling with orders, appeared insignificant and flimsy, as if he were only two-dimensional and would have looked as flat as the Knave of Hearts (whom he somewhat resembled) if one could have managed to view him end on. . . . Fervaques, greatly awed by the august company into which he found himself thrust on familiar terms, scarcely opened his mouth except to put food into it; while even Cateau, who generally found plenty to say to her brother-in-law, if only to dispute three out of four of his statements, felt little disposed to break the recurring edgy silences.

Magdelon alone, radiant in white satin and pearls, seemed to be at her best this evening. She said whatever silly things came into her head, laughing and turning her face first towards her husband, then towards her lover, as if her contentment were complete, now that she had them both under one roof. Cateau marvelled at her sister's sang-froid; then again, as at the beginning of her visit, she was forced to conclude that stupidity rather than self-possession was its keynote. Magdelon was happy because she was too dull to see that she ought not to be; she felt secure because she had not the wit to perceive her danger.

As dish succeeded dish La Ferté's humour, which at first had been meditative rather than lowering, became definitely sinister. He ate a great deal — he was at all times a heavy and terribly untidy eater, tearing his meat to pieces with his fingers and spilling his sauces recklessly down the front of his coat — and drank a great deal, in spite of his wife's pleading glances. Magdelon would not have dared to remind him of Doctor Pecquet's dictum, that stimulants were strictly forbidden; but Cateau, who recalled it quite as clearly as her sister, shrugged her shoulders as she beheld the huge draughts of strong red Beaune disappearing down her brother-in-law's gullet, and decided privately that tomorrow morning he would surely be in a terrific temper.

By the time the Maréchal had got to the end of the sweet, drops of sweat rained down his darkly flushed brow: he had worked himself up into a perversely aggressive mood, in which it was evident he intended to pick a quarrel, no matter with whom, no matter about what.... He had begun discussing the army with the Duke, and its prospects in the coming campaign against the Dutch; this naturally entailed a review of His Majesty's generals, whom La Ferté, with the scorn of an old trooper, dismissed summarily as a 'parcel of incompetent ninnies.'

'Damme, sir!' he shouted, pounding the table with his fist. 'I know what I'm talking about! I tell you, there's not one of the lot worth the powder it'd take to blow him up. Créquy — pah! Humières — faugh! Bellefonds — boo! A bunch of lily-livered amateurs! Zounds! It was a different story in the days when *I* was at the head of His Majesty's forces. We had some fighters worth mentioning then. There wasn't half so much silly chatter about strategy, or military science, or that sort of modern nonsense. No! In *my* time we simply went in and fought tooth and nail to the death — and Devil take the hindmost! By God, sir, we did! I tell you again, I know what I'm talking about. I've been in the service for nigh on fifty years. When I was scarce older than you are now I commanded the Comte de Soissons' regiment at La Rochelle — yes, and damned well, too, though I say it myself! I was at the siege of Privas in Languedoc — and in the wars in Piedmont — won my spurs as field-marshal at Hesdin for routing the Italian fox, old Piccolomini. Damme, sir! Don't try to tell *me* about the army! Didn't I win the Battle of Saint-Nicholas in Lorraine, where the enemies lost two thousand men on the field and all of their cannon? — and wasn't I in charge of the left wing at Rocroi? Damme, sir! And how about my record in the Fronde?'

La Ferté was well away now, full-sail, on the favourite theme of his military exploits, yelling so loudly that the flame of the candles before him fluttered at every explosion and emphasizing his points by a persistent pounding on the board, which caused the dishes to rattle uneasily. Cateau sat back with a look of well-bred boredom: she had grown very tired, in the last fifteen years, of the Maréchal's autobiography. Fervaques unfeignedly gaped at the quarrelsome old soldier. Magdelon, biting her lips, glanced anxiously from her husband to the Duke, and back again.

Monsieur de Longueville, as a matter of fact, behaved very much better in these trying circumstances than his uncertain disposition could have given grounds to hope. He listened politely to the Maréchal's tirade, tugging at his moustache to hide the amusement it caused him, but refusing to exercise the royal prerogative to interrupt until La Ferté paused in the middle of a sentence to gulp a mouthful of wine before beginning again. (For he had got only as far as the siege of Montmédy; there was a deal else to follow, as Cateau and Magdelon knew only too well.)

At this juncture the Duke set down the glass of ruby-red Burgundy he had been sipping reflectively and said, in a quiet voice: 'Sir, there is no doubt you have had an exceedingly distinguished career, of which His Majesty and the whole kingdom of France have a right to be proud as well as yourself. I warrant there *was* more excitement to be had in those old cavalier days you speak of; soldiers may have been braver because the risks they were forced to take were greater. But I'd fain not believe chivalry dead, nor that a young man of valour may not still find chances to prove his mettle. Besides, sir, are you not forgetting? — some of our former leaders are still in the field, no less courageous and capable than of yore. Monsieur de Turenne, I dare swear, has lost none of his skill in years of inaction, and — God be praised! — my good uncle Condé's yet to be reckoned with, as full of fire and natural genius as ever he was in the days of Rocroi and Nördlingen.'

Here, alas! in his well-meant attempt to smooth his host's irascible vanity, Longueville had inadvertently stirred up a hornet's nest. If there was one thing surer than another to goad La Ferté into a fury, it was to remind him that his two chief rivals, whom he had fought sometimes with, sometimes against, as the sides shifted in the long years of the civil wars, remained active and able-bodied, while he himself — prematurely, as he felt — was laid on the shelf.

'Damme, sir!' he bawled, 'don't you dare mention those nincompoops' names in the same breath with that of a serious professional soldier! Turenne may have his merits — I'd be the last to deny 'em — but he's always been as obstinate as a pig — and you know right well he's been whipped at least twice for every time he's come off on top. I call history to witness.... As for your uncle, sir — with all due respect to the blood of the Bourbons — he's had luck on his side, that's all. Luck — pure luck! He was sent to war when he was a mere stripling.... Don't I remember it? Didn't I teach him more than half what he knew? 'Twas but his rank as a prince gave him nominal command at Rocroi. Ask Turenne! Ask anyone who was there! Ask *me* — whose advice saved the day then and many another time for France, when his rashness would have tossed victory away for the sake of a little empty display. 'S death! Didn't I show him up in his true colours in the war of rebellion, when I chopped his army to bits at the Battle of the Faubourg-Saint-Antoine?... Yes, and I'd have captured him and all of his men if it hadn't been for that headstrong filly, Mademoiselle de Montpensier, who must needs play the heroine and turn the cannon of the Bastille on the forces of her own cousin, the King! Well, she's paid for that since.... No, sir! Don't prate to *me* of Condé's military prowess, for I tell you, it's a myth! Had he the smallest success in Spain during the years of his exile? You know he had not: he was only too glad to eat the bread of humble repentance when he was offered the chance, and slink back home like a beaten cur directly the King and the Cardinal gave him leave to do so. Zounds, sir! I say...'

As the Maréchal continued heaping insult upon insult, his temper rose and his voice assumed the querulous bear-like whine common to cranky old men.

The Duke suffered the angry monologue as long as he could. But at length his patience came to an end: he cared more, after all, for his uncle Condé than for all the rest of the family together. Springing up with white face and trembling lips, he drew his sword from its scabbard and flung it with a clatter at Magdelon's feet.

'Enough, sir!' he cried. 'Hold, enough! — or, old as you are, you shall pay for this! If it weren't for the respect I owe your wife, I'd not have put up with your insolence so long as I have. Now I hand my sword into her keeping, for fear I should no longer be able to contain my wrath. Madame the Maréchale, I beg your leave to retire. Madam' — to Cateau — 'I salute you. Sir' — to Fervaques — 'your humble servant.'

So saying, the little Duke strutted from the room with a parade of dignity so lofty that only the justness of his indignation saved it from seeming ridiculous. La Ferté, attempting to rise to head off his guest's retreat, lurched drunkenly and fell back into his chair. As he collapsed his elbow struck the goblet of wine before him, overturning it. The carmine pool spread over the damask cloth, ran down it to the end and began to drip from its edge to the floor like drops of dark blood.

Magdelon covered her face with her hands and burst into tears. Fervaques, doubtful what course to pursue, regarded the sobbing form with dismay. There was nothing to say to comfort her: whatever suggested itself appeared at once to be something far better left unsaid.

Cateau roused herself presently, with a small exasperated sigh, to take charge of the situation. She rang for Robert to haul his half-unconscious master off to bed; then summoned her sister's women, who, round-eyed with shocked curiosity, supported their weeping mistress to her own room. After that, she shooed away the remaining servants, who had naturally not had the delicacy to take themselves off; mopped up the stains on the tablecloth as best she was able; and, finally, blew out the candles and gave her hand to Fervaques, saying dryly: 'My dear, do you know, I believe we'd better go back to Paris tomorrow!'

Chapter VI

CATEAU HAD BEEN HOME LESS THAN TWENTY-FOUR HOURS BEFORE
discovering she had made a mistake in returning to town so precipi-
tately. For, during her absence, Maman and her suite had also returned from Vichy, which meant that Mademoiselle de Saint-Denis
was once more established in her post at the house in the rue Villedo,
and the problem Cateau had been at great pains to postpone had
finally to be faced with no further delay.

It became apparent immediately that deceiving a husband was
nothing, simply nothing at all, compared to the labyrinthine difficulties of outwitting one's lady companion. Olonne, say what one
would, had let his wife do what she pleased and go where she liked,
as long as he was not expected to follow. But Mademoiselle de
Saint-Denis never quitted her mistress for a moment. Naturally, it
was not her fault; it was what she was paid to do. Nevertheless, it
seemed terrible not to be able to shop or pay calls, go to Mass or the
play, or even take the air in one's carriage without that drab, discreet presence. Nor was Cateau safer at home than abroad. There
was no time of the day or night when she felt free from the possibility
of interruption. She might send the girl out of the room, it was true
— but who could deny her the door if she chose to return? . . . No, it
was unbearable! The Saint-Denis was eternally there, silent, unob-
trusive — but on that very account the more likely to be spying —
when Cateau ate her meals, or opened her letters, or had her hair
dressed. Did the latter raise her eyes ever so casually, they were
sure to encounter that other pair of eyes, brown and placid and unresentful; while the soft voice would murmur: 'Did you speak,
madam? . . . May I help you, madam? . . . Madam, do allow me to
go instead of you? . . .'

There was no putting up with such a mild but relentless determination to do one's duty. Worst of all, it was impossible for Cateau
to see Fervaques without running the risk of betraying their secret.
He could no longer call unobserved, for she could never be certain of
being alone. It was dangerous even to write. . . . Cateau had often
suspected Mademoiselle de Saint-Denis of inspecting her correspondence surreptitiously. . . . Of course, she could have made ap-
pointments outside the house and stolen away to join her lover. It
would have been hard, but with Quentine's expert connivance she

might just have managed it. In her younger days she had often been driven to resort to such stratagems. How many times then had she left home on the pretext of visiting the dressmaker or the drawing-rooms of her women friends, only to exchange her coach for a public sedan-chair, once she'd rounded the corner in safety! How often had these clandestine excursions found their goal in some anonymous suburban pavilion, hired for their trysts by Candale or Guiche or the Abbé Fouquet! What a web of mystery in those long-vanished times had surrounded her simplest comings and goings! What a tissue of elaborate subterfuges had protected her least blameworthy frailties! Indeed, she had grown so accustomed to depending upon them that she continued to practise her tinsel deceits years after she realized they were unnecessary. It was part of the game, that was all — merely what was expected of a professional coquette. And she had been young and reckless, and had greatly enjoyed seeing herself as the heroine of a series of breathless illicit romances.

But all that belonged to a chapter of life that was closed. In spite of her persistently youthful looks, Cateau's mind was beginning to grow old. The very recollection of her early misdemeanours ap-palled her now, at her age of fixed habits and methodical pursuits. To roam the streets in search of love seemed to her both improper and highly ridiculous. No, it would never do ... never. . . . Some dignified compromise must be found. . . .

Meanwhile, to Fervaques' utter dismay, she forbade him the house save at hours when she was at home to the world at large — and she retired to her cabinet every evening after dinner with a thoughtful look in her translucent eyes.

The solution, when at last she had hit upon it, was amazingly simple. Cateau was annoyed with herself for not having thought of it before. Since she could not meet her lover in Paris, she would meet him away from Paris — but not too far away. In this case one league would serve their purpose as well as one hundred. Cateau recalled the vague desire she had felt at La Ferté for a place in the country. Fervaques' duties at court often obliged him to remain at Saint-Germain for days at a time. Saint-Germain was in the coun-try, and a beautiful country at that, with its pure air and miles of green forests and wide, splendid views from the heights over the valley of the Seine. How delicious it would be, in this hot summer weather, to exchange the blistering cobbles of Paris for the streams and leafy solitudes of that convenient retreat!

Altogether, Cateau was charmed with her plan. She spoke about it to Maître Le Caron as her man of affairs, but to no one else — and spent the best part of two scorching July afternoons examining available properties in the neighbourhood of the palace. (For it ap-pealed to her as piquant to establish herself under the very nose of

the monarch who had forbidden her to appear before him.) When
at length she drove back to town, late in the second afternoon, she
held in her pocket a sealed parchment document designating Dame
Catherine-Henriette d'Angennes de la Louppe, Comtesse d'Olonne,
residing in the rue Villedo, parish of Saint-Eustache, as the legal
possessor of the Hôtel de Rouen, with its outbuildings and three
hectares of garden, situated at Saint-Germain-en-Laye, in His
Majesty's province of the Ile de France.

'My dear,' she wrote to Fervaques that very night, 'come to see
me tomorrow as early as possible. I am sure I have found a way out
of our troubles. . . .'

It seemed, in fact, that she had; for the Hôtel de Rouen, which
Cateau and her lover hastened out to view together the very next
day, appeared in every respect the refuge of their dreams. It was
near the palace, but not too near, at the end of a blind alley running
from the main square of the little town to the edge of the forest. It
was also small without being poky, standing in grounds which,
though much neglected — for the place had been vacant for several
years — were a riot of rosebushes and lilacs and undisciplined mazes
of shrubbery. . . . 'They want pruning, of course,' said Cateau,
as she picked her way along the overgrown path. 'I shall engage a
good superintendent at once. I've heard of a man at the Duc de
Luynes'. . .'

The house itself, tiny as it was, had distinct possibilities. Its proportions were good; it was a hunting pavilion that had been built for
one of the minor mistresses of King François I, a long low building
of buff-coloured stone, with a pair of tourelles rising like pricked-up
ears at each end of the angular slate roof to mirror themselves in the
miniature moat. Inside, there were two drawing-rooms, one large
and one small, both with handsome Renaissance chimney-pieces, and
an oval bedroom in one of the towers, whose walls were panelled in
yellow and gold. This bedroom Cateau decided at once would be
the very place for the carved gilt Chinese couch she had bought
some months ago at an auction sale and had been wondering ever
since what to do with. . . . 'And there are my Bergamo tapestries,'
said Cateau, narrowing her eyes and wrinkling her forehead as she
attempted to calculate the height of the ceiling. 'You remember —
the set of the *Pastor Fido* Aunt de Marville left me. My dear, I believe they'd fit those panels as though they were made for them!
Where did I put my notebook? . . .'

Fervaques sighed happily, and gazed out of the window at the
green tangle of bushes that was at present the sole view it afforded.

'It will be our paradise, my beloved,' he whispered, pressing
Cateau's hand to his lips in a transport of bliss. 'Where none but
ourselves may dare enter — not even the good Saint-Denis!'

'What do you mean — "not even"?' demanded Cateau, dropping her dreamy decorator's voice. 'I should say, "*especially not!*" Of all tactless idiots! But don't worry: she's told me times without number the country doesn't agree with her. It seems that grass makes her sneeze her head off! Isn't it lucky for us? Now tell me, my dear, I want your advice — should you place a console in this corner? — or do you think a glass cabinet? . . .'

There was nothing Cateau enjoyed more than furnishing a house and, to tell the truth, she needed very little advice from anybody. It had been some time since she had been able to indulge in her passion, for her places in Paris and Caen had long ago reached the ultimate point of perfection; not so much as a snuffbox could have been added without risk of spoiling the whole. She plunged therefore with eagerness into the delights of ordering furniture and materials — spent hours at the draper's and the cabinetmaker's, made innumerable diagrams on paper of alternative schemes of arrangement, even drew the design herself for a most remarkable bathtub of burnished copper, the outside of which was inlaid with panels of emerald-green velvet shaped like flowers.

She was busy all day every day, as she had not been in years. For the first time since she could remember summer was not a bore. How could it be, when there were such numbers of fascinating questions to be settled? — nothing to do with dull human beings and their tiresome relationships, but delightfully concrete objects like cornices and over-mantels, window-trims and door-trims, and panelling and paint?

Fervaques shared Cateau's enthusiasm. He was not permitted to see her in Paris any oftener than before, nor to accompany her on her excursions to the country; but if he happened to be at Saint-Germain when his mistress was there, too, it was easy to slip away from the palace to join her at the Hôtel de Rouen.

From his point of view the only annoyance was the time it took to get the house ready. July was long past; August, with its pitiless heat, gave place to a flyblown and dusty September. The first leaves were fluttering down from the tall beeches in the garden — and still the workmen remained in possession. At length Fervaques began asking when, if ever, they themselves would be able to stay there. . . . Cateau was soothing but evasive. The floors really needed refinishing — or that toilet-table she'd ordered from Venice hadn't come. . . . There was always some maddeningly reasonable excuse. . . .

It was October before everything was ready. The days had grown short, the nights frosty; most of the beech leaves had fallen now, and lay in neat rustling yellow heaps at intersections of the freshly gravelled paths. There was a smell of wood smoke in the garden, and the depths of the forest resounded with the music of hunting horns, in token that Saint Hubert's Day was drawing near.

Cateau had arranged to move while the court was in residence at Versailles, in order to avoid awkward encounters in the square. There were no difficulties of moment to be surmounted at the other end. She had no intimate friends in Paris; in fact, save for her servants and Maître Le Caron, Maman was the only person to whom she had confided her intention of living in the country. And Maman, fortunately, proved to be profoundly uninterested. After a first startled gape and a 'Jesus! My dear! Have you gone clean out of your wits?' Madame de la Louppe thought no more of the matter, except to express the pious hope that, if Cateau had more fresh fruit and vegetables than she knew what to do with, she would not forget the Carmelites in the rue Bouloi. . . . As for Fervaques, he was seldom at home nowadays. He had had for some months his own lodgings in town, and besides was often at Saint-Germain, or Le Mans or one of his other government seats; so that his mother and brothers no longer counted him a regular member of their household.

The Countess's measures had been taken well in advance of the move. A special staff was engaged for the new house, for she had decided to take none of her servants from the rue Villedo, who were to be left where they were under the temperate dominion of Mademoiselle de Saint-Denis. It seemed best to keep the two establishments entirely separate; and, as a matter of fact, the Hôtel de Rouen was so small that it could be run with very few people. . . . 'We shall be quite by ourselves, my dear, in our agreeable silvan sanctuary. How delightful!' Cateau wrote to her lover on her last night in Paris, as she sat at her desk trying to make up her mind whether three or four scullions would be needed, and if it were possible to do with fewer than the conventional half-dozen valets-de-pied.

Only the indispensable Quentine accompanied her mistress on the drive out from the city in the handsome new coach Cateau had bought to inaugurate her career as a country gentlewoman. Quentine was reflective, but not altogether disapproving. Her wages had been substantially raised, as a reward for her willingness to leave Paris. Privately, she feared that Madame d'Olonne had gone mad. . . . Still, one had to admit that Saint-Germain was not the same thing as the real country — it was a thousand times better than La Ferté, for instance — far more amusing even than Caen. There were markets and shops within walking distance, and the proximity of the court was likely to provide a certain amount of good company. So that, on the whole, if one could be sure that madam did not mean to stop there all winter . . .

They reached the little town just as dusk was falling, rattled across the broad square in front of the empty palace, down the blind alley leading to the forest, and in a reassuringly short space of time drew up in front of the entrance to the Hôtel de Rouen. Stars were beginning to twinkle in the powder-blue autumn sky, but their radiance was eclipsed by the welcoming blaze of candlelight brightening every window and streaming in broad beams down the garden path as the front door was flung wide at the carriage's approach. Fervaques, wearing his uniform as captain of the Queen's Light Horse Troop, was waiting on the steps to greet the Countess and lead her gallantly over the threshold. This seemed to Quentine a favourable omen for the future. She smiled to herself and nodded her head as she followed her mistress up the shining pathway to the great open door.

That night, to celebrate the beginning of their life together, Cateau had ordered a feast. The lovers dined at a round table laid in front of the fire in the smaller of the two drawing-rooms. There were fresh broiled trout from the forest streams, stewed ortolans, and an iced pudding shaped by a mould in the likeness of a snowy-white swan; likewise vintage champagne and some very rare rossolis from the cellars of Charles-Emmanuel, Duke of Savoy. A string quartet, hired for the evening from the leader of the King's private orchestra, played a pastoral symphony in a specially constructed bower of leaves and flowers that concealed the musicians from the eyes of the Countess and her guest. A cold wind had come up after nightfall and howled dismally in the half-bare branches of the trees outside the window. But inside by the fire all was cosy and warm. Cateau wore a most becoming golden dress made especially in honour of the occasion; she smiled across the table at Fervaques, whose grey-green eyes were dizzy with rapture, and responded to his slightly incoherent toast with a gay little one of her own (which had done duty at several similar ceremonies in the past — but there was no need of recalling *that*).

What a luxury it was to be able to sleep together, without fear or constraint, in the carved golden Chinese bed in the tower chamber! And, next morning, it was equally pleasant to wake side by side, to lie enlaced in each other's arms while the sun filtered softly through the amber damask curtains surrounding their couch, and birds twittered ... or no: come to think of it, birds did not sing in October: that must be a pump creaking somewhere in the garden. ... But there would be birds aplenty in May ... in May and June, when the roses bloomed. ...

Cateau drifted off to sleep again. ... After all, why not? There was nothing pressing to get up for in the country.

They breakfasted late, once more by the fire, for the morning was chilly, in spite of the sun. Then Cateau made a leisurely toilet, while Fervaques sprawled in an armchair and watched her, still with that

look of incredulous delight in his eyes. She donned a smart leaf-
coloured serge walking-costume and a pretty plumed bonnet, and as
soon as she was ready they set out to explore their kingdom like a
pair of excited children.

Fervaques was a most satisfactory companion on such an expedition. He thought everything Cateau had done absolutely perfect,
and cried out continually in delighted admiration over this and over
that, as if he really were unable to believe anyone could be so clever.

After exhausting the possibilities of the house there was still the
garden. Here Cateau moved about briskly amongst piles of yellow
leaves, pointing out the spot she had chosen for the sundial, the
allée she intended to line with the Roman marbles that were expected next week. There would be a fountain here, a trellis there —
and what did Fervaques think of placing an aviary in the sheltered
corner on the south side of the kitchen-garden wall? Aviaries,
Cateau opined, were becoming quite fashionable, since Madame de
Montespan had had one constructed at Trianon.

The young man assented readily to his mistress's suggestions,
marvelling at the energy and efficiency with which she marshalled
her projects for immediate execution. With Cateau nothing was left
to chance. She selected her spring bulbs and sketched out the
herbaceous borders in a concentrated quarter of an hour, besides
delivering to one of the under-gardeners a pithy lecture on the best
way to prune rosebushes that greatly impressed Fervaques. He
was so happy this morning that everything pleased him. He would
perhaps have preferred a little less planning on their first day together; but then, it was Cateau's own place; it was natural that she
should wish to arrange it to suit her excellent and very definite taste.
And presently, when all was settled, she led the way through a secret
gate in the wall into the forest, where they strolled for an hour under
the gold-and-brown-and-purple trees.

They returned to the house with formidable appetites for midday
dinner. Cateau's face was flushed a beautiful pink that could never
have come out of a box; they glanced at each other over the bones of
the roast fowl it had taken them scarcely ten minutes to demolish,
and decided that, really, what they had both always wanted more
than anything else — although, strangely, they had not known it
before — was to live their whole lives in the country.

This ideal existence continued for a week. The weather was unusually pleasant, sunny and mild, with just enough mist to lend a
note of heartbreaking beauty to the distant views from the terrace
overlooking the valley. And the lovers were always together from
dawn to dusk, except on the mornings when Fervaques went hunting on horseback. Cateau had never cared much for riding; she had
given it up years ago. However, she drove to meet him in the forest

with a picnic lunch; they would then come back in the pony-cart, while Fervaques' groom rode his master's mount home by another road. In the evenings they played chess by the fire, or Fervaques sat and smoked while Cateau strummed the clavichord and tried the airs from Cambert's new opera *Pomona*. Her voice was still fresh and sweet, and if her white fingers occasionally struck a false note, Fervaques was never the wiser.

Then, one morning, they woke to find the square at the end of the blind alley astir with new life. Hundreds of horses — black, white, and brown — were clattering over the cobbles; carriages of all sorts dashed importantly hither and thither; postilions halloa'd, whips cracked, harness jingled, dogs barked — and old people and children were got to the windows of houses in the town to watch the procession. It sounded like the victorious advance of an invading army — but it was only His Most Christian Majesty Louis XIV returning from a sojourn at Versailles to pass the winter in his castle at Saint-Germain-en-Laye.

That, of course, was the end of their idyll. Fervaques had no actual charge at court, but in his double capacity of cavalry captain and governor of one of the royal provinces it was expedient — this Cateau herself was the first to point out to her lover — for him to be seen as often as possible. Not only for his own sake, she was wont to add, but also for that of his family in general. Gallardon, his eldest brother, was supposed to be on the verge of securing the coveted post of first equerry of the Petty Stable, and was therefore surrounded, at this vital juncture, by a phalanx of interested relatives — all available Bonnelles and La Mothe-Houdancourts and their allies by marriage.

There were numerous opportunities of attracting one's sovereign's notice. One could attend the King's lever and coucher, his Mass and his hunt; and besides these daily fixtures plays were given twice a week in the palace theatre, followed by cards and refreshments, and midnight feasts every fast-day. Moreover, parties of a spectacular nature were in prospect, to celebrate the approaching marriage of Monsieur, the King's brother, to Princess Elisabeth-Charlotte, daughter of the Elector Palatine of Germany; and it was generally understood that those who paid their court assiduously now would be included in the lists of guests for the later festivities. (Who would have thought that Monsieur would marry? — *Monsieur*, Cateau's smart little field mouse of long ago! Yet Elisabeth-Charlotte was a replacement for his first wife, the English Madame Henriette, who had died very suddenly the previous summer.)

Cateau told herself reasonably that she would not have cared to appear at the palace even if she had been especially invited: she had long ago outlived her enjoyment, which had never been wholehearted, of the prosy routine of court life. No, there was nothing in it for her, though for Fervaques, it was easy to see, there was everything. She was only too glad he was willing to go without her.

At the same time it was undeniably irritating to reflect that his cousins, Doudou de Ventadour and that chit of a Toucy, were there, where she could not follow him. Also, his frequent absences brought her a new problem, of filling the void in her days — and this was much harder to do in Saint-Germain than in Paris.

She slept a great deal, which was good for her health, and walked a great deal, when the weather permitted. But there were hours every day when one could neither sleep nor exercise. Cateau had never liked reading, in spite of her strenuous efforts to be literary in the days of her affair with the Comte de Guiche. Nor did she take pleasure in sewing, nor sing and play, save to an audience. There were, of course, meals to be ordered. It was possible to spend a surprising amount of time considering food, even if, like Cateau, one were the reverse of greedy. She had long since conquered the aversion to good living engendered by her life with Olonne; it seemed to her now that things to eat were important, just as clothes and furniture and houses were important. Accordingly she began to fuss inordinately over her daily menus, hunted up half-forgotten recipes in favourite cookery-books, sent to Paris several times a week for divers out-of-season delicacies. She also worked tirelessly over the grounds, laying myriad schemes for the embellishment of her tiny domain, and consulting with the gardeners until the latter were reduced to a state of phlegmatic despair by her capricious chopping and changing.

As the weeks went on and the weather grew colder, even these pastimes failed to suffice. It was a pity, thought Cateau, that she had no tenants to care for: calling upon farmers and their wives was always one of her most dependable diversions in Normandy. Deprived of this resource, she took to driving into Paris with Quentine to consult Maître Le Caron on trifling matters of business, remaining to shop or attend the play, and often not returning till late at night. Fervaques once or twice got home before she did, and when this happened he was terrribly worried by her absence, pacing the floor until the sound of horses' hoofs on the frozen ground told him that the wanderers were safe.

Their personal relations continued as harmonious as ever. Indeed, owing to the enforced separation of their daily lives, their moments together took on a special quality of radiance. Cateau knew — and this knowledge sustained her through many tedious hours — that Fervaques would always rather have stayed with her; she might with impunity let him go where he would, safe in her assurance that he would never find anyone he preferred to herself.

When he came home from the palace, no matter how late it might be, she sat up in the gold Chinese bed, lighted a candle on the table beside her, and leaned on her elbow, while her lover regaled her as he undressed with a detailed account of what he had seen and heard during the day.

Cateau listened with inscrutable eyes in an attitude of marble repose, saying not a word until he had finished speaking. She was not really interested in court politics, for herself. . . . But Fervaques was young, untried, with his name and fortune still to make. It was most desirable for him to produce a pleasing impression, to form contacts for future use with the people who counted. . . . Had he played hoca tonight at the same table with the Montespan? Good! That was as it should be. Cateau had made up her mind that the reigning mistress was all-powerful, and that it was a waste of effort to be more than decently polite to poor La Vallière, whose day was done, though she lingered on like a tragic ghost at her rival's triumph-feast. Monsieur de Pomponne, the new Minister of Foreign Affairs, was by all means to be sought out and propitiated. Then there were Monsieur de Louvois, the Minister of War, and Monsieur Colbert, the Minister of Finance . . . and she had lately heard (never mind how) that the Gramonts were said to be coming back into favour. It might be wise to pay the Maréchal a compliment at tomorrow's lever — that wily old Gascon was vain enough to believe anything he was told. . . .

It seemed to her sometimes, as she proffered these bits of advice to the eager-eyed lad at her side, that Fervaques was more like her son than her lover: he was as truly her creation as though she had borne him herself, for he had been nobody until she took him in hand. Even now, there was a great way for him to go. . . .

One night, towards the end of October, he came home somewhat earlier than usual. Cateau had not yet quenched the candles; she was sitting up in bed, a white fluffy cape over her shoulders, having her nails polished by the drowsy Quentine, when she heard her lover's step approaching with unwonted briskness.

A quick glance at his flushed face and sparkling eyes caused her to lift her eyebrows in silent inquiry, which Fervaques answered by a jubilant nod as he flung down his hat and gloves and cast his sword on the bare floor with a clatter.

Cateau dismissed Quentine, who departed yawning, and then held out her hand to be kissed. (Such little formalities could not be insisted upon too often. What the youth at court were coming to . . . !) It was not until this ceremony had been performed to her satisfaction, and the young man was established in his privileged position at the foot of the bed, that she permitted herself to ask: 'Well, my dear, what has happened?'

YOUNG LOVERS

409

'We've got it!' cried Fervaques. 'We've got the place we wanted for Gallardon! It's to be announced tomorrow at the King's lever. He's first equerry of the Petty Stable, appointed over the heads of at least four chaps who have been in the service longer than he has.'

'Good!' said Cateau approvingly. 'I'm delighted to hear it. Who told you?'

'Colbert himself. I was standing near him at the card-table after supper — we both were, as a matter of fact, for Claude was with me: he came out from Paris late this afternoon in response to a note from Aunt de la Mothe. Well, I noticed Monsieur Colbert looking over towards us from time to time, and smiling and nodding his head as he talked to the Montespan, as if what he was saying to her might concern us. I'd not have dared press the point, for fear of being mistaken — but you know what Claude is! He's afraid of no one! So as soon as the opportunity offered, in a shift of the players round the table, he managed to worm his way next to the lady, kissed her hand, and got into conversation with her and the Minister. Well! It's true! It's quite settled, just as we hoped it would be, at the price we offered, three hundred and fifty thousand francs — and he takes over his duties on the first of the month.'

'It's an excellent thing,' remarked Cateau thoughtfully. 'Not that the post is so much in itself — but at least it will give him an official standing at court. And it'll help the family to get back the position they had in your grandfather's day, when Bullion was a name to be reckoned with. My dear, I'm very much pleased that this has turned out as it has. Pray give Gallardon my best compliments; I shall write him a letter tomorrow. Yes,' added Cateau, 'and one to your mother, too. It's only proper, in the circumstances.'

'Darling,' said Fervaques, after a slight hesitation, 'I wonder... There's something I've been wanting to ask you for weeks. I've only been waiting till this business was out of the way. Might I — I mean, would you mind very much if I asked Gallardon to dinner?'

'Here? In this house?'

Cateau looked surprised and somewhat indignant; Fervaques felt a sudden stiffening in her pose. But he went on hurriedly: 'Yes; why not? It's our home, you know. I think it would be only the friendly thing to do, don't you?'

Cateau was silent for a moment. Then she said: 'It is your right, of course, to have whom you please — Gallardon, or any of the rest of your family and friends. But not while I'm with you. If you care to ask him here in my absence, I've no objection. I can always spend the night in Paris.'

'But, my dear, that's not the point — that's not what I meant at all. I meant to have him dine with us *both*. You know I did. Are you ashamed to let him see we're living together?'

Cateau sighed: it was the old question, which she hoped she had succeeded in settling for good.

'You know that I'm not,' she said, 'but you must try to consider my position a little. Have you forgotten our bargain? I came here to live on one condition — that we were to keep this life of ours a strict secret, apart from everything else. That was the understanding from the very beginning. I've come and gone as I pleased, and allowed you to do the same. I thought you approved of the arrangement. Forgive me if I was mistaken.'

'Mistaken? Oh, no!' Fervaques exclaimed quickly. 'You can't think *that*. You know — you *must* know — how happy I've been. Naturally I want to respect your desire for privacy, to protect your good name with all that lies in my power. I haven't told anyone what we've done. Not a soul at court has the slightest idea.... Only Claude, my own brother, who's closer to me than anybody else in the world except you ... I'd so much like to share my good fortune with him — show him how snugly we're settled, you and I, darling! You could trust him to the limit; our secret would be quite safe with him.'

Cateau shook her head.

'That's what you think. No doubt Gallardon would think so, too. But a secret shared is a secret no longer. It's a miracle that we've been able to keep ours as long as we have. Every day I've been expecting it to leak out. I've been racking my brain to try to decide what I'd do when it did. For we can't continue this way indefinitely — you must see that as well as I do. Meanwhile, we simply daren't risk anything that might compromise us. I'm sorry, my dear. I like your brother, as you know. I'd be delighted to receive him in Paris, any day you care to bring him to call. But *here!* — oh, no, you're not serious! Or if you are, it's because you don't realize what you're asking.'

Here Cateau turned her head away slightly, as if to indicate that, in her opinion, the conversation was finished. Fervaques said nothing more for a moment; she supposed he had accepted her decision as final — as, indeed, he always had done, up to now. She was therefore surprised, and not a little displeased, when he burst forth afresh: 'But why? *Why?* I can't see why you need be so sensitive. It's not as if I were proposing that you should receive my mother or Aunt de la Mothe, or even one of my cousins. Claude is a man — he has a man's sense of honour. He knows what the world is, what men and women are. I'm sure he must have guessed months ago that I was in love with you.'

'You must have told him, then,' said Cateau pettishly. 'You've no more discretion than a baby!'

'Certainly I did not! But he's eyes in his head, hasn't he?'

'I wish, my dear, I could say as much of you. If you weren't blind to everything but your own interests, you'd never suggest ——'

'I can't see what harm there'd be in it. It's the first thing I've asked you to do. If you refuse, what can I think except what I've always feared? — that you're ashamed of me and my love! — we're not good enough for you!'

'Ah, I won't bear it!' cried Cateau, striving to avoid her lover's reproachful eyes. 'I'll put my fingers to my ears, so that I shan't have to hear what you say. There's no use in trying to argue with you, my dear.'

'No, my dear, I assure you there's not. For you'll never be able to convince me I'm wrong.'

'I'm well aware of that. I shan't even try. Why waste one's breath scolding a child?'

'Precisely. Why waste it? I'm sorry I ever mentioned the subject. But don't worry, madam, I'll not do so again.'

'I hope not, sir, with all my heart. For if you should, you'd find my mind as firmly made up as ever.'

'I'm glad to hear it, madam.'

'I'm glad that you're glad, sir.'

'Then we've no further cause for disagreement, I take it?'

'None whatever.'

'And can go to sleep in peace.'

'The sooner the better.'

Fervaques jumped up from the foot of the bed and stamped into the dressing-room to take off his clothes. He was biting his lips to keep from bursting into tears. While he was gone Cateau extinguished the candle and lay back on her pillows. The light of the hunter's moon, filtering through the bare branches of the beech trees outside the window, traced faint mysterious patterns on the wall.

Presently Fervaques came back in his nightshirt. He slipped into bed beside her, and after a minute touched her shoulder softly, and attempted to put his arm round her.

Cateau repulsed him without rancour, but determinedly. How strange men were! she thought. Women were never so fatuous. They might on occasion demand endearments out of season, but they were not simple enough to suppose that a quarrel might be set right by a kiss.

'I shall forgive him, of course,' said Cateau to herself, as she was falling asleep. 'But not for two or three days — perhaps even as long as a week. . . .'

As things turned out, it was longer than that before their relations were finally readjusted on the old trustful basis. And it took more than time to improve them. Fervaques left for Le Mans the following morning, on a business errand to do with raising new taxes for the war against Holland. When he returned, a fortnight later, he stopped first in Paris to spend a few days with his family. He wrote

to Cateau to tell her so, and to say he hoped to rejoin her shortly at
the Hôtel de Rouen. She received a second note from him, a day or
two later, from which she learned that he was remaining in town
longer than he had originally intended, owing to his mother's insistence. Gallardon had caught a feverish cold and was in bed.
Doubtless it was nothing to worry about, but Maman, who idolized
her first-born, was greatly alarmed, and had begged Fervaques not
to desert her.

Another week passed before he was able to go back to Saint-
Germain. When at length he and Cateau met they were perfectly
friendly, even fond, though a perceptible wall of ice had formed between them.

Cateau inquired politely after Claude's health. Fervaques replied, with equal politeness, that his brother was very much better,
thank you — in fact, quite out of danger, though the doctors had
ordered him not to quit his bed till the end of the week, merely as a
general precaution.

Affairs went on in this state for a number of days: then, one afternoon, a frightened, sweating lackey in the Bullion livery stumbled
into the palace, where Fervaques was attending a concert, to say
that the young Marquis de Gallardon was dead. It had been totally
unexpected . . . a sudden chill and rise of temperature, followed by
heart-failure. . . . Madame de Bonnelle was herself in the doctor's
care, and bade her son and her sister, Madame de la Mothe-Houdancourt, come with all possible dispatch if they wished to find her alive.

Fervaques was weeping when he told Cateau what had happened.
He buried his face, like a child, in her bosom, and sobbed aloud in
his grief. Cateau comforted the stricken young man as best she
knew how, stroked his hair and hands gently, said: 'There, there,
my darling!' many times over.

She was loath to leave him while he seemed to need her so much,
and therefore decided to drive into Paris with her lover to spend the
night in the rue Villedo. Braving discovery for the first time, she
waited up in her bedroom for his return from the house of mourning
— and that night they slept in each other's arms, as they had not
done for many weeks. But hours after Fervaques, worn out by his
emotions, had dropped off to sleep, Cateau lay wakeful, brooding
over the catastrophe that had befallen her. Their first quarrel was
over; perhaps in some ways it had left them closer to each other
than before. Still, she reflected gloomily, something divided them
now, and would continue to do so forever. Fervaques might not
wish to think it, but he could not help himself: he would not be able
to keep from believing, as long as he lived, that his brother's death
was partly her fault — that poor Gallardon might not have died if
only Cateau had been willing to ask him to dinner.

DURING ALL THESE MONTHS CATEAU HAD NO NEWS OF HER SISTER. She knew Magdelon was still in the country, and intended to stay there until after her lying-in. It was therefore not surprising to read in the *Gazette*, early in November, that La Ferté had come back to Paris without his wife. Fervaques, whose family's house was across the street from Great Senneterre, heard from his mother, and duly reported to Cateau, that the Maréchal was accompanied by young Henri. The lad had at last secured his father's permission to join the army as a volunteer. Although he was not yet quite fifteen, there was talk of fitting out an infantry regiment for him to command in the war against Holland. Cateau could imagine how excited he must be at the prospect. She would have liked to call to see him and to find out, if possible, how things were going with Magdelon; but the situation was delicate. She was not on good terms with her brother-in-law; moreover, she had private reasons just then for remaining out of sight. Hence, it seemed best for the present to let matters take their own course, trusting that if anything were seriously amiss, she would be apprised of it.

Then suddenly, about a week after the Maréchal's return, Fervaques told her that Magdelon, too, was in Paris. There had been no official announcement of her arrival; but Madame de Bonnelle, who now that she was again plunged into mourning spent most of her time spying upon her neighbours, declared that the windows of the state apartments at Great Senneterre, boarded up since June, had been opened. Besides, her cook had caught a glimpse of the Maréchale's four little maids playing Blind Man's Buff in the garden. So there could really be no mistake about it. . . .

Cateau, greatly mystified, drove into Paris early the following morning. It was true: the Hôtel de la Ferté-Senneterre appeared as it always did when its owners were in residence. Windows and doors had obviously been freshly painted, and flowers were blooming in jars on the balcony over the porte-cochère.

The Swiss who admitted Madame d'Olonne said, in reply to her eager question, that Madame the Maréchale had arrived from the country two days ago; he believed she was not receiving this morning — but naturally the Countess might be shown up directly.

On her way to Magdelon's rooms Cateau was struck, as never before, by the gloomy atmosphere of the house, which neither its noble proportions nor the lavish expenditures of the Maréchal could disguise. It was hard to see just what caused it: Great Senneterre was not especially old, nor in the least eccentric. Built on a regular classical plan, its rooms opened out in orderly rows, entirely lacking odd corners or surprises of any kind. There was perhaps something sinister in its very absence of imagination. All those square gilded halls with nobody in them!... Cateau shivered slightly, and told herself she was being ridiculous. Of course, no unseen eyes stared at her — there were no phantom voices whispering on the vast deserted staircase.... 'Come, now,' said Cateau, half aloud, 'you know, this really won't do!' She rapped smartly on the door of the Maréchale's antechamber; it was opened by the prettiest of the four maids, who smiled when she saw who it was.

Magdelon was alone in her enormous room, lying propped up by pillows in the great canopied bed, under a counterpane of olive-green velvet embroidered in gold-thread designs of fruit and flowers. The colour of the counterpane might have been unbecoming, or the morning light streaming in from the high windows overlooking the garden too harsh; for Cateau thought she had never seen her sister so nearly ugly. Her face was somewhat swollen and pasty — an effect only emphasized by the dabs of rouge placed too high on her cheeks — and her eyes looked as if she had been crying hard. Even the two long black braids on the pillow appeared strangely heavy and lifeless.

She smiled, however, as Cateau came in, and motioned to the little maid to leave them.

'Darling!' said Magdelon, quite in her usual voice — *that* was a comfort, anyhow! — 'I'm so glad to see you! How did you get here so quickly? I've let nobody know I was back.'

Cateau bent over to kiss the white cheek, and then seated herself on a tabouret close to the head of the bed.

'Fervaques told me last night,' she replied. 'I could hardly believe it, so, as you see, I've lost no time in coming to find out for myself. But, my dear! What on earth are you thinking of? Have you gone clean out of your wits? Or has an accident happened to change your plans? Perhaps you're no longer expecting ... I mean ...'

She paused to glance significantly at her sister's figure, which was concealed so effectually under the olive-green counterpane that it was impossible to tell whether what one could not help hoping for had actually occurred.

But Magdelon shook her head.

'No, dear; that's not it. I've been perfectly well.'

'Then *why?* Really, Magdelon,' said Cateau impatiently, 'sometimes I wonder if you've ever properly grown up! It's bad enough to be having this baby at all — but I certainly thought you had the sense to realize that your one hope lay in keeping out of sight till after you'd had it. If you'd stayed in the country, you might possibly have succeeded in saving your face. Here there'll not be a chance of it. What will La Ferté say when he knows ——'

'Darling,' said Magdelon, still smiling her stupid smile, 'I've told you over and over: he knows nothing whatever about it. He'll only suppose that I've come back to spend the winter in Paris, just as I always do. If I'd stopped away any longer, he'd have thought it much queerer, I'm sure. As it is, he's not even seen me yet.'

'No — but he will, sooner or later.'

'Not for some time. Not for a very long one, I imagine. The poor man's been dreadfully ill with gout all summer. He's not got out of bed for more than three weeks, except to make the trip home from the country. Poor dear fellow! I only wish ——'

'Well, then, if he can't come to you, he'll expect you to go to him. Magdelon, you *know* ...'

'Not for some time,' repeated Magdelon calmly. 'I've given out that I've had an attack of quartan fever — and you know how careful you have to be with *that*. I *did* have it once, the winter after Louis was born. It's really a perfect excuse, because it lasts for ever so long, and between attacks, as I remember, you feel quite well and look absolutely normal — so I can ask my friends in to see me as often as I like, and play cards, and amuse myself fairly well — as long as I take care not to get out of bed.'

'And what will your friends think?' sternly demanded Cateau. '*They'll* see you, even if your husband doesn't — and they'll guess at once what the matter is.'

'Oh, no, I don't think so. You yourself weren't sure when you first came in. If I don't move about, no one can tell. And I promise to be very careful, dear. I had to do what I did. I couldn't have borne to stop in the country all by myself another day!'

'Well, I suppose it *was* dull,' said Cateau, with a pinched smile more intimidating than a frown. 'But at least it was safe — or safer, at any rate, than you'll find yourself here. How long does the game have to last?'

'Another month, I think — or six weeks, at the most. Believe me, dear, I can manage it. I've planned it all out in advance.... La Ferté's rooms are quite at the other end of the house: if I screamed at the top of my lungs, he'd never hear me! Don't scold me, darling! I tell you, I *had* to do it.'

'But why? *Why?*' Cateau was so seriously upset that she spoke more crossly than she meant to do. 'To risk all you have just because you were bored ——'

'Ah, that's not it! You know it's not!'

Magdelon began to cry in her helpless, childish way — great round drops gathering on her lashes and rolling down her cheeks effortlessly, without spoiling her looks in the least.

'Longueville is going away.'

'Away? Where?'

'To — the war in Holland,' quavered Magdelon. 'With his uncle Condé.'

'Oh, *that!* . . . But that won't happen till next spring, silly! — and then everybody'll be going. So what's there to cry about now?'

'Ah, but it's different with Longueville! He'll never come back.'

'How foolish! What makes you say that? He's no more likely to be killed than anybody else — less likely than most, I should say. They don't expose Princes of the Blood to mortal danger any oftener than necessary,' declared Cateau unsympathetically, remembering how much greater the peril would be for Fervaques, riding proudly at the head of his squadron in the Light Horse Troop. 'My child, you're being absurd. If you weren't in this condition, you'd see it for yourself.'

'You don't understand!' cried Magdelon, making no attempt to check her tears. 'Charles is so rash; he'd rush up to a cannon's mouth, just to show people he wasn't afraid! I feel he'll be killed — I *feel* it, I tell you! There are ways you don't know . . . And if he's saved, I'll lose him all the same. His mother's determined to marry him off; she's given him no peace for months, poor boy! There's always the Grande Mademoiselle, old as she is, now Lauzun is out of the way — or the Montespan's niece, that Vivonne girl with her horrid thick ankles! And — and dozens of others, besides! He'll have to do what he's told. You know, the King's never done a thing for him — and the estate's been in debt ever since the old Duke died. Oh! Oh! We were so happy — and now it's all over!'

Magdelon sobbed harder than ever and beat her clenched hands despairingly on the counterpane. . . . Cateau glanced at her sister meditatively, and then looked away: she knew, from long experience, that there was no use in saying anything until the squall had passed. She sat perfectly still on the tabouret, holding her back very straight, and staring over the bed and out of the ivy-draped window. The ivy was full of sparrows: even from the other side of the glass their cheerful cheeping sounded louder than Magdelon's sobs. . . .

One could not help being sorry for Magdelon. Poor foolish child! She believed, as she had at eighteen, that love ought to last forever; she could not see at all what Cateau saw clearly, that the most romantic affairs ran their courses most quickly. Of course, if Longueville were to be killed . . . But he would not be killed. Princes never were. That was simply more of Magdelon's hysterical nonsense, for which her condition of health must be held accountable. As for marriage, it was another matter. There was no doubt that the Duc de Longueville was an astute young man, quite aware of his unique position as the sole adult single Prince of the Blood at the court of Louis XIV. He would certainly marry as well as possible. Cateau thought that the sooner he did so, the better it would be for his mistress; obviously, the liaison must be nearly at an end. Everything would conspire to spoil it: Longueville's station in life, Magdelon's volatile, imprudent temperament — but, most of all, the tragic disparity in their ages. No woman of thirty-six, however charming, could hope to keep a lover fourteen years her junior. The wonder was, really, that he had been faithful as long as he had. (And as to that, subterranean rumours had already reached Cateau concerning various other flames of the Duke. There were the Duchesse de Brissac and the Maréchale de Castelnau, who were said to have come to blows over his favours... to say nothing of Ninon de Lenclos, and that poor, silly little Madame de Coeuvres, who had been exiled last summer just in time to prevent fatal exposures....) Yes, Magdelon was lucky, whether she knew it or not. Longueville would leave her before satiety had set in — and, in after years, they could remember their ancient attachment with pleasure. If only there had not been this dreadful complication of the child-to-be-born!... Cateau shuddered as she drew her cloak more closely about her.... There was nothing one could do except pray that the shameful secret might remain a secret, and that the Duke's plan to provide for his illegitimate heir might go through without a hitch. Only a hare-brained dreamer like Magdelon could have been willing to repose her present safety, as well as all hope for the future, in the keeping of a houseful of servants, a word from whom, at any moment, might bring her to irrevocable ruin.

But what was the good in thinking of it any more?... Cateau shuddered again, and then patted Magdelon, whose sobs were trailing off now into a series of half-strangled hiccoughs.... Yes, she was quieting down at last. To assist in calming her, and also to divert her own thoughts from the dismal channels they had been following, Cateau began telling her sister about the Hôtel de Rouen. She talked on for some minutes, describing the charm of the little place and its matchless situation on the edge of the great wild forest. ... 'You must come out to visit me there, dear, as soon as you're well again — but mind, now! Not a word of this to anyone, not even to Longueville'... and by the time she had risen to go Magdelon was almost herself once more. The latter was even able to fetch a watery smile as she kissed Cateau good-bye and said: 'Darling, do come again — you've done me so much good!'

Cateau promised that she would, very soon — and her last memory of Magdelon's face was the tail-end of the smile bravely displayed on the pale, altered features.

She stole out of the room on tiptoe, as if it were important not to let anyone know what she was doing (why was this?); and then retraced her steps through the succession of antechambers and echoing corridors to the head of the grand staircase. Once again, the thought of those rows upon rows of empty gilded rooms depressed her — even more, the picture of the master of the house and the mistress lying in bed in their widely separated apartments, each alone and a prey to what melancholy fancies God only knew as the weary days passed. . . . Cateau all but ran down the marble steps, passing her startled attendant lackey halfway in her flight, and emerged into the open air with a sigh of relief. Dearly as she loved Magdelon, she feared it would be a long time before she plucked up courage to call at Great Senneterre again.

Her reluctance to see the La Fertés was abetted by the weather, which turned cold and wet in December and remained so for weeks. It had been years since Cateau had spent a winter in the country. She had forgotten how disagreeable it could be. The sun shone no more, and there was nothing in the chill opaque mists enfolding the forest and the little town on its border to compensate for its absence. The highroad to Paris was soon waist-deep in half-frozen slime, so that even if Cateau had wished to see her sister, it would not have been easy to go to her.

Meanwhile, she heard little of the household at Great Senneterre. The *Gazette* informed her that the Maréchal was still confined to his bed by the gout, and two or three brief notes from Magdelon mentioned the fact that their writer had not yet got over her 'tiresome fever.' . . . It was a strange situation. Cateau sometimes wondered how her sister had the heart to go on playing her part in the bizarre drama, and, even oftener, how, with all the determination in life, she could hope to deceive her whole world so successfully. In the old days it would have been utterly impossible. But times were so changed. . . . Paris seemed to be more than half empty even at the height of the season; for everyone who could afford it was at Saint-Germain for the fêtes succeeding the wedding of Monsieur and the German princess. And, as far as Cateau could discover, those who were left behind in the capital paid little court to the La Fertés. Neither husband nor wife was the kind of person who was called upon generally save on state occasions. The Maréchal was out of things now. He was no longer active in the army, and his governorship of Lorraine, once so important, had dwindled since the reconstruction of the duchy as a semi-independent state, some ten years ago, into a nominal control over Metz and Verdun and one or two other key cities in the east. If people were not forced to seek him on business, they not unnaturally preferred to leave the windy, disputatious old man alone.

As for the Maréchale, she had for years been too exclusively occupied with her babies and her lovers to have built up the phalanx
of female sycophants that, as a rule, surrounded ladies of her rank.
According to Maman, who went to call on her younger daughter
several times without being admitted — and afterwards wrote the
elder an indignant letter on the subject — Magdelon slept all day
and played cards most of the night with her pages and waiting-
maids. . . . 'I can't imagine *what* she's thinking of, dear,' wrote
Madame de la Louppe, who had evidently quite forgotten that she
herself had often followed a similar programme in her pre-Carmelite
period. . . . Hence, for one reason or another, the couple appeared
abandoned to a sort of splendid twilight isolation, which, dull as it
was, Cateau judged to be of inestimable value to her sister's scheme.

However, in the dark days before Christmas, knowing that the
baby must be expected at any minute, Cateau could bear the persistent dearth of bulletins no longer and therefore decided to spend the
holiday season in Paris. She could not explain to Fervaques her true
reason for the move, but luckily it was not necessary to do so. The
state of the weather made driving in and out of the city impossible;
yet, at Christmastide, one could scarcely avoid it. There were special
Masses daily in all the churches — Father Bourdaloue was, as usual,
preaching 'divinely' at Saint Paul's — and Cateau had attended
these services, as a matter of course, for so many years that it would
have seemed odd to omit them from her schedule. Besides, as she
truly remarked, Fervaques was busier than ever at the palace, going
to innumerable parties to which she had not been invited; so that he
would hardly have time to miss her.

On Christmas Eve Madame d'Olonne emerged from Midnight
Mass at the Minims of the Place Royale to find it snowing heavily.
Her eyes not yet accustomed to the darkness after the blaze of wax
candles within, she paused on the steps of the church, Quentine and
Lucie behind her, waiting for her carriage to enter the rue des Mi-
nimes from the angle of the rue du Parc Royal. As she stood there,
holding tight to her veil — for the wind was as sharp as the night
was dark — the crowd pushed past her into the street, bells tolled all
over the city, and snowflakes swirled down in millions from a low
prune-brown sky.

'Good evening, madam,' murmured a voice at her elbow. 'I have
news for you.'

Cateau wheeled round to find a man in a short fur-trimmed black
cloak standing beside her. He had his back to the light streaming
out from the open church door, but as he doffed his hat and bowed
before her a beam fell full across his face, and she recognized the
somewhat snub features and dark, heavy-lidded eyes of Gilette's
son, the young Comte de Fiesque.

Her heart gave a painful thump of alarm — for was not Fiesque Longueville's most intimate friend? and, therefore, what he had to tell her *must* concern . . .

She could not speak at once; but Fiesque, observing her anxiety, said quickly: 'Madam, your sister was brought to bed of a fine boy at six this evening.'

Cateau started. It was still hard for her to find words, but at length she managed to stammer out: 'And — and the Maréchale?'

The Count smiled reassuringly: he was, Cateau thought (she had not known him very well before), a most self-possessed young man. He took her hand without waiting to ask her permission, and guided her skilfully to a point just beyond her women's earshot. They were alone on the steps now; everybody had come out of church.

'All is well with Madame de la Ferté,' he replied. 'I saw her myself, not half an hour after the child was born. Clément told me he was perfectly satisfied with her condition.'

'Was the Duke there?'

'No,' said Fiesque. 'He wanted to be, of course — but both the Maréchale and I agreed that it would be wiser for him to stay away. No one was in the room when the birth took place except Clément, the accoucheur, and his assistant, old Madame Robinet. Your sister, madam, is a woman in a thousand. What courage! What devotion! Not a cry escaped her in the midst of her suffering — and as soon as possible, after her child was pronounced safely delivered, she sent word to me to come to her. (I was waiting in the antechamber with her maids.) We wrapped the little boy warmly in blankets and a robe of thick fur, and I drove with him to the house you have heard of, in the Faubourg, where Monsieur de Longueville was waiting, in his turn, with Porlier and the wet-nurse, to greet his son. All has passed off precisely as we hoped — the Maréchal heard nothing, suspected nothing — and within an hour after the baby's birth there was not a trace in the house of his coming. Madame de la Ferté begged me to find you, as soon as I had returned from the Faubourg, to tell you how matters stood with her. But they said at your house that you were in church: I've tarried here on the steps for you, celebrating the Feast of the Nativity in a double sense. Our Dear Lord is born, madam — and also an heir to the great name of Longueville!'

Cateau drew a long breath.

'I'm thankful it's over,' she said. 'But tell me, are you *sure* no one suspects? Is it really a secret? It would be fatal — fatal ——'

'Calm yourself, madam, I pray. Nobody knows — nobody ever will know, save those to whose interest it is to keep their own counsel. Tonight you may sleep in peace: your sister is safe, and your nephew as well. But I must not detain you further. The snow is falling fast, and your carriage is waiting.'

As the young man bent over her hand a second time Cateau saw that his face looked white and drawn and that there were deep circles under the heavy-lidded eyes.

'May I not take you home?' she asked gently. 'It is late; you must be very tired. Where do you live?'

The Count flushed with pleasure.

'I lie tonight in the Faubourg,' he answered. 'I promised the Maréchale she should have news of her child in the morning. It's a long way from here, madam; I would not trouble you to drive so far.'

'The distance is nothing,' said Cateau. 'And if it were twice what it is, it would make no difference. There's nobody waiting for me, alas! Come! The horses are here.'

She clapped her hands to summon Quentine and Lucie, who had been eying them with curiosity from a respectful distance.

Fiesque hesitated a moment longer.

'You are very kind, madam. It's too cold a night to argue. But — can your women be trusted?'

Cateau smiled.

'If they couldn't, I'd have packed them off years ago.'

She slipped on her mask and gave her hand to Fiesque, who helped her into her coach and took his place beside her, after muttering some instructions to the coachman.

On their way to the Faubourg both were silent. Fiesque leaned back against the cushions and shut his eyes, apparently spent with fatigue. And Cateau, seeing that her companion had need of rest, lost herself in her own thoughts as they sped through the wintry streets. Paris was gay tonight: candles were lighted in many windows, bells went on ringing, and each church they passed seemed to be standing in a golden pool, sending out streamers of light over the snow and darkness around it.

It was a long time since Cateau had been to the Faubourg Saint-Germain. She had lived there, of course, as a girl, and been married there, at Saint-Sulpice; and both before and after her marriage she had been a welcome guest in all the drawing-rooms of the neighbourhood. What wonderful parties there had been at the Luxembourg — the Orléans Palace, they had called it then — in the days of Monsieur, the Duc d'Orléans (Gaston, the present King's uncle) and his daughter, Mademoiselle de Montpensier! Madame de Choisy, too, Cateau's old friend (or enemy?), had assembled, night after night, the most amusing and elegant company the town afforded. And there had been delightful receptions at the Little Luxembourg, and the Hôtel de Condé.... How long ago all that seemed now! The Faubourg had changed a great deal. Though it remained outside the walls of Paris, it was not nearly so rural as it had been. More and more noble families were building houses and settling there, new streets had been cut, old gardens and landmarks were fast disappearing. Cateau was not even sure she would have been able to find her girlhood home in the rue Férou, though she would never forget the shabby red-and-gilt rooms, where Maman had received society during the Fronde, nor the tiny rectangular garden with its bosquet and the fountain that spouted a crooked jet of water, in which she had strolled on summer evenings with Magdelon, and flirted with the young Comte d'Olonne. . . . As for the Luxembourg, it looked much the same, but the gay crowds that had filled it with song and laughter were dispersed. The old Duke was dead; Madame de Choisy, also, was gone; while Mademoiselle de Montpensier, the Grande Mademoiselle, had turned into a prim, acidulous old maid. Oh, how could it be? How could so few years have wrought so many disastrous changes? And what, above all, had happened to the sweet young sisters La Louppe, the acknowledged belles of the quarter? . . .

Fiesque touched the Countess's arm.

'Madam, we are there.'

Cateau peered out through the falling snow at a high stone wall with a small door in it. Behind the wall was a garden full of trees, their branches white with flakes; behind the garden loomed the peaked roof of the house itself. As Cateau got out of the carriage she caught a glimpse, at the end of the street, of the twin towers of Saint-Sulpice squat against the sombre sky.

In response to a knock the door in the wall flew open. Fiesque gave Cateau his arm to conduct her through the gloom of the garden to the house, which was tall and gaunt and, evidently, very ancient. All was dark within save for a light glimmering faintly in the middle window of the first storey.

'It's an old place that belonged to the Montmorencys,' whispered Fiesque. 'His Highness inherited it from his grandmother, the late Princesse de Condé.'

He rapped three times distinctly at the front door, which was opened by Porlier, the Duke's secretary, a bent young-old man with a shock of greying hair and an anxious, gummy smile, who held a candle in his hand. Cateau had seen him several times with his master. She could not tell whether or not he had recognized her — probably not, as she was heavily cloaked and was wearing a mask as well. However, it seemed best not to speak unless it were necessary.

Porlier appeared to understand his part in the play perfectly. He nodded in silence to Monsieur de Fiesque, and straightway led them through the cold uncarpeted hall and up a flight of winding stairs to the first floor.

There were no tapers in the room into which they were ushered; the light that Cateau had observed from below came from a fire blazing away on the hearth.

A cradle draped in scarlet velvet embroidered in silver stood in the middle of the room, which was richly furnished and hung with tapestries; and in the cradle a baby lay sleeping. As they drew near, a figure started up out of the shadows, a plump, pleasant-faced young woman in a nurse's cap.

'All well, Marie?' inquired Fiesque.

'All well, sir. He's been sleeping ever since you left us.'

'I've brought a lady to see him,' said the Count. 'We'll stop only a minute. You may leave us, nurse.'

'Very well, sir,' said the young woman, dropping a curtsy as she went out.

Fiesque turned to Porlier.

'You've told her the child was mine, as I instructed you?'

'Yes, sir — certainly, sir. She's no idea whatever of the true state of affairs.'

'Nor need she have, if you continue to follow His Highness's orders. The Comtesse d'Olonne would like to look at her nephew, Porlier.'

Cateau fidgetted at the sound of her name; but of course, Porlier must have heard the whole story. She smiled as she held out her arms to receive the bundle of lace.

The baby did not wake up. He looked, his aunt thought, not too admiringly, exactly like every other newborn infant: the creased crimson face and slits of eyes were by no means appealing. But she stooped to drop a kiss on the minute wrinkled forehead before handing the bundle back to Porlier.

'Poor little thing!' she said. 'What a strange way to come into the world!'

'No stranger than his father's, madam. If you'll recall it, the Dowager Madame de Longueville — of course, she wasn't the Dowager then — was brought to bed of His Highness in the Hôtel de Ville, where she was living at the time as the head of the Parliamentary Party in the war of the Fronde. He was, so to speak, a rebel from the day of his birth — why, the Provost of the city was named as his godfather! That's why he was called Charles-Paris d'Orléans.'

'And the little one —?'

'He's to be Charles-Louis, madam — Charles for his father, naturally, and Louis for his great-uncle, Monsieur the Prince de Condé. His Lordship hasn't made up his mind, though, as yet, whether the boy will appear in public later as the Chevalier d'Orléans or the Chevalier de Longueville. That, I surmise, will be for his mother to decide.... Eh! Look, now, he's waking up!'

The baby stirred in its sleep and gave a faint cry.

'Poor little Chevalier!' said Cateau. 'May he live to do credit to his name!'

'I make no doubt he will, madam. Eh! He's a fine, lusty chap already! Only hear what lungs he has! Mayhap he'll be a monarch, too, some day, the same as His Highness. Please God, I'll be alive to see it, madam!'

'A monarch? What do you mean?'

'What, madam, have you not heard the news?'

'What news? I've not the faintest idea what you're talking about!'

'Why, then,' said Porlier, moistening his lips and glancing nervously at the Comte de Fiesque, 'perhaps I shouldn't have mentioned it. *You* tell her, sir, if you will. After all, the whole country is sure to know sooner or later.'

'I thought that His Highness might have informed you himself,' said Fiesque smoothly, 'or I'd have spoken before now. But, as a matter of fact, the Duchess Dowager had word from the Ambassador only last night. Monsieur de Longueville has been elected King of Poland.'

CATEAU FOUND IT HARD TO BELIEVE. SHE RECALLED THAT ONE OF the Duke's favourite boasts, last summer at La Ferté, had been of the offer of an all-but-mythical crown to the heir of the Longuevilles. But, at the time, the boast had seemed as mythical as the crown. How could a foreigner, however nobly born . . . ?

Well, said Fiesque, that was because Poland was not an hereditary monarchy like France. For a century or more its sovereigns had been elected by a Diet assembled in Warsaw, the capital. If the people did not like the king they had chosen, they were at liberty to dismiss him and find another. . . . As the Count expounded the matter, it began to sound less incredible. According to him, the Condés had already an entering wedge through the Duchesse d'Enghien, the old Prince's daughter-in-law, who was a niece of Marie-Louise de Gonzague, the last Queen of Poland. The childless Marie-Louise had adopted the Duchess as her heir; and after the death of the former and her husband, King Casimir, the throne had been secretly offered to the Prince de Condé, or, failing him, to his son Enghien.

They had both had to decline the honour, owing to Louis XIV's refusal to allow his cousins to leave France. . . . This had happened two years ago, since when the Poles had elected a ruler from the ranks of their own nobility and married him to the sister of the Emperor of Germany, and one had supposed the question settled for good.

But King Michael Wisniowiecki was young and flabby, in no way suited to the task of defending his realm against the frequent attacks of the barbarous Cossacks and Turks. There was much dissatisfaction among his subjects; affairs had come to such a pass that a delegation had been privately sent to France, urging the King to reconsider his decision and, if he could spare neither Condé nor Enghien, at least to give them the only other available Prince of the Blood, Condé's sister's son, the young Duc de Longueville.

His Majesty, Fiesque declared, had yielded at length to these entreaties less out of friendship for Condé than because, with a war in immediate view, it would be wise to make sure of as many friendly nations in Europe as possible. He could count on a French King of Poland, obviously, to swing that country's sympathies in the right direction.

So the deal was apparently as good as settled. It was not to be announced for some months yet, while the Poles and the French haggled busily over sundry bargaining-points. There remained a number of minor difficulties: the principal obstacle, in Longueville's eyes, being the necessity of wedding the present Queen, who could not, alas! be dismissed for fear of offending her brother, the Emperor, but would on the contrary be charmed to divorce King Michael (these little things could always be arranged, if one were in good odour at the Vatican) in order to marry the Duke. And with such a glorious future unfolding before him, the Count thought it hardly likely that his friend would be deterred by a wife more or less. . . . That, Fiesque concluded, was the whole story: Madame d'Olonne might take his solemn oath that every word of it was true.

Madame d'Olonne drove home to the rue Villedo with her thoughts in a whirl, so much excited that it was hours before she was able to sleep.

Next morning, when she came to reflect more calmly on what had happened, she decided that it was probably the best thing for everybody concerned. For the Duc de Longueville, without doubt, who for years had striven vainly to get a post at court, and would now, at one stroke, find himself lifted to heights dizzily above the heads of his rivals. For Magdelon, too, even if she were not clever enough to see it directly. Since her lover must eventually leave her, how much better for him to do so at once, at the flood tide of their feeling for each other! How much less humiliating, also, to have him depart to a distant land than to marry some wealthy French princess, as he otherwise must, and remain in Paris for the rest of his days! This way — though the wrench would be violent — he would be removed completely, not only from her life, but from his own as well, disappearing in a golden apotheosis that would reflect glory on his former associates. (It would be delicious — Magdelon ought, even now, to appreciate this — to be able to say, later, that one had been the mistress of a king.)

But, above all, it would be best for the child, for little Charles-Louis, lying unaware of the splendours in store for him in his scarlet-draped cradle in the Faubourg Saint-Germain. Charles-Louis would still be a bastard, it was true — but a royal bastard, which almost removed the stigma attached to the state. In years to come, when he was grown, he might seek his father and be acknowledged openly — nay, more, even Magdelon (who, it was to be hoped, would by that time be safely a widow) might without blushing avow the relationship. To give a child to a reigning sovereign was somehow not sinning. (Look at La Vallière and the Montespan!) Magdelon could be proud, then, of what she had done. Who could tell what illustrious rôle might be hers to play in the cloudy, uncharted future? . . .

Yes — yes — taking everything into consideration, Cateau was very much pleased at the surprising turn in events. She had been warned by Fiesque not to speak of it to anyone, as the King wished to keep the negotiations under cover until he deemed the time had come to reveal their result. It was especially necessary, too, to avoid rousing her sister's suspicions. Magdelon had not yet been told of Longueville's good fortune. The poor thing had, after all, been subjected to a great strain; Clément was afraid that, in her condition, the one aspect of the Polish affair to strike her would be the imminence of her parting with her lover.

Accordingly Cateau was careful, when she went to see Magdelon on Christmas afternoon, not to say anything that might provoke the slightest misgiving.

This was not difficult, for Magdelon, exhausted by her ordeal, looked so pale and pathetic as she lay on her pillows that Cateau scarcely spoke to her at all — merely contented herself with a kiss and a few loving words.

However, when the caller returned the following day, the patient was a good deal stronger; and though her mortal pallor persisted, she was soon sitting up in bed, taking a normal interest in life once more.

She still seemed to have no inkling of what had happened to Longueville. They talked instead of Charles-Louis, whom Cateau had been to see several times since the snowy Christmas Eve when he was born. She was made to describe in detail what he looked like, how he was dressed and had acted, what she thought of Porlier and the nurse.... (Were they really kind to him?) Magdelon's face grew wistful as she listened to Cateau's circumstantial accounts of all she had heard and observed at the house in the Faubourg. Charles-Louis was the first of her children she had not nursed; it seemed terrible to her that he should have been torn from her bosom in the very hour of his birth; but even Magdelon had wit enough to see it had had to be so. She was full of gratitude to the Comte de Fiesque for the devotion he had shown her and Longueville in their hour of trial; she dwelled often, too, on the Duke's happiness in his son....

'I told you, didn't I, dear? I'd not disappoint him! Ah, I knew it — I knew it! Charles says now that he's nothing left to wish for.'

'Does he, indeed?' remarked Cateau ironically. (Poor Magdelon!)

'Of course, it's dreadful we can't be together as we'd like to be,' Magdelon went on. 'But we've been careful so long, it would be foolish to risk discovery now that the danger's so nearly past. In fact, Charles says he believes, for the present, it would be well for him not to call here so often as he used to do. He's even going to pretend, for a while, to be having an affair with the Duchesse de Brissac — just to put people off the scent, you understand.'

'Oh, I understand,' said Cateau, still more ironically. (But irony was wasted on Magdelon.) 'It's very thoughtful of him, I'm sure.'

'Ah, I've always told you, dear, Charles thinks of *everything!*' cried Magdelon simply. 'There never was anyone in the least like Charles. He's arranging to take Madame de Brissac to the theatre — you know, Racine's new play, *Bajazet*, is to be given next week at the Bourgogne. We decided that would make an excellent beginning, because everybody'll be there for the first performance, and they're sure to notice whom he's with. If you've nothing better to do, dear, why don't you go to it with me? Bring Fervaques if you like, and I'll ask Fiesque to complete the party.'

'Thank you,' said Cateau. 'I'd like it, of all things.... But do you think you'll be well enough so soon, child?'

'Oh, I'll be well.' Magdelon's voice was determinedly confident. 'I'd not have stopped in bed so long as I have if Clément weren't a fussbudget. I gave him fair warning, though, yesterday, that I intended to get up on Sunday. I won't miss another minute of the winter if I can help it. I mean to enjoy myself now. There's so little time left.'

The last sentence was spoken in a whisper, more to herself than to Cateau; the latter wondered, as she went away, whether Magdelon had at last begun to suspect. . . .

The first performance of *Bajazet* at the Bourgogne, on the fifth of January, was an event of importance in social as well as theatrical circles. Since the triumph scored by his *Andromaque*, a few years earlier, Racine was considered the man of the hour; the King's marked preference for his pieces stamped the finishing seal on their success; and nobody now would have dared stay away from them or hint that they were not perfect without running the risk of being dubbed members of the 'old court' set. People professed themselves overcome by the tragic power of the new, incisive style — women not infrequently swooned during the more emotional climaxes of the brilliant tirades — and it had become the fashion to quote especially striking couplets, as in former days one had quoted Corneille or the sonnets of Voiture.

Cateau settled herself in her seat, well to the front of the Maréchale's box, with a gratifying feeling that everyone who was anyone had managed somehow to squeeze into the Hôtel de Bourgogne this afternoon. She smiled blandly as she turned her head slightly to one side, years of practice having taught her the precise angle at which her profile would appear to best advantage from the pit. It was delightful to find herself once more in the shabby old house, where she had spent so many happy hours in the past. She glanced with affection at the familiar smoke-browned tapestries on the walls, smelled the well-remembered smell of mingled patchouli and hot candle-grease, listened to the buzz of the assembling audience, the confused din of the hawkers' cries, as the fruit and sweetmeat vendors pushed their way through the crowd of lackeys and soldiers and bourgeois below, charmed by it all as in days long gone by.... Yes, it was fun to go to the play; she had missed it sorely during those dull months in Saint-Germain. And it would be interesting to see what she thought of Monsieur Racine's Turkish tragedy. (Privately — though she would not for worlds have confessed the weakness — Cateau preferred the old plays of Boisrobert and the brothers Corneille, in which the great speeches were punctuated by comfortable intervals of comparative boredom, when one might relax one's attention to spy out one's friends.) The Champmeslé, too, was said to be very fine. Cateau wondered if she would like her as well as the Beauchâteau and the Desoeillets, who had enchanted her youth. (Ah, and Jodelet — and Floridor! — Could the stage really be as good as it used to be?)

But there was another reason for being excited today: it was the first time Fervaques had appeared in public with Madame d'Olonne since becoming her lover. Cateau could scarcely have summoned the courage to try the experiment without another couple to silence possible gossip. She looked about nervously after taking her place, but soon decided that people were not noticing her particularly — perhaps not even so much as she had a right to expect. (Had Quentine been clumsy with her mistress's hair? — or was the new yellow satin a shade too sharp?) ... Maybe the true reason was that, for once, Magdelon was too formidable a rival.

Magdelon, Cateau admitted generously, was really superb this afternoon, in silver brocade and the Senneterre diamonds. Her figure freed at last from the defacing lines of approaching maternity, she looked slimmer than she had looked in years. (That was partly, she had confided to her sister, because she had so little milk, this time, which was a dispensation — it was almost as if Providence had known that poor small Charles-Louis was to be deprived of his mother's breast!) But in spite of her beauty Magdelon did not seem happy. She talked a great deal, even after the play had begun, and laughed loudly, coquetting with Fiesque in a heavy, unsubtle way. (The young man received her advances with imperturbable grace: nothing seemed to surprise him. But that one could forecast, in Queen Gilette's son....) At the same time her eyes remained restless and vague. Cateau saw that, whenever their owner felt she was not observed, they sought the box on the other side of the theatre, where Longueville was sitting with Madame de Brissac.

Cateau, too, stared at the pair very often in the course of the performance. They distracted her attention from *Bajazet*, which did not interest her so much as she had hoped. The story seemed rather far-fetched. There was a deal of talk about the Sultan Amurat, a character who obstinately refused to appear; and the Champmeslé had had, up to act three, disappointingly little to do. Nor was she so pretty as Cateau had expected her to be. In fact, she was not pretty at all, being sallow and rather squat, so that the Turkish costumes she wore as Roxane were distinctly trying to her figure. Her eyes were small, and she had a trick of screwing them up into pin-points when she delivered her lines that struck Cateau as affected. What men could see in a scarecrow like that... There was no doubt about it, the best of the drama today was in front of the footlights.

Poor Magdelon! Why would she keep looking at someone who would not look at her?... The Duc de Longueville held his eyes riveted on the stage as long as the curtain was up, while in the intervals he was all studied devotion to Madame de Brissac.... It was disheartening to be obliged to own that the Duchess was a very attractive woman. Her features were delicate and by no means imposing, but she had an appealing porcelain fragility and a demureness of manner that admirably suited her style. Moreover, she knew how to dress. So many Précieuses did not....

Between the third and fourth acts another man entered the Duke's box and, after bowing over her hand, took his place behind Madame de Brissac. Cateau did not at once recognize him. Then she saw that it was her old gallant, the Comte de Guiche. She had not beheld him in years — but, of course, nobody had: he had been exiled for court intrigues for almost a decade, during which a young generation had sprung up that barely remembered the bold young leader of fashion in the fifties and early sixties. Guiche was now — how old?... Dear me! Quite thirty-five, computed Cateau, who was even older. He looked his age, too. The sable curls were as thick as ever, but he had grown appallingly thin, and his face had shrunk so much that it was all eyes and nose.

Cateau felt sorry for Guiche. It must be hard for him to reappear, shorn of his posts at court and in the army, to start life over again. If reports one heard from reliable sources were true, the King had not really forgiven him yet, but had merely granted him permission to return because Guiche's father, the Maréchal de Gramont, had fallen ill last autumn and begged to be allowed before he died to see his eldest son once more. So the Count came back, and old Gramont pulled through, after all — which meant that there had been no inheritance to come into.... Poor fellow! Cateau, studying her former lover through a critical lorgnette, decided that he was still very handsome in a romantic, theatrical way all his own, though he had lost his aura of careless success, and his smile was now tentative rather than triumphant.

It was worthy of note that Madame de Brissac, at any rate, seemed very much pleased to see him. Surprisingly, the new arrival received a greater share of her smiles and glances than the little Duke, who was at length reduced to pulling his moustache and ogling the Champmeslé during the latter's thrilling soliloquy upon jealousy (when it should have been clear that she had no time to spare for him or for anyone else. The conceit of the man!).

Longueville never once left his box till the performance was over. It was Guiche who strolled across the house in the pause before the last act to present himself to the sisters. Magdelon was too deeply preoccupied by her own emotions to manage more than a flurried general-utility smile. Cateau, however, yielded her hand to the Count with all her old deliberate charm of manner. It was astonishing to find that she felt neither pleasure at seeing him, nor resentment at his treatment of her in the past. His presence produced simply no reaction whatever.

They chatted for a few minutes. Cateau inquired politely for the health of the Maréchal, and they exchanged opinions on the merits of the play. Had Madame d'Olonne heard Tallard's remark to the King that *Bajazet* was as far above the rest of Racine as the rest of Racine was above all of Corneille? That was perhaps hyperbolic praise, since one knew it could not fail to please His Majesty — but surely the Champmeslé was very fine! Guiche thought her unequalled in declamation. The tirade in the act just ended — could Desoeillets have touched such sublime heights in that? ...

When the young man — for he was still a young man, close to — bowed and took his departure, Cateau settled back in her seat with a sigh and flashed a smile of reassurance over her shoulder at Fervaques. (What a blessing he was not old enough to recall! ...)

On the whole, she told herself later, it had been a disturbing afternoon.

The next day Cateau and Fervaques went back to Saint-Germain, where they stayed for the rest of the winter. The court was unusually gay just then. It was carnival time; and the King was anxious to show his new German sister-in-law what that meant in France. Hence there were balls every night at the palace, masquerades, ballets, plays, and hunting parties in endless procession. People were so busy dressing for this and dressing for that, and undressing only to dress again, that, for the time being, even scandal was in partial abeyance. Cateau held her breath, during the first weeks of the new year, expecting to hear any day that the secret of poor little Charles-Louis' existence was out, and that the Maréchal had repudiated his wife. But, miraculously, not a whisper concerning the La Fertés fluttered the fans of the palace gossips. Monsieur de Longueville, on the other hand, was much in evidence. He continued to dance attendance on the Duchesse de Brissac, and was said to have become a serious rival of the Comte de Guiche for her favours.

Cateau met the trio one day as she was walking along the edge of the forest, inspecting the work on the great terrace Le Nôtre was building for the King. The men saluted her gaily, but Madame de Brissac drew aside her skirts, as if she had come across a slug in the path; and her malicious smile was more devastating than an outright cut. (Insolent hussy!)

Another morning, she ran into Madame de Richelieu, the recently appointed lady-in-waiting to the Queen (for Cousin Julie had died at last), and her bevy of maids-of-honour. It was droll to observe how the old lady hustled her charges together and drove them round the corner, for all the world like a flock of young turkeys. Cateau could hear their breathless exclamations of surprise after the encounter — 'My *dear*, did you *see* . . . ?' — and the high, spiteful laugh of their ringleader, her bugbear, Mademoiselle de Toucy.

On still a third occasion, it was the Prince de Marsillac whom she came across, in the midst of the wood — or, rather, the Duc de la Rochefoucauld, as he was beginning to call himself, his father having resigned the dukedom and the government of the province of Berry to his heir. Cateau had not seen Marsillac in more years even than the Comte de Guiche, though she had heard enough of the former since he had, inexplicably, become the King's best friend. She would hardly have recognized, in the stout, pompous bewigged courtier, the earnest, round-eyed boy who had loved her so helplessly, so inarticulately, fourteen years ago.

He was obviously not going to bow to her, so she pretended not to see him and walked serenely by, with her chin in the air — the best means, surely, of coping with an awkward situation! But she trembled afterwards for hours with mingled rage and fright, and blamed herself bitterly for having laid herself open to such insults. Fervaques, too, was at fault: he should have thought more of her reputation! Something would have to be done about their way of life, and that speedily. Cateau made up her mind to speak to him seriously at once. . . .

And then, suddenly, none of these things mattered any more. Cateau's social snubbings, her discontent with the country, Longueville's pursuit of Madame de Brissac — even the ever-present anxiety over Magdelon and little Charles-Louis — all faded into comparative insignificance in the face of the one grim reality, War.

One had known, of course, that it was bound to come sooner or later. And Heaven knew, it was not as if one hadn't become inured to wars in the past! Those four years of the Fronde and the weary struggle with Spain . . . As far back as Cateau could remember, life had been played to an accompaniment of shrilling fife and rolling drum and the tramp-tramp of marching feet.

But then peace had come with the King's marriage to the Infanta, ten whole years of peace, scarcely broken by a skirmish or two in Flanders and the slight flurry of the Franche-Comté campaign in '68. France was rich, France was mighty, France had everything it wanted. Gone, too, were the days of internal dissensions. There was no more religious strife, now that Catholic and Protestant were tolerated alike; and the King had become so powerful since assuming the reins of government in person, after Mazarin's death, that the very thought of the nobles' stirring up trouble was impossible.

Ah, it was so blessedly easy to grow accustomed to peace! After the long, cruel strain the whole country seemed to exhale a sigh of relief. Arts and sciences flourished, commerce expanded, peasants tilled their land and raised their crops; the King was pleasantly and innocuously busy building new houses and making his court and his capital the most splendid in Europe, which meant in the world. It appeared as if the millennium had been reached. What had anyone left now to wish for? . . .

But, almost overnight, the picture changed again. There began to be talk of Dutch 'atrocities' — of the unparalleled insolence of the Lowland merchants, of taxes and seizures and unfair commercial practices — then of border incidents and the like. It was all rather vague. Cateau had never been able to find out from anybody just what the atrocities were. What was clear was that France had been insulted — and naturally France was not going to stand *that*. She did not have to; she was too strong and well-armed, and possessed a powerful ally in England, who, it transpired, had promised, over a year ago, to aid in subduing the overbearing United Provinces. The English fleet was said to be invincible. . . . Dimly one suspected the real reason for all this unrest was that it was smart to make war. The greatest nation in Europe must impose its will on others because, if it did not, the others would not realize how great it was. It was part of the duty of a supreme monarch to conquer — so conquer he must, no matter whom, no matter on what pretext.

Apprehensively Cateau followed the news in the *Gazette*, and enjoined Fervaques to glean what he could in his daily attendance at court. Many of the items were contradictory. The Queen of Spain had promised to help the Dutch. The Queen would *not* help the Dutch, but had decided to stay strictly neutral. War was imminent. War was unlikely. War was inevitable. . . . The Dutch Ambassador, Mijnheer Grotius, had sought an interview with the King, in a last desperate attempt to stave off hostilities. Much was expected to result from this. Little was expected. Mijnheer Grotius asserted that negotiations were impossible. The King asserted that negotiations were impossible. Negotiations were already, in fact, in progress. . . .

So it went, seesawing back and forth for months, till finally, after a quiet week during which no particular pronouncement had been made by either side, Fervaques came home one night early in April with the news that war was declared.

Once the worst was actually confirmed, Cateau said she had known it from the first. After all, there was the army, two hundred thousand strong, ready and waiting for the fray: it could not just be told that it would not be needed and tamely sent home. Armies were useless unless they could fight; it would have been unthinkable to have spent so much money for nothing. For months, even years, Monsieur Louvois, the Minister of War, had been busy. He had prepared every detail in advance. This was to be a campaign like no other in history. For the first time the troops were to travel with their own supplies, like a nation on the march, no longer dependent on the forage they could find. There would be flour for everybody, meat and sugar, oil and wine — fodder for the horses — brave silken tents for the King and his officers — undreamed-of comforts for the men. At the same time it was announced that the Queen and her ladies would not accompany the warriors, as they had done in the past on various military expeditions to Flanders. Marie-Thérèse was pregnant — the Montespan, too, for that matter — and this was to be no Women's War, but a serious fight to the finish.

Cateau went to Mass the following Sunday, which was Palm Sunday, in the royal chapel at Saint-Germain, to hear Father Bourdaloue pray for the victory of French arms over the heretic Hollanders. The King was there with his whole court. Poor dumpy Marie-Thérèse, wearing a black lace mantilla on her frizzy blond curls, wept as she kneeled by her husband's side. The favourites, Montespan and La Vallière, together as always, were just behind her, praying ardently — hands clasped, lips moving, eyes turned up in ecstasy. But Louis was sublimely unconscious of his womenfolk. He bent his head out of courtesy alone — was even God to be mentioned in the same breath with His Most Christian Majesty? — looking proud and disdainful, as well he might. Doubtless his thoughts were already on the frontier.... A ray of yellow sunlight fell on his head, ennobling his urbane, sensual features, but also, alas! revealing the pockmarks that pitted forehead and cheeks....

In spite of her fears, Cateau's heart swelled with pride as she thought of Fervaques at the head of his Light Horse Troop, leading his men on to triumph.... For of course the French would win. They could not help winning. They were always stronger than anybody else; and this time they had a bigger, better army than ever before and the inestimable advantage of being led by the two greatest living generals — *pace* La Ferté! — the Maréchal de Turenne and the Prince de Condé, once more united, as in the days before the Fronde. With such commanders, how could they fail? The Dutch must be

all-a-tremble in their beds, these nights, as they beheld the frightful
vision of certain doom — Turenne approaching with half of the
army on one side of the Rhine, Condé, with the other half, on the
other, to combine at last and sweep down in full force on the luckless
land and its young, inexperienced leader, Prince William of Orange.

Yes, in those first raw, windy spring days, enthusiasm ran high in
Paris and Saint-Germain, as the old familiar pageant, so long absent
from the streets, began once again unfolding. Flags and flourishes,
trumpets and drums, and soldiers, soldiers, everywhere. . . .

On the twenty-seventh of April the King left for Charleroi. He
stole out of the palace early in the morning accompanied only by a
dozen picked bodyguards, having taken leave of no one save the
Queen and the Dauphin, his son. The Queen, it was said, cried bitterly, and vowed that she would never live through her lying-in, deprived of her lord's company. (Poor Marie-Thérèse! What a passion
she had for her husband, however unfaithful he might be!) On the
same day Madame de Montespan slipped away and drove in a heavily curtained carriage to the castle of Genitoy, which belonged to
Sanguin, the King's maître-d'hôtel, where it had been arranged that
the lovers were to say their farewells. It was whispered that her confinement, like the Queen's, would take place in June.

After that, everyone seemed to be leaving. Plumes nodded,
swords glittered, the roads to the north were filled with horses and
coaches and line upon line of marching men. And all the houses in
France held their complement of weeping women, brusquely awakened from the dream of picturesque pageantry to a sharp realization
that their loved ones were in danger.

Cateau repaired to the vantage point of a balcony overlooking the
square of Saint-Germain to watch the departure of the Queen's Light
Horse Troop. Fervaques looked very well at the head of his squadron riding his prancing grey horse; it was a pity only that he did not
sit straighter in the saddle. (He had been a trifle round-shouldered
since boyhood, and, lecture as she might, Cateau had not yet succeeded in correcting this fault.)

He smiled at her and waved his hat, as naïvely pleased as a child,
before saluting the colours and galloping off. Dry-eyed, his mistress
saw him go; she smiled back at him and waved her handkerchief to
the last. Unlike Magdelon with her little Duke, Cateau felt convinced that Fervaques would return. But after the soldiers had left
the empty square was depressing. And when she went home to the
deserted house, so strong a contrast to the cheerful bustle of the last
few days' preparations, it took all her self-control to keep from bursting into tears. Happily, it would not be necessary to stop there alone.
Her arrangements had been made some time earlier to move back to
the city as soon as Fervaques had gone: less than an hour later

she was in her carriage, jogging along the muddy highroad to Paris.

But the rue Villedo was not much better. Her servants received her with blank courtesy, in which she fancied she detected an undercurrent of sarcastic amusement. (Well, after all, it would have been strange if, in these months of shuttling back and forth between town and country, neither Quentine nor Martin, the coachman, had talked.) And there was no mistaking the careful complicity of Mademoiselle de Saint-Denis' unconcern with her mistress's actions.

Cateau felt she could not possibly face an evening alone with Mademoiselle de Saint-Denis. She therefore ordered the horses again and drove to Great Senneterre, hoping to find the family supping at home.

The Maréchal and his wife were already at table. At first Cateau thought that they must be expecting company, for the dining-saloon was swarming with liveried servants and ablaze with candles, whose flames fluttered in the soft spring breeze blowing in from the garden. But there was no one with them except Henri and Bonneville, the boys' tutor.

Magdelon rose with an exclamation of pleasure to welcome her sister, and insisted on having a place laid for her at once. She was wearing a glittering ballgown and looked thin and sad — there were dark circles under her eyes, as if she had been crying — but it was the Maréchal's appearance that most struck Cateau. Although evidently still badly crippled by gout — he could not get up to greet his guest, and one foot, swathed in bandages, remained on a stool throughout the meal — he was fully dressed in court costume, wearing his sword and the ribbon of the Order of the Holy Ghost. An immense black wig had been clapped on his head, beneath which his own sparse grey locks straggled out here and there in spite of Robert's ministrations.

'You see us, my sister, in ceremonial dress,' he began; 'that's in honour of my son. Young Henri here leaves us tomorrow, you know. He's off to Charleroi to join the King's regiment as a volunteer.'

'Yes, aunt!' cried Henri; 'and if I do well, Papa has promised me a regiment of my own in the autumn. What do you think of that?'

Cateau glanced smilingly at the lad's glowing face, and then with compassion at Magdelon's strained one. He was so young to go to war, scarce fifteen — she could imagine how his mother's heart must grieve at the thought of their separation. Still, he was tall and well-grown, with good broad shoulders and an air of assurance exceptional for his age. But for his beardless rosy cheeks, he might easily have passed for eighteen or twenty.

'What a lucky boy you are!' said Cateau. 'With the name you bear, you're predestined to success.'

'Oh, but I think that makes it harder,' said Magdelon. 'More's expected of a La Ferté than of the average soldier. I fear he may find the path to glory a steep one.'

'Nay, Maman,' protested Henri, 'only wait and see what I can do! I've wagered Brother Louis I'd swim the Rhine and bring him William of Orange's beard as a trophy!'

Magdelon sighed.

'Child, you're so rash, you've no idea what warfare means! Remember you've promised your father to be good and do as you're told ——'

'Don't worry, madam,' boomed La Ferté. 'Obedience is a soldier's first duty. Young Henri will have to carry out orders — no more and no less. Turenne's given me his word he'll keep an eye on the lad. I'll say that for the old rascal, if he says he'll do a thing, he'll do it, come what may! Ah, God, if only I were well enough to go, too! *I'd* show that handful of upstart Lowlanders what a Frenchman is worth!'

'Oh, Papa, why don't you come with me? Perhaps the doctor is wrong; perhaps what you need is exercise.'

La Ferté groaned.

'Damme! — when I can't put my cursed foot to the ground! I tell you, boy, my days in the field are over. I'm a worn-out wreck, fit for nothing now save to lie abed lapping up the nauseous brews of that villain Pecquet. Oh, that I were dead! Better death a thousand times than this hellish idleness!'

'Sir,' said Cateau diplomatically, 'you've served nobly in your time. Many a man would be proud ——'

'Zounds, madam! Do you think I don't know it! The past is cold consolation to a man who sees he's still needed today. Turenne alone hasn't enough authority. I suppose you saw in the *Gazette* this morning that the rest of the marshals refuse to serve under him — Créquy, Bellefonds, Humières — every one of the lot! What do you think of that? Rank insubordination! They say it's an insult to their office to take orders from a man who's no higher than they. 'S death! *I'd* insult 'em, I would! *I'd* show 'em who was master, if I had my way! The King's been criminally lax with such riffraff.... Ah, if I could walk! If I could walk!'

The old man buried his face in his hands in discouragement. There was a pause, broken at length by Henri, who piped up, in his high-pitched young voice — Cateau had not known before that he had so much tact —: 'Tell us about the time you were wounded at Chimay, Papa, in 1640, and led the charge of your troops with your leg strapped to your saddle-bow!'

Half an hour later, when a lackey entered to announce the arrival of His Highness the Duc de Longueville, La Ferté was re-enacting the siege of Gravelines — 'Damme, lad! It took just nineteen days to reduce the garrison, though everyone swore they could hold out all summer!' — while Henri watched his father with fascinated eyes.

Cateau regarded his sister and brother-in-law with interest as the Duke swaggered into the room. She was curious to see if a 'situation' were in prospect; but both La Fertés appeared perfectly self-possessed. Magdelon was so wax-white already that she could not have turned paler; and the Maréchal seemed pleased by his caller, seated him straightway at his right hand, and plied him with glasses of divers liqueurs.

The Duke's errand was to bid his friends good-bye. He had finally succeeded in buying the charge of colonel of a cavalry regiment, and was leaving the following day to join Turenne at Charleroi.

Whatever the young man might be feeling, he was in complete control of himself this evening. He sat for some time at table over his wine, exchanging military gossip with his host. The size and strength of the various citadels on the Rhine that would have to be captured before the two main divisions of the army could join each other were discussed in detail; likewise the difficulties of crossing the river into Holland, and the strange defection of the subordinate marshals. Who on earth would be competent to take the deserters' places? What did the Duke think of Chamilly? Surely he was too little experienced to assume much responsibility! How about Luxembourg? Could it be true that Enghien had inherited none of his father's military genius? And was it not mad to let Louvois, himself no soldier, meddle in the plan of campaign?

Soon the men were deep in their conversation, while Henri, who thought this side of war far less absorbing than Papa's accounts of delightfully gory battles, and besides had been plied by his oversolicitous mother with far too many good things to eat, struggled manfully to suppress his yawns. Cateau sat silent and bewildered. Never, she reflected, if she lived to be a hundred, would she be able to understand men's propensity to keep to impersonal subjects, regardless of what personal issues might lie between them.

It was past midnight when they rose from the table. La Ferté, leaning heavily on his son's arm, left the room, after bidding his guest a cordial farewell; but, late as it was, the Duke seemed to have no intention of going home. He proposed instead a stroll in the garden; and when Cateau would have excused herself, in an amiable effort to leave the lovers alone, he took her hand and insisted on her accompanying them.

The garden was dark, in spite of the lanterns set at intervals along the paths — dark, and very warm and quiet. It was the sort of spring night when one can almost hear things growing. Magdelon's tulips were in full bloom; they made chequered patterns of dimly seen colours under the canopy of the elms. Birds chirped sleepily in the shrubbery, fountains splashed, the church-bell in the monastery of the Little Fathers chimed once, and then was still. The scent of the orange trees in the tubs on the terrace — the biggest orange trees in Paris, La Ferté was never tired of boasting — was overpoweringly sweet.

Back and forth they paced; back and forth, three abreast; Longueville between the two women, whose silken skirts rustled on the gravel as the new leaves overhead sighed in the faint May breeze.

Cateau soon discovered why the Duke had wanted her to stay: he had, it appeared, only just broken the news about Poland to Magdelon in a letter, and naturally did not wish to be alone with her when the matter was first broached between them.

Magdelon, Cateau thought, behaved very well. She said little, but that little was unexpectedly sensible. Of course, Charles must accept his wonderful opportunity. What a chance in a million! Now at last the King would be forced to acknowledge what his cousin was capable of.... But was it certain that there would be no slip in the proceedings? Deposing a reigning monarch might prove a perilous task.

Longueville, too, was at his charming best tonight. He rather deprecated the whole Polish affair, laughed at himself in the rôle of ruler over a country of wolves and bears and wild horses — 'I swear, madam, they tell me there are more savage beasts in their forests than Christians in my capital city! Nay, though, if I really do manage to get there, I'll send you a hundred ermine pelts to make you a robe fit for a queen!' — and took it all so lightly that one might have thought it was merely a jest.

Nothing was said about a possible marriage with the Emperor's sister. There was no mention, either, of little Charles-Louis, asleep in his cradle in the tall, old house on the other side of the river. Cateau felt they *ought* to want to talk about Charles-Louis: she made several attempts to disengage herself and return to the house, but Longueville would not let go her hand.

At length, tired of walking, they sat down to rest in the grotto that was the Maréchal's latest addition to his garden ornaments. It was a quaint construction of rocks and shells, a copy in miniature of the celebrated Grotto of Thetis at Versailles. The somewhat mouldy interior was embellished by mosaic work in coloured stones and four statues of simpering sea-nymphs; a small illuminated fountain in the centre possessed a secret spring, which, when set in motion, made a most lifelike, if faintly asthmatic, imitation of whistling thrushes.

Here Longueville abruptly called for some music. On a beautiful evening like this... Besides, were they not celebrating his election as king? Nothing would do but that Magdelon must sing for them;

a lackey was dispatched to the house to fetch the Maréchale's lute.

While they waited for it to be brought Longueville sat in the middle of the bench by the fountain, still between Cateau and Magdelon. He was laughing a little and nodding his head as he pursed up his lips and tried to whistle in tune with the thrushes.

Magdelon was silent in the shadows. Her back was to the light, but when the lackey handed her the lute she turned round in order to tune it, and a ray fell upon her face. Cateau thought that her sister looked like a young girl, with frightened, mysterious eyes.

'I've not touched it in months,' said Magdelon, in a small, choked voice. 'I may have forgotten . . . What shall I play for you?'

'Madam, whatever you like. Psyche's air — something of Cambert's — I care not, so it be your choice.'

Magdelon struck a few rambling chords on the long cumbersome instrument, and then began to sing the words of an old song Cateau had not heard for years:

> '*To time's cold, cruel sway*
> *Your own coldness exposes*
> *Your charms. . . . Fickle its way,*
> *Changing all life discloses.*
> *Beauty lasts but a day;*
> *So, alas! do the roses.*'

Magdelon's tones were clear and true. They bore little resemblance to her speaking voice, being at once much higher and fuller, a common phenomenon among well-schooled singers. She sang the refrain bravely to the end, with her lover's smiling eyes upon her; she even repeated it, in response to his gesture of noiseless applause.

Then, suddenly she could not sing any more. Her voice did not break or falter; but there were no notes left in her throat.

She dropped the lute on the floor of the grotto and said, in an agonized whisper: 'Oh, do go! Go now! I can't bear it any longer!'

Cateau hastened on ahead, to give her companions a few last moments together; and when Magdelon caught up with her sister she was alone.

'Longueville's gone,' she said. 'He slipped out by the door next the chapel. It's better so.'

She clutched Cateau's hand: Cateau saw that she was trembling violently, and on the way back to the house she went on muttering: 'It's over! Everything's over! I always knew it!'

On the terrace by the row of orange trees the Maréchal met them. He had somehow contrived to hobble that far without Robert's help and stood at the top of the steps, flanked by two lackeys holding smoking torches aloft, as he peered nearsightedly into the darkness below.

'Ha, madam! Is it you? I thought I heard music in the grotto and was coming to join your revels. I've packed young Henri off to bed for one last good night's rest before he starts sleeping on straw. He must be up at dawn, you know, to join his regiment. But what's this? Tears? That will never do!'

Magdelon, unable to restrain herself, fell sobbing on the steps at her husband's feet. La Ferté stooped to lift her up and comfort her as gently as if she had been a child.

'Nay, I thought you braver than that. . . . I promise you, the lad will not come to harm. Turenne will watch over him like a father, and Robert, you know, attends him wherever he goes. He has his orders. . . .'

Magdelon raised a piteous tear-stained face to falter, with quivering lips: 'Sir, I know how good you are. But he's so young, my heart misgives me . . .'

She could speak no further, but, still weeping, gave La Ferté her arm as the couple passed on into the house.

THE DUC DE LONGUEVILLE REINED IN HIS HORSE AT THE TOP OF THE hill and sat at ease in the saddle, so that he might take off his hat and wipe the sweat from his brow as he gazed on the river beneath him. It had been a very warm day. Even now, when the sun was setting, round and red, over the edge of the flat, fertile plain on the other side of the Rhine, the air seemed heavy, almost stifling: it was filled with midges that gathered in clouds above the surface of the water and darting swallows in pursuit of the midges. The bank directly below the hill was marshy, overgrown with rushes and tall, thick-stemmed weeds with large lacy white flowers on them.

The opposite bank looked much the same, tufted with precisely similar weeds and rushes. But it was really another country: it was the island of Betuwe, a part of Holland. Here, on the right bank, higher and slightly rolling, Longueville was still on the territory of the Elector of Cologne, who was friendly to His Majesty's troops. That was why the men swarming about the rows of white tents in the camp, and between the camp and the Rhine, looked so comfortable and relaxed. They had had nothing to do all day for the first time since they had started marching north from Charleroi, over a month ago.

They must have been glad of that, thought Longueville, on account of the heat, though it had been an easy month, on the whole. It had not rained at all — rain was what made marching disagreeable — and there had been little fighting to do. Everything, so far, had gone according to schedule. After crossing Spanish Flanders the army had moved in leisurely fashion downstream, seizing various forts and fortified cities that belonged to the Dutch as they went. The garrisons of the forts put up a poor show of resistance. Condé took Wesel and Emmerich, on the right of the Rhine, while Turenne and the King were accounting for Buderich and Orsoy, on the left, with ludicrous facility. Scarcely a shot had been fired; the Lowlanders seemed paralyzed by the sight of that tremendous double army with banners, its guns and sabres gleaming in the hot summer sun.

Then — still according to schedule — Turenne and his troops had crossed the river at Wesel to join Condé at Rees, which also had fallen without a struggle. Now all their forces were encamped on the slopes of the low wooded hills between the latter place and Emmerich, while, to the north of them, the Duc de Luxembourg, who commanded the Swiss and German mercenaries and other allied regiments, faced the Prince of Orange across the Yssel, a tributary of the Rhine.

That was the situation on the evening of this torrid tenth of June. The French had got as far as they could get on neutral ground. If they did not cross the Rhine into Holland, there was only the narrower Yssel, on the other side of which Orange and his whole army were waiting for them. The Rhine was less well defended, a mere handful of men and cannon having been placed in the fort of Toll-huis, on the Dutch side — but there were no bridges across it and, in spite of the drought, the water ran deep and fierce; it was four times as wide as the Seine at Paris.

Therefore, for the moment, there was nothing to do but wait, while Turenne and Condé made up their minds how to solve the problem.

The soldiers did not mind waiting. In the city of tents on the hill slope they sat about in the shade, smoking and drinking and gossiping and staring idly at the pennants that drooped in the breathless air. Some, more industrious, polished their swords and their muskets, the smart new pieces with bayonets attached that were the boast of Monsieur de Louvois, Minister of War. Others combed the dusty woods of scrub-oak and beech in search of game, or wandered down to the river's brink to hunt for snipe in the reeds or fish in the green swift-moving waters. Occasionally they would meet a party of peasants, on their way to or from the hayfields, whom they tried to converse with in a mixture of French and the bad, guttural Low German of the Rhine provinces. The peasants shook their heads in return and scratched their ears, bewildered by the rapid speech of the foreigners. However, the latter's lively pantomime needed few verbal additions; the gold and silver coins, of which the strangers possessed an apparently inexhaustible supply, likewise spoke for themselves. When the soldiers went back to camp they were laden with fowls for roasting and flasks of the fine dry white wine of the region.

Altogether, it had been a pleasant recess in the strict course of military routine.

Only the Duc de Longueville, atop the hill, preening his curls and setting his hat to rights as the sun slid slowly out of sight, looked flushed, preoccupied, and out of humour with the world in general.

Longueville was bored. Like everybody else, he had had nothing to do all day, not much more the day before that — indeed, little enough during the whole of his month with the army. Of course, there was a good reason for this. He was the colonel of a cavalry regiment; up to now, the cavalry had played second fiddle to the infantry and the artillery, which were naturally more useful in besieging or storming a citadel. *Their* chance would come later, after they had actually got into the enemy's country. But no one could deny it was dull. Besides, Longueville could not help feeling that, if only he had wished, Uncle Condé might have made things more interesting for his favourite nephew. Uncle Condé had always treated him with paternal affection, excused his youthful peccadilloes, and straightened them out indulgently, time and again, when Madame de Longueville, from conscientious scruples, would have disciplined her idolized son.

Longueville had repaid the elder man with a slavishly fervid brand of hero-worship. Uncle Condé had been splendid about everything: he had settled his debts, more than once; got rid of importunate mistresses; persuaded the family, a year ago, to turn over the title and the estate that went with it to Charles-Paris, disregarding the claims of his elder brother, the addle-pated Comte de Dunois. Best of all, he'd undoubtedly had a great share in promoting the Polish affair. Oh, yes: Longueville had had every right to expect to be made a member of his illustrious relative's staff, directly the war with Holland had broken out. What a disappointment it was to find that Uncle Condé had no such intention! The latter had set out at once for Sedan, the rallying-point of his wing of the army, accompanied only by his son, the Duc d'Enghien, and the Comte de Guiche.

There was a peculiar annoyance, for Longueville, in his uncle's choice of companions. One understood the necessity for taking Enghien — poor Enghien! who, for all his father's anxious grooming, would never make a soldier. But it was not easy to forgive Condé's preference of Guiche to his own nephew — Guiche, that romantic dreamer, that ambiguous hero of a thousand alcove dramas, as heedless in war as in love. Longueville had even dared remark on the singularity of Uncle Condé's selection, only to receive the crushing retort: 'The Count's an old friend and a damned fine soldier. He'll be ten times more good to me than anyone else.'

Well, there was no help for it: Longueville had had to submit, and had trailed along with Turenne and the main part of the army, with no special duties or prerogatives, utterly undistinguished amongst a score of other young officers of equivalent rank. He had not complained, and he would not complain: he'd have scorned to betray the depth of his disillusionment. Besides, there was a grain of comfort in Uncle Condé's last words before departure: 'Remember, my boy, you'd better play safe this time. You've too much at stake to take risks now.'

That, of course, was perfectly true. Everyone lately had begun to suspect what only a few knew for certain, that the Polish envoys were even now on their way across Germany to seek their new king. Longueville was set apart from his fellows by the grandeur of his destiny. Meanwhile, what was there to do save conceal the bitterness of the pill he'd been forced to swallow, and hope against hope that somewhere, somehow, he might still win a laurel-wreath in his last campaign as a Frenchman?

Above all, it was useless to show temper towards Uncle Condé. Far from that, the Duke had actually arranged a little supper-party to be held in his tent that very night, at which Monsieur the Prince and his son, Monsieur the Duke (as they were officially styled at court), were to be honoured guests.

It was almost time for them to arrive. If Longueville wanted to be punctual at his own party, he would have to make haste. Letting Pegasus, his white battle-charger, pick his own way down the hill, he then urged the horse into a smart trot along the spongy path by the water's edge. As he passed them he flicked with his riding-crop the tops of the tall weeds lining the path, trying to cut off their white flowering heads. . . . After a little Pegasus turned off the road over the rough hayfields towards a cluster of tents, a kind of hamlet adjoining the city that sheltered His Majesty's troops.

There were ten or twelve of these tents, striped red and white and set in a semicircle, that belonged to the Duke and his numerous household. The open space between them was filled with a crowd of men and boys in uniform, horses and mules tethered in rows, and several large wagons bearing the crest of the Longuevilles embossed in gold on their doors. As the young man drew near the camp he halloa'd impatiently, to give warning of his coming. Swinging down from the heavy silver-studded saddle, he handed the reins to Bourgneuf, the chief equerry, who came hurrying out of the commissary's tent at the sound of His Highness's voice. The men and boys stood at attention and saluted their master: there were scores of them — coachmen and grooms, postilions and muleteers, lackeys and pages — for the Duc de Longueville travelled with a small army of followers. With the exception of the head steward of his estate and, of course, Porlier, who was busy in Paris taking care of little Charles-Louis, his entire personal suite went to war with their lord.

Inside his own tent, which was lined with cream-and-russet-brown satin, six valets were waiting to undress him. Longueville flung his hat, gloves, and riding-crop to the ground, fell on his camp-bed, and stretched out his legs, while Hervé, his favourite valet-of-the-wardrobe, kneeled solicitously to draw off the ducal boots. . . . David, the maître-d'hôtel, was sent for, to be interviewed concerning the menu for supper. His Highness was most particular about

every detail. Not that Uncle Condé cared a rap what he ate — not
he! In fact, the old Prince had been frequently heard to make fun
of the luxury Louvois had brought into fashion: he himself slept by
preference in a hayloft or in his filthy patched tent smelling of
leather and horses. As for meals, rough oaten cakes and a hearty
draught of beer were his usual diet, a sensible one since he, too, like
La Ferté, was now subject to gout.

Nevertheless, Longueville was determined to offer his guests
something out of the ordinary tonight. His royal cousin Louis
would have provided no less: could he himself lag behind, now that
he, also, was to be crowned king? . . . So there were grave and lengthy
consultations over the soup and the salad, the fish and the roast.
The Duke wrinkled his forehead at the choice of the sweet, stamped
and swore lustily till poor David trembled and broke into a sweat,
after his cringing confession that he had been unable to procure the
iced melons his master had ordered. . . . What was that? The local
fruit wasn't ripe yet? Good God, what difference did it make?
David should have known it would not be — he should have had the
wit to send to Cologne, if necessary, rather than let the supper-
party be disappointed. . . . 'Damn it all! What do I pay you for? . . .'

Longueville felt cruelly abused. There was no doubt of it, he was
the worst-served noble in France — in *France*, did he say? Nay,
why not in the world? With the ease of long practice he launched
into an ardent tirade against his household staff, accompanied by a
series of well-timed blows and kicks, which his valets dodged as best
they were able, considering the exigencies of their duties in assisting
His Highness's toilet.

The tirade was brought to a close by the entrance of the Comte
de Fiesque and the Chevalier de Montchevreuil, the first of the
guests to appear. As soon as Longueville spied them he stopped
shouting and kicking, quite effortlessly, in the middle of a sentence;
smiled charmingly instead, and gave the newcomers his hand.

The two young men smiled back and said: 'Good evening, Your
Highness,' respectfully.

The Count, very smart in his dress uniform of aide-de-camp to
the King, looked no less aloof and sleepy-eyed in the field than in
Paris. What could one campaign more or less matter to *him?* . . .
The Chevalier, whose family name was Philippe de Mornay, a year
or two younger than the other, was a round-faced, rosy youth, handsome — like all the Mornays — and obviously quite under the spell
of his admiration for the little Duke. . . . Good fellows both, Fiesque
and Montchevreuil! None better in all Turenne's army, thought
Longueville. They had been devoted to him always. . . . Well, he
would soon, thank fortune! be in a position to reward them. He was
resolved that no one should lose who had rendered him service in

the uncertain days of his youth. He had heard it said, it was even
traditional to say, that Bourbons were ungrateful — but here, at
least, was one Bourbon who knew what gratitude meant!... See
how easy he was with his friends! — the pains he took to treat them
precisely as if they were his equals in rank! That *proved* he had a
good heart, didn't it?... As a matter of fact, it was only subordinates whom Longueville treated as equals. With his peers he was
uncomfortable, unless he were able somehow to assert his superiority
— which doubtless accounted for his unpopularity with male members of the royal family.

Fiesque and Montchevreuil, however, had no intention of pre-
suming on their friendship with the future King of Poland. They
stood courteously while Longueville completed his toilet, the Count
handing him his shirt, the Chevalier clearly deeming it an inestimable honour to help his host adjust his lace collar and cuffs. During
these ceremonial operations the Duke laughed and chatted away
with cheerful familiarity. How simple it was to get on with a man
as long as that man took care to remember the value of their respective positions!

This hour at the toilet-table was the pleasantest of the day, the
only one in which one could entirely forget the trials and tediums of
military life. Longueville prolonged it deliberately, chaffing his
friends on their recent conquests amongst the Flemish beauties; displaying for their benefit a new shipment of uniforms that had just
come from his tailor in Paris, a gold-headed cane the Abbé de Choisy
had given him as a souvenir of the siege of Orsoy.... The Chevalier,
greatly daring, stammered a blushing reference to the latter's possible significance as a sceptre, which his idol received with smiling
complacency.

Before any of the three young men had the slightest idea how late
it was getting, the sound of horses' hoofs in the clearing outside betokened the arrival of the rest of the company. As they were supping informally, the Duke's gentlemen-in-waiting were not in attendance this evening; but the six valets lined up, three in a row, on
each side of the entrance, nervously conscious of their master's critical eye upon them. One of the lackeys hastily lighted the candles in
the portable carved wooden chandelier that swung from the centre
of the roof over the supper-table, and placed two black leather chairs
with arms (denoting the rank of Prince of the Blood) to right and
left of His Highness's own seat. Fiesque and Montchevreuil fell
back to a deferential distance, while the Duke, clad now in fresh
linen and laces, his curls brushed and shining, the blue ribbon of the
Order of the Holy Ghost slanting across his white-and-gold bosom,
advanced the prescribed three steps to the door of the tent to greet
his uncle and cousin.

The Prince de Condé stood for a moment, staring about him, before stalking in with stiff, rheumatic steps. He was wearing a worn leather jerkin and a pair of old boots that had certainly seen service in more than a dozen campaigns; his hat, adorned by a moulting cock's feather and pulled carelessly over one eye, gave him something the look of a brigand. This look was heightened by the general disorder of his person — the greasy, matted hair; the straggling beard grey with tobacco rather than age; his face even, alas! not overclean. (The Condés were proverbially a slovenly race.) But when he doffed his hat to salute his nephew the huge beaked nose and the bright untamed valour in his greenish eyes (much the colour of the Rhine water) reminded one irresistibly of an eagle — a dirty, shabby old eagle, it was true, but still dauntless and unbeaten.

His voice, too, sounded full of vigour — deep and brazenly male — as he clapped the foppish Duke on the back and cried out: 'And how's our young sovereign this evening? Eh, lad, I see you're rehearsing the Polish ceremony already!'

Longueville blushed hotly and looked a trifle foolish: Uncle Condé could always put him out of countenance! To restore his poise he turned off the jest with a laugh that he hoped sounded natural, and gave his hand to his cousin Enghien, then to Guiche and Marsillac, who followed hard behind the latter. None of the three was a member of his intimate circle: Enghien was a petulant pocket-edition of his father, devoid of Condé's genius and personality; there were half a dozen good reasons for disliking the Comte de Guiche; while Marsillac, dully correct, yet astute enough to have become the King's favourite courtier, was detested by everybody because everybody was jealous of him. (Besides, Longueville and he had a private excuse for their lack of ease in each other's society, since it was universally supposed that they were half-brothers — the old Duchess having been exceptionally gallant in her youth and La Rochefoucauld, Marsillac's father, her accepted lover through all the years of the Fronde.)

The young men saluted one another with glacial smiles and remarked what a hot night it was; then Longueville conducted his uncle to the table.

The Prince de Condé was often, without meaning to be, a difficult guest. His presence was so overwhelming that one could not, before it, embark on conversational trivialities. It was not his age that awed them: though he was already past fifty, he did not seem like an old man. No: it was rather the aura of his past triumphs, still unmistakably clinging to him, that abashed people. One could not look at him without realizing that here was the victor of Rocroi and Nördlingen and the siege of Mardyck, a born general who had led the forces of France to unequalled successes when he himself was scarce out of his teens. He had no need to deck his breast with medals to remind the youth of today of what he had done; it was implicit in every turn of his head, every regard of those piercing green eyes. 'Great Condé,' 'Monsieur the Prince, the hero' — so he would be called to the end of the chapter, whether he liked it or not.

At the same time, his attitude towards the younger men was endearingly paternal; and the young men returned his affection with interest. Enghien, his son; Longueville, his sister's son; as well as Fiesque, Guiche, and Marsillac, the sons of old friends — all adored him and felt that whatever he did must be right because he did it.

Tonight the hero appeared somewhat tired and dispirited: the heat of the day had been trying, and, though he did not complain, the rigid reluctance of his motions made it evident that he was suffering from an onslaught of gout, the one enemy he could not subdue.

He sat silent while David and his corps of subordinate lackeys served the soup and the Rhine salmon and filled the guests' glasses with pale gold German wine. His own simpler wants were catered to by his valet Pacolet, a disreputable old mummy who had been in his service for years and who invariably stood behind his master's chair, bending slightly forward, an unmeaning grin on his skull-like features.

The young men, meanwhile, chatted desultorily about the food and the climate and their horses — one could always talk about horses! — and exchanged sundry scraps of camp gossip.... There was the ridiculous plight of the Venetian ambassador, Michieli, who had insisted on following the King to war without proper funds or supplies, and now found himself, destitute of provisions, forced to beg for crumbs from his colleagues' better stocked tables. The strange passion of Monsieur, the King's brother, for making himself up every morning, as though for a ball at the Palais Royal, was also gone into exhaustively: naturally, as soon as the sun got at all hot, the poor little Prince's cheeks ran till they resembled a painter's palette. Guiche was especially acid on the subject of Monsieur, who had once been his bosom friend, in the days before the dashing Count's love for Madame, Monsieur's young English wife, had broken off their happy relations forever.

From these personal matters they passed to a lively discussion of army affairs — of Louvois' unheard-of innovations in the way of equipment and commissariat and the extraordinary measures of discipline in the troops introduced by the infantry leader, Colonel Martinet. Most of the older soldiers were opposed to such revolutionary changes, but, oddly enough, Condé broke his silence to put in a word in their favour.

'Discipline, lads, means nothing in itself, but it makes for a stronger army in wartime, and whatever does that, must be good. If I'd had disciplined troops at the Battle of the Faubourg-Saint-Antoine, they'd not have been hacked to pieces as they were. We're none of us so old we can't manage to learn a new trick or two. What my cousin's army lacks now is not order, but experience. Because they've not been up yet against real opposition, they imagine that every enemy they meet will topple over like tenpins. I fancy young Orange and his Dutchmen may have some surprises in store for us.'

'Perhaps so, uncle — but when shall we be able to prove it?' cried Longueville. 'Oh, sir, nothing's so hard to bear as inaction! My God, are we to camp here all summer like sheep, in very sight of the rich pastures we dare not make ours?'

'Papa, could a bridge not be built?' inquired Enghien, with an air of great wisdom. 'Surely Julius Caesar did not suffer himself to be vanquished by so simple an obstacle as a river?'

'No, nor Louis de Bourbon, either,' muttered Fiesque. 'Wait, my friends, and you'll see ——'

'But, my God! how can we fight, when we can't come to grips with the foe?' demanded Longueville impatiently; while even the more prudent Guiche observed: 'Was it not Silius Italicus who said: "Away with delay! The chance of great fortune is short-lived"? What's annoying to me is that the longer we do nothing, the more time the Hollanders have to build up their strength. I realize that the main Dutch army is waiting for us on the other side of the Yssel, but there are men arriving every day in the Fort of Tollhuis. I heard only this afternoon the report that was sent to Your Highness that Prince William had dispatched General Wirtz to relieve Montbas of the command. I know Wirtz of old; he's as sly as a fox, and twice as courageous! Sir, there *must* be some way of crossing the Rhine before it's too late to surprise the enemy. If only you'd give me leave to try to find it!'

Condé, who had paid little heed to the hotheaded remarks of the other young men, turned his glowing gaze on the Comte de Guiche with a measure of respect. Guiche had had a great deal of military experience in his comparatively short career, not only in France and Flanders, but in Holland and Poland as well, as a volunteer in the years of his exile. If he were seriously of the opinion that the Rhine could be forded, the venture might not be so foolhardy as it sounded.

'You know, of course,' he began slowly, 'that we have intended, all along, to build a bridge, directly the material for it arrived. I've been held up these last two days for lack of the promised wood and metal. It is a pity, I grant you, that the enemy should have wind of our plans and time to circumvent them — yet how dare I risk the lives of my men attempting to cross a river as wide and deep as the Rhine without a bridge of some sort? It's only too likely to prove suicidal.'

'Nay, sir,' exclaimed Guiche eagerly, 'with all due respect — and, naturally, I'd not dream of setting up my insignificant knowledge against yours — but when I was fighting in Poland we had often occasion to ford streams no less powerful than this one — and I assure you, we never let the lack of a bridge hold us back!'

'Ah, well, boy, that may be — but consider a moment the difference between the men at your disposal and mine. What half-wild Cossacks with none-too-full bellies would think all in a day's work might be an impossible manoeuvre for His Majesty's sleek, well-fed troops. I vow, a good third of 'em may not even know how to swim!' — And Condé threw back his head to emit the short, sharp bark that was his closest approach to a laugh.

Still Guiche was not discouraged.

'Sir, you may very likely be right — as, indeed, when have you not been? But remember this: your men need not swim if their horses can. My thought would be to leave the infantry here, and send only the cavalry across to rout the enemy's outposts and clear out the fort. You could cover the move fairly well from this side with your artillery, and then later, at your leisure, build your bridge — half a dozen bridges, if you will — to transport the rest of the army. Don't say it can't be done! There's no such word as "impossible" in the vocabulary of Monsieur the Prince. Haven't I proved it a hundred times in the old days? — when I was unfortunately in the forces opposed to Your Highness! Livy says, you know, that "necessity is the last and strongest weapon." There must be some spot where the water is shallow enough to permit us to cross in safety. There *must* — I am convinced of it! Only give me leave to-morrow to scout about by myself, and I'll engage on my honour to bring you before sundown the news you are waiting for.'

The Count spoke with an air of assurance that, Longueville could see, impressed Condé in spite of himself. Probably he had stolen a march on the rest of them and done a bit of reconnoitring on his own already. It would be just like Guiche to play a nasty trick like that. Damn the fellow's impudent, independent ways! Longueville had never been able to stand his superior smile — and his parade of classical learning, with his 'Livy says this' and 'Silius Italicus says that'! Was there ever more preposterous affectation? Who really believed his boast that he spent three hours a day, wherever he happened to be, conning the works of those musty old Greeks and Romans? As if anyone who cared to could not hunt up a few random quotations in some handy anthology to spice his conversation! None but women and priests were to be taken in by such flimsy pretensions. Especially women. Hang it all! Wasn't half Guiche's success with the little Brissac his ability to spout verses from memory by the yard? ... Yes, damn the fellow! ... All the same, though, it would not do to antagonize him now, when he was visibly on the verge of gaining his point with Uncle Condé.

The Duke waved to David, as a signal that the lackeys might remove the salmon and bring on the roast, and said, smiling (no one knew what an effort it cost him to produce that smile!): 'Sir, I think the Count is right. Have I your permission to accompany him?'

'And I?' — 'And I?' Enghien and Marsillac lost no time in speaking up, while Fiesque and the young Chevalier showed plainly by their faces that only their consciousness of inferior rank prevented them from following suit. If there were going to be some heroic surprise action, none of the four could bear the thought of being left out of the fun.... Damn them, too! Why, the whole army'd be in it, if one didn't watch out!...

Condé good-humouredly surveyed the eager circle of faces in the candlelight.

'What? All ready to volunteer? Ha, Guiche! You can take your pick of the lot. But I'll need you, Enghien, tomorrow myself, to ride to Cologne on a mission to His Excellency the Elector. And Marsillac, if I mistake not, has been detailed to take charge of the evacuation of Rees. As for you, Charles, my boy, as a member of the staff of Monsieur de Turenne, your duties lie outside my jurisdiction. Has he set you no task for the morning?'

Longueville frowned.

'I was to ride up towards Doesburg,' he answered sulkily, 'with the Comte de Roye and a small scouting party, to confer with the Duc de Luxembourg and see how the land lies in that direction. But really it's not at all necessary for me to go. Roye's quite capable of taking charge of the expedition alone. Besides, it's useless, isn't it? Since we all know perfectly well that the main enemy army is waiting there beyond the Yssel. Only a madman would think of trying to enter Holland that way.'

'Perhaps. Perhaps. But it might not be mad to persuade the Dutchmen that that's our intention,' remarked Uncle Condé mildly, swooping on his venison, as if Prince William himself lay under his fork and knife. 'My boy, you must obey orders. That's every soldier's whole duty. Guiche had better, I think, explore on his own, since I see he's determined not to give up till he's exhausted every possibility, no matter how faint, of achieving his end. That, too, is as it should be. Now, lads, let's forget the war for an hour, at least, and enjoy the admirable dinner our host has set before us. Lord, Charles, this roast is an excellent thing! Where in blazes do you get venison on the march, and at this time of year? My fool of a chef has sent me in overdone mutton every night for a week!'

'Why, uncle, 'tis no great matter,' replied Longueville, making once more a gallant attempt to suppress his rising irritation. 'These scrub woods hereabouts are chock full of deer, and the peasants, I find, are only too glad to break game regulations to get their hands on our good French silver. But come, sir, I see you are drinking nothing. Is this sour German wine too weak for your palate? If you can manage to choke down a glass, I'll call for a health to His Majesty — and death and destruction to the scurvy Dutch knaves who dare to resist him! The King, gentlemen, the King!'

The toast was drunk standing, with perfect solemnity; but afterwards, as if it were a signal they'd been waiting for, the guests grew freer in manner. To tell the truth, the wine had circulated fairly liberally already, judging by their flushed faces and the sweat that poured off their brows. It was appallingly hot in the satin-lined tent. Although the sun had been gone for some hours, the air was still heavy and brooding; it stirred just enough to set the wooden chandelier hanging over the table to swaying gently. The candles in the chandelier burned hard and clear: they were surrounded by scores of beetles and blundering night-flying moths, while in the dark fields outside crickets and frogs kept up a tireless chorus punctuated by distant rumbles of thunder.

The supper drew to its close in a merry mood. Chairs were pushed back from the table as their occupants relaxed into easier attitudes. Marsillac and Monsieur the Duke removed their wigs. Guiche unbuttoned his waistcoat with a laughing excuse for the necessity of the gesture. (As he did so, Longueville noticed that the Count's left hand was minus three fingers — grim reminder of his Polish campaigns.) Even Condé laid aside the hat with the moulting cock's feather and sat with his legs crossed, picking his long yellow teeth, looking more than ever like a benevolent vulture. And young Montchevreuil had apparently quite forgotten his fear of the illustrious company.

Only their host sat aloof and suspicious. He seldom perspired like other people, despite the luxuriant yellow tresses that must have been quite as trying to carry as any court peruque. He smiled punctiliously at everything that was said, and made polite rejoinders whenever it was necessary; but all the same he appeared to be suffering from some strange blight on his spirits. Under the conventional surface of his thoughts coursed a black current of doubt concerning Guiche and Uncle Condé. It was clear that the pair meant to trick him. More than likely, whatever they said, they'd already discovered a ford across the Rhine, and planned to take base advantage of his absence tomorrow to work up some brilliant manoeuvre between them, in which he, Longueville, could have no part. It was cursedly unfair!... And Enghien would be there, of course, no matter what his father pretended he meant him to do. Enghien always was there. That was Uncle Condé's invariable policy, to shove the poor chap into the limelight wherever possible, hoping that some day the latter would find glory thrust upon him, since he was obviously not destined to achieve it. . . . So far, the policy had failed. Enghien, clever enough about everything else, was a fool in the field. He could not understand the rudiments of military strategy, nor take charge of the simplest routine manoeuvre without making a muddle. In moments of crisis he was sure to lose his head completely and go galloping round in wild confusion. Why, damn it! the man could not even shoot straight! His handling of a sword was deplorable. For what reason, then, did Uncle Condé insist on pushing him ahead instead of Longueville, who was almost as close a relation and had twice his cousin's aptitude for the career? . . . It was not, Longueville added bitterly to himself, as though he had unlimited time to wait for preferment. No, it must be now or never, with the Polish throne in sight! . . .

The little Duke brooded, his chin in his hand, nursing his grievance, even after his guests had stopped talking about the war and fallen back on the soldier's second reliable topic, women.

Warm with wine, the young officers began exchanging tales of their exploits amongst the Flanders belles. Condé, though taking no share in their conversation, listened indulgently, half smiling, to their ribald boasts. . . . What, after all, did women mean in his life? Everyone knew that he had never loved his wife, who had been foisted on him by her uncle, Cardinal Richelieu. For years they had lived apart; now she was definitely relegated to one of the family's remoter estates, while the Prince's household, both in Paris and Chantilly, officially without a hostess, was more or less run by the Princess Palatine, Anne de Gonzague, the mother of Enghien's wife. Here was no matter for scandal: the Palatine and Uncle Condé were old and good friends, trusted allies since the days of the Fronde, now united more closely than ever by their children's marriage. But it was not clear that Monsieur the Prince had ever truly loved any woman. There had been talk of this one and that one in his youth — of poor, pretty Marthe du Vigean, who had fled to a cloister when her gallant deserted her — of the bold, handsome Duchesse de Châtillon. (But that had been mainly a political intrigue.) . . . No, even then, the hero's deepest affections had been reserved for his comrades-at-arms, the gay band of satellites known as Condé's 'little masters,' accomplished warriors and amorists all, who ran the army to suit themselves in the summer and spent their winters drinking, gaming, wenching, and strutting like peacocks before a prostrate court.

Longueville, who usually joined in talking bawdy with the best will in the world, found himself this time as silent as Uncle Condé. It was all he could do to force a smile as Marsillac, with lumbering impropriety, told several foul stories almost entirely lacking in point. . . . What was the matter with him tonight? Why couldn't he laugh as the others did? Was the sour German wine really to blame? . . .

Tongue-tied and miserable, he sat twirling the stem of the empty glass in his fingers, until at length his condition became noticeable to the rest of the company.

Guiche, who had approached the top of his form, leaned laughing across the table to say, with a significant glance: 'Your Highness seems distrait. Where are your thoughts, dear boy? I'll not offer a penny for them, for I dare swear I can guess where they are — with our little Brissac in Paris, eh? Have I hit upon it? Lord, sir! if you'll forgive my saying so, you're wasting your time there. My lady's a prim little taffeta doll, no more likely to come to life in a man's arms than if she were stuffed with horsehair and sawdust. Good God! When I think of the hours I've put in dancing hither and yon at young Madam's beck and call — and all without the slightest hope of reward — I vow my head needs examining! I wager Your Highness has had no better luck. Or have you perchance concealed your successes expressly to make us rage with jealousy? You're a sly fellow, we all know, a very sly fellow! Come, now, sir, no hedging — out with the truth! How goes the campaign? Has the little Brissac succumbed to your wiles?'

Longueville hesitated, blushing furiously against his will. He strove to turn off the question with a jest, as though it were of no consequence — which, indeed, was not far from the truth. But tonight, somehow, he could not: instead, to his horror, he heard himself mumbling, like any half-baked schoolboy: 'Ah, now, drop it! You know Madame de Brissac is nothing to me.'

But Guiche was not to be fobbed off so easily. He leaned even farther forward, his impish smile still more pronounced — those white teeth, after all, remained his best feature — as he cried: 'Well, then, my hero, if the Brissac isn't to blame for your sluggish humour, it must be old woman La Ferté. There, now, boys, haven't I got it this time? Gad, sir, as the poet says, "Neither absence nor time will be able to cure me"! And it's ancient history what the sisters La Louppe are capable of. Don't I remember, to my cost . . .? Why, when the Olonne was the toast of the town it took three gallants at once to keep her in trim! Hey, Marsillac, old fellow? No hard feelings, I hope? What's past is past, though not yet forgotten. But they tell me she's nothing at all compared to her sister — Messalina's completely eclipsed, and that sort of thing. . . . Well! Well! I've been away from court so long that my gossip is scarcely up to date, but the rumour's about that the Maréchal doesn't dare hire pages over twelve years of age — and that the reason his wife goes to the country so often is to get rid of certain tokens of her attach-

ments that might prove embarrassing recruits to the nursery at
Great Senneterre!... You're a brave man, my master — as brave as
I was, in my youth. But I freely confess that the little Brissac is
more to my taste in this sober autumn of my career as an alcovist.
More compliments than couch-work, so to speak!... No offence
meant, Your Highness! But tell us, do, how you left the old girl
when you came away from Paris. Did you clap a chastity belt on
her matronly form? I trust you haven't neglected that little precaution, for if you have, ten to one you'll find yourself replaced before the war's half over!'

Again Longueville made a desperate attempt to laugh, in order to
show that the gibe had not touched him. Guiche was a brazen,
mocking fellow, with respect for neither God nor man. But now,
when all was said and done, he was only joking. It was idiotic to take
his filthy insinuations seriously, for they were not meant to do more
than raise a fugitive laugh. And the Lord knew, Longueville had
taken part in enough debauches before this to know precisely the
kind of lewd banter that passed for wit: he ought by now to be able
to parry the thrust mechanically.

What. therefore, were his astonishment and dismay to find himself on his feet, crying out in a sharp, shrill voice: 'Shut your mouth,
you dog, or I'll damned well do it for you!'

Guiche paused in the midst of a fit of squalling laughter, his thick
black eyebrows lifted in sudden surprise. But he had had no time to
alter the rest of his features, which went on grinning unmeaningly,
though the excuse for it had passed.

Longueville gripped the edge of the table to keep himself from
trembling. A hard pulse pounded in his temples: he felt he would
burst if he could not manage to stop that senseless grin.... There
was his cousin Enghien, too, snickering into his napkin like an ill-
mannered colt. He hated him almost as fiercely as he hated Guiche.
God! How he hated them both!

Deliberately he reached for a decanter and poured out a glass of
the yellow German wine; then raised it, intending to dash the contents in the Count's mirthful face. But a hand fell unexpectedly on
his shoulder — a hand with a grip like iron — and a calm, cold voice
(rather like iron, too, that voice) whispered in his ear: 'Steady, old
chap, steady! Nothing's worth making a scene about any more. I
had word this morning that the envoys from Poland are coming tomorrow. You're to be crowned in Danzig, they tell me.'

Chapter X

THE THUNDER HEARD AT INTERVALS DURING THE COURSE OF THE
Duke's supper-party proved to be more than a sign of heat: not an
hour after the guests had gone home a short, sharp thundershower
swept with fury over the camp, drenching the tents and the wagons
and the rows of patient, unprotesting horses and mules that cropped
the grass in the open fields. Unfortunately, it did not last long
enough to do much good. Early next morning, when Monsieur de
Longueville set forth on his scouting expedition, the sun was as
fierce, the sky as cloudless as ever.

Before leaving he had given his staff detailed instructions concerning the Polish envoys, in case the latter arrived before he returned
from his mission. These dignitaries were to be received with full
honours, a special tent placed at their disposal, and an elaborate
dinner served them under the watchful eye of the Comte de Fiesque,
the Chevalier de Montchevreuil, and the Duke's eight gentlemen-in-
waiting. The Chevalier, of course, was rather young to assume much
responsibility, but he had begged so hard to be allowed to help that
Longueville had not the heart to refuse him. And, anyhow, with
Fiesque in command, nothing could possibly go amiss. Fiesque, in
his casual, unruffled way, was efficiency itself. He bore, as well, an
ancient and honourable name — those Polish chaps were sure to
have heard of *him*. Longueville was delighted to be able to leave the
execution of his orders in such capable hands. It was only a pity,
he thought, that the members of his suite were obliged to wear the
King's uniforms instead of the colours of his own ducal house, as
they would have done in the old days. This was another of Louvois'
newfangled notions that had found little favour with the nobles.
However, it could not be helped — nor would it, in any case, be for
long, now. Soon enough they'd be transferring their allegiance to a
new land and a new flag. . . .

Longueville smiled as he remembered the wonderful change to
come. He sat up very straight in his saddle and flicked Pegasus
lightly with the whip, so that the latter trotted briskly out of camp
to take the road to the north. Behind them arose a clatter of hoofs
as the Comte de Roye, who was the captain of a company in the
Duke's regiment, marshalled his thirty picked horsemen to follow
their leader.

Longueville paid no heed either to the Count or his men. Roye was an excellent officer, but a Huguenot, middle-aged and austere, and therefore not one of his affinities. This, on the whole, suited the Duke's plans very well, as it would spare him the necessity of making conversation during the long day they were to spend in each other's society. He could say as little as he pleased, lose himself, for hours on end, in his own thoughts — and he had need to do so, for since last night they had been tossing in painful confusion.

In that dark welter the promise of the Polish crown shone out as the one constant ray of hope. He dared not lose sight of it for an instant. It would help him to face the future as nothing else could; it was helping him *now* — just as, assuredly, it had helped him last night to conquer his temper. But for Uncle Condé's timely reminder, who knew what might have happened? Uncle Condé, of course, was right, as always: it would be the height of folly to risk spoiling things now, with the gleaming prize so nearly in his grasp. ... Just the same, Longueville would not soon forget the dastardly behaviour of the Comte de Guiche. No! By God! He'd pay him out for it some day — see if he didn't! — the slippery, insulting fellow!

All night the Duke's dreams had been fevered by an uneasy remembrance of his rival's taunting phrases.... '*Old woman La Ferté.... Tell us, do, how you left the old girl!*' went on echoing and re-echoing in his subconscious brain, only to spring once more to sharp immediate life when he awoke. Was that the way men spoke of Magdelon? Was that how they thought of his beautiful mistress, whose love had made him so proud?

For the first time in his life Longueville almost regretted his rank, which had kept him from learning what people really felt about his affair. Even now, if Guiche hadn't got drunk ...

The whole morning through, Longueville could not get the matter out of his head. He sat speechless and depressed all the way to Doesburg, following blindly the dusty road that wound among fields and vineyards, deserted save for colonies of larks and an occasional group of peasants. The peasants stopped work when they caught sight of the Duke and leaned on their rakes to watch the gay beplumed cavalcade jingling by. But Longueville did not see them, nor did he hear the fluting larks: his thoughts were turned in on himself, while his lips went on dully repeating: 'The old girl ... old woman La Ferté!' ... In the cheerless illumination cast by these devastating words he felt he must make a serious attempt to appraise his emotional life. What had happened to him? — and why had it happened? If he could answer those questions satisfactorily, he would have made at least a start at solving the problems that vexed him.

To begin with — he might as well admit it at once — he had always admired older women. But there were excellent reasons for that. How could he have helped it, given his queer, unchildlike childhood? . . .

'I never had my youth, like other boys,' thought Longueville, with melancholy complacency. 'I never had a family, like other families. . . .'

This last was undeniably true. Although not an only child, he might really better have been one. His half-sister Marie, Mademoiselle de Longueville, a cranky old maid with bookish tastes, detested children on principle and lived on terms of semi-veiled hostility with her stepmother, the Duchess. And Charles-Paris' brother Dunois, three years his senior, if not quite an imbecile, was certainly far from normal. Their father and mother, too, were in no sense average parents.

The Duc de Longueville seemed to childish eyes incredibly old. A careworn, bearded man, who seldom spoke, he looked what he was — an embittered noble, prematurely aged, not least by a clear realization that his failure was due to his own mistake. If instead of backing his rebel brother-in-law Condé in the civil wars, he had only held out for Mazarin . . . But there was no use, now, in raking up old scores. He had managed to save part of his fortune in the general crash of the party, as well as the governorship of Normandy. That was something to be thankful for. The Duchesse de Longueville, his second wife, was twenty-four years younger than he. Once so gallant, undisputed leader of fashion in Regency days, and a born intriguer, she had changed greatly in character after the ruin of her political hopes. In fact, in an agony of exaggerated repentance, she rushed to the other extreme — frequented Jansenist circles at Port Royal, gave up rouge and patches, wore hair-shirts under her silk gowns on fast-days, was birched regularly, and spent many hours confessing partly imaginary sins to her director of conscience, strict Father Singlin.

But, with all her parade of piety, Madame de Longueville remained a social queen. She was still beautiful, too. Every afternoon when the family was in town, at the Hôtel de Longueville in the rue Saint-Thomas-du-Louvre, her friends came to call, just as they'd done for years. Their hostess reclined on the bed of state, languid and lovely in a cloud of dove-grey silks and laces, smiling her enchanting new penitent's smile — whilst a circle of female toadies filled all the space in the alcove about her. At these functions Charles-Paris was invariably sent for, to be presented to the ladies. (There was no good in producing poor Dunois, with his shuffling gait and thick tongue and opaque idiotic stare.) But the little Comte de Saint-Paul was a charming child — rather small for his age — but with such keen blue eyes and sunny curls! His smile was as conscious as an accomplished coquette's as he was handed about from one toady to the next, to be petted and praised. His knowing complimentary speeches — thoroughly rehearsed in private — were pronounced perfection; and when, bowing quaintly, his hands on his heart, he passed a platter of sugarplums to the guests (sure in advance that the lion's share would be placed in his pocket before he trotted back to the nursery), a ripple of ecstasy swept through the room. Even Maman would raise her head to smile with flaccid approval and murmur (she never *said* things out loud): 'Ah, yes, Saint-Paul's the consolation of my declining years!'

These were the principal pleasures of Charles-Paris' early life. The Longuevilles, of course, were not always in town, but even in the country, at the castle of Trie, amidst the rain-soaked woods and pastures of Normandy, Maman's drawing-room was scarcely less full. Trie was not far from Paris; it was also on the road to Flanders and the Baths of Forges; and in those days few officers bound for the battlefields, or belles in search of a cure, would willingly miss a chance of paying court to the governor of the province and his famous wife.

So the petting and sugarplums continued. As the Comte de Saint-Paul grew older, however, he became gradually aware that, though he might be his mother's favourite, his father did not care for him at all. Not that Papa had said anything. . . . He was careful always to treat both boys with scrupulous fairness. Indeed, Charles-Paris had much more done for him than most younger sons. Because Dunois was too dull to share his lessons, Saint-Paul had a separate suite from the time he was able to walk — his own tutor and governor and gentlemen-in-waiting. Later, he was sent to the Academy to learn how to ride and handle a sword, while poor Dunois was banished to the Jesuits in the hope that he might take a fancy to the church, since it was obviously the best that could be aspired to in his case.

But Saint-Paul was too intelligent not to realize that he meant almost nothing to his father, and too inquisitive not to make up his mind to learn why. He got it at last out of his governor Fontenai, by dint of persistent questioning — the Duc de Longueville feared Charles-Paris was not his own son. It seemed that many people thought that Monsieur de la Rochefoucauld . . . 'Mind, now! Not a word of this to your family, nor to anyone else!' cautioned little owl-like Monsieur de Fontenai, wetting his lips and rolling his eyes apprehensively, as if he were afraid that the gilt-and-morocco-bound rows of books in the library at Trie might be listening. 'It's as much as my place is worth to tell you. But I suppose you'd find it out for yourself, sooner or later — you've a right to know, in a way, my lad. . . . No, there's never been an open scandal — and there's not likely to be one now. Heaven knows, there mayn't be anything in those old stories! It's all so long ago, isn't it? . . . Only remember this: it's no use your expecting anything from His Highness, outside of what it's his duty to give you. Your best chance, boy, lies with your poor mother. God be praised, she's a young woman still! — and you've the whole future before you. Just wait — and you'll see. . . .'

Wait — yes — he would have to do that! Often it seemed to Saint-Paul that he'd always been waiting for something. First, for his half-sister Marie to marry — that self-willed young woman's tardy match with the sickly young Duc de Nemours was, frankly, a deliverance to her family. . . . Then, for his father to die — because, while he lived, the Duchess could give little help to her younger son. After that, to grow up as quickly as possible, so that the question of 'What to Do with Saint-Paul' could be decided, one way or the other. Once the old Duke was gone, Uncle Condé had valiantly espoused Charles-Paris' cause; begged his sister to face facts, admit that Dunois would never be fit to inherit the dukedom, and settle the title on the logical heir.

But the distracted Duchess could not come to a definite decision. She wrung her hands and wept, yearning with her whole heart to yield to her brother's behest — still something held her back. . . . Dunois had revolted from the Jesuits' rule and was now at home again, asserting his right to his inheritance. And Madame de Nemours was supporting his claims — not that she cared a fig, really, what happened to any of them: it was merely an excellent chance to annoy her stepmother! . . . What to do — what to do! Would it not be wrong to steal Dunois' birthright? to bestow it on her ewe lamb, whom she was conscious of loving too well as it was? . . .

Madame de Longueville asked her friends for advice, wrote long letters to all her relations, badgered Father Singlin, her confessor, as well as the good nuns at Port Royal and the Carmelites' convent, until everybody was heartily sick of the subject. Meanwhile, the object of all this tender confusion stood aloof, waiting again, as usual — cynically aware of the secret motives underlying his mother's distress.

What would have happened in the end, it was impossible to guess — had not Dunois, surprisingly, taken matters into his poor, faltering hands and run away to Rome to be a priest.

Then, when one might have imagined that the worst of his troubles were over, began the dullest and longest waiting of all. Saint-Paul was Duc de Longueville at last — but he had nothing to do! His cousin the King refused point-blank to give him a post either in the army or the civil service. It had been made manifest from the beginning that he could not hope for his father's government — nor would he be considered for a military command.

Longueville understood well enough why. He read the look in his cousin's eyes clearly at their first meeting — the look that said, without need of words: 'Your mother was a dangerous and intriguing woman. Your father was dangerous, too. They tried for years to upset my kingdom — I'll take damned good care you never get a chance to follow their example!'

So that was that! The new Duke might fret as he pleased, make vain attempts to buy this charge and that, strut his way uneasily through various minor campaigns, meanwhile wasting his youth and gold and none-too-robust health on a round of aimless dissipation — until he met Magdelon de la Ferté.

Oh, there'd been women before — plenty of them! — for few were strong enough to resist the combined lure of a lustrous name and the youth's charming, insinuating manners. Young girls he despised, finding their conversation insipid and their dowries insufficient to tempt him. He'd paid court instead to a whole list of mature beauties, some of whom, truth to tell, he had met in his mother's own drawing-room. . . .

Magdelon was different. Hang it all! *Of course* she was, no matter what Guiche said, or anyone else! From the first day he met her Longueville felt that. It seemed odd now to think how nearly he *hadn't* met her, how close he had come to refusing his first invitation to the Hôtel de Senneterre, relayed to him by the Comte de Fiesque. He hadn't wanted to go in the least — he'd said so a dozen times —: in the end he'd given in, his inertia overcome by Fiesque's drawling insistence: 'I say, you know, my boy, you can't let me down — I've *promised* to bring you!'

The Maréchale, it appeared, had 'sent for' the Duke. She had said to Fiesque, with the easy arrogance of a beauty accustomed to having her slightest wishes regarded as orders: 'Why does Monsieur de Longueville not come to call? I see him everywhere with other women — in the Cours, at the playhouse, at the palace in Saint-Germain. Yet, I know not for what reason, he salutes me coldly, and leaves it at that.'

Fiesque had told her then that his friend's timidity was responsible for his negligent ways — which gave the two young men a hearty laugh. The truth was that Longueville knew the La Fertés only slightly. He had been a child in the days of Magdelon's early social successes; she was much older than he, yet not old enough to have formed part of his mother's circle. And he'd begun his career in the army just as the Maréchal was ending his. He admired Madame de la Ferté whenever he saw her, but he saw her seldom . . . and God knew, it wasn't women who were lacking in his life! . . .

So he went with the Count that afternoon expecting nothing, regretting nothing, even thinking of nothing in particular.

His first sight of the mistress of Great Senneterre changed everything for him forever. She was seated in a high-backed chair in one of the garden windows of the Gallery of Aminta — all in rose-coloured velvet, a cherry-red ribbon binding her curls. It was spring — he remembered afterwards, inconsequently — and thrushes were whistling in the garden.

Longueville stared and stared — he felt he had never seen her before, never, really, seen *any* woman! — There were other people in the room — indeed, many other people, for it was one of the Maréchale's reception days: she was surrounded by the usual crowd of vapid and noisy young men, each of them bent on securing as much of her notice as possible for himself. (Longueville spotted Effiat and Marsan and that insufferable ass of a Tallard — just the set of feckless riffraff he despised and particularly avoided at court.)

But somehow it was as if they had been alone together. As she gave him her hand her velvet-brown eyes met his blue ones in a long look — not challenging, rather thoughtful and gently questioning. Then she smiled suddenly — as though the question had been answered — a childlike smile, and said in a matter-of-fact tone, such as she might have used had they been in the habit of meeting every day: 'How do you do, Your Highness? You look very happy this afternoon.'

Longueville wanted to shout out: 'I *am* happy! Why shouldn't I be? I've just fallen in love with the most marvellous creature in the world!'

Naturally, however, being a well-schooled courtier, he did nothing of the kind. He stammered instead something noncommittal about the sun in his eyes having blinded him — then, in a moment, recovered himself sufficiently to turn the remark into a compliment on his hostess's charms, which Magdelon accepted gracefully.

The rest of their encounter passed in general conversation. They had no opportunity to talk in private: Magdelon would not let him stay when her guests rose to go, but dismissed him with the others, so that he was forced to content himself with kissing the tips of her fingers and receiving a conventional parting smile.

Yet she did not look surprised when he appeared at her lever next morning at an hour so early that none but intimate friends could have hoped for admittance. She was seated in front of her toilet-table, having her curls brushed by her waiting-maid. But as soon as Longueville entered she sent the maid out of the room, turned to her visitor, and said simply: 'I told the Swiss this morning I would be at home to one man in all Paris. Can you guess who it is?'

Within a week they were madly in love — within a month all Paris knew it — within a year she was expecting his child.

Longueville found peace with his new mistress, and contentment such as he had never dreamed of. Why would he not have been con-tented? Magdelon did everything in her power to please him. She was, thought Longueville, the most sensible woman he'd ever known — absolutely the only one to realize that the secret of success for lovers lay in the female's giving way to the male every time. How simple it was, after all! Why did not more women see...? Before the first month was up, Madame de la Ferté's little imperious airs, her front of self-assurance and self-sufficiency, had quite disappeared. They were not, as in her sister's case, an indication of character so much as a smoke screen thrown out to conceal her secret humility. She was no longer queen of a court: because Longueville objected to rivals, the vapid and noisy young men had all been banished.... She did not seem to miss them. With youthful intensity she gave herself utterly to whatever feelings possessed her — whether joy or pain — and, in those early days of their love, they had been almost pure joy. Magdelon was content to drift on from day to day, from month to month — from year to year, really — without asking what was to become of them. In the end, Longueville himself came to be affected by his mistress's carefree attitude. Something would hap-pen, of course — something was sure to happen before very long — that would decide things for them in spite of themselves. Mean-while, life was nearly perfect as it was.

When the Polish affair materialized out of a clear sky, two years had elapsed since the lovers' first meeting in the Gallery of Aminta, and the Duke was as deeply devoted as ever. The birth of Charles-Louis had forged even closer ties between him and Charles-Louis' mother. At the same time, he was too astute not to be beginning to see that the liaison must soon end. For one thing, he had to marry. The state of his fortune made it necessary. He could not marry Magdelon because she was not free — and even if she were, the match would have been impossible from every point of view. No doubt the crown of Poland was a blessing in more ways than one....

This did not mean that it would not be a fearful wrench to part from her, to say nothing of parting from little Charles-Louis. Longueville was full of tenderness for them both. Before leaving Paris he had taken steps to assure his son's future. In his will, drawn up just a few days before joining the army (it seemed odd, at his age, to be making a will — but, after all, when you were going to war, you never knew what might happen!), he left Charles-Louis half a million francs in cash, to be realized from the sale of his furniture and other personal effects, as well as the fine estate of Graville in Normandy. So that, in any case, the lad would not be a pauper.

He told Magdelon what he had done — and she had cried and cried, and clung to him, and said that he must not speak of such terrible things. He told his mother, also, begging her to use her influence with the court to have Charles-Louis legitimized, if it were possible to do so without naming Magdelon.... Madame de Longueville, who had not known before that there *was* a Charles-Louis, had been exceedingly shocked — she, too, had cried a great deal — but finally she promised to help her son; in return, to please her, *he* promised to make a general confession before setting out for Flanders. And he had kept his word — so *that* was all right. ...

Longueville thought about little Charles-Louis far more than he cared to admit. The idea of being a father fascinated him, the mysteriousness of the continuity of life! There was that other being, at once a part of you and quite outside of you.... How could it be borne to leave him, and never know? ... Well, he would do what he could to watch over his heir from afar. Not much, of course, was necessary yet. Charles-Louis' health and education would be safe enough in good Porlier's hands. Later, however, the Duke meant to see to it himself that the boy was launched on his military career under the best auspices. Perhaps he would do what his father had not done — perhaps he'd have chances that had passed Longueville by. At all events, France and Poland were allies, thank Heaven! so that some day they were assured of meeting....

It had been devilish hard saying good-bye to Magdelon. But he had got through it somehow — and it was better so, best for them both. In the future — though he would never forget his love — Longueville hoped he might be too busy to miss her as sharply as he was missing her now. Of course, that would be the way of it! Confound it! A king must have other matters on his mind of greater importance than a passion for any woman! Look at his cousin Louis — a model in that as in all other departments of a monarch's duty! ...

Well, to sum up, thought the Duke, everything would have been ideal — or not far from it — if it had not been for Guiche. His thoughtless, jeering words shed a new and horribly revealing light on the celebrated Longueville-La Ferté affair. In the beams of that light Charles-Paris saw himself all too plainly in a most unpleasant rôle, heretofore unsuspected. Good God! Could the Count be right? Was that really how people looked at him and poor Magdelon — as a besotted boy in the toils of a fading siren old enough to be his mother? ... It made no difference that to him she was not a fading siren: if the world thought her one, then, alas! for all practical purposes, she *was* one. There was nothing to be done about it.... 'The old girl — old woman La Ferté!' The cruel phrases stung his mind like a whip, drove the angry red high in his cheeks, started throbbing through his brain in torturing time with the pound of Pegasus' hoofs on the dusty highroad. He would never forget them — never — *never!* Damn Guiche! Damn *everyone!* It was spoilt now, that

Olympian vision of a noble farewell to his lovely and generous mistress. High drama had been turned into burlesque farce — Racine to Molière, at a moment's notice!...

Worst of all, his humiliation seemed to be strangely involved with his wrath at being 'left out of things,' as he expressed it, by Guiche and Uncle Condé. Easy enough, now, to see why they'd done it. They thought him a mere babe, an infatuated suckling, tied to a hag's apronstrings.... Well! He would have to prove they were wrong, and that as quickly as possible. Yes! More and more surely he saw that there was one way, and one way alone, to clear his honour and show them he was a man as good as other men — as good as *they* were, no less! He must perform an heroic deed — something fine and unheard-of and dashing.... But *what?*

All day long the Duke went on brooding over what had befallen him and the steps he must take to win back his lost esteem in the eyes of his fellows. He had plenty of time for these gloomy thoughts, as the journey proved quite uneventful. They saw no trace of the enemy the whole way, and little enough of their own men; when they arrived at the camp of the Duc de Luxembourg, on the Yssel, just across from the frowning fortress of Doesburg, where the Prince of Orange was, there seemed to be nothing to do save deliver the dispatch from Turenne and bow themselves out. Monsieur de Luxembourg received them agreeably, gave Longueville and the Comte de Roye an excellent dinner in his tent, and sent them back late in the afternoon with an answer to the message they had brought.

It was dull routine work.... On the way home, the sun felt hotter than ever. To avoid its rays Longueville decided to keep away from the shadeless river road, so they struck off instead through the comparative cool of the woods, on a wandering path that only once came within sight of the Rhine. This, as it happened, was directly opposite the enemy's fort of Tollhuis, which the Duke desired to inspect. Riding down over a sloping meadow to the water's edge they found Uncle Condé, who, also on horseback, was slowly following the course of the river.

Uncle Condé did not appear surprised to see his nephew, but at the same time, the latter noted suspiciously, he offered no explanation of his presence there alone so late in the day. After rapping out a few businesslike questions about the state of affairs in Luxembourg's army he handed his field glasses to Longueville and pointed out the enemy's camp on the other side of the river, where the Dutch soldiers were swarming about in the red slanting sunlight.

'Guiche tells me they've doubled their garrison since yesterday,' said Uncle Condé. 'But at that, I'll wager we've still treble their number of cannon and ten times as many men. Oh, if I could only get at them!'

Nevertheless, he maintained, in answer to Longueville's eager inquiries, that no means had been found of crossing the river except by a bridge, and it would take two days at least to build that.

'Go home, lad, and rest,' said the old Prince wearily. 'That's the best thing you can do. You look as white as a sheet, and your men must be fairly well fagged out by this weather. It's hard on us all, God knows! Perhaps you will find the envoys from Poland waiting in camp. That would prove some diversion for you.' (This speech caused Longueville to sputter inwardly.... It was terrible! Unbearable! Uncle Condé talked as though he were a child to be distracted by toys.... But there was nothing one could say.)

Monsieur the Prince rode back up the meadow with the troop and reined in his flea-bitten grey on the outskirts of the wood, where he bade his nephew good-bye. Longueville turned round in his saddle once or twice to find Uncle Condé still watching him, a quizzical smile on his lips. Slowly the older man raised his arm in salute....

The road back to camp through the forest, although somewhat cooler, was certainly longer than the direct route along the Rhine. It was late when Longueville's party at length crossed the crest of the hill and came in sight of the city of tents — so late that the sun had already set an hour before, leaving only a faint greenish-yellow tinge on the horizon. The swallows had deserted their hunting grounds by the river; here and there the dark, industrious shape of a bat flitted silently by.

Tired and discouraged, the Duke crossed the familiar stubbly field, letting Pegasus go as he pleased. There was no chance of missing the way, with the torch flares from the camp to guide them. Longueville was so deeply engrossed in his own reflections that he failed to observe there were fewer torches than usual; it was the Comte de Roye, dismounting to give his hand to his chief, who remarked on this and asked Bourgneuf, the Duke's equerry, what it meant.

'Why, sir,' replied Bourgneuf, 'half the camp's broken up and left. About two hours before sundown they went, six thousand horsemen or so, with the King at their head.'

The Count smothered an oath.

'Gad! You don't say so! Your Highness, did you hear that?'

Longueville pricked up his ears.

'Where were they going, Bourgneuf?'

'Well, Your Highness, I'm not sure — but I heard some talk from the ostlers of their taking the river road to the north along towards Tollhuis. It seems there was a message from your uncle Monsieur the Prince. They say he sent for the King to sup with him. There's a rumour, sir, of a surprise move against the enemy — fording the Rhine, or some such business — but no one here can rightly tell what is in it.'

At that, some string seemed to snap in Longueville's brain. Quite literally, stars exploded in front of his eyes, whole bouquets and constellations of rockets, like the fireworks let off for a garden party at court. In a blinding flash all became painfully clear, and remained so: the fruitless errand on which he'd been sent, the empty road they had travelled, Uncle Condé's odd behaviour by the river — most of all, the sudden, secret departure of the King and his cavalry.... Yes, mark that especially! Not ordinary foot-soldiers, who would be useless in this particular form of attack — but the Light Horse Troops and the Cuirassiers.... His worst suspicions, then, had been only too well grounded. Guiche had found a way to cross the Rhine, after all! God! What a master stroke. What a superb action of gallantry it would be! A heaven-sent opportunity, if ever there was one, for a man to distinguish himself in the field, and win his spurs before his sovereign for all the world to see.... And so he alone was to be left out of it — cheated of his chance for glory — wrapped in swaddling-clothes and kept safe from harm — all on account of those damned Polish envoys! To hell with the Poles, anyhow! What did he care for them and their paltry crown? His comrades were crossing the Rhine tonight without him. *Without him?* Well, he'd see about that.

'Bourgneuf' — His Highness's voice sounded thin and shrill — 'What time did you say the King left?'

'Some hours before sunset, Your Highness. Well, let's say about six o'clock, at a guess.'

'And they were bound for my uncle's camp?'

'Yes, Your Highness. So I was told. But indeed ——'

'Six o'clock. That means they can't get there before nine, at the earliest — and it'd have to be damned good going, at that! Nine o'clock — why, it's nearly nine now! But the troops will need rest, and Monsieur the Prince must confer with His Majesty. They'll hardly attack before dawn. I've still time, I think — I'm *sure* I have time!... Bourgneuf, saddle my horse at once!'

'Saddle your horse, sir! But he *is* saddled — you've just dismounted, sir!'

'Fool! I don't mean Pegasus. Another horse, of course! Lord! Of all the stupid...! Have a good strong one ready for me at — say, at ten o'clock precisely. I'm going to get a bite to eat — and then we'll see whether my uncle or I will have the last word concerning a little matter that lies between the two of us!'

Afterwards, Longueville could scarcely recall how he spent the rest of the night. He had lost the power of connected thought, but by some dispensation his actions appeared to take care of themselves. Though he could not command them consciously, his body obeyed his inmost impulses, as if his mind had passed into his muscles.

For instance, he did not know he was hungry, but his belly told him that he must eat — a hearty meal, too, for it had been long since he'd dined, and the blazing midday heat had allowed him small appetite for Monsieur de Luxembourg's sumptuous repast. Then, with automaton swiftness, a change of boots — clean linen — and a quick douse of cold water on his sunburnt cheeks. No questions answered — there was no time for questions! (Shut up, you idiots, and do as you're told!) He paused only for the briefest of interviews with Fiesque and Montchevreuil, who had been waiting in their friend's tent to report that the Poles had sent word from Wesel that they would pay their respects in the morning. With scrupulous exactness the Duke repeated his orders for their reception, in almost the same words he had used earlier in the day.... After that, tired as he was — but was he really tired any more? Longueville doubted it! — off to mount his fresh steed and gallop away into the night.... Alone? Of course, he was going alone! No, not even Fiesque and the little Chevalier should come with him this time.... Lost? Nonsense! How could he get lost? Why, damn it! he could find his way to Uncle Condé's camp blindfolded, if necessary! Hadn't he travelled it often enough in the last three days?... It was only a pity that he couldn't ride Pegasus, but the gallant beast was obviously played out by the heat and the long hours jog-trotting on the stony highways.... Well, this roan stallion with the Roman nose was not too bad. Strange, he had never tried him before. (Was he one of the last Norman lot?)

While his horse carried him on at a furious pace, Longueville's mind slid further and further into a coma. Now well beyond reasoned cerebration, one phrase kept repeating itself in his muddled head — later, he even found himself saying it aloud: '*I'll* show them — *I'll* show them! You see if I don't!'

In spite of the roan stallion's undoubted stamina and speed, it was long after midnight before the Duke drew near his uncle's camp. He had forgotten how dark it would be without a moon to guide him; several times the patches of forest, insignificant by day, proved confusing enough to force him to retrace his steps and puzzle out the path. When he emerged from the shadow of the last clump of trees to strike the open road again, the long straight stretch that led directly to the meadow opposite Tollhuis, cocks were crowing unseen in village farmyards and the sky had begun to turn grey. Stars twinkled palely remote — somewhere a church-tower clock struck three — a faint, cool breeze, surest sign of the coming dawn, blew through the reeds at the water's edge.

But now sounds of another sort started reaching his ears: the blare of trumpets, the rattle of sabres, shrill neighing of horses, an occasional gunshot — loudest of any, men's voices shouting hoarsely.

Longueville could not hear what they were shouting about, nor could he see what was happening, for the Rhine bent sharply here to the left, and the spit of sand forming the bend was covered by a screen of bushes and thick, untidy undergrowth. He spurred the roan stallion on to a supreme effort, crashed through the bushes he hardly knew how, and finally reached the meadow across from the fort of Tollhuis.

The scene before him sent a thrill of excitement mounting to his head. The French army was drawn up in full battle array, as was the enemy's on the opposite bank — but what was this in between them? The river was full of dark objects — moving black blobs in the swift, steely greyness — that resolved themselves into horses with riders — horses nickering aloud their alarm, plunging and churning the Rhine water to muddy foam. The animals were evidently frantic with fear, yet they continued to push forward towards the farther shore. To turn back was hopeless: those who did so were at once swept downstream by the force of the raging current. Longueville could see, as the light grew stronger, the Comte de Guiche on his chestnut charger at the head of the troop — hear his high voice screaming orders, telling the men to come on, not to be afraid; for the water was deep for a few yards only.

That was true. . . . In a minute or two the chestnut was already able to stand — soon a whole row of horses were floundering in the farther shallows. But just as the danger appeared over, the enemy's guns in the fort opened fire, to be echoed by the fire of the French artillery on the heights above the German bank of the Rhine. The battle was on in earnest. 'Hurrah!' cried Longueville. . . . For he had not got there too late, after all.

But what to do to get into it? The roan stallion was sagging beneath even its master's inconsiderable weight, its sides heaving and streaked darkly with sweat; obviously it was no longer fit to attempt the passage of the river. Longueville sprang to earth and glanced wildly about in search of a substitute. The bank on which he was standing was more and more crowded with horses jostling one another as their riders forced them down towards the water. By this time the advance guard had nearly all managed to get across — from the increased gunfire round the fort one could tell that the fighting was well under way — but they were being closely crowded from behind by other squadrons of the King's Cuirassiers. Prancing and whinnying in protest, pawing the soft mud of the brink in a last desperate endeavour to keep their footing, the heavy beasts splashed into the stream one after another, still others pressing upon them from the rear. Longueville saw no rider he knew. Help was not to be looked for here. Half crazy with rage and impatience, he began running up and down the field, wringing his hands and shouting to someone — to *anyone!* . . . But nobody noticed him.

Suddenly a small boat shot out into the river from the sheltering thicket of bushes on the sand-spit; it was manned by four peasants, who were pulling on their oars as hard as they could to stem the strength of the current. In the boat, standing muffled to the ears in their long military cloaks, were three officers. Even in the livid half-light Longueville recognized Enghien and Marsillac and, tallest of all in the bow, the hawk-like silhouette of his Uncle Condé.

The devils! Would they succeed in checkmating him to the very end?... Rapidly the boat made its way towards mid-channel, avoiding with skill the plunging mounts of the Cuirassiers.... Longueville hurried down to the brink once more and waved his hat to attract their attention. When that produced no result, he cupped his hands round his mouth and bawled at the top of his lungs: 'Uncle! Uncle! Come back! — or by God! I'll swim the river!'

This frantic move at length took effect. Enghien, at the end of the boat nearest the shore, heard his cousin's agonized voice topping the tumult and nudged Uncle Condé, who thereupon raised his right hand in token that he would answer the appeal. The boatmen reversed the direction of their oars; in a few moments the stern thrust itself in amongst the reeds, and Longueville — hatless, breathless, sobbing with relief — waded out through the shallow water and climbed aboard.

There was no time for explanations, even if they could have been heard above the noise of the firing, which by now had grown heavy and fairly continuous. Longueville crouched in the bottom of the boat, gasping to recover his wind.... Well, he was there at last! They hadn't been able to cheat him of his chance. Now for a horse! — and he'd be in the thick of the fray with the best of them!... Bullets spattered the surface of the water — but it made no difference to him. He did not even take notice of the screaming horses and riders around them. A soldier, swimming so close to the boat that the Duke might have touched him, groaned as a Dutch marksman shattered one hand — but with the other he still kept aloft the streaming silk of his regimental banner.... How long the passage lasted, the young man neither knew nor cared. He felt rather than heard the boat grounding on the mud bank; then, rallying all his forces, leaped to his feet and, pushing his cousin and Marsillac unceremoniously to one side, was ashore almost as quickly as Uncle Condé himself.

It was hard to tell what was happening here. Smoke from the guns hung in clouds round the fort, disclosing only brief glimpses of the battle in progress. Men on horseback galloped back and forth, drums beat, trumpets blared, Guiche went on shouting through the confusion. On the whole, it seemed that the French were in command of the situation, that enough of their soldiers to outnumber the enemy had succeeded in getting across.

In the other direction, however, to the right of their landing place, a small detachment of Dutch infantry appeared in a ragged, wavering line in front of a coppice of low-growing willows and alders. Their retreat to the fort having been cut off, the men were running aimlessly to and fro, obviously lacking a leader: one of their number, more intelligent than the rest, was attempting to fasten a scrap of white cloth to a stick, evidently feeling resistance to be useless.

Cowardly beggars! Wouldn't they even fight for their lives?...

'Come, boys!' shouted Longueville, to the last group of Cuirassiers emerging from the water. 'Let's cut 'em to pieces! Kill! Kill! And give no quarter!'

Looking desperately about him for a horse he could ride, he spied a groom in the Duc d'Enghien's livery holding a smart English pony in readiness for his master's use: they were both dripping wet, having apparently just swum the river. Longueville did not hesitate. Heedless of his cousin's protest and Uncle Condé's horrified exclamation, he seized the pony's bridle, vaulted into the saddle, and, repeating his cry of 'No quarter! No quarter!', dashed off at full speed towards the coppice.

His long yellow hair flying in the breeze, he slashed left and right with his sword, while the Dutchmen fell back dismayed. A thunder of hoofs behind him told him that he was not alone in his adventure. ... Nearer and nearer the willows they drew.... Now Longueville could see the Dutch soldier holding the flag on a stick — the fellow's eyes were wide with terror — he dropped the flag, flinging up both hands in a gesture of surrender.

Bullets sang past his ears, but the Duke did not care.... Faster and faster.... And then, without knowing how it happened, he found himself lying on his back on the spongy turf, staring up at the water weeds, whose white flowered heads nodded now, strangely, against the dawn-streaked sky, far, very far above him. The horses behind pelted by, missing his face as if by a miracle. In the distance drums went on beating, trumpets sounding, while, although he felt no pain, a great red stain spread over the white-and-gold front of His Highness's coat.

'Spoiled a damned good uniform,' he said lazily, to himself. 'I'll have to dig up another for those blasted Poles....'

And that was the last thought that Charles-Paris, Duc de Longueville, ever had.

BOOK FOUR

THE CHILDREN
(April, 1675 — January, 1689)

'OF COURSE, MY DEAR, I DON'T PUT IT IN WORDS,' SAID CATEAU, WHO
had done little else for the last six weeks, 'but say what you will, it's
an impossible match. I don't mean because Henri is my nephew —
naturally, that has nothing to do with the case! But he is — or,
rather, *was*, worse luck! — an excellent parti. You can't deny that.
Son of a maréchal of France, heir to a dukedom, colonel of his own
infantry regiment, to say nothing of being governor of all those towns
in Lorraine his papa turned over to him only last year — think of it!
Why, the Toucy's a nobody compared to him! *Her* father may have
been a maréchal, too; but he came of very plain people in Picardy
and hadn't a penny to bless himself with. And she certainly has no
beauty to boast of. Her sisters have some pretensions to looks, especially Doudou de Ventadour, though her figure's a fright and I've
never been able to see what you find to admire in her complexion.
But all the La Mothes have heads too big for their bodies — and the
Toucy's no exception to the rule. An ill-favoured, underbred chit, if
I ever ... Well, that's neither here nor there. She's got hold of
Henri, by what sly means I don't pretend to explain — after all,
she's three years older than that poor innocent! — and she'll be a
duchess some day, whether we like it or not. They're married now,
so I haven't a word to say. Not a solitary word. I've kept out of the
affair from beginning to end. But there are limits to even *my* patience. For instance, take this party Henri and his wife are giving
today. It's a matter of perfect indifference to me whether I go to it
or not. To tell the truth, I'd much rather not go. It's sure to be
deadly dull — that sort of duty-dinner always is! And I'd be willing
to wager that Gabrielle is a shocking bad housekeeper. But that's
not the point. The point is, I should have been asked. It's more than
a party, you see: in a way, it's a symbol — a young couple's first
entertainment after their wedding — for you might call it their first.
They were married in Lent; it wouldn't have been in good taste to
try anything spectacular then. But now Easter's over, as Magdelon
says, there's just time before the men go off for the summer campaign to put on a really good show — and I do honestly feel I ought
at least to have been given an opportunity of refusing!'

Madame d'Olonne set her coffee-cup down in its saucer, leaned back in her chair, smoothed the long, shining folds of her dressing-gown of honey-coloured satin, and glanced with intention across the depleted breakfast-table at Fervaques, who was pretending, unsuccessfully, to be immersed in the pages of the *Mercure Galant* for the month of April, 1675.

'My love,' said Fervaques, 'I'm sure I wish that you had been! As it is, you know the La Fertés would have been only too glad to include you. . . . It's on account of my mother. . . . After all, Gabrielle is her niece.'

But this did not serve him. . . . 'Well, Henri is *my* nephew — yes, and my favourite, too! He's been almost like a son to me always,' declared Cateau, with a ring of absolute conviction that did not falter before the mild astonishment in her lover's eyes. 'I stayed away deliberately from the wedding ceremony, because I didn't want to risk stirring up unnecessary trouble, and from the bridal feast besides. I didn't even show myself next day at the official reception at Great Senneterre. In fact, I did all I could to consider the feelings of your relatives. You can't deny it. But, as I say, there are limits to everything. It seems to me it's high time that somebody showed a little consideration for *me*. Why, it's disgusting for the family to plan a party of this size and ask everybody — positively everybody in the whole connection, down to the last little insignificant country cousin — except the bridegroom's own aunt! And then, to add insult to injury, haven't they even dared to ask you to come without me, when they know very well that we're living together?'

She began to beat a nervous, incessant tattoo with her fingernails on the bread-plate. Fervaques looked distressed. What had got into Cateau this morning? He could not understand it. There'd been one tremendous explosion, of course, a week ago, the day she heard for the first time about the dinner. That was inevitable; he'd been prepared for it; they had threshed the matter out once and, one could not help hoping, for all time. Since then neither had alluded to it again, and Cateau had reverted to her former practice of making small caustic sallies at the expense of her niece-in-law. This sudden burst of spleen was therefore as unexpected as it was unpleasant. What could have happened to cause it? . . . Five minutes before, when they took their places at table, all was apparently well. Cateau's smile, if not precisely lively, had diffused its accustomed pale beams of languid benevolence. Fervaques, who had not lived with her four years for nothing, was gloomily positive that no act of his mistress, however unreasoned it seemed, could be safely dismissed as inconsequential. He squirmed in his seat and cleared his throat tentatively several times before speaking.

'Dear madam,' he managed to get out at last, 'I do entreat you not to take it so hard! After all, isn't our living together just the trouble? I mean, most people do know now about us — and, naturally, from my mother's point of view ——'

'Bother your mother's point of view! I'm sick to death of hearing you quote her. If you're convinced she's right about everything, why in Heaven's name don't you go back to her? I'm sure I'd not lift a finger to stop you. All I must say is, I never expected to live to hear *you* reproach me for what I've done for your sake. Are these the thanks I get for my years of devotion? Don't forget, my dear, I was very well off when I met you — very well off indeed! I had a house of my own, plenty of money to do what I liked with, and a charming circle of friends who were all perfectly devoted to me. I was a decent woman in those days, and I led a decent and God-fearing life. I could have looked anyone square in the eye.... Well, of course, there may have been one or two little things in the past — I don't say there weren't — but that was *long ago*,' said Cateau firmly, 'and everybody'd forgotten about them. Then you came along and began making love to me. I held out as long as I could — I refused you over and over again — don't pretend not to remember how many times I refused you! But in the end I gave in, against my better judgement. Oh, I don't complain! I never have complained and I shan't begin now. I took the step with my eyes wide open. I gave up my home — my life — my social position — because I believed you needed me. I don't want to be thanked for that. All I ask is some recognition of my rights in the family. If you'd gone to Magdelon in the beginning and told her exactly how I felt ——'

'My dear, I did,' said Fervaques unhappily. 'You know I did— and she said she'd done her best to persuade the young people to invite you, but it was no use. Gabrielle wouldn't hear of it.'

'There you are! That's a proper answer for you! "Gabrielle wouldn't hear of it" — so of course it's not to be thought of! Who ever dreamed an upstart like that — Oh, if you were a man instead of a mollycoddle, you'd not stand by and let me be insulted so!'

'Dear love, what would you have me do? I've already told you a dozen times I'm more than willing to stay away from the damned party myself. Here! Let me send a note straight off to the Maréchal ...'

'Nonsense! What good would that do? It's not at all necessary.'

'Yes, but I will, though!' cried the goaded young man. 'I'd much rather! It'll put an end to this infernal business. I'll just ring for a pen and some paper ...'

'Nonsense!' said Cateau again, very loudly. 'I forbid you! Naturally, I expect you to go to the dinner and stay to the end. How else should I be able to find out who was there and what went on at it?'

She stopped tapping her plate for a minute and looked up, not so much at her lover as past him, towards a point above and a little beyond his head. Then she smiled suddenly, patted her hair, and began craning her neck this way and that. Fervaques, mystified at first by her behaviour, recalled presently that there was a mirror over the mantelpiece on the wall behind his chair.

This mirror was the Countess's latest acquisition; it had, in fact, arrived from Italy the night before and been hung by her orders only an hour ago. A handsome Venetian glass in a heavily carved gilt frame, it was the finishing touch in the octagonal chamber known as the 'Chinese cabinet' that Cateau had just created to serve as an upstairs sitting-room adjoining her private apartments. Her friends united in pronouncing it 'delicious' and 'highly original': the walls were panelled in lacquer — colonies of tiny men and women bearing lanterns and fans depicted in black and gold against a background of sealing-wax red — and the panels were joined by long strips of looking-glass in baroque shapes. The exotic note was further emphasized by groups of fine oriental crystals and porcelains standing on the mantel and the twin gilt console-tables that flanked it, while in the window overlooking the court, gay this morning with April sunshine, swung a scarlet lacquer cage full of bright-hued parakeets, whose discordant shrieks provided an appropriate obbligato to Cateau's matutinal tantrums.

Poor Cateau! Fervaques was really very sorry for her, though he did not know in the least what to do about it. These odd fits of ill-temper were growing more and more frequent lately. . . . It was all most perplexing. . . . However, once she'd begun admiring herself in the glass, one might feel reasonably sure that the worst was over. The young man relaxed with a sigh and returned to the *Mercure Galant* . . . while his mistress repeated her monologue with undiminished enthusiasm from beginning to end. At its conclusion three points remained clear: (A) that nobody knew what she'd given up for Fervaques; (B) that she had not the slightest desire to attend the La Fertés' dinner-party; and (C) that all the La Mothes had heads too big for their bodies.

Fervaques, smiling slightly, watched her narrow her eyes and shrug her shoulders and drum on the dishes as the effortless, expressive silver ribbon continued unfolding. There seemed to be no reason why it should not go on forever. . . . What finally stopped it was the entrance of one of the Countess's lackeys with word that Maître Le Caron had called to see Madame d'Olonne.

As the door opened to admit the lackey two huge shaggy grey wolfhounds bounded into the room, upsetting a chair in their passage, and rushed up to Fervaques, fawning upon him and licking his hands.

Fervaques patted their heads and scratched their ears....

'There, Cinna...there, Rodrigue!...Down, down!...Good dogs, I say!'

Cateau frowned and bit her lip, while the parakeets in the scarlet lacquer cage squawked their dismay.

'Show Le Caron upstairs immediately,' said Cateau, in a pinched tone, to the lackey. 'I'll see him in the library.'

She made no remark about Rodrigue and Cinna because she realized that it would have been useless. Fervaques gave her her way in everything else — but dogs he must and would have. As long as he was her guest, so to speak, at the Hôtel de Rouen, he had not made an issue of the matter; but directly they took this big house in the rue de la Sourdière on a joint leasehold he insisted upon it. There was nothing Cateau could do to prevent it. He was legally and morally within his rights. But she could and did show her disapproval, as now, when she rose from the table with deliberate disdain, picking up her train to avoid any possible contact with the great leaping animals.

'Sir, you'll forgive my leaving you?'

'Of course, dear, of course!'

Fervaques was sitting flat on the floor, frolicking with his pets.

Cateau eyed him with affectionate contempt. He was such a child, after all!...

'I shall be busy the rest of the morning, so I dare say I shan't see you before you set off for the Hôtel de Senneterre. Pray give my compliments to the Maréchal and my sister...'

'Yes, madam, certainly. But you? What diversion have you planned for the day? Will you be lonely in my absence?'

'Lonely?' said Cateau crisply. 'By no means! I, too, expect guests. Madame de Montglas and Madame de Montmorency are coming to dine.'

'That's all right, then,' said Fervaques, his brow clearing.

He jumped up from the floor and kissed Cateau's hand with respectful fervour.

'You know, my love, I could not bear to think of your being by yourself, today of all days.'

'I know,' said Cateau.

She gave him an amiable smile — her first of the morning — and trailed elegantly to the door.

'Don't trouble your head about me, dear friend. I shall be quite well amused. Mind you remember to tell me what everybody was wearing — especially Magdelon and the bride. I expect that snip of a Gabrielle will have on her sea-green velvet with the striped underskirt, the one that's so trying to her skin. Well, adieu, sir, once more...'

As she rustled out into the hall Fervaques caught a backward-floating murmur.

'...heads too big for their bodies,' fluted Cateau, in the distance.

For some reason she did not enjoy her interview with Maître Le Caron today so much as she had expected to do. This was a pity: it was also inexplicable, for the matter in hand should have been particularly absorbing: the lawyer had come to propose nothing less than a suit against her former husband, to recover the amount of forty-three thousand, seven hundred and seventy-seven francs. This substantial sum Olonne owed her, asserted Maître Le Caron, in part according to the terms of the financial settlement made at the time of their separation, in part owing to further accruements of principal inherited by Madame d'Olonne from the Marville estate. The Count was, of course, notoriously careless in business affairs; he was, moreover, at present in exile, together with a number of his cronies, out of favour with the King on account of their outspoken criticisms of government policies. The moment to attack him in court was therefore shrewdly chosen; Maître Le Caron was confident that his client would win her case.... 'A nice round nest-egg, madam, if I may say so — a nice round nest-egg for a rainy day,' he repeated several times, rolling the words round his tongue as if they were good to eat; while Cateau assented graciously.... 'But mind, now, *he* must be condemned to pay the costs as well,' she prudently added. (Cateau never named her husband unless it were necessary.) 'Else there'll be no profit in this for me. You legal men are all highway robbers!' ... And the little old lawyer grinned and rubbed his hands together and said that, naturally, that had been thought of, too — the Countess could rest assured that her interests would always be paramount with the firm of Gallois and Le Caron.

But all the time Cateau was examining parchment scrolls, and adding and subtracting endless columns of figures with lightning speed and deadly accuracy, part of her mind was vividly occupied with questions that had nothing to do with the snuffy black figure at her side or with Monsieur d'Olonne and his forty-three thousand, seven hundred and seventy-seven francs. She had almost forgotten, also, her annoyance over being excluded from the dinner-party, though, for form's sake, she went on muttering 'Heads too big for their bodies!' at increasing intervals for several minutes. Whatever she might say in moments of pique, she knew perfectly well the La Fertés were right: she and Madame de Bonnelle could not meet with propriety as long as she was living publicly as the mistress of Madame de Bonnelle's son.

As for Henri's choice of a wife — or, rather, the choice made for him by his father and mother — there was little point at this stage of the game in objecting to that. True, the Toucy was neither beautiful nor amiable; her dowry was small; she was older than her bride-groom; and her one claim to importance as maid-of-honour to Her Majesty Marie Thérèse had vanished, a year or so ago, when the flighty young maids were all dismissed and replaced by staid middle-aged matrons of the palace. But Cateau was candid enough to con-fess that her nephew was by no means so desirable a parti as he had been in the past. Though still very young, he had shown a head-strong obstinacy and a reckless devotion to pleasure that boded ill for his career in the army. His governments, too, if impressive on paper — the Town and Territory of Metz, Citadel and Bishopric of Verdun, Vic and Moyenvic, sounded imposing enough — together were worth very few francs' income a year. The Maréchal was old now, and definitely on the shelf; he and Magdelon, between them, had made a sad hash of their financial affairs. Worst of all, the lat-ter's position in society had been irreparably damaged by the birth of Charles-Louis.

The Longuevilles were in no way to blame for that. The dowager Duchess had respected her son's last wishes; she had even succeeded in getting the King to legitimize the child without naming its mother. (This had been astonishingly easy to arrange, since His Majesty was just then anxiously seeking a precedent that would enable him to do the same thing for his own bastards by Madame de Montespan.) But, somehow or other, the secret leaked out. In no time at all everybody seemed to have heard who was the mother of the or-phaned Chevalier de Longueville — everybody, that is, except the man who ought to have been most concerned in ascertaining his origin, old La Ferté himself. The Maréchal could not, or would not, admit the truth: there was even, in the period directly after the Duc de Longueville's tragic death, a kind of revival of romance in the conjugal relations of the couple, which resulted, to the general amaze-ment, in the birth of another baby whose parentage was not to be disputed. Small Cécil-Adelaïde joined the nursery at Great Senne-terre in October of the year 1673.

But though her husband might choose to condone her sin, for the public at large Madame de la Ferté was a ruined woman. And there was no doubt that most people felt she had done better than could be expected in securing so unimpeachable a daughter-in-law as Marie-Gabrielle-Isabelle-Angélique de la Mothe-Houdancourt, Mademoi-selle de Toucy.

So Magdelon and her family had no part in the preoccupied look that lingered in Cateau's blue eyes. Neither had her irritation with Fervaques, which had quite passed off and had never, in fact, been meant for him: it was merely his misfortune that he'd happened to be the sole target in sight.

Cateau was extremely fond of Fervaques. After four years of

domesticity that might just as well have been marriage, they were
still lovers. She no longer cherished illusions about the young man's
character; she saw now, quite plainly, that the Marquis was not destined to carve out a great career for himself, nor to bring back the
Bullions to the high estate they had enjoyed in his grandfather's day.
No: Fervaques was made of a different, more malleable metal than
his ancestor, the tough old finance minister. In spite of the many
battles he had fought, he had not advanced a single grade, but was
still only captain of a squadron in the Queen's Light Horse Troop. In
addition to his natural spinelessness, a kind of fatality dogged his
footsteps and saw to it that he was never in the right place at the
right time. At the very beginning of the war he had missed a golden
opportunity — through no fault of his own — by failing to take part
in the famous crossing of the Rhine de Tollhuis. That plum was reserved for the King's Cuirassiers; the Light Horse Troops were use-
fully, if ingloriously, engaged in protecting the artillery in the rear.
And since the first Dutch campaign, though the war had spread until now France was fighting Spain and Lorraine and the whole German Empire as well as the Low Countries, the poor boy had never
succeeded in distinguishing himself. One ray of hope there had been
last winter, after the Battle of Mülhausen in Alsace, when reports
reached Paris that Fervaques had ordered his squadron to march in
the nick of time to bring reënforcements to Turenne, thus turning defeat for the French into victory — but next week, alas! the truth got
out that somebody else had advised him to do it — and the last faint
flicker expired like the others.

However, he did his duty as best he was able — courage and
honesty none could deny him — and the mere fact that he was in the
army at all raised him above the rest of the Bullions. Besides, since
his brother Gallardon's death he had become the head of the family,
with a very large fortune at his disposal.

Cateau would never have been willing to acknowledge that this
sudden accession of wealth had anything to do with her decision to
cast her bonnet over the mill and live with her lover openly, but
nevertheless, when they took the house in the rue de la Sourdière together, it was pleasant to reflect that she would not have to shoulder
the expense alone.

It was the largest house she had ever lived in, and by far the
grandest, in a quiet, exclusive street of the Saint-Honoré quarter,
not a stone's throw from the church of Saint-Roch. They furnished
it with the utmost luxury; a greatly augmented domestic staff served
them in a style not unsuited to a prince of the realm. Here they
lived exactly as if they were married — but they were not married.
What would have been the use, now, even if she had been free? —
since no legal ceremony could possibly restore the Countess's lost

reputation. She felt that strongly; she realized, whatever she some-times said, that she had given up nothing for her lover because there had been nothing to give up. And after the first sensation aroused by their revolutionary step had abated, it appeared that she was really no worse off than before. People shrugged and smiled, and said: 'Oh, the *Olonne* —!' But they had said even nastier things when she'd been living a perfectly moral life by herself in the rue Villedo. It was not long before the excitement died down, and soon only Charlotte de Bonnelle's fulminations against the 'kidnapping,' as she wrathfully put it, were still occasionally heard as reminders that all was not as it ought to be in the handsome establishment in the rue de la Sourdière.

Nobody paid much attention, any more, to what Charlotte said. Then, too, Cateau and Fervaques were now so well off that it was hard to ignore them. They might not command the best company in Paris, but they were too rich not to be offered a fairly wide choice of the second-best — any men whom they liked, within reason, and any women not prudish nor so close to the court that they had to pretend to be.

Oh, no: Cateau's perturbation today had nothing to do with the life she led with Fervaques! She would have been greatly embar-rassed to put into words what it was that had upset her. But the underlying fear recurred several times during her conversation with Maître Le Caron. She could hardly wait till he bowed himself out to run back to the Chinese cabinet — now deserted save for Quentine, who was feeding the parakeets — and take her position once more in the precise spot where she had had the fatal first glimpse of that stranger in the glass.

Gingerly she seated herself in the chair she had occupied at the breakfast-table, gathered her gleaming draperies around her, and raised lovely, anxious eyes to the Venetian mirror in its gilt frame over the mantel. Was it possible? . . . Perhaps it was simply a fugi-tive impression — an unflattering effect of the morning light striking too crudely across her face, deepening the almost imperceptible lines about nose and mouth. Or it might be La Martin's last lotion was to blame; she had felt at the time that it was not altogether a success, and that her curls had displayed a slight carrotty tinge ever since. . . . A hairsbreadth alteration in her pose and the hateful picture was shattered in a trice. Full-face, Madame d'Olonne was still her be-witching, eternally youthful self. But she could not forget what she had seen. Preen and simper, revolve and strike attitudes as she might, the memory of the stranger must stay with her forever.

'Oh, Quentine,' cried Cateau, putting her fingers to her lips in the first unrehearsed gesture of her life, 'what shall I do? I'm an old woman!'

Chapter II

MADAME D'OLONNE'S DINNER-PARTY, THOUGH MUCH SMALLER THAN
the La Fertés', was no less important symbolically: it marked a mile-
stone in her life by renewing relations with two of her oldest friends.
One had had doubts at first about the wisdom of making the move —
old friends, thought Cateau, could be sometimes very embarrassing,
especially if their memories were good. And it had been years since
she had seen anything of Cécile de Montglas or Isabelle de Montmorency. The former, too, was a cousin of Monsieur d'Olonne's, an additional point of possible danger. She had not, however, espoused
the Count's cause at the time of his troubles with his wife, but had
remained neutral — poor Cécile! Doubtless she'd had troubles
enough of her own without taking on other people's.... Now, at
fifty-seven, she was a widow, having only a few weeks ago buried old
Montglas, who had left her two children, a son and a daughter; almost no money; and the manuscript of a volume of memoirs dealing
with the military and political affairs of his time. ('But they are
dreadfully dull, dear,' Cécile kept protesting. 'I'm afraid no one
will ever care to read them.')

Isabelle, in her way, had been equally unfortunate. She was ten
years younger than her boon companion, and had not yet lost her
husband — but really the Baron counted for so little that he might
just as well have been dead! She had two children, also, both boys,
born rather late in their mother's life, so that they were still of school
age. The Montmorencys were poor, grew poorer every year; and
though Madame de Montmorency toadied industriously to her great
friend, the wealthy Duchesse de Nemours, who was as unpopular as
she was eccentric — it was rather clever of Isabelle to concentrate on
a field she had practically to herself — her efforts, so far, had been
fruitless.

Neither of the ladies, it went without saying, had a rag of reputation left.

Cateau came across them one day at Mass at the Carmelites' in the
rue Bouloi. After the first startled stare they spoke to one another;
Cécile and Isabelle, indeed, waxed effusive; and at the end of a cordial ten minutes before the church door the Countess offered to drive
them home in her carriage. There was a moment of delicate hesita-

tion, but the offer was not refused. From that time on they met frequently, at the play, in the Cours, amongst the booths of the Fair of Saint-Germain. Whenever it happened gracious bows and smiles were exchanged; Cateau one day presented Fervaques, whereupon Cécile and Isabelle screwed up their eyes and screamed that they had not seen him since he was *so* high, but that they'd have known him anywhere for sweet Charlotte's son.

A suitable interval having elapsed — for it would not do to rush things — the matrons were bidden to dinner. This time there was no hesitation: both were 'enchanted' to accept. It couldn't, alas! Cateau explained, be a real party, in view of Madame de Montglas' recent bereavement — just the three of them, quite by themselves — that would be pleasantest, would it not? To which Cécile and Isabelle assented enthusiastically, protesting that this was precisely what would suit them best.

They arrived, nevertheless, on the appointed day dressed to kill in fashionable afternoon frocks. Cécile's, of course, was black, and she wore a widow's bandeau; but her air of mourning was confined to these conventional tokens of grief.

Cateau, even more elaborately gowned in a marvellous creation of lacquer-red velvet embroidered with gold (which would look wonderfully well in the Chinese cabinet, where she intended to sit after dinner), received her guests with unforced affability. She had prepared a Roman feast in their honour — Olonne himself, in his palmy days, could have done no better. Was it foolish to make such a fuss over two unimportant middle-aged women?... But she, too, was now middle-aged. Yes, best face the unpalatable fact as bravely as possible. No more definite proof was needed that they had all three reached — should one call it 'maturity'? — than the richness of the repast and the attire they had chosen to grace it. Old women who could afford it always lived too well — particularly, to be candid, old women who hadn't anything better to live for. They ate the best food, drank the rarest wines, wore the finest clothes they were able to get, because there was nothing else for them to do. Grooming and guzzling became ends in themselves.... It was horrible! horrible!...

Cateau shivered as she glanced from one carefully made-up, determinedly youthful mask to the other. Cécile and Isabelle were good-looking women still — especially Cécile, whom time had mellowed, and who was now quite distinguished with her fine dark eyes set off by a frame of silvery curls. Isabelle, more pronounced and aggressive — the school of adversity having sharpened rather than softened her militant angles — was yet handsomer than in her youth. She and Cécile returned their hostess's covert stares with interest, frankly appraising the changeless gold-and-white marble loveliness. (But ah, God! in spite of her splendid assurance, how perishable Cateau knew it to be! How grimly she fought nowadays to preserve what had once seemed a permanent blessing!) ... No doubt they were attempting uncharitably to compute her age. ... Well, try as you will, two-and-forty, my dears, is the most you'll be able to make it — and that's a point neither of *you* will be passing again!

The three 'my-dear-madam'd' one another scrupulously throughout the meal. It had been so long since the days of their early intimacy that they were shy of employing a more personal form of address. That would assuredly follow all in good time. Meanwhile, the guests politely praised every dish that was passed them, paid the Countess graceful compliments on her looks, her gown, the corps of well-trained lackeys that attended to their wants at table. And after dinner when they were shown about the house their admiration knew no limits.

Cateau displayed her new domain with complacency. She knew, she could not help knowing, that the hôtel in the rue de la Sourdière was a triumph, a crushing proof of the sureness of her taste and the length of her purse; in fact, a kind of private museum. The most unique item in her collection, however, the young master thereof, she took pains scarcely to mention: it was enough to wave her hand towards a door on the ground floor with a casual 'Those are Monsieur de Fervaques' rooms,' and to savour in silence the wry smiles of Isabelle (*her* husband was sixty, if a day) and the even less lucky Cécile (for hers was a corpse). ...

Having reduced both her friends to a state of speechless envy, Madame d'Olonne led the way to the Chinese cabinet, where a fire had been laid in the grate under the traitorous Venetian mirror. Here the ladies established themselves in comfortable armchairs, while a lackey fetched each of them a footstool and then a tray with glasses and decanters of rossolis and ratafia. The gaily-coloured parakeets shrieked their defiance, Madame de Montglas and Madame de Montmorency produced their embroidery, and Cateau took up a somewhat chewed-looking piece of tapestry she'd been working at spasmodically for years (because Fervaques had once told her her hands never looked whiter or slimmer than when so employed). And then they began to gossip. ...

It was not — to begin with, at any rate — especially ill-natured gossip, although they all said things they could not have said at table before Cateau's myriad domestics. There was a good deal to be touched on concerning the war — Cécile being confident that Turenne knew what he was doing in Germany, Isabelle quite as positive that he did not. The surprising retreat of Madame de Montespan to her castle of Clagny was also exhaustively discussed. On this point as well opinions were divided. Madame de Montglas (the most hopeful of the company) felt that the favourite's gesture of re-

pentance must be sincere and that she and her royal lover, swayed
by religious scruples, had definitely decided to give each other up.
Madame de Montmorency, on the contrary, contended that the
whole business was a blind, cunningly calculated to deceive the
court bigots and the nation at large.

'Oh, my dears, don't tell *me* —!' said Isabelle. 'The Montespan
knows what she's about. You can depend upon that. Look at the
way she got rid of that silly slut of a La Vallière — never said a word
against her, just sat tight and let the girl make an idiot of herself, as
she was bound to do, till there was nothing left for her but to go into
a convent! And there've been others since her day — I needn't name
them — who might have ousted a woman with weaker nerves and
less fertile intelligence. But she's got the better of them, one after
another, and outlasted them all — just as she'll get the better of this
pious fit of His Majesty's and be there in her place, long after it's
been forgotten. Louis is no saint, and she knows it.'

'Ah, but then, don't you see,' protested Cécile de Montglas,
'there's the more reason for her to fear while for the moment he's
out of her clutches! Even the King is putty in women's hands. And
it's at a time like this that the first pretty face is likely to snare him.
From *my* experience of men ——'

'Oh, as to that, my pigeon, I quite agree, they're beasts — purely
and simply, beasts! The Countess will concur with us there, I am
sure. I dare say, too, madam, your sister de la Ferté could supply
ample confirmation of my argument. What's this I've heard whispered lately about her giving ten thousand francs to the Comte de
Marsan to settle his gambling debts? I hope the report is false, for if
it's not, her troubles are only beginning. Marsan's a cad — he's incapable of keeping his mouth shut. Why, only yesterday at Madame
de Fiesque's he was boasting to everyone of his good fortune and
saying that, if the Maréchal could be gathered to his fathers — which
in the nature of things can't be very much longer delayed — he'd
half a mind to wed the goose that laid the golden eggs!'

Madame de Montmorency put down her sewing for a minute and
poured herself a glass of rossolis, which she sipped with unhurried enjoyment, her eyes round and deceptively innocent over the rim. . . .
She had not changed, then, in fifteen years, but was the same ser-
pent-tongued slanderer still!

'Madam,' said Cateau coldly, 'I know nothing of the matter to
which you refer. I doubt not it is a lie — and those who spread such
shabby fictions are little better than their authors!'

'Oh, my dear, I do so agree!' cried Isabelle, skilfully ignoring her
hostess's imputation and composing her own features into the semblance of a tenderly beaming smile. 'I am delighted to hear that the
story's without foundation. I told the Fiesque so directly. After all,

there's nothing so base can be said of a woman as that she's reduced
to paying her lovers. Once she starts doing that, I said, it's the end,
the absolute end. But I'm certain the dear Maréchale would never
be forced to stoop so low. Why, I said to Gilette de Fiesque, don't
you remember the rumour we heard, the very summer the Duc de
Longueville was killed, that Madame de la Ferté had pawned her
rubies to help young Tallard out of a hole? — and how it turned out
that, so far from being the truth, she was actually getting the most
marvellous presents of money and jewels from old Monsieur de
Béchameil the whole time? ... Oh, no, I've always claimed, and I
always shall claim, that Magdelaine is a clever woman, for all she
seems so simple! And she's a heart, too. I can testify to that, for I
saw with my own eyes how she acted after the poor dear Duke's
death. Why, she wept buckets of tears, my dear — positively buckets! When I paid her a call of condolence, the drops kept rolling
down her cheeks all the while I was with her. I was so affected by it,
I couldn't help sobbing a little myself! As I told her, I understood
exactly what she must be feeling — such a lover as Longueville
couldn't turn up twice in one woman's life! You can see how deeply
she must have cared for him by the way she let her figure go directly
he was gone. Why, she must have put on twenty pounds in the two
months after the news reached Paris — shouldn't you say, at least
twenty pounds, dear? — and what's more, she's kept 'em ever since!
And then her hair! All I can say is, I never knew before she'd been
dyeing it. (She must have got hold of a miraculous process: La
Martin can't do half so well for me!) I was thunderstruck when it
began to get streaky in front. As I remember, she refused to touch it
at all until she was quite finished with old Béchameil (who's far too
blind to have noticed what colour it was, anyhow!) and more than
half through with young Tallard. And since then, instead of going
back to her original shade, it's taken on a distinct reddish tinge.
That's smart of her, too, isn't it? for black, in the end, always gets
a horrid artificial look. Besides, auburn is perfectly charming with
her brown eyes and lovely fair skin. Say what you will, Catherine-
Henriette, no one ever had finer complexions than you and your sister. Yes, and you've managed to hold them in spite of everything.
As I said to Gilette de Fiesque, character is the answer to that.
There's nothing else so sustains one through trials in life. I admire it
more than anything myself. Ah, well, dear, we've none of us been
models of conduct exactly, have we? But one thing I claim — I'd
maintain it before a tribunal of justice, if necessary — and that is
that I don't know, and never have known, a single woman at court
who's been able to preserve so much dignity in adultery as Magdelaine de la Ferté!'

Madame de Montmorency threw her hostess a brightly benevolent look, which implied that only the hidebound conventions of polite society prevented her from including the name of the Comtesse d'Olonne in the same exclusive category.

Cateau continued stitching at her tapestry without saying anything, without looking up, even. She had no wish to meet Isabelle's eye, for she was certain that the bright benevolence would be in it — if she saw it, she would probably make a scene and order the benevolent one out of the Chinese cabinet — and what on earth would be the good of a scene? Isabelle was a viper — a toad — anything completely disagreeable and dangerous one might care to call her — but she was not, unfortunately, a liar. She never had been. Cateau knew that, to her own cost. She knew also, worse luck! that everything that had been said about Magdelon was only too true. Magdelon *had* got too stout, she *did* dye her hair — and no one who'd seen her at the time was likely to forget that she'd cried for weeks after Longueville's death, cried till her face was pink and pulpy and her nose swollen out of shape and her poor eyes almost disappeared in her cheeks — and then, suddenly, rallied her forces and started going to parties at court and giving parties at Great Senneterre and getting herself talked about with a number of men. Béchameil, the stodgy middle-aged councillor of parliament, and young Tallard, son of Cateau's old rival, Madame de la Baume of Lyon, were only two of a lengthy series. (It was a miracle, really, that Isabelle had not happened to hear of the others.) ... Cateau understood perfectly what had made Magdelon do it. She could relive at will, even now, the sharpness of her own grief for Candale, as well as the peculiar, but to her natural, means she had found to assuage it.

There was no point in raking up the past oneself — but still less in objecting to those who, like Isabelle de Montmorency, took a perverse and venomous pleasure in wielding the rake.

On the other hand, the report about Marsan was a different story. That might be important, because Marsan, Cateau was aware, was her sister's latest lover. Cateau herself did not like him — an adventurer, a horrid scheming little opportunist, she had pronounced him in her own mind, after their first meeting; greedy, as were all the members of the house of Lorraine; obviously out for everything he could get at the smallest possible cost to himself.

His liaison with the Maréchale de la Ferté must, almost certainly, have been inspired by interested motives. Cateau had not heard before about the ten thousand francs Magdelon was supposed to have given him, but she was dismally sure that it was as true as the rest of Isabelle's statements. Magdelon was always giving people things. All her life she had been used to making prodigal gestures. She wanted to be happy, herself, and everyone around her to be happy, too. If bestowing anything on her friends, from half of her income to the whole of her heart, could produce that result, why, Magdelon would not fail them! Poor, generous, misguided darling! The mistakes she'd made had never succeeded in discouraging her. It mattered not that she had lavished her trust and devotion again and again on the most ridiculously unworthy objects. She was ever ready to start anew, convinced that this time, at last... Poor darling, indeed! Who could help her, who was so pathetically powerless to help herself?

Cateau, lost in regretful musings, had stopped paying attention to her guests. She really did not notice that Isabelle had started gossiping once more till the sound of a name that interested her whirling by in the acidulous flood arrested her ear.

'... what the younger generation is coming to,' gabbled Isabelle. 'Lovers even before they are married, and liaisons of a most serious sort after less than a month in the nuptial bed! These modern young women! Look at Doudou de Ventadour, flirting like mad with "Charming" Villeroy! No wonder the Duke's always dragging her off to the country! And her little sister Gabrielle is even worse. Yes, Catherine-Henriette, if you'll forgive my mentioning it, your niece the new Marquise de la Ferté is exactly an instance of what I'm talking about. Everybody knows how she behaved while she was maid-of-honour to Her Majesty — men in her room morning, noon, and night — and it's been just as bad since she married your nephew. Well, of course, that's *his* business now — and if he doesn't give a fig for appearances, why should we? But what would he say if he knew that she was carrying on an intrigue under his very nose with her mother-in-law's lover?'

Cécile de Montglas gave a gasp of pure rapture.

'Isabelle, what are you saying? You don't mean — you *can't* ——'

The Montmorency tossed her head and smiled vaingloriously.

'Yes, dear, but I do! With Marsan himself! Oh, he's a worm, if you like — but you can't deny he's as bold as they make 'em! Imagine trying to drive *that* pair together in harness! Of course, we all know he admired Gabrielle very much when she was a girl; he'd have married her, I expect, if either of them had had a crown in their pockets. But you would think, wouldn't you, he'd be honourable enough to leave her alone, now that she's somebody else's wife? With such a delightful young man for a husband, too!... Catherine-Henriette, you needn't make those saucer eyes at me and purse up your lips, as if I'd said something I shouldn't! I'm simply repeating what's common gossip at Saint-Germain. I'm surprised it hasn't got to you before this. After all, Monsieur de Fervaques is a first cousin to Doudou and Gabrielle, isn't he? And they do say the girls are using his mother's name for their protection. I have it on the best authority that Madame de Bonnelle has given her nieces the run of her house for their rendezvous — that both pairs of lovers are in the habit of meeting there every afternoon in old Charlotte's private apartments, while poor Ventadour and La Ferté sit at the card-tables below without in the least suspecting ——'

'Stop it!' said Cateau harshly. 'Stop talking at once, Isabelle! I forbid you to say another word.'

Madame de Montmorency shrugged her shoulders.

'Very well, dear — as you like! I'm sorry — I hadn't any idea you'd take it this way. I thought you'd be amused. . . . After all, it's only what everyone ——'

'I don't want to hear any more. I don't care to discuss such things. If people have evil ideas,' said Cateau virtuously, 'naturally I can't prevent them. But at least I needn't listen to horrors. *Tell me, dear Cécile, where you got those delicious shoe-buckles!*'

For the rest of the afternoon Cateau held the conversation forcibly down to the reliable feminine fields of silks and servants, in spite of Isabelle's sporadic attempts to return to juicier subjects. This was partly due to her genuine distaste for scandal — like many sinners, Madame d'Olonne had an increasingly marked modesty of mind — and partly because she did not see the use in hashing over the La Fertés' affairs with her friends. Isabelle had said enough already. . . . That the thing itself must be so, Cateau had no doubt. Gabrielle had the morals of a tavern-wench — really, nothing was too bad to be believed of her! But why waste time in thinking of Gabrielle? As for Henri — favourite nephew or not — if he couldn't manage his wife, the more fool he! It was only Magdelon who mattered. . . . 'I can't bear this for Magdelon,' said Cateau to herself. 'If she hears what I've heard, it will break her heart.'

After her guests had left her she remained mantled in thought by the fire in the Chinese cabinet, waiting for Fervaques to return. The lackey took away the tray with the decanters and glasses, the parakeets in the window went on screaming and preening their feathers, the blaze on the hearth burned itself out till all that was left was a pile of hot hissing ashes — and still Cateau sat with her chin in her hand. Night had almost fallen when she heard the sound of carriage wheels in the courtyard below. This, of course, was natural, for the La Fertés' dinner-party would have been sure to have lasted a very long time.

Fervaques came directly upstairs to find his mistress. He looked flushed and cheerful, as if he had drunk a good deal of wine — but that, too, was natural: he was, as always, in command of himself.

He stopped to kiss Cateau and then stood in front of the fire, his hands clasped together behind his back in order to warm them. (The day had turned out cold and gusty in spite of the burst of spring sunshine that morning.)

'Well, my love,' said Fervaques, who was, understandably, a little more talkative than usual, 'I suppose you'll be wanting to hear all about it. Where shall I begin? There were forty at table — fourteen courses, and a separate wine with each. The Maréchal told me he'd attended to that himself — there were ten score bottles ordered especially from Crenet and Boucingo, besides the best champagnes and liqueurs from the family cellars. We ate in the Gallery of Diana, which has just been done over with a ceiling by Mignard. The table was covered with Flemish damask and set with the Senneterre gold service. The Maréchale wore her rust-coloured brocade trimmed with lace; she looked very handsome and sent you her love. The Marquise de la Ferté was in green, as you said she would be; but her complexion seemed brilliant today. She was much complimented on her appearance. The Duchesse d'Aumont was in blue. So was the Duchesse de Ventadour. She had a crown of white ostrich plumes on her head and was wearing the Ventadour sapphires and diamonds. Truly, our Doudou was a dazzling sight! The Comte de Marsan said he'd never ——'

'Marsan?' interrupted Cateau. 'Was *Marsan* there?'

'Madam, he was. Why should he not have been? He's one of the Marquis's best friends.'

'Best friends — phoo! That's all you know! If that Turkish rug on the hearth hadn't cost two thousand francs,' said Cateau trenchantly, 'I'd spit upon it! Listen to me, child; your tale can come later. I've something to tell *you* first.'

'... so you see,' she concluded, after five minutes of dramatic narrative enlivened by appropriate pantomime, 'it's our duty to find out how much there is in this — or, rather, *your* duty, for unluckily I can't very well force myself on the Bonnelles. I don't care a pin for that vixen Gabrielle, nor much more for her husband, if the truth must be told. It's Magdelon I'm anxious about. Poor Magdelon! She's been Marsan's mistress ever since Christmas, and I'm afraid she's really devoted to him — though how she can be! He's almost a dwarf — and the less said about the way he lives ——! But there it is: she loves him, and it will kill her if she learns he's deceiving her.'

'Oh, my dear,' said Fervaques, 'I don't think — do you? — Very likely Madame de Montmorency has made a mistake.'

'I wish I could agree with you. But you know Isabelle. She's had so many affairs of her own that her nose is unfailing for other people's. Oh, no! I'm afraid there is no mistake; but before we take any steps we must be sure of our facts. You've got to go straight to your mother and see ——'

'But how shall I see? What shall I do? Surely you don't expect me to ask her point-blank ——'

'No — but you've eyes in your head, I hope! There are ways and ways of doing things. Oh, if I were in your shoes, I'd show you soon enough how to set about it! If Doudou and Gabrielle are misbehaving under your very own roof, it won't be hard to surprise them. . . . I vow, it's too bad of Charlotte! She must have done this just to spite me. She's hated me, of course, for years, and since she can't touch me she strikes at me through poor Magdelon, who's never done anyone any harm. It's a nasty trick, that's what it is! You can tell her I said so, if you like.'

'My dear — my dear!' Fervaques began pacing up and down the room, his hands still clasped behind his back. 'Calm yourself, I beg of you! I can't believe this is as serious as you think. My mother wouldn't dream . . . and even if she did, it's impossible that Gabrielle — why, she's been married only a month! . . . And supposing it were true of *her*, surely *Doudou* would never . . . She's a prudent young person at heart and a well-conducted wife. That I could swear to! I'll not suspect her — or her sister, for that matter ——'

'Very well,' said Cateau; 'then prove it! You can — and I can't — or I'd do it myself, instead of wasting time talking to you. If Isabelle's wrong and there's nothing to the story, no one will be happier than I. But if she's right ——'

'Yes,' said Fervaques, pausing to face her and thrusting his hands in his pockets, 'what then? What do you suggest should be done if we catch them red-handed? What can *anybody* do, no matter what's happened?'

'Oh, well,' replied Cateau airily, 'let's think of that later. It'll be time enough to decide how to act when we see what we find.'

Unfortunately, as it turned out, it was impossible to put her plans into immediate execution, for on the following day they were engaged to go to the theatre to hear Monsieur Lully's latest piece.

Monsieur Lully — a new name for an old favourite, the famous Baptiste, to whose tunes all France had been dancing for twenty years — had now become a very grand personage indeed. He had taken over the Palais Royal, after Molière's untimely death, and persuaded the King, who admired him extravagantly, to give him an exclusive patent to produce operas there. And every winter he and his collaborator, the poet Quinault, brought out a work on some classical subject, replete with airs lively and tender, fine choruses, brilliant ballets, and stage effects of unparalleled originality. *Theseus*, their most recent composition, had been the success of the season at Saint-Germain. Fervaques, who had heard it there several times, had long promised Cateau that she should go as soon as it was played in town; and Cateau, in turn, had told her mother they would be glad to include her in the party.

This suited Maman, because tickets for the opera were very expensive: she saw no reason to pay for one herself, if she could get somebody else to do it for her. Maman had by this time got quite used to Fervaques' unconventional footing in the family, although in the beginning she'd made a fearful fuss about it. When Cateau first moved to the rue de la Sourdière her mother had wept and fainted and wept again, accusing the startled young man of seducing her daughter and dragging the ancient and honourable name of La Louppe in the mire, on purpose to bring its last most luckless possessor to what Maman strangely referred to as 'an early grave.' For some weeks she barred her door to the lovers, indulged in angry discussions with her confessor and the nuns at the convent, finally sent word to Cateau through her sister to say that she had only one child left and intended to remake her will directly.

Cateau, however, held her ground undismayed. She said nothing, having learned that, with Maman, actions were far more effective than words. But as soon as her house was fully furnished she gave a party, inviting everybody in the family except Madame de la Louppe. The reports of the Countess's new grandeur circulated speedily; Maman, as her daughter well knew, could not bear to be left out of the fun; and within a week the irate parent had forgotten her ire and asked herself to dinner.

She still, of course, occasionally made faces at Fervaques, slapped him with her fan, and declared that he was a naughty man, the naughtiest she had ever met; but as these kittenish reproofs were indistinguishable from signs of extreme favour, and as, moreover, Maman well knew that Fervaques would have married Cateau to-morrow if she had been free, their relations were soon of the happiest.

The old lady even consented to relieve them of their one outstanding problem by permanently annexing Mademoiselle de Saint-Denis — on condition, naturally, that Cateau continued to pay the young woman her salary. (That was only right, wasn't it? since everyone knew she herself could never have afforded to keep a companion.)

Today Maman was in high spirits, bravely arrayed in a new violet silk and a fearsome feathered bonnet made expressly for Henri's wedding. Not being in the least musical, she gave little heed to what was happening on the stage, fidgetting in her seat, patting her plumes, playing with a silver box of throat pastilles that had a lid that snapped open and shut, and whispering to Cateau throughout the noblest passages of the overture and the great air of Venus. But as soon as the first act was over, her glass ran busily round the circle of boxes in search of material for scandal. Perhaps scandal was the wrong word: unlike Isabelle, Maman was by no means malicious: she tore people to bits, conversationally, without harbouring resentment against them, merely because she had got so old that, like many old women, she no longer cared what she said. Kindness and unkindness, good and evil, truth and falsehood, even — what was the difference between them as one approached eighty? . . .

Cateau, absorbed in her own observations, did not hear what her mother was saying until the latter dropped her glass and exclaimed: 'Well, dear, see who's come in? directly across from us! My grandson and his bride! How do you like her coiffure, Cateau? Those little flat bows above her ears are ridiculous, don't you think? And I can't say I fancy her frock. Much too low in front! If I hadn't a better bosom to show, I'd keep a kerchief over it, wouldn't you? Shameless monkey! Have you forgotten how she sat, the very day after the wedding, bold as brass on her marriage bed? Staring everyone straight in the eye, as if being a wife meant nothing to her! Not a blush nor a sigh nor a modest word — she looked to me like an old hand at the game! Mark my words, child, the boy will live to regret what he's done. Poor Henri! He's very fat, isn't he, Cateau? Eats enough for three men, they tell me, and laps up half a barrel of Beaune every day. All the La Fertés are gluttons. But at least he keeps himself clean. Look at the Ventadours just arriving to join them — now *there's* a young woman I'm sorry for! The Duke's richer than Croesus, but he never gives Doudou a penny of pin-money, and besides he stinks like a fish!... Well! Well! If that isn't the little Nevers in her Aunt de Montespan's amethysts.... My dear, have you heard...?'

Madame de la Louppe went on babbling happily, as much for her own amusement as her daughter's; but Cateau had ceased listening. She stared intently, without appearing to do so — a minor art Madame d'Olonne had long since perfected — at the little party in the box on the opposite side of the house. Or, at any rate, at two of the party; for she was only vaguely interested in the Ventadours, and not at all in Madame de Nevers.... Henri, his aunt thought, was looking exceptionally well. He was a handsome youth, with his snapping black eyes and vivid colouring, though it was a pity that he had lately begun to grow stout. He appeared this afternoon to be in a high good-humour with himself and everybody else; the proprietary air with which he curved his arm round the back of his wife's chair was delightful, a droll assumption of insouciance that only showed, Cateau felt, how young he really was. It made her recall, she did not know why, the time he had acted in a play at the Jesuits' Academy.... Was it *Guzman* by Father Ridelle? No matter! It had been something swashbuckling and Spanish: Henri, aged eight or nine at the most, had swaggered about the stage in his cape and plumed hat, so naïvely enjoying his share in the proceedings that his mother, in the audience, was suffused in happy tears. There was still much of the infantile in the Marquis de la Ferté. He often seemed like a little boy pretending to be grown-up; his manner towards his wife strongly suggested a child with a new toy to play with.

As for Gabrielle, Cateau conceded, she was, if not pretty, certainly a great deal better-looking at twenty than she had been at seventeen. She was slimmer, her hair, though still red, was darker;

and the sandy eyebrows and lashes had been cleverly blackened. She had, however, in Madame d'Olonne's estimation, developed the intolerable manner of a great beauty in no wise justified by her appearance. Now, as she sat in the playhouse, she threw herself about in her chair — laughed too loudly, showing her pointed teeth — ogled her husband and her hideous little brother-in-law through the sticks of her fan — behaved, in short, as if bent on making her presence felt throughout the Palais Royal.

Her antics distracted Cateau, even after the second act of the opera began. The adventures of Theseus, winding a familiar course through a tangle of mythological monsters made of pasteboard and soprano Greek goddesses in modern court costume, seemed dull compared to the potential drama in the audience. The latter reached its climax during the stirring strains of the *Sacrificial March* when the Comte de Marsan appeared unexpectedly in the La Fertés' box. Though the theatre was none too well lighted, there was no mistaking that snub, self-assured profile. . . . He bowed in turn over his hostess's hand, then over Madame de Nevers' and Madame de Ventadour's; while Gabrielle smirked as blankly and odiously at him as at everybody else. But after discharging this official greeting she lowered her eyes, then looked up through her lashes towards the new arrival. Cateau was the only one in the theatre besides its recipient who surprised the look — it was no more than a momentary gleam of intelligence — but she needed no interpreter to tell her its meaning: she had used it herself too often in days gone by not to *know*.

She shared her discovery with no one. There was no object in mentioning it to her mother, and as for Fervaques, he was a man and therefore unlikely to be convinced by or even interested in such subtleties of conduct. . . . 'Though I'm as positive as if I had it in writing,' muttered Cateau to herself. 'Now to catch them in the act . . .!'

On the way out of the playhouse the Marquis de la Ferté and his wife accosted their relatives. They had not made a point of doing so — it was useless expecting a display of good manners from the new generation — but the press of the crowd brought them together in the colonnade outside the door. The young people, it developed, were invited to a supper and ball at Françoise d'Aumont's. . . . 'So it's no good trying to find out tonight,' thought Cateau, as she gave her hand to Henri with such formality that even that most negligent of nephews was obliged to kiss it; while Fervaques exchanged smiles and bantering remarks with pretty Doudou de Ventadour. (One could not help wondering whether he would have liked to go to the ball, too.)

At any rate it was clear that the Comte de Marsan had no desire to make one of the party. He took a prompt leave of the ladies before they were even stowed away in their carriage and flitted off on some mysterious errand of his own — which might, of course, have been perfectly ordinary: it was part of Marsan's charm that his most insignificant actions took on the aspect of an international intrigue. As the little man bent over his hostess's fingers Cateau admitted there was something attractive about him. Those strange deep blue eyes and that flashing white smile against his dark-skinned face gave him a vaguely Castilian look. . . .

Gabrielle's expression of pique as he left her was also delicious.

The next afternoon Magdelon asked her sister to go for a drive. It was a chill, sunless day with the wind in the east, and Cateau had lost her taste for the Cours, now that fashion had long since deserted it. But it seemed an excellent opportunity for Fervaques to visit his mother's at a time of day when, since Marsan could not be with one of the ladies de la Ferté, he must almost certainly be engaged with the other at the Hôtel de Bullion.

Fervaques was somewhat unwilling to accept his mission, but he fought only feebly against his mistress's much stronger will, and departed at length in a dejected frame of mind with his hat cocked at a do-or-die angle. Cateau, meanwhile, having promised to fetch him later in the afternoon, drove off in the Maréchale's big gilded coach.

Magdelon was alone except for little Cécile-Adelaïde (known as Chou-Chou), a rolypoly youngster not yet two, who was her mother's almost constant companion these days. (It was delightful to be able to exhibit so small a child to her friends, and took years off her probable age.) ·

The sisters greeted each other with affection, and Cateau patted her niece's round rosy cheek experimentally, as if the latter were a species of lap-dog. Then the baby was handed over to her nurse, while her elders settled down for a chat.

Magdelon, Cateau felt, though as sweet and smiling as usual, seemed a trifle preoccupied today. She made no reference to Marsan — which was a relief, as Cateau had with the years got very tired of hearing the virtues of her sister's current lovers catalogued at inordinate length. Instead she prattled gently away about the children — dear little Jules, in his first year at the Jesuit Academy, and clever Louis, who was ending his last in a blaze of glory, having made a clean sweep of the prizes in the classics. . . . 'His papa and I are so proud of him.' . . . The changes being made at Great Senneterre for the young married couple were also discussed in detail. . . . 'I suppose in a way, dear, they'd rather have had a home of their own. That's what Gabrielle wanted, I know. I'm afraid she thinks the house dreadfully old-fashioned and inconvenient, and perhaps it is. But there are such dozens and dozens of rooms in it — and besides, La Ferté had quite set his heart on having them come to us, just as we came to Monsieur de Senneterre when we were married. He's taken so much interest in getting everything ready for them — really, it's given him more pleasure than anything else in months — and I must say he's made it all look perfectly lovely. I fear he's spent two or three times the original estimate. It might have been cheaper to buy a new place, as Gabrielle wished. But La Ferté's so pleased — and dear Henri, too!'

How Gabrielle had succeeded in adapting herself to the arrangement, Gabrielle's mother-in-law omitted to say. Magdelon was too kind to make a critical remark about her son's wife, too loyal even (one could not help feeling) to harbour a critical thought. On the whole, she told her sister, she believed that the young people would be very happy. They were really quite attached to each other already — no matter what gossips said, it was a genuine love match! Of course, they quarrelled occasionally — but then, who didn't quarrel? For instance, only last night Gabrielle had flown into a temper over some trifle and boxed her husband's ears. Henri had retorted in kind, half laughing as he did so — and in less than an hour they were as good friends as ever.

'That's the modern way, dear,' said Magdelon comfortably.

During the rest of the drive she continued to talk cheerfully about family affairs, while Cateau, at her side, grew rigid with anxiety and suppressed indignation. ('What would she say if she knew what I know . . .?') When at last the latter was deposited at her door she could scarcely contain herself till the La Fertés' coach was out of sight to ring for her own and hasten, by a devious route she conceived it expedient to take, to her rendezvous with Fervaques.

Since Cateau thought it beneath her dignity to wait in her carriage outside the Hôtel de Bullion, they had arranged to meet in the garden of the Little Fathers, as the monastery of the Augustinian friars was popularly called, which almost adjoined Fervaques' mother's house. It was the sole public promenade of the quarter: a narrow, straggling garden with clumps of shrubbery amongst the vines and vegetable patches and a few stumpy rook-haunted elms bordering a gravelled path that ran behind the church. Twilight was falling as Cateau alighted and turned the knob of the garden gate. Spring this year had been late and reluctant: although April was far advanced, trees were only partly in leaf, and the ragged scraps of cloud racing across a sooty sky were driven by a wind more autumnal than vernal.

There was nobody there: Cateau was evidently the first to arrive. From the path she could see the slate gables of Great Senneterre against the dusk diagonally across the street. She recalled that Magdelon had told her how she and Longueville had been used to meet here in the early days of their liaison. There was a secret door under the ivy in the wall by the Maréchal's chapel, the door the little Duke had slipped through on the very last night he and Magdelon had been together. . . .

Well, it was foolish to think of that now. It was foolish to think at all of the past. Sometimes it seemed that it was foolish to think of anything, really. . . . Best reduce one's mind, if one could, to a comforting blank.

Cateau began to walk down the gravelled path under the elms, holding her hands tightly clasped in her muff on account of the cold. Slowly she moved, all in grey like the sky, her eyes cryptic and fathomless.

'I shall count one hundred by ones,' she announced aloud to the rooks overhead; 'then two hundred by twos; and then . . . if he still hasn't come . . .'

But she had paced to the end and back a dozen times at least, and was half through five hundred by fives, before Fervaques joined her. She saw him approaching some distance off; long before he was near enough for them to speak she knew by the way his shoulders drooped — though at the best of times he would never stand up as straight as she wished — that he had found what he most feared to find.

There was not much to be said, he told her. Maman had received him quite cordially, in the circumstances — the usual crowd had been there, including all three of his cousins. That, of course, was not surprising, as they had long been accustomed to do the honours with their Aunt de Bonnelle, who had no daughters of her own. Doudou and Gabrielle had appeared to be behaving in a perfectly normal fashion. They laughed and chatted with the guests, taking a hand here and there at the card-tables when it was required of them. True, their husbands were nowhere to be seen, but that could cause no particular comment as things went nowadays. . . . It was not until Fervaques was almost ready to take his leave that he remarked that the two young women had vanished without warning from the Gallery of Ulysses and that Marsan and Villeroy, who'd been amongst the noisiest of the gamblers, had also managed to slip discreetly away.

'Maman wouldn't tell me where they'd gone,' said Fervaques. 'She was ashamed to, I suppose. I got it at last out of Françoise d'Aumont. . . . Madam! madam! I never should have believed it! To think that my cousins should so far forget themselves in my mother's own house — that Gabrielle and *Doudou* ——'

'Bother Doudou!' exclaimed Cateau. 'I don't give a damn about her.' (She did, however, not fail to notice that her lover seemed to be far more upset by the elder sister's misdeeds than by anything the younger one had done. Would she have to be jealous now of that silly, simpering Ventadour creature? Heavens! What a waste of time!) 'Let Doudou have a dozen affairs if she likes! I shouldn't care either what Gabrielle did, if only she hadn't contrived to get her clutches on the one man in Paris who's necessary to Magdelon. Oh, if I could catch that unspeakable wretch, I'd claw his eyes out and no mistake!'

'But, my dear,' said Fervaques, 'how are you going to — I mean, I don't see, really, Cateau ——'

He eyed her, infinitely troubled, in the half-light; the homely diminutive, which he rarely used, sufficient proof of his perplexity.

'Do? There's only one thing to do. There's just one way,' said Cateau viciously, 'to get what one wants out of animals of that stamp. Money talks. Money's the only thing. We'll have to make it worth Marsan's while to leave Gabrielle. The question is, how much will it take?'

She expounded this theory for some minutes as they continued to walk up and down under the elms in the sober grey dusk. Her tones rose and fell dramatically, while she dwelled on the plight of poor Magdelon, Gabrielle's perfidy, and, most of all, the base venality of Charles de Lorraine, Comte de Marsan. Nature had given Cateau a resonant voice; she took no especial pains to moderate it, since no one seemed to be within earshot. The friars were at Vespers in their church, whence came a faint sound of chanting; the garden was deserted except for the plaintive rooks and one very old lay brother, who was weeding a patch of corn in a distant corner. So secure did they feel in their isolation in this lonesome backwater of the noisy city that neither of them observed the figure of a woman, wearing a black hooded cloak and long black gloves, that had entered the garden unseen and started to creep along the wall on a path running parallel to their own. She was not masked, but her hood was pulled up so high that her face was only half visible.

As the pair wheeled at the end of the gravel to retrace their steps the figure fell in behind them and followed them back to the church, while Cateau went on talking and talking, as she alone knew how to do. She was so wholly engrossed in her vigorous arguments that, finally, it was not she but Fervaques who gave an exclamation of dismay and pointed to the sombre black shadow in the rear.

Cateau said nothing: there was nothing to say. She ran forward to catch Magdelon by the arm, for the latter had halted, wavering, as if about to fall. (The thought flashed over her sister: 'Of course! *This* is where they've been meeting. . . . Fool that I was not to guess . . .!') But Magdelon did not fall. Neither did she burst into tears, as Cateau had been afraid she might do. She stood still, making strange dabbing motions with her hands, like a tightrope-walker striving for balance in the air. Her face was chalk-white, her eyes fixed and enormous. Then she began very softly to laugh. . . .

Cateau never forgot that evening in the garden of the Little Fathers, for, as she afterwards realized, it was the last time she saw Magdelon looking young.

Chapter III

IT WAS ABOUT TWO YEARS AFTER THE MARSAN CRISIS THAT CATEAU
began to be exercised concerning the future of her elder niece and
goddaughter, young Tinette. Two years ... or was it three? Neither
Cateau nor Magdelon had ever been good at remembering dates.
Besides, it was extraordinary how time seemed to fly, once one had
stopped being very young. Winter melted into summer, then froze
into winter again, almost before one got round to noticing the change
in the seasons; one thought of one's friends still as young men and
women, when they were actually grandfathers and grandmothers;
one spoke of events in the past as having happened 'the other day,'
only to realize, with a start, that one meant ten years ago.

However, in this case, several positive landmarks stood out to
serve as guides to faltering memory. Henri had been married in the
spring of '75; the following year, in November, his first child, Marie-
Angélique, had been born. Cateau would not soon forget Marie-
Angélique's birth, because it was just at that time that Fervaques
had decided to sell his commission of captain in the Queen's Light
Horse Troop to the Marquis de Sepeville for one hundred and ten
thousand francs — a paltry sum! But then, she had known Fervaques would be incapable of driving a good bargain. . . . Yes, that
must have been the winter of '76, surely. . . . It was the summer
after that that the Comtesse d'Olonne had gone to Orléans to attend to some business for Madame de la Louppe (poor Maman!
She'd grown too childish now to be trusted to handle the simplest
affairs). While there, Cateau drove out to call at the convent of the
Visitation in the country near by, where Tinette was a more or less
permanent boarder, and was so much struck by the child's pallid
prettiness as well as an indefinable air of dejection that she resolved
at once to 'do something about it.'

Prompt as always in the execution of her designs, she rushed to
the Hôtel de Senneterre when she got back to Paris to report her discovery to Magdelon. Magdelon agreed readily enough that it would
be wonderful if something *could* be done — but what had Cateau in
mind? Magdelon loved her daughter devotedly; she would gladly
have seen much more of her than she did. As it was, Tinette usually spent the holidays with her family at La Ferté-Saint-Aubin; it
was only this summer that the Maréchal's failing health had post-

poned their reunion. In the winters it had seemed best, up to now, for her to remain at the convent. Her chest was delicate; the climate in Paris was rather too harsh. Besides, said Magdelon, she supposed Cateau would admit that the atmosphere at Great Senneterre was hardly ideal for a growing girl. . . . 'Then, too, dear, don't forget, we haven't the money any more to give her a proper dowry, and I'm afraid she's not handsome enough to be sure of finding a husband without one. Have you forgotten how she looked at Henri's wedding? All arms and legs, poor lamb! — and I had so set my heart on her being flower-girl. . . . Gabrielle wouldn't hear of it, of course . . . and in the circumstances I couldn't blame her.'

Ah, said Cateau, swelling importantly, but had Magdelon seen her daughter lately? Tinette, it appeared to her aunt, was now safely past the awkward age. . . . 'Really, my dear, I was surprised! She was touchingly sweet in her simple little white gown, quite a type after Petitot — or should you say Nanteuil? I was strongly reminded of myself as I was at sixteen. Do you remember the miniature Maman had made of me, that last year at the convent in Caen — blue taffeta with a white underskirt and the Droué seed-pearls?'

Cateau was also willing to allow that life' at Great Senneterre might not be precisely exemplary for the young. (It was a toss-up, she thought — though she did not say it — whether the Maréchale or her daughter-in-law saw the worst company!) But might it not be feasible to arrange a presentation at court — say, next month, when the King went to Fontainebleau for the midsummer fêtes? Cateau stood ready to hire lodgings there for the whole month of August; and though she herself, alas! would be powerless to procure for her niece the entrée to the palace, surely Magdelon and Gabrielle between them ought to be able to manage it? Tinette was fifteen, quite old enough to be introduced to society. She had, too, a kind of unsubstantial snowdrop charm that might not last; it were wiser, therefore, for her to take her chances while she could. As for her dowry, girls of good family were married off every day with no fortune at all. Let Magdelon bear in mind that Tinette was a duke's daughter: La Ferté was likewise a maréchal of France, one of the most distinguished men in the country. And when it came to unearthing possible bridegrooms Gabrielle should be in a position to help. Whatever one thought of her, Gabrielle was a great deal at court; she must know any number of eligible young men. . . .

Magdelon sighed, and said gently that she feared Gabrielle was too deeply interested in eligible young men herself to be prepared to hand over even one of them to her little sister-in-law. However, she added, she would think it over and let Cateau know. . . . It was a perfectly lovely plan. . . . Cateau was really too kind. . . .

'Kind! Nonsense! How silly!' said Cateau brusquely. 'As a matter of fact, it would be a kindness to *me*. . . . I'm spoiling for some-thing to do. Don't say you will "think it over" — what on earth can there be to think about? Just send a line to that agreeable Prioress at the convent in Orléans to have the child ready to leave by the post-coach on Monday. She'll need a little time here to have some dresses made. Trust everything to me. It's as good as settled, dear.'

It appeared, in fact, that it was. In spite of Magdelon's feeble protests Cateau went straight ahead with her arrangements: in less than a week the house in Fontainebleau had been found, hired, and paid for; during the week after that, it was fitted out and fully staffed from the superabundant supply of furniture and servants in the rue de la Sourdière; and by the first of August the lessees were living in it.

The only hitch in the plan was occasioned by a note to Madame d'Olonne from the Prioress of the convent, stating that Mademoi-selle de la Ferté was suffering from 'one of her summer colds' and though not sufficiently ill to be confined to her bed, still in no fit con-dition to travel. (Cateau had an instant appalled recollection of a small girl perennially wiping her nose — or, rather, which was worse, *not* wiping it, but having this menial operation performed by her nurse or some kind female relative. One had hoped that by this time the child had outgrown . . .) Luckily, summer colds, as a rule, do not last long. The Prioress was soon able to write that her charge had entirely recovered and would be leaving for Paris on the first post-day; Tinette's arrival was preceded by her bust and hip meas-urements, which had been sent ahead, at her aunt's request, so that her new wardrobe might be ready to fit immediately; and Cateau, beaming with good-natured excitement, prepared to drive in to town to fetch her niece.

It was as she'd said to Magdelon: she really needed an occupation. There was far too little to do to fill up her days. She had no children; her house ran by clockwork; and although it was true that the well-oiled machinery was of her own devising, it had all been so perfectly planned that it took but a modicum of time and energy to keep it in motion. Then, too, though at first she had imagined she might be busier than before, since Fervaques was no longer away with the army a good half of the year, such had not proved to be the case. Now that he was free of military duties he felt obliged to visit the seats of his governments more regularly than in the past, as well as his principal country estates in the Ile-de-France and Normandy. And when he was in Paris he spent hours on end shut up in his own rooms, fiddling with his guns and his dogs and interviewing his bailiffs. . . . Also, he'd taken lately to paying a call every morning on Doudou de Ventadour. That was all right; Cateau quite understood about that. He and Doudou had always been like brother and sister. It was only natural that they should keep up the old ties of affection, especially as Fervaques was a bachelor and poor Doudou's marriage, it could not be denied, had turned out a flat failure. It often seemed to Cateau that her lover had an excellent and somewhat chastening influence on his pretty, flighty cousin. Far be it from *her* to object. . . . Still, there it was: the fact remained, she had much more leisure on her hands than formerly — so that this business of Tinette was really a godsend. . . .

What fun it would be if she succeeded in finding a husband for her little niece! Cateau was confident that the midsummer fêtes at Fontainebleau would provide a peerless background for the task she had set herself. They were, in point of fact, rather special fêtes. As a general thing the King went to Fontainebleau only twice a year, in autumn for the hunting and in spring for a few days while his principal residence at Saint-Germain was cleaned and put in order. Fontainebleau, lost in its deep green forest, was much farther from Paris than Saint-Germain or the nearly-completed new castle of Versailles. One could not journey back and forth between it and the city either quickly or conveniently. When the court was transported thither it was a real move to the country: people took clothes enough with them to last the whole fortnight, and those whose positions did not entitle them to an apartment in the palace were forced to hire lodgings in the town, while Louis chased stags and wild boar to his heart's content through the beech woods and across stony heather-clad uplands.

These elaborate festivities, scheduled for the first part of August, were therefore an exception to the rule. They had been planned perhaps because, after six years of almost uninterrupted fighting, peace was once more in the air — brushing its lovely wings so near, in fact, that, although it was the middle of the summer and should have been the middle of the campaign as well, the King and more than a third of his soldiers had already come back from the frontier. Turenne's death on the field of battle, two years ago, had been a terrible blow, and Condé's retirement, which closely followed it, another; but in spite of them, French successes had piled up impressively. The army in Germany under Créquy and the army in Flanders under Humières had won victory after victory; delegates to discuss the peace treaty were already in session at Nijmegen; and it was tacitly admitted by the allies that its terms would inevitably grant His Most Christian Majesty all he had asked for and more.

But there was also a private motive underlying the rejoicings. . . . Madame de Montespan, who had decreed them, was to be, in a very real sense, their heroine; for she had lately come with flying colours through a trying ordeal. Louis, never the most faithful of lovers, had basely taken advantage of her recent pregnancy — the latest bastard, Françoise-Marie de Bourbon, having been born in June — to embark on a short but violent intrigue with Madame du Ludre, one of the ladies in the suite of his sister-in-law, the Duchesse d'Orléans. This affair, intense enough while it lasted, had been nipped in its early stages by the fierce tempers and skilful manoeuvres of the official mistress. It was now over, and more than over — for the Ludre was disgraced, much worse off, poor wretch! than if she had never enjoyed her brief hour of triumph. As always, Louis was deeply penitent and decidedly inclined to give in to the whims of his favourite, no matter how much they might cost him. The Montespan enjoyed parties and loved spending money — as long as it came from the royal treasury. . . . Hence it was announced that an unparalleled programme of spectacles was being prepared. The best singers from His Majesty's opera were selected, and the best dancers from the corps de ballet; no fewer than thirty pieces from the general repertory were placed in rehearsal; while Lully and Benserade (the latter still the court's chosen poet) put their heads together with Vigarani and Le Vau, whose province it was to take charge of the staging of the plays, illuminations, fireworks, and other mechanical effects, in order to devise some novelties worthy of the occasion. Meanwhile, the great empty palace abruptly awoke from its Sleeping Beauty trance to an ant-like activity. Floors were frantically swept, rooms painted, beds aired, pictures hung, carpets spread, furniture polished, cornices regilded, and a hundred other household tasks performed by the most highly skilled workers in France. The quiet streets swarmed with vehicles filled with courtiers in gala array; for everyone who could afford it — in many cases accompanied by those who could *not* — seemed to have accepted their sovereign's invitation to the fêtes at Fontainebleau.

For Tinette, stepping with Madame Poussard, her duenna, out of the post-coach from Orléans one warm and thundery Paris evening in August, to find her aunt's pretty carriage awaiting her, it was as though the curtain had suddenly risen on the prologue to one of Monsieur Benserade's plays. Martin, the coachman, smart in his new summer livery with a well-powdered head, was up on the box, and a splendid footman sprang from his pose at attention to open the door for the ladies. He was so gorgeously dressed and looked so imposing that Tinette almost gave him a curtsy.

In the carriage, sniffling a little — for in spite of what the Prioress had written she hadn't altogether got over her cold — she blushed hotly to think how nearly she had come to compromising the family dignity. (How lucky it was that Madame Poussard, sitting beside her as prim as a poker with her hands folded in her lap, could not possibly guess what had not quite happened!) Dignity, thought

Tinette, was a hard thing to have. Some people, like Madame Poussard and the nuns at the convent, had it all the time; others — Maman, for instance — could at least count on it on occasion, only relaxing when there was nobody there to see; while still a third class, to which it appeared painfully likely that she herself belonged, were never able to achieve it at all.

To tell the truth, Tinette hadn't, she was afraid, many social graces. The lack of them, up to this, had not greatly worried her — in the schoolroom and, still more, at the convent, plural graces weren't considered half so important as grace in the singular; and grace in the singular meant things like saying your prayers and minding your book and doing what your elders told you to, without asking why. Even now, she was not really anxious, partly because she was too inexperienced to know how inexperienced she was, and partly because she was by nature a somewhat stolid child. In this she belied her looks, which were fragile and exquisite: in her fawn-brown taffeta cloak and bonnet she was a fairy-tale figure, with hazel eyes and long fair hair and delicate features that recalled her mother's and her aunt's. One would have had to glance twice to note that they were a trifle out of drawing — the nose too flat, the mouth too wide — like a pupil's sketch of an original masterpiece. But no number of glances could reveal her stolidity: that seeped through the exterior by degrees and became manifest only as one knew her better.

She was contented, too, as the stolid usually are, wherever she was — with her parents in town or country, with the sisters in Orléans — and now, she was sure, she would be equally so with her Aunt d'Olonne. Of course, it might take her a few days to get used to a house she hadn't lived in before, but Tinette felt undismayed by the prospect. In fact, so confiding was her trust in the future that, once over the flurry caused by the footman, she began, as they bowled along through the grey city streets, to hum under her breath a happy little tune that had neither beginning nor end.

It seemed queer, this evening, not to be going home. The carriage stopped first at Great Senneterre, to be sure, but only long enough for Tinette to run upstairs to embrace her family.... Papa, it developed, was ill in bed with a bad attack of sciatica — poor Papa! He was often ill, these days — and Maman, the Swiss said, was with him. That was not surprising: when Papa was laid up he invariably sent for Maman, though there was little she could do to help at such times, for his few personal needs were supplied by Robert, who would have relinquished the post of attendant to no one, not even Madame the Maréchale herself. Papa was a difficult invalid: he did not like to have his pillow smoothed, nor his linen changed, nor his forehead bathed with thousand-flowers-water. He refused to take medicines, and he hated being read aloud to, though his wife tried everything from the Scriptures to the new book of La Fontaine's *Fables*. No: all Papa wanted was to have Maman sit beside him, hour after hour, her soft white hand in his, while he devoured her with his eyes — those fierce, cavernous black eyes that used to terrify Tinette. ... They did not seem to frighten Maman. She did not grow impatient either, no matter how long she had to hold her rather cramping position at the head of the bed. Sometimes she sang to herself to while away the time, scraps of gavottes and sarabandes from her ballroom days, or the sweet old nursery songs she had crooned in turn to each of her children. But her smile was there always when Papa wanted it — she was never cross or impatient, never showed the slightest desire to stir from her place.

Tonight she welcomed her daughter with her usual tenderness as the latter tiptoed into the big darkened room. In animated whispers — for Papa was asleep — she explained the treat in store for Tinette, adding how sorry she was not to be able to go to Fontainebleau herself. She had planned to go, before Papa began feeling so badly.... 'But you'll be quite all right without me, won't you, my darling? I wish I could send Madame Poussard with you, but poor little Chou-Chou has a horrid cold, and her nurse isn't clever about taking care of her — she has to be watched, and I can't leave Papa. And you know Aunt d'Olonne has plenty of maids to look out for your clothes. You'll try, I am sure, not to make any trouble for Aunt d'Olonne. Do whatever she tells you to, and make yourself useful in any way you can, for it's very kind of her to spend so much money for your pleasure. Be sure to write to me every day — and remember the names of all the young men who ask you to dance!'

Tinette, somewhat bewildered, bobbed her head and replied that she would do her best. She and Maman conversed for a few minutes, still in whispers, for Papa hadn't yet waked up. Tinette told her mother about the journey in the post-coach from Orléans and the nuns at the convent of the Visitation — the Prioress sent her duty and most respectful remembrances to the Maréchale — also about the prizes she had won for spelling and sewing and the new white kitten with yellow eyes that Sister Marie-Louise had given her, which, alas! she'd had to leave behind, as it was too young to travel. Besides, she'd recalled in time that Aunt d'Olonne didn't care for animals.... Maman smiled approvingly, and patted her cheek with the hand that wasn't busy holding Papa's, and said she was a wise child — the kitten would wait — but of course she might take it with her next month to La Ferté-Saint-Aubin.

At this point Papa suddenly opened his eyes. He said: 'Eh!' and 'Hey!' and spat on the floor — and did not seem to know exactly what he was doing. He stared at Tinette as if she were a total stranger, even after Maman had told him who she was; and when it was announced that she was on her way to visit Aunt d'Olonne, who was taking her to the fêtes at Fontainebleau, Papa spat on the floor again — but this time as if he knew what he was doing perfectly well — and grunted something that sounded like ' . . . as-well-to-a-brothel-my-dear!' — whatever that meant!

Tinette was glad when Maman said she had better run along now, so as not to keep Martin and the horses waiting. She hugged her mother affectionately, dropped a curtsy and pressed a dutiful kiss on Papa's hairy hand — and then she tripped out, her last impression the bright gleam of Maman's parting smile. After that, she was off once more in the carriage, this time without Madame Poussard, to Aunt d'Olonne's house in the rue de la Sourdière.

During the drive, which was not a long one, she thought a good deal about her aunt. She had not consciously done so before, having taken her for granted, as children do take their relatives. But from scattered bits of conversation between the Prioress of the Visitation and Sister Marie-Louise, the Sub-Prioress, that were exchanged after the Countess's visit, Tinette had gathered that they did not approve of Aunt d'Olonne. 'A thoroughly worldly woman, my sister, if not *something worse*,' was one of the phrases she could not help overhearing. 'Can the Maréchale realize what she's doing?' was another — and even (in conclusion, with upturned eyes): 'God protect the poor innocent lamb in that den of iniquity! . . .'

Tinette had wondered at the time what a den of iniquity was. It sounded alarming. Nor were her fears allayed, on the last night before her departure, by the behaviour of Sister Marie-Louise, who had come to her before bedtime, her round red face puckered and solemn, to give her a rosary and a book of essays by Nicole, and to beg her to cling to the principles of her religious instruction in the great trials now ahead of her. . . . 'We had hoped, dear, to keep you safe here with us,' said Sister Marie-Louise. 'The world, I'm afraid, is a dreadful place. . . .' She had stayed with her pupil for more than an hour, weeping, praying, and exhorting by turns.

In the end, Tinette had cried a little, too, because it seemed to be expected of her.

But Sister Marie-Louise, with all that she'd said, still had not explained about a den of iniquity. . . . Could she have meant Aunt d'Olonne's house in Paris, which was large and very beautiful and not in the least like one's idea of a den?

If the arrival in the rue de la Sourdière were at all frightening, it was for reasons entirely unconnected with the Prioress and Sister Marie-Louise. Tinette was fond of her aunt. She was not really afraid of her — how could you be afraid of someone who was always sweet and serene, and fed you dragées out of a little gold box? . . . All the same, it was impossible to avoid a suspicion that Aunt d'Olonne might be different if you got to know her better. She smiled just as often as Maman — but somehow it seemed that, if people weren't looking at her, she might stop smiling. Then there was the way she treated her servants, ordering them about unmercifully and criticizing them in front of their faces. . . . You feared that Aunt d'Olonne might be quite as critical of *you*, if ever she took it into her head to examine your conduct. At any rate in her presence Tinette felt plain and awkward, tongue-tied and, worst of all, inclined to trip over her feet and drop things. (There was the terrible time she had let a glass fall that she had been given to hold — a wonderful carved Venetian goblet shining with all the hues of the rainbow. Aunt d'Olonne had said it didn't matter; she had told a lackey to sweep up the pieces — but she hadn't looked pleased again the rest of the afternoon, and the carriage was ordered to take the children home a good hour earlier than usual.)

It was quite dark in the street by the time Martin drew up at the front door. However, tall torches blazed away on either side of the entrance, and inside the house candles were lighted in every room, as if Aunt d'Olonne were giving a party. As Tinette followed the lackey up the marble staircase she stole interested glances to right and left of her path, for she had not been in Paris since Christmas, and there was always something new to admire in the way of a picture or statue or fine-woven tapestry.

The Chinese cabinet, on whose threshold the lackey left her, appeared to be full of people and parrots. Tinette, fortunately, was used to the parrots, and, even more fortunately, all of the people were persons she knew. The Comte de Fiesque, a great friend of Maman's, and Uncle Noël — whom the children called that because, strangely, he *wasn't* Uncle d'Olonne, and Uncle de Fervaques, he said, was too much of a mouthful — greeted her gallantly, and insisted on kissing her hand, just as if she were grown-up and married. Madame de Montglas and Madame de Montmorency, also, she had seen several times at receptions at Great Senneterre. The two ladies, who were standing together under the chandelier in the middle of the room, screamed shrilly: 'What a great girl you've grown to be!' The former then squinted in a curious manner she had and declared that the child was exactly — but *exactly!* — a replica of the Maréchale. 'Little Magdelon over again,' said Madame de Montglas, nodding emphatically. 'Come give me a kiss, love!'

Tinette complied willingly enough. She liked Madame de Montglas better than Madame de Montmorency (who stared hard, too, through a lorgnette, without saying anything further).

In her confusion, however, she forgot that her first duty should have been to seek out her hostess. That was doubtless because Aunt d'Olonne was the only person in the room not standing up. She was seated in the far corner of the alcove, scribbling a note at her writing table — the marvellous little desk inlaid with panels of mother-of-pearl she had once told the children had a hundred drawers in it. Although she must have seen that her niece had arrived and was standing before her, timid and blushing, she went on writing a moment longer, holding the quill firmly in her slim fingers and covering the sheet of paper with black sprawling hieroglyphics.

Then, suddenly, she dropped her pen, saying: 'There! *That's* done!' — and turned to embrace her niece.

Aunt d'Olonne looked just as she always did, all gold-and-white and graceful and gleaming. Her curls were brushed till they shone like satin — were they perhaps a touch yellower than usual? — and her clothes exhaled a faint familiar flower-scent.

'Dear little girl,' said Aunt d'Olonne, pecking the newcomer on both cheeks and producing what Tinette and her brothers secretly called her 'lady-come-to-see' smile, '*quite* over your cold, I hope?'

Tinette opened her mouth to make answer, and then saw that Aunt d'Olonne expected none.

'How glad I am you've come at last! Not a minute too soon, either, for we're off again in the morning to the country. Now that you're here our party for the fêtes is complete — or will be as soon as your Uncle Noël has carried this note to Monsieur de Bullion. Have you met Monsieur de Bullion, my pet? Well, he is Uncle Noël's brother, a very charming young man. I've asked him to spend a week with us in Fontainebleau, especially so that you and he may get to know each other — I'm sending him a line now to remind him ——'

'My dear,' interrupted Uncle Noël, who looked, Tinette thought, rather red and uncomfortable, 'remember I'm not in the least sure he'll be able to come.'

'And why not, pray?' Aunt d'Olonne tapped one gold-shod toe on the floor, as if she were annoyed. 'He can't have forgotten his promise ——'

'No — but I tell you, madam, this affair with the Rouillé girl has just developed. It may be something too good to be missed — an only child, I believe; her father's the Comte de Mêlai, who's a councillor of state and immensely wealthy, my mother informs me. Naturally, in the circumstances, she is most anxious ——'

'Pah!' cried Aunt d'Olonne rudely, tapping her toe so much harder that it was really a stamp. 'Those common parliamentary families!...' (And that, Tinette felt, was even ruder than saying 'Pah!' because Uncle Noël belonged to a parliamentary family himself.)

Whatever he might be thinking, however, Uncle Noël did not lose his temper. He flushed slightly, but he took the letter Aunt d'Olonne thrust upon him, saying in his quiet voice: 'Well, dear friend, I'll do my best — that, of course, you know.'

To which Aunt d'Olonne tossed her head and replied that she hoped so, indeed. . . . The idea of losing a chance like this for a guttersnipe's daughter! It was not as if money could be an object, either — when the Bullions had more already than they knew what to do with!

At this there was a general burst of laughter, and Madame de Montmorency remarked, with her queer twisted smile: 'Well, darling, some people like their nests double-lined, you know ——' which made everybody laugh again.

Then Uncle Noël kissed Aunt d'Olonne's hand — just as politely as if she'd been kind to him instead of quite cross — and bowed to the other ladies and Monsieur de Fiesque before leaving the room.

After he had gone Aunt d'Olonne jumped up, took Tinette by the shoulder, piloted her to the couch, made her sit down beside her, and plied her with sugar-biscuits and some strong-tasting spiced wine. Tinette drank two glasses of wine, which made her so sleepy that she had difficulty in answering the strings of questions concerning her age, tastes, and pursuits that were darted at her by Aunt d'Olonne's friends. Luckily, it did not seem to matter much what she said, for they laughed delightedly at her least sprightly remarks. Madame de Montglas, putting her tongue between her two front teeth (which were rather wide apart), pronounced her a 'delicious morsel' (whatever that might be — it sounded, didn't it, like something more to eat?).

Presently, in spite of herself, Tinette's head began drooping lower and lower, whereupon Aunt d'Olonne exclaimed that the poor lamb must be exhausted after her terrible journey. . . . 'What am I thinking of? Of course, you must be packed off to bed directly. Else you'll never be stirring tomorrow early enough to get through all we have to do!'

The visitor was forthwith handed about the circle once more, to be patted and kissed and called a 'dear little thing'; after which Aunt d'Olonne rang for her maid Lucie, who took Tinette away to a pretty rose-coloured bedroom directly across the hall from Aunt d'Olonne's own apartments; undressed her, bathed her, brushed out her long, straight, flaxen hair, which she plaited neatly and tied with ribbons; and when she had tucked her up in bed brought her a supper-tray laden with good things to eat.

Tinette, who at home was never allowed to eat in bed unless she were ill, was enchanted.

It was only a pity that she felt too tired to do more than sample the various dainties. To make up for this disappointment she asked Lucie to leave a plate of tempting small pastries on the table by her bed — 'In case,' said Tinette gravely, 'I should wake up hungry in the night, you know.'

'Bless the child! Of course!' said Lucie, who was plump and good-natured, with a pink face and very round, very blue eyes without many lashes.

She quenched all the candles save one, which was left burning for a night-light beneath a beautiful picture of Our Lady in a red-and-green dress with her arms full of lilies (Lucie had said it was Spanish), and then tripped away. Tinette, alone at last, curled up as comfortably as a kitten in her rose-scented sheets, wondering drowsily why Maman always said that Aunt d'Olonne had had a hard life. It seemed, on the contrary, that she had everything heart could wish for — beauty and charm, a magnificent house, heaps of money, a handsome young husband. ... At least, he wasn't really her husband, was he? Maybe it was because Uncle Noël was not married to Aunt d'Olonne that Maman thought people ought to be sorry for her. He was there all the time, though, exactly as if they were married — only Aunt d'Olonne had not to obey him, as she would certainly have done if they were husband and wife. Instead of that, it appeared that Uncle Noël was the one who obeyed ... so that, say what one would ...

'When I grow up,' murmured Tinette, watching the little candle winking in the soft night breeze under the picture of the Virgin in the red-and-green dress, 'I'd like to be just like Aunt d'Olonne. ...'

The next thing she knew, the sun was shining brightly, and Lucie was standing beside the bed, drawing back the damask curtains and crying out that it was past nine o'clock and mademoiselle had better wake up *this minute*, if she wanted to be ready to start for the country at ten.

As a matter of fact, no one was ready as early as that. It was nearly midday before Aunt d'Olonne had finished performing the last of numerous small tasks, all of which were asserted to be of the highest importance. Clad in a fluffy white dressing-gown, she vibrated between her own rooms and the Chinese cabinet (where she and her niece took breakfast), trying on hats, selecting shoes, rummaging through her chests in search of a certain diamond stomacher she maintained she could not possibly leave Paris without, and calling directions to Quentine and Lucie, who were packing their mistress's trunk. Between-times she would pause for a moment to sip her coffee or nibble a fragment of bread; twice she hovered, without actually sitting down at it, over the little desk inlaid with mother-of-pearl, to dash off notes that were said, like the tasks, to be 'very important.'

Tinette, round-eyed, ate a hearty meal as she watched these activities. Uncle Noël was nowhere to be seen. She would have liked to inquire what had become of him, but did not dare; and Aunt d'Olonne finally volunteered the information that he had spent the night with his mother at the Hôtel de Bullion and was to follow them later to Fontainebleau. 'That is, my dear, he'll come if he does what I've told him to do,' said Aunt d'Olonne darkly. 'If he *doesn't* do it, he might as well stop in town, that's all I can say.'

After breakfast Aunt d'Olonne's maids dressed her, and then dressed her hair — which took a long time — and after that, it was suddenly recalled that Tinette's wardrobe had been assembled and Maître Thomas was waiting to fit it. He was straightway admitted, followed by a row of pages bearing mysterious boxes and bundles. The boxes and bundles having been unpacked, Tinette was made to stand still for an hour by the clock, while Quentine and Lucie, on their knees, pinned and tucked and basted under the tailor's expert direction. Fussy little Maître Thomas walked in circles about his client, surveying proceedings with a critical eye; and Aunt d'Olonne walked in circles about Maître Thomas, equally ready to criticize *him* ... though, really, how they could find fault with anything ...

Tinette had never before in her life seen so many beautiful things. There were dresses of linen and satin and silk, hats trimmed with feathers and cloaks trimmed with fur, gloves and handkerchiefs, stockings and slippers in dozens. It seemed impossible that so much grandeur could be meant for *her*, but when she tried to express her thanks Aunt d'Olonne shook her head with a decided 'Nonsense, child!', not appearing to be in the least impressed by Maître Thomas' treasures. In fact, several of the prettiest frocks were dismissed as unsuitable, a number of bonnets barely escaped the same fate, being pronounced 'hideous,' though they would 'do in a pinch'; while one inoffensive evening cape was cast on the floor and might have been trampled upon, had not its creator boldly rescued it.

When Maître Thomas and his assistants had been shown out, a lackey came in to announce that Maître Le Caron had called to see the Countess about that property in the Brie she was thinking of buying, and Aunt d'Olonne dismissed her maids and sat down to a conference with her lawyer as tranquilly as if the whole day lay before her.

Tinette listened carefully to everything that was said, but found she could not understand more than a word here and there. Such phrases as 'rent of assize' and 'freehold with four per cent' were completely mystifying. How clever Aunt d'Olonne was, to be sure!

By the time the interview was over it was so late that it seemed best to dine before beginning the long drive to Fontainebleau. Madame de Montglas and Madame de Montmorency, who had also been bidden to join the house-party, had gone on ahead with the

Comte de Fiesque; so that there was no particular hurry, as long as they arrived in time to dress for the first of the fêtes.

When at last the travellers got into the coach — the best one, lined with bottle-green velvet — Aunt d'Olonne said she was a little tired; she leaned back in her seat, with her head against a cushion, shut her eyes, and soon was fast asleep.

Tinette, sitting bolt-upright beside her, stole a glance at her aunt and decided that she looked even more tired than she said she felt. In the strong summer afternoon light one saw a great many tiny lines round her mouth and the corners of her eyes that had not showed in the house, while her hair, almost startlingly yellow, had a strange dead look about it that reminded Tinette of wet straw. . . . Poor Aunt d'Olonne! Of course, she was really quite old — not fabulously antique, like Grand'maman, but still well past her youth; even older than Maman, Maman had said, and she ought to know, if anyone did.

The journey to Fontainebleau took a long time, and the sun was very hot; but Tinette enjoyed herself, all the same. She liked looking at the villages they passed through, with their neat houses and farm-yards and the surrounding orchards and vines filled with ripening fruit. And the last part of the road, which led through the forest, was delightfully refreshing.

Aunt d'Olonne woke up from her nap in the forest. She appeared much restored and not nearly so nervous as she had been in Paris. As they drew near the palace groups of soldiers in scarlet coats on horseback began to be seen, riding under the trees — some with gold-trimmed uniforms and on white horses, some with silver trimming and on black. These, Aunt d'Olonne said, were the King's Muske-teers. Tinette was rather disappointed in the size of the palace, which was rambling and low and did not look nearly so grand from the front as Papa's house at La Ferté-Saint-Aubin. But Aunt d'Olonne informed her that it was splendid inside — there were hun-dreds of rooms in it, almost enough to take care of the whole of His Majesty's court.

The square by the palace was also full of soldiers — more Muske-teers, as well as some members of the King's private bodyguard, whose uniforms were even more heavily trimmed with silver and gold together. There were numbers of carriages, too, drawn by prancing steeds with plumes on their heads; the noise of so many wheels was appalling. So was the dust that rose in thick clouds from the cobble-stones, for it had not rained hard in weeks. It was always crowded like this, Aunt d'Olonne said, when the King was in residence.

Aunt d'Olonne's house, the one she had hired for a month, was in the highroad, a little beyond the palace, but set back from the street and surrounded by walled lawns and shrubberies and clumps of tall trees. It was a square cream-coloured building, quite new, and,

Tinette thought, good-looking; Aunt d'Olonne, however, thought otherwise — so ugly, my dear, a positive horror, but it was all her fool of an agent had been able to turn up, and beggars could not be choosers!

The lackey who met them at the door told them that the Marquise de Montglas and the Baronne de Montmorency-Fosseuse had arrived some hours ago and were upstairs in their own rooms, resting in preparation for the evening's festivities. The Comte de Fiesque was stopping at the palace, but was expected to supper.

'And Monsieur de Fervaques?' asked Aunt d'Olonne, in a thin, cool voice, her head imperiously high.

'Monsieur the Marquis has not yet returned from Paris, madam. But he sent a postilion from the Hôtel de Bullion to say that he would surely reach Fontainebleau this evening, if not to sup, by all means in time to escort the ladies to the fête.'

'Yes, yes — of course! But was there no word concerning his brother? Is Monsieur de Bullion not also expected?'

'Monsieur the Marquis did not say, madam.'

Cateau tossed her head and flushed crimson; a steely glint appeared in her eye. She stood there in the hall, stiff and forbidding, while Tinette uneasily waited for an explosion. Then, surprisingly, she shrugged her shoulders, as if dismissing the subject from her mind, and turned to her niece. 'My dear, it's past six. We must start dressing you directly: the royal reception is scheduled for seven — and that's one place where one simply daren't be late!'

Now for the first time, as she ascended the stairs hand-in-hand with her aunt, Tinette learned she was to go to the palace alone. According to the programme laid out for the evening, the court was assembling in the Gallery of Henri II, thence adjourning to the gardens to witness an *al fresco* performance of Molière's *George Dandin* — 'Hardly the play I'd have chosen for a young girl's début in society, but never mind, dear, I dare say it will be over your head — and if it isn't, pretend that it is, anyhow!' advised Aunt d'Olonne.

After the play, supper was to be served in another part of the gardens, and then the ball and fireworks would begin. Aunt d'Olonne and her friends expected to be there for the fireworks, at which time the gardens were thrown open to all the gentry in the neighbourhood. But they had not been bidden to supper or the play, which entertainments were exclusively reserved for the inner circle of courtiers actually resident at the palace. It was really a great stroke of luck that Aunt d'Olonne had been able to secure an invitation for her niece: the trick had been worked through Gabrielle de la Ferté and Doudou de Ventadour, who were at court as guests of their mother, the Maréchale de la Mothe.... 'So you're not to worry, my love, about anything. The Maréchale will send her carriage to fetch you, and you've only to stay with your sister-in-law and the Duchess, and do what they tell you, and everything will be all right. They'll find you partners for the ball, and if there are any dances you're not particularly good at, you can always say that you'd like to stroll in the gardens instead. Mind, though, you don't leave the parterre on any account, nor step into a gondola, unless Doudou or Gabrielle should be with you. A well-brought-up young girl,' concluded Aunt d'Olonne sententiously, 'avoids gondolas like the plague!'

'But, aunt,' exclaimed Tinette, 'why can't you come with me? I'd feel so much better about it if only you would!'

'Goose!' said Aunt d'Olonne. 'There's nothing to be afraid of. The King and the Queen won't eat you, you know. I'll look for you after supper and bring you home, of course. No, I can't take you to the party, myself — that's for young people, child, and I'm not young any more. Think of the fêtes I've been to before you were even born! They're no treat to *me!* Now come along — don't dawdle — or I'll never be able to dress you in time! Quentine! Lucie! *Quentine, I say!* Where in Heaven's name are those wenches hiding?'

Tinette supposed it was true what Aunt d'Olonne said: she must have been to thousands of parties in her youth — and, of course, now she was too old to care about them in the same way. On the other hand, there had been an inexplicable tightening of her lips as she spoke, a faraway look in her eyes, as if, no matter what she pretended, she still would have liked to be asked. Poor Aunt d'Olonne! She was angry, too, with Uncle Noël about something. Perhaps, after all, her life was not so ideal as one had imagined. . . .

Dressing for the fête was a momentous affair, compared to which the fittings of the morning were but a faint preliminary rehearsal. The bewildered Tinette found herself immersed in a silver tub full of perfumed warm water, then dried with soft woolly towels and anointed with some fragrant salve, which Lucie rubbed into her skin until it had all disappeared. She was then clad in a silken shift and various frilled undergarments, a steel-ribbed corset and farthingale were clapped on her shrinking form, and, finally, the huge, billowing white and rose-pink brocade skirt dropped over her head, while the bodice was laced as tight as possible round her slim young waist. After that, she was turned over to the skilful offices of Quentine, who curled her hair before Aunt d'Olonne's glass and twined a wreath of roses in it.

Tinette was shy of Quentine, who was much older than Lucie and obviously felt herself a good deal too grand to wait on anyone except her own mistress. . . . 'I don't know how it is, madam,' said Quentine, 'I can't make those curls stay in place! Mademoiselle's locks are as straight as so much rope — I really can't think *why* — *your* hair, and Madame the Maréchale's, has always been naturally wavy!'

This was certainly depressing. However she grumbled, though, her round face creased and cranky, the deft fingers went on poking and patting and looping and contriving; and when the work was done Aunt d'Olonne pronounced it perfect. She herself dabbed thousand-flowers-water on her niece's ears, two tiny spots of colour on her cheeks, and clasped a small plain gold necklace round her throat.... 'No patches, child — they're bad style for unmarried girls, I think — and just a suspicion of rouge. After all, if you're a trifle pale, it's no more than proper at your first ball. That's charming. Here's your handkerchief, and your bouquet — I thought it would be better for you to carry flowers rather than a fan: a fan's no good unless you know how to use it! Now for pity's sake sit still and don't move till the carriage is here!'

Tinette felt like saying that she would not have known how to move, even if she'd wanted to. Her slippers were so high-heeled that they might almost have been stilts; the metal bones of the corset permitted her to breathe just enough to support life, and no more; while the tower of curls Quentine had erected — it was becoming very fashionable now to dress the hair up as far as it would go — betrayed a disconcerting tendency to wabble.

But there was no doubt that she was, as her aunt said, a creation. Much impressed by the gravity of her position, she sat demurely on a stool opposite the long glass, surveying with mild astonishment the glittering figure reflected therein. She thought, too, how kind Aunt d'Olonne was, how much trouble she had taken, and hoped that she herself would do nothing tonight to disgrace her.

The Countess, in the meantime, having made a triumphant success of her charge, had begun her own toilet.

Tinette marvelled at the amazing transformation that took place before her eyes. Only a few minutes earlier her aunt had looked her full age; she had been tired and fractious and wrinkled. Now, under the dexterous manipulation of Lucie, her skin became as soft as a rose petal, every tiny treacherous line smoothed away. Her hair, no longer the colour of wet straw, left Quentine's hands the same lustrous and rippling cascade of gold that Tinette had admired for years; her eyes, subtly outlined in black — perhaps even a little too much black? — took on depth and mystery. Precisely how the change was effected, it was impossible to tell; but after that half-hour at the mirror Aunt d'Olonne rose to shed the chrysalis of her dressing-gown and emerged the most splendid and youthful of butterflies.

She clapped her hands, well pleased by the result of her labours. 'Well, how do I look?'

'Perfectly beautiful!' replied Tinette, in all sincerity; while Quentine clasped her palms together, as she had done for a quarter of a century, and cried: 'Madam, there's no one at court can hold a candle to you!'

A lackey was scratching at the door.

'The carriage of Madame the Maréchale de la Mothe-Houdan-court has arrived to fetch Mademoiselle de la Ferté-Senneterre to the palace — and also, madam, Monsieur de Fervaques is but just come from Paris, and asks if he may be allowed to pay his respects.'

Aunt d'Olonne frowned.

'Is he alone?'

'Alone, madam.'

'Then Monsieur de Bullion is not coming later?'

'No, madam. Monsieur the Marquis requested me to inform you that Monsieur de Bullion was very sorry, but at the last moment he was unable to make the trip.'

Bang! Aunt d'Olonne hurled the hairbrush she had been holding straight towards the crack of the door.

'Tell the Marquis I'm too busy to be bothered. Tell him, if he wants to know when he may see me, that I can't say when it will be. Tell him — oh, tell him he may go to the devil if he likes!'

Tinette was frightened by her aunt's face, which was blank and flint-like; her voice was as cold as ice. But as the little girl jumped up trembling the Countess turned to enfold her devotedly — and she was smiling again, though her voice still sounded frigid.

'Darling, good-bye, and good luck! You're sure you're all right?'

'Oh, yes, thank you, aunt.'

Tinette tottered downstairs on her hazardous heels, holding her full flowing skirt high in one hand to avoid tripping over it, as Aunt d'Olonne had instructed her.

In the hall she spied Uncle Noël, wearing riding clothes; he had apparently just entered the house, and looked hot and dusty and out of spirits. Tinette intended to speak to him, but as she was on the point of doing so, a silver-clad figure, sparkling from head to foot in a gown of gossamer moonbeams like Cinderella's fairy godmother, glided out of the drawing-room and beckoned to him enticingly.

Tinette had to look twice at the figure to make sure that it was not some mysterious stranger, but only Madame de Montglas, in the dress she'd put on for His Majesty's fête.

Chapter IV

THE DRIVE FROM AUNT D'OLONNE'S HOUSE TO THE PALACE LASTED barely three minutes, but it took a good deal of time, after that, for Tinette to find her sister-in-law's rooms. To begin with, they were not in the palace proper, but on the top storey of an adjoining pavilion. Tinette had to toil up several flights of stairs and click down innumerable uncarpeted corridors before at last the lackey escorting her stopped in front of a door like all the rest and announced that this was the apartment of the Marquise de la Ferté-Senneterre.

He knocked; a peafowl voice from within screamed: 'Come in!'; and the door flew open on a chamber so minute and low-ceilinged that it appeared entirely filled by a tall looking-glass, a chest, and the figures of Sister Gabrielle and her two maids. The maids were on their knees, securing the flounces of their mistress's overskirt; Sister Gabrielle, in an orange-coloured satin gown whose train covered two thirds of the floor, was standing before the glass with her back to the door, fastening a black ostrich plume in her elaborately curled ruddy tresses. Her eyes met Tinette's in the mirror; she arched her brows without smiling, while Tinette made a brave attempt not to gasp at the torrid, heavily scented atmosphere in which she found herself.

'Oh, there you are!' said Sister Gabrielle, not too graciously. 'I was beginning to wonder what had become of you. It's just as well you're not late; the King makes a fearful fuss about being on time at his dull old receptions. Come in, child, and sit down; I'll be ready directly. Did you ever see such a hole in your life as this closet I've got to dress in? And Doudou, next door, is no better off. I must say, I do think Maman might have done more for us. What on earth's the good of a charge at court if one can't manage to wangle things for one's relations? But that's Maman all over! She's no more spirit than a sparrow — so here we are, tucked up under the roof with no air to breathe and scarce space to turn round in. It's a scandal, that's what it is! If La Ferté were with me, I'm sure I don't know what I'd do.'

'Oh,' said Tinette, her face falling — for she was fond of her brother — 'didn't Henri come, too?'

Sister Gabrielle made a face in the glass.

'No, thank goodness! He came back from Germany yesterday, but I've hardly seen him — and naturally His Lordship didn't condescend to tell me his plans! I've no idea where he is, and care less. As a matter of fact — no, Manon, *no!* How many times must I tell you —! Good God! These fools'll drive me stark mad!' (The exclamation was underscored by a smart cuff on the ear of one of the kneeling maids, that forced tears to the girl's eyes and caused her almost to lose her balance.)

Sister Gabrielle, however, paid no attention either to Manon's tears or to Tinette's puzzled stare. She stood twitching her train and ruffling her plumage, her olive-green slits of eyes unwinking in the small pointed face. Still without turning round, she commanded her sister-in-law sharply to come nearer, 'so that I may look at your frock. Let's see the back a minute — that's right! Well, I must admit you look very nice. Aunt d'Olonne dressed you, I suppose? . . . I might have known it. The old rip has perfect taste. Of course, if she's made up her mind to take you up, your fortune is made. She's filthy rich, with no children of her own, so if you play your cards well, there are really no limits . . . though I'm afraid you're too young to take full advantage. . . . Well, at any rate, it's a relief to know you'll do me credit, as long as I've got you on my hands this evening, whether I will or no. I've never chaperoned anyone before; it's a new rôle for me. However, I dare say you'll not be much trouble. Stand up straight, smile all the time, and don't speak unless you're spoken to — that's about all you'll have to remember! D'you understand?'

Tinette said she did, and that she would try to do her best. She was never comfortable with Sister Gabrielle, whose disposition was uncertain and who was apt to fly into a temper whenever she had five minutes with nothing to do. At the same time, it was impossible not to admire the Marquise's decision of character: she knew so well what she wanted, and went after it so boldly, with such ruthless disregard of obstacles in her path, that she was obviously destined to attain every goal she aimed for.

She was not beautiful, though she acted as if she were — and, in the end, aplomb served her purpose, for she received more extravagant homage than many a young woman with far stronger personal attractions. Neither was she rich, nor really important — but she had the grand manner (even if it took six-inch heels to help her achieve it!) that gave her an undeserved equality with her elder sisters, who were both duchesses and exceedingly wealthy.

As Tinette reached this stage in her reflections the door to the inner cabinet opened and Doudou de Ventadour rustled in, charming in gold-flowered brocade trimmed with knots of green velvet and Alençon lace. Doudou was much more amiable than her sister: she smiled and kissed Tinette warmly, exclaiming over the great improvement in the latter's appearance, with as much enthusiasm as if she herself were a member of the La Ferté family. Then a lackey appeared with the message that the court was assembling in the Gallery of Henri II, and the ladies gathered up fans, flowers, and handkerchiefs to depart. Sister Gabrielle had a page to carry her train; Doudou, a duchess, had two; while Tinette, as an unattached maiden, had to manage her yards of floating material by herself as best she was able.

Just outside the door they encountered a tall man in a smoke-grey steel-embroidered court costume, who cried out in affected rapture at his luck in finding 'three goddesses, quite by accident, as it were,' and begged leave to accompany them to the ballroom. Sister Gabrielle presented him to her sister-in-law as the Chevalier de Tilladet: she pretended to be very much surprised to see him, but it was only pretence, Tinette thought, as they seemed to be on intimate terms.

The Chevalier was rather good-looking, with a curly chestnut wig, blue eyes, and two bright red spots of colour high on his cheeks; but he was so thin as to appear emaciated; the skin was stretched so tightly over his jaw that the bony structure beneath it was unduly emphasized. He had, in fact, the kind of head that, even in youth, forecasts how its owner will look as a skeleton.

This impressive personage bowed to Mademoiselle de la Ferté with great ceremony, also to Madame de Ventadour — but his hungry smile lingered longest on Sister Gabrielle, and on the way down to the ballroom he kept close to her side, whispering compliments in her ear. He laughed, too, in a witless way, more than Tinette thought was polite; so did Sister Gabrielle, who when she opened her mouth showed so many teeth that the effect was carnivorous. It was not possible to hear what they were saying, except once, when the Chevalier nudged his partner with a meaning look and murmured: 'The hero's offspring, I take it? Or might the origin be of an even more interesting nature?' — to which Sister Gabrielle replied, with a shrug: 'Oh, no, quite genuine, I believe; the old bitch hadn't begun then to vary the litter!' — which Tinette didn't at all understand, though she thought it sounded even less polite than Monsieur de Tilladet's laugh.

The Gallery of Henri II was already quite full by the time they arrived there. It was an immense hall, about three times as long as it was wide, superbly panelled and painted, and illuminated by thousands of candles in sconces and chandeliers, which provided a piquant contrast to the red sunset light streaming in through the row of tall windows on the gardens. At one end of the room there was a loft, where the King's Twenty-Four Fiddles were playing a lively gavotte; at the other, in front of the gigantic chimney-piece, stood a gilt throne, large enough for two persons to occupy side by side, the back of which was carved in the form of a sun sending out rays of gold in every direction.

Tinette was disappointed to find the throne empty. The King and Queen had not yet made their appearance; the courtiers were busily bowing to Monsieur, the Duc d'Orléans, the King's brother, and to Madame, the German Elisabeth-Charlotte, who were seated next the throne, on tapestried chairs with both arms and backs. They were, Tinette decided, an oddly assorted couple: Monsieur was tiny and dark, with a long nose, almond-shaped eyes, and a wealth of perfumed curls; he was much rouged and sparkled with jewels. Madame, on the other hand, was severely unadorned — a tall, stout young woman with high natural colour and a cheerful expression. She looked uncomfortably constricted by her gown of purple brocade trimmed with ermine, as if it had been no mean feat to fasten her into her busk and her bodice — one could sympathize with her *there!* But though hampered in her movements by an invincible determination not to burst out of bounds, Madame seemed good-tempered, bowing affably to all who were presented to her and smiling a wide, pleasant smile that revealed her large, irregular teeth.

Tinette followed her sister-in-law and Madame de Ventadour up to the royal pair in the tapestried chairs, and copied their curtsies faithfully. She had expected to feel shy about making her entrance amongst such a crowd of elegant strangers, but the fact that there *was* a crowd was somehow sustaining. There was no need to feel embarrassed or conspicuous in a company where everyone was dressed more or less alike and was doing precisely the same things. A soothing sense of anonymity descended on the débutante as she rose trembling from her curtsy, and she said to herself, with pleased surprise, that the perils of court life were greatly exaggerated. What was there to be afraid of, really, as long as one had a chaperon to cling to (she had two of them, at the moment), and was reasonably certain that one's hair would stay up on one's head?

Sister Gabrielle and Doudou de Ventadour, having made their official obeisances, moved gracefully about the room, greeting and being greeted by their friends and relations. Court, it seemed, was like one big family, where everybody knew everybody else. But not knowing people, Tinette felt, might in some ways be an advantage, too.... The Maréchale de la Mothe, a handsome matron in black velvet and lace, spoke to her kindly; she and Doudou, between them, managed to introduce a number of youthful courtiers to their charge. The youthful courtiers bowed; and Tinette bobbed her head in return, and smiled and said nothing, as Sister Gabrielle had told her to do — which was all that was demanded of her.

Presently the music changed from a gavotte to the stately strains of the march from *Theseus*, heralding the King's approach. Upon this signal the courtiers lined up in two long rows from the door to the throne, the men bowing low, the ladies sinking all the way to the floor. A little procession entered, ushered in by a number of pages and lackeys as well as some soldiers from the royal bodyguard. Then came the gentlemen-in-waiting, walking two by two, and divers officers of the crown, in strict order of precedence, including the grand master of the wardrobe, who was the Duc de la Rochefoucauld, and the grand master of the artillery, who was the Comte d'Armagnac. Last of all came Sister Gabrielle's brother-in-law, the Duc d'Aumont, first gentleman of the bedchamber. At the very end of the procession walked the King, wearing a brown velvet suit embroidered with gold and clusters of seed-pearls and diamonds. Tinette had never been so close to her sovereign before; she could not help peering up at him as he passed. Louis walked proudly, as an absolute monarch should, but he was smiling agreeably, too — he looked pleased, thought Tinette, to see that so many handsome men and beautiful ladies had come to his party.

She was so busy admiring the King that she hardly observed that the Queen was there, also. Her Majesty appeared attended by the Duchesse de Richelieu, her chief lady-in-waiting, and eight middle-aged matrons-of-the-palace, all gorgeously dressed and made up quite shamelessly in stark red-and-white, to conform to their mistress's native preference. Poor Marie-Thérèse was not an imposing figure. After seventeen years in France she still looked what she was, a dumpy, frumpy little Spaniard, overloaded with gems, her blond hair unbecomingly frizzed, her small face worried and squinting as she waddled in the wake of her lord. Her lips were moving slightly, as though she were counting to make sure she was keeping in step with the music. ... Tinette was crestfallen: she had imagined that the Queen would be the loveliest lady there, just as the King was the finest man; surely she should have outshone all the others by divine right, because she *was* Queen!

The music stopped playing as soon as the procession was over. The King led the Queen to the golden throne, which she was apparently to enjoy alone, for he remained standing by her side, and after a minute or so drifted off to make a leisurely circuit of the room, distributing smiles and remarks here and there with an air of distinguished patronage. Tinette noticed that the people he spoke to, both men and women, turned pink with pleasure; after he had passed on they were at once surrounded by a knot of congratulating friends. Meanwhile, the Queen sat on her throne flanked by her ladies, four on each side, their ranks augmented by all the duchesses present, who sank into place with much swishing of silk on their coveted tabourets. Doudou de Ventadour and her elder sister, Madame d'Aumont, were amongst this favoured group; the former smiled encouragingly at Tinette as she settled her skirts with a practised hand. It seemed a pity that Sister Gabrielle could not sit down and be a duchess, too — of course, that would come to her all in good time, for wasn't Papa a duke? so that some day Henri must inherit the title. Whilst awaiting her august future, however, she had to stand up like the rest of the mob. Tinette was sure that this must annoy Sister Gabrielle very much, for she seemed suddenly out of sorts. Scowling, she seized the little girl's hand, saying pettishly (though Tinette was not conscious of having done anything wrong): 'Come on, for Heaven's sake! We must go bow again to Her Majesty.' Nevertheless, she was in no hurry to act upon her own words, for, instead of making straight towards the throne — where, to tell the truth, the press was not particularly great — she sidled about after the King, smiling and patting her hair and throwing herself into picturesque attitudes whenever there appeared the least likelihood that he might be looking in her direction. This was strange — but Tinette saw that a number of other women were copying Sister Gabrielle. They seemed to be afraid that, if they didn't do something to call attention to themselves, His Majesty might not know they had accepted his invitation.... But, as a matter of fact, Monsieur de Tilladet was the only man who took any notice of Sister Gabrielle — and *he* did not look pleased at the way she behaved. He kept on smiling the whole time, but the skin of his face grew tighter and tighter, as if it must positively crack under the strain.

Their wanderings landed them eventually before the throne, where the Queen was 'holding her circle,' as the phrase went. This she accomplished by sitting still, with an anxious look on her small red-and-white countenance, and saying nothing. Her Majesty had a box of sugarplums in her lap, which she was eating deliberately, one by one, holding each sweet up in front of her face in her little hands, like a squirrel devouring a nut. The ladies-of-the-palace whispered and tittered amongst themselves, while the crescent of duchesses held poses of conscious indifference, each aloof on her miniature private island of grandeur.

It was fearfully hot in the Gallery of Henri II under the blaze of those thousands of candles. Many of the courtiers were surreptitiously mopping their brows; the Duchesse d'Orléans said to her husband, not by any means in an undertone: '*Herr Gott!* But I sweat like six dozen pigs!'; and Tinette could not help casting longing glances at the sweet green of the gardens outside the windows. Why could they not sally forth to enjoy the last rays of the sunset in the shade of the trees? They seemed to be waiting for something to happen: what could it be? Had the fête then not really begun?

The question was answered by a commotion about the entrance to the ballroom, followed by more animated whispering amongst the ladies-of-the-palace and a general stirring and craning of necks. A very stout woman with bright red-gold hair then advanced into view, walking swiftly, glancing imperiously from left to right as she came. She was not old, in spite of her girth, and was handsome, with regular features, a fine white complexion (not spoilt by paint, like those of the Queen and her ladies), and keen dark blue eyes that seemed to be aware of everyone and everything in the room. But her physical charms paled before the aggressive magnificence of her gown, which was of silver brocade sewn so thickly with diamonds that almost none of the material showed through. She had sprays of diamonds in her hair, and was so laden with necklaces, bracelets, and rings of the same brilliantly unsympathetic stones that Tinette wondered how she was able to move so easily under their very considerable weight. The long glittering train of the lady's dress was borne, not by pages, as were those of the other women, but by two foppish young men in gala array, evidently beaux of the court.

This superb creature was greeted by low bows from all the gentlemen, while the duchesses rose from their stools and remained standing until she had taken her seat. The King himself came forward to speak to her; she swept him a splendid curtsy, then inclined herself with less ceremony before the Queen, who went on eating sugarplums as if nothing extraordinary had happened: she was the only person there who remained unaffected by the new arrival.

A special stool was placed for the Diamond Lady not far from the throne; the duchesses sat down again; and the party went on as before. Yet somehow there was a difference. An air of nervousness pervaded the stifling atmosphere — people talked just as gaily, and continued bowing and smiling to one another; but it was easy to see that they avoided, if possible, having to pass in front of the spot where the Diamond Lady sat with the King by her side. The King now looked bored by everybody except the Diamond Lady; the Diamond Lady looked bored by everybody, including the King. She surveyed the crowd with a stare in which insolence and utter ennui contended for mastery: her eyes looked weary, and her lovely disdainful mouth, whose short upper lip was curled back in a perfunctory smile. Whatever life there was in her concentrated in the fan she was carrying; it fluttered and feinted in her fingers like a restive dove. When she saw what the Diamond Lady was doing, Tinette understood for the first time what Aunt d'Olonne had meant when she said that it was no good having a fan unless one knew how to use it.

Tinette wondered who the Diamond Lady was. She felt reluctant to break in on Sister Gabrielle's conversation with Monsieur de Tilladet, but, curiosity at length gaining the upper hand of prudence, she ventured a whispered inquiry, which was answered by an impatient shrug of the shoulders and a still more impatient 'The Marquise de Montespan, *of course!*' that left her feeling humbled and adolescent, and nearly as completely in the dark as ever.

In any case, whoever the Marquise might be and whatever her title at court, there was no doubt that her coming was the signal for the fête to get under way. The musicians in the loft broke into a spirited refrain, pages and lackeys scurried to and fro in response to whispered instructions from the gentlemen-in-waiting, the King's bodyguard lined up, making an avenue of honour to the doors, which were flung wide open; and the procession formed once again to adjourn to the gardens.

Sister Gabrielle turned to Tinette.

'Come!' she said, in a peremptory tone. Poised to follow the duchesses, she cast an eye over her shoulder to make sure that her train was disposed in graceful folds and that her page was holding it properly. Then she beckoned to her sister-in-law and together, still with the Chevalier glued to their side, they marched with the rustling, dignified throng down the great staircase and out into the night.

Afterwards, when she came to think it all over at home, her first appearance at court remained in Tinette's memory a bright-hued medley of silk, velvet, and lace, lighted by rockets, set to music by Lully, the polite artificiality of its dialogue in sharp contrast to the scenery provided by the dark, whispering forest of Fontainebleau. Although her own rôle in the comedy could not well have been slighter, she enjoyed the whole spectacle thoroughly, with an objective interest. Parts of it, naturally, were more amusing than others.... The initial item of the programme, for instance, the play within a play, so to speak, was altogether delightful.... Aunt d'Olonne had been wrong about the play: Tinette understood *George Dandin* perfectly and found the story of the country bumpkin who married a snobbish society girl as funny as everybody else did. The little man who was George made such droll faces that she almost choked with laughter whenever he opened his mouth; it seemed hard to believe the Chevalier de Tilladet, who said that Baron (which was the name of the actor) was nothing at all compared to Molière, the creator of the part....

It was something to remember forever — not only the play itself, but its setting in an emerald glade in the forest. There were some odd outdoor accessory notes: the chirping of crickets, the murmur of the midsummer-night breeze in the oaks and the beeches, the white-and-buff moths blundering persistently round the footlight candles. . . . There was also Monsieur's pointed staccato laugh, and a fleeting impression of Madame de Montespan's red-gold head against a dusky background of leaves. . . .

Directly *George Dandin* was ended supper was served by the carp pond at the other side of the gardens. The whole company trailed across the parterre in their gay, light-coloured clothes — like moving flowers, thought Tinette. Only the Queen, who owed it to her dignity, and the Montespan, who was too lazy to walk an unnecessary step, were conveyed to the scene of the banquet in sedan-chairs. Tinette had never seen anything more sumptuous than the festal boards, of which there were three, long and U-shaped, laid with the royal gold service and decorated by pyramids of fruit and flowers, interspersed by mounds of moss, from the top of which miniature waterfalls trickled into shell basins set beneath them. The King and Queen, together with the Dauphin, their son, Monsieur and Madame, Madame de Montespan, and one or two others, sat in a row at the apex of the middle table, reserved for royalty and those of especially exalted rank. The table to the King's right was occupied by the next important guests, who were yet not noble enough to eat with their sovereigns; while the table to his left was given over to persons of no position whatever, like Sister Gabrielle and her Chevalier.

Tinette found herself opposite her sister-in-law, with several other unmarried girls: Mademoiselle d'Aumont and Mademoiselle de Luynes, who were also dukes' daughters, and Mademoiselle de Vardes, whose father was only a marquis (and exiled, at that), but who was, compensatingly, much the prettiest of the three. At their end of the U, Madame de Richelieu, the Queen's chief lady-in-waiting, had been posted, evidently for the purpose of keeping watch over giddy youth. This antique beldame, like a moulting parrot, sat hunched up in her chair, with a shawl over her shoulders to ward off the dampness, in a kind of sitting-up sleep, from which she roused herself at intervals to admonish her charges: 'Hold your backs straight, young ladies, I pray — remember, His Majesty's eye is upon you!'

But as far as one could discover, His Majesty's eye, which was in any case a long way removed from this particular end of the board, appeared to be fixed exclusively on his supper.

Tinette had never even imagined such a meal in her life. She identified fourteen separate courses before she got tired of keeping count, most of them cooked and served so elaborately that it was impossible to tell what they were without tasting. After holding back doubtfully once or twice, she decided to take a chance — and found what she ate to be excellent. After that, she took some of everything that was offered her. It was long past her usual supper-time, and she had a healthy natural appetite; besides, there seemed to be nothing else to do.

Mademoiselle de Luynes and Mademoiselle d'Aumont followed suit, but poor little Mademoiselle de Vardes, depressed perhaps by her consciousness of inferior rank, sat biting her nails and consistently refusing each dish.

Sister Gabrielle, across the table, satisfied her needs by nibbling a small crust of bread with an air of abstraction. However, she more than made up for her abstinence regarding food by the quantity of wine she drank. The footman attending her filled up her glass again and again, while the Chevalier was constantly sending him away to fetch another bottle. The Chevalier, too, seemed to find His Majesty's champagnes and clarets much to his liking. The more he imbibed the redder his face grew, and the more intently he stared at Tinette and her companions. He had developed a curious tendency, when he looked at any woman, of avoiding her face and concentrating his eyes somewhat lower down.... Tinette did not like it; she found herself blushing a little and distracted from her placid enjoyment of her supper; so that it was a relief when the repast came to an end in a stupefying series of sweets — ices and puddings, cakes and tarts, and silver baskets of petits-fours and sugar bonbons. (The bonbons were so delectable that she could not resist the temptation to fill her pocket with them when neither her sister-in-law nor Madame de Richelieu was looking: she forgot all about them until she got home, when she found them again, melted together in her handkerchief in a sweet sticky lump.)

After supper the ball began; and everyone trailed across the parterre once again, down some steps and along the torch-lined canal to a kind of pavilion constructed of leafy branches, where a floor had been laid for dancing. The Queen, who had a tendency to wax purple and stertorous after meals, had retired; and Madame de Montespan, growing bored by the revels, was carried away in her sedan-chair to some unknown destination; so, as the King did not care to dance, the ball was opened by Monsieur with his cousin, the Grand Duchess of Tuscany, and Madame with the Dauphin.

At the conclusion of the royal branle the dancing became general. Sister Gabrielle flitted off with the Chevalier, leaving Tinette alone in the middle of the floor; but Doudou de Ventadour, having evidently foreseen the contingency, at once sailed up with a youth in tow, whom she presented as the Marquis de Mirepoix — a rosy, lisping boy, whose patent shyness made Tinette feel adult and experienced by comparison.

'May I have the honour of a dance with you, mademoiselle?' asked the Marquis de Mirepoix, after some prodding from Doudou.

Tinette nodded and gave him her hand with a reassuring smile.

'I can do the gavotte quite well,' she said. 'Maman had me take lessons last summer — though I haven't practised for nearly a year.'

However, she soon discovered she had not forgotten the steps — and again, as in the ballroom at the palace, it was cheering to see so many other people doing what she was doing. Besides, the Marquis, in spite of his timidity, was a capable performer; after so many hours of sitting still the motion seemed delightful.

When the gavotte was over, Mirepoix led her back to Doudou, seated with the other duchesses near Madame at one end of the leafy pavilion.

Doudou did not fail her. She immediately produced a second young man, the Chevalier de Clermont-Chatte, also pink, also shy, also willing to dance.

After that, everything went smoothly. Tinette tripped through minuets and gavottes, courantes and sarabandes, with better than reasonable proficiency; while Doudou and her sister, Françoise d'Aumont (who was also chaperoning her stepdaughter, Mademoiselle d'Aumont), seemed able to marshal any number of possible partners. Tinette even achieved the delirious honour of dancing a courante with Monseigneur, the Dauphin himself.

The Dauphin's governor, the Duc de Montausier — who was a cousin of Maman's — led his pupil up to Mademoiselle de la Ferté and introduced the young people to each other.

Tinette found that during her dance with the heir to the throne she became temporarily as conspicuous as before she had been the reverse. Everybody stared at her hard, and she heard several men inquire who she was.

Monseigneur, on the contrary, differed in no wise from her previous partners, except that he was plumper and redder and even more silent, and, after a very few minutes, began breathing heavily in her face. He wheezed so continuously that Tinette became worried for fear he might be in pain; at last she plucked up courage to whisper: 'Do you not care for dancing, my Lord?' — to which Monseigneur replied, with a gulp: 'Nay, mademoiselle, I had far liefer hunt — but I must do as Montausier bids me!'

The poor Prince continued to perform his duty stolidly until the music ceased, whereupon he returned his lady to Madame de Ventadour with an air of relief, and took his departure with his father, attended by their pages and gentlemen-in-waiting.

It was shortly after this eminently satisfactory climax to her budding social career that something occurred that changed the whole quality of the evening for Tinette. She was in the midst of a minuet with the lively, agreeable Duc de la Trémouille (who had just informed her that he was her cousin, too — well, not really *her* cousin, but Aunt d'Olonne's cousin — well, not really *Aunt d'Olonne's* cousin, but Uncle d'Olonne's!), when a troop of young men made a noisy entrance to the pavilion. There were perhaps a dozen in the party, unaccompanied by ladies, and all laughing and talking uproariously, in violent contrast to the stately demeanour of the rest of the company; but their ringleader appeared to be a stout, ruddy young fellow with long curling black hair, to which he had attached a pair of yellow horns made of cloth and sewn all over with brilliants. This was supposed evidently to be the most exquisite joke, giving rise to gusty guffaws from his companions.

Tinette could not see what there was to laugh at in a pair of diamond horns, but she was surprised and shocked to find that the young man wearing them was her brother La Ferté.

So Henri had come to the ball, after all!

His arrival caused a commotion amongst the dancers, many of whom stopped in the middle of the floor to point and stare and whisper. Madame, on her throne, gave a loud neigh, and then looked away to hide her amusement; while the older ladies around her, scandalized, covered their faces with their fans.

Tinette stopped dancing, also, with a piteous look at her partner. She left La Trémouille, saying nothing by way of excuse; what was there for her to say? ... Doudou was dancing now, and Sister Gabrielle was still, luckily, nowhere about; so the way to escape lay clear. She had almost got out of the pavilion when a heavy hand was laid on her shoulder, and she looked up to see her brother before her. He was blinking at her, without being able to focus his eyes, and scratching his head in mock bewilderment.

'Bless my soul, little sister, is it you? Lord, but they've turned you into a beauty and no mistake! This is our aunt's work, I'll be bound! Well, well! Fine birds make fine feathers, they say — or do I mean that t'other way about? No matter! Come, give me a kiss, child, and tell me how I may find my coy Messalina. You must know where she's hiding, if anyone does. I told her in Paris that I'd get here in time to swing her through a courante before the ball was over, and I've come to keep my promise.... Nay, little one, don't look at me with such big frightened eyes! I'll do you no harm. Perhaps you're wondering what it is I've got on my head? Why, 'tis the latest fashion for husbands, child — a mode I'm launching at court this season in honour of my dearest, most dutiful spouse. Now lead me to the Marquise, I beg you! Take me to her this instant, d'you hear?'

Tinette threw Henri a terrified glance; then slipped from his fumbling grasp out through the door of the pavilion into the sheltering dark.

But it was impossible to be alone anywhere. The park had been thrown open to the public and was alive now with people. Couples were strolling along the path by the canal, whose black oily waters reflected the glow of myriad torches and lanterns; by their light was revealed a pair of startled white swans, surprised in their snug retreat, hissing and arching their necks in protest against the intrusion. ... It was while she was wondering, like the swans, where to flee that Tinette caught her first glimpse of Aunt d'Olonne and her party. (Why, she had almost forgotten about them!...) They were walking along the canal with the rest of the crowd, Madame de Montglas with Uncle Noël and Aunt d'Olonne (who would certainly never be the odd woman) on the arm of the Comte de Fiesque. Madame de Montmorency, a curious smile on her sharp face, brought up the rear by herself. None of the group saw Tinette, and the latter did not make her presence known to them, but shrank back under the shade of a giant beech tree to let them go by. Aunt d'Olonne looked exceedingly handsome; she was laughing and chatting gaily with Monsieur de Fiesque, who seemed pleased, if a trifle surprised, by these flattering attentions. But it was Madame de Montglas who made her audience of one catch her breath — Madame de Montglas with her silver hair and her silver gown, more than ever like Cinderella's fairy godmother. Her dark eyes wide and shining, two spots of brilliant colour in her cheeks, she appeared magically to have recaptured for the night the charm of her long-vanished youth. Down the path in the flickery torchlight she sailed with the undulating grace of the great ladies at the fabulous court of Louis XIII. Tinette watched her, fascinated; Uncle Noël, she saw, was fascinated, too — and no wonder! He followed the Montglas like a little dog — Aunt d'Olonne might shrug her shoulders and gesticulate as much as she pleased — he had forgotten, for the time being, her very existence!

Tinette, from her vantage-point under the giant beech, decided prosaically that there would be the devil to pay, later on — she hoped she might not have to be there when the time came to pay him!

After her friends had been swallowed up in the throng she turned to reënter the pavilion, which was safely deserted, as the music had ceased and Madame and her suite were streaming out onto the lawn to view the fireworks. Henri, thank goodness! had disappeared; the floor was empty except for a circle of men in one of the far corners — some of the same band that had come with her brother, Tinette feared. They were huddled together, laughing and applauding — about what, the little girl could not at first make out. Then she perceived a telltale flash of orange-coloured satin and heard an even more unmistakable giggle. The circle parted as she drew near and she saw, to her horror, Sister Gabrielle seated on one of the abandoned tabourets — Sister Gabrielle far from sober, with her dress in disorder and her hair much dishevelled. She had her head to one side, her eyes half shut, her mouth wide open; and she was singing, in an idiotic child's voice to the tune of a jig, while the men clapped their hands and stamped their feet to beat time to the refrain:

> '*La Ferté may hate me, he may be as rude as*
> *A boor, or as false and as scheming as Judas;*
> *He may tipple all night till he's drunk as can be!*
> *He may be the son of our greatest commander,*
> *He may be a cuckold, a fool, or a pander —*
> *I don't care a jot, dears — it's all one to me!*'

'Bravo, La Ferté!' cried one of the men — it was the Chevalier de Tilladet — and he leaned over to deliver a resounding slap of approval on the singer's bare shoulder. Tinette supposed that Sister Gabrielle would resent this cavalier treatment, but she only giggled the louder and started singing her song all over again, while the men went on clapping and stamping:

> '*La Ferté may hate me ...*'

For the second time that night Tinette fled from the rustic pavilion. She looked anxiously about for Doudou de Ventadour or Madame d'Aumont, but neither of her chaperons was to be seen. The gardens were more jammed with people than ever, as the guests coalesced about the canal to find places before the fireworks began. Gondolas were plying now on its sombre surface, and the King and Queen, who had returned from the palace, had just stepped aboard a festal barge strung with lanterns, which was slowly propelled to a chorus of cheers and the soft major cadences of a group of hunting horns sounding unseen from the shrubbery.

As Tinette emerged the first rocket shot into the air, bursting and falling in a shower of golden rain, while the crowd sent up a loud 'Ah!' of admiration.

Tinette had never beheld anything more entrancing. She stood still, forgetting where she was and what she was doing — forgetting that she was lost, really, and should be in search of her aunt or Madame de Ventadour. She forgot, too, all her recent distress — neither Sister Gabrielle's song nor Henri's stupid laugh echoed in her brain any longer. Breathless, she stared at the marvellous spangled patterns of light, uncaring how the time passed, as the acrid smell of powder scented the heavy night air and the swans on the canal, grunting reproachfully, scuttled out of the water to seek safety in the forest.... In the midst of the performance she was dimly aware that Uncle Noël and his lady had reappeared. Madame de Montglas brushed by her so closely that the child might have touched the gleaming folds of the silver gown.... They were stepping into a gondola, Uncle Noël smiling as he gave Cinderella's godmother his hand.... Now they were seated, drifting away on the dark secret waters before Tinette had really had time to take in what was happening.... With a bang the last rocket exploded, a great bouquet of roses and fountains of silver and gold. For one glorious moment it blazed against the velvet sky, while the people roared their delight — then it, too, collapsed in a welter of ashes, and the King's fête was over.

Tinette rubbed her eyes in bewilderment: it was hard to come back to earth!... But there was Aunt d'Olonne suddenly at her side: 'Child, I've looked for you everywhere. Where on earth have you been? It's time to go home!'

Madame de Montmorency and the Comte de Fiesque were there, too. But of the others there was no sign. Tinette wanted to ask if they were not going to wait for Madame de Montglas and Uncle Noël to come back from their gondola ride, but she did not dare. As for saying good-night to Sister Gabrielle, that was obviously out of the question.... 'Drunk as a guardsman, the slut!' she heard Aunt d'Olonne mutter to Monsieur de Fiesque, as they turned to retrace their steps over the trampled grass.

On the way home in the carriage Aunt d'Olonne was in a merry mood. She seemed, for the time being, to have forgotten her niece's affairs; no questions were asked about how Tinette had spent the evening. Instead she propounded, in fits of slightly breathless laughter, a most delicious joke she intended to play on the missing guests. Since Madame de Montglas and Uncle Noël had deserted the party, Aunt d'Olonne wanted to pay them out by throwing their luggage out on the steps and locking the doors in their faces. The servants would be instructed not to let in the truants, no matter how long they battered for admittance. Would that not be too amusing for words?... 'Too!' cried Madame de Montmorency. 'Darling, it's a stroke of genius!' — and she and Aunt d'Olonne and the Comte de Fiesque cackled aloud at the cleverness of the plan.

'But then, aunt,' objected Tinette sleepily, 'if they can't get in, they'll have to spend the night in the street!'

'So they will, pet! That's the point of the joke!' exclaimed Aunt d'Olonne, cackling more joyously than ever.

Tinette, tired as she was, felt disturbed by the turn things had taken. Really, really, it did not seem right, no matter what he had done, to shut Uncle Noël out of what was practically his own house! And poor Madame de Montglas, too, who had looked so lovely at the fête!... When they got home it became only too evident that Aunt d'Olonne meant what she'd said, for she sent a lackey upstairs directly to collect the Marquise's boxes. Uncle Noël's belongings, she remarked, she could toss from the window herself as well as not!...

Tinette crept off to bed unnoticed, thankful at least that her room was at the back of the house, so that she would not be forced to hear the racket that was sure to break out when the wanderers returned. Silently she let Lucie undress her, while through her drowsy mind whirled a succession of pictures of the evening just past. . . . There was Madame de Montespan with her fan — the old Duchesse de Richelieu nodding at the end of the supper-table — Monsieur de Tilladet smiling his queer tight smile — Henri with the diamond horns on his head — Sister Gabrielle singing her horrid song. . . . All these and more, strangely mingled with the hiss of the rockets and the hunting horns' gentle plaint, till at last Tinette's head touched the pillow and she fell instantly asleep.

Her last waking thought had been an uneasy 'Oh, *what* will happen in the morning?' — but whatever she expected, she could not have guessed the surprise that awaited her. Lucie roused her young mistress from heavy slumber at midday with astounding news. It seemed that a courier had reached the palace at dawn with the report that the Prince of Orange was besieging Charleroi. It was a sudden and devastating move, for Créquy and the Duc de Luxembourg had supposed the enemy to be operating in quite another direction, with the result that Charleroi, the most important French citadel in Flanders, had been left almost without garrison.

' . . . and oh, mademoiselle,' said Lucie, 'all the gentlemen at court are volunteering to go to their aid, whether they've got commissions or not! You never saw such a helter-skelter to get out of a place in your life! If the plague had broke out, it couldn't be worse. They say there's not a horse to be had in all Fontainebleau for love or for money. Monsieur de Fiesque is going, and our master, too — God save them both!'

Tinette listened with a shocked face, saying not a word; but as soon as Lucie had finished her story she jumped out of bed, flung on her dressing-gown, and pattered barefoot into her aunt's room.

Late as she had been up the previous night, the Countess was already dressed. She looked much as usual, elegant and beautifully coiffed, though there were two little lines at the corners of her mouth that were strange to her niece.

'Oh, aunt! aunt!' cried Tinette. 'What's the matter? What's happened? Is Uncle Noël really going to the war?'

Aunt d'Olonne did not reply; there was no need for her to do so, for just then a clatter of hoofs arose in the street — and the little girl, looking through the window, saw her uncle in travelling clothes, booted and spurred, astride Pyrrhus, the flea-bitten grey stallion that had been his favourite mount in his army days. Cinna and Rodrigue, the wolfhounds, were frisking joyfully about their master, and a train of postilions and lackeys on horseback were preparing to follow the Marquis as an escort of honour. Uncle Noël looked pale

and unhappy, his niece thought, as if he had not slept at all —
which, in view of the incident of the locked doors, appeared not unlikely! However, before riding off, he raised his plumed hat with a
splendid flourish and saluted his mistress — or, at any rate, the
window behind which he divined her to be — just as he always did
when he left her for even a day.

Aunt d'Olonne did not move from her chair, but Tinette waved
back energetically and smiled at Uncle Noël. Someone *must* wave!
It would never do not to, when the poor man was going away to
fight — to be killed, maybe! Who could tell? . . . A moment later
she felt herself unceremoniously pushed aside — saw the window
flung open and a blond curly head thrust out, while a high voice
screeched on a note of pure brass: 'Go! Go — *and be damned to you!*'

This, on the whole, thought Tinette, was the oddest thing that
had happened since she had come to stop with her Aunt d'Olonne.

THE EXCITEMENT OVER THE SIEGE OF CHARLEROI LASTED LESS THAN a week, but it ran high while it lasted. Having postponed his plans for the fêtes, the King hastened back from Fontainebleau to Versailles, where he would be nearer the zone of conflict and could receive news more quickly from his generals in Flanders. The whole court went with him.

For several days the bulletins were uncertain. Rumours came of a terrific battle in progress between the French and the Dutch — then there were exactly opposite rumours that there had been no battle at all. The siege was said to be on more strenuously than ever; it was said to be lifted; some authorities asserted finally that it had never been laid!... It was impossible to make up one's mind what to believe.

At last, however, towards the middle of the third week in August, it was definitely announced that the Prince of Orange had retired, at the approach of the Maréchal de Luxembourg with his greatly augmented forces — and the danger appeared to be ended.

There arose a universal sigh of relief, for no one had been really enthusiastic about this sudden disturbing postscript to the war. Now, with summer so nearly over and the peace treaty all but signed at Nijmegen, any further general engagement was unlikely. All the valiant young men who had volunteered for the siege came streaming back in a body, laughing and joking about the unlooked-for collapse of their 'hopes'; while a number of the regulars also began to disband, and there was talk of resuming the interrupted festival programme within a few days.

'It's really too good,' people were saying on every hand; 'even the Prince of Orange is on our side! He was told that the King was planning a party, and could not bear to spoil His Majesty's pleasure!'

It was in the midst of this atmosphere of relaxed nerves and public rejoicings that Cateau heard that Fervaques had been killed. He was shot at Mons, on the way home from Charleroi, by a detachment of enemy cavalry engaged in a quite unimportant scouting expedition.

As soon as she knew what had happened Cateau told herself she had felt all along that it would be so. The tragedy was inevitable —

assuredly she had brought it on herself by parting from her lover in
anger, for the first time in the six years they had lived together.
Always before, when he rode off to war, she had bidden him a tender
farewell. And every day during the weeks or months of his absence,
no matter how long it might be, she had prayed for him on her knees
in her oratory, and had Masses said at Saint-Roch — or at the Abbey
Church of Queen Mathilda at Caen, if she chanced to be in the
country — to ensure his safe return.

Season after season she had gone through this performance faithfully. It could certainly do no harm — that was the way Cateau
looked at it — and it might do some good. Above all — and this
seemed to her much more important than praying to God, who
might or might not be listening — she had enshrined Fervaques'
image in her heart; had held the *thought* of him close to her, with the
triumphant conviction that, regardless of who else fell in battle, *he*
must come back because she willed it.

That was what she had done for her lover gladly through the long
years of the fighting. She had had her reward, too, in seeing him
reappear every winter, with not even a scratch after the fiercest
campaigns.

And now — *this!* . . . Cateau was positive she was entirely to
blame for his death. Only her love had been able to pull Fervaques
through before — the moment she withdrew it he fell, pierced to the
heart by her cruelty no less certainly than by the Dutch bullets.
Oh, there was no doubt about it: she was a murderess!

She was so stunned by the blow that she could not even weep.
She felt turned to stone, too wretched to care what became of her.
Cateau did not know what to do with her grief. She had not had
one to live with for such a very long time — and this was the worst
thing that had ever befallen her. On one point alone she had made
up her mind: she could not stay any longer in Fontainebleau. The
place where she and Fervaques had quarrelled had grown utterly
odious in her sight. Besides, there was nothing to stay for — the
town was a desert. Cécile de Montglas had, naturally, taken herself off the day the men left for Flanders; and Isabelle de Montmorency, with unusual tact, did the same without waiting for someone to suggest it. So the villa was hastily closed, and Cateau and
her niece returned to Paris. Tinette, however, did not go back to
her family, but remained for the present, at her aunt's special request, in the house in the rue de la Sourdière.

It was rather strange about Tinette. On closer acquaintance
Cateau had been slightly disappointed in her: she was not really so
pretty as she had looked that day at the convent in Orléans, not
clever enough to win the social success one had hoped for. But the
child was a comfort, though one could not tell why. That round-

eyed, silent sympathy was somehow the only balm that soothed
Cateau's suffering; the latter had therefore begged Magdelon to be
allowed to keep her guest a few weeks more, and Magdelon, who
ached with sorrow for her sister, was only too glad to grant her wish.

The two settled down then in the big, lonely house — bigger and
lonelier than ever before — to await the return of Fervaques' suite,
whose duty it was to bring home their master's remains.

Cateau herself had had no direct word from Flanders. All the
information she had been able to glean came from Fervaques'
brother, young Denis de Bullion, now the last surviving hope of the
Bonnelles. Bullion was no soldier; he had made one campaign several years ago, but decided, in short order, that he was not cut out
for a military life. And since then he had taken a position as councillor of parliament in Metz, where he spent most of the year. It was
his newly announced betrothal to Mademoiselle de Rouillé — the
unfortunate first cause of Cateau's differences with her lover — that
accounted for his presence in the city at this time.

Denis was twenty-six, a small, neat, shy, rather literal-minded
fellow, whom not all the moneybags of the Bullions could make interesting. He had not been so close to Fervaques as the elder
brother, poor Gallardon: Cateau's acquaintance with him was so
casual that it seemed odd to find herself seated opposite him in the
Chinese cabinet, discussing her intimate tragedy with this precise,
vaguely hostile young man.

It was a stifling afternoon in late August, but in spite of the heat
the windows were all shut and darkened, and the room was draped
in black. Cateau wore black, also, a plain gown with high neck and
long sleeves, just as though she were really a widow; she had, however, not quite dared don the bandeau, conventional badge of marital bereavement; her uncovered curls, satin-smooth and scented,
were the only bright note in the scene.

Bullion, on the other side of the hearth, cleared his throat and began twirling his plumed hat with fidgety fingers — he was apparently
painfully embarrassed.

After all, there was little enough he could tell her. He himself had
not managed to gather more than the bare outlines of the story.
Fervaques, it seemed, had been shot at dawn on the fifteenth of
August, just outside the walls of Mons. Pyrrhus had fallen under
him, and he himself, mortally wounded in the breast, had been left
for dead on the field, the enemy having put the whole French detachment of cavalry to flight. When his friends returned later,
under a flag of truce, to claim the body, it was gone; only the car-
case of Pyrrhus remained as silent witness of the catastrophe. It
was to be presumed that the Dutchmen had removed the poor
fellow, either dying or dead, to the citadel.... However, said

Bullion, he was already in touch with his brother's chief equerry, who had been told to take up the matter with the colonel in charge of the garrison at Mons; they expected within a few days to be able to make arrangements for the transport of the corpse to Paris for burial.

'There's really no more I can say, madam,' ended Bullion, after his brief recital, 'except that I wish to offer you my sincere condolences. I know, too, that you must feel for us on this unhappy occasion — that you would like to express your sympathy for my poor mother, though, unfortunately, in the circumstances...I mean, as it's not possible...that is to say, I imagine...' He floundered awkwardly for a moment, colouring up to the roots of his hair; then made a manful effort to recover himself by a handsome conclusion: 'May I therefore be so bold as to take it upon myself, madam, to convey your appropriate sentiments to Madame de Bonnelle?'

Cateau bowed, courteously acquiescent; she felt for the first time a stirring of kindliness for the young man who was so like, and yet so unlike, her dead lover. Then she rose to take leave of him; there seemed to be little use in prolonging the conversation.

'Thank you for coming to see me, sir,' she said. 'I trust you will keep me informed as to the progress of this sad affair, and as soon as you have definite word from Mons ——'

'Of course, of course!' Bullion had also risen to stand, still twirling his hat in his hands. He cleared his throat again once or twice, having evidently not yet said all he had come to say.

'There's one thing more, madam...'

'Yes, sir?'

'About — about my poor brother's estate. I dare say you are aware that he died intestate?'

Cateau bowed again. 'Yes, I know.'

'And therefore, lacking a will, his fortune reverts to his family — that is, to his mother and to me.'

'Yes, I know that, too.'...Too well, alas! Cateau reflected; the subject had many a time proved a bone of contention between Fervaques and herself. She had tried, over and over, to get him to make a will, but always unsuccessfully. Whenever she chose to remind him, with gloomy persistence, that life was uncertain, that even the healthiest youth was in danger in wartime, he would chuckle and shake his head and reply that, if he died, he did not care in the least what became of his money — there was no one in particular he wanted to leave it to, since all the people he loved were too rich already. And no argument Cateau could devise had been able to shake him — there the matter had rested. It was now too late to do more than regret what seemed an almost criminal lack of foresight, and to

assure this indecently anxious young man and his mother, that
harpy Charlotte, that she had no intention of disputing their right to
what was legally theirs.

'I have small knowledge of the Marquis's financial affairs,' said
Cateau formally. 'When his household returns to Paris, his stewards
and bailiffs will doubtless be able to satisfy your curiosity regarding
his income; they will be answerable to you that all shall be found in
good order. As to the property he and I shared in common, this
house, as perhaps you know, we held on a joint lease only. The
Hôtel de Rouen in Saint-Germain belongs to me. As to the furnish-
ings of both places, they' — she paused for a second, to savour to
the full young Monsieur de Bullion's shameless eagerness — 'are of
course mine, also.'

'Yes, madam — that is, naturally, I have no doubt of your word.
But do you mean that all this...? We had always understood...
Had my brother no part...?'

'All mine,' Cateau repeated, with firmness. 'Except, of course,
such pieces as stand in the Marquis's private apartments. Whatever
is there is his, hence now yours. On the day I heard of his death I
turned the key in the lock of his rooms. That key I now hand over to
you. Use it as you will; your brother's belongings are yours to do
with as you see fit.'

She held out the slip of bronze to Bullion, who received it with
profuse apologies, the flow of which Cateau cut off with as curt a dismissal as was consonant with good manners. She had nothing further
to say to the young man; she hoped fervently she had done forever
with Fervaques' relatives. A pair of vultures, that's what they were!
hovering about to snatch what treasures they could, while the poor
boy's body was still unburied. A plague on them both!

As she conducted young Denis to the door of the Chinese cabinet
and gave him two fingers of her right hand to kiss, she said to herself
that, considering everything, she could claim to be fortunate. True,
she had not, unhappily, been able to induce Fervaques to leave her
by testament half, or at any rate a third, of his income — which, in
the circumstances, she felt would have been a fair disposition. But,
at least, it was entirely owing to her own prudence and powers of
persuasion that he had done, only last spring, what she had told him
for years was his duty and made over his share of the contents of the
house in the rue de la Sourdière — which had been as much his as
hers and were worth, at a moderate estimate, several million francs
— to his 'dearly beloved friend, the Comtesse d'Olonne.' The deed
of gift, duly signed in the presence of Maître Le Caron, lay safe this
minute in one of the hundred drawers of the mother-of-pearl writing-
table, scarce five paces away from where she and Bullion were standing.

On the way back from the door Cateau caught sight of her black-gowned figure in the glass. For a minute she hardly recognized the hollow-eyed woman with ravaged features and lustreless hair. Then she shivered and murmured pitifully, as if to some stranger: 'Poor thing! You look a thousand years old! Ah, if Fervaques were to see you now . . . !'

It was still early; she was faced with the burning necessity of finding some means of passing the rest of the afternoon. Whatever she did would be preferable to remaining indoors while that odious Bullion boy poked about, moving furniture and making inventories in Fervaques' rooms, which were just underneath her own.

She rang for Quentine to inquire the whereabouts of her niece, and when she found that Mademoiselle de la Ferté had gone for a walk in the Tuileries Gardens attended by Lucie, Cateau decided to go for a walk, too. It was hot, but not unbearably so; perhaps the physical motion would tire her sufficiently so that she could hope for a short sleep later, before supper. She called for Cinna and Rodrigue — who had accompanied their master on his last journey only as far as Paris — intending to take them with her; but a footman informed her that the dogs had gone out with the young lady and her maid. That was too bad: exercising Cinna and Rodrigue was a penance Cateau performed daily with fanatical regularity. Well, there was no help for it — very likely she would meet Tinette and her lumbering pets in the park, and they could then all come home together.

Cateau's house was so near the Tuileries that it was not worth while having the horses harnessed to carry her thither; she took a sedan-chair instead, and told her bearers to leave her at the west gate of the gardens. Casting a veil of black gauze over her head and hoisting a sunshade, she made her way slowly along the gravelled path towards the octagonal pool.

As she walked she thought how much the place had changed since her youth. In the old days the Tuileries had been a thick grove of trees, so wild and uncharted that one easily could (and sometimes did, with a lover!) get lost in it. The grove was gone now. So were the aviary and the menagerie and, saddest of all, the quaint little restaurant of Renard with its terrace overlooking the river, where it had been amusing to take an ice with one's gallant on fine summer evenings. These had been banished by decree of Le Nôtre, the King's landscape architect, who had laid out in their place a formal garden, with a profusion of neat paths and flower-beds. The big square weedy duck pond in the centre had given way to a number of handsome stone basins with fine jets of water. . . . It was all very smart and very correct, but Cateau sometimes felt a pang for the undisciplined charms of the past.

This was one of the times. While she strolled sedately between rows of late roses and flaming dahlias her mind travelled back to that day in June, so many years ago — Good God! Was it really *twenty?* — when she had walked in the Tuileries with the Duc de Candale and said farewell to him, all unsuspecting, for the last time on earth. She had thought — poor foolish girl! — that she could not suffer more than she was suffering then, tortured by love and jealousy. All the same, she had found later, when Candale was taken from her, that the pain she'd felt before was as nothing compared to that which came after. Life seemed to have come to an end. Ardently, endlessly, she had prayed to be reunited with her lover by death. But death would not come — she was too young and vital to die! — and after a while she had picked up the broken threads of the pattern once more, though she could not guess where she got the courage to do it. Still more time passed; in the end she grew used to the bitter business of living; she let men fall in love with her again, and even pretended to have fallen in love with them. From the day of Candale's death, however, to that other day, long afterwards — though it, too, was now buried six years in the past — when she had accepted Fervaques, she had not truly cared for any man. Fervaques was the gentle lover of her middle age, as Candale had been the fiery lover of her youth: she had been glad to find her repose in the tolerant, sympathetic understanding of the one, after the other's violent passion and egotism. Yes, Fervaques had been all and more than she had hoped he would be. He made up to her for the mistakes of her young womanhood, the disappointments of marriage. Child and lover in one, with him by her side she had not known what it meant to be really unhappy.

Now, as the sense of her present loneliness swept over her, together with the desolate vistas of the old age she would soon be facing with no hand in hers, her steps faltered and tears filled her eyes — the first she had actually shed, although ever since the terrible news had come she felt that her heart had been weeping unseen.

This would never do — *never!* Whatever happened, she must not cry in public — especially not in the Tuileries Gardens, where anyone in the world might see her. She feared she had attracted too much attention already; those Musketeers flirting with a pair of giggling nursemaids on the other side of the octagonal pool had sent several curious glances in her direction.

To distract herself and help calm her emotion, Cateau sat down on the first bench she saw, in the midst of the sun and the flowers, and fumbled in her pocket for a letter she had received only that morning from Madame de Montmorency.... Isabelle wrote from Bagnolet, where she was spending a fortnight with the Duchesse de Nemours, to tell her old friend how deeply she grieved for her loss.

Her pen was unskilled in expressing the softer sentiments, yet somehow a feeling of genuine pity contrived to make itself felt through the screen of conventional phrases. Nevertheless, it was not so much for the letter itself as for its postscript that Cateau reread it. Isabelle added, in an all-but-indecipherable scrawl at the foot of the page, that 'Madame de M.' had gone to the country because there had been so much gossip about her so-called 'affair' with poor Monsieur de Fervaques.

'You know and I know, my dear,' wrote Isabelle, 'how much truth there is in those ill-natured reports. No doubt Cécile is a foolish woman, but she is not, and never has been, a wicked one. For my part, I have always maintained she's spent her life doing the right things, but at the wrong moments. The one thing that distresses me now is that she's determined to justify herself; she has taken the stand that nobody in his senses could possibly have misunderstood her motives, and that it will be for me to "choose," as she puts it, which of my two friends I desire to keep. I cannot, apparently, retain both and her approval as well. I think there is no need to tell you, my dear, what my answer must be.'

Cateau let the letter fall back in her lap with a smile of listless irony. Yes, she could guess easily enough how Isabelle would decide — and, even more easily, alas! the causes determining her loyalty. But that made no difference now.... Poor Cécile, though! Poor silly creature, to risk losing the one friend she had for a point of petty personal spite. Cateau was very sorry for Cécile. She did not hate her any more — or, rather, it would be more correct to say that she had never hated her. She despised her, which was quite another thing, wasn't it? She had always considered the Montglas the stupidest woman of her acquaintance; that was the reason, of course, she had been so furious, the night of the fête in Fontainebleau — to think that Fervaques should choose, out of all the women there were in the world, to flirt with *Cécile!* — Cécile, who was old enough to be his mother, and who had had nothing on earth to recommend her then save her silver hair and her silver frock and the fact that she'd used her rouge-pot to more than ordinary advantage.... Cateau knew Fervaques had meant nothing by it — he had not cared in the least for the old hag! He had pretended to care, for an hour or two, only because he was angry with Cateau and realized that nothing else could so humble her pride.

It would have blown over in a few days at most. Cateau would have forgiven him. Oh, yes, of course she would! She despised the kind of mistress who watched her lover like a hawk, jealously refusing to let him out of her sight for fear he might break loose from his leading-strings. No! That type of narrow possessiveness was beneath her dignity. She had gone her way gaily instead, proud of her trust in her man. Look how broad-minded she had been about his friendship with Doudou de Ventadour, which many a woman would have nipped in the bud! In the six years of their life together this ridiculous quarrel over Cécile had been their only serious misunderstanding. That was why it seemed unforgivably cruel of fate to snatch him from her now, of all times — so that they could never kiss and make up and say how silly they'd been and how sorry they were. As long as she lived Cateau must remember that they'd parted in anger — it was no consolation to remind herself for how trivial a cause. 'And it's forever,' she thought. '*Forever!* (A horrible word and a horrible thing.) There's nothing I can do about it — nothing at all! That's what's so hard to bear!'

Tears welled up in her eyes again, and this time she made no attempt to conceal them. She did not even bother to draw the black gauze veil across her face. What did it matter how she looked or who saw her now? There was no one left to care — *no one!*

At the sound of a step approaching on the gravel she turned her blurred vision down the broad path between the flower-beds, wondering if it could be Tinette and the wolfhounds. Then, suddenly, she started and leaned forward in her seat, for she saw that instead of her niece it was Magdelon coming towards her — Magdelon, hatless and breathless, hurrying as fast as the heat and her voluminous seal-brown taffeta skirts would permit.

At first Cateau pretended not to see her — for who knew what had brought Magdelon to the Tuileries at this hour of the day and alone? Parks were lovers' rendezvous. . . . Besides, had one not heard lately that she and the Abbé de Lignerac . . . ?

But it was soon obvious that the Maréchale was in search of her sister. Cateau waved her black-bordered handkerchief in greeting, and stood up as the other drew near.

The two embraced: Magdelon, Cateau found, was distressingly out of breath; her dark eyes were big and expressionless, as though she did not see what she was looking at, but was staring at some dreadful vision within.

'What is it? What's the matter? There, child, sit down beside me, for pity's sake! or you'll drop dead of apoplexy in this heat.'

Magdelon collapsed and began fanning herself faintly with a small gold paper fan. She was still scarcely able to speak.

'My dear! The most terrible!' she gasped. 'I came as soon as I could. Oh, Cateau, you'll never guess! It's . . . Louis . . . !'

'Louis!' exclaimed Cateau. 'What in Heaven's name can have happened to *him?*'

For the Maréchal's second son was the best and most docile of all his children, the only one of the five who had never caused his parents a moment's uneasiness since the day of his birth. At the question Louis' mother grew so pale that Cateau was afraid she might be going to faint.

'Darling! Please tell me!' said Cateau, anxiously pressing her sister's hand. 'Has there been an accident? He's not ill or — dead, is he?'

Magdelon shook her head without speaking, and Cateau heaved a sigh of relief. As long as Louis was alive and well there must be hope. Life, thought Cateau sombrely, was the most important thing there was — the only really important thing. She pressed Magdelon's hand more warmly in hers and said, in her most matter-of-fact tone: 'Now tell me, my dear, as soon as you can, what it is that has happened and what we can do about it.'

Magdelon stared at Cateau for a few more minutes in silence — she was apparently still suffering from shock — but at last succeeded in finding the courage to begin. Her story, which took her a long time to tell — with many a pause for sobs — was sufficiently astonishing.

It appeared that Louis de la Ferté, who had graduated from the Jesuit Academy the spring before last with all possible honours, had begged as a special favour to be allowed to stay on after graduation to do some research work in the classics. His father had given him permission, albeit reluctantly: it seemed to La Ferté a great waste of time — the lad had been mulling over his books for years — surely it would have been better for him to join the army at once and try to make a name for himself quickly before the end of the war robbed him of the opportunity!... Louis was a likely young fellow, as well-grown and good-looking as his brother, and with twice as much common sense as poor Henri. The Maréchal had wanted to buy a regiment for Louis immediately, ill though he could afford it. It had been a deep disappointment to him to be forced to postpone the purchase, but he had given way, with unusual meekness, because both he and Magdelon felt the boy had earned a right to do as he pleased: the extra year's work was his due, if that were what he most cared for.

'But now, darling, we've discovered it was only a ruse,' cried Magdelon, 'on the part of those wicked men to keep him a prisoner with them. He's joined the Society of Jesus, without telling us or anyone else. He's going to be a Jesuit priest!'

Cateau made a small noncommittal sound of sympathy. She was surprised, and not a little disappointed herself — Louis, she felt, had been designed for better, or at any rate braver, things. But, after all, most noble families who had several sons gave one or two to the church. It was not in the least unusual: was it worth making such a fuss about?

She said as much to Magdelon; and Magdelon had replied: No,

oh, no — of course it was not! *She* would have been quite resigned to it, if only La Ferté hadn't minded so much. She always worried terribly when Henri was away at the war; it had often seemed that she would not be able to bear it when Louis grew old enough to fight, too — Louis, her darling, her best beloved boy. And he talked too beautifully about his vocation, saying that Ignatius Loyola had appeared to him in a dream and bidden him make teaching his lifework.... The Jesuits were very much excited about Louis' dream.... But La Ferté refused even to try to understand. He was raging with thwarted ambition. To think that *his* son — bone of his bone and flesh of his flesh — could have turned out a milksop, a pious, preaching eunuch in a skirt — oh, the words he had used! — those cruel, frightening words!... They'd found out what the boy had done a day or two ago, when the Maréchal sent to him to say that the year was up and his regiment waiting. But Magdelon had not told her sister directly because she knew that Cateau herself was in sore affliction.

'And oh, my dearest, I'd not have troubled you now, if I could help it! But of course you'd hear sooner or later, anyhow. La Ferté's been out of his mind, I think. He got up from a sickbed when he heard the news and drove straight to the college and talked to the fathers there as I've never known even him talk to anybody. He cursed them all — he cursed Louis, too, and the day he was born, and disinherited him. And then — it's so awful I can't bear to tell you! — today — just now — when we were crossing the Pont Neuf in our carriage, we ran into a group of boys from the college — novices, you know. They had sacks on their backs and were begging for alms and food from the crowd, to give to the poor. That's part of their work. But Louis was with them, and when his father saw him he cried out in a passion and cursed him again, and stopped the carriage in the middle of the bridge, and sent his lackeys to chase his own son. They'd have flogged him to death if they'd caught him! — Think of it, Cateau! I had to sit there and watch.... Only the boy managed to slip through the crowd and into a house in the Place Dauphine. I saw where he went, but my husband didn't, thank God!... I don't know how I got La Ferté home. As soon as I'd left him I drove to your house, but they said there that you'd gone for a walk in the Tuileries, so I came to find you as soon as I could. Oh, Cateau, Cateau, what shall I do?'

Magdelon burst into loud sobs.

Cateau comforted her in a quiet, unemotional way, as she had so many times before in their lives. She knew that Magdelon's griefs were soon over — like all storms, they must run their course — but though the victim might bend to the ground before their full fury, she would never break. And once they were past she would feel amazingly restored.

Cateau wished she herself might find surcease from her agony in physical violence of some kind. If she could weep wildly, as Magdelon was doing now, she would not feel the pain within her gnawing her heart away with terrible slow sureness. But she was not able to weep — she could only sit where she was on the bench in the park in the hot August sunshine, and thump Magdelon's shoulder and say: 'There, there!' and 'Never mind, dear!' and 'It'll soon be better' — just as she'd done years ago when they were little girls in the country and her sister stubbed her toe or bruised her shins in play. . . .

Presently, it *was* better: Magdelon sat up and wiped her eyes and put her curls to rights, and said (this, also, was according to formula!): 'Darling, forgive me! You're always so good! It was the shock . . . but it shan't happen again, I promise you!'

They sat there together a few minutes longer in the bright searching light amongst all those pretty, gay flowers — it was an incongruous setting for sorrow, thought Cateau; she was conscious of their two mourning figures, one in black, the other in sober brown, as tragic bolts on a scene made for joy. Then Magdelon kissed her sister and got up, saying gently: 'I'm going to Saint-Roch now, to burn a candle to Our Lady and ask her to watch over Louis. Come with me, dear, won't you? It will do you good, I know. I've talked so much about my troubles, I've almost forgotten that you've a much worse one of your own.'

'My trouble can't be healed by prayer,' answered Cateau bitterly. 'It's too late: there's nothing I can ask for now.'

'Well, come anyhow, sister,' urged Magdelon. 'It never does one harm to pray. After all, miracles can happen. Look how God saved Charleroi for the King! As long as Fervaques' body hasn't been found, you mustn't despair of his life. And remember poor Gilette de Fiesque — when her first husband Piennes fell at the siege of Arras, it was over a month before she had any news.'

'Yes,' said Cateau dryly; 'and don't forget, either, when they found him at last he had a bullet in his brain.'

As she spoke she gave the gravel at her feet a vicious prodding with the point of her parasol. But she rose after that and, arm-in-arm with her sister, walked to the west gate of the gardens, where she dismissed her sedan-chair and got into the Maréchale's coach.

Saint-Roch was deserted at this time of day, wrapped in a solemn mid-afternoon hush. The interior seemed gratefully dark and cool after the blaze of light and heat outside. Cateau and Magdelon bought candles from the drowsy sacristan and lighted them in the Lady Chapel, behind the high altar, which was even cooler and darker than the nave, and so quiet that one could hear plainly some sparrows twittering up under the eaves outside the tall stained-glass windows. Magdelon flung herself at once on her knees upon the bare stones and began to pray, with clasped hands and moving lips, her eyes upturned in devotional rapture.

After a moment's hesitation Cateau followed suit, a trifle self-consciously. Although she would never have admitted it to her sister, she was not used to going to church except on feast days. It had been years since she had attended either Mass or confession with regularity. There were excellent reasons for this. Cateau might not be pious, but she believed in God. That is to say, she knew there must be *Someone* up there, who looked down upon human beings and praised them or blamed, with impartial justice, according to their deserts. And there could, unluckily, be little doubt of the stand that Someone would take about the Comtesse d'Olonne: she was an adulteress, living in open and permanent sin. *Permanent* — there was the point to be emphasized! Other people were sinners sometimes. Magdelon — and Cateau herself, in her youth — had broken their marriage vows now and then, for a few days or weeks, or even months, maybe — at the end of which time they made a clean breast of their transgressions, did penance for them, and were duly forgiven. That was all right; there was a place in the church for occasional waywardness.

But Cateau's love for Fervaques was different. It went on and on: there was no stopping it. Worse, Cateau did not *want* to stop it. That she had somehow succeeded in rationalizing her conduct to her own satisfaction — that it did not seem wrong in *her* eyes — could not license the attachment in God's. As far as the church was concerned, she was a lost soul; and as she did not like being lost, she stayed away — it was really so much simpler — and sent Monsieur Coignet, the vicar of Saint-Roch, a substantial sum for the poor four times a year. She prayed, of course, at home, but less and less often as time went on, until there were days on end when she scarcely prayed at all.

But now, kneeling on the cold, slightly damp stones in the dusk of the Lady Chapel, smelling the incense, watching the light of the candles and Magdelon's streaming eyes and tremulous lips, Cateau began to feel, suddenly and uncomfortably, that she might have made a mistake. Perhaps it was not enough to treat God with respect, to retire from His presence when it appeared tactful to do so. Perhaps God did not just passively disapprove of her, but was actively angry instead. Perhaps He had sent her on purpose the worst punishment He could devise — the one blow that had the power to destroy her utterly. Perhaps, on the other hand, if she told Him now she was sorry for what she had done, He might relent.... No, no! That was hopeless! She was too steeped in habitual sin to expect His forgiveness. But Mary, Our Lady of

Sorrows, who was a woman and therefore merciful — what if one offered Her, in humility, all one's love and contrition? — and promised solemnly, if She would spare Fervaques' life, to recompense Her in whatever way Mary chose? ...

Expiation! That was it! It was a beautiful thought. For the present it would not be necessary to put into words precisely what form it ought to take. That could be left rather vague until one saw what Our Lady meant to do about helping.... '"An eye for an eye,"' thought Cateau, '"a tooth for a tooth"'... or no: that was from the wrong part of the Bible, wasn't it? That had to do with the vengeance of the Lord, which was not what was in question here. Besides, one must be properly polite in addressing such a very great lady as the Blessed Virgin.... 'Holy Mary, save my lover's life, and I'll do whatever You ask of me — I promise it — truly! Only save him — don't let him be dead for always! That's too long — I can't stand it! He's all I've got in the world.... Mary, *You* know it's not fair to exact such a sacrifice — anything else — I swear it — anything else on earth You want — only save his life for me! *Please, Mary* ...!'

She rose from her devotions stiff-kneed but greatly comforted. There were tears in her eyes again, but this time she was not ashamed of them; and when she took leave of Magdelon outside the church (for the house in the rue de la Sourdière was just round the corner), the latter whispered affectionately as they kissed each other: 'She's helping me, dear — and She'll help you, too — see if She doesn't!'

For three days in a row Cateau went back to Saint-Roch every afternoon and kneeled in the Lady Chapel an hour each time, her eyes fixed on the Virgin's image, her mind wholly concentrated on the bargain she hoped to strike with Mary. Yes, bargain — why not? There was nothing to be ashamed of in that. Mary was a lady, but none the less She could not be totally lacking in business sense. She must be made, somehow or other, to incline Her ear favourably to what Cateau could not help considering, quite dispassionately, an admirable proposition. Mary ought really to jump at it, Cateau thought. Think of the terms that were offered! Fervaques' life — the breath in the body of one insignificant human creature — in exchange for whichever of the Countess's lands or goods Our Lady might cast a covetous eye on. Yes, it was certainly a magnificent proposal! ...

On the fourth day Cateau did not go to Saint-Roch at all until late in the evening, and then only for a very few minutes; for she was too busy and too much excited to pray. The impossible had proved possible, after all — Mary had accepted the bargain — *Fervaques was alive!*

The news was brought to the house just as Madame d'Olonne and her niece were sitting down to midday dinner. It was contained in a brief note from Monsieur de Bullion, who said in it that he would do himself the honour of waiting on the Countess directly to give her the details he had no time to write. When Cateau read the note she turned red, and then white, and then fainted, for the first time in her life, sliding from her chair at the dinner-table to the floor in a limp heap; while Tinette shrieked aloud in terror, fearing that Aunt d'Olonne had dropped dead.

As soon as Cateau came to her senses she told Tinette the contents of the letter, whereupon they cried and hugged each other and indulged in a pleasant form of modified hysterics until Monsieur de Bullion was announced.

To do him justice, young Denis was beaming with joy over the tidings he bore. Interested considerations weighed nothing in the balance, apparently, compared to family feeling, of which all the Bonnelles had an inexhaustible stock. . . . It was almost incredible, was it not? Bullion himself had hardly been able to bring himself to believe it — but there was a line in his brother's own handwriting to prove it was true, as well as a letter from the colonel in charge of the Dutch garrison at Mons, where Fervaques was a prisoner. It seemed, amazing to relate, that he had not even been wounded: his horse had been shot under him, and as he fell to earth he was captured by the enemy, who had routed the French so promptly that there had been no one left to see what became of their leader. And at Mons he had been ever since, held a captive, but perfectly well and comfortable, having been given the best of treatment and made free of the officers' mess. The one trial had been that the colonel had refused to let him write to his family in Paris until it was certain the French troops had left the vicinity and there could be no further question of large-scale hostilities. Hence the stupid delay in assuring his dear ones of his safety. He hoped that they had not worried too much. Nothing remained now save to make arrangements, as speedily as possible, to pay ransom for his return to France. As ill luck would have it, there was no Dutch prisoner of rank against whom Fervaques might be exchanged. There was nothing for it, then, but to pay the price. Those greedy Lowland beggars were demanding one thousand pistoles. . . .

One thousand pistoles! Ten thousand francs! That was an immense, a breath-taking sum — still, little enough for a man's life and liberty. (Would the Virgin even stoop to consider it as part payment . . . ?)

'Oh, sir,' cried Cateau, 'I shall send the money at once! Only let me know how to manage it.'

But Bullion, smiling, shook his head.

'Nay, madam, that's *my* duty, not yours. I am my brother's heir, his nearest male relative. Naturally it devolves upon me to advance the money, until such time as he can reimburse me. As a matter of fact, my steward has already left for Flanders with the cash in hand.'

Cateau's face fell. How stupid she was! She had reckoned without Fervaques. She had become tragically used to doing that during this last week of horror. But of course, now that he was alive, he would want to pay his own ransom. So *that* would not serve as a means of requiting Our Lady! Something else must be thought of, to show how thankful she was. Meanwhile: 'You'll stay to dinner, sir?' said Cateau, remembering her manners. 'Jean, lay a place on my right for Monsieur de Bullion.'

During dinner Cateau, still almost hysterical with relief, made herself as agreeable as she could to young Denis. Denis, in return, was exceedingly polite to the beautiful Countess, who, no matter how many vile things were said of her (he himself had heard hundreds), must certainly love his brother very deeply, if her present behaviour were a criterion. Doubtless she was really a decent woman at heart; one had always known she was a charming one. It was quite possible that the world had misjudged her — why, look at her now! She was radiant, positively ecstatic, blushing and smiling like a young girl! And people called her hard and dissolute. . . . Well, that showed how little people knew. It was a pity only that she was not free to marry Fervaques — and that, even if she were, her age and the unfortunate notoriety of her career would have made the match unsuitable — for there was no question that she loved him with a wife's love for her husband.

Cateau, for her part, was feeling penitently that she had been wrong all along about her lover's young brother. Because he resembled a washed-out edition of Fervaques, she had too hastily assumed that his character was washed-out as well. She had supposed he must be calculating, because most Bonnelles were calculating — it was their inheritance from their ancestor, old Claude. Yet once he had established his claim to his brother's belongings, he had not pressed it, nor made the slightest attempt to remove what was, after all, his to take when he would. He had not disturbed anything — even refraining scrupulously from making use of the key she had given him to enter the Marquis's apartments. (That she had definitely ascertained by cross-questioning Jean, her maître-d'hôtel.) More than likely old Charlotte had put him up to the little he'd done to displease her. So that really . . . Yes, after all, young Denis was quite all right. He was not even so insignificant in appearance as she had thought him. Of course, he was puny and pale compared to Fervaques, but his features were pleasingly regular, and when he smiled — if the light weren't too bright . . .

All the while she was urging a second helping of fish upon him, and pouring him glasses of golden Ay with a hand that trembled ever so slightly (no wonder, tonight!), Cateau was studying her guest. Before the evening was over she had entirely revised her early unfavourable opinion and decided that Monsieur de Bullion was a most delightful young man.

She found no reason in the next few days to change her mind again. Bullion came to call every day: the more she saw him, the more she liked him — the more keenly, too, she began to regret his engagement to Mademoiselle de Rouillé, the councillor's daughter. For as often as she beheld him and Tinette together, as many times did she deplore her failure to carry through her original scheme. Cateau was so made that she could not view a youth and a maiden in each other's company without thinking of them at once in matrimonial terms. The match would have been ideal in every respect. Bullion was intelligent and good-tempered, well-behaved and rich, lacking only an illustrious family to be an altogether unexceptionable parti. Tinette's family, on the other hand, was excellent; what *she* lacked was a fortune. Cateau could not help reflecting what a good thing it would be for the La Fertés if someone belonging to them had not only money, but also a faculty for handling it.... Of course, Charlotte might have been obstinate — she might well have pretended that Tinette's birth and breeding were not dazzling enough to atone for a paltry dowry. But then, if that had been all that stood in the way, Cateau might easily have made up the deficiency herself. She had about come to the conclusion, anyhow, that it was her duty to provide financially for Tinette. After all, she had no daughter of her own — and the child was a dear little thing.... Oh, it was all a great pity! Bullion's betrothal had been already made public; he and his fiancée were only waiting for Fervaques' official sanction to make plans for the wedding. There was nothing Cateau could do about it now. Or was there...?

It was not until the night of her lover's return that she found the answer to the question that perplexed her — how to settle her niece and, at the same time, repay the Virgin for saving Fervaques' life. The solution, once she'd hit upon it, was perfectly simple. How queer it was she'd not thought of it sooner! Half an hour earlier, even, she'd not had the least inkling of what she must do. She had sat in the Chinese cabinet all evening, dressed in her best, waiting for the sound of wheels in the street. Tinette, dressed in *her* best, too, and much excited, was with her aunt. But Cateau was too deeply preoccupied to talk. She held her pose, tranquilly silent, her mind wholly bent on her problem, which seemed, as far as she could see, no nearer being solved than ever. Indeed, her train of thought was so undeviating that she was not as stirred up as she

ought to have been over the fact that her lover was coming home.
It was Tinette who bounced up to look through the window whenever a carriage rattled by below in the rue de la Sourdière, who
glanced at the clock with impatience at least every five minutes and
counted the quarter-hour chimes, very near, very clear, on this
warm August night, of the great bell at Saint-Roch. . . . 'Aunt, aunt,
don't you think now that *soon* . . .?'

When at last a coach, instead of passing by like all the other
coaches, did stop at the door, Cateau still sat on the couch as if
nothing had happened, even though Tinette tugged at her sleeve,
crying eagerly: 'He's here, aunt! He's here! Uncle Noël's come
home!'

The whole house seemed to be in a commotion. There were sounds
of feet running, of the door being thrown open, of cries of welcome
in half a dozen voices . . . then of a familiar step on the stair. . . .
And there he was on the threshold, the man she'd thought never
to see again! He looked the same as ever — he was smiling and holding out his arms — and she could not move from where she was,
could not fly to him as he must have expected her to, much less
dance about in triumphant circles like Tinette! And that was because it flashed over her, all of a sudden, what she must do for Our
Lady, who had done this for her. Her doubts were gone, her vague
premonitions took shape miraculously in the crystal clearness of
this dazzling revelation. She was so sure of Heaven's commands
that she spoke her thought aloud, while her lover stared open-
mouthed, fearing no doubt that she had gone mad from grief in
the weeks of suspense. But there it was: she *had* to say it! Throwing
Fervaques a glance charged with meaning over her niece's flaxen
head, she brought it out plainly, in a voice of inexorable conviction:
'My dear, *you* shall marry Tinette!'

Chapter VI

MADAME DE LA LOUPPE DIED IN 1679, AT MICHAELMAS. SHE DIED IN
her sleep at the Carmelite convent in the rue Bouloi — a peaceful
end, and not unexpected, as she was nearly eighty years old and
had been failing in health all through the summer.

Neither of her daughters was in Paris just then. Magdelon was
at La Ferté-Saint-Aubin, as usual, and Cateau had gone to Vichy
for a series of baths, as she had lately been troubled with rheumatism
in her hands. They returned to town, of course, as soon as possible
after hearing the news, to take charge of the funeral arrangements.
Rather to her surprise, Cateau found she was greatly upset by her
mother's death. It was hard to tell why, exactly; for Maman had
been a burden to herself and everyone else for some time. Her mind
had grown childish; she was a constant plague to the good sisters at
the convent with her caprices; it was certainly better that the Lord
in His mercy had taken her when He did.

Magdelon — as one might have known — went to pieces after
the funeral. She was in tears continually; and this was silly of her,
for she was her parent's chief legatee; in the present precarious
financial condition of the La Fertés the inheritance could only be
considered a godsend.

Maman, it developed, was richer than anyone had supposed. She
had spent next to nothing on her living for years. Even after the
death duties were paid, and various other sums handed over to
servants and charity institutions in which the old lady had taken
an interest, enough was left in both lands and actual currency of
the realm to provide a good income for her children. To Cateau,
who was already rich, that could make no great difference; but the
position of Magdelon, up to her ears in debt and saddled with a
large and demanding family, would undoubtedly be much improved.

After the will had been probated and each legacy duly paid, there
remained the question of what to do with La Louppe. The castle
itself and the adjoining estate came to Magdelon by right as part
of her marriage portion, but the furniture and other contents thereof,
of which no specific mention was made in the will, were to be divided
equally between her and Cateau, the two principal heirs.

There was nothing for it but that the sisters must go to the country to look over the property and perform the delicate task of apportioning their respective shares.

It would have been a good thing, Cateau thought, if the matter had been attended to at once, but several accidents intervened to postpone their journey. First, Magdelon caught a bad cold; then Cateau, too, came down with it; after they had both recovered, little Chou-Chou de la Ferté, who was always unlucky, cracked her ankle, and her mother insisted on nursing her herself. The Maréchal was by no means well, either; Magdelon could not make up her mind to leave him.

Time slipped away, autumn changed into winter, and still they had reached no definite decision. All Saints' Day came and went, and Martinmas, too; before one realized it hard white frost gripped the earth and Christmas was near.

It would not do to be away from home at Christmas. And, even after the holidays, for some reason or other, they found it hard to set a date for their departure. As a matter of fact, Cateau and Magdelon did not quit Paris till the third week in January.

They left on a dark and frosty morning, soon after dawn, for the way was long and the roads were sure to be slippery.

Fervaques got up early, also, to wish them godspeed. He wore a black-and-gold-embroidered dressing-gown and a nightcap atop his chocolate-coloured curls (not so thick now as of yore). Cateau bade her lover an affectionate farewell. She was sorry to leave him because she would miss him very much in the few days they were to be separated and, even more, because she knew how keenly he would miss her.

The two got on wonderfully well together, all things considered. They had not had a real quarrel in years — indeed, not since the famous one after Fervaques' return from prison in Flanders (and that seemed ages ago, now), when Cateau had tried to force him to marry her niece. To this day her face sometimes flushed as she recalled the details of that unfortunate misunderstanding. The battle had begun with arguments that lasted for days, growing more and more bitter as the chasm widened between them. After the arguments came out-and-out insults, and, after the insults, appalling fits of temper on Cateau's part, brought to a climax by slaps and stamps and even an occasional kick or two!... Fervaques had infuriated her from the start by refusing to take her idea seriously. He shouted with laughter over the tale of her vow to the Virgin, protested, in fact, that the whole thing must be a joke got up to tease him, until continued harping on one string convinced him that she was in earnest. Then, at last, he'd waxed as wrathful as Cateau herself; he'd even forgotten his manners so far as to box her ears as hard as he could — though he spoiled it by begging her pardon immediately afterwards.... In the end, Cateau could not tell how it was they had stopped. Perhaps it was only that they'd got tired of screaming and swearing at each other. Or it might have been Cateau's passionate resolve would in any case have been weakened eventually by Fervaques' lucid contention that it was absurd to say that Our Lady had brought him back to life. Had he died and then, like Lazarus, been raised from the dead by miraculous intervention, it would have been another story. But, as it was, to be childish enough to imagine that he must alter the whole course of his existence, take to wife a slip of a girl who was nothing to him, for the sake of a freakish whim — for it was no more than that! — Well, *really*, my dear ...!

By this time Cateau had arrived, though she would never have said so, at the same conclusion. Secretly she knew she did not want to give up her lover to Tinette or anyone else. Besides, she was beginning to lose the keen edge of her interest in her niece, who had done nothing, so far, to justify her relative's too sanguine hopes. Cateau had sent the child back to Fontainebleau in Doudou de Ventadour's care. Doudou duly chaperoned her to the fêtes at the palace, and reported later that her charge was docility itself: she had seemed to enjoy herself, too, in a placid way, and had danced with all the young men whom Doudou managed to persuade to the task. But nothing, alas! had come of it. Not a single offer of marriage, either brilliant or even just solidly worthy, had been made for the hand of Mademoiselle de la Ferté. Moreover, at this inopportune moment, Magdelon's affair with the Abbé de Lignerac became offensively public; so that there was really nothing to be done with Tinette except pack her off once more to the convent near Orléans.

There she had been from that day to this, apparently quite contented, poor little thing! Cateau had felt remorseful about her for a while, but after all, it was not as though one had not tried one's best to help! ... She consoled herself as well, with regard to Fervaques, by reflecting that it was not her fault if her project for marrying him off had failed. It was clear to her now — and, she felt, should have been from the beginning — that he was that rare type of man who was capable of falling in love only with older women. And on this point there was none to dispute her.

Peace had accordingly been re-established, and the two years following it were as happy as any they had known. Fervaques' victory proved ultimately to their mutual advantage; Cateau loved him the better for having conquered her once. It was a pity, she felt, to be obliged to upset the pleasant pattern of their domestic routine for even the short time required to make the trip to La Louppe. To console him for her absence she planned several small surprises, ordering from the chef special dishes that she knew to be his favourites, and even inviting Doudou de Ventadour to dine with him next Sunday after Mass.

Wifely solicitude, Cateau thought, could go no further.

Having done all in her power for her man, she was free to concentrate on the business in hand.

It was a pity the weather had suddenly turned nasty, so that the journey over rough country roads could not be considered an unalloyed pleasure. Nor, unhappily, was the prospect of two whole days in the winter coach spent in the unrelieved company of her sister as alluring as it ought to have been.

Cateau was as fond of Magdelon as ever — fonder, indeed, if anything. They had been through too much together not to be forged one to the other by links so strong that only death could break them. But Magdelon had not, worse luck! improved with age. That is, socially she had not. She was no less amiable than formerly, adversity having utterly failed to spoil the natural sweetness of her disposition. But with the passing of years she had grown almost incredibly discursive. That was perhaps to have been expected — all Angennes were active conversationalists. One must not forget poor Maman, who towards the end had babbled so incessantly it seemed sometimes as if she must have sprung a leak. Cateau herself was an admirably vigorous talker. But then, she talked about interesting things, whereas Magdelon, in her sister's opinion, was restricted to two topics only — her lovers and her children.

During the long hours side by side in the rattling, swaying carriage — their heads swathed in veils, their feet resting on charcoal footwarmers — Cateau made numerous attempts to introduce subjects of more general appeal. The war, of course, was over temporarily — the peace of Nijmegen having been signed now for more than a year — but the fascinating game of court politics offered a dozen different contemporary facets, each one worth energetic discussion. . . . There was Madame de Montespan's marked fall in favour, and Madame de Maintenon's equally marked rise. There was the appearance of a new star on the horizon in the person of the beautiful simpleton, Mademoiselle de Fontanges, the King's latest mistress. There were two royal weddings scheduled to take place in the immediate future, that of the Prince de Conti to His Majesty's eldest bastard, little Mademoiselle de Blois; and the even more brilliant nuptials of the Dauphin and the Bavarian princess, Marie-Anne-Christine-Victoire, who was the Elector's sister. There were — to descend a few rungs on society's ladder — really thrilling reports concerning the marital troubles of the hapless Doudou de Ventadour, who at last, after eight years of increasing infelicity, had been obliged to flee for her life from her husband and seek sanctuary with her mother at court. (Was it true that Ventadour had threatened to shoot her, and had actually put a few bullets through the door of her bedroom as a warning of worse to come?) ...

Nevertheless, try as she would, Cateau could not manage to decoy her sister away from the latter's twin preoccupations. Lovers and children. Children and lovers. Delightful and absorbing if they happened to be yours, hopelessly boring if they were other people's. (Oh, why didn't everyone see this?) Cateau found it hard to tell which of the two tried her most. Perhaps, on the whole, lovers were duller — at any rate, Magdelon's lovers. As she grew older and her charms began waning, the Maréchale had been forced by her insatiable search for pleasure into frequenting worlds differing widely from the court circles of her youth. Artists and actors, poets and playwrights, were her boon companions nowadays. She was forever running out to some rather shady cabaret in Saint-Cloud to attend a supper-party given by little Baron, the comedian, or the Chevalier de Liscouet (whose more respectable trade — he had two — was cardsharping). It shocked Cateau to hear of such performances, but there was no use in lecturing the culprit: Magdelon would only open her eyes very wide and croon obstinately: 'Darling, Baron's the most *adorable* ...!' or: 'You can't think what fun we had, really! Dancing till five in the morning, my dear — and the Chevalier swore he'd never seen anyone foot a courante so neatly! I felt just fifteen years old!' ...

Yes, whatever their faults, the young La Fertés were better than that! Magdelon loved her brood blindly, no matter what they did — and some of them did a deal they shouldn't! ... The girls were no trouble, of course, and Louis' career at the Jesuits' seemed exemplary. His piety edified the fathers; he was said, besides, to have developed a pronounced talent for teaching. But Jules was a spoiled and difficult youngster, and the less said about Henri and his wife, the better! ... Magdelon's eldest son had some excellent qualities; he was a very good soldier, having been wounded leading his men with great gallantry at the siege of Freiburg in '77. If only his character were more stable and he were not disposed, in moments of discouragement, to resort so promptly to drink! Not even the title of Duke and Peer, which his father had resigned in his favour two years ago in an effort to compel the lad to pull himself together, had been able to halt his dissipations.

'Poor Henri!' cooed Magdelon softly. 'There's a great deal of good in the boy. If his wife could be of some help to him ... I feel, then, perhaps ...'

But there was no use in counting on Gabrielle, as Cateau crisply reminded her.

Magdelon's face brightened when she came to speak of little Charles-Louis — Cateau's markedly did not. The latter's interest in the child, fairly strong at the time of the picturesque and dramatic circumstances attending his birth, had long since evaporated, unable to survive the flood of his mother's perpetual comments, speculations, vain wishes, and fancies. Since Magdelon could talk of her illegitimate son to no one save her sister, she indulged in her passion for doing so whenever she could, and so freely that Cateau groaned inwardly at the least mention of his name. It was Charles-Louis-this and Charles-Louis-that and Charles-Louis-the-other.... His eyes and curls and smile and likeness to his father were dwelled upon *ad nauseam*. Not even Baron's theatrical supper-parties or the outrageous remarks of that rascal Liscouet were so distasteful to Madame d'Olonne as the tale of the virtues of her youngest nephew, the Chevalier de Longueville.

Magdelon visited him in secret at the old house in the Faubourg as often as possible. Up till recently it had not always been easy to manage, but since the death last April of his grandmother, the dowager Duchesse de Longueville, there was no one left, except his tutor, the devoted Porlier, to care what became of the boy.... 'Chou-Chou and I go there once a week, regularly. It's so sweet to see the children play together. They're really getting very fond of each other. You should see how adorable they look taking turns riding on Charles-Louis' pony! Oh, he's the most entrancing child! He calls me Aunt Magdelon now, you know....'

'Aunt Magdelon' — of all things! Well, after all, why not? He'd have to call her something, wouldn't he?

Cateau sat up very straight on the back bench of the winter coach, and stared blankly out the window at the brown fields rolling endlessly by. It had begun, she noticed, to snow a little....

'I think we'll make Dreux by tonight,' she said, in a dead level voice, 'unless a storm comes up. As I remember, my dear, there's a fairly good inn at Dreux.'

No! It could not be said that this was an amusing trip. Cateau was unfeignedly glad when they reached La Louppe, about the middle of the afternoon of the second day.

It had been many years since either she or Magdelon had been there, but nothing had changed very much. The lone village street wore its familiar shabby, cosy aspect, as in their childhood. The drawbridge spanning the moat might be new, Cateau thought, as the coach rolled across it and up the drive towards the house, and some of the planting about the terrace. Otherwise all was as she remembered it, allowing for the alteration in her own vision, which made everything look smaller than it had looked thirty years ago.

She glanced about with a critical eye, observing that the roof was badly in need of repair and that the front door would have been the better for a coat of paint. But these were details. . . .

The coach had stopped; one of the lackeys had jumped off the box and was pounding for admittance. Why did no one come? Cateau had written well in advance to announce their arrival. She turned to see what Magdelon was doing and found her ecstatically contemplating a flight of pigeons, which had been startled by the sound of approaching wheels and rattled upward, their wings white against the grey slates of the roof.

'Pigeons!' cried Magdelon. 'Did you see them, darling? And white ones, too, just as they used to be. Perhaps they're the very same that were here when you and I ——'

'Nonsense, child!' said Cateau. 'I should think, at a moderate estimate, they must be their twenty-times-great-grandchildren! Now where for mercy's sake *is* everybody?'

She spoke crossly because she was more excited over the home-coming than she had expected to be — and one thing was clear: it would never do for the journey to degenerate, as it easily might if one did not keep a firm rein on one's feelings (more especially on Magdelon's feelings!), into a sentimental pilgrimage, a kind of retrospective wallowing amongst scenes and emotions of the past.

Nothing, thought Cateau, could be worse than thinking about the past. She granted that it was pleasanter than the present — everything one loved and lived by seemed sometimes to have retreated into its misty depths — but it was futile to dwell upon that, or one would fail to get on with the business of life.

It relieved her greatly to find, almost at once, that Magdelon was not going to be a trouble to her on this score. Not that Magdelon declined to look backward — far from it! Directly she crossed the threshold she was so steeped in the atmosphere of bygone days that she cast off the burden of years and became once more the little Magdelaine de la Louppe of long ago. The transformation was so complete that, curious to relate, it affected her powers of speech. Magdelon, the child, had not talked very much; Magdelon, the woman, reverted to her old, happy, inarticulate ways. She seemed in a trance, perfectly contented to wander about the old home that was now hers, dreaming in silence.

In silence — that was the best of it! She spoke scarcely a word for hours at a time, often gave the impression of not knowing where she was or what she was doing. Under the circumstances there was no obstacle to Cateau's performance of the duty that had brought her hither, which was to make a full and accurate inventory of the contents of the castle.

These, on the whole, proved disappointing. One had not hoped, of course, to find very much, but there was even less of value than

one had hoped. Most of the furniture was old and worm-eaten oak
— it would hardly be worth repairing — while mice and moths had
had their way undisturbed with curtain and carpet, leather and
tapestry. Even the sheets laid away in dozens were nearly all
mildewed beyond the rescuing point. There were trunks full of
clothes in the garret — outmoded satin and velvet gowns of the
time of Henri IV and Louis XIII, yellowed laces, quaint heavy
shoe buckles, ruffs that had graced the court of the Valois, tarnished
finery of all sorts. . . . Maman's real jewels, however, had been taken
to Paris and parcelled out amongst her daughters and granddaughters years ago.

It did not take Cateau long to dispose of such oddments. She
went through the whole place methodically, room by room, aided
in her labours by the housekeeper, a cross-eyed, ill-tempered young
woman with a black moustache, who had taken old Mahaut's post
at the latter's death, and by a flock of untrained serving-wenches.
('I never saw such slatterns in my life,' Cateau told her sister
privately. 'And there are dozens too many. If I were you, I'd
send 'em all packing!')

She would also have inspected the farms surrounding the castle
and the storehouses belonging to them — the really valuable part
of the estate — but there the Maréchal had got ahead of her. He
had dispatched his own steward and secretaries to take possession
of the property in his wife's name, within forty-eight hours of the
time Madame de la Louppe had breathed her last — and they
remained on the place, too firmly entrenched to be dislodged by fair
means or foul. Not that Madame d'Olonne had not tried her best
to do so — she'd sent for the whole troop the first morning after her
arrival and told them her sister had asked her to supervise their
accounts. But they had not believed her . . . nor, to be honest, had
Cateau really thought that they would . . .!

By the end of the third day she had succeeded in listing everything
on the premises with the exception of the picture gallery. This was
undoubtedly worth more to the heirs than all the rest of the furnish-
ings put together. There were a score of portraits of dead-and-gone
Droués and La Louppes, Marvilles and Rambouillets, a few of them
handsome still despite peeling paint and years of neglect, and none
lacking in associational interest for their descendants.

'We must play fair with the pictures,' said Cateau decidedly.

She divided them into two lots, appraising their values with an
auctioneer's eye and skilfully balancing the major items against one
another — the portrait of Maman by Philippe de Champaigne, for
instance, in exchange for a smudgy oil of incredible antiquity purported to represent Great-great-great-Grandpapa Denis de la
Louppe, original paternal ancestor of the barons of that ilk.

One canvas only was missing, the double portrait of Cateau and Magdelon as young girls that had been painted in Paris, the year of the former's marriage, by Juste d'Egmont. It was important to find it, for it was the gem of the collection. In the old days it had always hung in the Grand Saloon, but a blank space gaped now in its stead, nor could it be brought to light in any of the other reception rooms, though Cateau searched diligently the whole afternoon. She called Magdelon in from a walk through the frozen gardens to help her. They opened door after door, ransacked chests and cupboards and obscure passages in vain.

Finally the cross-eyed housekeeper with the black moustache recalled vaguely that, on the occasion of Madame de la Louppe's last visit, she had rearranged a small cabinet upstairs adjoining her bedchamber as a kind of private office and sitting-room combined. The housekeeper had forgotten to show the Countess this room; it had not been used since and, in fact, the door to it was now masked by the large pearwood chest that stood in the hall. Perhaps, it was barely possible, the missing picture might be there. . . .

'Idiot!' ejaculated Cateau. 'Of course it is! Why on earth didn't you tell me in the first place . . .?'

And there, to be sure, it actually was, on the wall over the mantel, as fresh and fine as they remembered it. It seemed to be the one spot of colour in the room. A pale yellow ray from the evening sun fell slanting across it, making lustrous the pearl pendants that hung in the painted Magdelon's ears, causing the rose in the painted Cateau's hand to glow as though it had started to bloom only now, instead of thirty summers ago.

There was a long pause, while the sisters contemplated this vivid reflection of their youth. After the first instant of startled delight Cateau began to feel a little uncomfortable. The picture was really too good, too lifelike altogether. It gave one an uneasy suspicion that the figures of those two girls, one in rose-colour, one in blue, must be alive — that somehow they had gone on living there all these years shut up in this dusty forgotten room, while the real Cateau and Magdelon were growing old in the world outside. But that was a morbid fancy; it was worse than foolish to indulge in such flights. . . . Cateau stole a glance at her sister to see how she was taking it, and found Magdelon staring wide-eyed, her hands clasped together like a wondering child's. She was saying something under her breath — Cateau had to lean forward in order to catch what it was.

'Sister,' whispered Magdelon, 'is it true? Can it be . . .? Were we ever as pretty as that?'

'Heaps prettier, I expect,' replied Cateau prosaically. 'To tell the truth, it never seemed to me that Juste quite got my mouth. Well, I'm very glad the picture was found. I should have been sorry to think it had been lost through someone's carelessness. It's a fairly good piece of work, on the whole, isn't it? — and not too impossibly old-fashioned either. How lucky it was that Maman persuaded us not to wear hats! I'll just attend to repairing the frame — I see it wants regilding in one or two places — and have it sent home to the rue de la Sourdière. You don't care, do you, dear? I've a wall in the gold cabinet where it would look rather well, I believe.'

'Oh, but, sister,' said Magdelon, still in a whisper, 'I want it, too! I want it very much indeed!'

Cateau raised her eyebrows in astonishment.

'Why, child, for Heaven's sake! what for, may I ask? Your house is so cluttered up with pictures already, I can't imagine where you'd find a corner for it. What with the Maréchal's family alone, to say nothing of the very generous share of Maman's collection I've allotted to you. And I've no husband, you know; I've nothing whatever of my own except what I've bought here and there. Besides, I'm the eldest — I've the best right to have it.'

'But the picture belongs in this house,' objected Magdelon sturdily, 'and this house belongs to me. And there's just as much of me in it as there is of you. It's both of ours, really. I've got every bit as good a right to it as you have, Cateau. And you can't want it so badly as I do!'

'I do want it, though. I want it much more than you know. As a matter of fact, it's the only thing in the damned house I *do* want!'

'Well, it's the only thing *I* want, either. If you'll let me have it, I'll give you the portrait of Grandpapa Denis and *both* silver trays in exchange.'

'I don't care a fig for Grandpapa Denis! Horrid old daub! — And I've more silver in Paris already than I know what to do with. No, dear, don't be obstinate — the picture is mine, I tell you.'

'The picture's *not* yours!' cried Magdelon, with unexpected spirit. 'Or only half of it is. The part that's of me belongs to me — you know it does!'

'I don't suppose you're suggesting,' said Cateau ironically, 'that we should cut it in two, like King Solomon's baby, and each take a share! Sister, how can you be so selfish?'

'It's you who are being selfish, not I. You've got everything in the world you want — you can't need this, too! And I — oh, you don't know how much it means to me, Cateau! You can't possibly guess. ... I'd give all I possess to own that picture. It's — oh, I don't know — it's all of our past!'

'Well, that may be, dear, but there's no particular reason, as far as I can see, to keep one's past about staring one in the face, so to speak. I shouldn't think you'd wish to be reminded every day of your life of what you were once. It isn't at all a good likeness now. You aren't in the least like that girl in the picture. If you think you are, take a peek in the glass! Your hair is bright red, and you're twenty pounds heavier than you were then. Now *I've* kept my figure, at any rate; it's not an impossible likeness of *me*.'

The moment she'd said it, Cateau could have bitten her tongue out for its cruel imprudence. Magdelon's eyes filled with tears, her chin quivered; still she withstood the attack, saying stubbornly, over and over: 'I don't care! If I've changed the most I've the most right to the picture! I'll not give it up, whatever you do!'

The quarrel continued for some time, while the light of the winter sunset faded over the canvas and the painted Cateau and Magdelon went on smiling sweetly from their tarnished gold frame on the angry, contentious real Cateau and Magdelon below. Neither would yield her position an inch. When a footman came to draw the curtains and light the candles they were still arguing; they kept it up during supper, and immediately afterwards flounced off to bed, for the first time in their lives omitting to kiss each other good-night, each to lock herself in her cold separate chamber and meditate glumly on the other's greed.

They felt that, whatever happened now, they could never really love each other again. . . . But in the morning a letter came from Paris that drove the dispute about the portrait quite out of their heads. Henri wrote to his mother to tell her that a fearful scandal had broken out in court circles. A woman of the lowest order called La Voisin and a number of her disreputable associates, who were in prison to be tried as sorcerers, had accused several well-known nobles of unspeakable crimes. Not much information had been made public as yet, but there was talk of poisoning and other offences of a capital nature. The Maréchal-Duc de Luxembourg was under arrest at Vincennes. The Comtesse de Soissons and her friend the Marquise d'Alluye had fled the country, barely warned in time to escape a similar fate. The Duchesse de Bouillon (who was Madame de Soissons' sister) and the Princesse de Tingry (Luxembourg's sister-in-law) were also gravely involved. They had been summoned to appear before a special criminal court of inquiry now in session at the Arsenal, by His Majesty's orders. And, worst of all, Henri advised his mother to come back to Paris at once, if possible, to clear her own name — for, horrible to relate, *she* had received a summons, too.

Chapter VII

'WELL, MY DEARS, I'M THANKFUL TO SAY I'VE NOTHING TO DO WITH
this shocking affair — nothing whatever! Why, I never even *knew*
the Comtesse de Soissons!' declared Isabelle, in the loud, overconfi-
dent tones of one resolved to convince herself that she was speaking
the truth. She paused for a moment in the midst of her denial to bite
off the end of her embroidery thread, which she proceeded to swallow with suspicious speed, as though disposing of a piece of incrimi-
nating evidence. 'Oh, I won't pretend I've not been to her house. . . .
Naturally, in the old days when her uncle the Cardinal was alive and
she was the King's best friend, I attended one or two of her receptions, like everybody else. *Like everybody else, I said, Catherine-
Henriette!* I used to see *you* there a good deal the winter you and
Candale . . . But that was years ago and I've scarcely laid eyes on
her since. As for her sister the Duchesse de Bouillon, and that horrid
little Madame d'Alluye, we may have met or we may not have met
— that I can't remember — but if I were to pass them now in the
street, I shouldn't know them well enough to bow to them — positively, my dear, I assure you! So you see I can't be blamed for wanting it distinctly understood that I'm in no way concerned in this
frightful business. Why, I've never seen a sorcerer in my life!'

Madame de Montmorency glanced nervously over her shoulder,
and then across the hearth at her hostess, the Comtesse d'Olonne,
and the latter's niece-in-law, the young Duchesse de la Ferté, who
were also sewing, or attempting to sew, in a spasmodic manner.

'Oh, neither have I, madam!' said Gabrielle promptly, wetting her
lips with her tongue; while Cateau, too, mechanically echoed the disclaimer.

The three women were seated in the Chinese cabinet, grouped
about the fire in the fading twilight of an afternoon in early February. The fire was not needed for heat — it was queer, warm, clammy
weather, the kind that in the spring of the year would have set
things to growing — but its light was useful. Although night had
almost fallen, Cateau had not yet rung for candles, and neither of her
guests had suggested that she do so. It seemed somehow safer to
stay in the dark. . . .

So they had sat for an hour or more, waiting for news from the Arsenal, where the judges of the criminal court were in session: this was the day on which the Maréchale de la Ferté had been scheduled to appear before them. She was to have been called at two o'clock. Two o'clock . . . and it was now nearly half past four. Surely there must soon be some word. . . .

'Sorcery,' continued Isabelle aggressively — she was talking, Cateau could see, against time, just to keep her thoughts quiet — 'is absolute nonsense. Everybody knows that. When we were young we used to hear tell about necromancers who hung about graveyards at midnight and alchemists who had discovered the secret of distilling gold from the elements, but those were nothing but old wives' tales to frighten children. I simply can't believe that sensible grown-up people — people who are our friends, like Monsieur de Luxembourg and the Comtesse de Soissons' — Isabelle had evidently forgotten her recent renouncement of the fugitive — 'in a word, my dears, men and women of position, could be so silly and credulous as to stoop to such mummery. It's beyond reason! Oh, I don't say they may not have consulted the crystal, or played at drawing horoscopes, or even, half in jest, bought some innocuous love philtres. . . . But as to anything serious, any real capital offences — why, the charge is absurd! When all is said and done, what does it rest on? Nothing but the word of a reckless, abandoned creature! Naturally, La Voisin's out to save her own skin. She'll say anything, anything at all, to escape the stake. Who puts the least faith in a professional criminal?'

Gabrielle shivered.

'His Majesty, madam, for one,' she replied. 'And La Reynie, the chief of police, for another. If there were nothing to these stories, why would Madame de Soissons have fled to Flanders? They say she tried for years to poison her husband and worm her way back into the King's good graces by all sorts of dreadful diabolical practices. As for Luxembourg, he's not in gaol for a bagatelle either. I heard only yesterday he'd been accused of feeding diamond-dust to the Maréchal de Créquy. And I've a very good idea that some other persons of far greater importance may yet be involved before the trials are over.' She lowered her voice and looked fearfully about to make sure no one was eavesdropping. 'Persons so close to the throne, madam — I mention no names — that not a soul dares predict what may happen when the truth is discovered. After all, who can tell how a particular lady has managed to keep herself first in her sovereign's affections through thick and thin? Haven't you noticed how each of her rivals has been destroyed in turn? — how none of them — no, not one — no matter how young and fair she might be, has been able to emerge victorious from that battle? Even Mademoiselle de Fontanges, the youngest and loveliest of them all. . . . I repeat, madam, I name no names, I make no definite accusations. . . .

But it's common knowledge that *her* child by the King died a fortnight ago, in mysterious circumstances, and that she herself is not
long for this world. I'm told at court she can't possibly live another
twelvemonth. I say it again, I make no charges — but we all know
that this certain person has visited La Voisin regularly for years!'

'Oh, my dear,' said Cateau, 'are you sure? I never heard ——'

'*For years*,' repeated Gabrielle, with emphasis. 'You needn't believe me, aunt, if you had rather not — but remember, I lived at
Saint-Germain as maid-of-honour to Her Majesty. I was at court
during the whole of the time when that vampire was fighting tooth
and nail to oust La Vallière as official mistress. You can't tell *me*
what was going on then — *I know!* Haven't I seen the Marquise
steal out of the palace at dead of night in a black shawl, with no one
for company but Suzon, her old serving-woman? Often enough she
didn't come back till late the next day, and we maids were hard put
to it to account for her absence at the Queen's lever. Do you suppose she was visiting the poor at the Hôtel Dieu, as she said she was
— washing beggars' feet in the charity hospitals? Oh, no, madam! I
know what I know; I've eyes in my head, and ears, too. There was
mischief afoot in those days. Witchcraft was the matter — Black
Masses were the matter — poisoning, too, for aught I know to the
contrary! It's horrible! horrible! To think that *I* should be involved in such infamies, in my present condition of health — three
months gone with child! Everyone knows how ill I was four years
ago, having Marie-Angélique. Well, if I die now — and I'm perfectly sure I shall — my blood will be on my mother-in-law's head.
Yes, the Maréchale will have killed me!... Not *too* near the fire,
darling! Come here, my own treasure, to your Maman who loves
you!'

The Duchess called her little daughter, who was playing on the
hearth amongst the rushes, to her knee, picked her up, and began to
fondle her emotionally, much to Marie-Angélique's surprise. (Gabrielle, as a rule, never noticed the child.) Cateau, who knew it as well
as young Marie-Angélique, decided that this sudden outburst of un-
convincing maternal affection was the best gauge of her niece's overwrought nerves. Perhaps it were wise to attempt to calm her: it
would not help anyone now for Gabrielle to indulge in an attack of
hysterics. They must all be brave, for Magdelon's sake.

'Now, my dear,' said Cateau, in a syrupy voice, 'pray don't excite
yourself! I fear you are taking the affair far too seriously. What the
Montespan's done or not done cannot concern us. That lies between
her and the King: His Majesty has his own dignity to maintain — I
warrant he'll not let anything come to light that might threaten it!
My sister was never a friend of the Marquise. As for the Comtesse de
Soissons, Magdelon used to go to her house to play cards once in a

while — we all did, as Madame de Montmorency told you. It was one of the meeting-places of our youth; everyone went there, because the King set the fashion for it. But I'm certain my sister has seen nothing of her for years. She told me herself she had not. She told me, too, that she had never been with the Countess to see La Voisin. *Never* — d'you understand? Magdelon says the Countess went once, she remembers, to have her palm read — but she herself refused to go with her. Now that's all she knows about the matter — she's sworn to me solemnly by our mother's memory that that's all she knows. They can't implicate her for so little. She'll have nothing to do but tell La Reynie and the judges what I've told you, and they'll let her off directly. So you see, child, there's not a thing for us to worry about. Nothing whatever, I say.... *Oh, my God, why can't those damned parakeets hold their noise?* Jean — François — take them away! Send for someone to choke them *this minute!*'

'There, now, Catherine-Henriette, you're a mass of nerves yourself!' said Isabelle gloatingly, 'and no wonder, poor lamb! The strain's bound to tell on you sooner or later. Of course, no one doubts the dear Maréchale's as stainless as snow — it's only too bad her name had to be mentioned at all in such an unpleasant connection. But it's an ill wind blows no one good: at least for once she'll have the satisfaction of hearing it said that she's innocent! which ought to be a great comfort to all her family.... Oh, by the way, loves, have I told you the latest about the Duchesse de Bouillon's retort to the judges? They say that when La Reynie asked her if she had ever seen the Devil, she replied at once that she had — she was seeing him *now* — and "he looks just like *you*, sir!" Isn't that delicious? The sweet Duchess is always so witty. All the same, I have it on good authority that she's to be exiled to one of her estates in the south. Ah, well ...! Did you hear, too, about the wife of the councillor of parliament who was accused of mixing love potions with her husband's soup? — he'd been straying from home all too often! But her husband didn't come home to dinner that night, and one of their servants drank it instead — so now she's having an intrigue with her own footman!'

Cateau and Gabrielle joined in the laugh, but a trifle edgily, and hitched their chairs nearer the fire. Paris was full of such stories these days. With one illustrious name after another being cited before the criminal tribunal, family after family amongst the finest of the realm becoming involved, it would have been no surprise to discover that one's best friends were murderers. People were too nervous really to stop at home. They ran about tirelessly from house to house, gleaning what scattered bits of information they could, while the list of those under arrest grew day by day. Nearly four hundred persons were said to have been seized during January, and the end of the terror was not yet in sight. One thing was clear, and that was that the King was determined, come what might, to get to the bottom of the noisome mystery. He seemed ready to sacrifice anyone — even Luxembourg, his best general, or an old flame like Madame de Soissons — for the sake of purging the kingdom of this sinister underground ring, which was evidently in league with the Devil himself.

Cateau was sure poor Magdelon could have nothing to do with these awful scandals. It seemed perfectly obvious her sister was speaking the truth when she asserted that she had never seen La Voisin, never even heard of the woman save on that one occasion when, fortunately, the Countess had been unable to persuade her friend to share her adventure. So Magdelon must be innocent.... *Of course, she must!* How could one suspect such a guileless, transparent creature? ... Cateau had said this to herself so many times during the last week that the words had almost lost their meaning. She felt, however, that it was important for her to go on doing so: she must continue to affirm her faith, as one might repeat a beneficent spell to exorcise evil; for if she did not, her thoughts would stray back, in spite of themselves, to a winter's day long ago and a certain queer old house on the Pont Marie....

It was hard, too, to forget Magdelon's face on the morning the news of her summons to court had reached La Louppe. She had turned immediately deathly pale, and deathly pale she'd remained ever since, with a frightened look in her eyes that belied her cheering words of self-vindication, her rather artificially tranquil manner. She'd *said* her one worry was keeping the matter from coming to her husband's ears — and that, with the Maréchal as ill as he was, had been easy to manage. But all the same ... Oh, sister, forgive me if I'm wronging you! thought Cateau, raising her eyes to Magdelon's eyes in the picture that hung on the wall just above their heads. (For in the midst of the excitement over returning so suddenly to Paris it had been simple for Madame d'Olonne to appropriate the disputed canvas unostentatiously. It looked very well, she decided, in place of the Venetian mirror — and, so far, Magdelon had not seemed to notice what she had done.)

'Ladies,' said Cateau, rousing herself briskly from her reflections, 'may I offer you a glass of rossolis, to cheer us while we wait for my sister? It can't be very much longer, you know....'

They had heard the wheels of the Duc de la Ferté's carriage so many times in imagination that when it actually stopped at the door it was hard to realize the waiting was over. Madame de Montmorency looked up curiously and began pluming herself as steps were heard on the stairs — one could not help feeling that, no matter how much sympathy she professed, Isabelle was enjoying this — while

Gabrielle set Marie-Angélique down on the floor once more and moistened her lips (she had been doing that, off and on, all afternoon) as she rose to receive her mother-in-law. Cateau did not move. She sat where she was by the fire, holding the half empty glass of rossolis before her and staring fixedly at the brownish liquor it contained. She was saying to herself in a whisper: 'I'll know as soon as I see her what's happened. She won't have to speak. When I see her *I'll know!*'

And then, all of a sudden, there they were at last — Henri puffing a little, young as he was, and exceedingly red in the face — he was perspiring freely, his aunt noticed, although the day was assuredly not warm enough to warrant it. Magdelon, standing behind her son in the doorway, was majestic in black with no jewels (she and Cateau having agreed beforehand that simplicity would be likely to have a favourable effect on the judges). She was very pale, but no paler than she had been at any time in the last few days: she and Henri were both smiling, so that everything must be all right. . . .

Cateau sprang up, almost dizzy with relief, as the young Duke cried in his loud, cheerful voice: 'Well, aunt, here we are, crowned with laurel, metaphorically speaking! All went wonderfully well, I am thankful to say. Dear Maman covered herself with glory!'

'Bravo, madam!' exclaimed Isabelle, her face obviously falling (the toad!). 'I am delighted to hear it.'

Gabrielle, after curtsying to the new arrivals, resumed her seat and began fanning herself very fast, as if she were faint. For a marvel, she seemed to have nothing to say. It was Cateau who demanded anxiously: 'Then you're sure there'll be no more trouble?'

'Sure — and more than sure!' answered Henri, with his gurgling laugh. 'Why, 'twas nothing whatever to be so stirred up about! Monsieur La Reynie was politeness itself — so were all the judges — and Maman was in the witness-box a scant ten minutes. They asked her first did she know a woman called La Voisin, at present in prison accused of witchcraft and other crimes. "Not I," said my mother: "never laid eyes on her in my life, sir." "But you've heard of her, at least?" "Oh, as to that, sir, who has not, this last fort- night?" replied my mother, as cool as you please. "You'll not deny, madam, you went for a drive on the sixteenth of August, 1664, in the coach of Her Highness the Comtesse de Soissons?" "Sir, after so many years it's a tax on my memory to be forced to recall a date so exactly, but to spare your trouble, I'll admit I was in Paris that sum- mer and that Madame de Soissons and I frequently took the air in each other's company." "But on this particular day, madam, you went to a house in the rue Beauregard with your friend the Countess and a gentleman. . . ." "I remember the occasion well, sir, now that you describe it in greater detail," said my mother. "The gentleman you refer to was the Abbé de Gordes, now His Grace the Bishop of Langres." (That, I could see, made a telling impression on the judges — there's nothing, after all, quite so respectable as a bishop!) "Well, madam, you went to this house, I say, in the rue Beauregard with the avowed intention of meeting La Voisin, the sorceress," said La Reynie. "How can you therefore deny that you know her?" "That's easily explained, Your Worship: *because I myself refused to enter the house!* Madame de Soissons went in alone to have her fortune told and her horoscope drawn. I remained in the carriage with the Abbé de Gordes the whole of the time. You can ask him yourself if I didn't; I am confident his testimony will agree with mine." And there, ladies, of course, she had 'em, for we happened to know that the Bishop's evidence was already on record. ... La Reynie did not like to let the Maréchale off so quickly — it's not often a man of his stamp has a chance to catch a glimpse of a great lady of hers — but there was little more he could do to detain her. He asked her rather lamely if she had not thought it her duty to try to dissuade the Countess from seeking the interview, to which she frankly rejoined: "I did not, sir. It was not my place to dictate to a friend in Madame de Soissons' exalted position" — and no one could take exception to that, for we all know she was Cardinal Mazarin's niece, wife to a Prince of the Blood, and Superintendent of the Queen's Household. So he shut up; there was nothing left to be done save confront my mother with the witch herself, who was held in chains in an adjoining chamber. They led her in, and naturally La Voisin did not recognize the Maréchale; she said so quite plainly before everybody; I'll give the wretch credit for speaking the truth on one occasion at least! And there was an end to the matter. ... Now could it have passed off better, I ask you? My mother's demeanour throughout the scene was in perfect contrast, so I was told, to that of the Duchesse de Bouillon and the Princesse de Tingry. Instead of insulting the judges and thereby needlessly incurring their ire, her manner was modest and candid — she maintained the truth and stood up for her rights, but gently, with dignity, as a noblewoman should. 'Tis certain she can have made no enemies by her appearance today, and we have every right to expect, so La Reynie assures me, that Madame de la Ferté will not be troubled again by the criminal court.'

'My dear, I'm delighted!' said Isabelle once more, with a false smile on her pointed features. ... Even Cateau and Gabrielle were smiling, too, now; the former placed a chair for her sister and almost forced her to sit in it. She then poured out a glass of rossolis and put it to Magdelon's lips.

'Thank you, dear,' said Magdelon, in a perfectly natural voice. 'I'm quite all right, really.'

But her eyes met Cateau's in a long questioning look, and when

Cateau turned away she said to herself: 'Whatever was the matter with her still must be the matter. We've not yet got to the end of this mess!'

Several weeks passed, however, without any occurrence that could alarm the La Fertés. The Maréchale's testimony had apparently been accepted as final in responsible quarters; she was not called again as a witness; and the report of her conduct at the Arsenal, circulated freely by relatives and interested friends, could only redound to her credit. It was generally said that she had made a most favourable impression. Thanks to it, her other sins of commission were temporarily forgiven and she enjoyed a gratifying, if transitory, success as the one really guiltless heroine of the great sorcery scandal.

Things did not go so smoothly for others amongst the accused. Madame de Bouillon was exiled to Nérac near the Spanish border, as Isabelle had predicted she would be; Luxembourg still languished in prison at Vincennes; while every day less exalted victims were arrested and brought to justice. Scores of seers and alchemists, witches and wizards and their apprentices, were seized and examined and sentenced to death.

Meanwhile La Voisin, the chief cause of the troubles, was being cross-questioned in her dungeon cell, and then tortured, when nothing more was to be got out of her by normal means. In the end, after she had told all she knew and invented a great deal else, in her desperate desire to bring down disaster on the heads of as many as possible of her former associates, she was condemned to be burned at the stake. February twenty-second was set as the day of execution. Enthusiasm ran high at the prospect, for it was hoped that, once the ringleader of the gang had been made do public penance for her crimes and expiate them with her life, the seething excitement might have a chance of subsiding at last. Everybody who could manage it wanted to be in at the death. A huge crowd assembled in the Place de Grève, where since time immemorial Parisians had watched executions. Householders in the square were besieged by their acquaintances for the loan of a window for family parties, and those who could trump up an errand to take them to the Hôtel de Ville on that fateful afternoon felt themselves fortunate, as the stake had been placed directly in front of its doors.

Others, fearful of the press in the street, were resigned to the second-best satisfaction of securing a glimpse of the tumbril with the sorceress in it somewhere along the line of march from Vincennes to the Place. Residents of the rue Saint-Antoine, the chief thoroughfare of the quarter, hastened to issue invitations to gay little 'days at home' on the afternoon of the twenty-second. (The procession was set for five o'clock, so that it would work out just right.)

The Duchesse de Sully, mistress of the largest and grandest establishment in the street, asked a group of her women friends to be her guests. Amongst these women were the sisters La Louppe. Ordinarily they would not have had an opportunity of attending so respectable a feminine assembly, but Magdelon was the centre just now of much sympathetic curiosity; and Cateau, as her sister, came in for her share of reflected fame.

The latter, poised for her entrance on the threshold of the Grand Saloon of the Hôtel de Sully, observed with pleasure that the crowd was an extremely fashionable one. The Duchesse de Chaulnes, wife of the governor of Brittany, was there, with her great friend, the Marquise de Sévigné (Bussy's cousin — such a charming woman, though she had a tongue to beware of!). The Comtesse de Guiche had just come in, too, and Doudou de Ventadour with her mother, the Maréchale de la Mothe. (Poor Doudou! It would be kind to make a point of speaking to her. She was all in grey like a nun; one had heard that she'd been shut up for good on a very small pension in some dreary suburban convent or other. Wasn't it in the Faubourg Saint-Marceau?) ... And Gilette de Fiesque, whom Cateau had not seen for centuries.... 'Good afternoon, madam,' said Cateau, bowing to her old friend so pointedly that it was impossible to evade the greeting.

Gilette flushed all over her tiny dark nut of a face, but, to do her justice, after a breathless instant she rallied her forces to return the bow.

Cateau smiled, and continued her placid progress towards the centre of the Grand Saloon. A babble of voices swept around her: 'My dear, how are you? Isn't this fun? I wouldn't have missed it for anything! ... Any news, madam? No arrests of note lately? I hear that Luxembourg's trial's coming up next week.... Well, such a nasty, vicious temper I never beheld! She's mad, they say, to denounce someone, only she can't think whom to denounce! ... Madam, you know my daughter, the Duchesse de Ventadour, of course? ... Dear Doudou, what a surprise! But I thought that you weren't — that you couldn't —— Oh, I was set on her coming with me today! What's the use in staying home forever and moping? A good witch-burning, I said, is just what the dear child needs to put her in spirits! ... I told my husband, don't come for me early; I want to be sure not to miss ... They say La Voisin's been drunk for a week, singing and shouting the most horrible obscene songs in her cell. I was told she ate a dinner like a dragoon's last night and spat in the face of the priest who came to confess her. I must say, I should think that now, when she's going to eternal judgement ... Ah, well, poor wretch! What's the difference? The Devil will claim his own, anyway. But my dear, have you heard ...' et cetera, et cetera.

It was a pretty, festive scene — the candles all lighted — lackeys in uniform passing cakes and sweetmeats, chocolate and wine — and the guests in their fine afternoon gowns forming in clusters, then shifting apart to cluster again, like a hiveful of bees preparing to swarm. . . . Cateau was reminded of the circles of the Précieuses in the old days. One had almost forgotten how amusing such gatherings could be! Here and there an elder woman glanced askance at the Comtesse d'Olonne, but others greeted her pleasantly enough; most of the younger ones probably did not know who she was. (Cateau was not sure whether this reflection were consoling or not.) . . . Oh, there was Magdelon! near the fire on one of the couches of honour, surrounded by a knot of satellites who were eagerly plying her with questions concerning her testimony before the criminal court. (Obviously she was going to be able to dine out on *that* all winter!) . . . Magdelon looked well, Cateau thought. She was still wearing black, as a general precaution, which was flattering to her figure; and her high frilled headdress à la Fontanges was most becoming. Her eyes, though, were restless. . . . As soon as she caught sight of her sister she signalled to her, and Cateau rustled over to join the group by the fire.

The Comtesse de Guiche was waving her fan with such energy that she appeared to be punishing it, and saying in her rapid, tripping little soprano: 'Well, God be praised! they're burning the creature, and perhaps when she's gone we'll be able to think of something else for a change. You remember how it was four years ago when the Brinvilliers was tried for murder: nothing else was talked of for weeks, and then, poof! once she was roasted to ashes she might as well never have lived, for all the mention was made of her name. Of course, I grant you this affair is more serious. To begin with, La Voisin's by no means the only poisoner in the case. I understand that the prisons are still crowded with 'em — there's her stepdaughter Catherine, and La Vigoureux, and La Dodée, and La Trianon, and I know not how many more of the same kidney, all awaiting their turn for the thumbscrew! Some say what we've heard up to now is a mere prelude to the dramas to follow. . . .'

One could only guess at what further revelations might be in store, for Madame de Guiche and her fan were arrested in full flight by a cry of 'They're coming! They're coming!' and there was a sudden rush to the row of long windows overlooking the street.

Cateau had meant not to look, but she could not help it: she was borne along on the wave of unanimous impulse and found herself, without knowing how she had got there, nose pressed to the glass, peering down into the murky darkness below.

It was a horrifying sight. She had no eyes to spare for the double line of soldiers marching by to keep order in the crowd as well as to guard their prisoner; nor for the rabble, whose jeering shouts rose in a confused roar as the tumbril bumped slowly along over the greasy black cobblestones of the rue Saint-Antoine. (It was raining a little, she noticed subconsciously.) Cateau's gaze was riveted on the white-clad figure in the tumbril, bound with chains, grasping a lighted torch in one hand. Her face red as fire, her eyes rolling wildly like a maniac's, La Voisin had yet the strength to repel with her free hand the priest who stood next her, holding a crucifix in a suppliant attitude. This woman, one saw, was a long way past common human emotions. She had been tortured into a mass of quivering desensitized flesh. But still she seemed to dominate the situation; her high squalling voice cut through the cries of the mob on a purely animal note of defiance and despair.

Cateau felt she could never forget the sound of that voice.

Even the little company of ladies, beplumed and bejewelled, in the Duchess's drawing-room, were overwhelmed by what they had seen and heard. They watched as if fascinated, either shocked into silence or conversing in tremulous whispers, until the short procession vanished from view.

Cateau could not make herself look any longer. She shrank away from the window and stood holding fast to the stiff brocade curtain, waiting until the slight feeling of nausea that had assailed her should have passed. It was then she saw Magdelon still sitting on the couch by the fire; she had apparently not quitted her place during the flurry of excitement over La Voisin. Cateau perceived at once that there was something wrong with her: her face was as pale as paper and she was trembling violently. Indeed, she was hardly able to speak. When Cateau hurried across to the couch to find out what the matter was, Magdelon just managed to gasp: 'Take me away from here!' before relapsing into her helpless shivering.

Cateau cast a quick glance about the room, noted that all the guests were still at the windows, and then almost bodily picked up her sister, supporting her firmly under both arms, half guiding, half carrying her down the stairs, through lines of goggle-eyed lackeys in the entrance hall of the Hôtel de Sully, out the door and into their carriage.

'The Maréchale's ill!' said Cateau to her coachman, partly for his benefit and partly for the benefit of the goggle-eyed lackeys. 'Drive her home directly!'

But in the carriage Magdelon appeared to revive. She neither fainted, nor went off into one of her seizures of hysterical tears, as Cateau had been afraid she might do. Instead she leaned back against the cushions with her eyes shut and said, in a very small voice: 'Oh, Cateau, it's dreadful — dreadful!'

'I know, dear,' said Cateau. 'I thought so, too. But — you didn't really see, did you? I hoped you wouldn't, because I feared that, after the ordeal you'd been through ——'

'No, no! — but her voice! that terrible voice! I couldn't — I can't . . . Cateau, I've something to tell you.'

'I thought so, child. What is it?'

'I — I wanted to say it before, but I couldn't. I've been so ashamed. Cateau, dear, you heard what she said . . .?'

'What *who* said?'

'The Comtesse de Guiche. She said there were other poisoners still in prison.'

'Well, what if she did? We all know it. I don't see ——'

'No, no! — but she said La Trianon was there. You remember La Trianon — that woman we went to see once years ago on the Pont Marie?'

Cateau's heart gave a sick thud of foreboding; she had an instant vision of the crooked old house built over the river — and of the winter sunshine on Magdelon's face as she listened to those preposterous fairy tales. . . . .

'Why, yes, I think I do,' she answered slowly. 'But that was ages ago, darling — and as I recall it, we only had our fortunes told. There could have been nothing wrong in that. If *that's* all that's bothering you ——'

'But it isn't,' quavered Magdelon. 'There's more to the story. I — I've been back to her many times since, Cateau. I've been to La Trianon once a week for years and years!'

It was Cateau's turn to look startled.

'You *have?* But what on earth for? *You* haven't been poisoning anyone, I suppose?'

'No — no — of course not!'

'Nor ridding yourself of superfluous infants? Then *what*, for pity's sake . . .?'

'Oh, Cateau, you'll think me too stupid. . . . I can't bear to tell you. . . . I went to La Trianon to keep myself young.'

'Keep yourself young! My girl, are you mad? How could she do that?'

'Oh, she said she knew how — she said it was very simple, really! Most of the time she just gave me ointments to rub on my face and brewed messes with herbs and told me to drink them. She said they couldn't fail. She said, if I did as she bade me, I'd be beautiful as long as I lived. I thought it might at least be worth trying. But then, later on, when it didn't seem to work, I — I got her to help me in other ways, too.'

'What other ways?'

Cateau's eyes were coldly compelling. Magdelon squirmed under their scrutiny, but made no attempt to evade the issue.

'Oh — love potions, and things like that. You can laugh, if you like, and think it silly. It *is* silly, I know. But I was so unhappy for

a while after Marsan left me, I'd have done anything — anything in
the world . . .! Of course, I didn't really believe her. How *can* you believe that if you seal a man's name with your own in a ball of tallow
and throw the ball into the fire, he's bound to love you forever? It's
a little like praying to God. You're not sure it will do any good, but
it can't hurt anyone, anyway. And I never would let her cast spells
against other people. Most of the women who went to her had wax
images made of their rivals and then stuck pins in them, which was
supposed to harm them somehow. I told her I wouldn't do that, no
matter what happened. And she was good to me, Cateau. She was
really a kind-hearted woman. I could always turn to her for advice
when I needed it. But now she's in prison, and it'll come out how
foolish I've been, and — and I can't bear it! Oh, I wish I were dead!'
    Cateau took her sister's hand gently and held it in silence for a
little. There was not much she could say by way of comfort. On the
whole, however, things were by no means so bad as she had feared.
Magdelon had been a fool, it was true — but a guileless fool! As she
herself said, she had hurt no one by her folly. What she had done
was ludicrous, incredible almost — but other women one knew had
done the same. Even granting that under the stress of the rack La
Trianon confessed all she knew, nothing could make Magdelon appear in a criminal light. People would think her what they had always thought her, a reckless, scatterbrained creature — never a designing one. . . . 'Oh,' thought Cateau hopelessly, 'if only she had the
wit to design something just once . . . instead of tossing this way and
that with every wind that blows!'
    But there was no good in saying that now. There was no use either
in scolding. Poor Magdelon had been through as much as she could
stand in one day. One must comfort her instead — tell her that
everything was all right, really — that nothing terrible could happen
— as one had done for years, as it seemed sometimes one would
never get through doing. . . .
    Before they arrived at Great Senneterre Magdelon had begun to
feel very much better.
    'I'll be good; I'll not worry, I promise you, darling!' she said, put-
ting up her face to be kissed; and she stood in the doorway waving to
Cateau and smiling a rather watery smile as long as the carriage was
in sight.
    But Cateau knew that her sister's mind could not be entirely at
rest as long as La Trianon's case remained unjudged, so when she
heard, some weeks later, that the woman had died in the dungeon at
Vincennes, she sent word to Magdelon at once to tell her the reassuring news.
    By this time, unluckily, Magdelon, in her anxiety to clear herself
in advance of all possible charges, had done so much talking to so

many people that her secret leaked out. Her reputation for spotless innocence in the great poison scandal became somewhat sullied. Indeed, when the Maréchal de la Ferté suffered a severe stroke of apoplexy that spring just before his eightieth birthday, there were plenty of uncharitable tongues to suggest that his wife's subterranean dealings with the sorceress were to blame.

Chapter VIII

LA FERTÉ WAS A LONG TIME ABOUT DYING. HE WAS SO STRONG, AND
had such a stubborn determination to stay in life to the latest possible minute, that he actually succeeded in rallying by degrees from
the effects of his stroke. When summer came he was well enough to
go to the country as usual, and after his return to Paris, on the eve
of Saint Hubert's Day, Cateau thought that in some respects he
seemed better than a year ago. His left side remained partly paralyzed, including the muscles of the mouth, which thickened and
slowed down his already turgid speech; but his appetite had improved, and his spirits, also.

Late in November, however, a comet appeared in the heavens, a
bright new one trailing spectacular tails of fire; and from the first
night he beheld it the Maréchal declared that it presaged his end.
No matter what was said to refute the theory, he clung to it with
tiresome tenacity. As the weeks passed his forces began to decline
visibly, and by the spring of '81 it became clear that, comet or no
comet (this particular specimen had been last seen in March), the
old man had only a few months to live.

As soon as the hot weather arrived he insisted on being taken to
La Ferté-Saint-Aubin, although his wife begged him not to squander
his fast ebbing strength on the trip. The doctors also did their best
to dissuade him — Pecquet and Daquin, the King's own physician,
who had been called in several times as a consultant, added their
pleas to the Maréchale's, but in vain.

After their departure Cateau heard nothing more from the family
until the first week in September, when Magdelon wrote, begging her
sister to come to her: La Ferté, she said, had had a second stroke;
the doctors now felt that death might occur at any time.

Cateau herself had just returned from Normandy. She did not
feel enthusiastic over the prospect of starting off again so soon, especially as the weather was exceedingly warm and she and Fervaques
had hoped to spend the early autumn at Saint-Germain. Besides,
La Ferté was no favourite with his sister-in-law, who had decided
long ago that his demise would be a general deliverance. It was only
a pity, Madame d'Olonne observed sourly as she turned the pages of
Magdelon's letter, that he had not died twenty years earlier and

given his wife her freedom while she was still young enough to enjoy it.

However, if Magdelon wanted her, Cateau could not disregard the appeal. It seemed particularly important, in view of the unpleasant rumours that had been circulated about supernatural forces being at work, to show the world that the Maréchale's sister did not believe them. Cateau packed her boxes the same day she received the letter; in the morning she bade her lover a regretful farewell and set off through the Porte Saint-Jacques on the long straight road to the south.

She reached her sister's castle late the same evening, hot, dusty, and out of temper after a blistering drive across the sun-baked wheat fields of the Beauce. But Magdelon, who was waiting up in the great hall with the three younger children, looked so glad to see her that Cateau was glad, in her turn, that she had made the effort to come. (Nothing was said of the rumours in Paris; Magdelon seemed not to have heard them; there was therefore no point in adding to her worries.)

In answer to inquiries it developed that La Ferté was feeling no worse. He rarely got out of bed, and slept a great deal of the time he was in it. In a way, said Magdelon, it was easier to nurse him than it had been before, when he was stronger; the difficulty now was that he would not let anyone wait on him except his wife and old Robert. He refused to allow the maidservants even to enter the room, and as for having special sickbed attendants, the very idea drove him into a frenzy, though the good sisters at the convent of the Visitation in Orléans had most kindly offered to supply any number.

The next morning Cateau was taken to call on the patient. He lay in bed supported by pillows, staring straight ahead of him, his grizzled hair and beard somewhat unkempt — but then, they always were! His speech seemed clearer, if anything, than before the second stroke, and he ordered Robert and a pair of startled lackeys about with so much of his old testy volubility that Cateau could never have believed the Maréchal was mortally ill if it had not been for his eyes. They had the superterrestrial purity of colour, the air of secret withdrawal from the world, that Maman's had had during the last months of her life. It was, one realized, a mere physical sign of approaching dissolution, having no connection necessarily with things of the spirit. While Maman had had it she had gone on gossiping and stirring up trouble in the convent as it was her wont to do, just as La Ferté shouted at his servants and grunted ill-naturedly at his wife and his sister-in-law. . . . Nevertheless, 'He'll not last out the fortnight, I expect,' Cateau said to herself, sagely nodding her head; and after they had tiptoed out of the bedchamber she asked Magdelon if she had sent for her two elder sons.

'I wrote to Henri weeks ago,' Magdelon replied, 'and told him I thought he and Gabrielle ought to be here. But he wrote back that he couldn't say for sure when they could get away: they're with the court at Versailles, and Gabrielle is dancing in the King's ballet — you know, the one she was in last carnival that everybody said was so pretty. It was called *The Triumph of Something-or-Other*.... Could it have been *Love*, dear, do you think? There's always such a lot about love in ballets. I danced in one once at the Palais Royal — do you remember, Cateau? It was during the second year of the Fronde, and the poor Queen of England was there; she'd just run away from the revolution; it was the first party she went to in Paris. Anyhow, that ballet had a title with love in it, too, and there was a troop of the quaintest little trained dogs from Vienna, and two of them did a pas de deux dressed as Cupid and Psyche.... But what was I saying, darling? Oh, yes, about Henri. Of course, I'd like him to come, but what can I do about it? He never pays any attention to me, and I can't ask La Ferté to write, because then he'd know I was worried about *him*. As for dear Louis, I'd have sent for him, naturally, in the very beginning, if I weren't afraid what his father might do. You know, he's never forgiven him — *never!* — for joining the Society. I can't even mention the boy's name in his presence — as if the poor fellow had done something disgraceful! Say what you will, it's an honour; the fathers all tell me that Louis is an inspiration to everyone at the college — and who knows what it may lead to, some day? Perhaps a cardinal's hat or even the tiara itself! After all, there *have* been French Popes, though it would be unusual for a Jesuit... And he would be such a comfort to me now, but there it is, dear, I daren't ask him — I simply daren't!'

'If he'd be a comfort,' said Cateau, firmly interrupting her sister's disjointed monologue — as one was forced to do if one had anything important to say — 'by all means let him come, then, and don't tell the Maréchal. As for Henri, I've no patience with the boy! Tell him you want him at once, ballet or no ballet! And if he leaves the Duchess behind him, so much the better! I'd hate to depart from this earth with *her* hand in mine!'

'Ah, you *do* see it, then!' cried Magdelon, her eyes filling with tears.

To this Cateau responded with a sober kiss and a reiterated 'Send for Henri, my dear!'

Magdelon left her sister and went to her room to write the letter. But it was fated never to be finished, for she was no more than half through when a footman came running to report that a coach was just crossing the drawbridge, a big gilded coach emblazoned with the arms of the Duc de la Ferté — and that in it were Monsieur the Duke and Madame the Duchess, their two daughters Mademoiselle de la Ferté and Mademoiselle de Menetou, and the whole of their noble suite from Versailles.

It was such a relief to Magdelon to know Henri was there at last that Cateau saw she was disposed to overlook the fact that there was something odd about his arrival. Why had he and Gabrielle appeared so suddenly, just after having written that they would probably not be able to come at all? Neither the young Duke nor his wife could offer a satisfactory explanation of the change in plan. Henri murmured unconvincingly he'd thought his mother needed him; Gabrielle added that they were not in the least alarmed about dearest Papa, but there'd been talk of postponing the ballet; both spouses later affirmed that nothing but their desire to seek seclusion and fine country air for the children was responsible for bringing them to La Ferté-Saint-Aubin.

'Fine-country-air-fiddlesticks!' thought their Aunt d'Olonne, who continued to entertain her own ideas on the subject. Divers small signs, according to Cateau, showed unmistakably which way the wind blew. . . . Henri's laugh, for one, was far too noisy and frequent to be natural. There was something, also, indefinably furtive about the expression in Gabrielle's green gaze. Most striking of all was the effect of uneasiness the young couple made in each other's company. They talked a great deal, sometimes both at once, but never *together;* more strangely still, they seemed to avoid meeting one another's eyes.

'Something's definitely wrong between them,' thought Cateau, with gloomy relish, 'though I can't yet tell what. Never mind: whatever it is, we'll learn soon enough. . . .'

The day after the arrival of the ducal pair the Maréchal insisted on getting up for midday dinner. Cateau and Magdelon both endeavoured to keep him in bed, but the old man was obdurate: since his son had come he seemed better and brighter; he had himself shaved, bathed, and dressed in full court regalia, and got Robert and one of the footmen to carry him into the great dining-hall.

As the weather was very warm, the place was in semi-darkness: most of the shutters had been closed against the searing September glare. However, even the subdued light could not disguise the shabbiness of the room. It had not been painted in years; some of the cornices were chipped, the gilding was tarnished, and bits of plaster were peeling off the handsome frescoes that had once been the family's pride.

As Cateau took her place at her brother-in-law's left she could not help thinking that he, too, appeared in need of restoration. His face was ghastly under the huge curled black wig — he looked like a dead man propped up in his chair.

Magdelon, opposite her husband, was in white, with a knot of her favourite cherry-red ribbons in her hair. She was rouged rather heavily, to counteract her prevailing pallor; unfortunately, the shade she had chosen did not harmonize with the cherry-red ribbons. Though her eyes were anxious, her smile was unflagging; and she was much preoccupied by her self-appointed task of selecting tidbits for her two little granddaughters, Marie-Angélique and Baby Catherine, who were seated with their nurse at the end of the table next their eight-year-old aunt, roly-poly Chou-Chou.

The meal began quietly: no one seemed today in a talkative mood. Tinette and Jules were constitutionally silent. Henri, who generally chattered away about everything and anything, was queerly glum. Even Gabrielle, as a rule less in search of lines to deliver than of an audience to attend to them, for once sat aloof, gnawing a chicken wing with haughty disdain.

Hence it was left to Cateau and Magdelon to see that conversation did not expire altogether. It was hard to know what subject to try. ... The presence of children precluded court gossip of a highly spiced nature; there wasn't a war at the moment; nobody seemed to have read much lately; and people were tired of saying that Lully's opera this year was not so good as last year's. The dialogue, therefore, soon degenerated into a series of lifeless comments on the new styles in hairdressing.... Had waterfalls gone out and palisades come in? And would the famous coiffure à la Fontanges have a happier fate than its poor young designer, who had faded out of life a few weeks ago in total obscurity at the convent of Port-Royal ... ?

No, it was not an inspiring occasion! Even the dinner, well prepared though it was, was too elaborate for such a hot day. The succession of heavy, old-fashioned courses, following the prescribed routine of a state banquet in the time of Louis XIII, progressed from soup through entrées and fish, roast, game, and salad, to pudding and pastries, iced fruits and sweetmeats. Despite the gruelling temperature each dish was accompanied by its appropriate wine. The Maréchal, whose former hearty appetite had deserted him, still made a show of sampling the beverages. Robert, standing behind his master's chair, was kept busy pouring out glasses of claret, champagne, and Burgundy to hold to the withered old lips: the two of them indulged in constant private mumbled remarks concerning the price and quality of various vintages.

The repast had almost come to an end when Gabrielle emerged from her trance sufficiently to engage in a low but spirited conversation with her neighbour at table, young Jules de la Ferté.

Cateau knew comparatively little of her third nephew, now sixteen and in his last year at school. He had attracted her less than his two handsome, agreeable elder brothers, being plain and snub-nosed, with a shock of straight blond hair and a sulky expression. He was said, too, to be clever — which further alienated his aunt — having composed a number of verses that were pronounced excellent by his masters and his brother Louis.

In company, however, he was shyly taciturn. Cateau could scarcely recall the sound of his voice. It was therefore surprising to note the animation with which he and his sister-in-law were conducting their argument — for it was an argument, evidently, that had sprung up between them. Whispers gave way to mutterings, mutterings to shrill, angry taunts: finally Gabrielle brought affairs to a climax by leaning forward in her chair and delivering a smart slap on young Jules' downy cheek.

The slap sounded loud because the room was so still. A moment of shocking silence succeeded it. Little Marie-Angélique, who was a high-strung child, began to whimper softly; the Maréchal ceased his half-maudlin mumblings and dropped his jaw in amazement.

Jules did not strike back. He looked at his enemy with a world of venom in his lustreless blue eyes; then he started laughing — his voice was hoarse and uncertain, being halfway through the period of mutation.

'Hit me if you like!' he cried, breathless with spite. 'You can't make me forget what I know about you. You're a nice one, you are, pretending you're here because the children look pale or your papa-in-law's ill, or I know not what more nonsensical reasons! You may be able to fool most of the family, but not me, Sister Gabrielle — *not me!* I knew the minute I saw you that there was something up, and I made up my mind I'd find out what it was. A fine row you had with my brother last night — eh, my lady? Henri is on to your pretty tricks at last, isn't he? Oh, now you're blushing, aren't you? Now you're afraid I may let the cat out of the bag and tell what I know! Well, it's too bad, Sister Gabrielle; you should have thought of that and locked the door to your powder closet before you began to fight with your husband!'

Gabrielle's face flushed brick-red; then her colour retreated, leaving her paler than before. She twisted her stumpy fingers together, as though she'd have liked to bury them deep in Jules' straw-yellow thatch. 'So it was you, you hateful little rat, I heard scrabbling about in the dark after I'd quenched the candles!' she exclaimed, in a fury. 'I might have guessed you'd be up to your usual dirty tricks. Well, go on, then: tell them all, why don't you? I dare you to! It makes no difference to *me* what you say. I've done nothing whatever to be ashamed of.'

'Very well, I *will* tell, Madam High-and-Mighty! What will Papa and Maman think of you when they learn that the real reason you're here is because you've been exiled? — yes, dear sister, exiled from court until further notice! — and for what? Why, for falling in

love with the King, no less! Oh, it's a lovely story! The dear
Duchess is distraught — she cannot eat or sleep — she is thinking
always of His Majesty, only of him! At the ball she reverses the
rôles of man and maid, and pursues her choice as though he were a
young girl and she the enterprising gallant! Everyone knows how
she feels and pities her plight. Such rosy blushes mantle her cheek
when her sovereign is nigh! Why, 'tis said that when she takes the
air in her carriage the lady carries in her hand a portrait of Louis the
Well-Beloved — a rare miniature on enamel framed in a circle of
sparkling diamonds — and that she lavishes her sighs and smiles on
the pictured image in lieu of the distant original. A touching romance, is it not, ladies and gentlemen? There's but one false note in
the music, and that is, that the royal lover refuses to return her
tender passion. What! Can he really be insensible to such selfless devotion? Alas! His heart, it seems, is flint. For 'twas only the other
day that our sweet Sister Gabrielle, meeting the august object of her
fancy in the courtyard at Versailles, on the point of taking the Queen
and some of her ladies to drive, pushed the Princesse de Soubise
roughly aside and attempted to enter the coach in her place. "You're
too old now, madam, to interest His Majesty," says she, as pert as
you please. "It's *my* turn now!" ... But woe is me! Instead of winning new favour by her boldness, she is cast into the depths of despair, for the very next morning comes a letter to her mother,
couched in delicate diplomatic language, but conveying its meaning
clearly enough.... So here's our amorous Phaedra dismissed to the
country to eat out her heart in secret for her ungrateful lord! Come,
madam, confess it: have I not made the most of the tale as I heard it
last night from your lips and my brother's? Won't you give your
family a treat and show them the exquisite miniature in its diamond
setting, as proof of the truth of my words? I dare swear it's somewhere on your person — mayhap on a chain of gold about your swan-
like neck? Now there's a dear, good girl, what do you say?'

The lad brought his sneering speech to a close with a burst of raucous laughter, as he thrust his blunt nose insultingly in his sister-in-
law's face.

For a second Gabrielle appeared too deeply outraged to reply to
the blast. She sat still in her seat, her cheeks an ugly greenish-
white, a mirthless smile contorting her pinched small features.
Cateau thought she had never in her life beheld two less amiable
young people. What a pair they were! There was nothing to
choose between them.... Then the Duchess slowly rose, took up her
wine glass full of saffron champagne, and poured the contents with
deliberate thoroughness over Jules' head.

The company sat aghast. Cateau, in particular, was shocked and
disgusted by her nephew's words. Little as she cared for her turbu-

lent niece, she felt that there was for once some excuse for Gabrielle's behaviour. Jules was a cad, and vicious into the bargain. There was so much concentrated malice in his tones that it seemed he could really not be quite sane. How else excuse the inexcusable attack on his own brother's wife? Yes, he was mad; that must be it; it was the kindest thing one could say.... There was no use in taking his charges seriously — though, worse luck! it was easy to see by Henri's face that Jules had spoken the truth.... Henri, of course, was never to be depended upon in a crisis. He blushed bright crimson, gave a nervous, indecisive laugh, but made no move to thrash the young cub, which was clearly his duty to do. No: one could not count on the Duke to protect the family's honour — that much was painfully certain.

Magdelon did not try to say or do anything, either — but this was not to be wondered at: how, after all, could she hope to remedy matters? She sat with her mouth open, the two red spots of rouge on her cheeks like a clown's patches, now that emotion had robbed her of her natural colour.

Little Marie-Angélique, at the far end of the table, went on crying from pure nervousness. For some minutes her sobs were the only sound to be heard in the great dining-hall.

At last, with creaking majesty, the Maréchal dragged himself up into a standing position. From his strategic position at its centre he dominated the whole table: Cateau had almost forgotten what a very big man her brother-in-law was. He stood there holding fast to the back of his chair in order to steady himself, and making agonized efforts to speak. For a while no words would come; then he uttered a few broken fragments: 'Disgraced — well punished — wouldn't have believed — you dog, I say!...'

He staggered a step or two towards the combatants, his fist clenched and raised to threaten — which one? It was impossible to tell from his actions whether he menaced his son or his daughter-in-law. But Gabrielle did not wait to see. With a startled parrot's screech she flounced from her place and ran the length of the room, holding her hands to her head in an unstudied gesture of terror. She ran so fast and screeched so loudly that she could not see the danger was past long before she had got out of range of retribution. The Maréchal hesitated, tottered uncertainly, and then fell flat. As he crashed to the floor he caught at a corner of the tablecloth to save himself, bringing a mass of glass and china down with him to splintering ruin.

After that, he did not quit his bed again. What had happened was not, as Magdelon feared, a third stroke — he had merely fainted — but the shock of the fall was severe. He had cut his face and hands badly, besides, on the broken pieces of glass.

For the next fortnight Magdelon scarcely left her husband's bed-side. It was not possible to persuade her to get her proper sleep — as for meals, she totally disregarded them, contenting herself with casual scraps from the patient's neglected trays. . . . 'He might wake and need me, dear,' she said, over and over, when Cateau tried, as she often did, to induce her sister to take a few hours' rest and relaxa-tion.

She sat hour after hour, day after day, in the darkened chamber, unconscious of everything but the quiet recumbent figure before her. She grew pallid and hollow-eyed during the vigil; still she refused to desert her post. It was her paramount desire to be there in the com-paratively short periods when the sleeper was awake, so that she might press his hand, and smile into the dark, troubled eyes, and mur-mur gently: 'I'm here, sir — what may I do for you, sir? — I love you, dear sir!' . . .

It was touching and tragic and, one could not but feel, completely absurd: more than half the time La Ferté did not even know his own wife!

But since Cateau was powerless to cajole her sister to reason, she sometimes joined her in her weary watch. . . . The Maréchal, thought Cateau, was an exceedingly unsatisfactory invalid. Ill as he was, he had yet strength enough to forbid his attendants to perform the usual sickroom rites. They might not smooth his pillow nor sprinkle him with perfume, and in his lucid intervals his taste in lit-erature was disconcerting. He had no relish for religion, though Magdelon tactfully avoided the prayers for the dying and tried some of the psalms instead. . . . '"The Lord is my shepherd; I shall not want,"' read Magdelon, in her low, musical voice — or, '"Judge me, O Lord; for I have walked in mine integrity. . . . Gather not my soul with sinners, nor my life with bloody men. . . ."'

But La Ferté's grimace of boredom forced her speedily to revert to the *Mercure Galant* or one of Molière's more ribald comedies.

Most of the time when he was awake he lay still, with wide-open eyes, neither speaking nor seeming to care whether he were spoken to. Vast and immovable he lay, his gaze fixed vacantly on the ceiling. Cateau wondered then what was passing in his mind. She fancied that his thoughts were with the armies he had led to victory in his youth — that he was reliving past triumphs — for he muttered fre-quent references to old battlefields in Flanders and Lorraine, names of long forgotten sieges, and soldiers who'd been dead more years than one could count. 'Montmédy,' he'd say, and 'Piccolomini,' and 'the night before Saint-Nicolas.' Then, again, he shouted aloud what they took for military orders, though these were too confused to be identifiable.

At other times he seemed to recognize Cateau and Magdelon and would stare at them hard, until the former grew restless under the piercing scrutiny. When this happened she would suppose uneasily that he was accusing them both of unmentionable sins: his eyes looked angry and malevolent. (Oh, could he have heard about La Trianon, after all ... ?) But she was unwilling to admit her fears, as her sister seemed unconscious of them. If Magdelon felt distressed at the thought that her husband was dying without letting her know he forgave her transgressions — without her even being able to find out to what extent he'd been aware of them — she gave no sign.

Magdelon, in fact, said nothing about herself, these days. She appeared to have forgotten her pain, which had been obvious at the time, over the unseemly dispute that had brought on the Maréchal's latest illness. For the present her children did not exist for her; they moved and breathed on another plane — one might almost have said, another planet. They were excluded from her thoughts as completely as they were from the sickroom; only Cateau, her sister, was welcome there where she brooded like a tender rescuing angel, intent on her task of keeping death at bay till the last possible moment. (If only the cruel gossips in Paris could have seen her now!)

So the long, hot September days wore on in a blaze of light and colour, all their mellow, bursting beauty shut away from the three sombre figures in the state bedchamber of the castle. Now and then a puff of warm wind blew through the darkened windows from the woods and meadows outside, bearing with it the sound of scythes from the cornfields and the distant voices of the mowers gathering the harvest. Once a great black insect blundered in, and darted about the walls in a frenzy while the women shrieked, until Cateau succeeded in driving it out. She was much astonished to see, as it took flight into the sunshine on shimmering wings, that it was only a dragonfly. . . .

This period of peace came to an end after about two weeks. The Maréchal grew suddenly very much more ill: he tossed in a fever, a prey to violent physical disturbances and, what was worse, mental delusions that tortured him without ceasing. He suffered horribly. His digestive processes were upset; he could eat little, and the little he ate did him no good. It seemed that the actual breaking-up of such a big, strong machine could not help being a fearful business. Cateau pitied him then more than ever before. It was terrible to see him suffering so, racked by misery none could ease. Death, one felt, ought to come with dignity to a doughty warrior like La Ferté-Senneterre; it should not have dared to strip him of his last remnants of pride and self-respect.

Nor was he even permitted the consolation of meeting it in private. From the moment that his illness took a definite turn for the worse La Ferté-Saint-Aubin was crowded with visitors. The Bishop of

Orléans and his Canons from the cathedral, the mayor of the town, the Seneschal of the province, all came to pay their respects and inquire how the Maréchal did. Deputations arrived from the seats of his governments in eastern France. There was, in fact, a constant stream of sympathetic callers, many of whom had travelled from so far that they had to be asked to stop the night. The house was thronged all day every day; the family often sat down to dinner twenty or thirty strong.

Naturally, Magdelon could not leave her duties in the sickroom to receive these people. Gabrielle, who should have done the honours of the castle in her mother-in-law's place, had shut herself up in her own apartments and refused to appear. It therefore devolved upon Cateau to deal with them all as best she was able. She made a determined effort to keep them from troubling the dying man, hoping to spare him as much as she could, and, in the main, was successful. However, once in a while someone more persistent than the rest contrived to worm his way through her defences, with dire results. . . . There was, for example, the unfortunate time that the Lieutenant-Governor of Verdun marched into the bedroom while the Maréchal was raving with delirium. On this occasion Cateau and Magdelon were both there, and Gabrielle, too. (She'd been sent for in a hurry, for fear her father-in-law should not survive the night.) They'd been discovered, regrettably, on their knees by the bed, chafing the sufferer's hands and crying out: 'My Lord! My Lord! Don't you know who we are?' To which La Ferté had opened a bleary eye in reply and bellowed: 'To be sure I do! You're three trumpery trollops!' (The story, of course, had got back to Paris in no time at all. It was no comfort, either, to be told later that old Madame Cornuel had said, when she heard it: 'You can see the poor man was still in his senses!')

Then there was another even more awful occasion, when the Bishop himself had been fetched to administer extreme unction, and Robert and one of the Maréchal's lackeys became involved in a quarrel as to who had the better right to hand their master the crucifix. In the midst of the tug-of-war that ensued it happened that La Ferté sat straight up in bed, pushed the horrified cleric aside, and yelled excitedly to his favourite servant: 'Go it, Robert! Paste him with it, why don't you?'

It could not, alas! be maintained that the Maréchal was making an edifying end.

Luckily he sank into a coma shortly after the Bishop's flustered departure: the last days of all were peaceful again.

On the evening of the twenty-seventh of September Magdelon shut the door of her husband's bedroom, walked along the corridor, and calmly descended the stairs to the great hall, where Cateau and the children were gathered together. Louis was amongst them, having arrived from Paris just before supper in response to a secret message from his aunt. His mother had not yet heard of his coming. When she saw him her deliberate composure was shattered: she tottered forward and fell into his arms, then raised a devastated face from his shoulder to say, in a small, choked voice: 'Oh, children, children, what will become of us?'

It was only then that they knew their father had left them.

Chapter IX

'PARIS, THIS TWELFTH OF AUGUST, 1683.

'The Duchesse de la Ferté-Senneterre presents her compliments to the Comtesse d'Olonne, and craves leave, if the latter be at liberty, to seek the honour of an interview.'

Cateau frowned as she identified the pointed, spidery handwriting, lifted her eyebrows superciliously as she read the message it conveyed, and then tossed the note across the table to Fervaques.

'Your cousin, sir, is at the door: shall we admit her?'

Fervaques sighed, and looked at the scrap of paper as if he could not bear to touch it.

'I suppose perhaps we must. Is she in trouble, madam?'

'Not that I know of.'

'But it's the third time this week...'

Cateau smiled, not very amiably.

'Ah, well, my dear, haven't you noticed? Our Gabrielle appears to have discovered me just lately. Since my slight illness in the spring she has begun to take a flattering interest in her husband's aunt — naturally I can't think why, can you? She sends me notes and flowers almost daily, and tells me every time we meet how deeply she sympathizes with someone in my position — a woman growing old alone, with no children of her own about her. I dare swear, too, she'll bring that youngest brat of hers to call today.... Dear little Catherine — *Catherine*, mark you! — is so devoted to her Aunt d'Olonne. The child prates of me continually, it seems. Oh, Gabrielle's no fool, believe me!'

'But why should she disturb us *now?* It's not a visiting hour — and I'm so comfortable, dear friend! Has a man no right to privacy in his own house?'

Fervaques set down his glass of syrup-and-water, mopped his brow with a rumpled square of silk, and sat back in his chair, surveying his mistress with good-humoured dismay. He was in his shirtsleeves, for the day was extremely warm — Cateau, in a loose, flowing housegown of some cool dark blue Indian material —: the pair were enjoying an after-dinner game of chess in the trellised arbour. The trellised arbour was the Countess's latest innovation at the house in the rue de la Sourdière. It occupied the whole of the small inner court. Screened by thickly growing large-leaved creepers, gay with flowering plants in pots, sweetly murmurous with the soft plash of a miniature fountain, it provided a refuge from the heat of the midsummer sun. What a pity it seemed to shatter the slumbrous peace of the atmosphere! On the other hand, 'If we don't see her this time, it'll have to be later. We may as well get it over,' said Cateau philosophically. 'Thomas, show the Duchess in.'

'Very good, madam.'

As the lackey departed she began raking in the black and white ivory chessmen, explaining laconically: 'There's no use in keeping them there, sir. One's never through with your cousin in less than an hour.'

For once, however, young Madame de la Ferté produced an impression of being in somewhat of a hurry. She made a fussy, portentous entrance in billows of her favourite sea-green silk and lace, accompanied — as one had feared she would be — by small Catherine and the latter's nurse. She kissed Cateau, as she had been recently accustomed to do, and held up her little girl inexpertly to receive a grudging auntly caress — this, also, in accordance with her unsubtle plan of campaign —; but somehow today her heart was not in her work. Her smile was mechanical, her manner abstracted; she refused her cousin's offer of iced wine or syrup-and-water, and scarcely seemed able to bring herself to settle, like a nervous taffeta butterfly, on the edge of a chair. And no sooner had she come to rest than she gave Catherine a push and bade her 'Go play in the garden with Nursey, there's a good child!' — turning finally to her hosts with a purposeful glint in her eye.

Cateau's heart sank. It was bad enough to be obliged to entertain Gabrielle when that young woman was in an agreeable mood, but there were distinct traces this afternoon of thunder in the air. She composed her features, nevertheless, into a courteously inquiring mask, though her glance had a tendency to stray beyond the Duchess's head to where small Catherine, whose legs were regrettably chunky, was doubtless wreaking her worst amongst the roses.

'Not *too* near the flower-beds, nurse!' called Cateau, in a wiry falsetto. 'And if I were you, I'd keep away from the fountain. . . . Yes, my dear ' — to Gabrielle — 'now what is it we can do for you?'

'Madam, I'm at my wits' end,' began Gabrielle boldly. 'God forbid I should come to you with complaints of my husband or his family!' (But that, reflected Cateau, was precisely what her niece best loved doing: it was her charming wont to bring outrageous charges against whichever La Ferté had last left the room!) 'You know what my life has been these eight years, the insults and indignities I've put up with since the day of my marriage. No other

woman could have stood it. I say nothing about the Duke's dastardly behaviour: you are sensible, I hope, what he is and what I've
been forced to suffer from his debauchery and extravagance. He's so
deeply in debt now that I doubt if he'll ever get out. Oh, I've warned
him of what was coming! I've told him, time and again, that he'd
end up in the Bastille, and that when it happened he needn't expect
me to squander my few remaining pennies in bailing him free! He
knows how utterly I despise him! If it weren't for my two helpless
babes — worse than fatherless, poor lambs! — I'd have left him
years ago.... But that's not the point, is it? I can't expect you to
reform La Ferté. What I am asking is your advice about what to do
with my mother-in-law — for unless you can help me there, I fear
we'll all be hauled off to prison, and no power on earth can save us!'

'My dear cousin, what do you mean?' cried Fervaques. 'The poor
Maréchale is devoted to her children; what can she have done to upset you?'

'Done? What has she done? Wait till you hear!' said Gabrielle.
'Madam, forgive me.... I realize the lady is your sister ... naturally, family feeling ... and all that.... But really, if you love her,
you must take care of her now, for she's gone clean out of her senses!
And if something's not done to stop her straight off, she'll ruin the
lot of us!'

'My dear,' said Cateau, 'try to calm yourself, I beg of you, and
explain what you mean.'

Her own tones grew colder and more measured as the Duchess's
rose excitedly: not even the silver voice of the fountain was more
gently remote than Cateau's.

'Wait till you hear!' said Gabrielle again, bridling offensively. 'I
hardly know where to begin.... You have heard, I suppose, that my
husband has received an offer this week to buy his town house?'

'My dear, no! How splendid!' said Cateau; while Fervaques
added frankly: 'Buy Great Senneterre! But who on earth'd want it?'

'Ah, that's what I said, too, cousin, when he told me! I simply
couldn't believe my ears.... A huge, outmoded monstrosity like
that! I never could abide the old place — as you know, I'd been
after him for years to see if he couldn't dispose of it. But he wouldn't
sell at first, and later, when he felt he had to, nobody'd even consider ... Only now, out of a clear sky, the Maréchal de la Feuillade's
taken it into his head to buy up all the property in the neighbourhood
and build a square in honour of the King. It's to be called the Place
des Victoires, I hear, and he's willing to pay a very good price — two
hundred thousand francs — for the mouldy old pile.'

Fervaques whistled in delighted surprise.

'Bravo, cousin! That's a jolly good sum! Why, you'll all be rolling in money!' — while Cateau, who'd have sold the gown off her

back if she'd been offered a round enough figure for it, immediately began to feel a spasm of keen regret that she did not own her own house, so that there was no use in trying to persuade La Feuillade to build his square in the rue de la Sourdière instead.... But what was Gabrielle saying?

'Ah, that's what I thought! I said to myself, Well, at least the worst of our troubles are ended — for with that amount, even after settling the family debts, there'd be plenty left over. But, my dears, you'd never guess... La Ferté can't make the sale without his mother's consent — and the Maréchale refuses to give it!'

'She *refuses?* Oh, but she *can't!* That's absurd! In Heaven's name, why?'

'Wait till you hear,' said Gabrielle, for a third time — as though they hadn't heard too much already! 'She's opened a gambling den!'

'A gambling den! Surely you're joking, cousin! What do you mean?'

'I mean what I say,' said Gabrielle. 'A gambling den in the Gallery of Aminta, if you please! Yes, madam, she's turned Great Senneterre into a resort for the lowest scum of the town. Oh, I'd never have believed it, if I hadn't seen with my own eyes! She's been fearfully restless and unhappy, you know, ever since the Maréchal died. You would have thought, wouldn't you, considering that some people said she had a hand in his death — but excuse me, madam! I'm sorry I mentioned ... There's no use going into those old stories now.... Well, at any rate, I've tried my best to interest her in good works, in visiting the charity hospitals.... My sister de Ventadour and I spend an hour every morning regularly at the Quinze-Vingts or the Hôtel-Dieu.... But it was hopeless; I couldn't induce her to come with us. And you yourself, madam, must be aware that my mother-in-law has no taste for sedentary pleasures. It's a matter of perfect indifference to her what she eats and drinks — she gave up her music years ago — and she's never, to my knowledge, so much as opened a book! Oh, it's not been easy sometimes to keep her amused! But really — really — in my wildest dreams I did not imagine she'd be capable of *this!* You know how she's always loved gaming — not so much for its own sake, for she's no head for cards — but just the excitement it brings! Well, madam, she's thrown the house open for play every night — and not to her friends alone: that'd be bad enough for a widow of her age — but to all the riffraff of the quarter besides! Anyone who cares to stake a louis or two on the tables is welcome now at Great Senneterre.... Then, not content with that, she's called in those awful cronies of hers to help her. You know whom I mean — Liscouet, the two Ligneracs, and that dreadful little toad Dupré (who was a midwife's son, or worse!). They've all manner of cutthroat methods of winning dishonestly.... The cheating that went on last night was simply abominable! I told the Maréchale so, and she only laughed and said, wasn't it clever of them? and she wished so much they'd tell her how they did it, so that she could make some money, too. I honestly believe she thinks she's going to pay off all our debts...! I'm in despair about it, madam! If you can't persuade her to stop these horrors and let the sale go through, we'll be arrested sure as fate before the week is up!'

Gabrielle brought her speech to a close with a gasp and stopped talking abruptly, her mouth still wide open as though she might have something more to say. Then she snapped it shut and reached weakly for a glass of Fervaques' syrup-and-water.... 'I think, dear cousin, after all ... ah, thank you!'

'But what,' Fervaques demanded, 'does your husband say to this? He's the Maréchale's son — it's his business to keep her in order!'

'La Ferté,' declared his wife wrathfully, 'thinks it's funny. What else would you expect from a fool like him? He doesn't seem to care in the least whether he sells his house or not — though he must know how important it is to us. He's fobbed La Feuillade off with evasive answers for days, and when I told him last night what went on at the tables he shouted with laughter and said he was delighted: perhaps Dupré would consent to teach *him* a trick or two as well: if only he'd known about it before, he'd not have lost five thousand crowns last week to the British Ambassador!... Oh, no — no one can help me but you! The Countess is the one person who has any influence over her sister. Dear madam, please try — not for my sake alone, but for the Maréchale's, too — for her children and grandchildren — save us from this terrible disgrace! Do what you can, I implore you — for if *you* cannot succour us, all will indeed be lost!'

While Gabrielle was making her plea her fingers plucked nervously at her hair, her necklace, the fringe of her gown, though her eyes remained fixed on the Countess's face. Cateau, meanwhile, had listened thoughtfully, chin in hand, to her niece's recital, allowing her own studied repose to throw into relief the other's fidgety mannerisms. She said nothing for a while; then she cast her lover a look full of meaning and remarked tersely: 'Yes, I see. Yes, of course. We'll look in tonight, Fervaques — shall we not, sir? — to see what can be done.'

'Thanks be to Heaven! Dear madam — *dearest* madam — you are our saviour!'

The Duchess set sail with confidence on a treacly sea of gratitude, all but flinging herself in her enthusiasm at her hostess's feet. This last extravagance Cateau was able to check by lifting her hand and saying, with one of her wryest smiles: 'Don't protest too much till we see what we can do! I promise nothing, mind you! All I've said is, that I'll look in tonight.'

Gabrielle seized her aunt's hand and kissed it.

'Beloved Countess! As if I weren't perfectly sure what that meant! Oh, we are saved! I feel it — I know it!'

The measure of her relief might have been gauged fairly accurately by the speed with which the Duchess brought her call to a close. Directly she'd extracted the promise she had come to secure she called her small daughter to her — the chunky Catherine now repulsively grubby, Cateau observed with distaste, after her romp in the rose beds — and almost scuttled away from the arbour. She did not even wait for her cousin to give her his hand to escort her to the door, but tossed a jubilant 'Till this evening, then, madam, we shall expect you!' over her green taffeta shoulder.

After Gabrielle had gone Cateau sat for several minutes in silence under the leaf-shaded trellises, while the little fountain went on tinkling in tune with her thoughts. Without paying heed to what she did, she took the black and white ivory chessmen out of their box and set them up on the board once more, so that she and Fervaques might begin a new game. She was thinking so hard that she did not even notice when they started playing again: mechanically she moved her pawns and pieces while Fervaques, on the opposite side of the table, moved his pawns and pieces, too, content to say nothing until she should give a sign that she wished to speak.

Cateau was more appreciative than ever of his mutely tactful sympathy. Nothing was too bad to bear as long as one could count on the support of such an intuitive partner. And yet ... and yet, this was perhaps the worst test they had had to face together. What could be done now to avert disaster? Poor Magdelon! Poor foolish child ...!

As Cateau left the forties behind her she thought more and more highly of privacy and peace, and all the solid, unspectacular virtues inherent in the better element of the class from which she came. She would have been the first to admit that she had not prized them sufficiently in the past — but what was the use in growing older if one did not grow wiser as well? It was shocking that Magdelon could not see things as she did; could not bring herself to realize that, once youth was over, nothing remained save to accept each stage on the way to old age as gracefully and gallantly as possible.

Magdelon, in fact, refused to grow old at all. She had behaved very well during her conventional year of strict mourning. Apparently crushed by grief, she had shut herself up in her black-hung halls and turned for solace, as was eminently proper, to her children and grandchildren. Louis, the young Jesuit novice, no longer an exile from his father's house, had been a comfort then.

But even this sorrow passed in time, like others that had preceded it. Soon enough the sable draperies were packed away, the doors of

Great Senneterre reopened, while its mistress emerged in the world once again, with nothing but the sacrosanct widow's bandeau on her brow to remind one of her loss. She began to live the same racketty, aimless life as before, except that, if possible, she was even sillier than she had been. La Ferté, after all, had served as a kind of safety anchor. Though he had never criticized nor even seemed to be conscious of her misconduct, the very fact of his physical presence, huge and impressive in the background, had kept her flighty fragility within bounds. Now there was no one left to control her. Louis could seldom be with his mother, and Henri, far from attempting to curb her silliness, actually seemed to encourage it. The Nemesis awaiting all much younger wives of old men had fallen upon the Maréchale: because she had been thirty-four years her late husband's junior, it was to be feared she supposed she must stay young forever.

Cateau, pained by these frivolous proceedings, had somewhat dourly stayed away from their theatre. In the last ten months she had seen almost nothing of Magdelon. She had not been very well. ... A minor operation in the spring had left her feeling languid and all the more likely a prey to the gloomy fancies that beset her in clouds concerning her sister. But none of her guesses came within measurable distance of the horrors revealed by Gabrielle. This was truly and dreadfully the end — unless somehow one could manage to dissuade...? A pallid hope possessed Cateau's heart, rather than her mind, that it might not yet be too late. She was still, as Gabrielle said, not without influence. In their lives together Magdelon had often bent her will to Cateau's — more often than not, really: she had been obdurate only where her affections were involved. And that, one must trust, could not be the case here.

'O dear God,' prayed Cateau, with ardour, 'please don't make it turn out that way. Spare us the last unspeakable infamy. Don't let Magdelon be in love with Dupré!'

But all she said, as she raised her clear eyes to her lover's, was: 'Look, my dear, I am taking your castle!... Now tell me, would it amuse you to run in for a few minutes tonight at poor Magdelon's? No doubt Gabrielle's story is greatly exaggerated — still, I'd rather like to see for myself how things are going, shouldn't you?'

And Fervaques replied simply, as so often before: 'My dear, you're quite right. I am ready to do whatever you think best.'

The coach was ordered for ten o'clock. In spite of the heat Cateau made an elaborate toilet. She wore a gown of pale straw-coloured satin to match her hair, which she'd lately stopped dyeing and was letting fade gradually into grey. The new shade was very becoming: Madame d'Olonne at fifty looked actually younger than Madame d'Olonne at five-and-forty.

At Great Senneterre every window was blazing with light, and there was an impressive crush of smart carriages about the door. Going up, the crowd on the staircase was encouraging, for it was full of familiar faces. Magdelon might have thrown open her house to the public at large, but so far most of those to avail themselves of the privilege appeared to be the same people, or others indistinguishable from them, who had had the entrée to her receptions for years. It was, Cateau thought, curiously like one of the La Fertés' official at-homes in the days of the Maréchal's lifetime. There were a number of councillors of parliament and their wives — one could always tell them from the genuine nobility by their too careful clothes and air of slightly overdone easiness — as well as a sprinkling of courtiers, particularly young ones like the Marquis de Biran and the Chevalier Colbert, who were Henri's friends. (Of course, one must remember that the court had just been plunged into strict mourning by the sudden death of the Queen, poor Marie-Thérèse: Versailles this summer was as quiet as a tomb.)

It was only by degrees, as she and Fervaques made a slow tour of the Gallery of Aminta, where play was in progress and the press was thickest, that Cateau observed there were some very odd accents here and there mingled with the more respectable elements. . . . Half a dozen pretty painted little women were drifting about from table to table, making themselves generally agreeable. What were they? — Actresses? Paid entertainers of some sort? Or worse? . . . Cateau saw Hippolyte, the Maréchale's butler, give one of them a playful slap on her bare bejewelled shoulder, but that might not mean anything — Magdelon's servants were notoriously the rudest in Paris. . . . No, on the whole, it was the queer men that one most objected to. Baron, the actor, and Liscouet were not to be found in decent folk's houses. Then there were the brothers Lignerac — the Abbé and the Chevalier — bleached blonds with affected, effeminate bass voices, whose reputations were certainly of the shadiest. And Dupré himself. It was when her eye lighted upon Dupré that Cateau became convinced that something was terribly wrong at Great Senne-terre.

When she and Fervaques came in he was holding the bank at the principal table of lansquenet. Cateau had never seen him before, but she was sure it must be he, he looked so exactly like one's idea of a professional gambler. Small and ill-favoured, with a mangy black wig and Mongolian features, he stood watching the circle of players about him, his rat-eyes darting obliquely this way and that as the bets were made. As Cateau drew nearer she perceived that his sallow face was deeply pitted with smallpox and that he was wearing two handsome diamond rings, one on each weazened middle finger.

His appearance was in one respect reassuring, for it was obvious that even the fatally susceptible Magdelon could not be in love with

Dupré! On the other hand, his black, blighting presence seemed positively evil: he looked like a beetle that ought to be stepped on: from the moment she spied him Cateau began to feel acutely uncomfortable. The low-voiced, shifting throng under the dusty chandeliers took on a menacing aspect. Even the room itself, with its garish, unimaginative magnificence — too big, too grand, too brightly lighted, as it always had been — looked suddenly evil, too. There was further cast over it the subtle atmosphere of a building condemned. Houses that were going to be torn down were like people that were going to die: the very stones of Great Senneterre seemed to know they might not be there, a few months hence. . . .

Cateau found Gabrielle, very pale and much powdered, and the Duke, very red and moist-handed, at the lansquenet table. They were not playing. . . . 'It seems better not, in our own house,' said Henri, adding frankly: 'Besides, if we did, we'd be sure to win!' . . . And in a moment or two up floated Magdelon, radiant in ice-grey satin and pearls, an aigrette perched precariously in her streaked auburn locks. She was holding her granddaughter, six-year-old Marie-Angélique, by the hand. The child, all white and gold like a little blond doll, curtsied when she was told to and blinked with sleepy solemnity at the company. Cateau was shocked to see her: nothing to her mind so clearly proved that Magdelon had taken leave of her senses!

But the Maréchale, in puerile high spirits, welcomed her sister and Fervaques delightedly.

'My dears, how sweet of you to come!' she cried. 'What do you think of my new little kingdom? Isn't it a marvellous idea? I've thought all along that something ought to be done to cheer people up this year — everyone's been so depressed since the poor dear Queen's death. To tell the truth, now that the Montespan's out of it, there's no one left at court to liven things up. Dear Madame and the Dauphine are Germans: need one say more? And though the Maintenon's an admirable person in her way, she hasn't at all what I call a real social gift. . . . Of course, I can't afford gaming with my dwindling small income, but what I say is, if I can't play myself, the next best thing is to watch other people! All my dear young friends have rallied round me superbly. I do truly think they're enjoying themselves, don't you? Young folk like a house where there's plenty of room to turn round in, and that I can offer them at Great Senneterre, whatever else may be lacking. To think when I came here as a bride I wanted the Maréchal to cut the big gallery in two! Of course, it does look a bit shabby, I know, but to be frank, dears, I believe, with our good Dupré in command, I'll soon be in a position to remedy matters. Don't breathe a word to a soul! — but he's the most wonderful system — it never fails, positively! I can't really think how

he does it. Isn't it clever of him! He's promised to show me next
week how it works. It seems that part of it's just the power of the
mind: if you *will* a card to turn up, it can't disappoint you!... Oh,
he's been the greatest help to me! I don't know what I'd do without
him. He has perfectly brilliant ideas about everything. Now last
night, for instance, when all those Swiss officers arrived unexpectedly
the house was fairly filled up with men, and it *did* look rather drab.
I felt it myself, though I couldn't think why it was. Well, Dupré
came to me in the middle of the evening.... I was having a bite of
supper in the green cabinet. I was really quite hungry, too; you
know, one develops an appetite sitting up so late! Remind me, Cateau, dear, to give you my recipe for stewed-peaches-in-rossolis....
But as I was saying, Dupré came straight to me and said: "Madam,
if you'll permit me to mention it, what we need is more ladies on the
floor." Well, of course, as soon as he'd said it, I saw that that was
what was the matter with the party. But I didn't know what to do,
because Tinette is in Orléans, and dear little Chou-Chou's in bed
with a cold, and my darling Marie-Angélique, for all she's so bright,
is perhaps a tiny bit too young to be expected to help. After all,
she's not quite seven. (Angel poppet, wait half a minute, and
Granny will find you a sugarplum!...) And you've been ill, Cateau,
and all the women at Versailles have gone away to the country
while the court is in mourning. So I explained that to Dupré, and he
said at once: "Never mind, madam. If madam is willing to rely on
me, it can be easily arranged." And — would you believe it? — he
was as good as his word. Tonight he's brought with him six or eight
of the sweetest young things! I can't imagine where he found them.
But they've lovely manners and are all perfect ladies, really. There!
That's one of them now, the pretty brunette placing a bet for Monsieur Colbert.... They seem to be touchingly pleased to be asked to
a house like this, and I must say I find them exceedingly useful.
They flit about from place to place, don't you know, keeping everything gay and cheerful. Speak to them, Cateau, dear, if you get a
chance; I know how much the little creatures would appreciate it.
... Oh, forgive me a moment, my loves! There's my favourite
Swiss guardsman, Colonel Sandoz, coming in. I must just say a
word...'

As she fluttered off, still holding little Marie-Angélique's hand,
Cateau's eyes met Gabrielle's in despair: had Magdelon, not content
with running a gambling den, decided to open a bawdy-house, too?

Ninon de Lenclos strolled by on the arm of her friend, the Chevalier de Méré; and Cateau seized upon her gratefully as a welcome
note of good breeding in the midst of much that was meretricious
(not to use a more sinister word). Good Heavens! What a pass
things had come to, when *Ninon* seemed less disreputable than one's

own sister! (But, after all, since the courtesan had given up having lovers and begun calling herself Mademoiselle de Lenclos, she was really quite generally received.) ... Ninon was a good ten years older than the Comtesse d'Olonne, but she had kept her teeth and her figure; moreover, she had taken care to choose in Méré, her escort for the evening, a man ten years older still than herself. She was charming tonight in swooning blue with a parure of opals, a mantilla like a frosted spider-web on her greying curls. Only her hands, tiny and claw-like and covered with ugly brown spots, betrayed her age.

Cateau was greatly relieved to see Ninon and the Chevalier, though she was wont to flee from the latter, a dried-up, dyspeptic old gallant as pedantic as the poetry he wrote. The three chatted together pleasantly: it was agreeable to be able to forget, even for a few minutes, where they were and what was going on around them.

Presently, however, Ninon looked up with a smile and pointed across the room. 'Look, my dears, at that funny fat little man with the very red face! What is the matter with him? Can he be going to have a fit?'

Cateau followed the direction of the Lenclos' folded fan and recognized, with consternation, Magdelon's friend, the Swiss guardsman Sandoz.

There was some trouble evidently about the play at the lansquenet table. The Colonel and a group of his friends, also members of the Swiss regiment, were arguing heatedly with Dupré: their voices, loud and angry, with the harsh, uncouth accent of their homeland, were a contrast to the Frenchman's oily tones.

Dupré faced his opponents coolly, his head to one side, his smile pacific and deprecating.

'I'm sorry, gentlemen,' he was saying. 'The luck of the game, you know.... See, I have nothing up my sleeve — no cards concealed, I assure you! Pray look for yourselves if you will....'

But in spite of his smooth excuses the angry murmurs increased. Colonel Sandoz, who seemed to be spokesman for his compatriots, stepped forward with clenched fists. He was as scarlet as a turkeycock, and his square blue eyes sparkled with slow but implacable racial truculence.

'Sir, it's an outrage!' he exclaimed. 'I demand to examine your pack! There's been foul play here. I say it, and so say my comrades. I've been watching you now for half an hour by the clock, and during the whole of that time you've won consistently, whenever the stakes on the table made winning worth while. Oh, you think yourself very clever, I know! You let the players pick up plenty of small coins to encourage their betting. But as soon as there's enough gold on the board to tempt you, you match the right card every time and pocket the lot. I can't tell how you do it — and I don't care to be told how

such dirty sleight-of-hand tricks are performed — but I say it's a
shame to cheat honest folk! Give me back my money, and give my
comrades' money back, too! Why, the place is no better than a den
of common thieves!'

'Careful, gentleman, careful, if you please! Remember where you
are, I beseech you. This is the house of one of the greatest nobles in
France, a duke and peer of the realm. Madame the Maréchale de la
Ferté-Senneterre is your hostess. Surely you would not stoop to ac-
cuse so high-born a lady...?'

'Lady or not, she's a thief! I say she's a thief! You Frenchmen
are all alike. Nobility's no patent of probity here. Why, there's not
an honest hair on your heads! Damn the lot of you, say I — with
your false curling periwigs and your false smiling manners! You
think you can pull the wool over our eyes because we're too stupid to
see what you're doing. But let me tell you this, Lord Lightfingers,
we crude mountaineers are cleverer than you think. We're by no
means the simpletons you suppose us to be, although we do live on
goat's milk and cheese instead of greasy ragouts and Burgundy wine!
Yes, by God! we know very well what our rights are as free-born
citizens of the free cantons, and we're going to see that we get them,
too! No pack of lousy lying French knaves can best us! How about
it, my friends?'

The shouts grew louder and louder. Emboldened by their support,
Colonel Sandoz marched up to the table and slapped his gauntlet
down upon it.

'There, fellow, take your choice! Either hand over our gold, or by
Heaven! we'll make you! If you're not man enough to fight me, I'll
call the police!'

Dupré looked terribly frightened; his sallow face had turned the
colour of celery, and his thin little hands twitched ceaselessly, as if
from a tic he could not control. But he stood his ground.

'Sir, it's a libel! Sir, I'll have your blood for this! Sir, send for the
police, do — the sooner the better! I've a tale to tell them, too....
Such insults ... I never ... in the house of a lady of fashion....'

Everybody in the Gallery of Aminta was staring at them now —
and an odd pair of adversaries they made, the stocky Swiss officer in
his uniform of scarlet-and-blue, and the squirming black beetle
Dupré. Ninon, with a gay, tinny laugh, put up her eye-glass the better to survey the scene. ('How deliciously primitive, my friend!' she
murmured behind her fan to the Chevalier de Méré.) Cateau,
gravely alarmed, looked about for Fervaques, with the intention of
bidding him appease the quarrel, if possible. But he seemed to have
vanished in the thick of the crowd. Magdelon was there, of course,
but there was nothing Magdelon could do. She stood in the middle
of the floor, a flat smile of pure fright on her poor painted face; she

was clutching her daughter-in-law's hand; and Gabrielle, strangely, was smiling, also. Cateau thought she had never beheld anything more odious than Gabrielle's smile. (Marie-Angélique, merciful to relate, had evidently been sent upstairs to bed.)

By this time Colonel Sandoz had unsheathed his sword and was preparing to use it to threaten his enemy. Henri then burst forward — where had he been? — as flushed and irate as the guardsman himself. His step was unsteady, his rolling eyes — tragic reminder of the Maréchal's — so glassy that it was plain to be seen he had been drinking heavily.

'Damme! You filthy Swiss swine!' shrieked Henri, in a high, cracking voice. '*I'll* teach you to bully your betters!'

Unarmed as he was, he flung himself bodily on the Colonel, who was so taken by surprise that he let his sword fall to the floor. The two men struggled together, each striving to upset the other's balance. They were well matched in strength, but the young Duke was in no condition to challenge the other's magnificent physical fitness. It might have gone hard with Henri, had the battle been a long one.

Magdelon, with a shriek, tore herself from Gabrielle's restraining grasp and tried to part the contestants. Cateau moved swiftly forward to aid her sister. But before she could reach her Fervaques had arrived — Fervaques grown suddenly greater than life size, armed with his quiet personal integrity (never more striking than now, in this dubious company) as well as the dignity of the law. He laid his hand firmly on the Colonel's square shoulder and said, in a low, level voice that carried throughout the room: 'Gentlemen — please! This is entirely unnecessary. As governor of His Majesty's provinces of Maine, Perche, and the County of Laval, I can promise you that justice will be done, sir, in the name of my master, the King.'

On their way home in the carriage, later, Cateau remarked (having first duly complimented her lover on his skill in settling the dispute without bloodshed): 'My dear, come to think of it, in a way I believe it's a good thing this happened! For now even Magdelon must see there's nothing to be done except sell Great Senneterre as quickly as possible.'

Time shortly proved the truth of her assertion. In less than a week the deal had been closed: Monsieur de la Feuillade, delighted after so many rebuffs to get what he wanted at last, paid the Duc de la Ferté two hundred and twenty-two thousand francs, which was enough to settle the family's debts and buy them a smaller, more modern house in the rue de Richelieu besides. And the latter, once he'd begun selling things, was so charmed by the idea of cash in hand that he decided to sell his regiment, too, and go to England with the Maréchal d'Humières, who was being sent on a special mission to the court of King Charles.

'After all,' said Henri to his Aunt d'Olonne, the day he called on her and Fervaques to discuss his new hopes, 'I've never cared much for the military life. As a matter of fact, I've always felt, don't you know, that what I was really made for was a career of diplomacy!'

Chapter X

WOULD IT EVER STOP RAINING?

Charles-Louis pressed his nose so hard that he made a white button of it against the windowpane, as he stared hopelessly out at the storm breaking with fury over the city. It had begun about dawn: when he waked up very early, before it was properly light, he'd heard the drops pelting on the shutters in his bedroom; and each passing hour had brought more and more of them in ever increasing strength. Now the wind had grown dangerously high; it lashed the tops of the trees outside the drawing-room windows, bringing down showers of leaves and here and there whole branches to litter the gravelled paths below. It howled in the chimneys, too, and shook the casements of the old house in the Faubourg till they rattled and moaned as if tortured by ghosts.

Of course, autumn in France was the rainy season. One could not expect anything better than this, from now on. But it was early autumn yet; summer had been lingering in Charles-Louis' garden no longer ago than yesterday afternoon.... Why, there were still hundreds of flowers in bloom, and the elms had not even begun to turn brown! It did really seem, then, as though the weather had broken on purpose to spite him. Surely, if it had wanted to, the rain might have held off today of all days, on this never-to-be-forgotten twenty-fourth of September, 1688, which marked the end of his old life forever.

Tomorrow everything would begin anew; tomorrow Charles-Louis would be a child no more. True, he was not yet technically of age; he had three months to wait for his eighteenth birthday. But times such as these made a man of one early. Had not his cousin Louis XIV declared war on the Germans just last week and issued a proclamation asserting that now was the moment for all brave and ambitious young nobles to prove their worth? Every chap at court was enlisting. Even Porlier, who for some reason had not been especially anxious for his master to follow their example, had admitted that. Monseigneur the Dauphin was slated to lead the army in person — he was leaving the very next day to take charge of the siege of Philipsburg on the Rhine. And, best of all, Charles-Louis d'Orléans, Chevalier de Longueville, was going with him.... Yes, it was almost too good to be true! He had bought the charge of ensign in the King's own infantry regiment. In Charles-Louis' eyes that was better than being the colonel himself, for it was the ensign's duty — or, rather, his illustrious privilege — to carry the regiment's banner proudly aloft when the army went into action — to symbolize, as it were, its undying glory in one's own person. Oh, it would be marvellous — *marvellous!*

No doubt the sun would be shining tomorrow when he marched off to war. . . . It *must* shine tomorrow! On the other hand, it would be nice if it could shine today, too, for just a little while. If it did not — if the storm kept up as it had been doing since daybreak — a great disappointment might be in store for him. Charles-Louis often felt that his life, so far, had been largely made up of disappointments — but this one would be particularly hard to bear. For Aunt Magdelon and her daughter Chou-Chou de la Ferté had promised to come to dinner to bid him good-bye. They had promised — and one knew that they would keep their word if they possibly could: Aunt Magdelon was very good about promises! They had said, though, hadn't they? that they'd be there by one o'clock at the latest — and it was already past two. For the last hour and a half Charles-Louis had been ready and waiting, clad in his ensign's uniform of scarlet and gold. It was so new and fine that he was afraid to sit down for fear of wrinkling his breeches. He'd wandered restlessly instead from room to room, peering out of this window and that, hoping each time to catch sight of Aunt Magdelon's coach. . . . Where could she be? What was keeping her?

If she were to fail him now, it would be for the first time in his life.

Charles-Louis had not many relatives to be kind to him, which made those there were seem peculiarly important. Grand'maman, of course, was dead — he could remember her quite well, for he'd been almost eight when she died. Papa was dead, too — and he had died so long ago that Charles-Louis could not remember him at all. Of course, there was Aunt de Nemours, Papa's sister, who came to see him once a month regularly, with a trying air of doing her duty. . . . But Charles-Louis could not say he cared much for Aunt de Nemours. She was tall and old and grim, with myopic, heavy-lidded grey eyes and two white curls like inverted question-marks on either side of her forehead. Also she appeared, for reasons best known to herself, to resent her nephew deeply. Charles-Louis could not have told how he knew this: it wasn't actually what she said — Aunt de Nemours talked very little, confining her efforts to a brief but searching catechism concerning his mental and moral delinquencies of the four weeks just past. However, he had a definite feeling that, no matter what happened, he could not hope to win her approval. There was no pleasing Aunt de Nemours! . . .

This morning, for instance, when she'd driven over to pay him a last visit before he left for the army, she had been by no means impressed by his newly-donned grandeur. She frowned alarmingly through her eyeglass while he revolved before her, and when he paused to glance up at her shyly she beat her ebony stick on the floor and barked out: 'Ha, young man, I suppose you think yourself very fine! Well enough — well enough — we'll see how you look later on, after a month in the German marshes! ... Such an insane time of year to start a war, anyway! My poor fool of a cousin Louis never had the slightest sense about military matters. If it weren't for his generals, he'd have been forced to shut up shop long ago. ... Well, my lad, give as good an account of yourself as you can — try, at any rate, to do as you're told — that's more than your father ever succeeded in doing. And whatever happens, don't spoil those new boots I've made you a present of! They're the best Russia-leather and much too expensive to be replaced in a hurry. Young people are always so careless. ... Porlier, I'll expect *you* to look out for the Chevalier's boots!'

By the time Aunt de Nemours had concluded her call she had managed to deflate her nephew's self-esteem completely: he felt seven years old instead of seventeen-and-three-quarters, and as he accompanied the Duchess to the door he studiously avoided meeting Porlier's eye, though the tutor was his best and most reliable friend.

After that, it seemed more vital than ever to Charles-Louis' well-being not to miss seeing Aunt Magdelon.

Aunt Magdelon — whom he called his 'good aunt,' to distinguish her from his cross one — was not in the least like Aunt de Nemours. For one thing, she wasn't really his aunt; she was no relation at all, but had been merely a very dear friend of Papa's. For another, though she, too, was old, she was not nearly so old as the bellicose Duchess: her face, it was true, was quite wrinkled, and her hair would probably have been grey if she'd let it be. (As it was, it ran the gamut all the way from bravest vermilion to an uncertain yellow — one of the fascinating things about meeting Aunt Magdelon after an absence of even a week was guessing what colour her hair would be now!) ... But her dresses were pretty and soft and shiny — unlike his cross aunt's crackling black taffetas — and she herself was as gay as a lark. She played with the children for hours on end, just as if she were one of them; sang them songs, told them stories, even — in their earlier days — indulged in an occasional game of Blind Man's Buff (if she were sure that the servants weren't looking!). And she could not have done more for Charles-Louis if he had been Chou-Chou's own brother. She always brought him a present when she came. Almost everything he treasured had been given him by Aunt Magdelon at one time or another ... his toy soldiers, his pony, his best bow-and-arrows.... Lately she'd not been able to be so lavish. Her gift nowadays was often only a spice-cake or a paper of sugar-plums.... But she never forgot to bring *something*....

Was it any wonder that Charles-Louis was fond of his good aunt? — fonder, indeed, than of anyone else except Porlier — and Porlier, of course, had been father and mother in one to him ever since he was born. He could not recall a time when the old fellow was not there, his constant companion, both in Paris in winter and during the long, pleasant summers at the castle of Graville in Normandy. Porlier made up to his little master for all that was lacking in his queer, lonely life, soothed his recurring impatience with what seemed unnatural restrictions. (For why, Charles-Louis sometimes wondered rebelliously, must he be shut away from his kind, deprived of all youthful society save Chou-Chou's?) It was Porlier who explained that it was by Papa's express wish as set forth in his last will and testament that his son had been educated in private instead of being sent to the academy.... 'And it's not for us to question our dear late lord's commands....' At all events, it was not for Porlier, who was faithfulness and devotion personified, who'd worked all his life for the Longuevilles and was never tired of telling tales about the gallant young Duke and his heroic death on the battlefield at the crossing of the Rhine. Charles-Louis knew that story by heart. How many times had he heard the invariable beginning: 'The eleventh of June, 1672, dawned fine and warm, and His Highness rose early to prepare for his scouting expedition to Doesburg...'?

The door to the hall opened now, and the tutor thrust in his long, lean horse's face — even if one loved Porlier very much, as Charles-Louis undoubtedly did, one could not help admitting he looked exactly like a benevolent horse! — to say: 'Sir, it's half after two. Don't you think, perhaps, in view of the inclement weather...?'

Charles-Louis straightened his drooping shoulders and lifted his chin.

'Certainly not, Porlier! We shall wait for my aunt and my cousin, as planned.'

'But it may be that Madame the Maréchale is not coming at all.'

'If she were not coming, she'd have dispatched a lackey to tell me. I dare say she has been unavoidably detained by the storm. No, no — we'll wait — of course we will!'

Porlier bowed.

'Very well, sir.... Though I feel constrained to add the chef has sent up word that the collation will be ruined if it is not eaten directly.'

Charles-Louis stamped. It was a very small stamp — but then, he had a very small foot. He flung back his yellow curls with an imperious gesture and exclaimed: 'How absurd! Tell Gabriel if the dinner is spoilt, I shall expect him to cook another. If he can't manage that, you may fire him at once.'

Porlier bowed again.

'Yes, sir; as you wish, sir.'

Charles-Louis held his pose of defiance until his tutor had left the room. Porlier was the one person with whom he occasionally put on airs. Far from chiding him for it, Porlier actually seemed pleased to have him show himself what he called 'a lad of spirit.' He would rub his hands together delightedly when his charge made an infrequent impertinent remark and mutter how like his poor father the Chevalier was growing to be....

Charles-Louis himself was not sure that Porlier was speaking the truth. He was not sure that he *was* like Papa — though, of course, nothing could have made him happier than to think so. His dearest possession was the full-length portrait of the Duke that hung over the mantelpiece in the drawing-room. It was not, according to Porlier, an especially striking likeness. It had been done by Mignard after the subject's death for his mother, the Dowager Duchess: like all posthumous portraits, it had a curiously set, smirking expression. Moreover, Monsieur Mignard had indulged his fancy to the limit in devising a suitably martial background, painting in rows of black, cloud-capped mountains (though the scene was supposed to be a plain somewhere along the Rhine), and also adding inches to Papa's stature, so that as he stood in a nonchalant attitude by Pegasus, his white battle-charger, he seemed to dominate the landscape, with its rows of cannon and marching men. The whole Dutch campaign, in fact, became just so much scenery to set off the superb blond, smiling figure of the last Duc de Longueville....

Therefore, although Charles-Louis admired the picture extravagantly, he was not really intimate with it. He had never, for instance, been able to talk to it as he sometimes talked for hours to Grand'maman's picture in the dining-hall. It was somehow much easier to visualize Papa away from his portrait, which had an invariably chastening effect upon his son and heir. Today, as usual, as his eye lighted on it after dismissing Porlier, he began immediately to shrink back into his natural diffidence, when the sound of wheels in the rue Férou sent him dashing to the window once again.... Yes, they were coming at last! Charles-Louis drew himself up to his full height — alas! only five feet three, but the heels of his new boots gave him almost another inch — and glanced anxiously in the glass to make sure that his buckles were buckled and his ribbons in order. It was a quaint little reflection that stared back at him — straight and smart in spite of its diminutive size, with blue eyes and golden curls that strongly resembled his father's. But the nose and mouth were too small and well chiselled for any Bourbon: the face in repose was gently melancholy, and, if he were not actually smiling, the corners of the Chevalier's mouth were apt to droop pathetically.

Aunt Magdelon and Chou-Chou came in with a rush from the rain laden with parcels; the former breathless and voluble. . . . 'My darling child . . . this tiresome weather . . . as fast as we *could* . . . some cinnamon buns in my bag . . . come here, let me look at you . . . my dear, did you ever see anyone so splendid?'

There were screams of excitement over the scarlet-and-gold uniform. Charles-Louis was spun round innumerable times till his cheeks were almost as red as his coat, while Aunt Magdelon threw up her hands admiringly and declared she had never beheld so fine an ensign in all His Majesty's troops; he was the image of his dear father at the same age. . . . All of a sudden, in the midst of her screams, her face crinkled up and she began to cry and protest that it was too much . . . he was too young to go to the war . . . he would surely be killed . . . the sorts of things women always said on such occasions.

Chou-Chou and Charles-Louis were greatly embarrassed by Aunt Magdelon's tears. They looked at each other helplessly; then the latter, who despite his shyness was socially the more resourceful of the two, took the old lady's hand and kissed it.

'Nay, my good aunt, do not weep, I beg of you! You would not have me stop at home, when all the men of my age are going. . . .'

But the expression 'men of my age' set Aunt Magdelon sobbing afresh; it was fortunate that just then a lackey scratched on the door to announce that dinner was served.

Charles-Louis led his aunt in gallant style to the table, where Porlier was waiting to join them — and with Porlier in the room conversation could be kept on a safely unemotional basis.

The dinner was good, in spite of Gabriel's warning. Charles-Louis was glad to see that the soup was not burnt and the roast had been done to a turn, but not overdone. He himself was quite hungry, as it was long past his regular dinner-time; Chou-Chou was hungry, too — she always was, in season and out of it! — ; so the two children ate heartily in comparative silence.

Aunt Magdelon, on the contrary, though she praised enthusiastically every dish that was offered her, did not seem to be hungry at all. She merely nibbled at things; even the caramel mousse with chestnuts and mounds of whipped cream, which was one of Gabriel's triumphs, could not tempt her appetite. Charles-Louis felt her gaze upon him while he ate. Whenever he raised his eyes from his plate there was her smile, valiant but tremulous, across the table.

After dinner the rain was found to have stopped. A watery sun came out through banks of torn clouds, and Aunt Magdelon sent the children for a walk in the garden, saying that she wished to have a few words alone with Monsieur Porlier.

Charles-Louis and Chou-Chou trotted off willingly enough.

They had always been friends, the slender blond boy and the round, smiling dark girl. Together they'd romped and run races under the elms, taken turns riding Charles-Louis' pony, played bowls and learned to shoot with bow-and-arrows under Porlier's good-humoured direction. Chou-Chou was more than a match for her cousin: she was a strong, active child, well-grown for her age, as tall at fifteen as Charles-Louis, who was nearly two years her senior. She was still as plump, though, and as cheerful as she had been as a little thing.

But — Charles-Louis could not tell why it was — he felt suddenly shy of his playmate. He felt, also, that Chou-Chou was shy of him. Only last week they had chatted and laughed like brother and sister: today they walked primly along the path, eying each other askance. Perhaps the new uniform was to blame; Charles-Louis was slightly awed by that himself. No doubt it was impossible for them to play as they were used to do, now that he had joined the army and was an ensign in His Majesty's regiment. He must remember that he was a grown man, Chou-Chou almost a grown woman. Still he was fond of his cousin. It was sweet of her to have come to say good-bye to him. He would not see her for a very long time; it would be pleasant if their last conversation could be a memorable one. ... But what to say? — *what to say?* ...

The garden was wet after the rain. The paths were strewn with wreckage from the trees, and whole rows of flowers in the flower-beds — mostly dahlias and Michaelmas daisies, so late in the season — that had been bursting into bloom a few hours ago, lay mown down before their time.

Chou-Chou held her buff quilted satin skirt high in one plump brown hand, to keep it from touching the glistening gravel. Charles-Louis strode behind her, listening to the proud clink of his sword in its scabbard that swung by his side. Chou-Chou glanced over her shoulder once or twice, her black gypsy eyes brimful of feelings she seemed unable to express. Charles-Louis thought she might be going to speak; he wished fervently that she would, for he could hit upon nothing worth saying to break the awful silence between them.

At last, when they'd got to the sundial at the end of the path and were turning to retrace their steps, Chou-Chou stopped short and rummaged in her quilted satin pocket till she produced a square gilt box tied with a pink ribbon.

'I'd almost forgotten, I've brought you some sweets,' she said. 'Here — take them!'

She made as if to toss the gilt box to him, as she would have done without thinking last week; then held it out instead, with a half-mocking curtsy.

'I bought them at that shop in the rue Saint-Antoine with my very own money,' said Chou-Chou. 'I hope you'll like them.'

Charles-Louis accepted the box and gave her a solemn bow.

'Thank you, cousin; that was most kind of you.'

'They'll be good to eat on the march, I expect,' Chou-Chou added sagely. 'Dear knows what you'll get in those foreign parts! Maman says they have very nice macaroons in Nancy — she used to stay there often with poor Papa, years ago when he was governor of Lorraine — but you're going farther than that, aren't you?'

'Oh, yes,' answered Charles-Louis. 'A long way farther. To Germany, you know.... May I have one now?'

'Please do,' said Chou-Chou, bobbing her head.

Charles-Louis untied the pink ribbon, opened the box, and selected one of the sweets. They were chocolate dragées, the kind he liked best. It was good of Chou-Chou to have remembered that, particularly handsome in view of her own preference for those that were covered with thick white almond paste.

'Will you have a dragée, cousin?'

'Oh, no,' said Chou-Chou, putting her hands behind her back. 'They are for you.'

But Charles-Louis kept on proffering the box; it appeared that it would be impolite to refuse. Chou-Chou took a sweet and put it in her mouth — Charles-Louis, she saw, had one tucked in each cheek.

They sucked them gravely for a minute, and then Chou-Chou remarked, with a sigh: 'They *are* good, aren't they?'

'Have another,' said Charles-Louis munificently.

'Oh, no,' said Chou-Chou again. 'They are for *you*, you know.'

But Charles-Louis insisted as before; finally Chou-Chou gave way and took another dragée; and after that the spell was broken — they did not feel embarrassed with each other any more.

Their tongues being suddenly loosed, they could talk about everything just as they always had done. Chou-Chou began by saying she supposed that her cousin was glad to be going to war.

'Of course I'm glad,' said Charles-Louis, his red-and-gold bosom swelling with pride. 'Why shouldn't I be? It's a very fine war. Everyone says so. That is, everyone except Aunt de Nemours,' he amended his statement, a trifle ruefully. 'She says we've no business marching into Germany. She says it's ridiculous trying to take Philipsburg at this time of year. She says the King's crazy — he doesn't know what he's doing! You ought to have heard her — she was here this morning to see me, and she went on like that for simply hours!'

'Oh, well,' said Chou-Chou, carelessly swinging her arms as she walked (which was something Madame Poussard, her governess, had earnestly enjoined her never to do), 'that old hag — who cares what she says? I dare say she's talking through her hat, anyhow. I wish *I* were a boy! I'd go to war with you. I'm sure it's going to be awfully exciting. I heard Henri talking with Maman about it last night; he said all the best men in France had enlisted. *He* wants to go, too — but the King won't let him.'

'Why not?'

'Oh, I don't know exactly,' replied Chou-Chou. 'It has something to do with his selling his regiment. He got rid of it three years ago when he went to England, and now he hasn't the money to buy it back, and the King won't take him as a volunteer — he says he's behaved too badly for that. Henri drinks, you know.'

Chou-Chou made the announcement as casually as though she had said that her brother rode to hounds every day or liked beefsteak for dinner. As a matter of fact, nothing seemed to shock or surprise the younger Mademoiselle de la Ferté, who lived in the midst of a family so large and untrammelled that she had long ago grown accustomed to all manner of temperamental vagaries. It was Charles-Louis who looked startled; Chou-Chou merely shrugged her shoulders, as if dismissing the subject.

'Anyway,' she concluded, 'it's a fine war, as you said, and the French are sure to win — they always do — so *that'll* be all right!'

'I hope,' said Charles-Louis wistfully, 'it will last long enough. I mean, sometimes we win almost too quickly, don't you think — and I am so anxious to do something splendid — win my spurs, as Papa did in Candia and Franche-Comté. Porlier's told me all about that; he says there never was a better soldier than the Duc de Longueville. Everybody thought — his Uncle Condé and all the other generals — that if only he hadn't been killed so young, there's no telling how far he might have gone. So I've got a lot to live up to. And then, besides, it's 'specially important for me to do well because — I've been thinking . . .'

He paused and looked doubtfully at Chou-Chou, who returned the look with candour.

'You won't laugh at me if I tell you what I've been thinking?'

'Silly! Of course I won't!' said Chou-Chou (though she had done so dozens of times in the past).

Charles-Louis stooped to pluck a dahlia from the path where it lay. He began twirling the great crimson head on the broken stump of its stalk; it felt as cool and soft and wet as a bath-sponge.

'Well, then,' he said, speaking rather fast and nervously, 'it's this way: you know, my father was Duc de Longueville, and I am his only son. But I am not a duke like him — I'm just the Chevalier de Longueville.'

'Yes, I know,' said Chou-Chou. 'I've often wondered about it. I never quite understood. . . . Maman's always told me I wasn't to ask you. . . . No matter what I thought, I wasn't to say. . . . I suppose it's because you're a bastard. You *are* a bastard, aren't you, Charles-Louis?'

Charles-Louis turned pale with indignation.

'Certainly not!' he said severely. 'What things you say, cousin! My father was married to my mother just as much as *your* father and mother were. . . . No, indeed! Porlier's told me about that, too. He always said he would tell me when I was old enough to understand. So the other day when I was joining the army I said I thought I had a right to the truth, and I got the whole story from him, just as it happened. My mother wasn't royal; she was a gentleman's daughter, but her father was only a knight. He had a farm in Normandy near Graville, my father's estate. Her name was Pauline — Pauline d'Arville. Papa married her secretly, against his family's wishes, so when he died they wouldn't recognize the marriage — and that's why they've never had much to do with me. Then my mother died, too, and her family moved away — Porlier doesn't know where. But of course they must have felt that it was best for me, because Papa left me his fortune.'

'Really!' said Chou-Chou, much impressed. 'Why, that's romantic, isn't it? I wish *my* father had been secretly married!'

'That shows what a child you are still,' said Charles-Louis loftily. 'It's not in the least romantic: it's very inconvenient. What are families for, if not to help one another? And I've never got a bit of good out of mine. Grand'maman was kind enough in a way, but she didn't take me to live with her as she ought to have done, and she died when I was so little that she hadn't got round to assuring my future. All Aunt de Nemours does is scold and say the bills are too high. And the rest of 'em have never so much as lifted a finger. . . . The Condés, the Contis . . . why, even the King is my cousin, you know!'

'So he is.' Chou-Chou was clearly more impressed. 'Dear me, I'd never thought of that! But I don't quite see . . . What is it you're planning to do?'

'Well,' said Charles-Louis, 'my idea is to make such a name for myself at the war that they'll *have* to recognize me, whether they like it or not. If I do that, they can't keep me from getting my title. After all, it's really mine by right. So if I can only do something fine enough . . .'

'Yes, yes; I see now, of course. But,' objected the practical Chou-Chou, 'it mayn't be easy. You're only an ensign yet. In the wars it's always the generals who get the glory. I ought to know about that. My father was a general.'

'That's not true!' cried Charles-Louis. 'My father was a colonel, and he was every bit as famous as your father. If he hadn't been killed ——'

'Well, but he *was!* And, anyhow, a colonel's not so important as a general. He *can't* be. Ask Porlier. Ask anyone who knows about soldiers. You're a stupid boy, Charles-Louis.'

'I'm not! It's you who are stupid. Women know nothing of war. My father was the bravest man who ever lived. Aunt Magdelon's told me so herself, over and over. So there!'

'Brave's not the same as important,' insisted Chou-Chou tenaciously: (That was the worst of Chou-Chou: she never would yield in an argument, and she had, besides, an uncomfortable propensity for sticking to the point.)

They began at once to quarrel, loudly and vigorously. In the end Chou-Chou, who was quick-tempered, slapped Charles-Louis' face; and Charles-Louis, disregarding his dignity, pulled Chou-Chou's fuzzy black hair. They raced over the lawn, one after the other, bringing up breathless and laughing at the door to the house — by which time they had both entirely forgotten what they had been quarrelling about.

Aunt Magdelon was standing on the threshold with Porlier watching them; she had been on her way to call her daughter; it was time, she said, for them to go.

Aunt Magdelon's face looked as if she had been crying again. The crinkles round her eyes were deeper than ever, and her red-lacquered mouth was puckered tragically out of shape. Charles-Louis was afraid at first that she might not be able to control her feelings; he hated to see women cry, and he was really very fond of Aunt Magdelon.

However, she seemed to have herself well in hand, for the tragic mouth twisted into a smile, and her voice when she spoke sounded quite strong and steady.

'I've a present for you, my dear boy,' she said. 'Something I've been keeping for you almost ever since you were born.'

Charles-Louis saw she was holding a sword in her hand — not a new one, though its steel had been burnished until it shone like silver — for the ribbons attached to the hilt were faded and worn. It was with a thrill in his heart that Charles-Louis recognized the pale blue satin band of the Orléans family.

'It was your father's,' said Aunt Magdelon — and her voice was even stronger and steadier than before: there was a proud, beautiful note in it that bewitched Charles-Louis. 'It was in his hand when he fell at Tollhuis. His good friend Monsieur de Fiesque brought it back to me, because he knew that I loved your father. Now I give it to you, with his blessing and mine. Wear it in memory of your dear Papa, and may it bring new honour and fame to the great name of Longueville!'

Charles-Louis stood very straight and still while she unbuckled his own sword and fastened his father's to his belt in its place. He was so much excited that he could scarcely find words to say what he felt, or to thank Aunt Magdelon properly for this wonderful gift. . . . Why, it was the very sword in the portrait that he had looked at every day of his life! To think it was his at last! Could there be a better augury for the future?

He was so deliriously happy that he did not even mind when Aunt Magdelon suddenly abandoned her noble pose, flung her arms round the little figure in scarlet-and-gold, and pressed him wildly to her breast. He kissed her with genuine affection, and said that yes, he'd take good care of himself — and no, he'd not run unnecessary risks — and naturally, he'd do what Porlier told him and would positively never forget to write at least once a week during the siege.

After that, he kissed Chou-Chou, too — very conscious of her nearness and of the wide black eyes that, strangely, had tears in them (he had never seen Chou-Chou cry) — ; then he conducted his guests to the front door, bent over Aunt Magdelon's hand, and helped her into the carriage.

When they were gone — with Aunt Magdelon's last smile and wave a poignant impression as the coach lurched round the corner into the rue de Vaugirard — Charles-Louis went back to the drawing-room by himself and stood for a long time underneath the picture of the gallant young man beside the white horse.

It seemed to him that the young man looked more alive than usual — there was a sympathetic gleam in the painted blue eyes that had never been there before. Of course, it might be pure imagination . . . but it was not impossible, was it, that Papa knew — wherever he was — what was happening to his son? . . . At all events, Charles-Louis found it a comfort to believe he did know.

'Good-bye, Papa,' said the young Chevalier softly, addressing the portrait directly for the first time in the years of their acquaintance with each other; 'I'll try to do what you would have me do. I'm going to be as good a Longueville as any of 'em — you see if I'm not!'

He started to go; then turned back abruptly and whispered: 'Oh, I almost forgot — and thank you for letting me have your sword!'

Chapter XI

'My good aunt:

'Today I take my pen to keep the promise made you in Paris and inform you that Porlier and I arrived here last night, after a safe and comfortable journey from Bar-le-Duc. We have now been six days travelling, and in spite of unfavourable weather have made good progress on our way to Germany. From Toul we go to Nancy, Dieuze, Sarrebourg, and thence to Philipsburg, a matter of another week at most. Monseigneur the Dauphin we found at Meaux, our first night's halting place; since then we have continued in his train, which is exceeding large, and includes many officers of the regular army as well as a great company of volunteers. I have not yet met my colonel, the Chevalier de Montchevreuil, for he is already at Philipsburg with the first two battalions of the King's regiment; I am to serve with the third battalion. Our coach rides well, the greys go admirably; yet I would fain exchange the luxury of a carriage for horseback: 'tis more befitting a soldier. Porlier has promised that I may do so later, as soon as the rains abate.

'Monseigneur the Dauphin is a very hospitable prince. He is attended by a fine suite of gentlemen, and as we are lodged here in the citadel, where there are splendid public rooms, he held court last evening after supper for all the nobles in his suite. Porlier took me and saw to it that I was presented to Monseigneur by the Duc de Beauvilliers. There were many princes there, my cousins Conti and Bourbon amongst them (the latter is grandson to the hero, the late Prince de Condé); likewise the Duc du Maine, who is the King's bastard by Madame de Montespan. It's sad that his birth is so disgraceful, for a fairer, pleasanter-spoken fellow I never met. He is but just eighteen years old, and has two twisted feet; still he is determined to make a name for himself and follows his half-brother as volunteer in the King's regiment, which as you know is my own.

'I was led up to the Duke, who rose to receive me — it was then I saw he was lame —; he greeted me courteously and said he'd heard tell of my father's bravery in the Dutch wars. We had a fine conversation together, the more agreeable to me as it happened that Monseigneur and his friends were at lansquenet, and neither the Duke nor myself plays cards.

'Monseigneur, in fact, was so intent on his game that he scarcely looked up to acknowledge my introduction; when my name was mentioned he slapped a card on the table and muttered something I could not quite hear. I was much disappointed both in his reception of me and in our host's looks: the Dauphin is by no means a handsome man — he is seven or eight-and-twenty, and tremendously stout for his age. Moreover, his face is smooth as wax and as pink as the skin of a pig, and when he looks at you he does not seem to see you. I do not think he means to be impolite; 'tis only that he's slow-witted by nature, and takes so long a-making up his mind to speak that, as Monsieur du Maine puts it, by the time his tongue is ready the talk has changed and what he says is no longer à propos. But is it not a pity all the same, dear aunt, that it's he must succeed to the throne, when his half-brother's so far the greater gentleman?

'I could write much more about all I have seen and done since quitting Paris, but 'tis past midnight, and Porlier has twice come into my chamber to bid me close my letter and make ready for bed. Tomorrow Monseigneur is to review the troops of the garrison, and the Lieutenant-Governor will give an afternoon party in his honour, to which I have been invited. I am very well at this present, my good aunt, as I pray that this letter may also find you. Give my love to my cousin, and tell her, please, that the sweets she gave me were most excellent. They lasted as far as Epernay only; I had meant to keep them longer than that, but at Meaux, the first night, I made the acquaintance of the young Marquis de Grignan, who is also bound for Philipsburg to serve as volunteer in the regiment of Champagne — we drove together the next day — and Grignan is monstrous fond of chocolate dragées.

'I remain, as always,

'Your most affectionate and obedient servant,
'CHARLES-LOUIS D'ORLÉANS,
'Chevalier de Longueville.'

'In camp before Philipsburg,
'This seventh of October, 1688.

'My good aunt:
'We reached our destination late last night, after a hard journey from Wissembourg. The roads are almost destroyed by storms, most of the bridges over the Rhine have been washed away (we succeeded in crossing by a new one of pontoons built by our soldiers

only a day or two ago) — and still the rain continues. But for the dismal weather, all has gone well with us. I rode horseback from Sarrebourg to Wissembourg in company with my friend, the Marquis de Grignan; we were very merry together, till the rain forced us to seek shelter in our carriages. Grignan is a splendid chap; he is a scant month my senior, but you would take him for twenty-one or two, to look at him — he is well-grown and not at all shy in assemblies. I envy him his figure and still more his wit, and only wish I could be like him — but Porlier says not to worry, that will all come in time — and why would the Marquis not be forward for his age, when he has been brought up at his family's castle in Provence, where his father is Lieutenant-Governor and they sit down daily twenty or thirty to table?

'Well, madam, we are now before Philipsburg, which is a town and fortress situated upon the river Rhine — or, rather, just beyond it — and surrounded by miles of swamps, so that our troops encircling the citadel are encamped some distance back on every side. The swamps are neutral ground; our men are busy there at night constructing trenches for the more active prosecution of the siege. There are forty regiments in all — twenty-two of infantry, the remainder of light cavalry and dragoons. I have never in my life beheld so many tents, so many horses, so many soldiers everywhere. It is very confusing, like a whole city in itself; I have thrice lost my way trying to find my own tent; but Porlier says I shall soon get used to that.

'Monseigneur and his suite arrived last night an hour after we did without their luggage, their train of wagons being mired in the mud near Wissembourg; the Prince was forced to seek lodging with the Maréchal de Duras. Notwithstanding the accident he was full of enthusiasm, and hoped to open the trenches at once — they have been digging hard all week — but so far the state of the weather has prevented it.

'Monsieur de Duras is the general in charge of the siege — a brilliant commander, I hear, but he is at present in bed with the gout (where Porlier says we shall all be soon, unless the weather relents), and leaves most of his duties to Vauban, the chief engineer.

'Later:

'I have but just returned from paying my respects to the Chevalier de Montchevreuil, colonel of the King's regiment, in which I have the honour to serve. Porlier took me to call on him directly after dinner. (N.B.: Tell my cousin that she was wrong about food in Germany. The people here talk an outlandish tongue, it is true, but they eat quite as well as we do. I sat down today to a fine cabbage soup, roast venison, and plum tarts as many as I could hold.) The

Chevalier is a noble fellow. How shall I describe him to you? About forty years old, very tall — full six foot or more — with keen grey eyes, a fine nose, and the brownest skin I ever saw. He looks as though wind and weather were nothing to him. In short, I was greatly taken with him. His name is Gaston-Jean-Baptiste de Mornay, he is a knight of Malta, and — only think, madam! — his late brother Philippe, who was also a knight of Malta and known as the Chevalier de Montchevreuil in *his* day, was the best friend of my Papa! He was with him all through the campaign in Holland, and was grievously wounded in battle shortly after the crossing of the Rhine. When he heard that my Papa had been killed he would not let the doctors dress his wounds, and so he died, a martyr to his love for the Duc de Longueville.

'Is that not a romantic story? My colonel told me it himself. When he heard that I was come he cried out at once: "Let me see this young man, whose father was so fatal to our family!" I was abashed, not knowing how to make reply; but the Chevalier was kindness itself, and promised me his friendship and special protec- tion. "Lad, you are strangely like the Duke," he said. "I was a boy in my 'teens when I beheld him, but I have never forgotten his face. May you be an honour to his name as he was!" ... The Marquis de Montchevreuil was in his brother's tent when I was there: he is the eldest of the family, already an old man, though hale and handsome for his years, and he is with the army as governor to the Duc du Maine. He greeted me most kindly, too, and said I must attend his master's lever every day — that I had the entrée there whenever it so pleased me. "The Longuevilles are our cousins and our friends," he told me; "and you and the Duke, whose situations are in some re- spects so similar, should find each other congenial, young fellow."

'I know not what he meant by that, dear madam — do you? For the Duc du Maine, King's son though he be, is a bastard, after all; whilst I am the lawful issue of a Prince of the Blood. Nay, I would not change places with him, were he twenty times as royal as he is!

'My good aunt, more of this anon. I am waxing exceedingly sleepy, and can scarcely hold my pen in my fingers. The cold fresh air and my sumptuous dinner are doubtless to blame for that. The world seems very big and full of things I do not always understand — but I am thankful to be here, and mean to do my duty as best I am able. Porlier sends his humble respects to Madame the Maré- chale. I embrace you and my dear cousin heartily and remain
'Your affectionate and obedient servant,
'CHARLES-LOUIS D'ORLÉANS,
'Chevalier de Longueville.'

'In camp before Philipsburg,
'This nineteenth of October, 1688.

'My good aunt:
'I trust you will forgive me this long silence. I assure you the neglect has not been voluntary; I have thought often of you and my cousin, but these last days have been amazingly busy. A siege, madam, is very interesting, but it is not in the least like a war. I thought, before I came, that there would be fighting all the time — and mostly what we do is *dig!* Monsieur de Vauban has been busy encircling Philipsburg with trenches; each regiment in turn has taken a hand at the task.

'The trenches were opened some ten days ago, but for all that there's been no real battle. It's most disappointing: all day long the enemy do nothing except fire an occasional cannon from their walls, that kicks up a bit of earth and lets us know they are still alive. But our men must sit idle till night. After dark things grow a little more lively. The enemy sometimes make sorties from the town in an attempt to break through our lines. So far, they have been repulsed each time with heavy casualties, whilst on our side we have lost very few soldiers and but an officer or two. (Today, for example, Maréchal-de-camp Le Bordage was slain: he had command of a cavalry regiment.) But our regiment has not had the luck, up to now, to be on guard in the trenches when a sortie was made.

'The men grow vastly impatient with so much waiting. They grumble continually, saying: "What are we here for, and why can't we get at those cursed Germans?" Indeed, madam, a siege is a slow business at best, and this one, I fear, is like to last half the winter, if the weather do not improve.

'We have rains, and rains, and nothing but rains. The trenches are greasy with Rhine mud and in places half under water. It is difficult under such conditions to raise our cannon to reply to the enemy. In truth, were it not for the fascines — these, tell my cousin (in case she is ignorant of the subject), are bundles of sticks tied together that serve to support our artillery and fill up the worst wet holes in the trenches — one could not manage to use them at all. And even as it is, after the guns have been fired several times they sink down once more in the mud, and 'tis all to do over again.

'Despite these trials I continue marvellously well, my good aunt — pray do not worry about me! I sleep sound and snug in my tent under my blankets and the great bear's fur robe you gave me, save when it's my night for trench duty — and I eat enough for a dozen men. Porlier says I have grown an inch since joining the army and gone up half a stone in weight. Would that were so, madam!

'I attend Monsieur du Maine's lever and coucher punctually

every day, as old Montchevreuil bade me do, and have been treated with kindness by everyone there. Papa's name, I feel, is the passport to their good will, but I study to deserve it on my own account as well. All the volunteers in the King's regiment pay their respects to the Duke — the Chevalier de Montchevreuil, our colonel, at their head — Lafayette and Valentinois, Biran and Brionne — fine fellows one and all. There is much good talk at these assemblies of war and politics and kindred matters, the Chevalier maintaining that we young men were born too late to see France at the peak of her glory. The greatest days, he says, are over, for now we're fighting not to gain new conquests, but to keep control of those we have. I'd fain believe him mistaken there, and so would most of our company. He vows also — and in this his brother, the Marquis, agrees with him — that we no longer have the generals we used to have. Such leaders as Turenne, my great-uncle Condé, and your late husband, the Maréchal de la Ferté — where are their like today? ... Though not a Huguenot, the Chevalier deplores the revocation of the Edict of Nantes, three years ago; he says France lost too many of her best men then, and blames it all upon Madame de Maintenon, the King's new friend (some say she's more than that). . . . But at this point the Marquis is wont to shut him up, for *he's* a member of the Maintenon's cabal at court, and will not hear a word against her, whom he calls the greatest Christian in the kingdom. The Duc du Maine will also take her part; she raised him, as you know, from infancy, having first come into favour as governess to the royal bastards. . . . When matters of such moment are discussed, you may be sure, dear madam, that I deem it best to hold my tongue discreetly! I listen as attentively as possible to all that's said, contradict nobody, and strive to wax wise whilst incurring no man's enmity.

'In truth, my good aunt, I have been pleased, and not a little surprised, to find how easy it is to get on with my comrades. You will remember that before I went into the army I was doubtful of my abilities in that direction. I had led so sheltered and solitary a life, owing to Papa's wish that I should be kept from school, that I was afraid I might be considered odd or affected merely through lack of experience. But in truth a man is always liked, I find, if he wants to be; there is naught so complicated in human relations that cannot be solved by tact and good temper.

'Withal I must confess there is one circle where I am not so easy in my manners, one man — or, rather, group of men — whose favour I have been unable to secure. And they, alas! compose the company in which I most aspire to shine, and where I feel I have the best right to be indulgently received — for are they not my relatives? If the Duc du Maine be gracious, why should his brother Monseigneur not be gracious, too? Yes — and their cousins Conti and Bourbon, who are my cousins equally: I ask myself if I am not as good as tney in birth and breeding, and why they have the right to treat me like an outcast from the family!

'My good aunt, I have consulted Porlier on this point; he tells me I am oversensitive, that it is partly an effect of my too active imagination — but it is not so: I swear it! Last night, for instance, I attended the Dauphin's coucher with the Chevalier de Montchevreuil, who remains as amiable to me as he was at the beginning, and loses no chance of putting me forward when he can. The Prince de Conti and the Duc de Bourbon were there, likewise a number of young officers from their regiments and the regiment of Champagne, including my friend, the Marquis de Grignan. It came time for Monseigneur to disrobe: the Duc de Bourbon, as the highest ranking Prince of the Blood, held his nightshirt — Conti, as the next highest, his bonnet. But there was need of another pair of hands to take charge of the gold candlestick that is lighted at this time; it is an honour highly prized and much disputed amongst the gentlemen in Monseigneur's suite. The Chevalier gave me a push from behind and whispered: "Go on, little Longueville, that's for you!" . . . But though Monseigneur saw I was standing ready, he turned his back on me — he has a very square back, my good aunt, and when he turns it the action seems final! — and cried out quite crossly: "What are you waiting for? Grignan, the candlestick!"

'Madam, I was never so taken aback in my life. I blushed and bit my lip and looked, I fear, as I felt, covered with confusion. The good Chevalier said afterwards that I was not to mind, it was nothing, the Dauphin had been dyspeptic all day — but I do not believe he can have been telling the truth, for I had it from Grignan that a whole sucking pig had been served at the royal dinner-table, and Monseigneur did away with most of it. No, the Prince does not like me, for what reason I know not; but his aversion confirms me all the more strongly in my desire to win renown, so that I may at least compel his respect, if not his friendship.

'Wish me luck, I pray you, my good aunt, in this honourable undertaking, and believe me

'Your very affectionate and obedient servant,
'CHARLES-LOUIS D'ORLÉANS,'
'Chevalier de Longueville.'

'P.S. There is a rumour abroad that the King will give the regiment of Le Bordage, who was killed today, to the Duc du Maine. This occasions much joy amongst the partisans of the Duke, particularly Messieurs de Montchevreuil, who declare that there will then be no reason why their favourite cannot show the world his true mettle. If this report be true, I am very happy for my cousin, and shall take the earliest possible opportunity of calling to congratulate him on his promotion.'

'In camp before Philipsburg,
'This twenty-ninth of October, 1688.

'My good aunt:
    'Our siege goes wonderfully well. There was hard fighting last night in the trenches, in which our regiment and the regiment of Anjou took the principal part. My battalion, the third, was unfortunately not allowed to go into action until towards the end of the engagement. 'Twas the first time I had been under fire, madam, and I was nervous for fear I should not comport myself in a manner to do credit to the family. But luckily I was not at all afraid, though one of the German bullets passed clean through the brim of my hat. (Aunt de Nemours will be wroth to hear it, as it was a present from her.) We have captured most of the enemy's advance positions on the side towards the Rhine and a number of cannon; their gunfire begins to grow feeble; and if all continues favourable, the Chevalier de Montchevreuil says that within a few days Philipsburg should be ours. He has just now sent one of his aides to summon me to his tent, so that I must conclude this epistle on my return. Adieu, my good aunt — believe me, I think of you often and tenderly. . . .'

    'Longueville?'
    'Yes, sir!'
    The Chevalier grinned. 'Eh, lad, you're puffing like a dolphin! Why so much haste?'
    'You — sent for me, sir! — I — didn't know ——'
    'Ever prompt to respond to the call of duty, eh? Well, that's right, that's right. Now listen to me: you are to go straight to the tent of His Highness the Duc du Maine and tell him, with my compliments, that the attack is scheduled to begin again within the hour and to continue in full force all night. Our second battalion goes into action directly, together with the regiment of Anjou — we hope to get possession of the enemy's crown-works before morning. D'you understand me?'
    'Yes, sir; certainly, sir.'
    'Furthermore — I have orders here from Monseigneur the Dauphin to the effect that inasmuch as the Duke is already in charge of the cavalry regiment His Majesty has been graciously pleased to present to him, he considers him ineligible for service as volunteer with the King's infantry regiment. That is Monseigneur's wish, d'you see?'

'Yes, sir.'

'He desires to spare his brother unnecessary dangers and recommends that he remain where he is until further notice. . . . However, you might say to Monsieur du Maine, also with my compliments — never forget compliments, lad, when addressing a prince — that, up to now, I have received no official notification of the transfer's having taken place, so that, as far as I am concerned, if His Highness chooses to return with you . . . You follow me, boy?'

'Yes, sir; of course, sir.'

'One thing more: as soon as you have delivered this message you are to report at your post, for it's quite possible that the other battalions will be needed shortly.'

'Yes, sir; at once, sir.'

'Oh — and Longueville?'

'Sir?'

'You'll take care, on your way, to avoid undue risks. The road is dark enough, in all conscience, but the German snipers are likely to be busier than usual tonight. Good-bye, Chevalier; good luck to you! I'm off to the trenches to see how matters lie with our men.'

'Good-bye, sir.'

Charles-Louis clicked his heels smartly together and saluted his colonel. Montchevreuil placed his hand for a moment on the young ensign's shoulder, much to the latter's discomfiture. Charles-Louis was grateful for his superior's kindness — he did wish very much, though, and not for the first time in the last month, that the Chevalier and the rest of the officers would stop treating him like a child. They acted often as if he were too young to know what he was doing — he, Charles-Louis d'Orléans, a veteran of nigh on five weeks in His Majesty's forces! No doubt they meant it well, but it was discouraging, to say the least. It appeared sometimes that there must be a conspiracy amongst them to keep him from exposing himself to danger. Take tonight, for example! when at last, after weeks of comparative idleness, a goodish scrap was in prospect — perhaps even a decisive action — who knew? For the French, having finally succeeded in taking the enemy's outposts, were advancing at full tilt against the main defences of Philipsburg. . . . How could he help suspecting that Montchevreuil had devised this paltry errand on purpose to get rid of him? Charles-Louis knew only too well what a long way it was from their own quarters to the Duc du Maine's tent, which had been shifted since his appointment as colonel quite to the end of the line where the cavalry regiments were stationed. . . . Well, there was no help for it; he must do as he was told. . . .

He bowed once more and then left the tent, a last vision of his chief's broad brown face and flashing smile following him as he retreated.

It was cold and raw outside, though not actually raining (one must be thankful for small mercies), and very dark — but not so dark that he could not see the citadel, looming vaguely against the lowering sky on the ridge opposite that on which the French were encamped. In between lay the marshes where the trenches were, brown with purplish patches by day, a yawning black chasm by night. Charles-Louis could see nothing now in the marshes, though he knew they were full of men. There was an occasional flash of flame from a musket, but for once the enemy's cannon were silent, after ten days of almost continual firing. (One had heard that they were beginning to run out of ammunition.) Tonight all was ominously quiet; it was so still that one could hear the crying of wild-duck and snipe below in the reeds.... The lull before the storm....

With a fervent prayer that he might be able to get back before the battle began in earnest, Charles-Louis muffled himself in his grey scarlet-lined cape and struck out into the night.

His path lay along the low, semi-circular rise of ground where the main part of the army had been quartered, less because it was out of range of the German guns than because it was the only solid earth for miles around. He passed tent after tent gay with striped silk, each flying the colours of its regiment. There was the King's own, and the Queen's and the Dauphin's; then Champagne and Normandy, Poitou and Touraine, and the rest. Most of the tents were deserted tonight, as their occupants had gone down into the marshes to man the trenches or the better to watch the impending engagement. The Dauphin's quarters, however, were brilliantly illuminated with a whole row of torches: Monseigneur was evidently giving a party to celebrate in advance the victorious end of the siege. Charles-Louis heard clinking glasses and squalls of laughter from within; even the guards on duty outside had got some mugs of ale and were quaffing them, uproarious with mirth.

Charles-Louis thrust his hands deep in his pockets and stalked on through the chill, empty darkness. *There*, at any rate, was one place he had no desire to be! — playing second-fiddle to a string of brainless courtiers better able than he to please their young master!... Lately it had become increasingly clear that Monseigneur had no use for his cousin, the Chevalier de Longueville; the latter had racked his brains vainly trying to divine the reason for it. He had fully expected, at first, to be thought a young cub through sheer ignorance — and instead his comrades had taken him in, treated him like one of them, praised his modest attempts to signal himself and win their approval till Charles-Louis glowed with gratitude for their kindness. Even Porlier had privately admitted his pleasure at his pupil's successes.... 'Though mind, lad, if you weren't who you are...'

Only Monseigneur and his satellites Conti and Monsieur the Duke, who might have done more for him than all the rest put together, withheld their favour. In fact, the one member of his own family who'd shown himself friendly was Monsieur du Maine, an outcast himself (though in *his* case it was easy to see why!) — poor Maine, sent to Coventry in the royal circle and therefore reduced to forming a rival circle of his own.... Well, there was no good in complaining. Porlier was right: one must be glad to have got as much as one had. ... Dear God, please don't make me be late for the battle ... and this time let me do something splendid!...

The tents belonging to the Duc du Maine were well beyond the last of the infantry regiments'. This part of the camp was lighter and less lonely, because most of the cavalrymen were off duty: there had been little enough for them to do during these last weeks. On a water-logged terrain, and under such appalling weather conditions, their duties had been confined to patrolling the outposts of the line and carrying messages from the Maréchal de Duras or Monsieur de Vauban to various officers of the troops. Charles-Louis was delighted that he had not joined the cavalry, as he had at first intended.

Monsieur du Maine's own tent was less brightly lighted than some of the others. At the entrance to it a hanging lantern glimmered wanly through the mist that was beginning to rise from the marshes; within, beyond a pair of red-faced lackeys dozing dully at their posts, their master was discovered reading alone by a solitary candle.

A brazier of charcoal made the tent almost suffocatingly warm. The Duke, clad in a long purple velvet dressing-gown edged with fur, lay stretched out on his camp-bed, leaning on one elbow. He looked up as Charles-Louis entered, but kept his finger in the book to mark his place in the volume of Tacitus.

'Those were days worth living in,' quoth Monsieur du Maine, just as if they had been in the middle of an already developed dialogue. 'The old Romans had the right idea about warfare. Gory pitched battles every day and plenty of action — none of this pestilential waiting and waiting for something to happen — eh, Longueville?'

'I don't know, my Lord,' replied Charles-Louis. (He had been cautioned by Porlier not to address the Duke as "cousin" too early or often in their conversations.) 'I never read much in the classics. Did the Romans not lay siege to their enemies?'

'Oh, ay — that they did — but not for so long at a time — no, nor in winter either! Here we've spent five cursed weeks in this swamp, up to our necks in half-frozen slime — and we're no nearer our object than we were on the day we first saw Philipsburg. Dashed if I know what my father was thinking of, packing us off at this time of year, just when the troops were supposed to be laid off till spring!... He's like to make monkeys of us all; and while I doubt if he cares much what becomes of me — or of Conti or Bourbon, for that matter —

he's stark mad for my brother the Dauphin to win his spurs in the field. The poor fellow's to be made look a hero, by hook or by crook — those are the orders from Versailles — even though the rest of us ordinary mortals must suffer for six months on end. . . .' Maine's lip curled disdainfully; he lifted his eyebrows in a way that brought them slanting together at an angle — they were straight and thick and dark brown, a good deal darker than his hair, and made the principal accent in a face that was otherwise handsome but not espe-cially striking. He had the usual big Bourbon nose — rather too big, in this case, for the remainder of his features —; the keen blue eyes of his mother, the Montespan; and an air of moody aloofness in-herited from neither parent.

He glanced quizzically at Charles-Louis, standing in his wet cape and muddy boots and shivering a little in spite of the warmth of the brazier — and then, abruptly, he smiled: the Duc du Maine had a charming smile.

'But come, boy, what am I thinking of, keeping you waiting there like this? Take off your cloak directly, and I'll have it dried at the fire. Jean! Gilbert! A chair for Monsieur de Longueville! Now tell me, my friend, what brings you here so far from home on such a dirty dark night?'

Charles-Louis divested himself of his outer garments, took the proffered tabouret next the camp-bed, and tried to sit down on it easily, as Porlier had taught him to do. He was acutely conscious, all the same, of the chilblains on his hands and the mud on his boots and the fact that his curls wanted brushing. (Charles-Louis was rather a dandy; one of the main trials in camp life, from his point of view, was the difficulty in preserving the niceties of his personal ap-pearance.)

'I've a message for you, my Lord, from our colonel,' he said.

'From Montchevreuil? So? And what's the old boy to say to me now? I had a rare dressing down from the good Gaston yesterday for doing trench duty with my cousin Bourbon's men. Pah! The red tape that exists in the regular army! It's disgusting! What excite-ment could possibly come the way of us poor volunteers if we didn't stir about a bit outside of our own bailiwicks? Well, what is it this time? Another lecture on the duties and privileges of a Prince of the Blood?'

'My Lord,' said Charles-Louis, rather breathlessly, 'our colonel has ordered a general attack tonight on the enemy's fortifications. He hopes to seize the crown-works and the escarpment before dawn. We're going into action at once with our second battalion and the regiment of Anjou — the first and third battalions to follow as needed. I was to say that if you cared to accompany Monsieur de Montchevreuil . . .'

Maine jumped up promptly from his recumbent position. The volume of Tacitus slid to the floor, the cushions of the camp-bed were scattered right and left in his eagerness.

'God, boy, why didn't you tell me at once? What are we wasting time for? Rouse my men! — Where the devil *is* everyone tonight? They swarm about me as thick as flies when I've no need of 'em — but if by some chance . . . Or no: what's the use? They're a lazy lot, anyhow. *You'll* help me, old fellow, instead, won't you? Of course you will! Damn it, I *would* be undressed at a moment like this! Look here — my shirt — my boots — my jerkin! A plague on these palsied legs of mine! I'm only half awake when I want all my wits about me!'

While he was talking Monsieur du Maine was hobbling excitedly about the tent, as fast as his poor deformed feet would let him, assembling sundry items of his wardrobe. Charles-Louis, who was passionately anxious to be helpful, found his fingers all thumbs; his hands were trembling so hard that he could scarcely manage to hold his cousin's shirt.

At last, however, by the combined exertions of the two boys the young Duke was dressed; it then remained only to call his chief equerry, the Chevalier d'Aunoy, and order the horses put to Maine's light carriage. . . . 'For I'd never be able to get there on foot!' said the Duke, with a grimace. 'Cousin, you'll come with me, won't you?' — and Charles-Louis accepted, glad not to have to tramp the long, cold way back and dizzy with rapture at the prospect of a quarter of an hour alone with his chief friend and patron.

They started off in a rush of wet wind; then the mist swallowed them up. It had grown so much thicker that they could see nothing save two will-o'-the-wisp gleams bobbing ahead that were the torches of the Duke's postilions, but the ridge road was familiar, and at this time of night they were not likely to meet other vehicles abroad.

Maine held the reins, driving with skill and decision. His first excitement had somewhat abated; he appeared to have his nerves as well in hand as the horses; but there was a novel light in the lazy blue eyes, and now and again he turned to his companion with a triumphant chuckle.

'Good old Montchevreuil!' he exclaimed, several times. 'He's said all along he'd see to it that I wasn't left out of the fun, but I couldn't believe . . . I should have trusted his word. What a sell for my brother! Monseigneur's *medianoche* will be just getting under way by now. How lucky it was I decided at the last minute it would bore me too much to attend it! You and I, little Longueville, are in luck for once in our lives. . . . Good old Montchevreuil! He's always been on our side. . . .'

This formula was repeated so often and so emphatically that Charles-Louis' latent curiosity was aroused. He ventured at length to inquire: 'But, my cousin, what *is* our side? Why *should* there be sides, when we're all members of the same family?'

'Oh, well, of course, strictly speaking, there shouldn't be,' said the Duke. 'But perhaps it's natural, you know, for them to resent us a little. After all, from my brother's point of view, we don't exist — we've simply no right to be here!'

'*We*, my cousin?' Charles-Louis was puzzled: he held on to his hat to keep the breeze they were making from blowing it off, and stole a side-glance from under its brim at the Duke's fine sharp profile.

'You and I, boy — the royal bastards! 'Tis an ugly word and an ugly thing — but there it is: we might as well face it. It's no fault of *ours* — *we* didn't ask to be born!'

A queer sick throb clutched at Charles-Louis' vitals. He felt breathless, hot and cold at the same time, and full of torturing doubts that seemed to take physical form as a lump in his throat. However, he swallowed the lump and said valiantly: 'I am no bastard, my Lord! I am not like you, the son of a double adultery. My father was married to my mother. Surely you are mistaken. . . .'

'Mistaken? Oh, no!' Maine gave a thin, mirthless laugh and laid his hand for a fugitive instant on Charles-Louis' arm. 'Don't resent what I say; it's for your own good.'

'But, my Lord, I *do* resent it! I resent it very much! I cannot in justice to my father allow the slur on his name to pass uncorrected. I am honest born and honest bred — as legitimate as any prince in France!'

'Legitimate? To be sure you are! So am I, lad, so am I! Our sires saw to that much. Paper's cheap, and parliament's not likely to refuse requests from exalted quarters. But we're bastards for all that!'

'Cousin, I assure you, you're mistaken,' said Charles-Louis again, with as much dignity as he could command, considering that his lower lip had begun to tremble perilously. 'You *must* be. I am no bastard, I tell you. My mother was a gentleman's daughter in Normandy. The marriage was never publicly recognized, but 'twas none the less legal. I've papers to prove it. Porlier says I have papers. Porlier told me the whole story. You can ask him if you wish. He swore to me . . .'

'Let him swear what he likes — 'tis all one — nothing can alter the case. The old codger's nourished you on fairy-tales far too long already. I've been meaning to speak to you about this for some time, cousin, ever since the Chevalier de Montchevreuil informed me that you were ignorant of your origin and bade us take care. . . . I don't want to hurt you, but you're old enough to be told the truth. I expect you'd have learned it long before now, if you hadn't been brought up shut away from the world. After all, there's naught to be gained through denying our plight. Being what we are, our only hope lies in admitting the facts — if we do, we've a chance to get something out of life, in spite of those who hate and despise us. It can't hurt me to confess that my dam was old Montespan, the King's whore — any more than it ought to hurt you to realize that you, too, were born out of wedlock. Your poor mother has suffered enough, as it is, in the past — why should you suffer now, after her, for what can't be helped?'

'My mother was an honest woman! Don't speak to me of her — she's dead and can't defend herself!'

'Dead! She's no more dead than you or I — that is, unless reports unknown to me have lately come from Paris. Why, lad, for God's sake, who do you think *is* your mother?'

'Pauline d'Arville,' answered Charles-Louis desperately. 'That was her name, Porlier said. . . .'

But even as he spoke he knew he no longer believed his own words. Rigid with misery, he faced the Duke, his eyes light and staring, his strained young face as pale as the mist outside the carriage windows.

'Pauline d'Arville!' echoed Monsieur du Maine. '*Pauline d'Arville!*' He pulled in his horses, as the sound of gunfire and confused shouting from the marshes below on the right gave indication that they were nearing the end of their journey. 'That's a pretty name, but unfortunately no more genuine than the rest of our friend's amiable inventions. Your mother wasn't Pauline d'Arville, boy. There isn't any Pauline d'Arville. There never was — except in the imagination of your tutor. *Your* mother was "Aunt Magdelon," as they tell me you call her — Madame de la Ferté, the Maréchal's widow!'

IT SEEMED TO CATEAU THAT EVERYTHING MUST HAVE HAPPENED TO Magdelon that *could* happen — that since her sister had been spared no misfortune, she ought by rights to have attained a state of bleak, bereft peace. Yet, incredible to relate, the late summer and early autumn of 1688 started a whole new series of domestic disasters for the family who were beginning to be called the 'unlucky La Fertés.'

Young Jules led off the list, in the middle of August, by losing his abbey of Saint-Jean-d'Angély. This benefice, near Rochefort in the province of Saintonge, had been secured for him ten years ago at the time he had joined the Knights of Malta, and was worth a good ten thousand francs a year. The King's revocation of his gift, out of an apparently clear sky and without compensation of any kind, was a heavy blow: young Jules, from being very comfortably off, suddenly found himself next door to penury.

His relatives were no less appalled than he. None of them knew what had caused the catastrophe. . . . At least, they professed not to know. Only Cateau was candid enough to admit that he had undoubtedly brought it upon his own head. Jules was a difficult, disagreeable young man, who kept very much to himself, never went to decent folk's houses, and had, as far as one could tell, not an atom of natural affection for any member of his family. He slept all day every day, and spent his nights in the shoddy cabarets of the Place Maubert quarter carousing with his boon companions, a set of impious, down-at-heel scribblers allied with the worst elements of the underworld. In these circumstances it was inevitable, his Aunt d'Olonne felt, that he should sooner or later have got into disfavour at court. The King, who was growing increasingly pompous and pious under the influence of that meddlesome bigot, Madame de Maintenon, had no use for young wasters like the Chevalier de la Ferté. . . . Cateau, who disliked her third nephew, was not particularly sorry for him. She did, however, pity his mother; she went to see Magdelon at once, to offer her help, and Fervaques' help. . . . 'If there were anything we could do, my dear, we'd be only too happy . . .'

'I know you would, darling,' said Magdelon gratefully. 'But no — no! There's nothing anyone can do. Poor boy! I'm afraid that he's taking it in just the wrong manner. He says it doesn't matter now what becomes of him — it's killed any spark of ambition he had. And Jules is so talented, too — his verses are perfectly charming, and Baron tells me that the first half of the comedy he's been working on lately is as clever as it can be. . . . The worst of it is, I haven't the least bit of influence over him. If only he cared for me as the rest of the children do! . . . He's so hard, so indifferent. . . . It often seems there's no way at all of reaching his heart.'

Cateau, being privately of the opinion that the Chevalier had no heart to reach, contented herself with a platitudinous murmur to the effect that, after all, he was very young yet. . . . Who knew what the future . . .?

She stooped to kiss Magdelon, who looked sombre and brooding in her long mourning veils; then she rustled away, equally sombre and brooding in *hers*. . . . For Cateau was now a widow too. She had been one for over two years, since that cold day in February, 1686, when the Comte d'Olonne, after a lingering illness, had come to a sudden and characteristic end at one of his own dinner parties. As the second entrée was being passed he had felt faint, asked to be carried out on his terrace to see the sun for the last time — five minutes later he was gone! After this dramatic exit Cateau had embarked on a spirited lawsuit, to compel her husband's heirs to restore her dowry. She had even — it was really most amusing — been able to force them to pay for her mourning expenses. . . . How angry Olonne would have been if he'd known! But he did not know: he had gone beyond the reach of emotions, pleasant and unpleasant; he was safe at last from anything that living could do to him. And there were, thought Cateau grimly, some fates in life a good deal worse than death. . . .

She was surer of this than ever, a week after her visit to her sister, when a new affliction, far harder to bear than the old one, blew the loss of Jules' abbey quite out of their heads. Tinette was caught at the convent near Orléans in the act of holding an illicit rendezvous with a man!

Here again, it occurred to the clear-sighted Countess that the event should have surprised no one. What *was* strange was that something of the sort had not happened before. Tinette was six-and-twenty; it was shocking that she had not been married off and settled long ago. Either that — or Magdelon ought to have insisted on her elder daughter's becoming a nun. But Magdelon was not made for such drastic decisions: she hadn't the money to provide a proper parti; on the other hand, neither could she bring herself to urge the girl, who showed no signs of a vocation, to adopt the religious life. A weak compromise, that suited nobody, had been reached, whereby Mademoiselle de la Ferté spent her summers at the convent and her winters in Paris at the house in the rue de Richelieu.

The Prioress of the Order of the Visitation was very fond of Tinette, who remained as docile and sweet as in her childhood: she was loath to believe that her charge was in any way to blame for the accident. Still, she wrote, there it was — she felt she would have been remiss in her duty if she neglected to apprise the Maréchale of the fact that her daughter had been conducting a clandestine correspondence with a gentleman for months. ... The Sub-Prioress, Sister Marie-Louise, had long entertained suspicions on the subject; she had remarked that Mademoiselle de la Ferté was in the habit of receiving a certain letter once a week regularly — that when it was handed to her the young lady blushed and gave evidence of great pleasure — now and then, when it failed to arrive on the accustomed day, she would betray what in a less well-poised character must have been termed extreme agitation. Under the circumstances Sister Marie-Louise had deemed it expedient to intercept and examine one of these epistles — with the result that Mademoiselle de la Ferté had been surprised in the convent garden, a day or two afterwards, in conversation with the Marquis de Villiers-Longchesne, a cavalry officer stationed at Orléans.

The Prioress trusted that the Maréchale would not allow herself to be too gravely upset by this information. As far as it was possible to ascertain, Mademoiselle de la Ferté had been foolish rather than frail. Her relations with the Marquis appeared to be innocent enough. Nothing had passed between them — at least, it was *hoped* that nothing had passed between them — except sighs and smiles and a fugitive kiss or two. ... 'But as I say, madam, I conceived it the part of wisdom to warn you. ...'

When Magdelon had got as far as that in the Prioress's letter, which she was reading aloud to the assembled family, she hesitated for a moment, overcome by painful emotions; whereupon her daughter-in-law Gabrielle, in whose private cabinet the assembly was taking place, seized the opening offered her to insert, with a sly, knife-edged smile: 'But, after all, how do we *know* that she's innocent?'

She ran her olive-green eyes round the circle, to observe what fruit her suggestion might bear. Henri — who, for a wonder, had consented to be present at the council to determine his sister's fate — was lolling back in his armchair, high-coloured and good-humoured, picking his teeth and whistling, and paying very little attention to what was being said. Louis, the Jesuit, a slight, black-clad figure with so strong a resemblance to his brother that he looked like the young Duke's better self — or perhaps his good angel — flushed warmly and appeared distressed. Fervaques, who was often included in debates concerning the La Fertés' affairs because the Duchess professed a high regard for his sagacity, was distressed, also — as well he might be; for Villiers-Longchesne was one of the Bullions, his own first cousin on his father's side of the house. The young man was ensign of Fervaques' old regiment, the Queen's Light Horse Troop, and, everyone had supposed up to now, a model character. . . . Cateau and Magdelon, seated side by side in their widows' weeds on the couch in front of the fire, as befitted their position as the oldest persons present, exchanged glances; the latter was crying a little, with her handkerchief held to her eyes. Since she seemed indisposed to speak, it was the former who finally said: 'What do you mean? Of course the child's innocent!'

Gabrielle made a face that expressed the inexpressible very neatly; she always took care, however, to be blandly polite to her Aunt d'Olonne.

'Madam, we may know it — but how about our neighbours?'

'Damn our neighbours! I'll take care of them, never fear!' (This, of course, was Henri's contribution.)

Gabrielle flung him a withering look, but instead of losing her temper with her husband, as she often did, she continued craftily in a smooth, purring voice: 'Very well, my dear, very well! All I wish to suggest, in this instance, is that it might not be wholly to our disadvantage to let people imagine things are worse than they are. Tinette's reached a great age already. You've never been able to catch her a husband. It seems to me that, unless you want the poor wretch to remain an old maid forever, now is the time to act boldly in her behalf. It might be the best solution for everyone to admit . . . Oh, I don't put it in words! You can see what I mean. . . .'

'You mean, we're to declare that she's been seduced, and get the fellow to marry her under false pretences?'

Gabrielle recoiled delicately and made another face even more expressive than the first.

'My love, how unnecessarily coarse! But yes, on the whole, I believe you apprehend my design. Cousin' — to Fervaques — 'you are, amongst us, Monsieur de Longchesne's sole relative: would you feel able to answer for his integrity in this perplexing affair?'

Fervaques squirmed in his seat; it was a little boy's trick he had never lost.

'Cousin, I know not. The matter's upset me more than I care to confess. We've always considered François a lad of high principles; I've taken, in fact, a particular interest in him. Why, 'twas I got him his commission as ensign of the Queen's Light Horse Troop! It's almost past believing that he'd stoop so low as to compromise a woman's honour — especially a young, helpless girl's. . . .'

'No one dreams for a moment that he's done anything of the

sort! Calm yourself, cousin, I pray! As I say, it's not what *we* think that counts — it's what the world thinks, or can be made to think. Brother Louis, I appeal to you, as a man of the church, to give us your unbiassed opinion. Are we not justified in taking any means within our power to achieve an end that can only be considered good in itself?'

The Jesuit eyed his purposeful sister-in-law without flinching, something few of the other La Fertés were able to do.

'Madam, you are very cunning indeed to cite one of the maxims of our society in your effort to gain me to your side in the argument. This thought, however, has occurred to me: why need there be an argument at all? I agree with our aunt that Tinette is undoubtedly guiltless of wrong. It is probable that young Longchesne, too, has no more heinous stain on his honour than a certain recklessness, to be excused by the strength of his attachment for our sister. Will he not therefore be glad to wed her? He is eligible, rich, of suitable age — best of all, a close relation of our valued friend Monsieur de Fervaques... Why, the match appears almost ideal! Surely it can be brought about through the gentlest persuasions alone....'

This shrewd insinuation appeared to have solved the chief difficulty: with a concerted rush all the family began talking at once, explaining that naturally there would be no argument, they had always known that everything could be arranged satisfactorily in an amicable way — the dear young people would be married directly — how clever Louis was, to be sure!... Magdelon and Gabrielle even launched into a lively discussion of the cut and material of the bride's wedding dress, and whether the Lady Chapel at Saint-Eustache would be large enough to accommodate the combined cohorts of Bullions and La Fertés....

It was Cateau who, with her habitual wry practicality, at length cut the conversation short by stating severely: 'The child has no dowry. And as far as I can see, there's no one to give it to her unless...'

Then, indeed, she was sorry she had spoken; for every pair of eyes in the room was fixed upon her, Gabrielle's radiating such hungry intention that it was clear that the latter had only now reached the point she had been aiming towards since the beginning of the family council.

In the end, it turned out as Cateau had all along suspected it might: she promised to find her sister the sum of one hundred thousand francs to assure Tinette's future.... Not to *give* them outright. Thank Heaven, she had sense enough still to avoid doing that! Besides, it did not do to give money to Magdelon, through whose inexpert fingers it trickled with frightening speed, leaving not a trace behind. (One might as well pour water down a drain.)...

No; this was an orderly business transaction, such as had taken place more than once before between them. The terms of the loan were drawn up by Maître Le Caron, the Countess receiving as security a lien on some of the Maréchale's properties in Normandy. (There were not, alas! nearly so many of these left as there ought to have been, poor Magdelon having despoiled herself recklessly in her attempts to succour her spendthrift sons.)

Everybody was exceedingly grateful to Madame d'Olonne, without whose timely assistance the project might well have fallen through. Fervaques was dispatched by his mistress to Orléans to interview his young relative, a startled freckled youth, whom he found sincerely attached to Mademoiselle de la Ferté and only too anxious to do anything in his power to make amends for the damage unwittingly done to her reputation. The marriage was arranged and performed as expeditiously as possible, and the bridegroom left shortly afterwards for the war in Germany. Within a fortnight the new Marquise de Villiers-Longchesne was at home once again in the bosom of her family. Magdelon was inclined at first to wax tearfully sentimental about the little bride, who had remained marvellously phlegmatic and philosophical through the whole of the trying negotiations, neither affirming nor denying anything ... so that 'even now,' as Cateau remarked to her sister, 'one can't really be sure. ...'

But Gabrielle scolded, and said that it was absurd to treat the minx like a heroine, when she'd been extremely naughty and tiresome, if not actually vicious as well — and, as usual, Gabrielle set the tone for the La Fertés in general.

It was astonishing to Cateau to observe, as time went on, how completely her nephew's wife had come to dominate the family circle. Of course it was undeniable that much of the strength of her position was due to the weakness of her husband's — or to put it more correctly, to his lack of any position whatever. Henri, at thirty-two, was a confirmed drunkard, an amiable debauchee, who had deliberately wasted his brilliant inherited military talents and found himself now unemployed, in disgrace, deprived of a future through no fault but his own. His career as a diplomat had been even more inglorious than in the field: he had been sent back from London with unpleasant speed, neither wiser nor richer than he had gone thither, his sole souvenir of the embassy a choice collection of English oaths he was wont to display for his cronies' amusement at convivial gatherings. There was nothing further to be done either with or for Henri. ...

On the contrary, whether one liked her or whether one didn't, it was impossible not to respect the combination of violent ambition and guileful persistence by which the Duchesse de la Ferté achieved her ends. She had survived her initial débâcle at court to become, if not precisely a favourite of the King, at any rate one of the members of his intimate circle. She was counted in everything; her name appeared with gratifying frequency in the *Gazette* on the lists of those present at races and concerts and lawn fêtes and, occasionally, even one of the breathlessly exclusive house-parties at Marly. The entering wedge, in her case, had been Doudou de Ventadour, who, after several years of social eclipse, had emerged from her convent in the Faubourg-Saint-Marceau to secure the coveted post of lady-in-waiting to Madame, the King's sister-in-law. Doudou and Gabrielle were devoted to each other: it was only natural that the former should invite the latter to visit her at Saint-Cloud and Versailles. Gabrielle, a clever actress when need arose for it, played the prude so successfully that Madame de Maintenon found her charming — and the rest was merely a matter of patience and tact, in neither of which the Duchess was lacking when the object in view seemed to warrant their exercise. . . . She still, Cateau was perfectly sure, had lovers in secret and drank too much whenever she could (Monsieur's court was far more dissolute than his brother's, and his suppers at the Palais Royal were sometimes scandalous performances); but on the surface she was all that was circumspect. In fact, it was thanks to Gabrielle alone that the La Fertés were still accounted members of respectable society.

Their somewhat questionable status was further impaired by the third of the winter's tragedies — the worst of them all for Magdelon —: the death at Philipsburg of the Chevalier de Longueville. Cateau could scarcely believe her ears when the report reached her. . . . Charles-Louis had gone unscathed through the whole of the siege; he had written such happy, confident letters to his mother (all of which she had read aloud to her sister, swelling with pride as she read). Philipsburg had fallen on the twenty-ninth of October. Count Starhemberg, the officer in charge of the fortress, had led his garrison out to surrender to Monseigneur the very next day — and all over the kingdom of France the hearts of mothers and wives and sweethearts rejoiced that the peril was past and their loved ones were safe. It was too late in the season now to expect any more actions of consequence. . . .

Then, suddenly, word came to Paris that the Chevalier de Longueville had been killed 'by mistake.' It was a peculiarly unfortunate accident. . . . After the siege was over the soldiers were put to work filling in the trenches; an officer in charge, bored by the hours of tedious duty, had borrowed a rifle from one of his men and fell to taking pot-shots at the snipe and wild-duck that fed in the marshes. Just then the Dauphin and his suite arrived to inspect the operations. The officers rose to receive him; the Chevalier, who for some inexplicable reason was slightly out of line, was pierced through the chest by the soldier aiming at snipe. (It was afterwards found that, unknown to its user, the gun contained several bullets in addition to the small-shot intended for game.) ... The victim had lived less than twenty-four hours. ... 'The shock was severe to the members of the King's regiment,' it was said in the official bulletin describing the disaster, 'the Chevalier de Longueville being a general favourite. The fatal accident that cut short his life in the flower of his age caused universal grief amongst his comrades.'

Magdelon was prostrated by the news. She took to her bed at once, laughing and crying by turns. Cateau was sent for, and did not quit her for a week, at the end of which time Porlier returned from Germany with his young master's body. He came at once to call on the sisters. ... 'It was very affecting,' Cateau told Fervaques afterwards. 'The poor fellow sobbed like a child, and Magdelon had to comfort him, which no doubt was an excellent thing, as it kept her from going to pieces herself. But I cried, too — indeed, my dear, you'd have done the same if you'd been there, no one could have helped it — though God knows the Chevalier was nothing to me. ...'

Porlier related the whole story as best he was able. He did not attempt to conceal the fact that Charles-Louis — one could not say how, for the boy had refused to divulge the source of the information — had learned the truth about his origin, with startling suddenness, at the very end of the siege, and that this truth had greatly upset him. ... 'Poor lad! Poor lad! To my last hour on earth I'll never forget how he stared at me with his big eyes and kept on saying, over and over: "Now it's all spoilt, Porlier — I can never be Duc de Longueville!" He blamed me, too, quite severely for not telling him long ago — but oh, madam, madam, how could I have done so? In the early days it was my duty to keep silent to protect your good name; and later, after the Maréchal's death, when the same precautions were no longer necessary, I couldn't bring myself to disillusion him. You know, I've told you often, he clung so hard to his pride in his birth. ... It seemed, in a way, all he had. ... But I fear I did wrong, old fool that I am! — for if I'd acted differently, our dear little lord would be with us today. I make no doubt, madam, 'twas nothing but shame at the thought of what he was that caused him to break ranks unexpectedly when Monseigneur came. If he hadn't made that sudden wild rush to the rear, he'd never have stopped the hunter's bullet!'

There was no need for the La Fertés to take official notice of Charles-Louis' death. As far as they were concerned, he had not existed: how could they be expected to regret someone they had not even seen, who ought really never to have been born, and whose disappearance relieved them of a cause of considerable shame and anxiety? Only Chou-Chou mourned her lost playmate in secret.

Nevertheless, when it became known, as it very soon did, that the Chevalier de Longueville had left a fortune of half a million francs to his tutor Porlier, Gabrielle pricked up her ears and expressed her opinion that her mother-in-law would be a fool if she did not lay claim to a part of it. Porlier did not need the money, nor want it — he had said so himself — and it was manifestly ridiculous to let it fall into the clutches of the Chevalier's natural heirs, the Condés and that hateful, grasping old Duchesse de Nemours, who, disgustingly rich as they were already, were preparing to go to law to fight for the prize. (One had heard they contended that the boy had been too young to make a legal will.) ... 'Besides,' said Gabrielle cleverly, 'if you come down to it, who has a more natural right to the estate than his natural mother?'

She pleaded with Magdelon for several days in this strain; approached every member of the family in turn, to demand that they use their influence to persuade the Maréchale to her duty. The house was filled from morning till night with the sound of her fluent, metallic arguments, till even Chou-Chou de la Ferté realized, with a shock, that her 'cousin' had in reality been her brother, all along. But Magdelon stood firm under the onslaught, shook her head silently, and refused to discuss the matter.

During the sad weeks before Christmas Cateau came daily to see her sister. She was so sorry for her that she would have done anything on earth to cheer her — but for the moment Magdelon appeared to be past cheering. She sat for hours apathetic and dumb in the chimney-corner, staring into the fire, seeming neither to know nor to care what went on around her. Then again, she would feel impelled to talk about her little dead son. She would recall incidents of his childhood, read and reread the letters from Philipsburg, speculate fruitlessly as to what would have happened if Charles-Louis had lived to come home from the war and confront her with his knowledge of their real relationship. Porlier had not had the wit to conceal from her that, at the end, his pupil had suffered a revulsion of feeling — natural enough in the circumstances — towards his 'Aunt Magdelon.' Of all the heavy sorrows Magdelon had to bear, that, Cateau divined, was the worst.

Besides her sister, Magdelon's most constant company at this time was supplied by her granddaughter Marie-Angélique, now a pale, pretty child of twelve, very small for her age, with long golden curls that recalled her great-aunt d'Olonne's and a sweet manner not unlike Magdelon's in her youth. Gabrielle thought little of Marie-Angélique, who was shy in public to the point of being considered backward, if not quite mentally deficient; the Duchess's fondest hopes were centred on her second daughter, eight-year-old Catherine. Mademoiselle de Menetou, as the latter was called, was a forward chit, with a nimble tongue and a marked talent for music, which was being assiduously cultivated by Maître Colasse, the late great Lully's most brilliant successor. She had already played the clavichord before Monsieur and Madame at the Palais Royal, and her mother planned to present her early in the new year at a chamber music concert in Versailles.

Marie-Angélique, on the other hand, having no perceptible gifts, was often left at home to her own devices; and so it fell out that almost every afternoon her timid knock was heard on the door of her grandmother's room. Magdelon invariably made the little girl welcome, and seemed glad to have her with her. Indeed, Marie-Angélique made no trouble for anyone. She placed her small three-cornered stool near the hearth and sat still upon it for as long as she was permitted to stay, stringing beads or playing wordless, mysterious games with her dolls, of which she had a great number. Cateau and Magdelon sometimes forgot as they talked that she was there; but when her governess came at length to fetch her away the gentle presence was missed.

On Christmas Eve, as the sisters were seated as usual by the fire with their youthful companion, a lackey brought a message that the Duchesse de la Ferté had just returned from Versailles and would like the Maréchale, if convenient, to join her directly in the mauve cabinet.

'Darling, don't mind me — I was going home in a minute, anyhow,' said Cateau.

But the lackey declared that his mistress was aware of the Countess's presence in the house and had particularly requested that she also be invited to attend the gathering.

'Another council of war! My dear, what can it be this time?'

Magdelon made no reply; she stooped to kiss Marie-Angélique, saying gently: 'Run away, baby, back to the nursery; I'll come to say good-night to you later when you're tucked up in bed.'

As she stood in front of the fire the light from it struck her hair, which she'd lately stopped dyeing, revealing plentiful white streaks amongst the mottled sunset glow of the auburn tresses under her black mourning bandeau.

The mauve cabinet was the smaller of the two principal drawing-rooms in the new Hôtel de la Ferté. Like the rest of the house, it was over-elaborate and far too full of furniture, Gabrielle's ideas of decoration being even more exuberant than those of her mother-in-law.

When Cateau and Magdelon arrived they found that the former was right, for the family was assembled and waiting: the Duchess was there, and her two brothers-in-law, Louis, the Jesuit, and Jules, the Knight of Malta; also Tinette, whose position as a matron made her eligible for admission to the conclave. Only Henri was absent, but that could occasion no surprise, as he was seldom at home these days. (His irritation at being left off the list of forthcoming promotions in the sacrosanct Order of the Holy Ghost was well known. Worse still, the King had taken the trouble to inform him in a private audience *why* his name was excluded — since when the Duke had embarked aggressively on a new programme of orgies, and none of his relatives had laid eyes on him for more than a week.)

In spite of her husband's defection, Gabrielle appeared in high feather this evening. She had, it developed, just returned from a concert at Trianon, where her darling Catherine had performed before Madame de Maintenon and a select group of ladies with overwhelming success.

'Dear poppet! Everyone said she was simply adorable — that Baptiste himself in his heyday never did better,' asserted the Duchess, glancing about the circle with a steely eye, as if challenging contradiction.

She was gorgeously dressed in a creation Maître Baudelet had designed especially for this auspicious occasion, a gown of rich reddish-brown velvet, the skirt of which, adjusted in graceful folds, was held up by six butterflies made of Dresden china. The front of this remarkable garment was an apron of cloth of silver, upon which was embroidered an orchestra of musicians arranged in a pyramidal group of six ranks of performers with instruments wrought in raised needlework. Reddish-brown ostrich plumes fastened with garnets nodded in her reddish-brown hair; she looked smart, and hard, and capable to a degree unusual even for her, as she rose to greet the elder ladies with a ceremonious curtsy, and then resumed her seat in the geographical centre of the group.

'My dears,' she began, speaking very fast, 'I've the most wonderful news for you all! Wait till you hear! You'll never guess ——'

'La Ferté has fallen and cracked his skull,' whispered Jules, in a sepulchral tone; whereupon Tinette, who never could tell when her brother was jesting, gave him a horrified stare.

'The old Marquise de Senneterre is dead and has left you a fortune,' hazarded Louis.

'The King's reconsidered and given the Chevalier another abbey,' contributed Cateau.

'Whatever it is, there must be money in it, sister,' added Jules; 'else 'tis certain you'd not be smiling so sweetly!'

'Money? I should think so indeed!' said Gabrielle, who was far too much excited even to stop to quell her old enemy. 'More than you've ever dreamed of, or'll be likely to manage to get your hands on, between now and Doomsday, I'll warrant! Oh, you can say what you like, but money's the most important thing there is in the world! All of you need it — all of you want it — all of you spend it as fast as you get it. In fact, you're quite powerless without it — but do any of you lift a finger to bring it your way? You know very well you do not! There never was such a hopeless, helpless lot as the La Fertés! I ought to know: I've lived with you now for nearly fourteen years.... Well, let bygones be bygones; there's no use in recalling the past — though I must say, when I think of the chances you've muffed ...! I make no charges — I blame no one — but the fact remains, as a family we're ruined!'

'Oh, come, my dear sister,' said Louis, 'you're exaggerating! Surely it can't be as bad as that!' —; while Jules muttered: 'There are always Papa's pensions....'

'That's just what there are *not*,' said Gabrielle ruthlessly. 'By far the larger part of the Maréchal's income stopped with his life. All he left unentailed were his governments in Lorraine, worth exactly twenty-two thousand francs a year. There were also his houses in Paris and the Orléannais. Great Senneterre was sold, as you know — though by no means so soon as it ought to have been — but the money from the sale went to pay the Duke's debts and to buy us this house that we're living in. Your mother's properties are all mortgaged; Jules has lost his abbey; Tinette's husband will be practically penniless till his father dies — even then, as he's a younger son, he'll get only a fraction of the estate. And you don't need me to tell you that there's little likelihood at present of Henri's being able to help, even if he should want to, which is most improbable. The King has refused him a post in the army; he's even been turned down for the promotion to the Order, for which, as far as I can make out, every stable-boy in Versailles has managed to make himself eligible!... No, we'd best face the truth: we are ruined, utterly ruined — unless something drastic is done.... Oh, I've thought, and thought, till it's a miracle, really, that my hair's not gone grey, trying to hit upon some plan to save us! Finally it came to me: if we can't make money, we must marry it! An alliance will have to be arranged. Then I fell to pondering who would be the best available parti at court. I reviewed in my mind the whole list, balancing this one's income against that one's influential connections. In the end, it seemed to me that there was no one so suitable as the Marquis de Mirepoix.... *You* remember young Mirepoix, Tinette? As I recall it, he was one of the most attentive of your swains that summer during the fêtes at Fontainebleau. A charming fellow — and most excellently situated for our purpose. His father's just died, and his mother was a Puy-du-Fou — nobody is richer than the Puy-du-Fous! They say that when his grandmother goes there'll be another considerable fortune coming to him from her. Meanwhile, he's the head of the family, young, but not too young; in the army — he's ensign at present of the White Musketeers, but they tell me he's treating with the King for the commission of second lieutenant of the Blacks. (I always think, don't you? that the Black Musketeers are the smartest regiment in France!) In short, from any point of view, there couldn't be a more nearly ideal bridegroom. To tell the truth, I made up my mind months ago not to let him elude my clutches! Proposals were made to his family in our behalf by my mother — dear Maman! She's always the soul of tact! — and when I heard last night that they had been favourably received, I resolved to speak to the King today on the subject myself. His Majesty could not well have been more polite. His sole objection was on the score of age. "The child's very young to be married," he said. "True, Sire," I replied, "but the matter is pressing: if we wait a few years, till Your Majesty's perceived and rewarded the rare merit of Monsieur de Mirepoix, 'twill be too late — the quarry will escape — for he'll have nothing to do with the likes of us!" ... His Majesty laughed and laughed — I can always amuse him, you know — he was vastly diverted when I told him that what I really wanted was a son-in-law to suit *me* — that, in a manner of speaking, it was I who was marrying my son-in-law! ... Oh, we had a very droll conversation, I assure you! And the result of it was that he's given his permission for the marriage — it's as good as settled already!'

'But, sister,' said Louis, when Gabrielle had been forced to pause for breath, 'I don't understand.... What is this talk of "sons-in-law"? Surely, 'tis "brother-in-law" you meant! For you've no daughter of nubile age as yet, while our sister Cécile, though young enough herself in all conscience, might perhaps be deemed ripe for a husband.'

Gabrielle tossed her topknot of ostrich plumes and smoothed her bodice with nervous fingers.

'Now upon my soul, Brother Louis, I gave you credit for more intelligence! Why on earth should you suppose I'd waste my breath and weeks upon weeks of patient effort arranging a match for that lumpish Chou-Chou? Whether *she* finds a husband or not is no concern of *mine*. Her mother is welcome to the task of settling her as she chooses, for aught I care. No, no — I see you don't follow me — I perceive I've not made the matter sufficiently plain. Naturally, it's my *own* child whose future I've been taking such pains to assure. It's Marie-Angélique who's going to marry the Marquis de Mirepoix!'

A dead silence followed the shock of this announcement, broken at last by a cry from Magdelon — the first sound she had uttered since entering the room — a long, low, involuntary wail like that of an animal in distress. She slumped forward in her chair, saying no word, incapable evidently of making an articulate protest. Cateau, seeing her thus, felt that her sister had reached the limit of human suffering. At least, one could hope that, from now on, nothing would have the power to hurt her as she had been hurt in the past: poor Magdelon's heart must really be broken.

During the next three weeks all the La Fertés, the Maréchale included, were busier than they had been in years.

Marie-Angélique's engagement to the Marquis de Mirepoix made a sensation at court as soon as the news became public. The solid wealth and position of the bridegroom, the extreme youth and poverty of the bride — more especially, the cynical determination with which the Duchesse de la Ferté engineered the whole business, and succeeded in putting it over against the will of every member of both families — caused a good deal of gossip, most of it highly unpleasant. But Gabrielle appeared impervious to what was said of her. She rallied her relatives to her side: her mother, the old Maréchale de la Mothe, came in from Versailles to attend the official receptions and visits of ceremony; and her two sisters, Françoise d'Aumont and Doudou de Ventadour, who, whatever their past reputations, were respectable now, lent their noble names and decorative persons to the lists of guests at the series of elaborate entertainments given to celebrate the marriage. The Hôtel de la Ferté and its owners, as well as the entire staff of servants (the latter greatly augmented for the occasion), were in a perpetual state of brilliant, nervous disorder. Meals were irregular, people wore their best clothes all day, nobody seemed to go to bed at ordinary hours. . . .

Marie-Angélique was called away from her beads and her dolls, dressed in silks and velvets, hung with jewels, and perched on the highest high-heels procurable, in order to increase her Lilliputian stature. Thus attired, she was produced in drawing-room after drawing-room, to be smoothed and patted and handed about admiringly, rather as if she were a doll herself. She had very little idea, Cateau imagined, what all the stir was about: she seemed pleased, though, in a mild, undemonstrative way, at her sudden importance, and her delight, when she found that henceforth she would not be required to do any more lessons, was pathetically unstudied.

Her sister Catherine came in, too, for her share of prominence in the proceedings — possibly, Cateau thought, even more than her share! Bedecked and bedizened like a miniature idol, she made her appearance at each of the parties, where Gabrielle was wont to call attention to Mademoiselle de Menetou by asking the child to perform on the clavichord at the drop of a hat. So much excitement, together with unavoidable dietary indiscretions, soon brought about a decided reaction: Catherine grew shrewish and dyspeptic after a week of late hours and an unwholesome régime of pastries and ices and sweet champagne. Finally she became such a nuisance to everyone that even her mother agreed that the one thing to do was to banish the small offender permanently to the nursery.

In the meantime, the financial aspect of the marriage gave rise to disagreeable differences between the Mirepoixs and the La Fertés. Henri, it transpired, had not been consulted concerning his daughter's matrimonial plans. That, Gabrielle contended, was perfectly natural, considering her husband's notorious carelessness of his family's welfare — why, he was not even sleeping at home at present, but was living quite openly with Louison d'Arquien, one of his mistresses, in a house on the other side of the river!... However, he was not so detached from his duty as not to raise a tremendous fuss over the question of a dowry; he hurled insults at Gabrielle and Madame de Mirepoix alike, declaring that he had no money to spare, and that, if he had, his future son-in-law should have none of it. Gabrielle, in her turn, insisted she was destitute; she had leased a house for the young couple in the rue Sainte-Croix-de-la-Bretonnerie, on the furnishing of which she averred she had spent her last remaining resources.... 'I'll not have a penny to feed myself and the chicks, much less provide a nest-egg for those mercenary Mirepoixs, who've got more now than they know what to do with!' said the Duchesse de la Ferté sweetly to her friends and acquaintances.

When the case was examined by the notaries of the respective parties, it appeared that the bride had been promised fifty thousand crowns by her family, one-third in cash, two-thirds to be left her in her mother's will. Gabrielle made a shameless attempt to extort the sum from Cateau; but Cateau, though willing to assure her niece's future, felt that it was needless to extend her liberalities to grandnieces, also. She therefore returned a polite but unequivocal refusal, and sent Marie-Angélique a diamond pendant with her love and good wishes.

The Duchess acknowledged the gift in a stiff little note; several days later, the two ladies happening to meet in the street, she took occasion to upbraid Aunt d'Olonne for her stinginess. At that, something snapped in Cateau's brain: she told Gabrielle what she thought of her and her works — called her a 'slut' and a 'harpy' and a 'cold-blooded schemer' — unloosing the resentments and inhibitions of years — and retired victorious from the fray thoroughly pleased with what she had done.

On the very day before the wedding — which was scheduled for the sixteenth of January, 1689 — the dowry had still not been paid. Scandalous scenes had occurred between Gabrielle and the Mirepoixs and their legal representatives; it seemed more than likely that the ceremony would not take place at all.... Then, late that evening, Cateau heard that Magdelon had raised the money required by turning over to her daughter-in-law her last unmortgaged piece of property, La Louppe.

Cateau stayed away from the wedding. She had no wish, as she expressed it trenchantly to Fervaques, to attend the massacre of the innocents — he might go without her and welcome!

It was a cold, snowy day. As she sat on the couch by the hearth in the Chinese cabinet, listening to the crackling of the fire and the soft thud of snow-flakes against the window, she thought how many times in how many places she had waited for him, as now. The time of waiting might seem long, but at least it was a comfort to know that she could count on his return — that he would come back to her without fail because there was nowhere else he'd rather be. That was a great deal to be sure of in life! Cateau hoped she was properly grateful for it.

She fell into a reverie, chin in hand, as she reviewed the eighteen happy years — they seemed, now that they were over, each and every one to have been reasonably happy — that she and Fervaques had lived together. In fact, she was so lost in her thoughts that she failed to hear a step on the stairs; it startled her when the door was pushed open and she looked up to see her lover, splendid in his festal crimson velvet and gold braid, standing before her.

'Oh, there you are,' said Cateau, rather unnecessarily. 'My dear, how well you look!'

So he did: that was no more than the truth. Her Noël at forty-four was still a brave figure of a man. His face was as smooth and unlined as a youth's, and though his body was older than his face, having thickened somewhat with the years, no one would have taken him for anything near his real age.

Cateau, too, had stayed astonishingly young; her radiance had paled, even altered indefinably in quality — but it had not yet gone out....

'We are still a handsome couple,' she thought, with quiet satisfaction, as Fervaques bent to kiss her hand before establishing himself in his time-honoured post at her feet.

She took his hand in hers and stroked it.

'Well, now, about the wedding...?'

The wedding, replied Fervaques, who had been schooled by the exigencies of his mistress into becoming an ample and accurate reporter, seemed, on the whole, to have passed off successfully. There had been a great many people at the church. Poor Marie-Angélique had lived up to her name and looked ravishing as an angel in silver tissue and a wreath of white myrtle. Gabrielle, triumphant in cloth

of gold, with one of the new bonnets called commodes on her
head, had maintained to the end that she had 'saved the family'
by the only possible means. The Mirepoixs were glum, as was only
to be expected. (Madame de Mirepoix had told Fervaques flatly that
she did not intend to appear at the bride's reception the following
day.) Henri, on the other hand, had behaved better than one could
have hoped. He had saved the situation at the last minute by appearing in time to bestow his daughter's hand on the Marquis,
though he had rather spoiled the effect of his yielding by being so
drunk that he could scarcely stand in the chapel while the ceremony
was performed. And afterwards he declined to attend the feast at
his own house, and lurched away, with a bottle of brandy under
each arm, to his carriage, in which the notorious Louison d'Arquien
was plainly seen to be awaiting him.

'And my sister, sir?'. . . Magdelon, said Fervaques reassuringly,
looked exceedingly well. She had had on a magnificent new gown of
black velvet embroidered in seed-pearls; she had sent her dear love
to the Countess and bidden Fervaques tell her how sorry she was not
to see her at the wedding. Her behaviour was perfect — that is,
most of the time it had been perfect. . . . No, she had not cried at all.
On the contrary, she had smiled the whole time. Never, asserted
Fervaques, had he beheld so persistent a smile. He had thought,
indeed, that, if anything, she had smiled a little too much.

'There are moments, you know, my love,' he remarked, 'when a
certain gravity of demeanour is perhaps more in keeping with the
solemnity of a rite such as marriage. It occurred to me that the
Maréchale might well have checked her mirth in the chapel — she
laughed out loud while the priest was blessing the bridal pair — and
when I asked her afterwards what made her so merry, she replied
that the snow coming down outside the windows reminded her of
her own wedding, four-and-thirty years ago (it had snowed that
day, too), and how you had told her then that when one was married
one had reached the end of everything. "But indeed, indeed, sir,
my sister was wrong: marriage is really the beginning of a great
many things: I can't keep from laughing when I think how much
lies in store for Marie-Angélique!". . . Whereupon she burst out
again with such lack of restraint that everyone stared at us strangely,
till I was quite put out of countenance, I assure you. Now tell me,
my dear, do you see anything droll in what your sister said?'

Cateau pressed his hand without speaking, and then went on
stroking it gently.

EPILOGUE

THE GRASSHOPPER AND THE ANT
(Ash Wednesday, February 6, 1704)

Epilogue

AS SOON AS MAGDELON WOKE SHE SAID TO HERSELF: 'THERE'S
something on my mind, something I've got to do today — I was
thinking about it last night, just before going to sleep — now, what
can it be?'... But of course it was gone: her mind was a jumble,
as it always was when she first awakened: she lay still in bed, trying
to bring order out of chaos, and forcing her thoughts to go back....
At least, she had plenty of leisure to try to remember, for it was
early yet, very early, not nearly time to get up. Her bed-curtains,
which she knew to be rose-coloured, hung grey and lifeless in the
dead, still air; the faint light filtering through them was grey, too....
What could have roused her at this hour of the night?... In a
moment that question was answered, for all the church bells in the
quarter started to ring.

The Feuillans began it (Magdelon always could pick out its thin,
fussy note from a dozen others); then the Jacobins and the Capuchins took it up, and the church of the convent of the Conception —
where her granddaughter Marie-Angélique lived. Finally the great
bell of Saint-Roch, almost next door, added its voice to the chorus,
loudest and most imperative of all. When Magdelon heard the bell
of Saint-Roch she rolled over in bed, and gave up hope of trying to
go back to sleep.... Bing-bang! Jingly-jang! Oh, dear, what a
racket it made! For almost a minute she could not think why the
bells were tolling; then the mists cleared from her brain and she
recalled what day it was. Lent was beginning today; there were
Masses all morning from five o'clock on.

Really, Magdelon reflected, as long as one could not be quiet any
longer, it would have been just as easy to get up and go to the five
o'clock service. But Cateau said that was too early: she had gone to
Mass at seven o'clock all her life, and had no intention of changing
her custom *now*. And as Magdelon lived with her sister, she had no
choice in the matter — she had to do what Cateau did, or else attend Mass by herself. The alternative of having it said in the Countess's oratory, with its pretty pink and white stucco decorations and
the Carlo Dolci Madonna over the altar, did not present itself to
either of them, since Cateau would not, and Magdelon could not,
pay a priest to officiate privately.

Cateau, unfortunately, kind as she was about big things, was sometimes most unreasonable about little ones. Take the question of breakfast, for instance. Magdelon liked to have it as soon as she woke, on a tray in bed. It heartened her wonderfully, as nothing else could, if she swallowed a draught of hot coffee before getting up. But Cateau preferred to have *her* coffee served later in the blue cabinet, after she'd put on her dressing-gown and half made her toilet. And she insisted on Magdelon's joining her there; she said it was ridiculous not to breakfast together — think of the wicked expense of making two fires in the kitchen, when one would do perfectly well for them both!

So there it was — Magdelon had to give in on that as on so many other things. Beggars could not be choosers, and Magdelon could not forget that, if it had not been for Cateau, she would have been a beggar, or something very like it. Yes: if Cateau had not helped her in her hour of need, she did not know what she would have done — hopeless and friendless, with no money left and no place to lay her head. . . . Magdelon often thought about her life; now that there was not much else to do, she relived in imagination for hours at a time every day all that had happened to her and to those whom she'd loved. She supposed that that was a sign of age — old people were said always to dwell in the past — but she did not really feel old. She had lived day by day, one at a time, till the tale of the days reached the impressive total of seventy years — the biblical three-score-and-ten — but still she did not seem to herself like an old woman. What were white hair and wrinkles and the loss of a tooth or two, if one's heart remained almost uncomfortably young? Why, when one came to think . . . 'Come, now!' Magdelon admonished herself severely, 'this is too absurd! You're letting your mind wander, which is just what Cateau has told you dozens of times not to do.' . . . Very well, then: to prevent its flying off at a tangent first that way and then this, she would concentrate with firmness on the miraculous fact of her rescue by her sister. And perhaps, if she did that, it would come to her what it was she must remember.

Of all the horrors from which Cateau had saved her, homelessness was surely the worst. Magdelon had not had a real home of her own since Great Senneterre was sold, twenty years ago. The house in the rue de Richelieu had never been home. It was an Hôtel de la Ferté, but not *her* Hôtel de la Ferté. It had belonged to Henri and his wife; Gabrielle at least had made it quite clear that her husband's mother was allowed to live there on sufferance only.

Magdelon had hated it — but she had stayed on because there was nowhere else for her to go, and because it seemed to be her duty to give Chou-Chou the best background she could, in the circumstances.

She might, it was likely, have been there yet, if Chou-Chou had not got herself engaged to be married, quite on her own and totally unexpectedly, in the summer of '93, to the young Comte de Rabodanges. Everybody was pleased and surprised.... It was not an especially brilliant match, the Rabodanges being nobody in particular and certainly not overburdened with money. However, they did own a fine place near Argentan in Normandy, and César was a handsome lad and devoted to Chou-Chou; so that there could be no doubt that it was a love match. (It *must* have been, when one considered the pitiable dowry that was all her mother could manage to give her!)

With Chou-Chou married and settled, Magdelon felt that there was no further reason for her to remain in Paris. She could not afford to live there alone — and people told her that the provinces were cheaper.... So she tried Normandy for a while herself, going to Caen, where she settled at first at the Hôtel de Beuvron — which Cateau kindly lent her —; then, later, at various convents, when it seemed wiser not to attempt to keep house at all. But the experiment had not been a success. Money appeared to be quite as necessary in Caen as in Paris; debts and taxes had a way of following her wherever she went. And Magdelon was bored and lonely, so far from her family. Moreover, the damp Norman winters were bad for her health; she suffered a great deal from rheumatism.

After a few months she began writing letters to everyone, to say how unhappy she was. She wrote to her sister, her sons and her daughters, her few remaining old friends; to her creditors, also, and the tax collectors; in the end, even to Madame de Maintenon and the King — throwing herself on their mercy, complaining, explaining, luxuriating in her expression of her sense of self-pity. These letters became her chief interest. During the years that she spent in Caen she wrote literally hundreds of them — more than in all the rest of her life put together.

Cateau, she knew, had been troubled by those that came her way. It had been reported to Magdelon by her daughter-in-law — who loved spreading unpleasant news — that the Countess had said to Fervaques: 'My dear, it's too dreadful — they're just like the letters of a professional beggar! But what can we do? There's no use sending money....'

Nor was there. On that score, in her heart of hearts, Magdelon was obliged to agree with her sister. She realized that Cateau's insensibility to her pleas was not caused by an inherent unwillingness to help her financially. She *had* helped her in the past, over and over again — with the same result always: Magdelon spent at once what was sent her, or gave it away to her family, and within a few weeks was as badly off as before.

The only real solution seemed to be for the sisters to join forces; and that Magdelon steadfastly refused to do, in spite of Cateau's repeated urgings. She might never have changed her mind, if something had not happened to alter Cateau's manner of living, with dramatic swiftness. Fervaques died in May, 1698, very suddenly, at Cosne, on his way back from the Baths of Bourbon, where he had been taking the cure. The blow was entirely unexpected: he was only fifty-three years old and had been enjoying his usual health, as far as anyone could tell, up to the end. . . . Cateau was completely broken by his death. It was her need of Magdelon, rather than Magdelon's need of Cateau, that finally brought the two together.

The Countess gave up her house in the rue de la Sourdière — she could not bear to continue alone there, where she and her lover had lived for so many years — and hired an hôtel in the rue Neuve-Saint-Honoré instead, in the same quarter, only a few doors away from her old home. The new house was enormous, much bigger than she needed; but she was used to big houses. Besides, she had by this time acquired so many possessions — such limitless stores of furniture and pictures and statues and tapestries and art objects of all kinds — that she had to find place for them somewhere. However, she had no sooner signed the lease than the air was filled with wails about the extravagant size of the premises . . . and how she was ever going to be able to afford to live there, in what she dourly referred to as 'straitened circumstances.' For Fervaques, much to her chagrin, had not made her his chief legatee. He had, to be sure, turned over a good deal of his property to her during his lifetime — more, in fact, his lawyers contended, than he should have done or than she had any right to expect. But after his death, when the will was opened, it was discovered that the lion's share of his estate had been left to Doudou de Ventadour.

Cateau was furious. For a time her anger at having been 'cut off with a penny' almost outweighed her grief at her lover's death. . . . 'I can't imagine *what* he was thinking of!' she exclaimed, with acidulated violence; and, 'A hussy like that!'; and, 'I'll be driven into the street, that's what'll be the end of it!'

Of course, the end had been nothing of the kind. Madame d'Olonne was one of the wealthiest women in France. Immediately after Fervaques' decease she had engaged a competent steward, Hubert Letors, to manage her affairs; and his first act in her employment had considerably eased her fears of future penury: he had leased one whole wing of the house in the rue Neuve-Saint-Honoré to Madame de Puyssègue, a rich widow from the country. Nevertheless, it was undeniable that, even after that, there was much more space than the Countess could use. She wrote to Magdelon to that effect, saying that her sister would really be doing her a kindness by coming to live with her. She was so lonely and unhappy. . . .

Hence, at last, Magdelon gave in and came back to Paris to join Cateau. Cateau gave her a charming apartment at the back of the house on the same storey as her own. There were six fine rooms, handsomely furnished. Cateau had spared no expense on them. She asked no rent, either — no compensation whatever — the sole stipulation being that her tenant should sign a paper before the steward Letors and Maître Le Caron, stating explicitly that the contents of the rooms belonged to the Comtesse d'Olonne. That, Cateau maintained, was unfortunately absolutely necessary, since Magdelon was so careless of her possessions, and had such a fatal propensity for giving things away, that, unless stringent precautions were taken, the apartment would be as bare as a bone in less than a twelvemonth. . . . Magdelon had understood. She had been very grateful to Cateau for taking her in and giving her such a beautiful place to live in, and unutterably glad, after the dreary years of exile, to find herself once more with her sister.

Naturally, it was not all plain sailing. There were various small difficulties to be smoothed over here and there. Cateau was growing old, and set in her ways: she had done what she liked with everyone about everything for so long that she had become a trifle despotic. Magdelon was old, too — but it had been years since she'd had her way about anything at all. Besides, she was gentle and yielding by nature: she would always, or very nearly always, rather give in than fight for her rights. So, on the whole, they'd got along well enough. They were alone together at the end of their lives, as they had been at the beginning. That seemed right, somehow, for sisters who had always been as devoted to each other as she and Cateau. . . . Time passed. . . . One . . . two . . . it was going on three years now since Magdelon had come to live at the house in the rue Neuve-Saint-Honoré. . . .

(Was it time to get up? The bells had stopped ringing, and the light coming through the bed-curtains was no longer grey, but a pale, cold ash-blue. But there were still no steps to be heard in the adjoining chamber, where Marton, the Maréchale's maid, was sleeping. If Marton were not yet about, then Magdelon might as well relax for a few more minutes' rest. And she must think again, think as hard as she could; for she had not, up to now, succeeded in remembering what it was that she had to do today, that had seemed so important the night before. What could it be? . . . It had evidently not to do with Cateau, or her life with Cateau. Well, then, there was the rest of her family. . . .)

During these difficult years there had been no let-up in the succession of calamities that pursued the hapless La Fertés. Marie-Angélique, the doll wife, was now a doll widow, having lost her husband in 1699, when he was not yet forty and she was barely twenty-three. She was left childless and very badly off. Owing to some legal quirk in the wording of her marriage contract she had been unable to recover her dowry, and therefore was forced to retire from the world. She lived, from motives of economy, at the convent of the Conception, not a stone's throw from her great-aunt and her grandmother.

Shortly before this bereavement Marie-Angélique's sister Catherine had got married — and that marriage, both Cateau and Magdelon considered, was the worst disgrace that had yet befallen the family. It was all Gabrielle's doing, of course. Despairing of snaring a suitable husband for the portionless Mademoiselle de Menetou, the Duchess had cooked up an infamous plan, with the aid of her friend Monsieur, the Duc d'Orléans, whereby an alliance was to be made between her daughter and La Carte, the captain of Monsieur's body-guard. La Carte was a cipher, with neither money nor family behind him; he was merely the latest in the long series of pretty painted young men infesting the Palais Royal, who owed their rapid advancement to the peculiar tastes of the King's brother. But La Carte was assuredly the most presumptuous of the lot. He not only aspired to the hand of a duke's daughter, but saw no reason why he should not succeed to his fiancée's family title as well: he was to change his name, forsooth, and be known henceforward, by royal decree, as the Marquis de la Ferté!

Raucous and shrill were the cries of dismay amongst Magdelon's children when this terrible news was announced. Henri, the bride's father, threatened to horsewhip the insolent puppy in public; Jules, her uncle, used such abusive and menacing language to his sister-in-law that Gabrielle, quaking with fright, had recourse to the law to protect her: she had the Chevalier bound by the chief of police to hold the peace. In the end, in spite of frantic opposition from the whole family, the shabby deal was put through. The wedding was held in semi-regal state at Saint-Cloud; the new Marquis and Marquise de la Ferté were formally presented to the King; and Monsieur promised to settle a fortune on his perfumed pet and to further all his ambitions both at court and in the army.

'You'll see,' Cateau predicted sourly to her sister, 'no good will come of this shocking affair.'

In a very short time they *had* seen: Monsieur, sole mentor of the bridal pair, fell flat to the floor of his palace, one warm evening in June, 1701, stricken by apoplexy. He died without recovering consciousness, leaving Gabrielle raging and Catherine in an anomalous position — with an impossible husband and no discernible social or financial future.

Could anything more happen to sadden Magdelon's old age? . . .

Yes, it could: within a year she lost both her eldest and her youngest sons.

Jules was the first to go. He'd always been a burden to his mother — a worthless and dissolute young man, whose chequered career had contained all manner of discreditable adventures, beginning with the dreadful time he'd been arrested at the castle of Nantes in Brittany, in the midst of his military service, accused of stealing his commandant's table silver!... From then on Jules had gone steadily from bad to worse. His violent actions at the time of Catherine's wedding led his mother to fear that he was not quite sane. At last there seemed to be nothing to do except ask the King to take him into custody. The poor fellow was kept for a while in Dijon, then sent to the south of France, whence he embarked for Malta in October, 1702.... The felucca in which he set sail was lost in a storm in the Straits of Messina — and that was the end of the Chevalier de la Ferté.

Even Magdelon, though her heart ached for the fate of her wayward son, could not help feeling that perhaps it was for the best.

The following August, Henri died of dropsy at the age of forty-six: failing male heirs, the duchy became extinct at his death. (That was one thing Magdelon meant to do today: have Masses said for the souls of her sons.... 'Dear God in Heaven, forgive them, and show them Thy mercy!'...)

Magdelon had great faith in God's forgiveness. See what He had done for *her!* He had sustained her through all her misfortunes. Again and again, in the last dozen years, when human consolation proved unavailing, the Lord had come to her aid as no one else could.... Cateau had at first been scornful and incredulous. She had not been able to understand what was happening to her sister.... 'Poor Cateau!' thought Magdelon tolerantly. 'If only she could be brought to see things as I do! If only religion could be a comfort to her!'

It was so simple, really, when you came to think of it. Magdelon was a child of light. *Everyone* was a child of light. Whatever became of you, that much you could count on, to the end of your days. To be sure, Magdelon had strayed from the path of righteousness — but at least she had known at the time that she *was* straying — had realized dimly, in the midst of her worst transgressions, that she would some day be sorry for what she had done.... Now she *was* sorry; she had told God she was sorry; and He had accepted her act of contrition and forgiven her. Oh, the bliss beyond measure of being at peace with your Maker at last! There was nothing to regret, nothing to be afraid of any longer. You had only to accept what came as meekly and bravely as possible, conscious that you were in God's hands, that He alone knew what was best for you; that all your doubts and perplexities would vanish when you got to Heaven (as you would, assuredly, quite soon), and everything was made radiantly clear forevermore.

Meanwhile, the infinite charm and variety of the religious life enchanted the penitent. For the truly devout, there could never be a dull moment. Why did not everyone see this? ... Magdelon's delight dated from the early days of her conversion, when she recounted her sins (as it was her duty to do) to her father confessor. Once she'd begun there was no stopping her; she went on for hours and hours, always recalling some new enormity when she feared the interest of her audience might be flagging — until finally poor Monsieur Coignet, the vicar of Saint-Roch, had all but fainted, there in the confessional, from sheer fatigue.

But that was only the beginning. Thenceforth she indulged in numberless soul-probing, soul-satisfying talks with the vicar and with her son Louis, now a full-fledged Jesuit, Father de la Ferté, and one of the glories of the Order. She had entered, also, with enthusiasm on a programme of acts of contrition and mortification; fasted and feasted in strict accordance with the laws of the church; wore hair-shirts during Lent; even had herself birched occasionally. (Cateau had screamed with laughter when she heard of the birchings; then said scathingly that perhaps it might be good for the circulation.) Magdelon spent much time, too, working for various societies for the alleviation of poverty in the parish and missions for the propagation of the faith. In fact, she became so passionately interested in these that she gave them the greater part of her income, sometimes even more than she had to give. Cateau complained frequently that Magdelon was far more extravagant now than she had been in her worldly days — that she squandered much more substantial sums on 'those wretched sodalities' than ever she'd done on gowns and jewels and lovers.

Be that as it might, Magdelon had no regrets for the past. Religion made up to her for all else that was lacking in her life. She was sorry only that Cateau persisted in holding aloof from the church. Cateau gave to God what she conceived to be God's due — not a penny more! To God's steward, who was Monsieur Coignet, she handed over divers amounts at stated intervals, to be disbursed as he pleased to the poor of the parish. But beyond these amounts she refused to give rein to charitable impulses. Magdelon thought she was wrong about that. Cateau was so rich, she had such masses of gold stored away in vaults at the bank, that she could not possibly spend it all. Why, in an ordinary year, the income alone of her income sufficed for her needs! Magdelon had often heard her sister boast of that fact. It was really rather frightening to think of all that gold. What on earth could she want with so much? She had neither chick nor child to bequeath it to! Surely it would be better to lay up treasure in Heaven instead of the savings-bank and let Monsieur Coignet have the little he asked for to buy that new organ for Saint-Roch! — Ah — and *there* it was at last, the thing she'd been trying so hard to remember, the thing she'd told herself she must do that day without fail! It was the organ, of course; she'd promised Monsieur Coignet she would help him persuade her sister that it was her duty to give him the splendid new instrument from Holland he had heard about, with its hundreds of pipes that could simulate every musical sound in nature, from the singing of birds to the crashing of thunderbolts.... Magdelon had been bold enough to broach the subject at supper last night: she would not soon forget how Cateau's mouth had tightened at the corners, and her eyes had looked cold as steel as she rapped out her answer: 'What nonsense! The old organ's quite good enough for me! And what's good enough for me ought, I presume, to do for your friend Louis Coignet!'

After that, Magdelon had not dared say any more, though she was longing to do so. But she would return to the charge today, never fear. She would keep her word to dear Monsieur Coignet.... 'I mustn't forget, though, again, what it is ... I simply *mustn't* forget ...!'

Now the church bells were ringing again. The light through the curtains was growing stronger and stronger. And there, at last, was Marton's step on the parquet.

Marton entered the room on tiptoe, for fear her mistress might be sleeping, and drew back the draperies of Magdelon's bed deftly with one hand; in the other she was holding a lighted candle in a silver candlestick.

'Good morning, madam,' said Marton. She smiled as she said it: Marton was a pretty creature, and young, not more than eighteen. Magdelon had always liked her maids to be young and pretty. She grew fond of them, too; when they married, which invariably happened before very long, she cried as she bade them good-bye and gave them fifty gold-pieces to invest in their trousseaux.

'Good morning, Marton,' said Magdelon, eying the maid kindly and thinking, with a touch of melancholy, that *this one* would surely be announcing her betrothal any day now, she had such bright eyes and plump rosy cheeks. 'Is my sister awake?'

'Oh, yes, madam — she's been up for an hour or more, going over the household accounts by the fire in the blue cabinet.'

Magdelon shivered. That was another of Cateau's pet economies: she would never have a fire laid in her bedroom, no matter how cold the weather might be, but dressed by preference in a freezing apartment, and then sought sanctuary in the room where she intended to spend the morning.

'My child, is it very cold today?'

'Well, madam, the sky's quite clear, as far as I can tell; but the trees in the court are all covered with frost — you'd best wear your fur tippet to Mass.'

Magdelon shivered again, and told Marton to dress her as fast as she could. She did not dare have a fire in *her* bedroom either — if Cateau had come to hear of it, there'd have been a fearful scene — but the charcoal brazier Marton fetched in provided a modicum of heat. By the time she was dressed the slight exertion had warmed Magdelon enough so that the pink had deserted her nose, where she didn't want it, and invaded her cheeks, where she did.... She put on her best black serge gown and a black lace mantilla with a high starched frill in front that only partly covered her abundant white curls. (Widows did not wear bandeaux any more. Magdelon thought that it was just as well. They had never become her... Besides, if one had good hair, why not show it?)

When she was fully attired Quentine tapped on the door to say that the Countess was waiting in the blue cabinet for her sister: they would drink a cup of mint-tea together before proceeding to church. It was, of course, rather daring of them to drink anything at all. The rules prescribed a strict fast on communion days, but Cateau had declared roundly, in the beginning of their life together, that, communion or no communion, she would *not* go out in the cold without something hot in her stomach; and Magdelon had succeeded in getting a special dispensation from Monsieur Coignet.... Kind Monsieur Coignet! He'd understood at once, and had pronounced their favourite beverage a 'medicine necessary to the maintenance of health.'

Magdelon followed Quentine through the chilly hall to her sister's rooms at the front of the house on the other side of the court. She walked a little stiffly, as she had a right to do, having passed her seventieth birthday. But Quentine, who must certainly be much younger — probably not more than sixty-five — was scarcely able to hobble. The gay little Norman soubrette of fifty years ago had turned into a shapeless and hideous crone. Not even Mahaut, Maman's old servant, had ever appeared so impossibly ancient as poor Quentine.

The fire in the blue cabinet was burning briskly; Cateau, sitting beside it, was already sipping her tea. She was dressed exactly like Magdelon, and she looked exactly like her, too. After years of comparative individuality the sisters had strangely recaptured their lost identity with each other. Cateau had gained a little weight, Magdelon had lost a little; now that they were old the fine bone structure of the heart-shaped faces stood out with striking similarity. Even their hair was the same.... Who could say which mass of high-brushed snowy curls had once been molten gold, which black as the raven's wing? . . . But for the colour of their eyes, it would have been impossible to tell the Comtesse d'Olonne from the Maréchale de la Ferté.

Magdelon bent to kiss her sister, and then sat down on the opposite side of the small square table in front of the fire. She had meant to say something immediately about Monsieur Coignet's new organ — in fact, all the time she was being dressed by Marton she'd been repeating to herself: 'The organ — the organ — don't, whatever you do, forget about the organ!' But no sooner had she entered the room than she received a shock that drove the matter quite out of her mind.

From the moment she came in she realized that something was missing from the blue cabinet, though she could not tell at first what it might be. The blue cabinet was a kind of comfortable refuge from the vast gilded wilderness of the rest of the house. It was the only one of the Countess's rooms that was not filled with chairs that weren't sat in, clocks that weren't wound, carpets never stepped on, and books never read. Cateau really lived in this cosy oval chamber. Here she had gathered together a few of her most cherished possessions: the mother-of-pearl writing-table from the Chinese cabinet in the rue de la Sourdière, a quaint old couch that had been her mother's, the Bergamo tapestries once displayed on the walls of the Hôtel de Rouen. She had also assembled a fine collection of oriental porcelains, a favourite picture or two. . . . Ah, that was it! It was a picture that was missing! Where was the likeness of Cateau and Magdelon as young girls, the famous double portrait that had once proved a bone of contention — the only one they had ever known — between them? For years now it had hung over the mantel in this little room, to Magdelon's profound satisfaction. She never passed beneath it without admiring it, wistfully but happily. . . . It was their most precious souvenir of the past; naught else save that canvas remembered their youth. . . . And now, overnight, it was gone, in its place a stiff, oily Flemish flower-piece the Countess had bought at an auction only last week.

'Sister,' cried Magdelon, 'our portrait — what's happened to it?'

'Nothing's happened,' replied Cateau, tranquilly continuing to sip her mint-tea.

'But where is it, then? Where else did you hang it?'

'I didn't hang it anywhere else,' said Cateau, with a touch of tartness. 'I gave it away.'

'Gave it away!' echoed Magdelon blankly. 'To whom? Oh, Cateau, to whom did you give it?'

'To President Foucault,' said Cateau. 'He was here yesterday afternoon to see me about some business connected with my properties in Caen, and admired it extravagantly. He's been useful to us more than once in our affairs, so I told him I'd make him a present of the picture if he liked — and last night I had it packed up and sent to him with compliments from us both.'

'But why, dear, *why?* How could you let it go?'

Cateau's lip curled in scorn.

'That 'old thing! Did it mean so much to you?'

'You know it did! Oh, Cateau, you know it! Why, I cared for it more than for any picture we had! Darling, how *could* you?'

Cateau shrugged her shoulders in affected bewilderment — at least, Magdelon felt that it must be affected. 'Child, how foolish you are! What in Heaven's name was the good of keeping that silly, simpering daub about to remind us of what we were once? I've no children to leave it to; there's no one to come after us who'll care how we looked when we were young. Best get rid of the thing and all our old memories!'

She spoke so curtly that Magdelon feared she might be going to be angry — and that, the doctors said, was at all costs to be avoided. The Countess had lately been troubled with giddy spells and accessions of great fatigue; her physicians had cautioned her to rest as much as possible and to eschew undue emotional stress. . . . Magdelon therefore forbore to mention, as she might otherwise have done, that the portrait was as much hers as her sister's — *she* still had heirs who might have been glad to inherit it — Cateau really hadn't had the right to give it away on an impulse without permission.

Magdelon opened her lips, and then shut them again.

'I mustn't say anything,' she thought.

After all, it did not do to forget that Cateau was already in her seventy-second year, which of course was very, very much older than just past seventy. Besides, something in the tight, drawn expression of her mouth smote Magdelon's heart even more poignantly than her deep concern for her sister's health. As she looked at that mouth and at Cateau's hands — which the latter kept covered with black lace mitts, less to ward off the cold than because she could not bear to see what time had done to them — Magdelon realized, as never before, that she herself was the luckier of the two. Yes, in spite of all . . . for, to her, beauty had been simply a means of achieving life; while, to Cateau, it had been an end in itself. In losing it Cateau had lost everything.

Thus Magdelon mused as she slowly drank her tea, keeping her silence unbroken until she had mastered her feelings, for fear of upbraiding the sister who had done so much for her. It would be better, she felt, to dismiss the subject of the portrait altogether and change to something more cheerful.

'Louis is dining with us today,' she said, after a little.

But that did not appear to be a fortunate choice.

'Then we'll have to order a fish,' said Cateau, clucking with dismay. 'I wish you'd told me before; I'd planned a light meal of eggs and cheese for the two of us. Louis is always so monstrously hungry. He's just like his brother — I maintain that Henri would be living today if he'd been willing to curb his appetite. Whom else have you asked, sister? You'd better make out the list at once, instead of springing the names on me, one by one, the whole morning through.'

'You know I never spring people on you,' retorted Magdelon, with some show of spirit. 'And anyhow, even if I wanted to, whom would I spring? There's nobody but Louis I *could* ask.'

This was only too true. Marie-Angélique, who observed the strict rule of her convent, never left it for meals. Tinette and Chou-Chou and their husbands and children lived in the country. Gabrielle and her idolized Catherine were generally at Versailles — and, in any case, seldom deigned to pay a call on their antique relatives. But, worse than that, Cateau and Magdelon had no one left outside their family. Being slightly younger than most of their generation, they had managed to outlive the lot. All their friends and their rivals were dead — all the brave and gallant young men who had loved them — vanished as completely as yesteryear's snows. The house in the rue Neuve-Saint-Honoré was peopled largely by ghosts. . . .

Magdelon liked these ghosts; she thought of them fondly and often. She loved to recall this one's face, that one's voice — a turn of phrase, a characteristic laugh, that had endeared their owners to her in life. Her mind, too, forgetful of most things, was a matchless necrologist: she was forever saying: 'Cécile de Montglas died eight years ago last Tuesday,' or, 'It'll be four years next October 16 since Gilette de Fiesque left us.' . . . But that, also, was a subject best avoided today.

'Well, of course, darling,' she said pacifically, 'I *had* thought a little of asking the vicar, dear Monsieur Coignet. But I'm afraid . . . that is, if you'd rather I didn't . . .'

Cateau tossed her head.

'Coignet's an ass!' she said tersely. 'I told him so yesterday, when he came whining to me to try to coax me to give the money to buy that damned new-fangled organ. He knows what I think of him and his puling, puttering ways. Why, there's not a parish in Paris as badly managed as ours! If I've said it to him once, I've said it a hundred times. I've told him over and over: "*I* could put things on a businesslike basis. Leave it to *me*, and, with my steward's help, in a month we'd eliminate your ridiculous waste and stupid duplication of effort." But do you think he will listen? Oh, well, my dear,

never mind: if you want to ask him to dine, it's a matter of indifference to me. Have him by all means, if it would give you pleasure. I
suppose perhaps Louis would be glad to meet our vicar.'

'Oh, yes, dear, he would!' cried Magdelon happily. 'He thinks
Monsieur Coignet a splendid Christian. And so he is — and a good,
kind man as well — truly, Cateau!'

Magdelon clasped her hands together eagerly, just as she had
done ever since she was a very little girl.

Cateau gave her a softened glance. 'Well, have it your way, child
— perhaps he is! You really like everyone, don't you?'

Magdelon considered a moment.

'Why — I suppose I do!' she answered, with gentle surprise.
'Don't you, dear?'

'Everyone but fools!' was the Comtesse d'Olonne's crushing re-
joinder, as the bells of Saint-Roch began pealing a third time to call
the faithful to the seven o'clock services.

There was a flurry of excitement getting the ladies ready for
church. Cloaks and veils, muffs and prayer-books, fur tippets and
footwarmers were rapidly collected. Pretty young Marton and ugly
old Quentine fetched candles to carry, for it was still quite dark outside. Cateau issued commands in a shrewish soprano, made a
frightful scene in the midst of the bustle when Quentine inadvertently let a drop of candle-grease fall on her mistress's foot. . . . Then,
just as they were on the point of leaving, the Countess decided that
it would be better to order dinner before they went. Félix, the chef,
was summoned in a hurry, and a detailed discussion ensued concerning the menu. Finally it grew so late that Magdelon was emboldened
to remind her sister that they would be shut out unless they made
haste. As they descended the stairs Cateau was still calling over her
shoulder minute directions about the best way to boil carp in Cha-
blis. . . .

It was cold outdoors, bitterly cold, although no air was stirring.
Their breath went straight up in small frosty puffs; the flames of
the candles the maids were carrying scarcely quivered in the blue
morning gloom. They were late, too, as Magdelon had known
they would be; they had to scramble along as fast as they were able.
That was all right for Cateau, whose wind was good; but Magdelon,
who suffered somewhat from breathlessness and nervous flutterings
of the heart, had trouble keeping up with her indomitable sister. As
she pattered down the cheerless street she could not help thinking
how pleasant it would be if Cateau sometimes ordered the carriage
to take them to church. She always said, when Magdelon suggested
it, that Saint-Roch was too near, it wasn't worth the bother of having the horses harnessed; but Magdelon knew the real reason was
that Cateau did not want to go to the expense of keeping her coach

in commission during the winter months.... Not that she wouldn't, on occasion, alter her policy. She had driven all across town, four Sundays in a row, the year when Father de la Ferté had preached during Advent at Saint Paul's in the Marais.... Dear Louis! Magdelon would never forget her pride in him then, which Cateau had shared to the full. (They had even, one Sunday, persuaded poor Henri to go with them — though that had been hardly a successful experiment. The Duke had snored out loud in church; and when his mother asked him afterwards how he liked his brother's sermon, he had replied, with a graceless grin: 'The actor was fine, but the play was rotten!')

That was all nonsense, though: nobody preached better than Louis. Hadn't the fathers once wanted to send him to Canada to convert the heathen? (Thank fortune, their project had not gone through! Magdelon felt she could not have borne it if Louis had been taken from her.) It was only a pity that he could not be in the pulpit this morning, for Monsieur Coignet, the best and most pious of men, was by no means an impressive speaker. Those cheerful, prosaic little homilies, delivered in his high nasal bleat, went in one ear, Cateau was wont to declare, and straight out the other — and Magdelon reluctantly agreed with her....

Here they were at last — not hopelessly late, after all. The doors were still open, even though the bells had stopped ringing.

Cateau and Magdelon paused on the threshold to adjust their black veils.

'And what's to be our friend's subject today?' inquired the former, with a gleam of sardonic amusement.

'I believe, dear, we're to have a talk on repentance,' answered Magdelon, stooping to dip her fingers in the font of holy water that stood just inside the entrance.

'Repentance!' said Cateau. 'Ha! That's very good. Repentance, indeed!'

She snapped her mouth shut on the word as though it were something she had caught in a trap; and her eyes as she led the way up the aisle were bright and mutinous with mischief.

Magdelon never knew afterwards how they got home. She had no clear recollection either of walking herself, or of Cateau's walking.... Yet they must have done so, for when at length they came to themselves, so to speak, they were back in the blue cabinet, staring at each other like spectres across the square table where, only an hour before, they had drunk their mint-tea. The fire on the hearth was still burning briskly; the room looked precisely the same, except that the candles weren't lighted any more, and the mysterious light of dawn had given place to the clear, discreet all-over-greyness of a

Paris winter day. How could it not have changed, too? . . . when one thought . . .

Magdelon found she was crying slightly. She put her black-bordered handkerchief to her eyes.

'But, my dear, it was terrible — *terrible!*'

She felt shaken to the roots of her being; she could tell, by looking at her, that Cateau was shaken, too.

The best indication of this was the latter's silence. Cateau, the fluent — Cateau, the voluble — who never lacked the right word in the right place (and sometimes the right word was a euphemism for several thousand of them) — was gazing speechlessly at her sister. Her face was blanched as white as milk, her large light eyes, wide with horror, seemed fixed, not on Magdelon, but at some hideous vision that lay behind and beyond her. Magdelon, however, knew well enough what the vision was: it was the same one that she herself saw, just as she was sure that Cateau's horrified expression was merely the duplicate of the blind terror stamped full across her own countenance. (To regard each other now was more than ever like looking into a mirror.) . . . Oh, would they ever be able to see anything else as long as they lived? How could they hope to escape the remembrance of the dire prospect the priest had disclosed of the tortures lying in wait for sinners like them?

Magdelon would have given all she possessed to forget what she had heard, to return to the comforting prosiness of dear, dull Monsieur Coignet. Why had he been absent this morning? And who was the stern dark young stranger that had taken his place and thundered such relentless denunciations from the pulpit? Merciful God! What a picture he had painted of the punishments in store for the damned! . . . They would burn in dreadful Hell fire, till they could not bear the agony of the flames another moment, yet there would be no release: even unconsciousness could not save them, who were all-conscious forever. Or perhaps they would freeze with a cold beyond human imagining — a cold as much worse than the cold on earth as the heat in Hell was worse than the heat they knew — and this torture, also, would be endless. There was no alleviation in sight, there could be none, to the end of time, and beyond it. . . . Time was not in Hell. Only Eternity existed there, Eternity compared to which life on earth was the briefest of spans, a fugitive flash, a breath drawn and exhaled in a moment. But the worst pain of all, the preacher had said, would be the recollection of their sins committed in life. They would remember each and every one, with searing clarity; and so would the demons who scourged them, and the other damned souls who shared their suffering. Everybody would know everything they had done; there'd be no place to hide from the cruel, revealing glare; they'd be exposed as the sinners they were, and reviled for their

sinning gibed at and taunted by mocking voices. And that punishment, like the others, was to be limitless. There could be no
respite from the stabs of conscience — no possible penitence — no
chance to go back and set right the wrongs one was guilty of — in
fine, no faintest ray of hope anywhere!

'Too late! Too late!' The preacher's cry echoed in Magdelon's
brain. She put her hands to her ears to shut out the sound — but the
accusing roar only increased in volume.

Ah, what should they do? For they were sinners, she and Cateau
— there was no doubt of it — the stern dark young priest's sermon
might have been meant for them alone. Magdelon realized it only
too well; she was sure Cateau realized it, too. They had been imbe-
ciles to suppose that God would overlook their transgressions. How
could a few prayers, some paltry bits of gold doled out to this convent, that church, be expected to compensate for the years of deliberate wickedness that lay behind them? God was not mocked; He saw
that their hearts were not penitent — that pride and self-love still
lurked there. (Magdelon felt almost like blaming dear Louis and
Monsieur Coignet for allowing her to dwell so many years in a facti-
tious fool's paradise . . . when all along, if she'd been shown reality
and made to face it . . .)

She and her sister had been given good gifts — how had they used
them? It was hard to say which of them was most to blame: Cateau,
who had made her beauty an idol, sacrificing virtue and honour and
truth itself on its altar — or Magdelon, who had used hers wilfully
to secure all the love and excitement she wanted, beyond reason or
measure, till her store was quite spent?

Both of them, she now saw, had been led into grievous error by
their own compelling desires. Their lives, each in its way, were
monuments of vice and corruption.

Was it too late to repent? Was it useless to throw themselves on
their knees and cry out to Heaven: 'Lord, we have strayed from Thy
ways like lost sheep! We confess it. But we truly repent. Hear us,
Lord! We truly repent of our sins. Therefore, save us, in all humility we implore You, from the torments of everlasting damnation!'

The priest thought not. The priest thought it was never too late.
He had said positively that there would still be time, if one turned to
God on one's death-bed. There was the one bright beacon to follow;
for though they were old, Cateau and Magdelon were strong; life
abounded in them yet; they did not intend to die — but of course
they did not! — for many years to come. So perhaps . . .

Magdelon glanced at her sister again. She perceived that Cateau's
lips were muttering something she could not quite catch. (Strange
how people had taken lately to mouthing and mumbling, instead of
talking out loud!)

'What is it? Did you speak, dear?'

'Sister,' said Cateau solemnly — and this time she was plainly to be heard — 'we must repent, or we are lost!'

Magdelon nodded her head, with equal solemnity. So Cateau saw it, too . . .!

'Sister, I know it — but what shall we do? What *can* we do? If only I knew! . . .'

She began sobbing afresh and wringing her hands in despair.

Cateau raised her hand: she looked, Magdelon thought, like an admonishing sibyl, with her flowing black veils and pale, widened eyes.

'Don't go to pieces, whatever happens! That won't help matters. We've got to face this thing squarely. We're in it together, you and I. If I'm a sinner, Magdelon de la Ferté, so are you!'

'Oh, I know it! I know it!' Magdelon sobbed harder than ever. 'I've been far the wickeder of the two!'

'I don't know about that,' said Cateau, whose voice sounded stronger now and more controlled. 'You've been a deal more foolish than I, perhaps — but that's because you've no head. On the whole, I dare say I've been more to blame than you. I'm the elder — I had a better idea of what I was doing — and, say what you will, there's no blinking the fact that I lived twenty-seven years with a man who wasn't my legal husband!'

'But think of Longueville!' moaned Magdelon, rocking herself to and fro in an ecstasy of grief. 'Think of Longueville, sister, and my poor, beloved little Charles-Louis!'

'I *am* thinking of them,' said Cateau. 'And I'm thinking, too, of all the other men we loved, or who loved us — a cloud of witnesses to our misdeeds! They've gone to their judgement already. It's too late to save them. But it's not too late yet to save ourselves. We must give up everything we've got, Magdelon, and yield ourselves to God.'

'Give up everything?' quavered Magdelon. 'How do you mean, dear? Must we stop living in this house?'

'Certainly,' replied Cateau, who appeared to be regaining her poise with marvellous speed at the prospect of immediate action. 'At once! Who ever heard of penitents in a palace? I can cancel the lease at any time; there's a clause in the contract. . . . We'll move directly to the convent of the Conception, where Marie-Angélique is. I think it might be well for us to join the Order, too — though, come to think of it, I don't particularly care for their rule. Perhaps the Carmelites or the Feuillantines would be better.'

'Oh, I'd like to be a nun,' said Magdelon, nodding her head again, this time more hopefully. 'That's a lovely idea, Cateau. God would surely know we were sorry then, wouldn't He? But what would you do with your money, darling, and all the beautiful things you own?'

'The contents of my houses can be sold and the proceeds of the sale turned over to charity. As for my personal fortune, that must be given to the church, of course — or, rather, to whichever convent we decide to belong to. It's rather a ticklish question, isn't it? We want our gold to go where it will do the most good — and most cloistered women have no talent for business. I shall never forget that utter fool of a Superior at the convent in the rue Bouloi, where poor Maman died; their affairs were in such a shocking tangle that she never knew where the money was coming from to feed the sisters, from one week to the next. Twice when I was living there, I remember, I offered to straighten out her accounts. It took Maître Le Caron and me each time the better part of a fortnight.... Maybe it would be wiser not to join an Order ourselves. We could give the whole of our property to the sisters, and reserve an apartment in their house for our own use, so that we could come and go as we pleased, as the Duchesse de Longueville used to do in the old days at the Great Carmelites, and her mother, the dowager Princesse de Condé.... Yes, on the whole, I think that an excellent plan. Then, as we'd still be in the world, though not of it, we could control the disposition of our funds and make sure that they were spent in a sensible manner. I could even retain Letors in an advisory capacity. His judgement on investments is exceedingly sound.... You follow me, dear?'

'Yes, darling. At least, I think I do. You mean, you'd give all your money to the convent without actually entering the sisterhood. But then, if you had nothing left for yourself, how would we manage to live outside it?'

'That's true, Magdelon — perfectly true — why, I never thought of that! How stupid I am! Well, of course, we'd have to keep something back. Perhaps one-fourth of our capital, or a third ... Well, even *half* of it wouldn't be too much, do you think? After all, we've a certain position to maintain in society. People expect something of us. And if we'd nothing whatever of our own, we'd become a charge on your children, who could ill afford any added expense, as we very well know. Then, too, I've always found that you're much more apt to be regarded favourably if you've some money in the bank. As long as the good sisters think that they stand a chance of inheriting further bequests, they're far likelier to show us proper respect and to consider our wishes in the disbursement of funds. And, as I say, if we have our own rooms in the house — I think, don't you, we'd be entitled to ask for them, since we're prepared to be generous? — we can stop there as much as we like, make the retreats, and follow the rule whenever it suits us, besides keeping an eye on what goes on.... If only, my dear, I felt absolutely sure that our money would be properly used! Nothing does more harm, to my way of thinking, than misapplied charity. The prioresses I've had the ill-luck to meet since the turn of the century have been without exception poor creatures at best, as lacking in charm and personality as in sound common sense. Ah, the church has sadly degenerated, these last fifty years! Where are the successors to the great spiritual leaders we used to know — women like Mother Agnès de Jésus-Maria at the Carmelites, and dear, wonderful Angélique Arnauld of Port Royal?... My child, the more closely I examine the matter, the less certain I feel that we'd be doing right in abandoning what we have to the kind of weak-kneed, mealy-mouthed opportunists that clutter our convents nowadays. I really believe, if we want our resources to be employed to the fullest advantage, we'd best remain where we are and distribute them in person.'

'You mean — not give them to a convent at all? Not leave home at all? But, dearest, I don't quite see what ——'

'Why, the thing's simplicity itself! We can continue to give to charity as much as we like — even double our contributions, if necessary — though I must say, for the moment, I feel I am doing as much as I can afford, if not more. The harvest last year was wretched, you remember, and we've had so much cold weather since Christmas and so little snow that, unless the spring's unusually early, I fear most of my corn will be winter-killed. I get such discouraging reports every week from my bailiffs in Normandy!... But there, dear, I don't want to depress you unnecessarily. All I mean to suggest is that, for the present at any rate, it might be more prudent to draw in our horns a trifle, instead of reversing the process. Our duty actually is to regenerate our souls: it's a question, it seems to me, of spiritual rather than material change. I am positive we ought to be able to make ourselves over without altering our status in society. We can fast and pray — every day, if need be...'

'Oh, yes!' exclaimed Magdelon. 'We can fast and pray! Let's begin at once, shall we, Cateau?'

'Certainly, child; whenever you like.... Not perhaps till tomorrow, though, since Father de la Ferté is coming to dine and the carp-in-Chablis will go to waste if it's not eaten directly. But tomorrow we can start afresh on a régime of bread-and-water...'

'Every day?'

Cateau considered.

'Well, perhaps, not just at first. The transition might be too sudden, I fear. We must not forget, my love, we're neither of us so young as we once were. We must take care not to lose strength too rapidly, or we'll be very little good to God or anyone else! But I don't see why every *other* day... or at least once a week! Yes, by all means let us subsist on bread-and-water once a week regularly! It can not hurt us, and it will be splendid discipline for the servants. Naturally,

as far as you and I are concerned, we eat little enough, anyway. I
often think that a bird has a bigger appetite than I! A cup of beef-
broth and a crust are all I can stomach, more often than not. And I
must say, dear, you eat a great deal less heartily than you used to
do.... But if you could see what goes on in the kitchen the minute
our backs are turned! I went down there on purpose yesterday, just
when the chef was returning from market; for I'd heard rumours
from Quentine of the shocking extravagance below stairs. All I can
say is, you'd never believe what I found! Game out of season —
three brace of partridges and a hare — and a whole roast sucking-
pig, if you please!... Well, I'd half a mind to throw the fellow out
then and there! I fancy I'd have done it, too, if it hadn't been
Shrove Tuesday — I suppose people have a right to make merry
before Lent begins. But within reason! And really, with game at the
price they're asking this year, I was surprised and very angry to see
what Félix had bought. I told him so, too. I said quite plainly I
could tell he intended to ruin me as fast as he could. The rascal was
insolence itself. He knows he's the best cook in Paris.... I suppose
he thinks he's sure of keeping his post, whatever he does. But just
let it happen again ...! My dear, do you know, this thought occurs
to me. (It would pay Félix out, too, in the only way he'd understand!) ... Would it not answer just as well, to make peace with God,
if, instead of fasting ourselves, *we made our servants fast?*'

Cateau was delighted with her proposal; she seemed to feel that
she had hit upon the ideal solution of their dilemma. On the strength
of the brilliant new idea she even managed to rally her forces sufficiently to make a substantial breakfast, when Quentine, grumbling
and mumbling, brought a tray of coffee and rolls to the square
table in front of the fire.

After breakfast she read the weekly *Gazette* — or, rather, had it
read to her: Magdelon, who had the stronger eyes of the two, gabbled
the news aloud to her sister.... The *Gazette* was not always gay
matter for gossip, these days. Although the century was young, the
court had grown old; its circular lately had often been little more
than a series of death notices. Military bulletins, too, were less
encouraging than in the past, Louis XIV being, alas! no longer
invincible, while his enemies were more numerous and powerful
than ever as twilight fell over his long, proud reign. Magdelon was
thankful this morning to have neither deaths nor defeats to report.

When the reading was finished, Cateau retired to her bedroom to
change her dress. Before going she kissed Magdelon with her usual
warmth, then made for the door with more than usual briskness and
disappeared down the hall, followed by Quentine, who was still
grumbling and mumbling.... A minute later, Magdelon caught a
glimpse of her sister through the window on the other side of the

courtyard. Cateau saw Magdelon, also, and waved her hand almost blithely. Then Quentine drew the curtains, and the courtyard was grey and empty once more.

Magdelon, left alone, felt bruised and bewildered by the agitating events of the last few hours. She was still suffering from the effect of the words of the stern dark young priest; one did not quickly recover from such a shock. Nor was she perfectly satisfied that Cateau's great decision had succeeded in calming her fears. Cateau, she knew, had been frightened — almost as badly frightened as she was herself — yet within an incredibly short space of time she had managed to rally her forces and salve her conscience by what, when one came to examine it closely, was merely a trifling adjustment of diet. Could real salvation be purchased so cheaply?... Magdelon was troubled, unhappy, unsure of the future.... It would be good to talk it all over later with dear Louis, who would know how to settle her doubts, as he always did, and help her reconcile her moral scruples with the exigencies of daily life.

All the same... how splendid to be like Cateau, ever confident of oneself and one's ability to choose the right course of action! Cateau never seemed to have doubts like other people. Magdelon thought that that must be because she was so rich that she did not have to worry about anything or be afraid of anybody. It must be wonderful to be as rich as that — to be lifted, once and for all, above the necessity for shabby contrivances and still shabbier fears.... Magdelon did not want money so much for herself as for her children and grandchildren — all of them poor — all harassed by debt and petty, day-to-day anxieties. There was no end to the good things she would have done for them if she could.... But she was helpless, her hands were tied. Cateau, cannily foreseeing just such contingencies, had refused to give her even a tiny allowance to spend as she liked....

Then, suddenly, the thought flashed through her mind unbidden: What if Cateau should die and leave me her fortune? Not now — O Heaven! *not now!* — but some day far in the future.... Cateau had no heirs but her sister. She had no one else to inherit her gold; as a matter of fact, she had told Magdelon once that a will had been made in her favour....

But that was bad and disloyal — that was something not to be thought of — how could she hope for the death of the person who was closest to her in the world? God forgive me! said Magdelon to herself. She whispered a heartfelt prayer of remorse, made the sign of the cross; then rose creakily from her chair, dusted the crumbs from her black serge lap, and stacked the breakfast dishes on the tray Quentine had forgotten to remove: Cateau disliked above all things a table left in disorder.

Before leaving the blue cabinet she glanced once again through the window that gave on the court. It was empty no longer: some pigeons were fluttering there in the soft grey light. As she watched them idly one of the birds flew onto the window-sill, looking up at her with pert amber eyes with its head to one side, cooing as though pleading to be let come in.

Magdelon stretched out her hand to it involuntarily. She had always loved pigeons; they reminded her of her childhood and the old, happy days at La Louppe. But there was another memory somehow connected with them — something less clear and less happy, but almost equally remote.... What could it be? Once before in her life she had seen a pigeon through a window — not a white bird from the castle, but a plain, sooty Paris pigeon like this one.... Dimly she recalled a night at Cateau's house, the Hôtel d'Olonne in the rue Neuve-Saint-Augustin — oh, years and years ago it must have been! ...What...where?... No: it was gone now. She couldn't remember....

With a regretful shake of her head, that caused the lace frill of her bonnet to flutter like the pigeons' wings, Magdelon slowly quitted the room.

Cateau, meanwhile, in her own chamber had by degrees settled down into the peaceful rhythm of her morning routine. She had got out of her black church gown and bade Quentine dress her in a smart dead-leaf taffeta trimmed with Alençon lace. She hesitated for a moment over her jewel-box: there was a parure of topazes that went admirably with the dead-leaf taffeta. But, recalling the words of the preacher concerning the snares of vanity, she let the glittering chain drop back into its velvet-lined cubby-hole and turned the key in the lock.

After she was dressed she had a spirited quarrel with Quentine, who had forgotten to dust Madame d'Olonne's priceless collection of Dresden china — worse still, on detailed inspection one of the figures, a round, rosy cupid with bow-and-arrow, appeared to be slightly chipped!... The Countess scolded her serving-woman shrilly, though she got as good as she gave: all domestic tyrants have at least one person in their household who refuses to be afraid of them, and in Cateau's case Quentine was that person.

She enjoyed the fight, though; by the time the maid had stamped off to the china-mender's the mistress was her old self again. She had quite got over her strange accession of weakness. How glad she was that she'd not allowed the sermon to stampede her into a panic! For a moment, indeed, she'd gone dizzy with fright, like poor Magdelon. There was no harm in admitting it, now it was over. At the stern young priest's words horrid black abysses had seemed to open beneath her trembling feet. It had taken all her courage and resolution and native good sense to struggle back to sanity. But she *had* struggled, and she had won. With the victory hers, she was able to view the incident calmly in its true perspective.... Yes, incident; nothing more. Cateau suspected that it might well have been a put-up job, all along. Very likely Monsieur Coignet had hired that explosive young man on purpose to frighten her. There was no doubt that the latter's incendiary phrases had appeared to be aimed straight at her and Magdelon.... Yes, the longer she thought about it, the more thorough was her conviction that that ass Coignet had hoped to get even with her and settle old scores with his enemy in this new and devastating fashion. He knew only too well his own tiresome twaddle would have no effect, so he had fetched that young firebrand to do what he himself was unable to.... Very well, *very well!* But if he supposed he could conquer her thus, he was finely mistaken. Cateau d'Olonne was no coward to collapse at the prospect of Hell fire and brimstone! Certainly not! She had stood her ground gamely and was able, now, to laugh at his clumsy manœuvres.... 'Well, I don't say I won't give him his silly old organ,' said Cateau to herself. 'But not to please *him* — no, never! — not in a million years! It would make poor darling Magdelon so happy....'

Having settled it all to her own satisfaction, she trailed across to her bedroom windows at the front of the house, flung back the casement, and stood there looking down on the city below. The church bells were ringing again. Loudly and insistently they chimed, an accusing chorus, filling the air with their clamour — the air that was so still and dead that, for all the bells' noise, they might have been sounding under the sea.

Cateau paid no heed to their accusation. Proud and erect she posed in her taffeta gown, her white head unbowed, her eyes wide and unfocussed. Her breath rose and fell in little gasps, no longer from fear, but merely because the February day was cold. She was not thinking any more of the stern young man and his terrible sermon, nor of the ignoble machinations of Monsieur Coignet. She had forgotten Quentine's clumsiness and the incredible insolence of Félix, the chef. Even Magdelon's muddles retired to the background, as well as the uneasy suspicion that sometimes assailed her, when she reflected on them, that in spite of all her mistakes and misfortunes her sister had got more out of life than she herself had. The past was erased no less completely than the present. As for the future, she faced it stoically, incuriously, unwilling to ruffle a single page until time made her do so. In fact, as she stood gazing over the grey roofs of Paris, Cateau's mind was not far from a blank — she was really thinking, as nearly as possible, of nothing at all.

Postscript

Extracts from the Journal of the Marquis de Dangeau

FRIDAY, MARCH 16, 1714, AT VERSAILLES
    ... The Maréchale de la Ferté died yesterday in Paris. She had passed her eightieth birthday, and had not appeared at court in many years; she leaves a very small estate. The Comtesse d'Olonne, her elder sister, who is very rich and from whom she hoped to inherit, is still living, but she has been childish for some while. . . .

FRIDAY, JUNE 15, 1714, AT RAMBOUILLET
    ... Madame the Comtesse d'Olonne died in Paris a few days ago; she was more than eighty years old, and in her youth was considered the greatest beauty of her time. . . .

THE END

A Note About Sources

'THE IVORY MISCHIEF' IS A NOVEL, NOT A BIOGRAPHY NOR AN historical work. At the same time it should be reiterated that every character in it actually lived in France three hundred years ago. Virtually, all the incidents, too, really happened just as described; the author has invented only where it was necessary to link together beads in the chain, and has in no case trifled with the dates or facts of public events, or of private ones either, so far as they are definitely established. The sole liberties permitted were an occasional simplification (not alteration) of the details of some court intrigue, and an even less frequent substitution of one minor personage for another, whereby the first was empowered to take over the duties of the second in addition to his own (this in order to set some limit to the almost numberless secondary characters in the novel).

The seventeenth century in France is one of the best documented in the whole history of the country. To give an idea of the bibliography of THE IVORY MISCHIEF would require many pages of citations and the titles of several hundred books of reference, chiefly contemporary, which have been consulted at one time or another before the actual writing was begun. Most of these books are entirely unknown to American readers. Besides the four great guides to the Grand Siècle — Tallemant des Réaux, Mademoiselle de Montpensier, Madame de Sévigné, and Saint-Simon (the last of whom composed its mordant obituary) — there are innumerable other sources of information, less celebrated but almost equally useful.

After a hundred years of comparative neglect — if we except the sophisticated ironies of Voltaire — French writers of the nineteenth century subjected the personalities of the Louis XIV period to renewed scrutiny. Old letters and half forgotten memoirs were dug up in family files and the great public libraries, and a whole fresh crop of critical and biographical works resulted from this revival of interest in the past, which has continued to be cultivated assiduously up to the present. The majority of these works were also consulted, but apart from manuscripts of value published therein there is little real worth in their pages. Modern historians have been incredibly careless in their methods of research, cheerfully scrambling dates and misidentifying numerous characters. To be exempted from this general charge of inaccuracy are the annotators of the texts published in the two splendid standard series, *Les Grands Ecrivains de la France* and *La Société de l'Histoire de France*, as well as some of the newer men, particularly Emile Magne. Special mention should be made of Monsieur Magne's *La Comtesse d'Olonne* for furnishing useful dates and addresses.

The facts of the story were then all on record, to be gleaned and assembled in chronological order. But there the task of the novelist had only begun: he found himself in the peculiar position of knowing exactly what happened to his characters, without having been given any idea *why* it happened. In other words, it was necessary to reverse the usual procedure of the novelist of manners and work backwards — given the plot, to invent plausible motives therefor. It must be admitted that the responsibility for the characterization of the dramatis personae rests solely with the author. Anyone can discover what these people did — why they did it, what they were really like, must be inferred from their actions. In only a few instances have the memoir-writers left a definite portrait as a guide. Such an exception to the rule is the Comtesse de Fiesque, who appears so vividly in the autobiography of her friend, Mademoiselle de Montpensier, that all that was needed was to clip her without further ado into the pages reserved for her. The same thing is true of the Duc de Candale, whom Saint-Evremond analyzed, briefly but brilliantly, for all time. . . . Saint-Simon knew some of these men and women, but only when they were old: his paragraph on the Comtesse d'Olonne and her sister, the Maréchale de la Ferté, which serves as the basis for the epilogue to the novel, is justly renowned as a triumph of concentrated malice. (The anecdote on which it turns has been thrice recounted, in his memoirs and in two separate corners of his voluminous notes to the *Journal du Marquis de Dangeau*.) And when, having credited the Countess with a great deal of wit in spite of her ignorance of religion, he adds of the Maréchale that she was *gueuse, libérale, douce, et avoit beaucoup moins d'esprit*, have we not found out all we need to about poor Magdelaine de la Ferté? (Especially when Bussy-Rabutin contributes, further, with his usual malice, that she was *belle et de bonne intention*. . . .)

But there it is — we know everything about these people, and we know nothing. For one who has spent years brooding upon them and their lives, which were so extraordinary, it is impossible not to reach the conclusion that the men and women of the seventeenth century were amazingly vital and tough-fibred. They lived lives of ceaseless activity, beginning in extreme youth and continuing often, in spite of the awful hygienic conditions and dangerously rudimentary medical knowledge of the day, to extreme old age. Most of them lived to be old, many of them died octogenarians, and they were vigorous to the end. We can never be sure what it was like to be them, to live in their world, which has vanished forever; but it is no bad idea to try to recapture something of their clear-eyed vision, their unfettered grasp of reality as they saw it. All of them — saints and sinners, soldiers, statesmen, poets, philosophers, mystics, eccentrics — were enthusiastically, passionately themselves, with the whole of their physical and spiritual energy: they lived with brio, and they seemed to die only when there was nothing left for them to do. Opportunities they were always in search of, sometimes mishandled, but never let slip. The lesson, to the tragically bewildered individualists of today, may not come amiss. ·